Praise for *Screams from the Dark*

"*Screams from the Dark* crackles with ferocious energy and ravenous delights. A thrilling feast for we who love monsters."
—Hailey Piper, Bram Stoker Award–winning author of *Queen of Teeth*

"There is a darkness in these pages that leaks out and shows you worlds you never dreamed possible. Not even in your worst nightmares."
—Philip Fracassi, author of *Boys in the Valley*

"This epic volume, with its impressive table of contents, will satisfy the hordes of readers looking for new takes on the monster trope."
—*Library Journal*

"Any horror fan will be glad to check this out."
—*Publishers Weekly*

"This is a treat for horror fans."
—*Booklist*

Praise for Ellen Datlow

"Ellen Datlow is the tastemaker, the greatest, most respected, and most prolific horror anthologist who's ever lived. Every Datlow anthology is a gift to the genre."
—Christopher Golden, *New York Times* bestselling author

"When I see Ellen Datlow as editor on an anthology, my first thought is always, that's a must-buy."
—Tim Lebbon, author of *The Silence*

"Ellen Datlow is the empress of the horror anthology—enviably well-read, eagle-eyed for talent, eager for originality; she's one of the glories of the field."
—Ramsey Campbell, author of *The Searching Dead*

T0006519

ALSO EDITED BY ELLEN DATLOW

SCREAMS FROM THE DARK

29 TALES OF MONSTERS AND THE MONSTROUS

edited by

ELLEN DATLOW

NIGHTFIRE

TOR PUBLISHING GROUP
NEW YORK

SCREAMS FROM THE DARK

Copyright © 2022 by Ellen Datlow

A Nightfire Book
Published by Tom Doherty Associates / Tor Publishing Group
120 Broadway
New York, NY 10271

www.tornightfire.com

Nightfire™ is a trademark of Macmillan Publishing Group, LLC.

The Library of Congress has cataloged the hardcover edition as follows:

Names: Datlow, Ellen, editor.
Title: Screams from the dark : 29 tales of monsters and the monstrous /
    [edited by] Ellen Datlow.
Description: First edition. | New York : Tom Doherty Associates, 2022.
Identifiers: LCCN 2022008025 (print) | LCCN 2022008026 (ebook) |
    ISBN 9781250797063 (hardcover) | ISBN 9781250797070 (ebook)
Subjects: LCSH: Monsters—Fiction. | Horror tales, American—21st century. |
    Horror tales—21st century. | LCGFT: Monster fiction. | Horror fiction. |
    Short stories.
Classification: LCC PS648.M54 S37 2022 (print) | LCC PS648.M54 (ebook) |
    DDC 823/.010837—dc23/eng/20220410
LC record available at https://lccn.loc.gov/2022008025
LC ebook record available at https://lccn.loc.gov/2022008026

ISBN 978-1-250-79705-6 (trade paperback)

Our books may be purchased in bulk for promotional, educational, or business use. Please contact your local bookseller or the Macmillan Corporate and Premium Sales Department at 1-800-221-7945, extension 5442, or by email at MacmillanSpecialMarkets@macmillan.com.

First Nightfire Paperback Edition: 2023

Printed in the United States of America

0 9 8 7 6 5 4 3 2

COPYRIGHT ACKNOWLEDGMENTS

*Thanks to Fritz Foy for asking for a BIG monster anthology,
and thank you to Kristin Temple for shepherding it into reality.
And to Stefan Dziemianowicz for saving my bacon as usual,
by advising me on my Introduction.*

CONTENTS

SCREAMS
FROM THE
DARK

29 Tales of Monsters and the Monstrous

INTRODUCTION

by Ellen Datlow

What is a "monster"? What is monstrosity? The definition depends upon who is doing the defining.

The etymology of the word "monster" is complicated.

"Monēre" is the root of "monstrum" and means to warn and instruct. Saint Augustine proposed the following interpretation, considering monsters part of the natural design of the world, deliberately created by God for His own reasons: spreading "abroad a multitude of those marvels which are called monsters, portents, prodigies, phenomena . . . They say that they are called 'monsters,' because they demonstrate or signify something; 'portents' because they portend something; and so forth . . . ought to demonstrate, portend, predict that God will bring to pass what He has foretold regarding the bodies of men, no difficulty preventing Him, no law of nature prescribing to Him His limit."

In Old English, the monster Grendel was an "aglæca," a word related to "aglæc": "calamity, terror, distress, oppression." A few centuries later, the Middle English word "monstre"—used as a noun and derived from Anglo-French, and the Latin "monstrum"—came into use, referring to an aberrant occurrence, usually biological, that was taken as a sign that something was wrong within the natural order. So abnormal animals or humans were regarded as signs or omens of impending evil. Then, in the 1550s, the definition began to include a "person of inhuman cruelty or wickedness, person regarded with horror because of moral deformity." At the same time, the term began to be used as an adjective to describe something of vast size.

The usage has evolved over time and the concept has become less subtle and more extreme, so that today most people consider a monster something inhuman, ugly and repulsive and intent on the destruction of everything around it. Or a human who commits atrocities. The word also usually connotes something wrong or evil; a monster is generally morally objectionable, in addition to being physically or psychologically hideous, and/or a freak of nature, and sometimes the term is applied figuratively to a person with an overwhelming appetite (sexual in addition to culinary) or a person who does horrible things.

Since humans began telling stories, monsters have figured in them. There's a rich tradition of monsters in literature. In Greek myth there are many monsters, a good number of them created by the gods as punishment for perceived slights. For example, Medusa was raped by Poseidon in the goddess Athena's temple. Athena then punished her for desecrating her sacred space by cursing Medusa with a head full of snakes and a gaze that turns men to stone. The Minotaur was born of human and bull from a situation fostered by Poseidon to punish King Minos for backing out of a sacrifice. Minos' wife Pasiphaë was cursed to feel lust for a bull and mated with it. From that union came the Minotaur. Lamia was the daughter of Poseidon, and her exquisite beauty drew the attention of Zeus. Lamia eventually became Zeus' mistress, much to the displeasure of his wife, Hera. The jealous wife cursed Lamia, and the curse is what led to the queen becoming known as a child-eating demon. Etc. etc. etc. So should we be surprised that we might feel sympathy for some monsters when they so often seem created solely to punish women for male transgressions against them?

Less morally objectionable with regard to their origins are Arabian fire demons known as Afrits and Ghuls (which became Ghouls, when Westernized); Japanese Fox-maidens; the Mesopotamian Ekimmu, which are said to suck life force, energy, or sometimes, misery; the Inkanyamba, a huge carnivorous eel-like animal in the legends of the Zulu and Xhosa people of South Africa; and huge Ogres that are a staple in African folktales. Bad fairies, evil witches, crafty wolves, and nasty trolls that terrorize and/or eat humans in fairy and folktales from Europe fit in perfectly with this crowd of international monsters.

There are many different kinds of monsters represented within these pages—including vampires, werewolves, shape-shifters, changelings, human monsters who are unaware of the pain they cause, and the other kind all too well aware, yet indifferent to it.

Sometimes the monstrous requires a shift in perspective. Who is the worse monster in Mary Shelley's *Frankenstein*? The creature abandoned to his own devices by his creator or the prideful Victor Frankenstein? What if you have an ethical choice to make in order to survive? If a child is murderous and isn't aware of what she is doing, is she monstrous? Outside circumstances or pressure can create monstrous behavior. Does that behavior make the perpetrator a monster?

Even our most insightful critics are divided in their appraisals of monsters and the monstrous. Noël Carroll, in his study *The Philosophy of Horror, or Paradoxes of the Heart,* writes of an "entity-based" scheme of horror, in which beings that defy neat cultural categories of what is "known"—in other words, the monstrous—arouse a sense of threat, or feelings of disgust. Conversely, as David J. Skal writes in his chapter on monsters in the popular culture of the 1960s in *The Monster Show: A Cultural History of Horror,* "Monsters . . . provided an element of reassurance. They were transcendent resurrection figures, beings who couldn't die." The monsters of television and film were appreciated as cultural touchstones because we all shared in our experience of them together: at the movie theater or drive-in; on television; and in magazines like *Famous Monsters of Filmland,* whose readers, mostly teenagers, may even have identified with them.

Stephen King, in his now-classic study *Danse Macabre,* may have put his finger on how we define the monstrous, and the hold of monsters on our psyche, but not with regard to the usual channels horror provides us. He considers the sideshow attractions of Tod Browning's film *Freaks;* the polymorphous villains of Dick Tracy cartoons; and even the supposed "abnormality" of the overweight, or the left-handed. Why do such examples pique our interest, he asks, indirectly, before answering, directly: "We love and need the concept of monstrosity because it is a reaffirmation of the order we all crave as human beings . . . and let me further suggest that it is not the physical or mental aberration in itself which horrifies us, but rather the lack of order which these aberrations seem to imply."

What's most interesting to me as a reader is the range of monstrousness that exists within ourselves and that we impose on the creatures unlike us that we name monsters. Monsters are our mirrors: in them, we see who we hope we are *not,* in order to understand who we are.

YOU HAVE WHAT I NEED

by Ian Rogers

Tamsin was stitching up an adulterer's arm when the woman came in with the bite wound.

Just another night in Chicago Hopeless, she thought.

That was what the emergency room staff called North Chicago General. Not because things there were particularly hopeless—the death rate at North Gen was no higher than that of any other hospital serving a major metropolitan area. It was just the gallows humor common among doctors and nurses who worked in a high-speed, high-stress environment. Being able to laugh at the unpleasant things they saw on a daily basis was as much a survival technique for themselves as the medical care they administered to their patients.

The adulterer's name was George Morse. He had come to the ER with a long gash on his arm and started talking a blue streak. That's what some people did when they were scared and in pain. Usually Tamsin didn't mind—sometimes their patter worked as a distraction that enabled her to complete her work—but in Morse's case, she wished the man was a mute.

"It was my wife," Morse said. "She cut me when she found out about Bettina. Grabbed the biggest knife out of the block." He chuckled to himself. "I bought her those knives for our fourteenth anniversary. She was waving it around and I was trying to get it away from her before she could cut me, and well . . . she cut me." He chuckled again. "She wouldn't take me to the hospital, so I had to call a cab. Probably could've driven myself, but I didn't want to bleed all over the upholstery in my car. It's not leather or anything fancy like that, but I . . ."

Tamsin let the words wash over her as she worked the needle through the skin of Morse's arm. She remembered something one of the attending physicians had said during her residency: *Tune out the drama, focus on the trauma.*

After she was done and Morse had been sent on his way, Tamsin went over to the triage desk, where a nurse named Joan Cuno was working on a crossword puzzle. "Slow night," Joan said, stifling a yawn.

"Famous last words," Tamsin said.

They both turned and looked at the automatic doors leading into the ER. They remained closed.

Joan shrugged. "I guess not."

"Night's not over yet," Tamsin said.

Joan's mouth stretched wide in another yawn. "Don't remind me."

"I was going to grab a coffee. You want one?"

"How about a caffeine IV drip?"

Tamsin laughed. "I'll see what I can do."

As she turned away from the desk, the automatic doors shushed open and a woman stepped into the ER. She was holding her left arm out in front of her, her right hand clamped tightly around the wrist. Blood seeped out between her fingers and dripped onto the floor.

Tamsin turned to Joan. "Now look what you did."

The woman's name was Rosalie and she said she'd been bitten by a vampire.

"A vampire?" Tamsin said. She swapped a look with Joan, who glanced up from typing the woman's information into the computer. "Are you sure?"

The woman, Rosalie, frowned. "Well . . . no. But how often does a guy jump out of an alley and bite you? Usually they go for your purse or knock you down so they can . . ." Her cheeks flushed a bright red. "Well . . . you know."

"Can I take a look at your arm?" Tamsin said. She was already reaching into her pocket for a fresh pair of latex gloves.

Rosalie hesitated, then held her arm out toward Tamsin. Tamsin held the woman's arm gently in both hands and leaned in close to examine the wound.

It was definitely a bite, and definitely human. The only other bite wounds they got in here on a regular basis were from dogs, and the marks they left were markedly different.

"It was good that you came to the hospital," Tamsin said.

Rosalie gave her a funny look. "Of course I came to the hospital. Why wouldn't I?"

Tamsin stared at the woman, unsure how to reply. She didn't want to tell her that most people who thought they'd been bitten by a vampire wouldn't have come within a hundred yards of a hospital.

"Why don't you come with me and we'll get this looked at properly." Tamsin turned to Joan, who was watching all this with wide, avid eyes. "Joan, could you tell Dennis that the drain in the break room is still clogged? I meant to tell him earlier, but I forgot."

Joan nodded and picked up a Motorola radio. After Tamsin had taken

Rosalie by her uninjured arm and led her off down a hallway, Joan keyed the mike on the radio and spoke in a low, breathless voice:

"Dennis? This is Joan. We've got a bite."

Tamsin hated this part. *Maybe she's not infected,* she told herself. *Maybe it really was a crazy street person that bit her.*

But they didn't deal in "maybe"s at Chicago Hopeless. Anyone who had been bitten by a supernatural creature—or thought they had been bitten by one—was taken down this hallway. Sometimes they had to be dragged kicking and screaming. Tamsin took small comfort in knowing she never had to do that part. That's what Dennis Nunez was for.

The hospital's head of security was already waiting for them when Tamsin and Rosalie reached the door at the end of the hallway. Dennis was tall and broad-shouldered in his tan uniform, his shaved head gleaming under the fluorescent lights. Tamsin felt better the moment she saw him. There was another guard with him, a young man named Anthony Tam, whose mouth was usually quirked in a flirty grin. He wasn't grinning now.

Rosalie looked warily at the two men. "What is this? What's going on?"

Dennis hooked his thumbs into the top of his garrison belt and tried to strike a casual posture.

"Ma'am, we understand you were involved in an incident this evening. You said you were bitten by a supernatural?"

"Yes," Rosalie said carefully. "Or . . . I don't know. I think so."

"Can you tell us what happened?"

"Well," Rosalie said, "I was walking home from work when a man came out of an alley and grabbed me."

"That must have been terrifying," Dennis said. "It's pretty late to be walking home. Where do you work?"

"I'm a barista at Cosmic Coffee, over on Pine Street."

Dennis nodded. "I know the place."

Tamsin liked watching Dennis work. She admired the way he spoke to the patients, the calm, even tone of his voice that managed to sound both interested and sympathetic. It was as much about putting them at ease as it was to gather information. Dennis used to work for the Chicago Police Department, and in moments like this Tamsin could see how he must have been in the interrogation room, playing the role of Good Cop to cajole a suspect into telling him things they didn't want him to know.

"I don't usually walk home alone," Rosalie said. "Normally I get a ride with Cheryl—she's one of the other baristas—but she's been out all week with the stomach flu."

Dennis crossed his arms. "The man who attacked you, do you remember anything about him? What he looked like? What he was wearing?"

Rosalie shook her head. "It was really dark. All I remember is him grabbing my arm and pulling me into the alley. I thought he was trying to take my purse, but I was holding it in my other hand. It wasn't until I was able to pull away from him that I realized he had bitten me."

"Then what happened?"

"I ran." Rosalie looked at the three people standing around her. "What would you have done?"

"You did the right thing," Dennis assured her. "Now, what made you think this man was a vampire?"

Rosalie's cheeks had filled with color as she talked about what had happened to her. Now, as Tamsin watched, it drained out like a plug had been pulled.

"He didn't say anything," Rosalie said. "Not a word. He was making a sound. Low, in the back of his throat, almost like a growl. Or maybe that's just how I remember it. And he bit me! Who would do a thing like that? It's not normal. I started to think that *he* wasn't normal. That maybe he was . . ."

"A vampire," Dennis said.

Rosalie nodded.

"It was probably someone with a mental health issue," Tamsin said. "Or maybe a drug addict. But it almost certainly wasn't a vampire. You know what they say: you're more likely to be struck by lightning . . ."

"Than to encounter a supernatural," Rosalie finished. "Yeah, I've heard that before, but . . ." She raised her wounded arm. ". . . I thought it was best to be sure."

"That's very responsible of you," Dennis said. He gave the other guard, Anthony, a brief look before turning back to Rosalie. "Now why don't we get you into the examination room so we can get that bite looked at."

Dennis placed his hand lightly against Rosalie's back and guided her toward the door. Anthony swiped his ID card through the electronic reader to unlock it and held it open.

Rosalie went inside, taking small steps and looking all around like a frightened child.

The examination room, as Dennis had called it, was a room with another, smaller room inside it. This inner room was an enclosed chamber composed of four thick glass walls, with a tempered-steel ceiling and floor.

Rosalie turned to look at the three hospital personnel standing behind her. "What is this?"

Anthony moved around her and used his ID card to open the door to the inner room.

"This is the hospital's paranormal biocontainment chamber," Dennis explained. He ushered Rosalie inside as he spoke. "It's where we treat people who have been attacked by creatures from the Black Lands."

Tamsin followed them into the chamber, the tension thrumming under her skin like low-voltage electricity. She knew if there was going to be a problem, this is when it would happen. She watched as Rosalie looked around the chamber. There was nothing inside except a stainless-steel toilet bolted to the floor in the corner. It looked less like a hospital room and more like a prison cell—which, in a way, Tamsin supposed it was.

Anthony stood in the doorway while Tamsin went over to Rosalie and asked to see her injured arm. Rosalie held it out toward her. Tamsin cleaned the wound with an antiseptic wipe, then bandaged it with a dressing. It was the bare minimum of treatment, just enough to stop the bleeding and hold things over until they could determine if Rosalie was infected.

When she was done, Tamsin met Dennis's eyes and said, "We're good." Then she left the chamber and Dennis took her spot in front of Rosalie.

"Now, ma'am . . ." Dennis began.

"Please stop calling me that," Rosalie said abruptly. "You make me feel like an old woman. My name is Rosalie Lewis."

"Ms. Lewis," Dennis said. "Since you may have come into contact with a Black Lands entity, we have to keep you under quarantine until we can determine that you haven't been infected with a paranormal pathogen."

Rosalie's face fell. "*What?*" She turned and looked through the glass wall at Tamsin in the outer room. Tamsin saw the hurt and betrayal in the other woman's face and quickly lowered her eyes.

Rosalie turned back to face Dennis. "What do you mean 'quarantine'? I was only . . . I was bit. I didn't . . . I'm not sick!"

"Ma'am . . . Ms. Lewis, we can't take any chances. If you were attacked by a vampire, there's a possibility that you have been infected. Until we can make that determination, you have to remain in this chamber. For your own safety as well as that of everyone else in the hospital."

Dennis stepped around Rosalie and took Anthony's place in the open doorway. Rosalie turned to follow him, but was halted in her tracks when the security chief's hand moved to the butt of the pistol holstered on his hip.

"But . . . there must be some test," Rosalie stammered. "A blood test or something."

"They aren't conclusive," Dennis told her. "The only way to know for certain is to wait."

"Wait?" Rosalie said. "For how long?"

Tamsin stepped forward. "The incubation period of the vampire virus is about twelve hours."

"*Twelve hours?*" Rosalie said loudly. "You can't keep me in here for twelve hours!"

She moved quickly toward the doorway. Dennis stepped back and swung the door shut. There was a sharp click as the electronic lock engaged. Rosalie pounded her fists against the door, then grimaced in pain and cradled her injured arm.

"You can't do this," she said. Her voice was muffled through the thick glass, but Tamsin could still hear the fear and hurt in her voice. "You can't . . . you can't . . ."

While it was true that the vampire virus—or VV, as it was commonly known—had an incubation period of approximately twelve hours, Tamsin knew that symptoms usually manifested much sooner than that. But in twelve hours, they would know for certain if Rosalie was going to turn.

Dennis and Anthony left the room. Tamsin started to follow them, then turned back to Rosalie. She was still standing on the other side of the glass door, tears streaking down her face.

"I'll come back in a bit and check on you, okay?" Tamsin hated the weak tremble she heard in her own voice. "I'll bring you something to help pass the time. A magazine or something."

Rosalie stared back at her in silence, her chest rising and falling, her lower lip trembling. She sucked in a big gust of air and screamed: "*Get OUT!*"

Tamsin recoiled as if struck. She turned around on shaky legs and stumbled out of the room.

An hour later, Tamsin was filling out paperwork and trying to keep her eyes from sagging shut. She needed coffee, then remembered she'd been on her way to get one when Rosalie had come into the emergency room. That reminded her that she had to check in on her patient.

Tamsin sighed deeply. She didn't need the reminder. The truth was she had been putting it off. She wouldn't have admitted it to anyone, but she was nervous about looking in on Rosalie.

As a doctor, she was used to giving people bad news. It was part of the job. But telling someone that they had a paranormal disease, that they were going to turn into a monster, was something she had never gotten used to.

She told herself that the vampire virus was really no different than cancer. It was a malignant agent that invaded the host's body, changed it, corrupted it, and ultimately destroyed it. But the fact was the vampire virus was worse. It didn't stop at killing the host, it brought them back, transformed them into a demonic version of their former self that cared about only one thing: blood.

The only thing Tamsin could think of worse than that was to go through it all alone.

With a sigh of resignation, she put down her pen and started down the hallway that led to the PBC. Then, remembering she told Rosalie she'd bring her a magazine, she detoured over to the waiting area and picked up a copy of *Newsweek* and *Us Weekly*.

She glanced over at the triage desk and saw Joan Cuno talking to a woman and her young son. The boy was five or six years old and had a pained look on his face. He was holding his left arm close to his stomach, like a bird with an injured wing.

Tonight seems to be the night for arm injuries, Tamsin thought. She started to yawn again, then suddenly found herself gagging on a smell so horrible she seemed to taste it. She covered her nose and mouth with one hand and looked around for the source of the offensive odor.

The woman and her son went over to sit in the waiting area. Looking past them, Tamsin saw a man in ragged clothing standing in the entrance of the ER. His brown hair was filthy and fell to his shoulders in long greasy snarls. He wore an old army-surplus jacket with holes in the elbows and a pair of faded jeans. Tamsin's gaze dropped lower and she saw he wasn't wearing any shoes. One of his socks had a hole in it and his big toe stuck out, the nail long and yellow.

Homeless people sometimes wandered into the ER, especially late at night, looking for food or shelter, drugs or alcohol. Something to keep them warm. Something to stop the shakes or ease the pain.

Tamsin was moving toward the triage desk to tell Joan to call security—the man was probably harmless, but it was always best to play it safe—when the automatic doors slid open and two more men stepped inside. Although they bore no physical resemblance to the first man, their frayed clothing and looks of general uncleanliness made Tamsin think they were together.

She got another waft of that awful smell and covered her mouth again. The stench was so strong it actually stopped her in her tracks. It wasn't the smell she normally associated with the homeless people who came into the ER—the reek of old sweat and unwashed bodies, the sour stink of stale wine. This was a much more pungent odor. The cloying, sickly-sweet stench of roadkill baking on a hot asphalt road.

It seemed Tamsin wasn't the only one who noticed the smell. Over at the triage desk, she saw Joan wrinkle her nose and look up from her computer. In the waiting area, the woman made a gagging sound and covered her nose, while her son's face twisted in a look of almost comical disgust.

Tamsin turned back to the three men. They tilted their heads back and started sniffing the air, as if they were suddenly aware of how badly they smelled. One of them curled back his lip like a dog about to snarl, and Tamsin saw his teeth.

They weren't homeless people.

They were vampires.

I'm dead, she thought. *We're all dead.*

The other two men opened their mouths to reveal their own pronounced canine teeth.

Fangs, Tamsin told herself. *Those are fucking* fangs.

She tried to take a step toward the triage desk, but found herself unable to move. There was a panic button under the counter that would bring a STAR team on the double. Response time was about ten minutes. At the present moment that seemed about nine minutes too long.

Joan was staring at the three men standing in the entrance, but she seemed to be as frozen by fright as Tamsin was, and didn't appear to be making any move toward pressing the button.

Tamsin was trying to think of a way to signal her without drawing the vampires' attention when the woman sitting with her injured son suddenly started screaming.

She had also noticed the men, and, like Tamsin and Joan, seemed to know that they weren't human.

To the vampires, those screams were like a dinner bell ringing. One of them leaped through the air, slamming into the woman and her son and knocking them both to the floor.

"Joan!" Tamsin shouted. "The button! Press the button!"

Joan turned toward the sound of her voice, then one of the vampires dove over the top of the desk and tackled her. Her screams joined those of the woman and her son.

Tamsin looked over at the third vampire, the one with the long filthy hair, and saw he was staring right at her. She felt the magazines she was holding slip out of her hands and fall to the floor.

The vampire took a step toward her and Tamsin's paralysis broke. So did her bladder. Hot urine spilled down her leg as she took a step backward.

The vampire's nostrils twitched and Tamsin knew he was smelling her piss, smelling her fear. He took another step forward, arms extended, fingers hooked into claws, getting ready to strike.

Tamsin glanced over at the automatic doors, but there was no way she'd be able to reach them before the vampire was on her. The part of her mind that was on the verge of full-blown panic told her to try anyway, but she knew that would be a mistake. The last one she'd ever make.

She had to run, but not outside. There was only one place she could go. One place she knew she'd be safe.

Just as the vampire was about to pounce, Tamsin spun on her heel and went sprinting down the hallway. She turned down a connecting corridor, but was going too fast and bounced off the wall like a pinball. She managed to stay on her feet but couldn't make herself slow down. She could hear the vampire close behind her, panting and snarling, as if angry that she hadn't stood still like the others and let him feed on her.

There were rooms on both sides of the hallway, but it never entered Tamsin's mind to duck into any of them. She didn't have time to properly barricade a door, not with anything that would keep out a vampire.

She came around another corner and collided with a gurney parked against the wall. The gurney went rolling across the hallway, struck the opposite wall, and crashed over on its side. Tamsin hurdled it and kept running toward the door at the end of the hallway.

She took out her key card and gripped it tight. If she dropped it, she was dead. If she didn't get the door open fast enough, she was dead.

She timed it as well as she could, slowing down enough that she slid to a stop in front of the door instead of freight-training into it. She slid the card through the reader on the first try and slipped inside. She dashed across the small anteroom to the glass-walled chamber, used her key card to open the door, and threw herself inside.

She got the glass door closed just as the vampire burst through the outer door, striking it with enough force to knock it off its hinges and send it cartwheeling across the room.

Tamsin backed up until she was standing in the centre of the chamber, as far away from the four glass walls as she could get. She was confident the vampire couldn't smash his way inside. The chamber had been designed explicitly for that purpose . . . although the vampire was supposed to be the one on the inside.

A timid voice asked, "What's going on out there?"

Tamsin snapped around and saw Rosalie cowering in the corner next to the stainless-steel toilet.

Before she could answer, the vampire slammed into the chamber door. Rosalie screamed. The glass panel trembled in its steel frame, but didn't shatter. The vampire howled and flung himself at the door again. Rosalie screamed again. There was a loud cracking sound as the vampire's body rebounded off the glass and went tumbling to the floor.

Rosalie said, "Is that . . . ?"

"Yes," Tamsin said.

Rosalie stood up and took a tentative step forward, peering at the vampire with a mixture of curiosity and fear. "What happened?"

Tamsin shook her head. Not because she didn't know, but because she couldn't believe it. She had seen it with her own eyes, but was still having trouble processing the reality of the situation. She had been trained on what to do if someone came into the ER with a paranormal infection. She had not been told what to do if a vampire—much less three of them—came in and started attacking people. Tamsin wondered if Joan had managed to push the panic button before the vampire had attacked her. She supposed she'd find out if the cavalry showed up. They had to show up eventually, right? The question was how many people would be dead before they finally got here.

The vampire was back on his feet and walking around the perimeter of the chamber. Sometimes he would come close to one of the glass walls, start to reach out a hand toward it, then pull it back quickly. Like he was distrustful of the glass for keeping him from his prey.

Tamsin turned to Rosalie and said, "Is this the man who bit you in the alley?"

Rosalie stared at the vampire for a long moment, then shook her head. "No, I don't think so."

There was a scream from out in the hallway. Both women turned in unison, but they couldn't see anything beyond the open doorway. There was another scream, this one higher in pitch, and the vampire went running out of the room.

"How many of them are out there?" Rosalie asked.

"Three," Tamsin said.

"Three?" Rosalie paled visibly. "Why are they here? Why would they attack a hospital?"

Tamsin shook her head. "I don't know. I've never heard of them doing anything like this before."

"Do you think they came for the blood?"

Tamsin turned to her. "What blood?"

"You have a blood bank or something here, don't you? For transfusions and surgeries?"

"Yes," Tamsin said, "but I don't think *they* know that. Vampires aren't supposed to be that smart."

"Is that . . . ?" Rosalie gestured with her chin. "Is that what's going to happen to me?"

"I don't know," Tamsin said. "That's the honest truth."

"But you've seen vampire bites before, right?" Rosalie started to roll up her sleeve, then remembered the bandage covering her wound. "You've seen what happens to those people? Do I look sick to you?"

"No," Tamsin said, "but that doesn't mean you aren't infected. That's why we put people in quarantine. To be sure."

Rosalie blew out a frustrated breath and leaned back against the glass wall, sliding down it until she was sitting in a squat.

Tamsin walked to the other side of the chamber, cursing herself for the insensitive way she had spoken. Rosalie was only looking for reassurance, for some hope, and Tamsin had replied with all the warmth of a Wikipedia entry. She tried to tell herself it wasn't her job to dispense hope, but another part of her said that was exactly what she was supposed to do. That hope was just another type of medicine in a doctor's repertoire. Sometimes it was the only thing they had to give.

"It's funny," Rosalie said.

Tamsin turned to face her. "What?"

"This." Rosalie spread her hands. "You came in here because you thought you'd be safe. Only now you're trapped with someone who might turn into one of those things out there."

Tamsin crossed her arms. "If you're looking for an apology . . ."

"No," Rosalie said. "You're just doing your job. I get it. I just think it's ironic."

Tamsin sat down on the floor, positioning herself so she could talk to Rosalie and keep an eye on the open doorway at the same time. Nothing seemed to be happening out there, but she knew the vampires were somewhere in the hospital, causing bloody mayhem. The silence that had descended was somehow worse than the screams of a few moments ago. So Tamsin started talking . . .

"In medical school they told us about a man who was attacked by a vampire. He managed to escape, but instead of going to the hospital—where he knew he'd be put in a chamber like this one—he decided to go home. To his wife and his three children." Tamsin let out a weary sigh. "Less than twenty-four hours later, after the infection had taken hold and the man had turned, he had killed his entire family, the elderly couple who lived next door, a mailman, and a woman who happened to be passing by on the street as she walked her dog. Someone called the police, who in turn notified the PIA, and a STAR team came and killed the man. Only by then he wasn't really a man anymore, and they didn't really kill him. The man was already dead. He had died the moment he was infected. And when the STAR team staked him, they weren't ending his life, they were putting him out of his misery. The same as you'd do for a rabid animal."

Rosalie sat silently for a moment, digesting Tamsin's story. Then she said, "Is that what I am? A rabid animal?"

"Not yet," Tamsin said. "Maybe not ever. But if you're infected, you *will* change. I've seen it before." She lowered her eyes. "Too many times."

"The man in your story," Rosalie said. "You would have put him in here, wouldn't you? Locked him up and let him sit in here to die?"

"Yes," Tamsin said. "Better he die in here alone, than out there with his family's blood, and the blood of those other people, on his hands."

"I heard there were shots."

"The antivirals?" Tamsin shook her head. "They're just rumors. I don't know who started them—the medical establishment as a way of preventing panic, or the government to trick people into going to the hospital if they're infected. Either way, it's bullshit. There are no shots, no antivirals. No cure."

"Except a stake through the heart."

Tamsin looked her straight in the eye. "That's right."

Rosalie was quiet for a long time. Then she said: "This wasn't how I expected this night to go."

It was Tamsin's turn to stare in silence. Then she snickered. She couldn't help it. Rosalie managed to keep her composure for a few seconds, then a smile broke across her face and she started to laugh, too. It was completely inappropriate to the situation at hand, but that didn't seem to matter. Laughter and the vampire virus had at least that much in common—they were both contagious.

After their laughter tapered off, Tamsin turned solemn and said, "Can I ask you something?"

"Sure," Rosalie said.

"What did you think would happen?"

Rosalie frowned. "What do you mean? From the bite?"

"No," Tamsin said. "Coming here. To the hospital. You must have known we weren't going to just stitch you up and send you home."

Rosalie looked off toward the open doorway. "I don't know," she said. "I guess I was in shock. I didn't know where else to go and I thought . . ." She gave a small shrug. "I thought someone here would be able to help me."

After another long silence, Tamsin said, "Maybe it wasn't a vampire."

Rosalie started laughing again. Tamsin stared at her in confusion until she finished.

"I'm sorry," Rosalie said, wiping at her eyes. "I just remembered something. From when I was attacked."

Tamsin raised an eyebrow. "Something funny?"

"I told you I didn't know I'd been bitten until after I'd gotten away."

Tamsin nodded.

"That's not exactly true. I did feel it, but I didn't want to say because it made me angry."

"Angry?"

Rosalie nodded. "All I wanted was to go home and sleep, and here was this guy biting my arm. I should have been terrified, but the thought going through my head was *How DARE you!*"

"That's probably why you survived," Tamsin said. "You didn't just break down and curl into a ball. You fought and ran for your life."

"I did more than that," Rosalie said.

"What?"

"I bit him back."

Tamsin stared at Rosalie, waiting for her to start laughing again. When she didn't, Tamsin said, "You bit him. You bit a vampire."

"He bit me first!" Rosalie blurted.

The two women looked at each other, then they both burst into laughter.

Tamsin didn't know how long they went on like that, but it was long enough that tears started to leak out of her eyes and she started to feel a little breathless. It was startling to think that anything could be funny at a time like this, sitting in the biocontainment chamber with someone who might be VV-positive while vampires roamed throughout the hospital.

They stopped laughing when the vampire came back.

Tamsin didn't see him at first. She only became aware of his presence when Rosalie suddenly stopped laughing and went scurrying back into the corner next to the toilet. Tamsin turned and saw the vampire circling the chamber as he had done before. It was the same one who had chased her, looking as filthy as ever, only now there was a wide bib of blood staining the front of his shirt. Tamsin wondered if that blood was from one person or a dozen. She wondered if it was from anyone she knew.

The vampire came around to the glass door, and Tamsin felt her fear go up a notch as he tilted his head to the side and scrutinized the electronic card reader. How smart were they? she wondered. Smart enough to take an ID card off one of the people he had killed? Smart enough to know how to use it?

The vampire pressed his hands against the door, then leaned forward and peered into the chamber. Tamsin found herself drawn into the vampire's eyes. She couldn't seem to tear herself away from them.

She took an unconscious step toward the door, and was about to take another when there was a loud blatting sound and a spray of blood splashed across the glass.

Tamsin was so startled that for a moment she thought the blood was her own, that the vampire had somehow managed to pass through the door and sink his teeth into her throat.

But the blood had come from the vampire. He didn't look pained by this sudden turn of events; he looked mildly annoyed. Tamsin watched as he turned away from the glass door. She was trying to look around him to see what was going on when there was another angry burst of sound—gunfire, she realized now—followed by another splatter of blood across the glass wall of the chamber.

The vampire was thrown backward by force of the blast. He slammed into the chamber door, then fell forward onto his hands and knees.

Three men moved quickly into the room. They all wore black body armor and tactical gas masks. STAR was stamped in white letters across their chest plates, which Tamsin knew stood for Supernatural Threat Assessment and Response. Two of the men carried M4 submachine guns, which they had trained on the vampire. The third was holding something that might have been a gun, but it was oddly shaped. Tamsin was trying to get a better look at it when the vampire leaped back to his feet.

One of the STAR officers raised his M4 and fired off another burst that sent the vampire stumbling back into the chamber door. Rosalie screamed and Tamsin looked over to see her lying flat on the floor. Tamsin figured that was a good idea—she didn't know if the glass walls were bulletproof—and dropped down to join her.

Tamsin raised her head and saw the vampire's body slide down the glass, leaving a thick blood trail behind like a bug smeared on a windshield. But he wasn't dead. No amount of bullets would do that. The vampire's wounds would already be healing—broken blood vessels repairing themselves, new tissue forming, all at a rate that could only be described as supernatural.

The STAR officer slung his submachine gun and knelt down on top of the vampire, pinning his legs and one of his arms to the floor. Another officer—the one holding the strange-looking gun—knelt on the vampire's other arm. The third STAR officer remained in the doorway and covered the other two.

The vampire hissed and tried to get up. The two STAR officers managed to keep him pinned to the floor, but Tamsin could tell it took a great effort. The man holding the vampire's legs and one of his arms spoke in a strained voice to his partner. "Do it! Punch him!"

The STAR officer pressed the barrel of his strange-looking gun against the vampire's chest. He hesitated, moved it two inches to the left, and pulled the trigger. The vampire's body bucked off the floor with enough force that he almost threw off the two STAR officers. Watching this from inside the chamber, Tamsin was reminded of the way a person's body jumped after getting a blast from a defibrillator. Except a defibrillator was used to shock a person's heart back to life. The STAR officer's device had done the opposite—it had fired a wooden stake directly into the vampire's heart.

The two STAR officers stood up and looked down at the vampire's unmoving body. Tamsin could see the top of the stake protruding from the creature's chest. A little blood welled around the wound, but not as much as she expected. As she continued to watch, the skin on the vampire's face began to tighten and draw back from the sharp planes of his skull. The body seemed to shrink inside its clothes as flesh, blood, and muscle tissue disintegrated rapidly. *Accelerated cellular decay,* Tamsin thought. The virus attempting to save itself by feeding on the host's body until there was nothing left to eat.

When it was over, the STAR officer stationed at the door lowered his M4 and said, "Clear."

Tamsin climbed to her feet and approached the door. She looked out at the three men. They looked back at her, their faces unreadable behind their gas masks.

"Sit tight," one of them said. "We'll be back."

Dennis Nunez had two black eyes and a tic-tac-toe board of scratches on his face. His left arm was in a cast, the right one was in a sling. In addition to a broken collarbone, he also had three broken ribs and a mild concussion. He was lucky to be alive, and Tamsin told him so.

"I know," Dennis said. He winced in pain as he eased himself into the folding chair in front of the containment chamber. "I keep telling myself that. Maybe one day I'll believe it."

"I'm sorry about Anthony."

Dennis nodded, staring at the floor. "I don't know why the vampire bit him instead of me."

"You didn't exactly get off scot-free."

"Fucker used me like a punching bag, then threw me out a window. I woke up outside on the lawn with a bunch of STAR guys standing over me. I laid there waiting to see if they were going to stake me. But I wasn't infected." He raised his left arm in its cast and pumped his fist weakly in the air. "Yay me."

For some reason they would never know, the vampires had remained on the first floor of the hospital. Maybe because they couldn't find the stairs and they didn't know how to operate the elevator. Or maybe they wanted to stick close to their hunting ground in the ER. It didn't matter. By the time it was over, seven people were dead, including Joan Cuno, Anthony Tam, and the woman and her son in the waiting area. Two of the others were patients in the ICU. They were so drugged up they probably didn't even know what was happening when the vampires ripped out their throats and started lapping up their blood. The last victim was a cardiologist named Victor Freeburg whom Tamsin had flirted with on occasion. She had been giving serious consideration to one of his frequent dinner invitations.

After the vampires had been dispatched by the STAR team, one of the officers had come back to the containment chamber to speak with Tamsin. When they found out that Rosalie might have been infected, they took her out—at gunpoint—and led her away to another containment chamber in the mobile control center they had parked outside. Since she'd been in close contact with Rosalie for a long period of time, Tamsin was told she would have to remain in the chamber to undergo quarantine herself. Tamsin understood, and even if she didn't, she was too exhausted to argue.

"Why do you think this happened?" Dennis asked her.

Tamsin looked at him. "What do you mean?"

"Why would three vampires come into the ER like that? It doesn't make any sense."

"I don't know," Tamsin said. "I've heard of hospitals being attacked in the past, but it's very rare. They usually don't bother because the security is too good."

"You think these vamps were just desperate?"

Tamsin considered his question for a long time, then said: "I think we had something they needed. So they came and took it."

There was a knock at the door. Dennis rose from his chair with a grimace and went to open it. It was Rosalie. She and Dennis exchanged some words too quietly for Tamsin to hear, then Dennis ducked out with a small wave at Tamsin.

Rosalie approached the chamber. She held up her left hand to show a slip of green plastic looped around her wrist.

"I just got cleared," she said. "They said I could stop in for a minute."

Tamsin nodded. She didn't know what to say.

"I'm not infected," Rosalie said. "That means you aren't either. But they said they still have to keep you in quarantine."

"It's okay," Tamsin said. "It's protocol."

"You kept me calm," Rosalie said. "You kept me from freaking out. That wasn't protocol. I wanted to do the same for you, but I didn't know what to do. So I brought you these."

She held up a stack of magazines.

Tamsin smiled. "You're going to have some trouble sliding those under the door."

Rosalie saw the chair in front of the chamber. She sat down in it. "That's okay," she said. "I can read them to you."

"You don't have to do that."

"I know," Rosalie said.

She opened one of the magazines and started to read.

THE MIDWAY

by Fran Wilde

When the latest Saturday-night blackout hits the boardwalk, Alan Staley's so hell-bent on making me come in to feed the Midway before dawn, he hardly stops talking.

I have a good view of the coastline going dark, because Alan, my boss, took me to the benches overlooking the dunes, away from the staff and crowds inside Staley's by the Sea Amusement Arcade, just in case I freaked out. He says some people do. But I just stare straight ahead as the sparkling curve to our north disappears into the night, the surrounding hotel air conditioners fall silent, and Alan tells me exactly what I need to do. After a minute, a few generators trudge on. Behind us the arms of the Staley's by the Sea Tilt-A-Whirl, the light-pricked Freefall stanchions, and the sparkling canopy of the historic carousel keep spinning bright and fast above the ring of try-your-luck games that border the amusement arcade. The laughter and screams of the crowd at Staley's never misses a beat, Alan keeps talking, and my ten-minute break from the bumper car station slowly slips away.

Though it's only my second week on staff, everyone at Staley's knows the place stays bright no matter what happens to the rest of the electrical grid. Back when Pops Staley started the place, the locals had a few questions as to why, but now they love Staley's because it's reliable, when the rest of the world isn't. Which is why the arcade is still hiring into the off-season, and—in light of my prior failings—I should be grateful for the job, according to my cousin, Mara.

Sure, when the lights go out, Alan's Adam's apple does bob up and down a little faster, before he takes a long drag on his cigarette, flicks the ash at the darkened horizon, clears his throat, and gets back to business. I can mostly hear him over the crash of the waves and the noise from the Skee-Ball machines. "It's your turn this time, Skyla. Yes, or no?"

I need to pee, and Alan's holding out a damage waiver for me to sign. He stops talking and lights another cigarette. To get to the staff restroom, I have to cross the crowded boardwalk, push my way through the crowds playing

Whac-A-Mole and Skee-Ball, then weave through lines for the bumper cars, carousel, and spinning teacups, take a sharp left at the ticket booth in the center of the arcade, and duck behind the haunted house. The restroom's next to the cooler where they keep the dry ice. Once I'm done, I have to do it all again backwards, to get back to my spot at the bumper cars before I'm late, and Staley's is strict about breaks. But I'd rather wait to go back in until the Lloyd family leaves the bumper cars, so I half-read the waiver while I play with the pink and white Staley's by the Sea pen.

"Why not someone who's done this before?" I click the pen and try not to squirm on the bench. Alan had said "this time," and that means someone among Staley's dozen staff has more experience. "Why not Mara?" She moved up to bumper car manager when I was hired. "Or Kathleen, or Cyrus?" Those are the only other staff I know so far, and not well.

"Last hired, first right of refusal," he says, voice jaunty like he's working a ride. "Your choice: triple overtime or turn in your uniform."

When she got me the job, loaning me money for the pink and white Hawaiian shirt and pink baseball hat embroidered with STALEY'S BY THE SEA, plus the regulation khaki shorts, Mara promised I had nothing to worry about at Staley's. She'd said Alan was a decent boss. That he'd kept the arcade going just fine when Pops Staley took ill at the start of the summer. But Alan's maybe a few years older than me and Mara, and looks nothing like the jovial, bearded man in the cowboy hat on all the billboards. Alan's wiry voice breaks when he feels like the staff's not listening to him, which is a lot of the time. He chain-smokes and gets mad when people ask when Pops is coming back. Even though they should be happy with Alan, according to Mara: "The arcade's running better than ever. The place hasn't eaten a single kid this year, for starters."

At the time, I thought she was joking, like those UNATTENDED CHILDREN WILL BE FED TO THE SEA posters in stores around town.

The lights flicker two towns up the coast, but don't hold. The lamps buzz and click, then stop. I squirm. Four minutes until my break ends. The rest of the area's dark, but Staley's gleams. People stream down the boardwalk toward us, eager for something to do until the grid fixes itself.

Alan grins at them, waving families toward the arcade's gates. "Everyone's welcome!" But then, under his breath, with the kind of chuckle that always makes me angry, he says, "Best time to feed the Midway is the first Sunday morning after Labor Day. That's tomorrow. Go too far into the off-season, or try to change its diet, and the locals start disappearing. Yes, or no?"

I think about how even Mara looked nervous when the boards below the bumper cars rumbled out of sync with the haunted house ride, late at night. How the skin prickled on the back of my neck and I felt like I was being watched while we locked up. About the stories my oma used to tell back home, after the war, but before I left, while we pedaled electricity with her rusty bicycle generator, about the monsters in the sea long ago. About the power in their tentacles and pincers. Their hunger. About how they're all gone now, she'd say, just like everything else good.

A long while back, the Staleys must have got themselves a monster. A big one. And now they want me to feed it.

Alan shakes the waiver as he takes another long drag on his cigarette. Time to decide, then pee, then rush back to my station. Still, I hesitate, my eyes on the horizon. Clicking the pen: out, in, out, in.

"Mara said you'd be chicken." He jerks his chin at my saint's medal. "Doesn't that protect you, or something?"

I pass my thumb over the rough etched medallion hanging from the thin chain around my neck: a woman heading out to sea in the grip of a wave or tentacles, it's hard to be sure. "Or something." Saint Silvana—a very minor saint with a following of two, me and my oma—might know what to do with someone like Alan, or something like the Midway, or she might not. She'd never thought to use a monster to power Oma's apartment, for instance. "Mara's wrong." I sign *Skyla Arkantik* fast, angry at my cousin for talking about me to the boss and embarrassed because I can't wait any longer for the bathroom.

He takes the waiver back. "Great. The fish are in the haunted house cooler, behind the dry ice."

I must look upset, like I won't actually show. Alan grabs my wrist, hard, as I turn toward the bright amusement park. "I'll be here too, so don't be late. Just do this once and you're done."

With two whole minutes left, I run through the crowds toward the staff room stall, angry that I had no real choice, but he still made me say *yes*. On my way back, the power comes on again outside, and families with younger kids begin to leave. *Bedtime.* I breathe relief when I see the Lloyds swinging Lucille between them out to the boardwalk, one hand held firmly by each parent. She's wailing. Lucille's a runner, but the four-year-old hasn't seen me, I'm sure of it. Mr. Lloyd? I'm not so sure.

"Did they ask about me?" I don't use English as I swap stations with Mara, who's been silently, obviously watching the digital clock atop the ticket booth as her own break approaches.

"Why would they ask? You were only with them a month." Mara replies in English. My language skills are as good as hers, my accent as thick. I just don't want to be overheard. She doesn't care. "Anyway, I kept to the back of the rink, alone, so I didn't have to talk to them. Did you sign? Or did you leave me hanging again?"

My shoulders hunch, but I remember the trusting pressure of Lucille's hand as we walked through this arcade weeks ago, the curl of her small fingers over my thick palm. How she'd clutched the stuffed animal we'd won at Skee-Ball. How I'd abandoned her, and my first job, and the belief my oma had placed in me, because I was scared. "I signed."

"Good. You don't *always* run away like your mother, then." She flicks my medallion, then gives me an uncharacteristic hug and slips away from the ride. Alan meets her by the Skee-Ball game and slips an arm around her waist.

Ten weeks since Mara convinced Oma to let me come over and join her, saying she'd handle everything. I owe her so much. I look away.

The noise from the haunted house swells and the floorboards beneath me rattle again. I shiver as I walk across them during the reset to wipe down a fouled bumper car seat, since Mara hadn't bothered. Spilled ice cream and soda and who knows what else greet me. *Gross, Mara.* My nose wrinkles. *You always save the worst jobs for me.*

Before dawn the next morning, I prepare to feed the Midway.

I'm already late because Mara's got the phone with the alarm, and she didn't come home last night. A loud cloudburst woke me almost in time, and I get ready while shaking loose the tendrils of a nightmare I've had since I was a kid. Shadows crossing overhead, forming grasping hands, and, this time, yanking me from the caved-in, secondhand sofa, through the small, hungry window, and out to sea.

I pull my hair into a Staley's regulation ponytail beneath my cap—over the strap, not under, like the manual says—and make sure I look presentable, because the boss will be waiting. I look ready to take tickets, not drag a mechanical trolley loaded with hundred-pound fish toward the Mad Hatter's Spinning Teacups.

I've had something like that nightmare since my mother, Silvana, was swallowed by the ocean, and my oma made her a saint, just for me. The nightmares made sense on that distant gray shore by the seawall. Here, they leave me feeling simultaneously empty and ready for a fight. And I can't fight here. I must work, or Oma's bills will pile up, and eventually crush her. So I sprint the five blocks from my cousin's basement apartment, past fading rental signs on sagging porches, to the wall of hotels punctuated by Staley's empty parking lot, and out onto the boardwalk. My skin itches as sweat drips and cools down my back.

Unlike last night, the ocean is predawn quiet, like the tide is holding its breath. Outside the amusement arcade's locked gates, the salt-rimed wood creaks beneath my weight. The stilled curve of the Tilt-A-Whirl hangs darkly overhead, blocking out the last of the stars.

"Do this once, and you're done," I whisper. The wind picks up, warping my words and sending them out to the horizon. The sun's leading edge slices ocean from sky, before the fog overtakes its glow. The lights along the boardwalk begin to turn off with soft gasps. A sucking sound tugs at my consciousness. *Just the tide going out. Definitely.*

The keypad on the gate that's been pulled across the gap between the Whac-A-Mole and ring toss stands is a wrestle; it's crusted with the breath of the sea and the last of the chill night air. I hurry, fumbling the code Alan gave me. *Before dawn.* The metal gate finally takes the code and screeches open to reveal stilled, darkened rides. The arcade smells like stale sugar and old sweat.

Leaning inside on tiptoe, my sneakers firmly planted on the boardwalk and my Saint Silvana medal cold beneath my shirt, I call to my boss. "Alan?"

Staley's by the Sea waits silently. I'm not used to the quiet; usually the Staleys play a long, looping laugh track all over the park: under the music and children's high-pitched squeals, familiar giggles and hoots rise and fall each evening like waves. With everything powered down, there's a hunger to the place that sucks the sound of my voice from the air.

Come on, Skyla. I shake my head at my own stupidity.

Puddles from the early rain seep into my knockoff Converse. The thin black canvas is going to stain my toes purple again, matching the goose bumps on my legs. The shoes and my silver Saint Silvana medal are the two things I've still got from home. Everything else—passport, work documents—are still at the Lloyds', because I was afraid.

Today, I will be brave.

The gate squeals as I pull it shut from the inside, as instructed. I shiver again. It's colder at home, I know. Here, new houses are still rising, on stilts, by the shore. On home's distant coast, my oma's apartment tower crumbles beside the seawall, the constant offshore wind helping prop the state-owned building upright, but only just. There, the ice comes early, even now, and the chill will stay. Here, the day will heat up just fine. There, the few creatures like the Midway are long gone, driven far from land by the war. Here, I'm starting to suspect, one's worked at Staley's by the Sea for an awful long time.

My fingertip brushes the warm pewter oval commemorating Silvana Going Out to Sea, and I make a wish to my highly questionable saint. "Help me see this through."

The ocean waves begin to boom as if they've been turned on by a remote switch, but Silvana doesn't answer. She never does. Alan doesn't answer either.

Oma, in an apartment by the sea, waits for me to send money home, like Mara promised I would. She knows that I'll do the right thing, that I won't disappear on her. Not like my mother. Sometimes saints are enticements to the rest of us to be good. Same as monsters.

I bounce on the balls of my feet to try and get warm. "This is miles better than working for the Lloyds," I remind myself, but don't believe. *Just feed the Midway, Skyla. Get the overtime bonus, pay back your clothes, and rent for Mara's lumpy sofa, and send something home.*

A low growl from beneath the boards reminds me: the Midway waits, hungry.

I recite the steps Alan told me last night. First: "Latch and lock the gate." *Done.* Now: "Get the boat hook and the harpoon from the beams over Skee-Ball Alley."

I heave the ladder from behind the ticket booth and haul it past the carousel to the Skee-Ball court. Salt roughs my hands and the hinge shrieks when I straighten out the ladder. But it holds steady when I climb up to push at the water-stained ceiling panel high above the Skee-Ball games' wooden troughs. I reach into the darkness until my fingers find two cold metal bars, the sharp ends wrapped in a rust-stained and torn Staley's polo. When I try to lower them slowly to the ground, they slip and clatter.

The boards below the ladder rattle, pushed from below.

"Easy." There's a wobble to my voice. "Stay calm." I'm not sure whether I'm saying this to myself or the Midway, but the noise stops. The growling doesn't.

Still no Alan. I descend the ladder slowly, struggling to remember what he'd said to do next. *Fish. Haunted house. Behind the dry ice.* Logical enough.

But I'm going too slow. The clock on the ticket booth next to the security camera says Alan is twenty minutes late. The boards rattle again.

Saint Silvana, help me. I wrack my brain. "Ready the gear and the fish before you open the boards." I can do that.

The fish, when I find them, are enormous, crammed into the extra-large walk-in freezer behind the haunted house, with just enough dry ice to keep them out of sight. Tuna, maybe. Or swordfish. Whatever they are, they're big. Enough to sate what's below the boards? I hope so. Wrapped in plastic, the fish feel cold and slick against my arms, shoulder, and cheek as I wrestle the first one onto the trolley.

I'm strong. I've been fishing another shoreline my whole life, like Oma before me. Like Silvana, before she left. I'm not small like Mara. Or skinny like Alan. Still, I struggle with these fish, alone. *How am I going to get three of them to the teacups by myself?*

A board lifts off its nails beside the haunted house. Something dark and slippery reaches. I shiver, then growl back and stomp as hard as I can. "Wait." I hope I'm doing this right.

Oma might know what I should do to see this job through. Why hadn't I asked her advice when Mara let me call yesterday morning?

Because I'd been so relieved to hear her voice. To hear her say that she was well, that the neighbors were taking care of her. That, so far, she had enough coins for her medicine meter. Because I'd been too proud to admit I'd left my last job, and the child I was supposed to mind. Too afraid to hear the ruinous "You can always come home," and to have to say that I can't, not just because I lost my passport and my ticket home.

"Don't worry, Oma," is all I'd said. And then Mara took the phone back. And I gave her a grimy dollar for the time. Mara charges me for everything.

As I heave and pull three of the huge fish onto the trolley, I realize Mara knew what Alan was going to ask me. And she still made sure she got my dollar. My uniform grows dark with sweat and grease. By the time I'm done, I've wiped my eyes so many times, my makeup's probably slid halfway down my cheeks. I'd been dumb to wear it, knowing what I had to do, but it made me feel like I was going to normal work. Besides, it was Mara's mascara, borrowed when she hadn't been home to say no.

The sun is halfway into its trek over the ocean. Light ripples against the boards, beyond Staley's by the Sea's closed gates. *Too slow. Go faster.* Next: Make sure you have the harpoon before you lift the boards.

Where did I put that?

Searching and finally shoving at the first of the fish, I spot the metal pole sticking out from a gap in the boards. I yank it free. *Careless, Skyla. You could have lost it entirely, and then had to pay that back too.*

When I shoulder the harpoon strap so that the trigger is in reach, I miss my oma so much it hurts. After I grew big enough to learn to swim, she'd showed me how to work the apartment's just-in-case harpoon, kept by the seawall, telling Saint Silvana stories all the while. "She never understood monsters, not really. They are different from us. We don't communicate in the same ways. A harpoon is good communication, Skyla. Monsters don't know anything beyond their own wants. Or that what they want may keep you from being alive. They might all be gone now, but it's good to know this anyway. Understand?"

"I understand," I whisper to the harpoon.

The ticket booth security camera clicks, and its light turns green. "You're running late, Skyla." Alan Staley's tinny voice coming from the speaker sounds very far away. "I've got the flu, so you'll have to keep going without me. Just lift the boards and stuff the fish in, like I told you."

"Yes, sir, I'll try." I shiver with cold and frustration, but I lift the boards with the hook one by one. Something helps from below, speeding my work. I bet Alan's got *Stolichnaya flu,* and Mara's probably "sick" too. *Great.*

Below the boards, where a sturdy base of sand and concrete slabs should be, pilings stretch down into liquid darkness. Stars seem to ripple between the supports. A splash echoes beneath my feet. I think I can hear the ocean.

"You have to be firm with the Midway," Staley's voice cautions from the speaker above the ticket booth. "You can't show fear. But don't worry. The thing's been pescatarian for decades now. Pops trained it like that, to keep the town officials happy. Just toss those fish down, don't look, and we're done."

When one of the stars opens wide—a giant eye—I do show fear. I can't help recoiling, thinking of my dream. The tip of a slippery tentacle breaks the dark surface and reaches—

"NO!!" I smack the water with the harpoon.

The tentacle pulls back.

"It's very well trained, Skyla. Don't be scared. Pops did it all himself. Carrot-and-stick stuff. And don't use the harpoon unless you have to." The camera's green light glows silent approval.

There's a distant rattling at the gate. I ignore it as the dark water swirls. Whoever it is, they'll go away.

But they don't.

"I lost my toy!" An insistent wail, a voice too young to be out alone this early, comes from the boardwalk.

"Leave the gate locked," Alan whispers. "Don't answer."

Had I locked the gate? I thought I had. I steel myself to silence until another tentacle reaches from the water, glittering with electric charge, like a giant eel. The arm brushes a contact pad that Pops Staley himself must have wired below the boards. The pad, one of several, has deep grooves and dents, like Pops trained the thing to grab all night, every night. When the arm curls around the pad, the laugh track starts up, suddenly, startling me. There's silence outside the gates. More thick graspers with their pus-colored suckers reach past the contacts, straight for my ankles.

"No!!!" I slap the water again with the pole. The tentacles splash and then recoil. The canned laughter stops.

The voice from outside comes again. "Skyla!"

Dammit. I can't not answer. I know that voice. *Why isn't she still in bed? Where are her parents? Doesn't she have a new nanny by now?*

The Midway is awake, there's nothing I can do about that. And Alan's not here, even though he's watching. There's just me. I roll a fish in fast and try to push the boards back, hoping that will distract it. The tentacles fight me, so I put the harpoon down to shove things into place. "Hang on, Lucille."

"Skyla, don't!" Alan whispers.

When I reach the gate, it's already open a crack. I hadn't locked it. Just dropped the latch that barely holds. Good thing I'd answered. I lean against the door with my sweat-soaked shoulder. "You have to go home, Lucille."

Lucille pushes from the other side. "My stuffie. The octopus you gave me.

I left it by the teacups." The child, an insistent bright smile beneath tight curls and a familiar blue and green tutu, slips between gate and frame and evades my grasp.

"Get back here!" The words come back to me, well-practiced, even as I lock the gate for real this time. But Lucille is four and will not get.

The security camera's light goes off. Hopefully Alan's suddenly over the flu and is speeding here now to help. Then he's definitely going to fire me.

I'm running for the teacups when I hear the splash. The deep kind. In front of the ride, the boards are up, and water laps below. Lucille is nowhere to be seen.

Fuck. I want to run away. I've left a bad situation before. This is the Staleys' problem and the Lloyds'. I'm just supposed to feed the Midway. Mara would walk away. Saint Silvana too. But I cannot.

I have to distract the Midway. I grab the tail of a plastic-wrapped fish and shove it into the water like Alan said to do. A tentacle rises toward the fish, holding a small, blue Croc sandal.

I stop thinking. Speed to the edge. Yank my own shoes off, tearing the canvas.

When the fish begins to sink, I dive in after, exactly like he didn't say to do.

Salt crackles my lips; my skin drinks it in. The cold is a shock, but I open my eyes and start to search the depths for the girl. I must work fast.

A tentacle wraps my arm. Soft. Tight. Drawing me forward. *Monsters don't know anything beyond their own wants,* Oma had said. I can barely keep from screaming as another grasps my ankle and flips me around. Struggling only makes the slick flesh wrap tighter. My skin puckers and itches where it touches the Midway.

Toys, says the Midway. I can't tell if its high-pitched voice is in my mind or a trick of the water.

I nearly do scream, but instead I press my lips tight to keep from drowning faster. I wait for the pressure to build in my chest.

Just ahead, sequins trail like bubbles, sprung from Lucille's tutu. Where is she? *Saint Silvana, please don't let her drown.* I wish this, even as I wait to drown. *Oma, I'm sorry. I didn't understand.*

Pressure builds in my ears, becoming painful, and I let out a breath. Bubbles trail up like the sequins, and don't stop. My skin pulses, flush with oxygen where the tentacles hold me, and my lungs remain filled with air. In the deep, a bubble pops near my ear and I hear the toddler, giggling.

Lucille, I shout. The water ripples. The girl keeps giggling. Another slick arm, holding the plastic-wrapped tuna, passes between me and the sequins. I grab hold with my free hand. Then I kick hard against the tentacle's grip and push the fish before me, toward the giant body of the Midway.

Here's your food. Let her go. I yell again, bubbles shaping the sounds deep in the water.

No, the Midway answers. *Mine.*

And then all the stars go out, and I cannot find which way is up, and the strong grip tightens around my ankle and pulls me, the fish, and Lucille down so fast my ears pop.

In the darkness, I hear Lucille's laughter again. For a moment, I'm back at the Lloyds' fancy beach house, in the nanny's basement room. "Just for the summer," Mara had said. "It's by the sea. It wasn't for me, but it will pay enough to help your oma."

The Lloyds' kid was sweet and very fast, the nanny's room windowless, and when Mr. Lloyd's footsteps began stopping outside my door in the darkness, late, I'd been afraid.

Oma had worried about this, even though Mara had promised no one would dare. Behind the door, I dreamt of grasping, grabbing, pulling. I'd woken wanting to fight. Growing up with a mother who might have run away to sea, or turned into a saint, but who was also definitely very gone, made me afraid: not just about monsters, but about what I might do, who I might let down, who I might become.

So I fled the Lloyds' house while they were at church. I left everything—my phone, passport—kept locked in the beach house safe, everything but my saint's medal and the clothes I was wearing, in my panic to get to the safety of Mara's apartment.

The space beneath the boards and the water is as dark as the nanny's room at the Lloyds'. But it breathes.

I can hear my heart beating. A heartbeat means I'm still alive. I want to escape, to stay that way. But Lucille.

I kick again at the darkness. An eye opens beside me in the thick, cold water. It blinks too, sun-gold and flecked red, shot round with blacks that layer deep. The water grinds and scrapes at loose shells far below as a maw opens.

No, I won't kick, I'll behave, I whisper fast. Bubbles carry my words into the darkness. The grating stops. I steel myself: Panic later. I must be strong, like Saint Silvana, and live, now.

Behave, the Midway replies. I think I hear it chuckle.

What had Alan said? That Pops Staley trained the Midway. Carrot and stick. Could I do that? How? I'd dropped the harpoon. The Midway wouldn't listen to *NO* for very long.

How much longer before Alan reaches the arcade? Before he grabs the harpoon and saves us from his dad's not-so-well-trained monster? Where the hell are the Lloyds?

Questions build up and emerge as a slow underwater sob. The red eye glares, until a bubbly giggle rises from below. The eye gentles, the Midway seems to sigh. This is not the canned laughter from the park. It's the laughter of a real child, nearby, while caught in the Midway's grip. *She's alive.*

My skin crawls as I realize the Midway's grip—which pulses and makes my skin feel like a runner's, flush with oxygen, right where the tentacle makes contact—must also be pumping life into her. Just like the creature pumps energy into Staley's by the Sea.

The Midway's silent now. I watch the eye watch me.

Though it's definitely not as well trained as Alan said, it has learned, over time, to love what we love. Toys. Us. Our happiness. Floating deep beneath the amusement park, I burst into hacking, bubbly laughter, and the Midway begins to spin with delight.

As we rotate, I spot two things swinging wildly past. One: a metal grate covering a distant pipe. Two: in the dark, the Midway's tentacles glitter with power when they brush against the walls and contact pads. The Staleys didn't so much train it as cage it, back when the Midway was much smaller.

The third thing I notice—and when I do, I bite my lip to keep myself from panicking again—is Pops Staley's trademark cowboy hat from all the billboards, wedged between two of the Midway's enormous teeth. A few bones lie scattered on the dark floor of the cage below, lit up each time we swing past.

"Hasn't eaten a kid all summer," Mara said. And yet, no one has seen Pops since he got sick. And now Alan's in charge.

No one's coming to save us. Once I think it, I can't un-think it.

The maw grates again and I look up, still panicked, right into a school of small fish swimming upside down. A tail fin smacks my cheek. It's me who is upside down. A dark tentacle reaches past my ear and I shudder while the Midway delicately picks three fish from the group, shoves them down its gullet, and chews messily.

When the maw closes, the school of silver fish shuffles itself to fill its gaps and swims out through the far-off grate. The water tastes like the sea. Through a spray of fish scales and guts, I realize these are ocean fish. *There is a way out.*

I keep myself from screaming as fish scales stick to my skin. *Panic later. Think, Skyla. What would Saint Silvana do? What would Pops have done?*

He'd trained the Midway to hold the charging pads, in return for music, sound, and food. *The Midway has food. It's ignoring the tuna in favor of the smaller fish. What does it want now?*

The Midway shifts, swinging me through the water, and I see Lucille, laughing below. Her face isn't happy, but she's laughing all the same. Lucille falls silent when she spots me.

Laugh, the Midway says. It twirls the child gently through the water, at the speed of a toddler ride. Lucille laughs.

Two arms tighten painfully around my wrist and ankle. *Laugh.*

I press my lips together tight. The red-streaked eye draws close, the tentacle on my arm squeezes tighter. *Laugh.*

I laugh again, at first a slow *ha,* and then more hysterically, hiccuping. My lungs refill with air, but painfully slow, as the Midway swings us around. The maw doesn't open. *It is pleased? It likes the sound? Did it keep Pops Staley here, laughing, until—*

I don't want to think about that.

My leg scrapes against a rough wall and I cry out. The Midway slows but doesn't release me or Lucille, even when its giant eye closes. Laughter *must* be one of the carrots the Staleys use. It's soothed, I can feel it. But why does the Midway stay?

On the next spin, I see the grate again. It's a fish weir. Bottle-shaped, meant to look closed from the tank side. Small fish don't care about the barbs and the narrow passage, but the Midway must have been here for far too long and grown too big. It's stuck.

The arms relax their grip as it sleeps. *I could slip away.* The thought comes fast, and I force myself still, so I don't wake the Midway. It's harder to think now. Less oxygen coming in makes me feel light-headed, even as an ankle still itches, flushed from a tentacle's tight hold. I feel like a prize for a monstrous child.

If the Midway loves laughter, and it's found a source that doesn't get shut off each night when the amusements close, it may never let go. Worse, if the Midway ever does release us, taking the air-giving tentacles from our skin, we'll both drown.

"Lucille." My whispered word forms bubbles that drift toward her before they rise to the surface, somewhere above my feet. Lucille looks at me, eyes wide, still slowly laughing. "Don't be scared."

I've been telling myself not to be scared, not to panic for so long, but I know better than to say that to a toddler. This one specifically. Lucille begins to wail straightaway. Enormous bubbles of fear. Being scared is all she can think of.

The Midway growls, its eye rolling red again.

"Easy now," I whisper. "This is just a ride."

"It's Not. A. Ride," the child screams. Her bubbles fill with snot and tears, then pop in my face. "I want Mommy."

The Midway's eyelid flutters. "It's a new ride." I chuckle while I speak. That seems to work. "I work here, see?" I point to my shirt. My hat's floated away.

"It's called the Silvana ride. You get to be the first to try it. Want to hear another story of Silvana?"

Lucille nods, her face a small moon in the water. I reach for a story to tell her, trying to recall the cadence of Oma's voice when she told me about the Saint. How much that calmed me after a nightmare.

"Can you help me tell it? I'll need you to laugh while I do."

Lucille is quiet for a long time. "It likes for people to laugh. It told me."

"Can you help me?"

The toddler nods her head so emphatically, her curls swirl in the water.

I shiver harder as the Midway's grip tightens again. "Once upon a time, a girl made friends with a sea monster," I begin. "Her name was Silvana, and everyone she loved had gone to fight a war. But she'd stayed home, and kept her mother and her baby safe, and when she discovered the baby sea monster, she didn't tell anyone."

I'm not sure whether this is true, but my oma had decided it was. Lucille's eyes are as big as saucers. She laughs a little when I pause, to keep me going. "More!"

"They played until the sea monster got too big, and then the people in Silvana's town were afraid of it. So Silvana told it she wanted to leave, and rode it out to sea, laughing."

Lucille laughs. The Midway's growls quiet.

How do you tell a monster what you need? Lucille and I have been laughing for hours; our throats are raw. I need to figure out a different way to communicate.

Pops Staley's hat drifts past again. Then the plastic-wrapped, thawing fish.

"Shut your eyes, Lucille," I say. I grab the fish, and slowly unwrap it.

"Why?" she asks, her words all stubborn and bubbly.

"Or don't, I guess." Something in my voice convinces Lucille to shut her eyes. Plastic wrap spools away from the fish's frozen tail.

I bite back a scream. Hysterical laughter bubbles through my teeth. I can't help myself. The fish has feet.

This is not a tuna or swordfish. It's the rest of Pops Staley.

Alan killed his dad. So no, he's definitely not going to rescue us. The half-unwrapped body, pale with tentacle marks on it, floats from my grasp. Lucille stops laughing. The Midway growls.

"Lucille, keep your eyes closed. Keep laughing."

Lucille doesn't argue now.

The water is growing darker. What time is it, exactly? Upside down, underwater, with the Midway's demands rippling around us, I can only guess it's time for Staley's by the Sea to open. Four o'clock, even on Sundays after Labor Day.

But the arcade can't open without enough power. If the Midway's holding on to too many things to grab the conductor panels, maybe Alan will have to help us, after all. I laugh, slowly, and wait. We spin through the dark water.

A boat hook pounds on the boards far above. With a click, the canned laughter starts up. I breathe relief for the first time in hours. Alan is here to fix this.

But the Midway doesn't let go. It doesn't reach for the contact pads. It doesn't want anything right now.

After a long pause, more noise: the rattling of a generator that catches and roars. *Dammit.* The smell of gasoline makes me feel ill, and I realize the scent is coming to me through the Midway's grip. The slow pulse of the haunted house and the bumper car motor shakes our limbs.

Lucille groans, then retches from the gasoline and the motion. She cannot laugh anymore. I can't reach her to comfort her. "You have to let us go; we can't survive."

The Midway extends two curious tentacles upwards, drawn by the beat. *Mine,* it whispers. I can hear it speak in my bones. I shiver, my skin as prune-cold as the water around us. What exactly had the Staleys done to this monster? What had Saint Silvana promised hers?

The generator begins to sputter, like it's running out of gas. The music above goes flat, and the gears that turn the rides slow.

"*No.*" The Midway tightens its grip on me, as it reaches for a charging pad with its nearest free arm. The generator stops entirely just as the tentacle connects to the underside of the amusements' power system. I feel the pulse of Skee-Ball and the whir of the rides on my skin, then in my bones and brain. Lucille laughs. "We're on the rides! All of them!"

And we are—the teacups, the salt and pepper shakers, the parachute, the Viking ship—all of it spinning and swaying at once. The Midway's eye begins to whirl beside me with pleasure and its grip tightens and relaxes with the pulse of the rides. *Laugh.*

The Midway hums along with the beat above. *Laugh.* The sound of the park invades my mind and I grow dizzy, while somehow Lucille and I keep up our thready *ha ha ha*s. The Midway sighs, pleased.

Above, I hear Alan arguing.

A man's voice shakes, angry. "My daughter, she slipped out and disappeared. She hadn't wanted to leave here last night. You can't open until we find her." Mr. Lloyd.

"Mommy? Daddy!" Lucille shouts. But her bubbles pop underwater. I bite down on my confusion. I still don't want to see the Lloyds, and I do.

"There's no kid matching your description on the security tape, or anywhere in the park. Your daughter's not here, sir. I've checked the whole place for her myself. And we must open. It's nearly time. You can put your poster up in the staff room. We'll keep an eye out."

I groan as Alan's voice tickles my inner ear like a spider. I can't stop laughing, but now it's more like crying. Of course he can't have people poking around. Not while the amusements are lit. Not when his father's down here too, and not coming back. The rides spin faster.

Where is Mara? If Alan's back, Mara can't be far behind. She's helping me help Oma. She'll help us. I press my pewter medal tight with my fingers. Whisper another wish. Wait for what feels like forever. But when Mara's voice comes, it's a whisper, to Alan alone. "I guess you were right to be worried it wouldn't want fish anymore, after Pops." She sounds sad.

"Yup, Dad was dead wrong about that. We'll go back to the old ways from here on out," Alan whispers back. "Last in, first eaten."

I wait for Mara to shout at him. To tell him to fix this. But instead, she chuckles. "Then we'd better hurry up and hire someone. There are more like Skyla at home."

No. I let the motion of the rides and the hysteria of my laughter take me for a moment, as the Midway spins, until I am sick with dread and loathing. Everything Mara said was lies. She's happy to sacrifice everyone else if it means she gets to survive.

But that's not what Oma would do. She stayed with me, and I won't let her down. And I won't let Lucille down either. She deserves a chance. I force myself calm again, even as the Midway spins faster. Send a bubble the toddler's way. "We're going to get you out, I promise."

The noise from Staley's by the Sea above us increases. Alan has succeeded in opening the park, despite the Lloyds' protests. I can hear happy laughter and shrieks. The spinning teacups grind their circuits just overhead, churning the water to thunder. Attendants at the haunted house and the bumper cars begin to go through their patter. "Three tickets, one ride, two people per car, keep your hands inside at all times. Miss, you'll need to finish that drink. No, I'm sorry, you're too small."

The Midway grips the charging panels. Its nearest eye is closed, like it's listening to music. And Lucille and I drift in its clasp, slowly becoming lightheaded again. Lucille's whispering *Mommy,* in between laughs.

How do you talk to a Midway? Or a child?

Saint Silvana, the night you and your sea monster disappeared, what did you do? Did you and Oma fight? Did you run away? Or did you do something braver?

With the last energy I have, I push at the tentacle wrapped around my wrist and it slips off. I swing loose, still caught by the ankle. The Midway's spun us close to the bars and the fish-trap grate, and the tunnel dug deep into the shoreline. The water's much saltier here. As I drift upside down past the grate, I imagine stars sparkling in the distance, over real ocean waves. A way out.

Is it possible? How far, and how fast, can I swim?

Below, in a swirl of sequins and tired, flat giggles, Lucille begins to tug her own foot loose, just like I did.

"No, Lucille, you'll drown."

"I want Mommy," she replies. She's not laughing now.

I can't leave her here. I drag at the tentacle holding my ankle, and it slips. I swim closer to the toddler. "Hold your breath, okay? Let's go find your stuffed octopus."

She, still in the grip of the Midway, holds her breath. Her cheeks balloon pale in the water.

"When I say ready, you have to kick as hard as you can. Okay?"

She nods.

"Ready!" I yank my ankle loose and grab her small hand, pulling her from the Midway's grip. The creature clings to the contact pads, then slowly twitches its emptied tentacles, and reaches for us again.

I'm already starting to run out of air, to sink. My Saint Silvana medal floats and glints in the light. No running away. I kick hard and Lucille kicks too and we find the loose board by the haunted house, the one where a sliver of light has slipped through. There's a gap between the water and the wood there, and we breathe and gasp in the stale-sugar air.

"Hold tight to my shoulders," I whisper, making sure Lucille's got a good grip on me, and then I push hard at the boards. One lifts a little more. "Your octopus toy, it's by the teacups," I say as I kick and push, and she scrambles over me and squeezes through the opening. I shove her up into the bustle above. Her breath wobbles. "Mommy!" When there's no reply, she sits down hard, wailing, and the boards slam shut.

The light disappears, and I'm treading water, my chin just above the waterline, hoping someone will lift the child away. Take her to safety. Let me out.

The Midway grabs my leg mid-kick and yanks me under again. Pulls me back toward the giant eye. Its enormous mouth opens. *Mine,* it whispers. *Staley promised.*

Lucille! I hear the woman's voice through the Midway's contact. The little girl cries and a wave of relief mixes with the push of the Midway's hunger. She's free.

The need I felt through my feet while I worked the amusement arcade presses all around me. So much *want*. Now I panic only for me. *Time to feed*. There's no one left to save, nowhere to go, but I keep trying to fight. I flail and kick, then grab the bars of the grate and try to pull myself through, scraping skin and yanking at the leg the Midway's grabbed. More tentacles reach for me.

I can't make it. I know I'm not going to. My shoulder's stuck. I'm running out of air. And then I slip through, howling at the pain of the rough iron. I won't be like Pops Staley. I won't die laughing here. I yank and scrabble for a handhold on the barnacle-encrusted side of the pipe with my fingers. The sharp shells cut my skin and the water tastes of blood, but I hold fast. I pull harder, against my still-caught leg, as the Midway's teeth close over the bars. There's a dull clang as bone hits metal, but it's missed me. I pull myself farther away.

The Midway screams in frustration, splitting pain against my ears, and then the water goes completely black and silent as the kraken disconnects from the amusements above. It grabs me tighter. It won't let go this time; I know that now. Its thoughts wrap around me: *Mine*.

When the boards lift again, Alan calls down to us. I can hear his voice ripple through the water, the way the Midway hears it.

"You useless, antiquated thing!" he yells. "You cost more to keep fed and entertained than you're worth. I had to send everyone home! Do you know what that means? No more rewards for you!" He lifts the harpoon.

"This time don't miss and make me help you pull half a body out," Mara whispers. "If this makes the news, my oma's neighbors may stop wiring me money to keep an eye on her."

Alan chuckles, "You're hot when you talk money." And he steps back, taking a deep drag on his cigarette. Turns on the security camera. "Let's make it look good then."

And Mara reaches an arm into the water, shouting, "Skyla! Can you hear me? Grab hold, Cousin, I'll get you out of there!"

I admit, I consider it for a minute. Her pale fingers dangling far above. Her offer of help. The kind I don't need anymore.

The Midway, with most of its arms stuck through the bars of the intake pipe, senses what I want. It reaches back, fast as a whip, and pulls Mara into the water by her ankle.

Distracted by Mara's thrashing and kicking, the Midway's frustration floods my mind. It isn't at all ready for Alan's first shot with the harpoon. But Alan's not ready either. The shock of metal-pierced water enrages us, even as the barb goes wide, hitting Mara. It pulls her from the Midway's grip and pins her to the floor of the tank. She doesn't make another sound. Her feet twitch, pale in the shadows. We hear Alan's "oof" as he falls back, hard, on the boards.

A tentacle peels Mara off the harpoon. Gently it whirls her, limp and bloodied, through the water. *Laugh*. It waits. Then again. *Laugh?*

Mara does not laugh; her stare is fixed, her jaw slack. The Midway's mouth grinds open, and its arm tucks her head and shoulders neatly between giant teeth. I feel the grind, the chew. The damping of hunger. The Midway's mouth makes terrible sounds. *More*, it says, swallowing, as the rest of Mara rises to the surface, leaving a trail of red bubbles.

From the blood-muddled water, the Midway reaches for Alan next. I laugh, trying to get its attention. I think about what I want, and what the Midway wants, and weave both feelings together. Maybe a common enemy is a good point of communication.

"Mean," I say, thinking hard about Pops Staley, and Alan too.

Mean, the Midway agrees. *Sharp.*

I think about how terrible Alan would taste, with his cigarettes, his wiry voice. Bile rises in my throat, but I laugh harder. At the sound of Alan trying to reload the harpoon. At the thought of him explaining more missing staff, and Lucille's story, to Mr. Lloyd, to the police. I begin to laugh hysterically and the Midway laughs too. There's more than one way to escape.

I pull myself painfully backwards, tucking one knee to my chest and yanking at my caught ankle as best I can. The Midway mimics me, folding itself smaller in pursuit. Arms scraping against barnacles, eyes closed, it squeezes close to the fish trap's opening and, bulging and wriggling, compresses and begins to slip through. The monster has obviously not tried this in a long time, because it nearly lets me go in surprise when its biggest section emerges on the other side.

Then the Midway laughs—a delighted, high-pitched scree from the laugh track—and tries to reel me in. But now I can see the end of the pipe, and the moonlight above the waves, and I'm starting to see stars on the periphery of my vision. Maybe a monster is kind of like a saint. You can wish on them, and they might answer, they might not. As I wish for a ride home, I can hear the Midway humming happily in my head: music from the carousel.

There's no more hunger. The Midway's curious. About me, about the ocean beyond the pipe. That's dangerous too, but in a different way.

"You can do it," I laugh. I lure the Midway to me, and back to the ocean. I think hard about the sea, and distant shorelines, where they might need a monster. There's nothing left for us in the arcade above, and we're ready to go.

At the end of the pipe, the Midway overtakes me, and then we're racing through the water, toward the depths. I start laughing for real and the Midway laughs with me. We surface once, far from the beach. The coastline glitters around a pitch-black gap at Staley's by the Sea.

In the moonlight, my Saint Silvana medal gleams, and I'm giddy with the idea of home. Or perhaps that's the Midway. We've gotten so I cannot tell our thoughts apart.

WET RED GRIN

by Gemma Files

Imagine a lady, old as dirt. Kind of old where there don't seem to be much left of her but bones, wrapped in a loose, wrinkly bag of skin. Cataracts on her slitty blue eyes, so thick they make 'em throw back light; she stinks of vinegar and baby powder, adult diaper rash and Clorox bleach. Goes without saying she's white, too, but I will anyhow, just to set the scene.

Chart down the bottom of her bed says CAMP, MRS. WILLENA, plus a bunch of meds and a few more diagnoses—DEGENERATIVE DEMENTIA; ALZHEIMER'S DISEASE. And on the *very* last line, there's this, just in case: HAS SIGNED A DNR.

Most old ladies, they got yellow teeth, stained from years of smoking, coffee; some got off-white or ivory, meaning they come out at the end of the day, go in a cup and get cleaned with Polident if you're well provided for, baking soda if not. Dip and no insurance gives you brown teeth, or black, or none. Mrs. Camp, though—she had something different, something I never saw before or since. Bitch was closemouthed in general, had a scowl on her, like knotted purse strings. But sometimes . . .

. . . sometimes, Mrs. Camp, she let slip with a kind of wet, red grin, 'specially if she thought you weren't looking. Thin in the lips but with way too many teeth for comfort, all dyed dark as stewed beetroot somehow, and crooked with it, too. That's how I first knew she was a wrong 'un.

My mawmaw knew conjure, grew up with it. And my auntie Fee grew up with *her,* so she knew it, too—maybe not as much, but enough.

So: "What makes somebody's smile that shade?" I asked her, one day, as we sat in her room down the end of the DNR unit. "It don't seem natural."

Auntie Fee laughed a bit, just a bare hissing sketch of the way she used to, and blew a little smoke out through her tracheotomy scar; janitors'd been good enough to unplug the fire alarms in that part of the Home a while back, 'cause when you got Covid and you're upwards of eighty, who the hell cares?

"Ain't much natural 'bout *that* one," she whispered, and I nodded. "But them choppers of hers . . . they 'mind me of something your mawmaw used to mention, back when. You ever hear of reddening the bones?"

"Never."

"Well, you go home and look it up on that Google of yours, Lainey. Thing knows more'n I've forgot, or so I hear."

Didn't have the internet at home, so I went to McDonald's instead. Google showed me pictures of graves from Paleolithic times, skeletons dyed with ochre and madder root, sprinkled with the dust of ground-up rowan-tree berries. The idea was to bring vitality back by colouring them the same shade as blood, so you could consult with your elders if things got bad enough—uncover 'em and ask 'em for advice, same way you would've back when they were alive. Found a couple of sites said you could make totems by cleaning roadkill, disarticulating the skeleton and boiling it, then stewing beetroot mush, red wine, and red chalk dust to make a paste with it. You mixed it with your own blood to "feed" 'em, then rubbed the bones all over, buried them, dug 'em back up when the moon was dark, and washed the paste back off: Hey presto, nice and red.

"So you think she's a conjure lady?" I asked Auntie Fee, the next morning. She stared at me sideways like she didn't remember a thing about it, which maybe she didn't. "Or used to be, I guess."

"Who?"

"Mrs. Camp, Fee."

"Oh, *her*. Hm, wouldn't put it past her; sure is haughty enough, not that she's got any good reason to be, these days. Now she's stuck in here waitin' to die with the rest of us, I mean."

"True enough, I guess. How would a person go 'bout reddening their *own* bones, though?"

"Oh child, how would *I* know? Pass me another one of them cigarettes, 'fore that other nurse comes in."

It was Covid times, two years on. Got a job in Dawson's Care Home, mainly to check up on Auntie, and 'cause they were short-staffed enough they sort of stopped remembering to check up on whether or not a person had the exact kinda experience they claimed they had, on their résumé. Though from my point of view, wasn't like I *lied* to 'em, exactly; was halfway through my paramedic training when they slapped me up in Mennenvale Female for a five-year bid, and I probably spent at least three-quarters of that playing trusty in medical, drug bust or no drug bust. Kept my head down the whole while to rack up good behaviour, and they needed people already knew where to stick a needle wouldn't kill a bitch outright, so old Doc Rutina didn't have to fuck around with anything entrance-level while they were bringing in somebody with a shank between their ribs.

Anyhow. Doc's character testimony came in handy later on, when the M-vale board had to figure out if it was worth letting me out on compassionate after my mother passed—Second Wave was all over that place already, 'specially in gen pop, so they decided what the hell. Kind of hilarious in hindsight, considering I hadn't seen that sorry whore since she dropped me off at Maw-maw's and skedaddled, back when I was five.

Guess Mawmaw must've had enough of men altogether by the time she hit fifty, so she took up with Auntie Fee instead, her best friend since childhood. They raised me up both together, sharin' a truck, a house and a bed 'til Maw-maw got cancer and Fee nursed her through everything after—two surgeries, two courses of radiation, three trips to the hospital that all but cleaned 'em out, broke 'em so bad I had to give Fee my tuition just to keep the bank from evicting her after she paid for Mawmaw's funeral. *No baby, that's so you do better'n either of us* is what she told me, with tears in her eyes; and *Naw, Fee, I'll be just fine* was what I told her, folding it back into her hand.

Well, what else was I gonna say?

But I was out of M-vale now, just like Auntie Fee was in Dawson's, penned up with Mrs. Camp and the rest of them wheezing biddies on the DNR unit. She needed me, same way I needed that job—bad enough to lie for, or obfuscate, at least. Didn't know just *how* bad, though, not back then.

Not as yet.

Dawson's was a bleak place, overall—worse than M-vale's infirmary by far, and that was saying something. Didn't help they were sticking to no family visits, or all the staff went double-masked, hair-netted and gloved-up like they was treating Ebola, smiles hid behind face shields we had to disinfect thirty times a day. Some nurses wore those clear plastic glasses underneath, like dental hygienists; janitors and us newbies, we mainly got by with dollar-store swim goggles and wraparound sunglasses, if that. Nobody wanted to get too close, on either side.

Auntie Fee was fast asleep when I came in her room that first time. They'd took her wig off and hid it somewhere, her face gone all white and slack under a mess of baby-fine hair; had to take her pulse and study her breath awhile, to convince myself she wasn't dead already.

Eventually, she cracked one eye open. "Hello, ma'am," I said, at last. "I'm new 'round here, thought we should probably get acquainted. My name is—"

She stirred and snuffled a bit, grimaced, then went off in a surprise coughing fit once she recognized my voice. "Lainey, child, that you?" she managed, finally. "Gal, I thought you still had . . . six months to go, last I checked. What-all you doin' up in *here,* for Christ's own sake?"

At that I gave a quick look 'round, just in case anybody else might be bothered to listen in. "Well, now," I told her, quietly, "Jesus can look after himself, if the Bible's anything to go by. Bad bitches like us, though—times like this, we got no choice but to look after each other."

That got her eyes all bright again, thank God, even under those too-thin, bleared-up lids. "You go on and speak for yourself, Elaine Ann Merrimay," she hissed at me. "And wash your damn mouth out, too, while you're at it."

"Yes, ma'am," I replied, smiling, under my mask. One thing a job like mine teaches is that people say all sorts of things when they're dying. It's like the process breaks something open inside them, some long-buried infectious reservoir, a quick-draining sick-pocket. They don't even have to know what's happening, let alone accept it; might still be entirely convinced they'll survive, but it doesn't matter. A sort of punch-drunkenness takes over, when it comes home that the walls around 'em are probably the ones they're gonna die inside; not despair, exactly, just a kind of stillness, a waiting. The ones without that look, they were either new, or checked out completely: dementia, psychosis, amnesia, catatonia.

Mrs. Camp wasn't any of that, though, whatever it said on her chart. Didn't know what she had goin' on inside her, either, any more than what she might've done to make her teeth so red . . . but it made me shiver.

The night nurse, Ke'Von, said she liked to tuck cutlery up her sleeve and sneak it back to her room, which was creepy, even if she never cut anybody with it but herself. For all her bag-of-bones gauntness, she moved on her own, not fast but steady; never needed hearing aids or glasses, either. Sometimes I saw her whispering to other residents, right close up in the ear—one day I had to take her back to her room when I saw the lady she'd been talking to was crying, but Mrs. Camp wouldn't tell what she'd been saying, and the other one just blubbered, lying how she couldn't remember. One way or the other, that same lady died a day or so later, which wasn't exactly a surprise. Didn't like how Mrs. Camp grinned as they wheeled her body past, though.

About a week later, I swapped shifts with Ke'Von, 'cause his boyfriend was sick of 'em only ever meeting up over breakfast. Not like I had anybody at home, and besides . . . I sort of wanted to know what went on at Dawson's every night, 'specially in Mrs. Camp's room.

"That bitch is odd with a capital 'O,'" Ke'Von agreed, when I asked him how she seemed, from his angle. "You know she cuts herself, right? All over, where she thinks nobody's gonna see?"

"Yeah, 'Von, I know—with the cutlery."

"Okay, sure . . . but did I tell you *what* she cuts on herself?" I shook my head, folding another towel. "Looks like words, but not in any language *I* ever saw. No, seriously—took a snap while she was asleep one time, ran it through a bunch of translation apps. That shit ain't even Cyrillic, sis."

"What's it look like?"

"Um . . . Arabic, maybe, with a little Pinyin thrown in on top, but like if worms wrote it underneath a tree's bark, or some shit. And you *know* I know what I'm talkin' about, so don't give me that stink eye, either."

"Yeah, yeah. You higher-education-havin' motherfucker, you."

He struck a pose, like he was rolling his Languages degree out for all and sundry to admire. After which we both smirked at each other, high-fived, blew each other a kiss and got the fuck back to work.

Soon enough, I was walking in on Mrs. Camp herself. I knew she'd seen me; caught the eye-flicker, even if she didn't react as I went through the routine spiel: *How're-we-today-time-for-your-sponge-bath,* and the rest. I was the one lost my place, shocked still, when I slid her robe down her shoulders. On her front from breastbone to waist and all down both arms, not to mention the tops of her thighs and inside both her legs, her skin was scar-etched with signs like vévés or alchemy, all woven together in a sagging web—some red, some pink, some white as sin. Must've taken all her life to make. And looking at it . . . maybe it was the way the wrinkles bent those scars out of shape, but just for a second, the whole of it made my guts twist, and my head hurt.

Then she looked over her shoulder at me, and grinned, like she was ready to bite a chunk out of my arm, right there. Don't mind admitting it, I jumped. She laughed.

"Be careful when you put your hand under the pillow, dear," she told me, like it was a secret. For the first time, I heard her accent—Kiwi, maybe, or South African; *kayuh-ful, hend, pillah, deah.* "Sometimes there are *things* under there. And they might not always let you go."

The fuck? I thought. But: "Thanks for the warning, ma'am" was all I replied. To which she simply chuckled, then looked away as I sponged her down, stripped the mattress, checked for night-sweat and other fluids. No need to clean the rubber covers, thank God—Ke'Von was good about that, not like some—but I still had to check, which meant steering her to a chair while the air finished drying her. Which was harder than it'd been a minute ago. I couldn't get my hands near her without the skin on my arms trying to yank itself away.

It got a bit easier once I'd helped her dress, and she didn't look at me again, either, which also helped, so I sighed to myself slightly when it was all done. Almost made it out the door, too, before I heard her mutter something.

"Sorry, Mrs. C.—what's that?"

"I *said,* 'You and Miss Fiona over there have a bit of a bond there, don't you?'" She nodded toward Fee's room, thin lips twitching. "Oh, not by blood, I mean; can't smell *that* on you, not quite. But something, nevertheless." That grin blooming back out, even as I tried my best not to look. "A certain care, on both sides. It's very—'sweet' would be the word, I suppose."

"Think you got me confused, ma'am. Maybe it's just 'cause Miss Fiona and me, we're . . . from the same stock."

"Why, what a way to put it, Nurse Merrimay! Sounds positively archaic."

"Not sure what-all you mean by that, ma'am."

"Really? You surprise me."

High-nosed, gutter-minded bitch. I couldn't stop myself from shaping back inside my jaws, where nobody should've been able to see—or hear—it. Her head whipped around, though, like I'd said it out loud. And she just smiled the more, 'til I felt like I was going to puke with it.

Vinegar in my eyes, prickling at 'em; vinegar in my nose, making it itch, making me want to sneeze and retch at the same time. Shouldn't have been able to smell her breath, but I could—it was rank with meat, and peat. Dead vegetable matter. A bog-stink, hot like a breeze from hell.

And then she looked away, suddenly, blinking at the window—the way people do, they got what she's got. They disconnect. Needle skips in the brain, and they're somewhere else. Somewhen.

"Suboptimal conditions," she said, abruptly, scowling up at the dark sky outside. "Oh, I should have prepared better. Why is there never enough time?"

Since I didn't think she even knew I was here anymore, I could pretend like I hadn't heard. Never any good answer to that question, anyway.

Last time I ever saw her, alive. But not the last time I ever saw her.

It shouldn't've been me who found her; wouldn't've been, Ke'Von's man-at-home hadn't gotten a positive test result that sent 'Von off to line up for most of the day before to get *his* ass tested. But he did, and whoever covered 'Von's shift did the usual half-assed job, probably just knocking on Mrs. Camp's door and moving on when nobody answered.

Between paramedic training and M-vale, I've seen my share of the shit people can do to each other, and I can handle it—mostly. That room, though; that night. It's the only thing that's showed up in my nightmares, since.

I remember walking in, flipping the light and thinking, *Shit, who painted the place red?* Then my foot went out from under me and I went down, *splat*, in a cold, viscous puddle; scrambled back to my feet, wiping myself down, swearing. Wasn't 'til I saw the limp, shredded thing all over the bed and realised how the stuff dripping off me was blood that I punched the alarm and swore even harder, if only so's I wouldn't start screaming.

The worst part was how I could still make out Mrs. Camp's scars on the torn remains of her skin, surrounded by a spill of deflating organs. They made weird channels for the blood leaking everywhere, guiding it into patterns on patterns on patterns, a whole new design.

Doc Dawson and a couple of orderlies came running, took over, set me aside to wait for the cops. I remember Dawson himself wrapping a blanket 'round my shoulders and saying, quietly: *Sorry, Elaine, can't let you wash 'til the CSIs say it's okay.* Poor little Nurse Sarah, who thought she could handle anything just 'cause she'd bagged upwards of fifty patients when the ventilators wouldn't give 'em enough oxygen and gotten quick enough at slipping a bronchoscopy tube down the throat to clear the lungs of gunk, she just about tore out of the building, wailing—never saw her again. And that one detective, a lady, saying: *No one saying* you *did this, Miss Merrimay, though if you did have to remove all the bones from a body, you'd know how, right?* Not to mention the residents and the rest of the staff alike, rubbernecking over the yellow tape like this was hands down the most interesting shit ever happened to them.

Dawson drove me home, afterwards. "Might want to think about preparing for the worst, Elaine," he told me, at my door. "I mean, I'll do my absolute best to avoid the topic . . . but if the police happen to ask me why I hired an uncertified ex-con on compassionate parole as a nurse, I'm going to have to tell them we had no idea you falsified your résumé, so we're letting you go; you understand. Just can't afford to keep the Home operating if we lose our liability insurance."

So he knew the whole time, obviously. Asshole.

"I get it," I said, finally. "Thanks for that, Doc. G'night." And closed the door on him, right in his face. Then I took a hot shower, burned my scrubs in the sink and passed out.

Last thing I remember is wondering just what the fuck *did* happen to old Mrs. Camp's bones, let alone the rest of her.

I took the day off, then switched with 'Von again for the night shift, 'cause I felt like I really might as well rack up as much time with Auntie Fee and money as I could, considering. Helped I actually kind of liked the hands-on work—reading a chart all the way through, getting the routine and the meds down, trying to catch issues might've got skipped over . . . like solving a puzzle, in a way.

So when I opened the door to a resident's room I'd never visited before, the bloated size of the woman in bed didn't throw me any, or the restraints— she was another dementia case, prone to wandering, and people on permanent rest get heavy. The faint sour stink in the air was . . . familiar, somehow, though I knew I didn't know the name: AZZARELLO, MRS. JOY, 8/10/41. Then I read further enough something *did* hit me wrong, and frowned. *The fuck?* I mouthed.

"Language, dear," croaked the woman in the bed, without opening her eyes.

I froze. "'Scuse me, ma'am?" I asked, after a moment.

"Oh, sorry." Mrs. Azzarello gave a close-lipped smile, eyes crinkling open. "That's what I have to tell my grandkids, when they visit. Shocking how young folks talk these days, isn't it?" She took a deep breath, looking around, like she'd never seen her own room before. "Still, shouldn't complain. It's a miracle just to be alive, on a beautiful night like this."

"Guess so." My brain did the thing brains are supposed to do, telling me: *'Course you thought she sounded like Mrs. Camp—you were thinking about Camp and she said something Camp used to say, 'cause most folk her age say the same things, sooner or later.* "Mrs. Azzarello—"

"Call me Joy, dear. And I'll call you Elaine."

But my first name's not on my badge, I thought.

"Um—sure. Well, Joy . . . don't remember the last time we updated your chart, do you? Offhand."

Those eyes of hers flickered, and though my brain still had no idea what was going on—wouldn't admit anything *was* going on, for fear it might make it true—my nerves and my guts, they knew.

"Oh, I don't pay attention to all that," she said. "That's what my family pays for, don't they? Elaine."

And she grinned at me: Wet. Toothy. Red.

Dark brown red, like peat. Like meat.

Hello, Mrs. Camp.

Made myself smile after that, say some happy nurse-y bullshit—I don't re-member. It was straight-up reflex, taking over. Meanwhile, I checked the chart again.

Wt Admit: 104 lb 7 oz / 47.732 kg, I read on Mrs. Azzarello's chart, doing my level best to look dumb as paint. *Wt Last: 99 lb 14 oz / 45.303 kg.*

The words kept on repeating in my head, while I strained and grunted her puffy, malformed body upright for a sponge-down; couldn't be less than two hundred pounds, now. Close to her, that vinegary stink was worse, the skin drum-tight, full of weird protrusions and hardnesses. Her round, weirdly cheerful face had marks all down the cheeks and forehead: faint, wavery, pur-ple. Bruises from the inside, spread out thin and long as cellulite, tapering into scars.

Stretch marks, I thought, numbly. *Fuckin' stretch marks.*

"See you later, ma'am," I sang out as I opened up that door again, glancing back. She grinned at me again, even wider.

"Do say hello to Miss Fiona for me, dear," she said.

(*Deah.*)

I slammed the door, ran down the hall and barely made it to the john.

"What would be the point of reddening your own bones?" I asked Auntie Fee, a few days later. Didn't necessarily expect her to answer, but she did—it was a good day for her, least in *that* way.

"Your mawmaw would've said the *point* was to keep on living," she told me, whispering, wheezing. "The soft parts go, but the hard parts survive. Bone has a long memory, you know, longer by far than flesh. Think about all them old kinds of human beings they're always finding in caves and such—all that information they can get ahold of now, and from nothin' more than a bunch of dust. They can boil it down, tell you exactly what that person might've looked like when they were alive . . ."

"That's from DNA, Auntie Fee."

"Sure, but where-all does DNA live, exactly? In the bone, the marrow. In the smallest of all small things, just like God willed it to do."

I moistened my lips. "Auntie Fee, you ever notice how Mrs. Camp used to smell like vinegar?"

She snorted. "Hardly coulda missed it."

"Well . . . Mrs. Azzarello, she smells like that, too, now. Why you think that is?"

"Oh, Lainey. And I thought you were so smart." She chuckled. "Need a *lot* of vinegar to make your bones soft, red or not. That's so's you can slip 'em out through the mouth and into the skin of the next person you want to pretend you are. Break out of this whole waiting-to-die nuthouse in stages, one dead old lady at a time."

Granted, she said it like she couldn't imagine it being anything but a joke. And yet.

After my shift, I went surfing on my phone, reading about things like the *penanggalan,* the *kephn,* the *obayifo, adze,* and the *loogaroo,* who leave their skins behind to go hunting as floating sacks of organs or balls of fire, fireflies even, soaking their guts in vinegar-tubs to shrink 'em back down for reentry. Then I ordered some stuff off of Amazon, splurging on next-day delivery. And finally, I called Prisha, who'd be on the front desk by now, and handled a lot of the admin. She cheerfully filled me in, without even asking why I needed to know.

Maybe people 'round here could stand to ask a few more questions, every once in a while, I thought.

Mrs. Azzarello hadn't talked, though she made a point of grinning whenever no one else was by, teeth like an open gash. All the mysterious bloat she'd suffered was shrinking away fast, leaving her gaunt as before, or gaunter. The orderlies didn't think she'd last much longer, offered me a chance to get in on the betting pool. I declined, but asked 'em to do me a favour: Could they put this Love U Grandma teddy bear in Mrs. A.'s room for me? Somewhere she can see it, and it's facing her; even if she don't remember who it's from, it'll make her happy. They agreed.

Nannycams in those bears don't send a signal very far, but Ke'Von's boyfriend was one of those IT geeks builds fiber-optic networks for fun; he set up an app under my user ID on the Home's network that picked up the cam signal via Bluetooth, so I could log in from my phone to watch it.

This is federal-level privacy violation, he warned me, in a text. Easy to find if admin goes looking. U sure u need to do this???

Yup, I texted back.

¯_(ツ)_/¯ was his only reply.

Traded shifts with Ke'Von again, which pissed him off 'til I made him promise not to go into Mrs. Azzarello's room, and to stay off that corridor as much as he could—then he got all interested. So I said I'd show him what I came up with, once I had it. "Bitch, you better," he told me; *Might be you think again if it's what I think it's gonna be,* I thought, but didn't say.

Tried to stay up and watch, but I fell asleep two hours in and yawned all next day, so I switched to skimming through each night's video on my break the next morning, deleting it if nothing happened. And four days later, I got my proof.

"Well, technically Mrs. Camp's file's still private" was what Prisha had told me, when I called. "But there's no next-of-kin listed and she's *super* deceased, so—what'd you want to know?"

"Oh, just where she came from, who she was. Stuff like that."

"Well, says here she was born in Rhodesia, this place that used to be next to South Africa; trained as an anthropologist, wrote a lot about various Indigenous folk religions. Oh, and her husband was in Doctors Without Borders, just like Dr. Dawson—a lot younger than her, too, when they hooked up. Doesn't say how he died, just it was a few years ago, and . . ." She paused. ". . . uh, maybe I shouldn't get into this, but—hell, the bank records are right there."

"What?"

"Turns out, Mrs. Camp had her a *lot* of money set aside. Like, not to be shitty about it, but enough to afford a *much* better home than here. Huh." I could almost hear her shrug. "Could be she was being nice to Dr. Dawson, since him and her husband were friends? I guess?"

"Guess we'll never know," I said, and hung up.

Okay, so . . . what I saw on that file was bad. Worse than. Like the first time I got beat up so awful I didn't recognize myself, after. Like that other time I woke up bleeding, hurting from north to south *down there,* and couldn't remember anything about it—just laughing at some shitty country bar, things getting dimmer, getting small, flicking off. Like that one night in M-vale I heard someone bumping against the wall over and over, moaning, and I banged back 'cause I thought they were enjoying themselves just a little too much—but in the morning Guard Winslow went in to find out why they weren't lined up for count, only to discover someone'd fucked 'em to death with a hammered-out bolt from the kitchen stove fan hood.

No sound or color, thankfully, but the nannycam had an infrared setting, and didn't need light to see: grainy black and white, except reading white for various shades of gray, and what have you.

It starts with Mrs. Azzarello in bed, slack, barely seeming to breathe. A rattle deep in her chest. Then she spasms, jolting back and forth, like somebody with an invisible set of defib panels is trying to revive her: mouth open wide, arms whipping. Black mist abruptly sprays, falling to darken the sheets, painting scattershot patterns over floor and walls.

The body writhes, twisting. It opens its mouth again, wider, wider. More mist sprays from splitting skin. The head twists and twists again, corkscrewing itself upwards. The hair parts, shows what must be skull. The gray bedsheets have gone almost completely black; great splotches drip down, soaking the mattress. And something sharp-edged, black as the blood it's shed, rips free, reaching upwards. I catch gleams off slick tendons, peeling away like string cheese; at the end of fleshless fingers, somehow still strung and reaching, dim nails shine.

The rest of the skin tears away with ease, like it's already rotten. Both hands pop back the scalp, shred and shed the upper body from skull to thighs; knees and feet kick free of the bottom half, like a pair of crotch-ripped pants. Organs spill out the rib cage as the thing inside curls back, clambers into a crouch, crawls to the end of the bed, and sits there waiting, a cat on the lookout for prey. Can't listen, 'cause it's got no ears; can't *see,* not with those empty sockets. Doesn't seem to matter worth a damn, though, on either point.

Then something blurs and jerks, almost too fast to register—it's down on the floor all of a sudden, spider-crawling, limbs bent back and unnaturally high. *Scuttling,* to the door, and through it. And just before the light outside blots out the camera's IR vision, you see how it's nothing but bones, and all its bones are black.

But in color, you just *know,* there's no way they'd be anything but red.

Knowing what to expect when I walked into Mrs. Azzarello's room the next morning didn't make it any easier, 'specially the part about how once I hit the alarm, I'd inevitably end up in a room with that same lady cop asking me what I thought the odds were on the same person finding this kind of mess twice in a row. Not to mention why I hadn't seen fit to tell anybody, last time, how I was not only a former adoptive ward of one of the patients, but a former resident of M-vale.

"'Cause I knew the whole place'd get shut down, if I did," I said, bluntly. "You tell *me* what's more important—fucking my life up even more and gettin' my auntie thrown out on the street, or figurin' out who did this. And *how.*"

That got her to blink. Cops don't like admitting they don't know something, but the smarter ones don't like lying, either; getting caught at it wrecks cases, makes the whole job harder. In the end, she just told me they might come back to me on the topic, so don't skip town—best I could've hoped for, really. Fuck your worst-case scenario, Dr. Dawson.

When it was finally over, I cornered Ke'Von at the end of his shift and dragged him out to my car. He didn't want to come—was already freaking out over having been grilled by the cops for the second time in a month—but I insisted. "Got something to show you," I told him, and cued up the recording.

"The fuck's that," he asked, afterwards, a lot more toneless than that reads. More like: *The fuck. Is that.*

"Mrs. Camp," I answered. "Them weird-ass bones of hers, anyways."

Never seen a guy that big make a face like that before, and I don't hope to ever again, if I'm lucky.

"Lainey, no," he said, finally, kind of pleading, like he thought I could do anything about it. "I mean . . . c'mon now, *no.* That is some seriously ill sort of bullshit, right there. That just . . . can't happen."

"Well, I kind of think it *can,* 'Von," I pointed out, "if only 'cause we both of us just *watched* it happen, in real time. Shouldn't, I do agree with you on that one, for sure. But . . ."

He nodded. "You could've faked this, though, somehow, right? For—a joke, or a prank, or whatever. A . . . sick, *sick* . . . joke."

Now, that did get me annoyed, just a tad. "Seriously? If I *did,* your boyfriend must've been in on it, 'cause everything I know about computers could fit in a fuckin' Dixie cup. Who you think helped me set up this shit, in the first place?"

"Aw, man." He thought about it for a minute, and I watched emotions chase each other over his face. "Okay, so—ugh, Christ. So. What do we do about it?"

I had to think. I mean . . . conjury, at least according to what I'd heard, didn't truck too much with stopping things. It was more all about rerouting what was already happening, turning it toward or away from the people you wanted to hurt or to keep safe. There was always this sense that motion made for more motion, that the world followed a set of laws mostly based on energy and nothing ever really came to an *end*, as such. But then again—I ain't my mawmaw, nor yet my auntie Fee, and some things are just bad, rotten, inexplicably so; need to be done away with, or close as makes no never-mind. Just like some people do things that put 'em beyond the pale forever, making it so there's no forgiveness for them, just regret and penitence at best, eternal exclusion from being trustworthy-'til-proven-otherwise at worst.

"I think we gotta kill it," I told Ke'Von. "Break it down real small, burn it and piss on the ashes, bury it out in the goddamn desert . . . something like that, anyways. So it can't do something like *that* anymore, to anyone."

"Suits me. Can we, though? I mean—that's fuckin' *magic*, right there."

Well, he wasn't wrong.

"We can try," I offered, which was all I had. "Don't have to help me do it, you don't want to; I'd understand. Can't claim I wouldn't appreciate it if you did, though."

"I just bet you would. Bitch."

"All day, every day."

I gave him a smile, most probably of the wan, small variety. To which he just kind of nodded again, sighing.

". . . Yeah, okay," he replied, at last.

Whole Home was afraid, now, staff talkin' amongst themselves, surly, *too* quiet. Overheard Dawson *begging* one orderly named Wojciech not to quit, and if he couldn't afford to let even *him* go—same asshole I knew for a fact liked to slap patients 'round on the sly—then things really were getting tight around here. Then again, plenty of people were looking at me cross-eyed as well, like they thought the cops might be right, and *I* was doing this shit. Like it was *my* fault Mrs. Camp had chosen me to fuck around with while she was making her slow-motion escape from death.

Late that afternoon, Ke'Von found me in the office, on the computer. "Mrs. Waltham," he murmured. "On the second floor, few doors down from your auntie Fee. Lisbeth had to get me to help her change the sheets, 'cause suddenly she's too heavy for her to move, and looking like ten tons of sick in a two-ton bag." He hesitated. "Might have to go slow, though—Beth swears she's gonna make sure Dawson knows something weird is going on with Mrs. W., and she's a good one. She means it."

Maybe, I thought. But would Dawson do anything about it?

"Go slow, we may not get another chance," I said.

At that, Ke'Von gave up trying to be subtle; still kept his voice low, thank God. "Lainey, I don't wanna kill an old lady, no matter what the fuck's inside her! You get me?"

"Look, me either," I told him. "So . . . we wait 'til the bones come out, give it a few days for it to finish—eating her, I guess. Absorbing her. Whatever."

"Aw, shit." He looked away. "Man, we're supposed to *help* people."

I sighed. "'Von, Mrs. Waltham's gonna die anyway—just like Camp, and Azzarello. If it wasn't Covid it'd be Alzheimer's; matter of *when,* not *if,* this unit. We both know that."

Ke'Von scowled at empty air. "So what's this all *for,* then, anyway?"

I'd asked myself the same question, truth told—wasn't sure how long Mrs. Camp had been thinkin' on this, but just hopping over and over from one DNR-havin' end-of-lifer to the next didn't sound like any kind of long-term strategy, to me. Then again, maybe there was less and less Mrs. Camp every time she let those red bones rip, 'side from the parts that remembered how she liked sneering at other people.

"Really don't think that matters now, 'Von," I said, at last.

"Shit, probably not." He grimaced. "The hell you looking up the cleaning inventory for, exactly?"

"Just checking on something Prisha told me," I said.

Ke'Von and I'd already both switched back to night shift, which wasn't hard because—surprise, surprise—people were *really* eager to get off that shift, they only could. We snuck the bear into Mrs. Waltham's room, and Ke'Von's man put a script on my app to send us an alert if it picked up any motion. "Looks to me like that thing takes at least a minute, minute and a half to finish completely," I told him. "So long as one of us stays nearish, we should be able to get there quick enough."

Ke'Von shook his head. "We really doing this?"

"Brought your bat, didn't you?" He had, and we weren't the only night staffers who'd started carrying for self-defense, be it knives, Tasers or tire irons—anything they thought they could hide fast if Dawson dropped by, which he was doing a lot less of. Wojciech had started wearing a full tool belt, with a wrench *and* a hammer. "Just keep moving, look busy, even if you have to let things slide. Gotta pray there's no code blues, when that thing goes off."

"Christ Almighty." Ke'Von offered his hand; I gripped it tight. "Stay safe, okay?"

"You too."

That was one long fucking night. Some of it I spent watching Auntie Fee sleep, through the little window on her room's door; the rest I spent trying to stop myself from checking on Mrs. Waltham, while Ke'Von tried to do the same. Every noise—the buzzing of lights, slow tick of wall clocks, creak of opened doors or the squeak of cleaning bucket wheels—sounded ten times loud as normal, the silence between noises ten times as deep.

One of the former caught my attention when I was passing by Mrs. Waltham's room for what must have been the twelfth time, eventually: a different *kind* of wheel-squeak, one I didn't recognize. Looked down the hall to see Wojciech hauling an empty cargo cart away from a residence room. As the door clicked closed behind him, every muscle in me went instantly cold and stiff, faster than my brain could figure why. "*Hey!*" I shouted. "Wojciech! The fuck you doing?"

He looked up, startled. Then his eyes narrowed, and my guts clenched up. He stepped away, hand falling to the hammer on his hip, and I took a step back . . . which is when the phone alert from the nannycam went off, a shrill shriek I'd intentionally picked to be painful as possible. Made me jump like a rabbit.

I turned, grabbed up the bat I'd brought from home—hidden behind a supply-closet door—and ran, forgetting Wojciech completely. Pulled up in front of Mrs. Waltham's room, panting. "'Von, *get on over here!*" I yelled, hard enough to scrape my own throat. Then I flung the door open, and lunged inside.

The upper half of Mrs. Waltham's body looked like it'd exploded: blood all over the bed, the walls, dotted by shreds of skin. Mrs. Camp's shiny red-brown skeleton sat up amid the wreckage and clicked its teeth at me, tilting its head, like it was flirting. Words seemed to leak out between its jaws, buzzing inside my head: *Why, hello, deah! So pleased you could joy-en me! I do hope you—*

Well, fuck *that* shit.

If I hadn't right then realized which door Wojciech must've opened, not to mention what he must've left in that room, I'd probably have stood there frozen a lot longer than I did. But I wasn't losing anyone else—not that night, anyhow. So I just swung my bat as hard as I could, aiming straight for her skull. That fleshless arm came up, but I'd moved too fast. The bat struck the skull's temple dead-on, with a deafening *crack,* and spun right the fuck out of my hands, leaving my palms stinging in agony. I staggered backwards. The skull grinned at me, utterly untouched.

And: *Oh my deah, deah, deah.* The click-buzzing voice sounded almost fond. *Didn't really think that would work, did you? After all, this is* magic.

Right that same second, Ke'Von appeared in the doorway, own bat held high like he was ready to try for a grand slam. Then he saw Mrs. Camp, and dropped it. The skeleton's jaw flapped like it was laughing. It reached down, ripped away the tissue left over its legs, and leaped at him. Ke'Von screamed. They went down together. I jumped in, grabbed my arms 'round the rib cage—those red bones were hot and slippery, almost steaming—and tried to pull her off, feet skidding on the blood-slick floor. Ke'Von was still screaming, trying to push Mrs. Camp's naked skull away, but it had its teeth into his wrist now and was biting down, grinding; I shoved one hand up inside her jawbone, hooked the fingers of my other into her eye sockets and pulled 'til her grip broke, twisting upper from lower like I was Steve Irwin punching a crocodile's ticket. As Ke'Von yanked his mauled wrist back, I rolled my whole body, hard as I could. Whatever let the thing move like it still had muscles, it sure didn't give it any extra mass—Mrs. Camp's skeleton went flying down the hall like a discarded puppet, clattering to the floor in a heap. An instant later it was straight upright again, crouched in that same hunting-spider pose.

This was fun, children, I heard, in my head. *But I haven't the time, right now. See you soon . . . you in particular, Elaine.*

Faster than a snake, the thing leaped over our heads, bone feet rattling down the hall. By the time I could make myself roll over to look for it, it was gone.

Ke'Von was twisting on the floor, meanwhile, desperately holding his wounded wrist shut. The size of the blood-puddle slapped me back to reality—he needed emergency care, *now.* I stumbled back into Mrs. Waltham's room, hit the alarm.

Then I ran.

When the cops realized I wasn't first on the scene for once, they searched the building, but I'd worked here long enough to know spots like that place behind the boiler where the basement wall went back three extra feet. Thing was a sweatbox, but I gritted my teeth and sat it out, turning on my phone every few minutes to check the time. *Please, God,* I thought, *let them finish up and clear out before it's too late.* If I was right, I had at least a few hours . . . but there was no way to know, really.

At last, around five in the morning, I took my chance.

Creeping back up, I found Mrs. Waltham's room taped off and the blood already mopped up off the linoleum; whatever Ke'Von had told the cops, they'd apparently decided they didn't need to leave officers in place. I let out a breath I hadn't realized I'd been holding, went to the supply closet, unscrewed the handle from one of the mops.

Then I opened the door to Auntie Fee's room.

Fee was snoring. Her room looked exactly like usual, except for the big blue plastic barrel that asshole Wojciech had left in a corner; I could smell its vinegar stink from here. Faint gurglings echoed from inside it; shadows moved, like they were settling.

Just to confirm my guess, I shook Fee's shoulder, gently first, then harder. When she didn't move, I skinned back her eyelid; her pupil shrank, but the eye stayed still. My stomach went cold again. Of *course* Wojciech had probably pumped something extra into Fee's IV, to make sure she stayed down—for all I knew, she was dying already.

A dull *clunk* echoed through the room, then a whirr, a dropped coin edge-spinning, about to fall flat. The stench of vinegar billowed out; I choked, bracing myself on the bed to keep from puking. It took everything I had to make myself turn around.

Mrs. Camp's skeleton grinned at me as it rose slowly from the open barrel, teeth wet and red and shiny as always. Vinegar ran down its skull's smooth sides; I heard static in my head yet again, buzzing.

Deah, we're not really going to bother with this, are we? You already know how fighting me ends, for you.

"Just tell me one thing," I managed, trying to spit out the taste. "Dawson . . . was he in on this from the beginning?"

The skeleton's skull tilted. *Well, when I realized those nasty plaques in my brain were going to make it difficult to focus, I had to improvise. Dawson offered the perfect environment, even if I had to settle for distinctly substandard material. And I was going to take your auntie, there, just to teach you a lesson, but—no amount of old bodies can ever provide as much power as one young, healthy one, you know.* It clapped its jaws, smacking nonexistent lips. *Which is why, though I'd have preferred a different, what did you say?—stock?—you'll do, dear. You'll do.*

The dripping digits came up, curving into claws.

This will hurt quite astonishingly, dear, the skeleton told me, pleasantly. *But not for long.*

And: *Yeah,* I thought, *that's true. If I just stand here and let it.*

In hindsight, I think Mrs. Camp might just have forgotten how fragile her bones had to be, now she'd spent hours soaking in vinegar. Soft enough to get down a woman's throat without killing her, right? I mean . . . she *was* magic, that's true. But if magic could cure senility, this would be a whole 'nother sort of story.

When she leaped at me, I didn't try to duck out of the way; just let her grab on, fingers clasping 'round my throat. My breath choked off for a second, 'til I stretched my head back and locked the muscles hard, and the bones bent like rubber. I shoved one hand up to wedge my fingers between hers, loosening her grip; jabbed my other right between her ribs to grab her spine, then ran straight at the wall. The skeleton crumpled between my body and the wallpaper, black rips tearing mushily open in the smooth red surfaces.

The buzzing static in my head skirled upwards, into a shriek. While the rubbery arms beat at me helplessly, I grabbed at the joints in hip and shoulder and yanked them apart, threads of sinew stretching like taffy, hurling arms and legs into each corner; they whipped over and over themselves, began humping back toward me like blind snakes, while I threw the rib cage down and trampled on it in a frenzy. Vertebrae separated; ribs spun away. My head was splitting with those silent screams. And then I stamped down hard on the neck, separating skull from spine; crouched and jumped, both feet landing square on the skull, weight of my whole body behind 'em. Crushed instantly flat, the skull split apart like a rotten melon.

The shrieking stopped. The limbs stopped moving. A second later, whatever held them together dissolved, and every bone not already torn free tumbled away from its neighbours. Suddenly I was standing amidst a scattered fan of pieces, red and damp and lifeless. I dropped to my knees, panting. "Don't throw up," I gasped to myself, "don't throw up, don't throw up . . ." *It's over,* I thought. *It's done.*

Except it wasn't, quite.

I made myself get up, soon as I could. First step: Gather up all the pieces, dump them back into the vinegar barrel. Lid on, lock shut. Then down to the basement, find a cart—thank Christ this was the deadest hour of the day, just before shift change at six A.M.—and wrangle the barrel back down to the basement, in the service lift. That gave me privacy, and time, to separate what was left of Mrs. Camp out into twenty different medical waste disposal bags, double-wrap them, and put 'em all in the bin for next week's pickup.

After that, one last meeting.

When he opened his office door and found me waiting in his desk chair, Dawson boggled, but only for a moment. Then he came in and closed the door.

"Miss Merrimay," he said, dully. "I'd say I'm sorry, and it's the truth, but somehow I don't think you care."

"Got *that* right, Doc." I folded my arms, not getting up. "Did you know? When you admitted her? That all this shit was going to go down?"

Dawson closed his eyes. "I'd seen her do amazing things," he said. "She spent her life learning how. It was like having a saint for a sister-in-law—Edward was as good as my brother. Then he died, and she couldn't save him, or stave off the Alzheimer's, and she offered to leave me enough to keep the

Home going for decades if I'd just . . . accommodate her." He gave me a desperate look. "You have to believe me, even after everything I'd seen—what she planned? I just didn't think it could be *possible*. Would you, if you hadn't seen it?"

"Still ordered the vinegar drums, didn't you?" I said, tonelessly. "Don't lie, Doc, I saw your signature on the order. Passed them off as cleaning supplies. Got Wojciech to haul one into every target's room, and haul it away afterwards. And went out of your way to get a good selection of candidates in your intake. Dementia patients, no kin left who cared about 'em . . . they couldn't remember if they saw anything, and who'd believe 'em if they did?" I got up, then, walking 'round the desk to glare in his face. "So you can tell yourself it was all for the Home, but I'm gonna bet she told *you* what'd happen to you, if you didn't. And you believed her."

Dawson took a shuddering breath. "I have no excuse for what I've done," he said. "But if you want to punish me for it, you're going to have to come up with a much more plausible version of events, if you don't want the Home shutting down after I go to prison. Not to mention how I could provide an equally plausible version that would present you to considerable disadvantage, as well." He moistened his lips. "So it seems to me we can either ruin each other, or walk away and not throw more of the living after the dead. Which would you prefer?"

I sighed. "Doc, I'd be a lot more pissed off about that kind of ultimatum, I hadn't already thought of it." He blinked. "So here's what we're going to do."

The cops marched into the Home a week later and arrested Jan Wojciech right in the middle of his shift, charging him with the murders of Mrs. Camp, Mrs. Azzarello, and Mrs. Waltham, as well as multiple ongoing cases of patient abuse, theft, and trafficking of medical pharmaceuticals. Dawson made sure there was enough evidence available on the smaller stuff that the circumstantial murder case looked a lot more convincing, and the court denied bail. Trial's still in progress; I haven't really cared to follow it. In the meantime, Mrs. Camp's will was cleared by the lawyers, and things have improved a lot around the Home: better staff, better food, better class of care. I even got a pay raise.

Never told Ke'Von about the deal I worked with Dawson, and he didn't ask. But then again, it was never the same between us, really. About a month and a half later, he quit. We haven't talked since then.

I did ask Fee, once, if I'd done the right thing. She took a long time answering. At last, all she said was *Would you do the same again, Lainey, you had to?*

Absolutely, I said, and she shrugged.

Then there you go.

And I would. If somebody's got to suffer shit they don't deserve, better assholes like Wojciech than the people in the Home, even if it means weasels like Dawson get to put off their reckoning awhile.

Nobody gets to put it off forever, after all. Mrs. Camp could tell you that, and so can I.

So *will* I, no doubt.

THE VIRGIN JIMMY PECK

by Daryl Gregory

It was just before the lady with the crazy eyes plunged the knife into his chest that Jimmy Peck thought, Maybe I shouldn't have skipped my shift at the 7-Eleven.

It was a week ago that the guys he knew as Rolo and Winston convinced him to come out with them. Jimmy wasn't comfortable making small talk with customers, especially ones that came in after three A.M., but these guys were regulars, and really friendly. They stopped in every Tuesday night—well, Wednesday morning, technically—after their bowling league finished up. He liked their matching forehead tattoos. They were just temporary ones that looked like they were drawn in Sharpie, but cool for a couple of middle-aged guys. It was some kind of team thing.

That night they stomped in from the cold looking exhausted and worried. Jimmy tried out what he thought might be typical guy-to-guy small talk. "Tough game?"

Winston, the skinny one, frowned as if he didn't understand the question. Jimmy quickly added, "Or is that not what they call it? Match?"

"Definitely a hell of a match, Jimmy," Rolo said. He was shorter, chubbier, and the talker of the pair. "The coach, she wasn't too happy with us tonight. Really reamed us out."

They knew Jimmy's name, but he only knew them by their brands: Winston Red kings for the skinny, quiet one, and Fierce Green Apple Gatorade and a pack of Rolos for the talker. Jimmy put the cigarettes on the counter and started scanning the items.

"Tough coaches are good, though, right?" Jimmy said, winging it. "If you're going to be competitive?" He'd never been on a team outside of gym class.

"Oh, she's a tough one." Rolo slid a ten across the counter. "Women, am I right?"

"I'll take your word for it," Jimmy said.

"What, no girlfriend? No Mrs. Jimmy?"

Jimmy felt the heat in his neck. Rolo raised his eyebrows, wrinkling his forehead drawing. It was either an eye with thick, squiggly eyelashes sprouting all the way around it, or a panicked amoeba.

"Let's go," Winston said. Probably anxious to light up. Smoking wasn't allowed in the store.

"Just a sec." Rolo leaned across the counter and quietly asked, "How old are you, Jimmy?"

Jimmy didn't want to say. But he also didn't want to lie. "Twenty-three."

Winston made a surprised sound. How young did Jimmy look?

"Have you ever had a girlfriend?" Rolo asked. "Or a boyfriend?" Jimmy shook his head. Rolo said, "What, a handsome guy like you?"

He was being polite. Jimmy knew he wasn't close to handsome. He'd never had the money to fix his teeth, and the acne that tortured him throughout his teenage years had erupted again. He hated looking at himself.

"Come on," Rolo said. "There had to be someone."

"Um, I liked this girl back in high school."

"Have you ever done the deed?"

"Deed?"

"Sex, Jimmy."

Jimmy's hand went to the zipper of his hoodie, pulled it up. "Sure."

Rolo smiled forgivingly.

"Well," Jimmy said. "Mostly hand stuff." Sophomore year, coming back on the bus from the Field Museum field trip, Madison McKinnon grabbed his hand and put it on her boob. He thought it might have been on a dare, because she immediately jumped up and went to another seat. And her friends were laughing.

Rolo looked at Winston. The skinny man tapped the hard pack against his palm, thinking. Finally he spoke. "Worth a shot."

Rolo beamed. He clapped once and spread his hands, like a magician who'd just made a coin vanish. "Jimmy, you're coming to our next meeting of the League. No argument, end of discussion."

"I don't know, guys." Jimmy found his hoodie's zipper and moved it up until the metal bit his chin. He wanted to go with them, but were they just pitying him? They probably thought he couldn't find a girlfriend without their help, which, okay, history was not on his side there. "I've got to work on Tuesdays."

Rolo blew out his lips. "It isn't going to kill you to take one night off. Is this how you want to spend your life? Chained like a galley slave to a cash register?"

Jimmy laughed in surrender. "Okay, okay." Then he felt a twist of guilt. "I do have to tell you something, though."

The men exchanged a look.

Jimmy said, "I don't know how to bowl."

Winston put his hand on Jimmy's shoulder, and Jimmy's eyes drifted up to his forehead tattoo. Definitely less an amoeba than an eye. It seemed to be looking straight into Jimmy's skull.

"We have a confession of our own," the skinny man said. "The League is not really about bowling."

He got back to his apartment building at 5:30 A.M., feet cold and sneakers wet from the Chicago slush, but he didn't mind; he was still buzzing from the conversation with Rolo and Winston. (They'd told him their real names, but their brands were hardwired into his brain.) They'd asked all about his life, where he lived, where his parents were (good question, especially regarding Mom), who he liked to hang out with (outside of work? Um . . .). The longer he talked the more determined they were to change his life next Tuesday. "The League's a social club," Rolo told him. "And by God, you'll be social. People are going to see you for the special person you are."

Jimmy slipped through the building's front door, trying to keep quiet. Mrs. Yogovich's apartment was the first on the right, and her door, as always, was ajar. He pulled up his hoodie and slunk past. Before he reached the safety of the stairs, the door banged open behind him. "Hey! Dipshit!"

The old woman stepped out in her winter usual: housedress, puffy vest, Bears sweatpants, and Ugg boots. "Where do you think you're going?" She always asked this, as if his range of options were limitless.

He tried to throw out a cheery good morning but she steamrolled over it. "You been feeding the rats again, Jimmy! Leaving food out! I can hear them fucking in the walls—eeee! eeee! eeee!—like a God damn Roman orgy." He backed away, explaining. He kept his food in the fridge, he told her. He vacuumed. Took out the garbage every chance he got.

"Don't lie to me," Mrs. Yogovich said. "You've got a God damn pizza sitting in front of your TV."

That stopped him. "You've been in my apartment? I don't think you're supposed to—"

"I have to check for violations, don't I? You could be keeping a pet down there!"

If you let me have a cat, he thought, we wouldn't have a rat problem.

"Clean up and grow up, Jimmy Peck, or I will evict your ass, don't think I won't."

He didn't think she had the power to do that—she was only the resident manager, not the landlord—but didn't want to antagonize her. He fled down the stairs with her voice hammering at the back of his head.

Only Mrs. Yogovich could make him grateful about entering his tiny, dank apartment. Rolo and Winston had asked him if he had roommates and Jimmy had laughed: Where would he put them? The "garden-level studio" had barely enough space for the minifridge, TV, and futon. A narrow, high window allowed headlights to rake the opposite wall. There was no garden.

He sat on the edge of his futon, staring at the remains of last night's pizza, a couple of waxy slices decorated with crumbles of Italian sausage. Rolo was right. Jimmy needed to put himself out there. Was Madison McKinnon on Facebook? He should check his phone's data allowance and send her a friend request. Not yet, though—five thirty in the morning was too creepy. Later, after a nap. That way, if she wrote back right away, he'd be alert and ready to make conversation.

He reached for a slice of pizza, frowned at the brown crumbles atop the cheese, and then remembered: he hadn't ordered sausage.

A week later, Jimmy was waiting outside his apartment when a bright orange car pulled up to the curb at 8:00 P.M. sharp, Rolo behind the wheel. Winston, looking glum and under-nicotined in the passenger seat, stared out through the windshield. Neither of them were wearing their eyeball tattoos.

"Subaru Crosstrek," Jimmy said appreciatively. "Nice ride."

"Looking good yourself," Rolo said. Jimmy was relieved. He'd put on his best jeans and washed his hoodie, but he was pretty sure it wasn't social club attire. He climbed into the back.

They drove out of the city blasting Steely Dan's greatest hits. Rolo yelled back things like, "What did you tell your boss about taking a night off?" And, "What did your friends say when you told them you were going out with us?" Which seemed like trick questions; Rolo and Winston had made it clear the social club was private and hush-hush, and Jimmy had promised not to tell anyone about it.

Eventually they reached the woodsy northern suburbs. The houses got bigger and bigger, yet farther and farther from the street, like an experiment in perspective. Finally they turned in at a gate which swung open for them. The Crosstrek glided up a long, curving driveway, past a dozen parked cars, and rolled straight into a three-bay garage. Jimmy had barely glimpsed the size of the house before they were inside it.

The garage door came down behind them as silent as a theater curtain. Jimmy didn't know garage technology had progressed to that level. It was the clearest sign yet that he'd entered another world.

Rolo and Winston went to the hatchback and pulled on long, forest-green robes. Then Rolo produced a paint stick, and Winston stooped to allow Rolo to draw on his tattoo. "Do I need . . . anything?" Jimmy asked.

Rolo said, "Kid, you're perfect as is." He finished the last eyelash/tentacle and handed the stick to Winston, who started on Rolo's forehead.

"But what do I do in there?" Jimmy asked.

"You don't have to do anything," Rolo said. "Just be yourself."

"You can stop playing with your zipper," Winston said. "It makes you look nervous."

Jimmy dropped his hands.

"And we're going to need your phone. No social media posts."

They led him through a series of rooms which kept getting larger, until they reached what seemed like a giant aquarium—glass on three sides, more candles than a Bed Bath & Beyond, the flames throwing crazy reflections against the glass. Twenty or so people in green robes milled around, sipping drinks. Under every hood was another guy wearing a hand-drawn amoeba. They seemed to take note of Jimmy without making eye contact.

Jimmy pulled his zipper up higher. He thought, Is this a gay thing? He'd assumed because of the coach that there were women in the League—hadn't they brought him to meet women? Or maybe strippers were coming. He really should have asked more questions.

Rolo led him toward a cluster of robes. They stepped back as Jimmy approached, revealing at their center a redheaded woman in a silky green gown.

Rolo said, "Madame van den Dreissche, this is the—Jimmy Peck."

The woman stared at him. Her left eye was normal, but the pupil of her right eye was so big and black it looked like an eclipse. In two years working nights at the 7-Eleven he'd never seen someone who looked exactly 50 percent high.

Rolo elbowed him, and Jimmy stuck out his hand. "Hi, Madame Vander—Vandashush—"

"Please. Call me Heather."

Her face was very beautiful and very pale. At least, that's how her thick makeup made her look. Her face was spiderwebbed by fine cracks, like the Epcot Center decorative plate Jimmy had dropped when he was seven and Mom had glued back together, after she'd beaten him.

"I hear you're old enough to drink," Heather said.

"Born before the Baleful Ascendancy," Rolo said.

"I confirmed his birth record," Winston added.

"Baleful what?" Jimmy asked.

"You're at least twenty-two," Heather explained. "What can we get you? You look like a Red-Bull–and–vodka kind of guy."

"Sure?"

She waved a hand, and Rolo and Winston stared each other down, until Rolo broke and hurried off.

Heather put her arm through Jimmy's. "Walk with me," she said. "Tell me all about yourself. What makes Jimmy Jimmy?"

They drifted out of the aquarium, into smaller, darker rooms populated by hulking furniture, while he told her a lot of the things he'd already told Rolo and Winston. Hearing them a second time made his life sound pathetic, even to himself.

Heather reached out and put a hand over his—stopping him from moving the zipper. "You don't have to be nervous," she said. "Look, here's your drink."

Rolo was carrying a large bronze cup with a stem as thick as a hammer handle. "All out of glasses," he said. "Down to just the ancient goblets."

"I really need to stop by Crate and Barrel," Heather said.

The goblet was heavy, and whatever was inside it didn't taste at all like Red Bull. But it made his mouth fizz, so Jimmy didn't complain.

"So tell me," Heather said. They'd reached a dim room where bookshelves lined the walls. "Is it true you've never been with a woman?"

"Or a man," Jimmy said, remembering Rolo's follow-up.

"Spent any time on farms?"

"Pardon?" He took another sip. This goblet juice was good.

"I have to ask. The people who made the rules generations ago had very regressive ideas on sexuality. And race. And women. And, well, pretty much everything. The thing you have to remember is that they're not so much rules as recipes. You can't skip the fundamentals, but if you know what you're do-ing, you can make substitutions. I mean, who has that much turmeric in the house?"

"What's . . ." He tried to pronounce it like she did. "Turmeric?"

"I thought it was toomeric," Rolo said.

"Too-mare-ic?" Winston offered.

"It's a metaphor," Heather said icily. "Sit down, Jimmy, you look dizzy."

He did feel a bit light-headed. He plopped onto a weirdly small couch, and liquid sloshed from the goblet. "Oops, sorry."

"I'll get it later with some baking soda."

"What's in this?" Jimmy asked. "I wanna know the—I wanna order it later."

"It's destiny, Jimmy." Heather sat beside him and put a hand between his shoulder blades. "Have you ever wanted to be part of something great? Some-thing world-changing?"

Jimmy thought hard, and finally came up with: Nope. He never wanted anything great, he just wanted . . . okay. Okay would be nice. A one-bedroom apartment. A job where he wouldn't be robbed at gunpoint. A sporty yet reli-able car with great gas mileage. Or a cat! One of those cats with a sweet disposition but some kind of medical problem that he could post about all the time. Madison's public profile pic was of her holding an aged tabby with a milky eye. Last week he clicked on the photo and sent her a friend request.

"Jimmy? You still with me? Hello?"

Darkness rushed in from all sides.

"Madison never friended me," Jimmy said.

"What did he say?"

Jimmy lay flat on his back, staring up at a constellation of huge, glowing eyeballs. The couch he'd collapsed upon was gone, replaced by something flat and hard and very cold. He tried to hug himself but his arms wouldn't move.

"Can you hear me, Jimmy?"

He squinted. It was that nice lady, Madame Heather. And the eyeballs floating beside her belonged to Rolo and Winston and several other League members; the tattoos looked as if they were etched in neon.

"What's up?" Jimmy asked. His tongue felt thick.

"That's a good boy," Heather said. "You've got to be awake or it won't take. One of the fundamentals." Her voice echoed. He was in some kind of cave. The air was chilly, despite an abundance of small torches, whose flames illuminated some dramatic rock formations.

He tried to lift his arm again and failed. Both wrists were tied with ropes. When did they do that? And where did his clothes go?

"Ready the malovulum," Heather said. She looked at Winston, who held the goblet Jimmy had been drinking from. Winston reached in and fished out something pale and glistening about the size of a mozzarella ball.

"Ready," he said.

"Start the chants," Heather said. "Hello, chants?"

"Just a second, I've got to connect to Bluetooth."

"Damn it, Chuck, you had one job. Somebody take care of this."

There was a lot of scuffling and arguing. People really didn't like Chuck. Then, voices boomed from a speaker somewhere in the room, real medieval soundtrack stuff.

"And finally," Heather said, raising her voice. "The Rifting Key." Rolo held out both hands. Balanced across his palms was a long knife with a fancy handle and twisty blade.

"Whoa!" Jimmy said. "Whoa!" No better argument came to mind.

"Jimmy, settle down," Heather said. "Look at me." Her right pupil had expanded to fill her entire eye socket. "Breathe in through your nose and out through your mouth, okay?"

This has to be a prank, Jimmy thought. One of those frat-boy hazing things. In a minute they'd cut him loose and everyone would laugh and laugh . . .

Heather lifted the knife. "And a one and a two—"

Jimmy bobbed into consciousness a few minutes at a time, over the course of several days, until one morning he broke the surface and stayed there. He was thirsty. Somehow he'd been moved yet again, this time to a strange bedroom, surrounded by floral print wallpaper, pinned to a hospital bed by an aggressive shaft of sunlight.

He tried to sit up, but a lightning bolt of pain made him go rigid. He breathed shallowly for several minutes. Then, slowly, he lifted his head. He wore a cotton gown, light blue with yellow ducks, fastened with Velcro tabs. He pulled open the first tab, and the second.

Thick bandages, stained pink, lay along his chest like a chain of gauzy boxcars. They started at his collarbone and ended just above his crotch. He picked at the top bandage. It was taped to his skin, and every tug was painful—but he had to see. Finally he glimpsed the wound, a bloody line, stitched closed with bright silver thread. He touched the thread, and his belly lurched.

A tall, robed figure walked into the room and stopped, surprised. It was Winston. "You're up."

"What did you do to me?" He sounded panicked, even to himself.

"You'll be fine."

"Fine?" It hurt to speak so loudly. "You cut me open."

"And put you back together again. Don't try to get up. I'll be right back."

"Wait! I need water. Water and . . ." Something. He tried to nail down the craving. "Hamburger."

"You want a hamburger?"

"No. Raw hamburger. Can you get that?"

"We'd planned on it."

Jimmy woke again. He hadn't realized he'd fallen asleep. Madame Heather sat beside him, brushing his hair away from his forehead. He jerked away from her. He intended to shout something like "Get away from me" but the pain flared and he couldn't finish the sentence.

She made a pouty face. "Don't be that way. We're all done with the stabbing." Her red hair was pulled back, and she was dressed in yoga pants and a stretchy tank top. Her biceps were amazing. "I just wanted to stop by and tell you, first, thank you for your service. Second, we're all proud of you."

Rolo and Winston stood behind her. Rolo gave Jimmy a thumbs-up.

"But . . . why me?" Jimmy's hand went automatically to the bandages. His fingertip touched the silver, and his stomach turned again. "What did I do to you?"

"Oh Jimmy," she said. "You were just the right person when the stars were wrong. But isn't it nice to finally have a purpose to your life? Some people work all their lives and never do anything that makes a bit of difference. But you, you'll be famous."

"Historically," Winston said.

"I'm supposed to be at work," Jimmy said feebly. Tears prickled his eyes.

"Your only job now," Heather said, "is to take it easy and be kind to yourself. And stop playing with your stitches."

"Sorry," Jimmy said.

"We'll roll a TV in here, you can finally take some time to binge something fun. The equinox will be here before you know it. All you have to do is hang on for . . ." She checked her Apple Watch. "Ten days, minus about seven hours. Have you seen *Goliath* with Billy Bob Thornton? I haven't found a single person who can tell me what it's about."

"I want to go home," Jimmy said. "Please."

"Oh, we can take much better care of you here. Such as . . ." She held open her palm and Rolo put a package in it, a lump wrapped in butcher paper. Jimmy's stomach rumbled loudly. "Ta-da! Ground Chuck."

Everyone laughed as if this were a terrific joke.

The cravings continued. Jimmy wolfed down a lot of raw ground meat, but also sushi, whole fish, bowls of sweetbreads . . . any uncooked protein. The meals came four times a day and he snacked constantly, popping down chunks of organ meat while he watched baking shows and season after season of *Survivor*. Occasionally nausea would sweep through him, but in a few minutes he'd be hungry again. He started putting on weight, and the stitches felt tighter every day. The silver thread—real silver, he was told, nothing but the best for Jimmy—itched constantly, but he could only scratch when one of the guys wasn't paying attention.

Jimmy was rarely alone. Rolo was there most often, but Winston and a few other guys took their turns sitting with him. So Jimmy would have to sneak. He'd idly rest his hand on his belly, and when something exciting was on the TV, he'd quietly slip a hand inside. Oh, it felt so good to scratch. And sometimes, the thing inside him would feel Jimmy's movement and do a little flip. It was as if they were talking to each other.

It was alive.

It hadn't taken him long to realize they'd put something inside him the night of the party. Every day he felt it growing under his skin, getting stronger, more active. Sometimes he felt a spike of pain, as if his little passenger had grazed a nerve, or a thump as it shoved his kidneys out of the way. It was hard to sleep. But throughout all the nausea and itching and discomfort, he was buoyed by a constant low-rumbling joy, a rightness he'd never felt before. Also, his acne had cleared up.

One day he said to Rolo, "I wish you could feel what I feel."

"Good chemicals, huh?"

No. This was no Red Bull and vodka. This was real.

"Enjoy it, kid." Rolo suddenly looked sad. "I'm glad it's not . . . worse." He sucked in his breath, looked away. "I think it's about time for lunch, yeah?"

He patted Jimmy on the leg and walked out. He left the door to the hallway open—that was standard—but this time there were no other League members out there. Jimmy lifted the sheet and opened his gown.

The wound had stopped seeping blood a couple days ago, and yesterday they'd removed the bandages—"giving it air"—so now all the silver stitches were visible, a zipper that ran down his chest and over the hill of his newly chubby belly. Gaps had developed between many of the stitches near his navel. He gingerly poked a finger into the wound. It stung a little, but not as bad as he'd expected.

He pressed deeper. His first knuckle disappeared, then the second. He was fascinated by the feel of muscle and fat. How far could he go? He pressed further, pushing through rubbery tissue . . . and yelped in pain. Something sharp had pricked his finger. He looked up in alarm, but no one was in the hallway.

The tip of his finger was bleeding, perforated by a half-moon of pinpricks. He rubbed his thumb across the injury, smearing the blood. Had he touched a bone or something?

His stomach lurched. Something pushed up between the stitches—a dark, wet bulb, on a thin stalk. It rose an inch into the air, then another, swaying, like a plant tendril seeking sunlight.

"Hey there, little guy," Jimmy whispered. He let his finger hover over it. He didn't want to scare it.

The bulb slowly unfolded, revealing a bright red center ringed by a dozen white needles. It shied from the bulk of his hand.

"Don't worry," Jimmy said. "I won't hurt you."

The bulb snapped upward. The needles plunged into his finger. Jimmy stifled a shout—and held his hand steady. The tiny mouth held fast to his finger. Jimmy breathed in through his nose, out through his lips. The pain subsided.

"It's okay," Jimmy said. He felt its tiny body tugging on his own. "Take what you need."

He was surprised to feel tears in his eyes. He wasn't crying from the pain, though the needle teeth still hurt. It was that the pain was such an insignificant thing compared to his love.

He heard Rolo coming down the hallway, singing "Deacon Blues." Evidently his mood had recovered. Jimmy pulled up the sheet, over Little Guy.

Rolo stopped in the doorway. He looked at the bed, the white mound under the sheet, and at Jimmy's closed fist. His eyes narrowed. "What were you doing?"

"Nothing," Jimmy said.

"Nothing?" Rolo marched forward. "Don't lie to me, Jimmy." He yanked down the sheet.

Little Guy had disappeared. The wide spot in the wound where he'd emerged was bloody.

"You were scratching again, weren't you?" Rolo asked.

"Guilty," Jimmy said.

The more his body swelled and transformed, the less Jimmy slept. The itching made it hard to fall asleep, and now he was getting night sweats. If he lay on his back, Little Guy would plop onto some internal organ. Shift onto his side, and his passenger would go quiet for ten, twenty minutes—and then start moving again. Doing laps, Jimmy called it. Sometimes Little Guy would kick so hard that the metal stiches would bite into Jimmy's skin. And if Jimmy did manage to doze off, his dreams were filled with startling images: broken skyscrapers, black skies, tiny figures running through rainy streets.

Parenthood! he thought. How does anyone survive it?

And yet . . . Jimmy had never been happier. Little Guy was thriving. Everyone in the League was happy about that. Madame Heather stopped in at least once a day to touch his growing belly and tell him he was doing a fabulous job.

One night, Winston came into Jimmy's room carrying a huge white pillow that was almost as long as the bed. "Husband pillow," Winston said. "My wife used to use one, when she was—you know."

"You have a wife?" Jimmy said.

"Not anymore," Rolo said. He slouched in his usual seat by the television. "She ran away with the pillow."

"Funny man." Winston tucked the pillow in beside Jimmy. "Just put it under your belly. You'll work it out."

"Thanks, Winston," Jimmy said. "I really appreciate it."

Winston's eyes narrowed. "What did you call me?"

Jimmy blushed. "Sorry!" He tried to explain about the cigarettes, the guys' regular orders at the 7-Eleven. That dead-end job seemed so long ago.

"Forget about it," Winston said. "You just have to get through one more night."

"Oh, right," Jimmy said. "The equinox." Ten days ago, before he met Madame

Heather, he thought that was just a car. "Do you really think it'll all be over to-morrow?"

"We're counting on it," Winston said.

That night, Jimmy awoke to a gargling noise. Was that his stomach? He leaned away from the husband pillow and touched his belly. No, the sound wasn't coming from inside him. He looked over his shoulder.

Two robed figures wrestled quietly in the middle of the dark room. The taller one stood behind the shorter one, his arm around his neck—and it was the shorter one, Rolo, who was doing the gargling.

"Guys! Guys!" Jimmy said. "What are you doing?"

"Shut. Up," the tall one said in a strained voice. Rolo stopped struggling. Long seconds later, the tall man loosened his grip, and Rolo slid bonelessly to the floor.

The tall one pushed back his hood. Jimmy had never seen him before. He was TV handsome, but in an angular, quirky way, less CW series regular than British guest star. In a low voice he said, "James Peck?" It wasn't really a question. "I'm getting you out of here."

"Out?" Jimmy repeated. "Why?"

"Why?" The man was keeping his voice down, but the condescension was full volume. You don't have to be snotty about it, Jimmy thought. Yet he still didn't call for help.

The stranger shrugged out of the robe. His clothes were fancier than Jimmy expected from your standard robber/rapist/murderer: a crisp white shirt, gray vest, shiny black combat boots. Pinned to his vest was a large, silver brooch. Maybe "badge" was a better word. The man said, "You don't have any idea what they're doing to you, do you?"

"I'm doing what I want to do," Jimmy said. The Little Guy roiled beneath his skin. The stranger's badge was hard to look at directly. It had many com-plicated surfaces, and seemed to catch what little light there was in the room. The sight of it made Jimmy nauseated.

"You ever see *Rosemary's Baby*?" the man asked. "They're Rosemary-babying you." He fiddled with the rails at the side of the bed, bending close to Jimmy—and Jimmy didn't like how close that badge was to his face. Little Guy was doing frantic laps.

"You think these bastards care a whit about you? *They're going to cut you open and throw away the husk.*" The rails suddenly dropped. "Come on, we don't have much time."

"I'm going to hurl," Jimmy said quietly. "Could you put that away?"

The man grabbed Jimmy's arm. "Now, you idiot."

A stitch popped like a guitar string.

The man paused. Turned his head, trying to place the sound.

Jimmy grabbed the badge and yanked it from the stranger's vest. The metal was surprisingly hot, and Jimmy tossed it away from him. The motion made a second thread go. *Plink!*

The man looked down at his vest. Then he looked into Jimmy's eyes. "What did you do?"

The tentacle burst from between the gown's Velcro snaps and jammed into the man's eye socket. He screamed and lurched backward, but the tentacle pulled him back like a bungee cord. A second Little Guy limb embedded in his cheek. The stranger's thrashing nearly pulled Jimmy off the bed.

"Stop it!" Jimmy yelled. "Both of you!" He gripped the top of the sheets and tried to brace his legs, but his footies provided little traction.

The man seized the tentacle attached to his eye with both hands. White barbs sprang up from the Little Guy's skin, porcupining him. He screamed again. Shouts erupted from down the hall.

The man threw himself backward. The tentacles popped free, and the man collapsed to the floor, moaning. Little Guy's not-so-little limbs reeled themselves back into Jimmy's chest with a loud *thwip*!

Robed men rushed into the room. Winston was second or third through the door. He rushed to his friend's side. Rolo moaned.

Someone flipped on the lights. The stranger writhed on the floor, holding his face. An alarming amount of blood pumped between his fingers.

"Holy shit," one of the Leaguers said. "It's Doc Jameson."

They started kicking him.

Madame Heather strolled into the room wearing a silk robe—and Ugg boots. Mrs. Yogovich would have approved. A couple of the League members were sitting on the stranger's back, though he'd stopped moving minutes ago.

"Well, if it isn't Jameson Jameson," Heather said. "You don't look so good, Doctor."

"Physician heal thyself, am I right?" one of the Leaguers said.

Heather snapped her head in the speaker's direction. "Hey. I make the witticisms."

"Could someone please tell me who this guy is?" Jimmy asked.

Rolo was sitting up now. Winston squatted beside him, patting his back. "He's her nemesis," Rolo said. His voice sounded rough.

"I don't have nemesises," Heather said.

"Nemesees?" Rolo asked.

"Nemesi," Winston offered.

Heather glanced about the room, taking in the distance between Jimmy and Doc Jameson, the blood spatters on Jimmy's smock. Then she saw something on the floor and hissed. "The Amulet of Shu'garath."

It was the hunk of jewelry Doc Jameson had been wearing. "Somebody pick this up and put it in my study," she said. "Wrap it in foil first."

"What about Doc Jameson?" asked one of the Leaguers sitting atop the man. "Do you want us to kill him?"

"No, not yet," Heather said. "Take him to . . . the guesthouse."

Several of the League looked shocked. Jimmy pictured a stone pit. Something with knives at the bottom.

"But Madame," one of the men said meekly. "We're not allowed to use that. The rental agreement says—"

"Fuck the rental agreement. And fuck Airbnb!"

The man gasped. But behind him, Leaguers obeyed; they hoisted Doc Jameson and dragged him out of the room.

Heather shook her head, calming herself, and turned her asymmetrical pupils on Jimmy. "And how's our number one patient doing? Did the bad man hurt you?"

"I'm okay," Jimmy said.

Heather parted the fabric above his belly and winced. "Hmm. Doesn't seem worth it to stitch you up now. Think you can keep our spawnling inside for a little while longer?"

He had no idea. But the Little Guy had gone quiet. Maybe sleepy after all the action. And snacks. Jimmy nodded.

"That's the spirit," Heather said. She kissed him on his forehead. "Big day tomorrow."

The next evening, Rolo and Winston were waiting when Jimmy stepped out of the shower. He didn't try to cover himself. They'd seen him naked a dozen times by now.

"Thought you were going to run the hot water out," Rolo said. Jimmy had recently started taking long spells with the water massager to ease his aching lower back. The heat and humidity also seemed to calm the Little Guy. Tonight's shower had been extra long because Jimmy was hoping for a little calm himself. It hadn't worked.

Rolo held up a League robe. "Just for you. Your very own team uniform."

They had to help him slide it over his head. It barely fit over his huge belly.

"Do I get my own forehead tattoo?" Jimmy asked. Both Rolo and Winston had applied fresh paint jobs for the evening.

"That would be redundant," Winston said.

The guys had also brought a wheelchair. Jimmy told them he didn't need it, but Rolo insisted. "Safety first. And don't dawdle. Everybody's waiting."

They rolled him to a tiny elevator that didn't have room for all three of them. Winston took the stairs. Rolo pulled the gate shut and pressed the lowest of four buttons. "So what do you call me?"

"What?"

"I bet it's Gator, isn't it? Because of all the Gatorade I drink."

"Nailed it," Jimmy said.

Rolo wheeled him into a huge, unfinished basement: cement floors, unpainted drywall, fluorescent lights. A hundred feet away, a League member stood behind a camera on a tripod, filming Madame van den Dreissche talking to a dozen other Leaguers. They'd gathered around a wide granite countertop. Behind them were high walls of obviously Styrofoam boulders, and rows of unlit tiki torches. It looked like the set of a cooking show called *Baking with Neanderthals.*

Jimmy put his hand down on the wheel and the chair jerked to a stop. "This is where we . . . did the thing? I thought it was real."

"You know how hard it is to find a decent cave in the suburbs?" Rolo said.

Jimmy could see now that extension cords connected the torches to the wall. Not even the flames had been real.

Winston caught up to them, and Rolo wheeled Jimmy forward. The camera swung toward them, and Madame Heather started clapping. The rest of the Leaguers immediately joined in. He waved back, bashfully.

Heather sashayed toward him. Her dress was somehow even fancier than the one before, this one made of some elaborately scaled material. "Ready?" she asked him, and leaned forward to stare into his eyes. Staring back was like looking at a tricycle from the side.

"I guess," Jimmy said. He rose awkwardly from the chair. Little Guy tumbled inside him, waking up. Jimmy shuffled to the granite countertop, and looked around at the dozen League members and their thirty-six eyes.

They're going to cut you open and throw away the husk.

Jimmy's knees went weak. Winston caught him before he could sag to the ground.

"I want to go to the hospital," Jimmy said.

"No you don't," Heather said. "They'd kill the youngling in a heartbeat, then the government would lock you up and do medical experiments. No, you're better with us."

His hands were shaking. "Can I at least have the goblet juice?"

Heather looked around her for effect, then made sure the camera was on her. "I think our boy is asking for an epidural!" Everyone laughed. Except Jimmy.

Heather touched his cheek. "Sorry, Jimmy. Not this time. Pain's a major ingredient. The Curse of Eve and all that."

"Fundamentals," Jimmy said.

"You're really picking up on this stuff! You would've made an excellent member of the League."

"What are you going to do to him?" Jimmy asked.

"Him? You think the spawn of an interdimensional elder god has a gender?"

Jimmy's hand rested on his belly. Little Guy was more than doing laps, he was bouncing on the diving board. "Just tell me."

"We're not going to do anything to him—it's what he'll do for us."

"You're going to . . ." He struggled to understand. "Control him?"

A bark of laughter escaped her. "Somebody's got to! You have no idea what that thing could do if it got off-leash! But controlled, channeled, made to use its power on our behalf? The sky's the limit."

"But what about what he wants? His goals and dreams?"

She rolled her normal-sized eye. The dinner-plate one didn't shift position. "Get on the table, Jimmy."

He didn't move. The men around the circle had gone silent, and Jimmy could feel their animosity. *You think these bastards care a whit about you?* They'd tear him apart if Heather gave the nod. And Rolo and Winston would do nothing to stop them.

"Fine," Jimmy said quietly. The table was a little high, but he didn't want any help from the League. He managed to get his butt onto the top, then rolled onto the surface. The stone was just as hard as he remembered. At least this time he wasn't naked.

Madame Heather started shouting out instructions. When she demanded to know who was working the boom box, someone said in a low voice, "We know it ain't Chuck," and another man snickered.

Jimmy stared at the drop ceiling. How had he not noticed that the cave had white ceiling tiles?

Oh yeah, he answered himself. Drugs.

"Who's got the Rifting Key?" Heather asked. No one answered. "Jesus. Nobody's got the fucking dagger?" Finally someone spoke up, and they handed the knife to Rolo. "Stay here at my left," Heather told him. "Just like we rehearsed. And what the fuck is that noise?"

Everyone froze, and gradually everyone's eyes turned to the ceiling. A high-pitched beeping was coming from the floor above.

Someone said, "Do you smell smoke?"

Before anyone could answer, a sound like a clap—followed by two more. Jimmy recognized the sound from one of his nights at the 7-Eleven. The pistol that time had been a .38.

The Leaguers all started shouting. Heather raised her voice above them. "I said, how many people were guarding Doc Jameson?"

That's when the lights went out.

The shouting and general panic went on so long that Jimmy thought they'd forgotten about him, but no: Heather shouted, "Get Jimmy to a secure location! Now!" And Rolo answered, "Where?" Heather told him to stop arguing.

Jimmy felt a hand on his arm. "Come on, kid." Rolo reached across Jimmy's chest and pulled him from the table.

The smell of smoke had grown stronger. A few of the Leaguers had managed to fumble phones out from under their robes and turn on their flashlights. The wildly swinging lights, cutting through the slight haze, made the basement look like a low-rent rave.

Rolo was holding the dagger—the Rifter thingy. He waved it at a far wall and said, "Head that way. Hurry the fuck up."

Jimmy waddled as fast as he could. Finally they found a doorway. Rolo pushed Jimmy through and slammed the door shut behind them.

The secure location seemed to be a closet. Rolo found his phone and turned on the light. Yep, closet. Metal racks held kitchen supplies: canned food, serving trays, cooking gadgets.

"Hey, an Instant Pot," Jimmy said. He'd always wanted one. It would have been perfect in his tiny apartment.

"Shut the fuck up," Rolo said. "And it's Instapot." He pressed his ear to the door.

"I agree that it should be Instapot, that sounds a lot better, but it says right here—"

"Jimmy! For fuck's sake! Doc Jameson is hunting for us, and all I've got is this fucking dagger."

"Let him find us," Jimmy said.

Rolo stared at him. "He'll kill you. You get that, right? That's his only way to stop this thing from happening."

"So? He kills me, you guys kill me . . . whatever. Come on. I know I wasn't going to survive whatever this ritual thing was tonight."

"But then he'll kill me!"

A gunshot, sounding as if the shooter was just outside the door. Though it was hard to tell; the sound really resonated in that empty basement. Rolo started whispering, "Fuck fuck fuck." He was trying to turn off his phone light, but the dagger kept getting in the way, and he wouldn't put the knife down.

Jimmy reached up, straining his stitches, and accidentally rattled the metal racks.

"Quiet, damn it!" Rolo whispered.

Jimmy lifted the combination pressure cooker / slow cooker off the shelf, and squinted to make sure of the name. Then he slammed the pot down on Rolo's head. The man fell to the floor, and the dagger and the still-lit phone skittered out of his hands. Jimmy had to squat awkwardly to pick them up.

The knife was surprisingly heavy.

Jimmy played the phone light over Rolo's body. He wasn't sure if the man was dead, but he sure wasn't getting up soon.

"Instant Pot," Jimmy said.

No one stopped him; in the dark and the smoke, Jimmy was just another robe running for the exit. He found the tiny elevator but that seemed too much like a one-size-fits-all coffin, so he took the stairs, one arm supporting his belly, the other gripping the handrail. His eyes were stinging.

The ground floor was thick with smoke. Fire roared from nearby rooms. A man's voice called out, "James Peck! Where are you? Walk toward my voice!"

Jimmy did not walk toward his voice. He covered his mouth and nose with the sleeve of the robe and hurried away in the other direction. He didn't know the way out, but he figured that any hallway not on fire was a good choice. Chunks of flaming ceiling kept falling in his path, and sparks burned his feet. He really should have stolen Rolo's shoes.

And then, suddenly, he was in the garage. Two of the three bay doors were open, and the air was clearer. One vehicle remained inside, a black SUV. Not the car he was looking for. He hurried through one of the big doors, into the night air, and as soon as he got a dozen feet from the house he bent over, coughing hard. He thought of his mother. How had she managed to keep smoking through her pregnancy?

A sound like a thunderclap. He looked up at the mansion, and the third story collapsed into the second. Flames whooshed up to engulf the new fuel. A pair of Leaguers rushed past Jimmy and hoofed it down the driveway. They hadn't even glanced at Jimmy, or the dagger he was holding.

Jimmy followed them down the drive, and then spotted the bright orange Subaru Crosstrek. He studied the key fob he'd fished out of Rolo's pants pocket, holding it to catch the light of the burning building, and found the unlock button. The Crosstrek beeped in welcome.

He climbed in, pushed back the seat to accommodate his belly. Thank God the car was an automatic. Jimmy didn't know how to drive stick.

Jimmy also didn't know where the hell he was, exactly. He rolled through the gate (open and hanging crookedly, evidently knocked open by a previous escapist) and drove through the fancy neighborhood, making turns on gut instinct. His gut, being 90 percent Little Guy by this point, had no idea where he was, either.

Eventually Jimmy pulled over and punched buttons on the infotainment screen and found that the Subaru did indeed include a built-in GPS. What a car! After this was all over he really should go online and give the Crosstrek five stars.

Little Guy rumbled and stretched. The stitches pulled painfully. "Don't worry," Jimmy told him. "Daddy's going to take care of everything." It was the kind of thing he imagined good parents saying when the shit had hit the fan and they didn't know how to turn off the fan. The important thing was to not alarm the child.

He put the car in gear and turned up the stereo. Steely Dan asked if he was "Reelin' In the Years." Jimmy didn't understand the question, but for the sake of Little Guy he sang along with gusto.

A little after midnight, he parked illegally in the alley behind his apartment building. The building seemed quiet, with few lights on. He went over the mental list he'd made during the drive: clothes, bathroom stuff, pillow, blanket, the forty dollars he'd hidden in his mattress . . . Just the basics, enough to survive until, well, things had resolved one way or another. He couldn't go to the cops, or to an emergency room. What Madame Heather had said about hospitals and the government made sense. He was on his own.

His bare feet hit the icy pavement and he yipped in surprise.

The back door of the building was locked, as always. He walked around to the front, almost tiptoeing on his stinging feet. He pushed through the metal door and glanced back. A black SUV was pulling up to the curb. Shit! Had they seen him?

He shut the door, his heart thudding. He'd given Rolo and Winston his address, so they knew his apartment number—and his apartment had only one exit.

Mrs. Yogovich's door was ajar.

He slipped inside her apartment and closed the door behind him. Seconds later, he heard Madame Heather's voice: "Find him." Heavy steps hurried down the hallway.

"Hey! Dipshit! What the fuck are you doing in my apartment?"

Mrs. Yogovich had stepped into the room. Jimmy put up his hands and winced—the age-old "please shut up" gesture. Unfortunately he was still holding a giant dagger. "They're right outside!" he whispered. "Please."

She scowled. "Who? The cops?" It was late at night yet she was wide awake. She seemed to be wearing the exact same clothes as a week ago. "And where the fuck have you been for a week? Rent is due."

Jimmy stepped away from the door. She stopped him. "Drop whatever that is."

"Oh, right." He dropped the Rifting Key to the rug. "Here's the thing," he said quietly. The words came out before he knew what the thing was—and then, suddenly, he knew what to say. "I owe them money. If I give it to them, I can't cover my rent."

Mrs. Yogovich's eyes narrowed. "Bullshit. What's really going on?"

"Nothing."

"You're wearing a monk robe, carrying a knife, and you've got no shoes. Your eyes are all sunken in, but you've got a beer belly. What do you got, fat cancer?"

Someone pounded on the door behind him. Jimmy jumped.

"Hell no," Mrs. Yogovich said. "No one fucking pounds on my door."

"Please," Jimmy said.

"Stand over there." She pointed to an armchair out of view of the doorway. It was wedged between a chest-high pile of newspapers and a bookcase crammed with knickknacks. She kicked the knife in that direction. "Don't touch my stuff."

Jimmy lowered himself into the chair. Sitting on the bookshelf at eye level was a photograph of a young Marine in dress blues. Jimmy felt like he was intruding on his space.

Mrs. Yogovich opened the door. "It's after midnight! What the hell do you want?"

"We're looking for Jimmy Peck." It was Madame Heather. "Have you seen him tonight?"

"That dipshit owes me rent. Who the fuck are you? And what's with all the fucking robes?"

"We're friends of his," a male voice said. Winston. "We know he was here, because he borrowed my friend's car, and it's parked out back. We just want to talk to him."

"Because you're friends," Mrs. Yogovich said derisively. "Well if you're such great pals, are you going to pay what he owes me?"

"You're an unpleasant person," Madame Heather said. "But I like the Uggs."

"Get out of my building, you old bitch."

"What did you call me? Old?"

Mrs. Yogovich slammed the door and jammed home the deadbolt. "I'm calling the cops!" she shouted.

She looked at Jimmy. "You joined a cult, didn't you?"

"Kinda," Jimmy said.

Mrs. Yogovich wasn't bluffing about the cops. She called 911 to report that "religious fanatics in robes" were breaking into her building.

"It'll take 'em an hour to show up," she told Jimmy. "You're sweating like a pig. You're not going to throw up, are you? You better not vomit on my rug."

"I just need to sit for a while and warm up." Little Guy was kicking again with what felt like fifty tiny steel-toed boots.

She disappeared and came back five minutes later with a cup of tea. Stood over him, hands on hips, until he took a sip. It tasted like bark, but in a good way. He didn't know what to say, so he nodded at the photograph and asked, "Is that your son?"

"That moron. I told him not to enlist, but did he listen? Second tour he got blowed up."

"I'm sorry, is he . . . ?"

"He's right there. In that white box next to the picture."

He'd thought that was a Chinese take-out box.

"Like I said," Mrs. Yogovich said. "Dipshit."

Several hours later, Mrs. Yogovich had fallen asleep sitting up, and Jimmy was back in the armchair, breathing in through his nose and out through his mouth. The pain was tremendous. Little Guy seemed to be trying to claw his way out of his stomach.

The police had come and gone. Jimmy had hidden in the bedroom while they interviewed her. They called her Mrs. Y, and it was clear this wasn't the first, or even tenth time she'd made a report. Jimmy's apartment had indeed been broken into, they told her, but they'd found zero fanatics in the area. Wasn't it time she had the landlord put a lock on the exterior door, as they'd advised? She'd told them to mind their own business. And no, she hadn't seen this Jimmy Peck person in a week. Her willingness to lie for him was a mystery.

But Jimmy couldn't hide in her apartment any longer. During the equinox, he'd learned, the night was the same length as the day, and this night was almost over. Little Guy, he understood, needed to be born in the dark, and Jimmy didn't want to ruin Mrs. Yogovich's rug.

He pushed himself out of the chair, stifling a groan that might have woken the old woman. He took the dagger, then unlatched the door and slipped out.

Yellow police tape covered his door. One diagonal piece had already fallen off. The wood around the lock had been smashed apart, and the door no longer sat flush with the frame. He cut the tape with a flick of the knife—the blade was sharp, not just decorative—and pushed his way inside.

The only light was the smeary streetlamp glow leaking through the window above his bed. He walked to his bed, braced one hand against the wall, and lowered himself to the mattress.

"I knew you'd show up," a voice said. The light snapped on. "I could feel the Rifting Key was close."

Doc Jameson was looking rough. A bloody rag covered one eye at a rakish angle, but his cheek wound was uncovered. His vest was undone, his white shirt was stained with blood and soot, and the combat boots looked like they had seen actual combat. The only thing that looked clean was the shiny pistol in his hand.

"Can't you just leave me alone?" Jimmy asked. "It's been a long night."

"Van den Dreissche and her boys have this place surrounded, James. They're waiting for you. They think they can control the dark spawn, but they're wrong." He was nervously eyeing Jimmy's big belly. "Sooner or later it would have broken through whatever half-assed foulbond they created. After that, the spawn would begin killing, growing with each death, and committing unspeakable horrors."

The Jameson guy went on like that for a while, which seemed like a lot of talk for the unspeakable. Jimmy was more focused on the waves of pain rolling up from his thighs to his collarbone. And why was it so hot?

"James. Look at me."

Jimmy looked into his unbandaged eye. Yet another asymmetrical face.

"I'm not going to lie to you," Doc Jameson said. "The spawn has already consumed much of your insides. You're not going to survive this. But if you act now, you can save the world. And if you don't . . ."

"What?"

"Everyone you love will die. Everyone. Is there anything worse than that?"

Jimmy took a moment to go through the list of everyone he loved. "No," he said finally.

"Thank God," Jameson said. "I thought I might have to shoot you, but that was likely to trigger the exanthemus, and then, hoo boy." He held out his hand, but kept his face—and remaining eye—far back. "We don't have much time. Give me the Rifting Key."

"No," Jimmy said firmly. "It's my responsibility." He pulled the robe up over his belly. Nakedness still meant nothing, even in front of this stranger. Two of the stitches had popped when they'd attacked Doc Jameson the night before. There were five left, and all them were painfully tight. The wound had widened several inches since Jimmy had last looked at it, in the shower.

"Wow," Jameson said. "We really cut it close."

Another wave of pain rolled up through his body. Jimmy gritted his teeth.

"The key has to go straight in, between the threads," Doc Jameson said. "There, right above your navel. You're going to have to push deep, okay? That's the only thing that will destroy the spawn and seal the rift."

Jimmy gripped the dagger. He thought of Mrs. Yogovich, and her dead son. *Everyone you love will die.*

He flicked the knife. The top stitch popped with a familiar *plink!*

"Yikes," Jameson said. "Don't do that. Straight in."

Jimmy plucked the next one. The wound split open like a red mouth.

Doc Jameson jumped up. "What the fuck!" He pointed the pistol at Jimmy's head.

Jimmy ran the knife down his chest, easy as unzipping his hoodie: *plink plink plink!*

The gun went off. Jimmy arched his back. A furious mass exploded from his chest and launched into Doc Jameson. The man screamed and was engulfed in a storm of tentacles.

"Hey there, Little Guy," Jimmy said. He slumped to the floor.

The dozens of limbs suddenly contracted around Jameson, squeezing him. The man emitted a high-pitched squeak. His face turned red, his head jerked back, and then . . . popped.

Blood sprayed the ceiling.

The tentacles cinched tighter, and the many saw-toothed mouths went to work. Little Guy seemed to be swelling in size with every bite.

"Oh my God," Madame Heather said. Jimmy's vision was spotty, but he recognized her silhouette in the doorway, and that of the tall man looming behind her.

"Isn't he beautiful?" Jimmy said.

"He is," Heather said. "He really is."

"We should go," Winston said.

Too late. Little Guy had spotted them.

Soon the screams moved out of the building and onto the street, where they joined other sounds in the apocalyptic orchestra: screeching tires, sirens, gunfire.

Jimmy lay on the floor. The waves of pain were gone, replaced by a numbing cold spreading across his body. He was very tired. And also a little sad. Little Guy had rushed out of the room so quickly, without even a backward glance. So hungry, and so eager to do what he loved. Wasn't that always the way? They grow up so fast. The malovulum he'd nurtured belonged to the world now. Or maybe the world belonged to him.

Jimmy gradually realized that someone was in the room with him, talking. He opened his eyes. It was Mrs. Yogovich, kneeling beside him. Poor Mrs. Y, he thought. As blue as Jimmy felt, he knew she'd had it worse. No parent deserved to see their child die before them.

"You dipshit," Mrs. Yogovich said gently. She brushed the sweaty hair from his forehead. "You absolute fucking moron."

THE GHOST OF A FLEA

by Priya Sharma

I have made the Flea my business since that first night with John Varley.

I searched out Robert Hooke's *Micrographia: Some Physiological Descriptions of Minute Bodies Made by Magnifying Glasses with Observations and Enquiries.* Micrographia. Small Drawings.

Hooke's work is an exquisite endeavour but his rendering of the flea is larger than any other creature therein. So much so that the page folds out as if Hooke is trying to communicate something. Why else would he elevate the flea so?

Hooke made his study in 1665. One hundred and fifty-three years ago. He writes with obscene interest of the flea's *curiously polish'd suit of sable Armour, neatly jointed, and beset with multitudes of sharp pinns, shap'd almost like Porcupine's Quills, or bright conical Steel-bodkins; the head is on either side beautify'd with a quick and round black eye, behind each of which also appears a small cavity, in which he seems to move to and fro a certain thin film beset with many small transparent hairs, which probably may be his ears; in the forepart of his head, between the two fore-leggs, he has two small long jointed feelers, or rather smellers . . .*

That we could be terrorised by something so minute is both woeful and laughable. Unlike Hooke I see nothing to admire in this parasite. I've seen the Flea's ghost and he doesn't look like Hooke's drawing. No, not at all.

John Varley came to the rented room on South Molton Street that was our kitchen, bedroom, parlour and workroom. A bear of a man, he had to duck to avoid the prints that Kate and I had hung like drying laundry on washing lines.

"It's a pleasure to meet you Mrs Blake. Mr Linnell is full of praise for your skill as a printer."

Kate scoured his face for mockery, as did I, but there was only geniality in his ruddy complexion. The examination was mutual. Age and care had worn Kate down but her hair was still dark and her black eyes lively.

"Mr Linnell's too kind." Her smile told me she thought John Varley genuine. Her judgement was rarely wrong.

"Rot, Kate." Christened Catherine, she was always Kate to me. "She's much more Mr Varley. She has a hand in every element of the work you see from design to execution."

I reached out and we shook hands.

"Come, sit."

The chair creaked under his weight. He laid a folio, fat with papers, on his knee.

"Are you here with a commission Mr Varley? That would help me enormously. I have to pay the butcher."

"And the greengrocer," Kate put in. "The money is going Mr Blake."

"Oh, damn the money Mrs Blake!" I barked. "It's always the money!"

Varley looked alarmed until we both burst out laughing. Our small income was a running theme in our jocular arguments. We'd vowed to be unashamed in our deprivation.

"I'm not here on a commission. Do you know my work Mr Blake?"

"Your watercolours? They're very fine."

"No, my other occupation. I understand that we both have certain sympathies for other realms."

John wasn't only an artist, but also an astrologist, known for the accuracy of his predictions, his poor head for business and his large brood of children.

"Yes, I've heard. How can I help you?"

"Mr Blake, I need to know if your visions are real. I'd understand if they were," he searched for the right word, "cultivated."

Kate put a hand on my shoulder and I lifted mine to meet it. We would always remain unified. Kate's reply was calm. Her most dangerous state.

"My husband is publicly ridiculed. His work overlooked by the Royal Academy. He's mocked as the happy madman for his gifts and we barely scrape a living. He's not a liar Mr Varley, not for publicity or anything else."

"My sincere apologies." He flushed. "I meant no offence. I wouldn't ask unless it were crucial for me to know."

"I saw angels in the trees at Peckham Rye when I was four years old." They bespangled every bough like stars. "I've had the sight ever since. What do you want from me?"

"I've been reading the constellations." He pulled at the ribbon securing his folio and it fell open. "May I?"

He motioned to the workbench which had been cleared for the night. I nodded. He divided up the stack of papers and laid them out. There were charts of the heavens, a map of London, newspaper clippings, and scrawled lists.

"Mr Blake, there's a blot on the sky so dark that it devours all light and hope." He stabbed at the celestial chart with his forefinger. "The stars are emphatic in their message."

"Which is?"

"Death is here."

"Death's always been here." Kate's gaze was a deep well. "We live in a time of atrocities. Of blockade and famine. Slavery. Riots and revolutions."

"Not like this. May I show you?" He started to spread out the clippings but paused and looked at me. "Perhaps this isn't for Mrs Blake's eyes."

"Mrs Blake's eyes are her own," I said gently. "She decides what she sees with them."

"I'll stay." Kate was resolute.

"The stars signal certain days going as far back as 1811. They turn their eyes to us in pity. I searched the newspapers from all over the city. I believe this is the first one."

The cheap paper was brittle and yellowed. The ink was smudged. The sketch lurid. A man in shirts and breeches sprawled on a bed. A dark stain spread from the cut at his neck and soaked the sheets beneath him. The window over the bed was open, framed by billowing curtains.

Joseph Tarvin, aged 28, formerly of Cheshire, was found cruelly slain at his lodgings on Sugar Street, Putney. His landlady, Mrs Jones, hearing a fracas went up to his room on the third floor. When she knocked the room fell silent. Other lodgers broke down the locked door.

On entering they found Mr Tarvin dead and his assailant gone. The window was open. It overlooks Banks Yard and from there it is impossible to escape to the rooftops.

"There's more."

John put two more clippings alongside it and waited for us to read them.

"They were all bled like slaughtered pigs." Kate couldn't read when we wed but insisted I teach her. Now she was faster than I. "Tarvin and this one at the neck. This third one at the neck and groin. He was interrupted with Tarvin, which is why there was so much blood. He had time to finish with the other two, hence no blood."

"I came to the same conclusion." Varley grimaced at the thought.

"And they're all in rooms several floors up and the windows were left open." I didn't want to be outdone.

"The only event I could find on the next date was this."

It would have been easy to miss. It was the report of a suicide. Jacob Sorenson had jumped from his window.

"I went to the home he shared with his elderly father. He said Jacob was a happy man."

"It's not unheard-of though, is it? Some people hide their inner demons."

"You think he jumped rather than stay in that room." Again, Kate was ahead of me.

"Yes." John nodded.

I imagined the young man plummeting to his death, more afraid of who was behind him rather than the darkness below.

"The next one was four weeks later at the Egremont Hotel. He'd become bolder by then. Ready yourself."

"We heard about that dreadful business." It had been on the front page of every paper. There'd been two deaths that night. Newlyweds.

"I bribed the porter for more information. The couple had been placed on the bed, side by side. Naked." John mumbled the last word. "Their wounds were deep, made with some sort of thin knife, but there was no blood on the sheets. The groom had been tied at his wrist and ankles. They think his wife had been killed first."

"Terrible."

"You've not heard it all. Their bodies had been there for two days. The maids didn't want to disturb them but when they didn't vacate the manager went up there."

"Don't fear for my sensibilities." Kate saw John was hesitant. "Just tell it plainly."

"The porter said they looked most foully used and worse, they looked like they'd been dead for weeks, not days."

"How is that possible?"

"I don't know. And look at these dates."

He passed over a list in his long, looping handwriting. The murders were getting closer and closer together. First months apart, then weeks.

"We only have seven days until the next."

"Have you told the constables?"

"They laughed at me." Varley looked like an embarrassed schoolboy despite his size. "One told me to go back to reading *The Vampyre* or *Frankenstein*."

"I had no idea they were so literate."

I was glad to make John laugh. It drove the shadows from his face.

"I still don't understand how I can help."

"I want you to help me stop him."

John returned the following night.

"Will the angels come?"

"They're not hounds I can call to heel. They sometimes send other souls. Voltaire. Moses. Joseph of Arimathea."

"William, are you sure you should do this?"

Kate had already asked me this. She was my rudder. Woman isn't man's subordinate, no more than the chimney sweep is subordinate to the king. No soul should be silenced or yoked.

Kate is my wife. She is my equal.

No. She is my superior.

"I've never really understood the reason for my gift. Perhaps this is it."

John looked relieved. Even then he thought I might change my mind. "What now? Do we chant? Pray?"

"Nothing so difficult. Sit. We leave a fourth chair at our table for our guest."

"You won't see anything John, but you might feel something." Kate moved around the room with a taper, lighting candles. "Say nothing. Be still."

She joined us at the table. I matched her breathing, our chests rising and falling in unison. I submerged myself in the calmness. The candles were at the edges of my awareness.

Mankind shouldn't look directly at the angels. It's like staring at the sun.

There came whirring wings. The yellow flames became golden. They shifted like flowing robes or hair. Who would come forward?

The world carries on around my visitations. I could see Kate as if at a distance, her gaze concerned. John stared at the empty chair, unnerved by the invisible.

Something was wrong. Darkness was gathering in the right-hand corner of my vision, behind the chair. I jerked my head to see better. Kate motioned to John. *Keep still.*

The room dimmed. The light couldn't fight the night as it poured in. The shadow grew. I never knew darkness had a shape. It unfurled.

The angels' screams were piercing. I covered my ears with my hands. Winds tore through the spaces between us. God's golden warriors fled.

The empty chair moved. John's eyes widened.

"Who are you?" I asked.

The dark shape sat down.

"I am the Flea." The voice was rich and deep. Almost a purr. It vibrated inside me. "Rather, I am the Ghost of a Flea."

"You've done terrible things."

"You'll have to be more specific or am I responsible for everything terrible?"

"Those people, locked in their rooms, all the blood drained from them."

"Yes, that *was* me." The Flea had the glee of a child who'd done something wicked and delicious. Then, "Look at me, William Blake."

Please don't make me.

"I said look at me."

I did. His bulk rivalled John's. I saw the creature in pieces that were hard to assemble. A forehead that sloped straight down to the tip of a small nose. Little nostrils. Deep-set eyes. Segmented flattened ears. Thin lips. A thick neck.

His physiognomy was neither beast nor man.

"You're no flea."

His smile revealed animal teeth.

"I am *the* Flea. This body is a vessel."

"For what?"

"The souls of men who were bloodthirsty to excess in life. I'm the progenitor of their crimes. I am the worst of them."

Its breath stank of old meat.

"What do you want?"

"The same as anyone. The freedom to pursue my true nature. The real question is what do *you* want, William Blake?"

Its laugh was a rumble, its open mouth a gaping grave. I scrambled from my chair, falling in a bid to escape. I landed on my back, winded.

"Help me get him up John."

Kate and John were beside me, arms through mine. My teeth chattered. The candles were either smoking stubs or flickered in fits. Kate wrapped me in a blanket while John stoked the fire.

"Our murderer's not of this world. Pass me paper and pen."

I blew on my fists, trying to warm my joints and make them move. It was hard to grip the pen. I sketched the Flea's head. His wide, near-lipless mouth and row of teeth.

I dropped the pen, ink splattering over my hands.

"I've seen him before."

"Where?" John asked.

The memory was an unravelling thread.

"Years ago. We lived in Hercules Building in Lambeth." I turned to Kate. "It was the day I saw James."

Kate did what she always did at the mention of my older brother. Her expression became smooth and guarded, keeping her self-imposed promise never to influence me against him.

James, by contrast, never hid his distaste for her, illiterate daughter of a market gardener. James inherited our father's ambition and haberdashery.

"My brother James and I are estranged," I explained to John. "I saw him on the street for the first time in years, so the day was already marked in my mind."

I'd gone to fetch a pot of porter to have with my dinner. On my way home I stopped to admire a mapmaker's window display. Then I saw the reflection of a man watching me from across the street.

Everything James thought of me was in the wrinkling of his nose. He took in my knee breeches, gone shiny with age, my mended stockings and shabby hat. I looked more workman than an artist. A poor man with no servant to fetch his ale.

"When I got home I stood at the garden gate, trying to calm myself. That's when I saw it."

Seeing James destroyed my contentment. There was a seed of hate where once there'd been brotherly devotion. He encouraged my parents to disown me for marrying Kate. I tried to guard against that hate because of my love of God but the seed germinated. I felt it root. It would become a tree bearing poisonous fruit.

An apple of bright wrath.

"A man raced toward me with such purpose. I thought him a Beau Nash sort, in a frock coat of shifting colours. As he got closer I realised it wasn't a man in silk but something covered in speckled scale. It was him. He calls himself the Flea."

"What did you do?"

"I dropped the tankard and ran for my life."

I was relieved to see John at the door the next afternoon. I was scared he might not come back. He sat opposite us at the table, puffy eyed. He'd slept as little as we had. Daylight didn't dispel what I'd seen. I'd been burnt by a malign sun.

"This is where he'll strike next."

The map reduced London to lines and blocks. He'd circled a spot at the end of Courtney Avenue.

"That's very precise. Who lives there?"

"Lord Bartlett-Cole."

The Flea craved richer blood.

"How do we warn them? John, perhaps you should go to the constables again." I chewed my thumbnail. "We could keep watch ourselves."

"No." Kate was sharp. "It's come too close to you already."

"What then?"

"Are they in residence?" She looked at John.

"Yes. I asked their footman."

"We don't know who the Flea wants. We write four separate letters. One each to both Lord and Lady Bartlett-Cole, one to the butler, and another to the constables, explaining everyone in the house is in danger." Kate's skirts swished as she paced.

"Saying what?"

"We're a Royalist spy who remains anonymous for their own safety. We've infiltrated a secret organisation who wishes to bring revolution to England."

Revolution. When I was twenty, with more fire in my blood, I'd worn a red bonnet myself and applauded the French Revolutionists. That united they'd abolish slavery, monarchy, and the subjugation of woman. Abolish churches, leaving us to speak with God directly. Jerusalem here on Earth. But no, blood ran in French gutters, drowning all humanity.

"They can't ignore that." John lifted his head. "What should we advise them to do?"

"Close up the house and leave. Send the staff to safety." Kate grimaced. "John, I'll deliver them in case they recognise you."

We talked about the wording of each letter. John got up, stretched and went over to the mantlepiece. He picked up the small portrait resting there.

"Who's this handsome young man?"

"Robert, William's youngest brother. He died. Consumption."

"I'm sorry."

I took it from him. "Robert was a fine artist himself. He lived with us for many years. We made a happy family. He adored Kate."

"And I him." Kate slipped her arm around me.

I sat beside him for two weeks as he faded. Kate and I bathed him and trickled in broth when he could manage it. I watched his spirit ascend with great joy and my heart felt unburdened of the pain I'd watched him endure.

But not my anger at James. I begged him to come and see Robert to say goodbye but he refused.

Early in the morning, following the night marked for death by the constellations, I woke and slipped from our bed, leaving Kate to sleep on. I lit the fire for her and went out. The previous day I'd watched the mansion of Courtney Avenue being closed up, trying to seem indifferent to all the bustle of a household departing.

All my angels had deserted me. I was lost without the advice of my visionary heads.

Angels aren't to be found in churches, which are the artifice of priests, the pedlars of these false temples. It was a long walk to Peckham Rye, where I hoped to find them again. I'd been with James that first time, when I was four.

I'd fallen over and he put his arm around me. The love of innocence. The comfort of children. When I looked up into the branches they were suffused with divine light.

So I sat on a bench at Peckham Rye, staring at the boughs. The memory of James brought an angry stab in my chest.

My poison tree was in flower.

I tried to set it aside and concentrate on the rustling hymn of dry leaves and air in my lungs.

When the angels came they weren't clean and bright. I saw them as if through a dirty glass. I couldn't hear their vital counsel, only see mouthed words through a veil of silence. They gave me a vision instead.

I saw a room at dusk. A charming mural covered three walls. On one side cattle grazed in fields. There were fields of stacked sheaves of corn which gave way to a fine park. Ancient oaks sheltered grazing deer. A stag sat in the long grass, proud head high, antlers spread like branches. Then the grand house itself, with columns and a grand pediment.

I realised it was a nursery when I saw the shelves of children's books, a hoop and painted wooden blocks. Embers glowed in the grate.

There was a boy in the bed, writhing in his sleep. He sat up suddenly, howling like a dog. His face glistened with sweat. He was no more than four or five. A woman rushed in.

"Nanny."

"Ssshh, Harry, I'm here." She clutched him to her. "It's just a bad dream. Oh darling, why did you open the window? You'll catch a chill."

I don't want to see! I wanted to shout at the angels.

The Flea's shadow went before him across the room.

Harry saw him first. A whimper escaped his lips. The woman turned and when she saw the Flea, she stood to block his path.

"Take me, not the boy."

The Flea caught the brave lady by the throat, stifling her words. The Flea was strong. He kept the struggling woman at arm's length, raised off the floor. His shoulders and arms were sculpted from stone. He leant over Harry. I couldn't see but heard sucking and slurping. The boy groaned. It went on for a long time.

The Flea drew back and smacked his thin lips together. Harry was silent, eyes closed, pink skin now grey. His dark curls were the colour of ashes. Open-mouthed, I could see his gums had already receded. He looked not just dead but desiccated.

The Flea turned sharply toward me. I shrank back but he wasn't looking at me.

"Was he your brother?" The Flea addressed a boy in the doorway.

The older boy nodded.

"Will you miss him?"

The boy considered the question, then shook his head.

The woman had stopped kicking. She hung, limp, in the Flea's hand.

"Do you want to see?" The Flea laid her on the floor.

The boy went to him. He didn't give his brother's body so much as a glance. The Flea stretched a hand and something appeared in it, like a magician producing something from thin air. I thought it was a knife but it was a giant thorn.

He paused.

"What's your name?"

"Jack," said the boy.

"A good, strong name. Shall I show you how to rip them?"

The boy nodded, eyes round.

"Shall we be brothers one day, Jack? Would you like that?"

I didn't need to see Jack's face to know he'd be the Flea's disciple forever.

The thorn was the instrument of the woman's fate. The Flea slit open her dress, then made an incision that revealed her innards. He sifted through them like they were auguries, handing each piece to Jack, whose hands were red from his instruction.

The only certainty about getting home was that I must have put one foot in front of the other to get there.

Kate was slumped in a chair. She'd let the fire burn down. *The London Gazette* was folded on her knee. She must've gone out especially for it.

"William, the Bartlett-Coles went to their house in the country. Their son . . ."

"I know. The angels showed me. I wish they hadn't."

"That poor boy. He must have been very afraid." Her face contorted. "It's all my fault. They thought they were fleeing to safety, not death."

"The blame is mine."

I'm not sure how long we sat there. The silence was broken by a knock on the door. It was John, grim faced. Seeing Kate he went straight to her. She covered her face with her hands.

"Don't despair dear friend." He gently prised her hands away and held them in his. "The only one to blame here is the Flea."

"The letters were my idea."

"Listen, both of you. I checked my calculations over and over. I'm convinced I was correct. Don't you see? Whatever we do the Flea will find its quarry. God help me, I've got a son the same age as that boy. And that poor girl, Eleanor Morton, was only nineteen."

Brave Eleanor. *Take me, not the boy.*

Kate wept openly. I knew it wasn't just for Harry or Eleanor. It was for all the children that we never had because we couldn't.

I lay awake studying Hooke's work by the light of a single candle. Kate was beside me, in the companionable snores of deeper sleep. How one body accommodates another. How what was once charming becomes an irritation to be tolerated and then, with time, essential to our comfort.

Hooke's drawing of the Flea spanned eighteen inches. Its bristle-jointed legs looked fragile against its bulbous abdomen and plated back. Its head was disproportionately small.

I put the book down, feeling Kate stir, then settle. I leant back, enjoying her warmth against me. Comfort is beguiling. It lulled me into a sacred space. The flame flared and then guttered, leaving a column of smoke in the moonlight.

It heralded the Flea. He no longer needed to slink in after the angels, if he ever needed them at all. I reached out to wake Kate but he wagged his finger at me as if I were an errant child.

The Flea was different in the flesh. He was power personified. Bigger than when I last saw him. Bigger than any man. He had swagger. He stalked across the room like a player on a stage. Naked and shameless. He glimmered with unholy light, that gave him a reptilian iridescence. His musculature was part man, part animal. A prowling tyger. The run of his spine was gnarled and his neck bull-like. He had a murderer's profile.

"You interfered with my pleasures, William Blake. I had to go out of London because of your meddling."

Only the thought of brave Eleanor Morton stopped me from screaming.

"You said your purpose is to kill. The wolf doesn't toy with the lamb. You take pleasure in cruelty."

"I thought you understood me." He shook his head. Even monsters desire understanding. "I am becoming."

"Becoming what?"

"What I should've been. When God made me He intended me to be as big as a bullock but changed his mind. He told me I was too powerful in proportion to my bulk and would be too mighty a destroyer, so He diminished me."

"He limited you for a good reason."

"He *belittled* me." The Flea's rage was swift. "He *betrayed* me. Am I not magnificent? I should walk as a God upon the Earth."

My blood curdled.

"The darkness can't hold me. Nor the Land of Nod. Mayhem's delicious. I'll reach my true proportions and the streets of your precious city will be strewn with corpses."

"Why are you here? To kill me?"

The Flea paused by the fireplace and picked up Robert's portrait.

"Who's this?"

"My brother."

"Brothers." He looked from me to Robert. "You loved him deeply."

He put the picture down and came to the foot of the bed, looming over us.

"Your wife still has fire, even though the world's worn her down. I can see why you still might want her."

The Flea slowly pulled the sheets from us. *Micrographia* fell to the floor with a thump. Kate's nightgown was tangled around her thighs. His gaze wandered along her contours. He slid over her, his body close to her bare legs, without touching her. He inhaled the scent of her hair. I couldn't call out. I couldn't move. I couldn't stop him.

The thorn appeared in the Flea's hand. In the other an acorn cup as large as a chalice. He trailed the thorn's tip from her stomach to her throat. Then he pierced the skin at her neck, the spot I'd kissed that morning. Kate moaned. He caught the pulsing blood in his ungodly grail, which he lifted to his lipless mouth. His tongue flicked in and out, running around the rim. Then he tipped back his head, the muscles of his throat working as he gulped.

He hadn't finished. His weight shifted and rolled to the edge of the mattress. It was my turn. I tried to draw away.

"Why so coy? There's nothing shameful here. Only the mingling of your blood in me, here on your marriage bed."

The engorged degenerate was closer than a lover. The dome of his head had the same shifting colour as the rest of him. His hot breath on my groin made me tremble. Then came the sharp penetration of the thorn and the wetness that followed.

"Don't make me your enemy, not when we could be allies."

He lapped up my blood like a voluptuous connoisseur. Each stroke seared my skin. I thought I'd be sick.

When he finished he went to the window. I thought of Hooke's flea, those jointed legs. The Flea folded up his legs so that he fitted in the window frame. Such power. He sprang out on an impossible trajectory, higher than the buildings, than the city, than the sky.

The following morning Kate and I sat on the edge of the bed, unable to look at one another. I wrapped my arms around myself.

"The Flea's been here, hasn't he?"

"Yes."

Kate sighed heavily and stood up, face flushed. She pulled her nightgown over her head. I stood too, my own gown dropping at our feet.

We examined one another. We were both marked with painful, itchy bumps, red haloes around their centre. They ran in lines over us, on our ankles, waists, armpits and groins.

Flea bites.

I dragged out the tin bath while Kate lit the fire.

Hot water and soap would never eradicate the Flea's touch. I'd never understood what it is to be in another's power until then. I cried as Kate covered me in suds. I bathed her in turn and afterwards we sat together in clean clothes.

She forced me to look at her. "William, tell me everything."

"I can't say the words."

"You must. Tell me every detail while you remember it. Our life may depend on it."

"How?"

"He didn't kill us. There must be a reason."

So I told her, stumbling over the difficult parts.

"Did he ever seem afraid?"

"No. Why would he be?"

"Then why threaten us?" Vertical lines of consternation appeared between her eyebrows. She looked at Robert's portrait. "Tell me again what he said about brothers."

"He mentioned brothers before."

"When?"

"When he spoke to the Bartlett-Coles' boy."

"That poor child."

"No, not Harry. His brother Jack."

"You'd better tell me about that too."

"It's too dangerous," John said when Kate and I told him our intentions. "I'm afraid for you."

"We're willing to risk everything to stop him."

"How do you know he'll come?"

"I'm offering him what he craves most. A brother in his endeavours."

"A brother?" He looked at me with disbelief.

I was aware of the pressure of Kate's knee against mine. I'd told her about Jack. We decided not to share it with John. Perhaps if we ended the Flea the lamb might regain its innocence.

"John, we're doing this tonight." Kate pressed his hand. "Hold your family close. Pray for us."

"Will it be here?"

"No. I'd be grateful for your advice. Where's London's most Godly spot? Not a church. Nowhere sanctified by man but somewhere truly holy. Somewhere outside."

"This I can do!" John was glad of a task. He worked at it for a full hour, his nib scratching at the paper. When I looked up I knew he'd finished from his smile.

"Where?"

"Peckham Rye."

We stood in the clearing, surrounded by the long-lived trees of Peckham Rye. We hadn't dared light flares for fear of drawing attention. I was rooted to the spot where an oak stood when I was a child. I was nine when it was felled by lightning. I watched as it was chopped up and hauled away. I was sad to see such a stalwart laid low, England's history written in its rings.

John insisted on coming with us. "I brought you into this. If you're right then all of London is the Flea's hunting ground. And when the city's empty, where next?"

Kate and John dribbled lamp oil in a wide circle around me. I tried to fix my wandering mind. My greatest wish was that Kate were beside me so I could kiss her again one final time. Even the stars wander, so I turned to them, losing myself in their transition.

Come to me Flea.

"You called me, William Blake."

He sprang from the sky and landed beside me. Eager tongued, the pink point whisking in and out of his mouth. My bitten skin itched. He looked brighter than before, glistening green, glistening red, glistening blue and dusty gold. His splendour was terrible.

"I did. I've been considering our last meeting." I stood up, as tall and proud as I could manage, hoping to be larger than my five feet. "You haven't been honest. You want something of me."

"You're intriguing, William." The Flea was amiable. "You're the antithesis of this age of reason. When men like Newton measured the world and made their calculations they were always looking down. You look up. Your talents are prodigious, your imagination sublime. You would be my herald and prophet in the world's new dawn."

"Why would you need a prophet?"

"God does. Why not I? And to kill such a man as you would be a waste. You have a pure vision and a skill for necromancy and transcendence."

"And what do I get in return?"

His laugh was the roar of the beast. "That's delicious."

He was upon me so quickly that I had no time to register anything but those glowing eyes set against mine. His rasping breath was hot, as if from an inner furnace. It was a feat of self-control to meet that glare with my own.

"Very well, William. You will have greatness in your own lifetime. All those puffed-up sniggering men will laud you. They're your inferiors. Your name will be praised throughout history."

How Gainsborough and Reynolds mocked me. They'd reduced art to obsequious portraiture to flatter their patrons. They'd forsaken divine imagination for filthy lucre while I remained uncompromising and impoverished.

The Flea read my mind.

"You'll have riches as well as renown."

"I'm weary of poverty," I said with feeling. To have money is no small thing. To not worry about rent or have to choose between being cold or hungry.

"You could have a fine house. Servants to light your fire in the morning. A studio with assistants and pupils. Humble origins are forgotten where money is involved."

Kate was hidden in the trees, listening. Her loyalty to me had been repaid with worn, leaking shoes. She's never asked for anything for herself. Not once.

The Flea hadn't finished. "I know what you crave most. A big house should be full of children. You'd be an excellent father. There's no reason why you still shouldn't be."

"We're past childbearing age."

"*You* are not." The oaks held their breath. "What if you were widowed?"

I baulked.

"That would be up to you." He gave me a conciliatory smile. "We can remake the world as we want. Why shouldn't you have as many wives as you wish? You could be a father a dozen times over."

A whole flock of lambs of my own. I could feel Kate's eyes upon me.

"Pledge your loyalty to me."

"How?"

"An act of good faith. Something to align us."

"What?"

"Brotherhood has marked us both irrevocably. There's nothing else like it."

"Born of the same womb. Bosom rivals. Beloved foes."

He nodded. "One must always dominate. One is always held above the other. A story that goes as far back as Adam and Eve."

"How do I prove myself?"

"Smite the brother who has wounded you."

James.

"Your wrath is what freed me all those years ago. I've been waiting all this time and gathering my strength. Now is the time to free yourself of it. Come to me. I will be your balm."

"Yes. For what he did to Robert."

James cut Robert from his life when he came to live with us. All Robert wanted was to see him one last time to say goodbye.

The Flea was as intent as a lover. My every thought was on display. He sensed the fulcrum at my centre and he only needed to apply a small amount of pressure.

"He's hurt you at every turn. Over your wife. Over your brother. Over your work, which he despises."

"We were forever at odds." It wasn't always so.

"And he was always favoured over you and you loved him anyway. Our love for them is what scarred us the most."

There. What I'd been waiting for. The Flea to reveal himself. Brotherhood was a personal story for him too. A story all the way back to Adam and Eve.

I am the Flea. This body is a vessel.

For what?

The souls of men who were bloodthirsty to excess in life. I'm the progenitor of their crimes. I am the worst of them.

"You're Cain."

Cain, brother-slayer, who poured Abel's blood into the waiting earth. Cain, banished for the first murder to the Land of Nod.

The Flea bowed, as if for an encore.

"You loved Abel once."

"He was set high above me no matter how hard I tried. And I didn't mind that for the longest time. And I missed him until your soul called out to mine."

"We're truly the same."

The Flea came to my open arms willingly. His embrace was gentle, for all his strength, as if I were something precious. I drew back and plunged the knife I'd carried in my pocket into his chest. I clung to him, pushing the knife up to the hilt. He didn't cry out. He bent his head back, his face anguished.

Do it now, I willed.

There was a flash of light as Kate lit the oil. She called out my name. John was behind me, doing the same thing. Fire encircled us. It glowed with a blue flame.

The Flea struck me, the blow sending me over. I felt my cheekbone crack. He pulled the knife from his chest and blood trickled from the wound. He stood over me, panting. I waited for the killing blow. His breathing slowed in an agony of what seemed like hours. The fire grew higher, a wall that trapped us. Blue light reflected on his skin.

"Why?" The blade slid from his palm.

"I'll not put my faith in a flea, no matter how large."

"Better that than the shadow of a man. You'll die penniless and obscure. Your memory will come to naught, without even a child to curse your name and no headstone to mark your passing."

"My concern's not for this lifetime but the next."

"Do you think you could end me with a kitchen knife? You mock me." The ground shook as he stamped his foot. Wrath inflated him. "I'll gorge myself until I'm colossal. I'll be the blackest of deaths. No one will escape."

The Flea reached down and picked me up. He shook me like a rag doll. I thought I'd break. He flung me down but the world continued spinning around me. Each breath was like a knife. I'd cracked ribs when I landed.

"Your brother despises you. So do I."

"It doesn't matter. For there to be such enmity, there must be love first."

"Love is meaningless. I loved Abel too much."

"You'll never be free of him because you didn't love him *enough*. I loved James enough to forgive him. And I will." James, who held me once, on this very ground when he thought I was hurt. "I forgive my brother."

Forgiveness. Finally. It was an explosion in my chest. It shattered the dark veil keeping the angels at bay. The Host rushed in with a furious battle cry. Wings brushed my skin. Their swords and armour flashed in the blue fire-light. Their hair glowed gold. The world was on fire and it burned with a cold light that filled my vision. In that cold light I saw eternity. Its perspective was blinding. Everything was simultaneous. Time was all at once. Robert dying and being born in the same moment. Grazing my knee, over and over, James kneeling beside me ad infinitum. Meeting Kate for the first time and our final day together.

Then I was lying in the grass, the burning circle now charred, Kate and John running toward me. The Flea and the angels were gone.

"We've put it off too long."

We excused the delay at first to gathering money for materials. Then planning. Then Kate and I spent an entire week considering the composition. We decided on the sketch of the Flea as I first saw him in the flesh that night, when Kate and I were in bed. To the viewer he'd be an actor on stage, our curtains theatre drapes. He'd carry his thorn and cup. A star would fall behind him to represent the angels.

It began with the image mapped out on a hardwood panel. We applied white gold foil beneath the curtain folds, the stars, his flesh.

We ground the pigments on marble. Indigo, cobalt, gamboge, vermillion, Frankfort black. One of us worked while the other mixed the powdered colours with egg yolks. Speed was essential for this fresco style, as the paint dries rapidly. Our necks and backs ached.

We used our finest brushes to pick out details with powdered gold and then sealed it with a layer of a mixture of sugar, gum, and carpenter's glue.

And of course, he was painted in miniature, as befitting a flea.

THE ATROCITY EXHIBITIONISTS

by Brian Hodge

A Tuesday, another typical day with Logan, but let's be clear about one thing. There's not much consistency from one typical day with Logan to the next, other than the reality that everything he does, everything he has me do, however ordinary it may seem, arises out of his bottomless pit of need.

I'm okay with that. It feels good to be needed, a trait my mom insists makes me the perfect daughter, but at least half the time ends up feeling like a character defect in the predatorial hunting grounds of L.A.

For me, it was early to rise, hours before Logan dragged himself out of bed, making the commute from Los Feliz and letting myself into his mission-style house a few blocks north of the Santa Monica Freeway. I fielded phone calls—always that—forwarding a few I knew he'd want to take ASAP and cockblocking the rest, who were after his hot bod for one self-interested reason or another.

The latter included a cold call from a clothing label floating an endorsement deal. This one peeved me because it should've come through his manager, but somebody got my number and thought they'd try to squeeze in one layer closer. Just for that they could wait; in the end, they'd still be happy. Logan would want this, of course, and not just for the money. There was no such thing as enough free merch. He could be suffocating under an avalanche of distressed denim and leather chewed on by designer wolves, and still wave for the dump truck to pile on more.

What else . . . ? A quick jaunt to the Walgreens up on West Pico for his Claritin, because it was allergy season, and to replenish my stock of medical-grade latex gloves. Later, to establish a chemical theme for the morning, I took a delivery from his dealer, just weed. For several months he'd been off the recreational hard stuff.

Much later, after Logan worked on some new riffs, the session concluding with him marinating in squalls of feedback, we hashed over his fret of the day: what to do about the new tattoo he wanted. The design was a rip-off of the symbol Prince wanted to be known by during his Artist Formerly Known As phase, melding the male and female symbols with other swoops and curlicues. Logan figured gender fluidity was here to stay, so he might as well stake a claim to all points along the continuum. All things to all people, as long as they were fans, or might be.

None of that was the fretting part. Talent borrows, genius steals, and to the shameless go the spoils. No, his turmoil was where to put it. The new tat had to be visible and his shoulders were already at capacity. For a normal person, the obvious choice would've been somewhere on his less occupied lower arms.

"Except that's prime real estate I can't clutter up." He traced a fingertip between elbow and wrist. "If I get inked here, that can only distract from the bruises."

When you front a band called the Damaged Goods, people expect a certain degree of truth in advertising.

I pointed at the inside of his wrist. "How about here? The good bruises don't even happen here, hardly."

We've been having conversations like this for so long, 99 percent of the time I never stop to think how weird they are.

Logan wagged his head no. "Not enough room. It would turn out too small there. With this one it's go big or go home."

For every suggestion, a rebuttal. We couldn't resolve anything and ended up tabling the matter for tomorrow. Which left one final item on the day's agenda.

Logan drummed on his thighs to amp himself up. "Okay! Let's do this!"

We'd been in the living room, which always seemed a misnomer, because it was the scene of so much playing chicken with mortality. The overstuffed sofas and comfy chairs looked to me like coffin linings bursting into bloom, plus there were so many tabletops for whatever paraphernalia friends, associates, and random dirtbag hangers-on brought over that the place could, on a moment's notice, transform into a pop-up lab for tampering with the forces of nature and personal biochemistry.

While Logan shoved aside a few things to clear space on the dining room table and put down a runner of aluminum foil, I went for a fresh, single-edge razor blade, rubbed it with an alcohol swab, and snapped on a pair of the latex gloves I'd bought earlier.

He didn't look. He never looked. He just held out his arm on the foil and turned away as if the limb were no longer part of him. He hissed a loud in-breath at the first shallow slice I made across the back of his forearm, then let it out, yelping "Ow! Ow! Ow!" at the second cut as blood welled in the first. Number three paralleled the others as he held his breath, a whine grinding in the back of his throat.

I held the blade poised as blood trickled down his arm. "Want to go for four, or is this it?"

He inspected and pondered. Tough call. Finally, "Three is good."

I dropped the razor blade into the trash and opened the camera app on my phone. "I keep telling you, anytime you're ready to do this with makeup, just let me know. I can get good stuff. My roommate's boyfriend does a lot of horror film work."

Logan hit me with a look of dyspeptic offense. "It wouldn't be authentic then."

"He said, in the plastic surgery capital of the world."

"All the more reason to keep it authentic."

"Right," I said. "Just testing you."

He lifted his arm so the blood would stream lengthwise and around. When it seemed unlikely to drip anymore, I snatched away the foil and angled the camera down at him. With his uncircumcised arm, he reached out, just past the phone, so the end result would look like a selfie.

"Say 'Joy Division,'" I told him, then shot half a dozen as he looked appropriately mopey, counterbalanced by a whiff of never-say-die. "And there we are . . . one for the Gram. Anything in particular you want to say with it?"

Logan began mopping the blood with a wet paper towel. "You write it, just say whatever, I trust you."

I AirDropped the pix to my iMac in the kitchen, otherwise the least used room in the house. I decided on the best shot, spruced it up in Lightroom, then handed it off to Photoshop for a patina of grime that didn't call attention to itself as an obvious filter effect. Some photos are born authentic, others have authenticity thrust upon them.

Final stop, Logan's Instagram page for the upload. What to say, though? It had to reflect the, ahem, sanctity of the process, right? Because talent borrows, I decided to crib from someone who was always going to be way better than Logan even at his most genuinely inspired.

I hurted myself today, to see if I could find the feels.
But no. The search goes on, and not even this seems real.

I know bands borrow all the time but do you lame shitheads have to be so flagrant about it? Grunge, stoner metal, industrial, shoegaze, you've stolen so much I can't tell what it's supposed to be. The 90s called, they want their suck back. (via Facebook)

When people find out what I do, they always ask me what it's like being the personal assistant to Logan Elliott. I pause to give the impression I'm considering this, like, wow, I've never heard that question before, you must be so insightful.

It's not for everybody—that's my go-to if I like the person, or they're neutral. If they're annoying they get the truth, blunt and unfiltered: *It's not for you.*

Sometimes, the blissfully ignorant want to know how to get a sweet gig like this. *Personal* assistant? That sounds so glamorous! And I suppose it is, if you're not qualified to, say, take care of the experiment rats in a pharmaceutical research facility.

It's not like I had some master plan to get here. It's all about who you know, two degrees of separation meeting opportunity. I was semi-dating a guy who'd been in a band with Logan before the Damaged Goods, and they'd remained friends. Also, my predecessor died in a car crash. I keep trying to forget that part. The tragedy was unrelated to working for Logan, although the question stands: Would she have been flying down Laurel Canyon Boulevard with a blood alcohol level of 0.23 if she'd gone into some other line of work?

Still, why me? We clicked when introduced—nervous sarcasm for the win—but I was vetted by his handlers, who then lobbied for me. Honestly? I have a crushing suspicion they figured I was someone with whom he'd be unlikely to get into trouble. I would *last,* without drama. Musician meant groupies, and, more recently, getting roles in indie films meant actresses. Years earlier, he was the crown prince of his high school theater department and baseball team, which meant artsy chicks *and* cheerleaders. My school years were spent as the phlegmatic girl who was always being drafted to serve as secretary-treasurer of the Latin and physics clubs. So if Logan were ever to go to an awards ceremony, I might make it into the limo, but never onto the red carpet. I'm functional, not ornamental.

Discreet, too, by default. The other reaction I get when people find out what I do? They try to weasel gossip out of me. What's he like, they want to know. *Really* like? You can tell me, Dana. I'll bet you've *seen* some things, too, haven't you, Dana? They're stuck in middle school, huddled by the lockers, eager to talk shit about the freaks and weirdos.

I always politely decline to comment, but on the inside my scorn is plugged into a Mesa/Boogie Dual Rectifier amp: What's he really like? What sort of things have I seen? Are you KIDDING ME? I mean, have you actually watched him, any of his antics? What makes you think there could possibly be more you're not seeing? Does he seem as if it's within him to hold back any grotesque thing that occurs to him to do if he believes it will bring him fame, fortune, instant gratification?

What's he like . . . ? Oh god.

Sometimes he's a sweetheart and sometimes a monster—not interpersonally, just in pursuit of the currency of the realm: attention.

This much is indisputable: With his tousled dirty-blond hair and teardrop-shaped eyes that downturn at the corners, Logan naturally looks crushed by the world, like someone rescuers have dug from beneath a collapsed building and all anyone can do is wrap a blanket around his shoulders and offer him a bottle of water. It's part DNA and part calculated cultivation, but I have no idea what the ratio is. I only know it's astonishing how many lovelorn people are slain by this image, female and male and all nonbinary points between—as big a mess as he is, maybe bigger, but convinced they're the one kindred soul on earth who can take this fixer-upper and make him happy, for real.

Bitches, please. He laughs. He smiles. He jokes, in private and in public. All the time. But face value isn't good enough for you, is it? You think you're able to peer deeper, to the frowny-faced truth, and maybe there are people with whom you can, but in this instance you're being conned. You look, but you don't really see. Or you see, but you don't register. Or you register, but refuse to accept.

Here's the joke, and it's on you: He's plenty happy . . . and nothing makes him happier than your certainty he isn't. Your conviction that any expression of joy from him is forced, thrashing upstream like a wounded salmon against a river of misery only you can alleviate.

He's doing fine.

You followers, though. How much more pathetic could you be?

I know—I should never pose such a question. Because there are legions of you clamoring to be seen and heard, giving the most degrading answers possible.

Most of my sorority sisters think you're gross, but to me, every time you have a birthday, the maximum age of a guy I'll sleep with goes up by one. (via Twitter)

A Friday. The heavier duties began early, when Logan had me whack his limbs several times with a sand-filled length of rubber hose. The impact zones would purple up into lovely photogenic bruises suffered while rolling in his latest Brazilian Jiu Jitsu session.

By now I'd learned the life cycle for Logan's bruises, and how the window for catching them at their most vivid seemed unusually narrow. Cuts, bruises, black eyes—since he'd started down this masochistic road, I had repeatedly witnessed that his recuperative faculties operated at an infuriating speed. Like, no fair, you take worse care of yourself than a rodeo clown.

Another thing to resent, if one were so inclined.

Even though I've always played along, delivering whatever damage he requests, I try to serve as a moderating influence, encouraging him to limit his focus to stunts that won't end in septicemia and the emergency room. But then there are times he comes up with some new idea for clawing further attention out of the world and I have no idea what he's talking about.

"How do you think it would go over if I started doing mukbangs?" he said.

Stall for time, Dana. "Think? You've told me more than once you don't pay me to think."

"If I have no recollection of that, then it doesn't count." So cheerful! Well, okay then, all forgotten, I guess. "Anyway . . . mukbangs. What do you think?"

I thought it sounded like something disgusting. Out of ignorance, I went for the obvious. You . . . do what? Have consensual yet nauseating sex while wallowing in muck? Like Jell-O wrestling, only hardcore? I thought I should keep silent. Maybe he would take that as disapproval so stern it merited no further comment.

Which he saw right through. "You don't know what it is, is that it?"

I seesawed my hand. "We better make sure we're on the same page here."

To Logan's credit, he's never made me feel like a remedial student when coming out with something that catches me by surprise. Instead, it delights him that he can. Because then he gets to assign me homework and observe my reaction.

Next stop, the Urban Dictionary and YouTube. Okay, so mukbang wasn't what I thought. But his pronunciation was off, which helped give the wrong impression. Still, I wasn't much relieved, because it seemed like porn of a different kind. The term was a portmanteau of Korean words that meant *eating broadcast* . . . so, binge eating, only done not in your own shameful privacy, but in front of a camera for an audience to see.

Soon after Logan suggested two stars in the mukbang firmament for me to check out, I wondered if his ears were sufficiently sensitive to hear bits of my soul drop off and die.

I was already aware there were men who got off on watching morbidly obese women gorge on smorgasbord quantities of chow. But I'd never seen an actual demonstration, gluttony become seduction as Princess Puddin' lolled on a sofa and gobbled a giant slice of pizza rolled into an edible funnel, pausing every few chomps to pour M&M's down the tube. I marveled at how prissy her bow mouth appeared, until I realized it only looked that way in context, centered in the pumpkin-head dimensions of her cheeks and jowls and the rolls of her neck.

Next was a guy who called his channel The Great Gutsby, and liked to jiggle his belly in shrieky anticipation of his feast. For this exhibition he plowed through a serving platter as big around as a tire, heaped with fast-food bacon double cheeseburgers. He lubed them with deep dunks into a tub of warm cheese sauce. He made sure his face got slathered, christening himself as the guest of honor at a nacho cheese bukkake.

We compare human ruination to train wrecks for a reason—all that ungodly noise and unstoppable momentum. Mesmerizing. Just try looking away. You have to know: How bad can this get?

With the burger mound down by a third, Gutsby careened into a fit of self-loathing and began to blubber. It didn't seem to slow him down. He could sob and eat at the same time, explaining that he would keep going, it's what we expected from him. He'd promised to get to 350 pounds and nothing was going to stop him.

To prove his commitment, he seized a burger in each hand and submerged them in liquid cheese up to his wrists. The cheese glistened, but I couldn't spot a sheen of tears above the yellow slick across his cheeks. I found it impossible to discern how much of this spectacle was genuine and how much was put-on.

Behind me, Logan raided the fridge for a bottled mocha, then peered over my shoulder. "So now what do you think?"

Finally, an excuse to look away. "I think my first impression an hour ago was more wholesome. I'd rather watch you bang a crack whore in chocolate pudding than sit through any more of this."

Logan cackled. "That'll be next on the list." He pointed at my screen. "Look at that subscriber count. Two and a half million! For this. It doesn't even take talent. Just endurance."

"A knack for being a raging drama queen helps. But look at the dislikes. That's almost all it is. Everybody's hate-watching this."

"They're still watching. I had our accountant check. The guy's a millionaire from this. The genius of the whole thing is that, on some level, people understand they're watching other people kill themselves. It's just happening really slow."

While the audience gets to feel instantly superior. There but for the grace of better life choices go I.

"You can't aspire to this, Logan. This is how you turn into Fat Elvis. Nobody wants that."

With his most disarming grin, he thumped his ribs, his flat belly. "Skinny people do mukbangs, too. They manage to stay skinny."

"Yeah? How much of the chum ends up back in the bucket?"

Over the next few days, there was no talking sense to him. Gastrointestinal distress, lethargy, the groaning misery of pounding that much food into his organs . . . none of the consequences discouraged him. It was like caring for a toddler who wanted ice cream for every meal and being powerless to enforce a no.

He started with several dozen hard-shell tacos. Everybody loves Taco Tuesday.

While I edited the video, I counted it a small mercy that every time Logan barfed, he leaned out of frame. But the mic was still hot, so I had to mute the sound, because hurling gets contagious.

> I appreciate almost everything he's done. A lot of his music and lyrics have helped make me a better version of myself, and when I couldn't manage that, they got me through some rough times. (via YouTube)

He wasn't always like this, not even at the start of my tenure three-plus years ago. On his way, maybe. But not like this.

For *this,* I blame the pandemic.

I blame the quarantine, the lockdowns, the screeching halt the live music industry came to. I blame the shutdown of studios, the limbo that paralyzed film productions, the locked doors and dark, empty stages of performance venues.

Necessary measures? Okay, no argument.

But I blame them anyway, as sure as I blame the generations of parents who failed to teach coping skills to their horrid offspring, then scooted them into the world with a sense of entitlement so feral it would shame a Roman emperor.

Poor, poor pitiful we . . . all the attention whores cut off from their live-supply pipelines and forced to stay home.

By the time I was several months into this gig, I'd identified three operational modes for Logan and the band. There were the creative cycles of writing, rehearsing, recording. There was the external grind of touring, the repetitive daily interviews . . . plus, for Logan, the periodic film role, which meant he had to make like a grown-up and arrive at the set on time, day after early-rising day.

Finally, there was downtime—restorative, sometimes lifesaving, but only to a point. Then it starts to turn dangerous. When you no longer have any idea what to do with yourself, just about anything starts to look good.

Suddenly, disaster: After COVID-19 hit, it was *all* downtime. Doing nothing had never felt so weird. But, remember, when the going gets weird, the weird turn pro. And, I would add, the narcissists turn malignant.

The Damaged Goods already had their social media accounts for the band as a whole, and the guys each had individual accounts, as well. Logan had always been too distracted to bother with them himself. That's what people like me are for. Post-pandemic? He got interested. Of particular significance was his Logan Elliott Official channel at YouTube, a potential cash cow he realized he could milk much harder. Because it was the rare thing that was 100 percent his own.

He'd had the misfortune of ascending during the era of the 360 Deal, which means if you're signed to a label with enough machinery to make you a star, they'll expect you to be cool with them scooping their fingers into every slice of your pie, and they have more arms than a Hindu god. Live performances and touring, merchandising, music publishing, endorsement deals, TV and film, and so on . . . they take from it all. I know his percentages. Yeah, I'm nerdy about details.

Because it's good to lob your dogs an occasional bone, Logan's reps got the label to exempt his personal YouTube channel from their indentured servitude profit-sharing plan. Within a week of Logan realizing it was the most viable public outlet he had for the foreseeable locked-down future, it went from an afterthought to a lifeline to the meaning of life itself.

His efforts started out normal enough. Here's a new song I'm working on. Here's an old song I could never figure out how to end. Here's the time I fell off the stage at a Lollapalooza festival, and for a second, you can see my ass crack. Here's a walkthrough of my home, with the legally questionable debris stashed out of sight. Oh, and here's my personal assistant Dana, who's my brilliant external brain, say hello, Dana—

Which pleased me not one bit. I could instantly imagine the judgments. What's he doing with *her*, and can't somebody start a GoFundMe to get her a nose job?

I'm more of a behind-the-scenes person. Respect the boundaries, please, Logan?

Soon, I got him focused on how clever he'd be if we started approaching his socials as an integrated whole. Our vocabulary lesson of the day: S is for synergy. He already had decent subscriber bases, and over those first months growth was good, steady, better than linear but not yet exponential. Until we began analyzing views and likes and other engagement metrics, and could only conclude Logan's most popular content was the stuff that made him look like more of a hapless, hopeless fuckup than he actually was.

So the cuts, the bruises, their associated angst and ennui . . . they seemed a natural progression. *I bleed for you* has always been a winning stance. Bruises? That's just bleeding on the inside.

The feedback, though? We really weren't prepared for that.

I grew up listening to a song my mom loved, "Message in a Bottle." The gist is, one lonely message goes out into the world, a flood of them comes back in response. Oh look, how heartwarming, he's not alone after all. It gave Mom hope. The song was okay, I guess, but it was easier for her. Mom kept the looks in the family. What adolescence taught me was that my hopeful bottle was more likely to come back full of pee.

So I wonder what Mom would think about this. A message going out in blood, the return tsunami coming back the same way. Logan, can you see me? Logan, can you hear me? Logan, can you read your name carved adoringly into my skin? Can you find your way to my heart from this topographical map of scratches, burns, and scars? They posted their tribute pictures for him with the wounds still fresh. They posted updates to prove the permanence of what they'd done. They revised and edited themselves in his secular name. Logan, you give us the courage to loathe ourselves just as much as you, and how we love you for it.

"I never asked for this," he told me one afternoon, in hushed and hesitant awe.

I nearly laughed, but come on, Dana, read the room. "Well, I think it's too late for you to give it back now."

If Logan continued to have qualms, he didn't bring them up again. Nobody likes an ingrate. What's a poor boy to do, then, but continue to feed the beast he's created to worship him?

After the world's grand reopening, with lockdowns lifted and quarantines over and renewed claims on his time, he wouldn't be giving any of this up. It gave back too much.

Not even Amazon could deliver this fast on immediate gratification.

Cutting on yourself, sooo edgy. Get a proper knife and do the job right, edge-lord. (via Instagram)

There's an observation attributed to Aristotle, which goes to show how long the complainers have been a bother: If you don't want to be criticized, then do nothing, say nothing, be nothing, make nothing.

Logan had no such reservations in this quest for attention. He was wholly sold on the logical extrapolation: that the more haters and whiners he attracted, the more this proved he was doing things right. He cultivated haters like valued relationships. He dreamed up better reasons for them to hate him. He dedicated a luau roast pig mukbang to vegans. For the Damaged Goods fans who liked their heavy stuff, he came up with sappy ballads. To the fans who actually liked the ballads, he dedicated unholy compositions of distortion and noise. For people who said he couldn't sing for shit no matter what he played, he performed in falsetto. For those who said he couldn't act, he deliberately massacred Shakespeare: "Now is the winter of our disco tent!" After he voiced an opinion and someone told him he was talking out his ass, he made a video in which he took the accusation literally, wearing a lab coat and stethoscope to explain in deadpan earnestness why rectums are medically incapable of speech.

Overall, people loved it. At least when the mockery wasn't directed at them.

He also drew fire for the personal habits he put on public display, or hinted at. He was a terrible role model for his reputed drug use. He wasn't defiantly open enough about his drug use. He was emotionally disturbed and should seek help. He was pathetic and boring and the more irrelevant he got, the more he acted out, so stop, just stop, go away and die.

"I need a fight. I need an enemy with an actual face," Logan told me one day. "I should give one of these haters some airtime. And do it as a livestream, so nobody can accuse me of making them look bad through editing. What do you think?"

"I think there are all kinds of ways that could go wrong."

"It only goes wrong if nobody's watching." He went through his standard ten-second deliberation routine, cocking his head one way, then another, as if listening to voices. A devil on one shoulder, an angel on the other, only they're both on bath salts. "Let's make this happen. Find somebody. Find me a worthy foe."

Okay, then. On it.

Never read the comments is the closest thing to Ultimate Wisdom I've ever heard, but duty called. I toted a laptop out back for the countervailing balm of fresh air, sunshine, and orange trees, and took the plunge into the ick. Anybody could mindlessly hate. Anybody could spew venom. I was looking for a point of view that went beyond YOU SUCK.

I began by focusing on names that showed up on a recurring basis, and narrowed from there. Which eventually led me to Katrin Coolidge. She'd been dogging Logan from site to site for months, not to spit at him so much as audition as a nagging conscience—think about what you're doing, consider the messages you're putting out. Other times she tried to communicate with Logan's followers, pleading with them to ignore him, he wasn't healthy for them. She was like a religious nut without the religion part. Instead of the Holy Bible, she quoted from the DSM-5, the bible of the mental health profession.

Her spelling and grammar? Chef's kiss. Her favorite word? *Toxic.* Katrin belonged to something called the Social Media Ethics Initiative, a wannabe watchdog group whose ultimate aim was . . . oh, what is it they always want? Control. Imposed values. A world remade in their own humorless image. An avatar photo showed a youngish woman with a choppy plume of hair the pink color of Darvocet, a sharp nose, and a demeanor that went more with the nose than the hair.

She. Was. Perfect.

And understandably reluctant when I emailed her. Framing was crucial: a public dialogue with Logan, I called it . . . not a debate. Not an argument. Definitely not a screaming match. After two rounds of email, Katrin suggested we advance to a FaceTime call.

"Before I make a final decision, answer something for me," she said. "How long have you been his assistant?"

"Four years." Barely three, but call it a rounding error. I was curious to see if she already knew and would challenge me on it. Apparently . . . not.

It soon became obvious how she'd sculpted the worry-crease between her eyebrows. "Why do you do this job?"

"Umm . . . flexibility? Connections? It's never boring, because no two days are the same? Because I, umm . . . like to be useful?"

Hearing that last one slip out surprised me. It was probably the truest among these reasons, but the thing I would have least intended to share if I'd taken a moment to think, rather than blurt. It felt like admitting to weakness. The truth is always easier to use against you than lies, and this was true. So much of my life had been spent semi-visible that to feel useful to someone, even indispensable, was really, really rewarding.

"Look," I said, "I'm not sure what you're going after here."

The room behind her was everything her glorious hair wasn't—sparse and drab, a room where someone would merely sit and exist. Shudder—I *knew* that room.

"People like him, they chew other people up and spit them out. Everywhere they go, it's another trail of carnage behind them. I'm questioning if you even see that."

"Well, what do *you* see? After four years of him, do I look all that masticated?" I figured her for someone who appreciated a big word where a little word would've done fine. "This carnage trail you're talking about . . . eleven years along, the band still has all five original members. Same management team. Logan's never been pointed at in anybody's MeToo story. He's worked with one film director three times already."

Katrin seemed to be loading counterarguments, then returning them to the rack.

"You know how it is with anybody who has any degree of fame," I said. "They have a public face and a private face. I'm acquainted with both, but it's the private face I see most of the time, and I'm still here. All in one piece. It's his private face that thinks you're promoting some misconceptions about him."

Annnd . . .

Done. Landed. Delivered. Katrin was in, agreeing to this live dialogue with, of all things, an expression of relief. Oh, poor lamb, she looked as though she might be thinking there was something in Logan worth salvaging, if she could reach it. That she could appeal to the better angels of his nature. That lost-boy look was his superpower.

I don't know how Katrin prepared, beyond the quick, helpful briefing I gave her in confidence. Logan spent an exuberant week pimping and promoting the upcoming clash across all his socials.

And then it was ON.

There's a vicious part of me that wants to watch the archived video of their train wreck livestream again, to see if I can pinpoint the moment Katrin fully comprehends the nature of the beast sharing the other half of the screen with her, angling to pounce for whatever jugular he could find.

Her determination to stick to whatever game plan she had wobbled early, when after some opening pleasantries, Logan, loopy grin in place and looking as disarmingly crushed by the world as ever, said he would like to establish her qualifications.

"I mean, you've been quoting the DSM-5 about me," he said, making a smooth transition into Lab Coat Logan. "For everyone out there who doesn't know what that is, it's the fifth and latest edition of the *Diagnostic and Statistical Manual of Mental Disorders.* This isn't a layperson's book. It's for professionals, from the American Psychiatric Association."

Had Katrin even considered this would come up? Signs point to NO.

He morphed again, into the Logan you'd get if he was onstage and someone hurled a bottle at him. But not the eruption of fury. It was the sly, seething Logan gathering force just before the eruption.

"So I'm thinking here's a chance for me to get some free help. But I at least should know what your credentials are, that you weaponize this professional manual against me," he said. "Psychiatrist? Psychologist? Licensed Practical Counselor?"

He let each one land barely long enough for Katrin to give a tiny lunge forward, as if attempting to grasp for control, before jabbing with the next one.

"Or, a B.S. in Media Studies from Arizona State University, wasn't that it?"

Like we weren't going to research this?

"If I'm wrong, *mea maxima culpa,* wave that medical diploma in my face and set me straight."

From determined to defensive, within five minutes. Logan sat back as if letting a bandmate take a solo, seeming to possess every confidence she would make the worst of it. First person to yell loses.

"It doesn't take a degree in *anything* to see through you. I've been to—I've had my—" Wherever Katrin was headed, she thought better of it and decided more volume and treble was the answer. "I don't know what's worse, that you think self-harming is something for public entertainment and actually inspire people to follow your sick lead, or that you're such a pitiful fraud about it!"

Logan's puzzled expression? Genuine. You're welcome, boss.

Katrin believed she had him and pressed the advantage. "Yeah, that's right! I have it on good authority that the sharpest thing you cut yourself with is a sponge. It's just makeup. Stage blood. You get your little pictures and it washes off."

Oh my. Wherever had she gotten *that* idea?

Logan appeared dismayed as, slowly, he pushed up the sleeve of his shirt and held his left forearm close to the webcam. Pretty scabs, all in a row. He got a fingernail under one and worked it until the wound wept a red tear.

"Look. Ms. Coolidge," he said, quiet and contemplative. "How I deal with my issues sometimes . . . I know it makes things feel better in the moment, and we could probably have a valuable discussion about whether that's really helping or just making them worse in the long run. But if these are the kind of therapeutic techniques they teach you in Media Studies, I don't think I'm ready to go there."

Whatever else was going on at the other end, in Katrin's drab room, I could imagine a director hunkering just out of frame, coaching her through maybe the worst minutes of her existence.

Show me regret for every bad decision you've ever made, all at once.

From determined to defensive to desperate—that's what the blood sport section of our audience was waiting for.

Show me a look of betrayal, after trusting the wrong person.

They'd watch this again and again, in froth and fury.

Show me floundering.

Logan's mob would mobilize for the counterattack and launch it on a thousand fronts, a screaming hydra with a million mouths and ten million fingers on keyboards.

Show me despair.

They might even marvel at how someone could argue so hard to regain the upper hand and keep making it worse for herself, enraptured that this un-masked pink-haired bully has given them so much to punish.

Show me the soul-crushing understanding that you know enough about the internet to realize life as you know it is over.

But Katrin needed no director, and couldn't have played this better with a script.

Okay, so she did have one, sort of, being written in real time. All she had to do to consult it was glance toward the right edge of her screen, at the live comments pane. An avalanche of live-scrolling hostility, every corrosive line aimed at her. All the greatest hits, all the worst names to be called, all the old reliable threats.

It would follow her everywhere. Poor lamb.

oh so your creatively blocked well boo fukking hoo some of us have to work you know so two words SHOTGUN ENEMA try it that should clear you out. (via YouTube)

A Wednesday. Or was it? Really, it's whatever day I say it is, isn't it? It's not like you're going to check.

When I let myself into Logan's house at the usual time, he was up already, a disturbing ripple in the natural order. He wasn't doing a movie. His eyes were clear, with none of the mania of a pharmaceutically assisted all-nighter. His exhilaration seemed entirely natural. High on life.

"No pictures today. You look too healthy," I said. "They'll hate that."

"I can't help it, I feel amazing."

You can work with someone a long time without really looking at them, and that's how it had been lately. I didn't *want* to look at him. The livestream had been a success by any standard . . . unless, of course, you were Katrin Coolidge. I'd totally set her up. For ambush. For failure. For humiliation. For whatever the trolls and orcs of the internet could throw at her, and they were delivering, with a fervor that horrified even me. Three years ago I never would've done something like this. Now? What . . . all in a day's work? So I didn't want to look at Logan, didn't want him looking at me.

But I was looking at him now.

And had to ask: "Are you losing weight?"

He didn't own a bathroom scale, but it was obvious, and he didn't have much weight to spare. It had been eleven days since the last mukbang, which, so far, hadn't had a noticeable effect on him. But then, most of the shitty food ended up jetting back out the intake pipe anyway.

I poked around. The fridge was nearly empty, but that was nothing new. No food wrappers or cartons in the trash, though. No dirty plates anywhere.

"How long has it been since you've eaten anything you've actually kept down?"

"I'm past that. I don't have to anymore." He looked like he was in on some joke I wasn't, and lifted his hands skyward. "You can't feel it, can you?"

"I don't think you want to know what I'm feeling right now. So that's a no."

He leaned toward me, his confidante, keeper of his secrets. "It's *them* feeding me now," he whispered.

I didn't get it, but he was eager to elaborate: Out there, all of *them,* all around the world. Them, and everything they were sending him. The love, the hate, the blood, the bile—he wasn't particular, it was all good, and all he needed now.

I tried to fathom this from his perspective. He bled for them, for show, and they bled right back, for real. And the blood is the life, wasn't that the bottom line?

Except, in the telling, he looked like one of those starry-eyed lunatics explaining how they live on breath and sunshine alone, and sounded like any dictator, convinced his subjects' adoration would keep his regime in place for a thousand years.

The way Logan began staring at me then, it felt as if he were pitying me for reasons I didn't deserve. Modest, unremarkable me, diminishing from his ever-exalted level, maybe. Whatever, I hated it—nobody needs such condescension first thing in the morning. You trust me to cut you, you asshole. You trust me to beat you with a hose. You've trusted me with everything. So don't look at me like that.

"There's something you have to see," he said, and steered us toward the dining table. "Cut me. Make it good."

Oh come *on*. I should be allowed to finish my coffee. But he insisted. No pictures, just a cut or two, we'd be done in no time. So I did it, one slice, then another. Once he got over the ouchie part, he sat back with a complacent grin.

"Now what?" I said.

"Just wait."

So we waited. Watching the blood run.

"It's going to heal. Right in front of your eyes."

Watching the blood dry.

"It's going to be amazing, like you never cut me at all."

Watching the scabs congeal.

"Just a little longer."

Watching the daylight swing across the room as the sun climbed the sky.

The thing that hurt the worst was knowing where this was headed for him. Here's the joke, and it was on him: Junkies never see the crack-up coming.

I can tell you why you're still around. You're 32 years old and the good ones try to die at around 27. (via Twitter)

A confession. Starting when I was a sophomore in high school, my guilty-pleasure reading was heroin memoirs. If they'd known this about their secretary-treasurer, the Jane Austen Reading Club would've been scandalized. The stories always ended up in the same horrible place, but before that, there was this phase where it was mostly fun and euphoria, and I'd have this vicarious yearning: if only they could keep it poised right there, ten feet before the edge of the waterfall.

It's why I found this gig so easy to say yes to, because it sure wasn't the pay. I thought I could help. I hoped I might be useful.

While he was still engaged with his days, Logan obsessed over his phone, locking into a cyclical loop through his accounts, starving for the only sustenance that mattered now. Whatever the addiction, it's always the same unsustainable story—the craving for more, more, ever more, until all it's doing is keeping the addict functional, but the high is gone, and no amount of more can be enough. Where are you supposed to fit more, anyway, when the vessel itself has begun to wither and his leaky cuts won't heal and the bruises no longer fade?

He'd have me shoot pictures of him, shirtless and sallow, stark studies in ribs and unfillable hollows, and looking appropriately mopey was no longer a put-on. Each one for the Gram, and for captions I raided his lyrics, prophecies that had come true.

> Where are you tonight,
> where are you right now?
> I can't feel you anymore,
> no way, no how.
> Fill me. Fill me. Fill me. Fill me.
> And if that's too much now, then just fucking kill me.

At last, he'd become everything he'd wanted them to believe he was. Fans called him beautiful and starved themselves in alliance.

So when Logan resumed his heroin journey—twice-daily deliveries, nothing recreational about it, needling himself into vacancy on a regular basis—it seemed redundant, is all.

He'd already given his soul over to something so much worse, and I wasn't feeling hopeful about my own. Both of us, willing servants to this malign intelligence that seduced us through our pockets and at our desks . . . this voracious parasite, this incubator of inhumanities that rewarded us for being our most grotesque. It squatted over our lives like some gargantuan toad-god, ravenous for blood and souls, only we were part of it, too, a couple more warts on its pulsating hide. It drained its appeasers to husks and made more.

Heroin seemed the logical alternative, Logan using one high to numb himself to the failing of another. Or maybe it was guilt. He'd started shooting up again after learning that Katrin Coolidge killed herself, weeks of unrelenting savagery by his most rabid defenders having taken one final toll. How does that work, Katrin—after enough death threats, you decide that denying the cannibals their chance is a win?

All of us in Logan's closest orbit made excuses for him to the world beyond, although nobody came around more than they had to. He'd gone from hot mess to plain old disgusting mess.

But I'd signed on to be useful to the end.

I kept the pictures flowing with discards from earlier sessions, plus new ones, because authenticity is important and here's what authentic looks like today. The stupor, the unfocused eyes, the hazy grin, the drool. Every day, another one for the Gram, and the captions came effortlessly now.

For a bathroom close-up of a box of stool softener from the Walgreens up on West Pico, acquired because of what opiates do to the bowels: *Breakfast of champions.*

A thousand likes before lunch.

The stats, however, left Logan unmoved.

"You picked a weird time to grow a conscience," I told him. In the fetor of his bedroom, my voice sounded unnaturally loud, even as it was muffled by the dust. "I *would* say better late than never, and I'm proud of you . . . but maybe it would've been better if you never had."

No answer.

What day was this again? I honestly don't remember. Just call it another typical day with Logan. They used to all be so different, and now they were exactly the same.

Doomsday, then.

Call it Doomsday.

A few hours later, I caught up with him in the living room, Logan slouching into the puffy couch that reminded me of an open casket. He'd put the Damaged Goods' first album on repeat and was staring at the curtains as if trying to see beyond them to the window, to the sky, to those airborne energies he'd convinced himself were better nourishment than food. He kept a laptop open beside him, browser tabs full of his socials, and every so often he would refresh them, then come away as blank as before.

"Anything?" I said. "Are you getting anything from them at all?"

As if on a delay timer, he shook his head no. It was like he was suffering from the ultimate service outage. There were times I loved him, other times I hated him. But most of all, I hated seeing him like this. We could at least give him a proper send-off.

"I know what the problem is for you. I know how to fix it, too."

I had his focus. His attention. Of course—everything was about him.

"The way you told me about how the craziness used to feed you, you made it sound like Wi-Fi. You just picked it up. It charged you. But sometimes Wi-Fi goes out. There's interference, or the signal sucks."

I waited to make sure he was following me.

"So what you have to do then is change to a wired connection. You have to plug directly into the source. That boosts the signal back up again."

I dangled a network cable in front of him, then stepped close enough to touch.

"The jack should be right about there. Under your liver. It's been growing inside there all along. You didn't know?" I pointed beneath the inverted V of his rib cage. "You love cyberpunk. Well, this is the kind of enhancement you can expect when you're an evolved being." I probed him with my fingertips. "Yeah. There it is. Can you feel it?"

So susceptible. He'd always trusted me with everything. And when they hurt bad enough, addicts will believe anything.

"We'll have to go in through there."

I set a fresh razor blade on the sofa, next to him. MacBook on one side, blade on the other. He looked at one, then the other, and nodded.

"Cut me."

"Not this time. This time you have to do it for yourself. Any other way, it wouldn't be authentic."

He let every word sink in, putting one fact in front of the other, then took up the razor blade and got to work, making his first slice from breastbone to belly button. All that anesthetic, he didn't appear to feel much pain. But it did make him sloppy, and his fingers got slippery. Whenever he needed it, I guided him, encouraged him. A little higher, Logan. There—no, the other way. Now cut deeper, you really need to be able to get your hand in there. You've almost got it.

When he lost the first blade inside himself, I gave him another.

It can take so little to be useful.

As he worked, I reflected on my Aristotle. If you don't want to be criticized, then do nothing, say nothing, be nothing. It sounded appealing to me, but while maybe this was true in Aristotle's time, it isn't now. Now you'll have the human-potential cheerleaders after you: Who are you to deny the world the wonderful light of your being, you socially crippled selfish monster, you? Get out there and atone for the mortal sin of your insignificance.

I made myself watch Logan until his red hands stopped moving and felt at peace with this decision for the greater good. His fame could only grow from here. He would get to retain a certain dignity that some stupid overdose would've eliminated. His legend would resound, like that of a warrior who fell on his sword rather than surrender, or a samurai who slumped into his own entrails after honor was gone.

THE ATROCITY EXHIBITIONISTS 119

Useful—who would dare say I wasn't?

I joined Logan for a few selfies, because it was time to stop being so self-conscious and claim a little of the spotlight for myself for a change.

Feeding the beast, it never ended. No caption, I'd just put this out there to see what happens. A thousand likes before dinner. Maybe see if we couldn't inspire a few of these venomous trolls we'd helped spawn to do the same.

"THE FATHER OF MODERN GYNECOLOGY": J. MARION SYMS, M.D. (1813–1883)

by Joyce Carol Oates

I saw everything, as no man has ever seen before.
—J. Marion Syms

(1836) Exile to Alabama
Meigs Plantation
Mt. Meigs, Alabama

"Doctor Syms!—you must come with me at once."

The astonishment of my life—the very day to determine my Future—at last!

Swallowing all pride, summoned like a common tradesman—yet—no choice but to acquiesce—brought on horseback to the Mt. Meigs Plantation—the largest cotton-growing plantation in eastern Alabama.

Obliged to confess—I was trembling badly. (Retired) General Matthias Meigs was known through all of Alabama as a harsh master of both White and Colored in his service—(nearly) as tyrannical with his White staff as with his Colored slaves—a man to respect!

Other physicians had been summoned to Mt. Meigs, I knew; others had been dismissed if they failed to please the Master, with but minimal payment. Yet—my fortunes were such—I had little choice but to leap at the offer; & not much pride remaining.

(& it did occur to me, even on that first adventure, I might continue my surgical experimentation, that had been rudely interrupted in Headley, in this new purview where lurid tales of my malfeasance had not reached.)

Arriving at the great plantation covering thousands of acres—the grand white-column'd house on a knoll which I would see only from a distance—a

Greek temple rising amid the steamy heat of May—a vision of such beauty, it seemed to me a mirage; but, as a lowly hire of the Master, I was invited nowhere near the house on this first occasion—but was brought at once to the Colored quarters where a powerful odor arose of infected & unwashed flesh, pinching my nostrils and bringing tears to my eyes.

Ah!—was this not a descent to Hades, a shameful descent for a White physician from a good, genteel South Carolina family!

On a makeshift cot on the ground lay, on his side, a Colored man insensible from his wounds—broad muscled back shining with blood, & buzzing with flies—face contorted with pain & covered in sweat. A fine physical specimen in the prime of life, looking to be well above six feet in height, and two hundred pounds of solid flesh—yet, a shadowy ribcage was visible through the sleek sable skin, like the peeking of a skeleton. All that I was told was the murmured explanation *Samson been whipped bad*—it was shocking to me to see, for the first time, the effect of a whip on a man's skin, transforming it into raw festering flesh upon which great horse flies were alighting, to torment him further.

"My God! What has the man done, to merit such punishment?"—the naïve question sprang from my lips, and was met with expressions of blank bafflement and incredulity among the Colored gathered about the injured man.

One of the women, a very dark-skinned person of about forty years of age, with large glaring eyes and well-muscled arms, and little evident respect for the White physician in her presence, fixed upon me a gaze of particular scorn and, startlingly, laughed aloud—a response that seemed to me particularly inappropriate, in the very presence of the injured man.

As if to say—*Merit? What is "merit" on the Plantation?*

In a fever delirium the injured man looked up at me with an expression of terror in his widened eyes—seeing (I supposed) a White demon in my place, akin to the foreman who had whipped him within an inch of his life—baring teeth big and discolored as a horse's teeth, and shrinking with fear at the sight of me. & so it happened that, to this afflicted person, I might be something of a Savior, & not a demon, or a mere hireling.

A wild happiness seized me in that instant—quite unlike any I had felt in my life before this—a sensation of *joyous righteousness*—beyond even pride. That I—J. Marion Syms—scorned in certain quarters, & made to feel an outcast—might *be of use* to this luckless Slave—& to his demanding Master who would pay me a decent wage—as I had been paid but a pittance in my past life as an apprentice to an elderly, tyrannical physician, & treated with contempt.

& another surprise: *I was not uneasy in this patient's presence* as I had been in the presence of White patients.

For indeed I was not uneasy in the company of the Colored, decreed by God as our inferiors & servants. & unless it was a misconception of mine, it seemed to me that the Colored respected *me,* including even the woman who had laughed in scorn.

Bathing poor Samson's wounds with my own hands, not only those wounds fresh that morning from a vicious beating of fifty lashes but older wounds, that had not healed but had opened anew with the whipping—a criss-crossing of piteous wounds, festering & maggot-infected—dreadful to see. All of which awakened much sympathy in me for Samson, that he had behaved in such a way to incur upon his body the righteous wrath of his owner, as a blundering child might behave, who does not comprehend his own welfare; of course, I did not cast blame at him, as I would not have cast blame upon a child, or an animal. It did not fail to touch my heart that Samson fairly wept in gratitude for my physician's care—and did not wince, shudder, and moan at the slightest touch, as White patients are wont to do.

Thus, it seemed to me likely, that the Colored do not feel pain as White persons do—by nature they are stoic & resigned—perhaps they are the truest Christians, who understand that pain is to be borne, like the wounds of our Savior.

This day, my first at Mt. Meigs, changed the course of my life. Not only did I succeed in bathing and dressing severe wounds, such as I had never done in Headley, but chance provided me with a "nurse"—the very Colored woman who had laughed at my question—who turned out to be the most skilled midwife at Mt. Meigs, named Corinthia.

Usually, Corinthia followed my orders capably. This too was gratifying to me as I could not imagine an impertinent White girl obeying with such alacrity; yet, if I seemed hesitant, or frankly had no idea what I was doing, Corinthia would learn, in time, to modify the treatment according to her own judgment; for she had been, indeed, a midwife for many more years than I had been a physician.

That day, however, I made the brave pronouncement: "I have come to 'heal'—I have come a long distance just for *you.*"

A harmless fib, which leapt so readily from my lips, it scarcely registered as a *fib* at all but rather a mysterious sort of *truth* the Colored were avid to hear as the Gospel.

Indeed, even Corinthia seemed to be placated by these words, and did not glare at me scornfully any longer.

Having brought with me my valise of medications, to administer to Samson liberal doses of echinacea, hawthorn, St. John's wort, and a potent solution of laudanum, all of which hasten healing as well as suppress pain and induce sleep.

Seeing that I had fared unexpectedly well with Samson—(who, it was revealed, had been declared "past mending" by a previous physician summoned to the Plantation)—I was requested to attend to other incapacitated persons in the slave quarters, of both sexes, and of all ages from mere children to the elderly; misfortunates suffering from divers maladies (badly infected wounds, from lashings; sunstroke, from picking cotton in blazing sunshine; boils, festering sores; bunions, hernias, cysts and tumorous growths; ingrown toenails; fevers, and chills; intestinal flu, constipation, diarrhea; dropsy, gout, wheezing lungs & calcified breasts that did not allow for nursing; complications of pregnancies, shortness of breath, "pains all over," etcetera). Of these, several, like Samson, had been "given up for dead" but who revived, to a degree, from my ministrations, and were able to return to the cotton fields, to some degree.

My heart was greatly moved, as well as my pride restored. Not only did Samson thank me profusely once he was able to speak but others as well— even those who had not been ill themselves, but had been fretting over the ill, fearing that they would die. & all this wonderfully astonishing to me, for no White patients had ever thanked me, in Headley!

Yet, the greater surprise was that *I was not nervous in the slightest, in treating either the male or female Colored.*

Most astonishing, and with much significance for the future (as you will see), in Mt. Meigs I discovered that while the mere prospect of examining a White woman terrified me I was soon at ease with Colored females of all ages, whether young & shapely, or older & disfigured; whether "beauteous" or very plain, or even ugly.

Why was this?—it is unmistakable that the female body is, in certain respects, repulsive to examine too closely, a curse of the (female) flesh.

Yet, with the Colored women, as with the men, I did not feel as if I were trespassing in a forbidden place but rather that, as a White physician, it was my privilege to do as I wished, without regard for any judgment. I have come to think that the tincture of skin is everything.

For the White skin is "my own"—the Colored skin, "their own." As God has set His children above the race descended from Ham, I could summon Christ's strength as my strength in ministering unto them, as one might minister unto an animal lacking a soul; for, if the physician failed, and the patient expired, it was not nearly such a loss as if a White patient had died. Still more, the White female has so sharp an eye, she *sees* who I am, and may scorn me; while the Colored female is obsequious, obedient, uncomplaining, and likely to be grateful for my attention, knowing that she is not inherently worthy of it, but has been granted it as a gift.

From this Day of Miracles onward, through years of faithfully attending the Colored at Mt. Meigs, and rarely failing to acquit myself well, Dr. Syms was the Savior of the Colored, & not their scourge; they soon learned not to fear me, as they feared other White men. For when the overseer's whip lacerated their bodies, it was I who treated them; anointed by their Master as by God himself, I staunched their bleeding wounds, & cleaned their infections; with the help of Corinthia, I bandaged them as they had not been bandaged before; if it was *their time* & nothing more could be done, it was I who gave them a final dose of laudanum, to deaden their pain and quell their pained hearts. As one might speak to children, I spoke calmly to them, showing only kindness, patience, and Christian fortitude.

My heart was suffused with deep emotion many times, as a Colored patient expressed gratitude to me, sinking to his knees on the ground—*Thank you, Doctor!* The rumor was, I had journeyed a long distance, thousands of miles, from "up North"—& I was gifted with "special powers."

Even when I could not save a gangrenous limb from amputation, or remove with a forceps a stillborn baby virtually impacted in its (often very young) mother's womb, nor successfully staunch the hemorrhaging that followed like a geyser—yet it was evident that my presence made some difference, at least; where in the past, as it was told to me, nearly all the stricken died without medical intervention at all, or were forbidden to be fed and were made to starve to death, since they were too ill to be restored to work.

Instead, as a result of my diligence, an impressive number of the afflicted soon recovered sufficiently to return to the cotton fields & resume their backbreaking work—so much so, the Master himself began to take note; and also, that I saved from certain death wenches in the throes of childbirth, and little black babies that would surely have expired before drawing a breath.

Soon then, General Meigs requested that I be brought to him, to be thanked in person; & to my surprise, the Master paid me with his own hand, and not through the usual intermediary, indeed in excess of what had been promised.

"You have saved me a considerable sum of money, Doctor! Having to go to auction to replace these brutes would have cost me many hundreds of dollars, as well as the aggravation."

I was deeply moved by General Meigs's generosity. No one in Headley had recognized my worth, certainly not that ignorant old man Strether, or indeed any of the wealthy and purblind McIntyres. Harsh things I had heard of this stalwart Christian gentleman, and all of them mere jealousy and envy.

It seemed fitting for me to present my full, formal name to General Meigs, "J. Marion Syms," and not the more plebeian "James Syms," which I had outgrown.

In this way "Dr. J. Marion Syms" was baptized, where the mere "James Syms, M.D." had been in ignominious exile.

Following this, through the patronage of the General, my life was changed utterly.

Most wondrous, my fear of White patients, especially my terror of White women of a genteel class, began to subside, in my confidence with Colored patients; my fear had been that of a young novice, shrinking from the judgment of others, where it was made clear to me, with my Colored patients, that I had little to fear if I maintained an air of self-assurance and never betrayed anxiety, dread, or despair. It is not the Hippocratic oath that guides the physician—*Do no harm;* but, rather—*Do not falter in your decision, whether you do harm or no.*

Quickly I should amend: I would never be fully at ease examining White women, as I was with Colored women; nor did I examine White women unclothed, while with Colored women it was a matter of no significance whether they were part or fully naked. The repulsiveness of the female body is not, I realize, a matter of race or skin-color, but an inheritance from Eve, accepted as such by the wisest females; not so much the mammalian features which can be made to appear sightly to the eye, if properly corseted and clothed, as the nether features, between the thighs and upward, a hellhole of unmitigated filth, yet, paradoxically, the very *birth canal,* with its sacred mission.

I was rarely in any examination room alone with any White woman, but always with a nurse or assistant, it scarcely needs to be said. (Not Corinthia, of course: for Corinthia was of use to me solely at the Plantation, not in my home office.)

When it was unavoidable I would "listen" to a pulsebeat (at a wrist) with my fingers or lay my hand against a seemingly fevered forehead, but such touch was never prolonged. If a White woman suffered from a rash, cyst, a lump, or a tumorous growth in a "private" part of her body, she would not ordinarily wish to speak of it to a (male) physician but would confide in a nurse or assistant, who would then report to me, to determine how best to proceed. Most of my consultations with White women were a matter of careful inquiry, my questions and their replies, a listing of symptoms, of which many were familiar to the physician: breathlessness, fainting spells, no appetite, an excess of appetite, rapid heartbeat, slow heartbeat, night-terrors, motiveless weeping, excitation, extreme fatigue as did not allow them to rise from bed on some mornings, and lace themselves into their whalebone corsets, etc.; usually then, I would treat the patient with a healthy dose of *blood-letting,* to quell the tremors of the nervous womb; sometimes, if there appeared to be a swelling of the gums, with my lancet I cut the gum back to the teeth, following up with proper medications to staunch bleeding and hasten healing, specifically extract of echinacea. Another frequent treatment was new to me—*mustard plaster.* (Smelling most loathsomely!—but good for the morale of the patient.)

Back home, the convalescent would be prescribed medicines appropriate to her condition, usually drops of cocaine, or laudanum, which proved agreeable with genteel ladies who did not have to exert themselves over-much through the day, unlike Colored women, who had not that luxury; for the Colored, a solution of nicotine extract might trigger a more rapid heartbeat, and a rush of strength in their limbs, generally so much more "muscled" than the limbs of White women.

It was rare that I did not closely consult with a husband, a father, or a brother, after having examined a White female patient, and before revealing to her my diagnosis, like any other responsible physician of the day. Every aspect of the White woman's treatment which I undertook was with the approval of a husband or a relative, of course, for it would be he who would be paying my fee, and it would be his satisfaction I would have to provide, particularly in the case of certain "controversial" surgeries with which I was entrusted: requests by husbands of women concerned for their well-being, whether extreme agitation in the woman, or lassitude; manic laughter, or helpless tears; "frigidity" of the lower body inhibiting conjugal relations, or, perversely, an unnatural "avidity" of the lower body during conjugal relations; all these, forms of *hysteria.*

Removal of the ovaries was frequently prescribed for these afflicted women, in more extreme cases the removal of the entire uterus (thus, "hysterectomy"); another frequent request was the surgical removal of the vaginal "clitoris," like the appendix a mysterious but useless part of the body with a dangerous latency, described in Galen as hyper-sensitive to any touch, with a propensity to exacerbate excitation, anemia, sleepwalking, hyperventilation, overeating, anorexia, morbid thoughts, migraine, insomnia, madness, and certain unspeakable habits of a degenerate nature more often associated with the male of the species, in his looser behavior.

The usual stratagem was to invite the (unwitting) patient to the physician's surgery, and converse with her on pleasant, innocuous subjects while providing her with a hot liquid, usually tea, containing a strong soporific, that would soon cause her to fall heavily asleep, without the slightest suspicion; when, hours later, she was capable of being roused, the surgical intervention in the nether region of her body would have been completed, and, apart from inevitable pain, and occasional complications requiring further treatment, the patient would be carried home to heal in quiet, sequestered circumstances. (Rest assured that these surgeries were carefully executed to protect the modesty of the patient: the head and torso of the comatose woman were chastely draped in a white cloth, to render the circumstances impersonal, as in an anatomy lesson, while the thighs were propped up, and spread, exposing to the surgeon's clinical eye the nether regions of the woman, i.e., the vagina, labial lips, birth canal, etc. Steely nerves were required of any surgeon who ventured into such territory, that presented a hellish spectacle to the eye; truly, beyond the power of language to describe, nor have I attempted to describe except to say, in the *Journal,* humbly, and without vanity or pride, that indeed *I saw everything, as no man has ever seen before.*)

According to my carefully maintained physician's log for these years, in no cases did one of my White woman patients complain of the purifying transformation of her body; rather, the removal of ovaries, uterus, clitoris, was scarcely registered at all, in those who survived, most of whom continued on a daily regimen of laudanum. Only one instance stands out disagreeably, the case of General Matthias Meigs's seventeen-year old daughter Bettina, a lively, ginger haired young woman with an outspoken, often contradictory manner, suspected by the General of an unclean habit, as well as a propensity for headstrongness and disobedience; when Bettina was brought to my office by her father she was immediately suspicious, and did not smile at my playful banter; balked at drinking the sweetened cocoa that was offered to her, and demanded to know why she'd been brought to "this nasty place" when there was "not a thing wrong" with her; eventually, after cajoling by both physician and father failed, headstrong Bettina had to be forcibly restrained, strapped screaming to a table and sedated, to a degree, by a forced ingestion of cocaine drops, that I might be able to practice a sort of debridement in the girl's nether region, with my razor-sharp surgical instruments—a shocking sight to behold, in one so young and presumably virginal, that the offensive little organ appeared to be inflamed, as with an obscene fire lit from within.

However, this obscene fire was soon quenched—the slight bit of flesh tossed out like garbage amid medical waste, and the bleeding wound expertly staunched, and stitched with tough black twine.

As it happened, I did not see this recalcitrant patient again, nor did General Meigs inform me of the fact that, not many weeks after the procedure, the ginger-haired Bettina attempted to run away from Mt. Meigs, in hysterical despair, but was captured and returned; still later, the unhappy creature was reported to have taken her own life by drowning, in the mosquito-infested paludal marshes at the outermost border of the Plantation, where, from time to time, rarely successfully, a Black slave fled, with the delusional hope of making his way North to freedom.

If only General Meigs had brought Bettina to me earlier, that I might have executed the procedure when the girl was a younger adolescent, thus less rebellious and habituated in her degenerate ways!—but it does no good to contemplate what might have been, as General Meigs conceded, with a heavy heart.

Not surprisingly, with God's blessing, and the imprimatur and support of General Meigs, my practice, once so humble, began to flourish through the entire state of Alabama. Soon then, in 1840 I had accumulated enough savings to purchase a property with house and outbuildings, within a decade to become the site of my first "back yard hospital" near Mt. Meigs; and, not least, to marry a good, Christian woman from a family of some substance in the vicinity, a helpmeet who would prove devoted to me, unquestioning in her loyalty and to every demand of our soon-increasing family—in all, nine children.

Hopeless—it was said of those females afflicted in a certain, scarce-describable manner.

Filthy, abominable, disgusting animals—it was cruelly said of them, who had no control over the afflicted nether regions of their bodies, thus should not have been *blamed*.

Rarely was the condition discussed in respectable company. Rarely did a White company know of it at all; a White gentleman-physician, never. For it was, overwhelmingly, an affliction of the Colored female, and not of the White; it was the luckless Colored females who, for reasons specific to their race, and their conditions in life, were first impregnated at very young ages, before their pelvises had time to grow sufficiently, to allow for a safe delivery of an infant of normal size. (It was not uncommon on the Plantation for Colored girls as young as twelve to become impregnated, certainly thirteen or fourteen were indeed commonplace; rumors of impregnation at even younger ages came to my ears, but were not within my personal experience.)

As a result of protracted, torturous labors lasting as long as seventy-two hours, it often happened that the young mother suffered tears, lacerations, and extensive abrasions in her nether regions, which caused a ripping of the bladder so that the excretory fluid (urine) flowed directly into the vaginal canal, and out of the body in a near-continuous trickle; thus rendering the afflicted young mother a virtual pariah among her kind, who could not bear her uncleanness, and the perpetual stench of her affliction. Even those who felt strong emotion for the afflicted, as close as a husband, a parent, or a sibling, could not abide the afflicted one for very long; the consequence being, young women injured in this way, with a "fistula" (as the wound was called), were not only banished from living with their kind, forced to live and eat like animals at some distance from the dwelling places of the others, but were susceptible to open sores, festering infections, and terrible raging fevers that soon brought their miserable lives to an end, sometimes before their babies were weaned.

(Indeed, these infants were often victims of the "fistula" as well—abandoned by their mothers who were unable to nurse, too frail or afflicted to flourish with other, surrogate breasts offered to them.)

And even in death, the afflicted body of the young mother so terribly stank of excrement, it was useless to attempt to wash it, according to custom; a Christian burial was executed in haste, within hours, with little time to mourn. Over all, when one of the "fistula"-afflicted women died, it was counted as a blessing, however sad to those who had known the afflicted in happier days.

Why, then, did young girls not resist impregnation?—one might reasonably inquire.

At such an age, and usually out of wedlock, such sexual precocity is baffling to the more civilized White society; a genteel White woman would shudder at the very thought, though it is not likely that a genteel White woman would have much occasion to think along such lurid lines.

A certain laxity in morals is the reason, most likely; an inheritance of the race, in which marriage is not so sacred as it is among White Christians. As pagan Africans become converted to Christianity, we may see a diminution of such wanton behavior; that is a hope for the future, but not a very plausible hope for the present time in which poverty, and filth, and laziness, and the intellectual faculty is stunted amid the Colored population. Wealth, a cultivated intellect, a refined mind, an affectionate heart, are exempt from the ravages of such maladies, but such lay in the future, for descendants of the enslaved.

Still, as a physician to the Colored, I would often ask in exasperation, of one of these afflicted girls, "But why would you allow such a thing to happen?"—and was met with tear-filled eyes but stony reticence.

Most impertinently, Corinthia intervened, laughing scornfully at my question and telling me that it was not possible for any girl or woman to say "no" to any male—"Colored, or White, or brindle."

I did not appreciate the woman's sharp tongue. I did not like her speaking so rudely of a *White man* behaving in such a way, nor of her joking reference to "brindle"—by which Corinthia meant *mixed-race*.

"Not possible! Surely you are joking, Corinthia."

I may have blushed at the thought of a White male impregnating an enslaved Colored female, which was very distasteful to me, as a Christian; the mingling of the races being an insult to the purer race, and an omen of degeneration to come, if it were not thwarted. The situation at the Plantation was most awkward for one could see, amid the very Black slaves, numerous slaves of much lighter skin, including a virtual bevy of children who clearly did not have a wholly Black parentage, some of these, the more attractive, with startlingly fair skins, fawn-colored hair, and blue eyes!—but of course, the discreet reaction was to say nothing, never to express surprise or dismay.

Corinthia took note of my unease, adding, in her way of rough teasing: "Of course, Doctor Syms, it could only be White men from elsewhere, not from Mt. Meigs, who would stoop so low. In Mt. Meigs White men, like General Meigs, are gentlemen, we know."

Hotly I retorted, "Certainly, yes. Indeed—*gentlemen*."

Stiffly I chose to confront the impudent woman's sarcasm with a flush of indignation, and a sincere rejoinder. It is a truism that, if you do not insist that Blacks *keep their place,* they will push out of their place, and take advantage of your Christian charity, mistaking it for a softness of conviction.

Corinthia laughed heartily at my words, and at the look on my face, but understood, with the cunning of her kind, that it were wisest to cease her effrontery at this point.

"Doctor! You are summoned to Mt. Meigs, please come in haste."

Once again, this imperial summons: on a very warm morning in late September 1845. Such words never failed to stir in me a sensation of ecstatic expectation, yet the most visceral dread: the expectation that my medical services would prove beneficial to the afflicted of the Plantation, yet my dread at what I would encounter.

Always I hurried to obey as I was commanded, to come at the bidding of General Meigs, to the Plantation—a summons to the Plantation was likely to be a dire emergency situation, for General Meigs would not have called me otherwise; routine medical care did not exist for the Colored, as it did not exist for "poor whites" in Alabama.

Corinthia hurried me to a hovel in the Colored quarters, distraught and grim-faced, explaining that there was a girl of sixteen struggling to have a baby, in labor for three days, steadily weakening, and in danger of bleeding to death.

Of all medical situations it is such horrors of childbirth that physicians most dread for sheer disgust: the grotesquely swollen belly of the pregnant woman streaked with blood, the strained, stretched blood-glistening vagina rawly exposed, a hideous organ in normal conditions but the more unspeakable when turned virtually inside-out as it is at such an awful time; the luridly contorted face of the woman, scarcely identifiable as human, and not a trace of femininity remaining, to lend some charm to the gruesome scene. (Of the head of the fetus/infant impacted between the blood-smeared thighs, seemingly clamped within the straining vagina, a mere glimpse of which so shook me that I feared fainting, I cannot bring myself to speak in any detail; the reader must rely upon his own imagination.)

So agitated was the pregnant girl, she seemed but scarcely aware of the White physician, standing hesitantly above her; I had a mere glimpse of her grimacing face, mask-like in ugliness, seeing nothing human in the glaring eyes, that rolled back in her head as she panted, grunted, whimpered like a stricken animal.

Ah, the feculent odor of the earthen-floored hut, abuzz with flies! Except for determined forbearance, I would have been sick to my stomach.

It was clear that the girl lacked the pelvic girth for childbirth, and being very young and seemingly terrified; and the baby, sired by who knew what brute, was too large for the birth canal. For some seconds I stood unnerved by the spectacle, paralyzed with dread, pity, horror, and the knowledge that I did not truly have the first idea what to do in this emergency, for I had never "delivered" an actual baby, only a dummy-baby in medical school, with several other medical students, and that several years ago; the delivery of babies fell to the responsibility of midwives like Corinthia. A skilled surgeon could perform a "Caesarian," I supposed—but I had only the vaguest idea what a "Caesarian" was.

Corinthia had already boiled water, and had a fresh pail prepared for me, along with numerous cloths, of which some were clean, while most were already blood-splattered; I saw that I had no choice but to behave as if I knew what I was doing, or the girl would die a hideous death, nor would the brute baby survive.

In my distraction I had forgotten my physician's satchel, which I gripped tight in my hand, and this, politely, but resolutely, Corinthia detached from my fingers, and opened to discover therein the curious instrument known as a "forceps."

All this while, Corinthia was thinking clearly enough to be fitting me, as best she could, with a protective cloth like a sheet, to cover my clothing; for I was wearing, on this warm September day, my usual attire—a somber dark suit of a light woolen fabric, with a white cotton shirt and a proper tie, befitting my visit to Mt. Meigs, but impractical in a situation involving surgery.

By holding her down, and by spreading her legs farther apart, Corinthia prepared the patient for me, all the while instructing me what to do: to maneuver the forceps inside the straining vagina, to close about the head of the impacted infant which was horribly visible, a pale scalp with strangely coarse dark hairs, and bulging blue veins, and to give the head a tug—a gentle tug at first—then more forcefully. By now I was kneeling between the Colored girl's legs, in a position I could not have imagined myself in, ever in my life; with inheld breath moving the baby's head from side to side, as if to wriggle it free as the mother screamed, and Corinthia called encouragement to her—"Push! Push!"

How long this hellish struggle persisted I would not know afterward. A red mist came over my brain, my heart pumped in desperation, yet the baby would not budge, and so, at last, Corinthia put into my hand a knife with a long, sharp blade, seemingly a butcher knife, and told me that I must use it, to free both the mother and the baby, which, God help me, I did, for I had no choice, cutting somewhat haphazardly and desperately in the swollen pelvic region until at last the brute infant was freed in a torrent of blood of which some splashed up onto my heated face.

But following this, it seemed that the baby was *born*, to cries of relief and rejoicing, lifted in triumph, and taken aside to be washed, while we attended to the now-unconscious Arelia lying amid the filthy rags of the childbed limp and unresisting as a corpse, as we tried to staunch the flow of dark blood from her.

Only dimly was I aware, the brute baby was, indeed, a *he*. Filling his lungs with air and crying lustily, borne away by others out of the feculent hut.

My impression was, beneath the ruddy flush of the infant, his skin was many times lighter-complected than the skin of the young mother, a feature that could not have gone unnoticed among witnesses.

I was concerned that the young mother was so very exhausted, and her injuries extensive, she would require further medical care; yet, it seemed that my services at the Plantation were ended, somewhat abruptly.

"But there is more to be done," I protested, "—the girl will die, I'm afraid, if . . ."

Somber-faced Corinthia did not disagree with me, I could see, but neither did she protest, that I was to leave the Plantation, by wagon, as I'd been brought; with the deft motions of a much-practiced servant, she removed the filthy sheet from me, that had protected, more or less, my clothing; as thoroughly as any mother, Corinthia washed my face and hands, and even attended to my hair, into which blood seemed to have splattered. Someone came to lead me away from the hut, and away from the Colored quarters, to hand me a flask of Scotch whiskey sent by the Master himself, which, though I am not a drinker, as I explained, I accepted with gratitude, in these special circumstances.

On all sides it was being told me: "Doctor! Thank you."

Somewhat weakly, I rejoined: "But—my work here is really not done . . ."

No one seemed to hear. On all sides the cry was taken up: "Doctor! God bless you."

These were White-skinned persons, presumably in the hire of General Meigs. In vain I looked for Corinthia who, I hoped, was attending to the stricken young mother, from whom I had been removed so abruptly.

On all sides congratulations as, unsteady on my feet, I was led back to the wagon that had brought me to the Plantation: "Doctor! God bless you."

Though I was not invited to the manor house this day, nor did General Meigs speak with me in person, an intermediary told me that the General would be very pleased with the outcome, as any new boy-baby, among the Colored slaves, was a great boon to him, saving him hundreds of dollars; and so his payment for my services was generous, twice what I had expected.

When I tried to explain that the exhausted mother would very likely not live unless she received further medical care, which I would be happy to provide for no extra fee, no one seemed to hear; it was forcibly iterated that General Meigs would be pleased with the outcome—"That is all that matters, Doctor."

Belatedly, a muted joy rose in my heart, that jubilation which came to me only at the Plantation, in circumstances like these I could not foresee, beyond my control: that, though a failure elsewhere, I was something like a success at the Plantation, and should rejoice in what success I have, and not pine after more.

A picnic basket of the most delicious fried chicken, and other specially prepared foods, was presented to me, to devour on my journey back home, for which, in my famished state, I was grateful.

Doctor! God bless you—these words would echo in my ears, even as I sank into an exhausted sleep despite the jolting wagon bearing me away from the Plantation into the dark.

From "The Story of a Physician's Life" by J. Marion Syms, M.D. (posthumously published, 1888)

HERE COMES YOUR MAN

by Indrapramit Das

"Can I buy you both a cup of tea?" the man asks them in Bengali, his smile too lazy to not be genuine. Dressed in a shawl, his hair long and wild, he looks like one of the bauls. Aditya and Megha take him up on his offer, since they've come to Santiniketan to mingle with the bards and townsfolk during the winter harvest festival. The locals treat the two of them like tourists, but then, they are—city people from a world away. Everyone they've met has been friendly, welcoming. They don't think twice about talking to another stranger.

The bearded man buys them tiny, shot-glass-sized plastic cups of sugary cha from one of the stalls selling snacks and drinks. There is a turtle-like placidity to him, the careful way he hands them the cha, his shawl wrapped tight around his neck so his head seems to emerge from hunched shoulders.

"Are you both from Kolkata?" he asks, probably because it is the nearest big city, and their clothes and accents always give them away.

They say that they are. "Where are you staying?" he asks. "In one of those new lodges?"

Aditya hesitates because his Bengali is rusty from his years abroad, and it embarrasses him. Megha glances at Aditya and takes over. "We're staying in town. My family has a house here."

"They are here also?"

"No, they're at home in Kolkata. They don't like to visit during Poush Mela, too crowded."

"I've been visiting the Mela here for many years, you know," the man says. "There weren't so many people coming for the festival, even ten years ago. This town was once full of field and forest that is now getaway houses for people from Kolkata. There used to be nothing but snakes underfoot. Now people can step a little less lightly." He smiles at them.

"You must be here to sing—you're a baul?" Megha asks him, hurriedly, to fill the silence between them.

He laughs gently. "Oh no, I'm just a fellow festivalgoer. I play no instrument, I could never be a bard. I am here because I like to make friends. I think it pays to treat people well. Some of my friends are over there. We are just here to enjoy it all," he says with a nod to a circle of men a few feet away, sitting on the grass and drinking tea amid the passing legs of the crowd. The blue smoke of bidis wreathes their heads.

That languorous smile rolls across the man's face again. "It brings people together, the harvest festival," he says, waving his hand. He's right, of course. There are thousands of people packed into the field, from all over the vast countryside that fills the spaces between Indian cities. Their heads bob like a sea, bathed in jaundiced neon from light murals and the flashing decals of cheap fairground rides.

"Like you two, all the way from Kolkata," the man says, lilting the name of the city as if it were a distant, exotic land out of reach instead of three hours away by train. "I can see that you are not brother and sister. That's all right. You are a good-looking couple. It makes me glad to see such happy, good-looking young people together."

They thank the man with polite smiles, downing their cha. Aditya coughs, his tongue and throat burning. The man crumples his little plastic cup, now empty. There is a crackle as he tosses it to the grass.

"Can I make a prediction?" he asks, poking a large, bony hand out of his brown shawl, which hides his lank body like a cloak. They don't even need to nod before he decides they've agreed.

"Give me your hand, my dear," he says. Aditya watches as Megha does. Her hand lies small like a chocolate in the man's joined palms. The sight is oddly disturbing. He makes her hand disappear within his before flipping it, exposing her palm and running a thumb across it. Aditya gets goose bumps. The man nods, sage-like, his long hair bobbing. "Now yours," he says to Aditya. Aditya flinches slightly when the man takes his hand, though he doesn't expect to. The man repeats the motions he went through with Megha, but quicker. The man's fingertips are coarse and dry, as if the whorls at the ends of them are etched into wood. He touches lightly, lets go. Aditya pulls his hand away.

"Yes." The man grins, lids sliding over his eyes slowly as he blinks. "You're an artist, aren't you? You both are." Megha isn't, exactly. She works as an editor for a small academic press. But Aditya's nod is enough. "I can tell that you're an artist, you have the look," he says, looking at Aditya. "You will fail her financially, because of this. Husbands cannot be artists. This you will have to live with, if you marry him," he says to Megha. "You must marry, of course. You don't look like the kind of girl that goes around with a boy without getting married. A girl like you, such light skin, from a good family, is a pride of this nation. You are destined to be a good wife and give us healthy children. There is trouble ahead for you both, though."

Megha glances at Aditya, one hand going to the small of his back. He knows what her fake smile looks like, and it makes him uneasy in the best of circumstances. She's wearing that smile.

"We should go now. We've had a long day," Aditya tells the man.

"Hmm. You must have been exploring the town? Let me tell you something. You shouldn't go to the groves beyond the maidan. There are people who fuck there in the evening, under the trees and in the bushes, out in the open, as if they don't care who sees them," he says, face wrinkling in sudden revulsion. "Young men being men, getting carried away by their nature, them I can understand. But these shameless girls with them, they have no modesty. Imagine, doing such things in the open, none of them even married. It's filthy. Such women cannot be the future mothers of this land. You are good young people, you would be disgusted if you saw it, I know. Stay away from there."

Aditya feels Megha push her shoulder against his arm. Her hand stays at his back. He can feel her fingertips through his jacket.

The man licks his lips. "Let me buy you both another cup of tea."

"No. Thank you. We really are feeling very tired," Aditya tells him.

"Then what's the harm in more tea, yes? It will wake you up. You cannot retire this early when the Poush Mela is going on. You're young and from the city, how can you be tired? Look at all these people, they are hardworking countryfolk who are all awake long past their bedtimes. Just to enjoy." His teeth appear from behind the oiled curls of his moustache and beard. "Tell me something. You don't speak much, but when you do your accent is different from hers. Did you go abroad?" he asks.

"I went to America, I did my studies there," Aditya tells him. He can't tell whether he should be rude and insist on leaving. He feels a dull throb above his genitals, a fresh urge to urinate.

"I knew an American, once," says the man. "White as an eggshell. I speak very good English, you know. So this lonely man could talk to me. He gave me lots of money to show him around in Delhi. He paid me to be his friend. So I lived in Delhi off the money he gave me. I didn't like it there. I didn't like him. I left soon enough. My true home is in the mountains in Rishikesh, the holiest of places. It is a long and rugged road up to it."

He looks at Megha.

"You must visit me there. Yes. Yes, you will come to Rishikesh, and ask the guides to take you to cave forty-two. But do not trust the dark-skinned guides by the paths. They will carry you up the mountain on their shoulders. It is an uncouth thing, for a girl like you. If you're not careful, they will take you to their own caves, and you will never leave. No, come to my cave, my beautiful girl, and I promise you I will put a wild tiger cub in your lap."

Megha grips Aditya's forearm. "We really must go now, I'm sorry," Aditya tells the man, and takes a step back, eyeing the men sitting in a circle not far from them.

"Oh, you're tired. Don't worry." The man flashes his widest grin yet, his hands hovering around Megha's and Aditya's shoulders, as if about to touch them. "I will buy you some more tea, and you will come sit with my friends," he says, and walks between them toward the stall.

"Take me back to the house," Megha whispers.

"He's getting more tea for us, we can't just . . ."

"Take me back to the house. He just touched me. He touched my ass."

"What?"

"I told you, he . . ."

"What the f—"

"Don't. Don't."

"What?"

"Please don't. Just. Let's get the fuck out of here."

"Okay. Okay. Let's go. Come on."

Aditya holds Megha's hand and leads her away, past the circle of men, the stranger's friends, into the swirling throng. They don't look behind them, don't see whether the stranger and his friends saw them leave, whether they are following through the crowd. Aditya knows what happened to Megha when she was a child. She takes her hand out of his, and walks alongside him rapidly.

"Are you okay?" Aditya asks. She walks, not nodding, not shaking her head, arms crossed against her chest. He touches her shoulder. "Megha. Are you all right?" She shrugs his hand off quickly. Flinches. His hand a spider.

"Please. Please don't touch me. I'm fine."

"Okay. I'm sorry," he tells her. They walk through this endless sea, with its own humid gravity of bodies seething in the mist rising from the grassy earth. Eventually, they come to its shores, escape its claustrophobic tides, walk back across the empty ground, the sparsely lit country roads of Santiniketan, the stars a thousand eyes open now above them. The lights of distant bungalows and houses twinkle between black trees, a far-off warmth. There is salt in Aditya's mouth, a residue of that tide of humanity left behind. "I can't believe I just stood there. I'm. I'm so sorry." Megha is silent.

Every muscle in Aditya's body is tense, painfully so, his heart clenching rigid with adrenaline. He feels sick, only his penis curled flaccid amidst the storm of hard, burning body parts sliding under clothes in the darkness. Megha next to him.

"I'm sorry," he says.

"Stop saying that. It's not your fault," she says.

He feels so, so very terribly, like a man.

The road is silent, empty. No one else walks with them. There are only occasional pools of streetlight in the night, bathing dew-speckled leaves, dusty side road. The rest of the world is wrapped in mist and darkness. The thin curve of the waning moon is lost in cloud. Bats flutter above them, just sound in darkness. There is faint music from the fairground in the distance. They are far from the centre of Santiniketan, with its tarred roads and university campus, its shops and dhabas. Out here, it is all fields and groves, interrupted by houses.

Megha looks behind them often. There is nothing in those pools of light they leave behind. It's difficult to see anything else on the road. The houses leading up to Megha's family's place are dark. Their owners could be asleep inside, or far away in the city, no one behind those shut windows.

Their throats are silenced by the inability to comfort each other. They're surrounded instead by the billion-limbed rasp of insects singing around them, the squelch and crunch of their sneakers on damp leaves and twigs and, finally, gravel as they open the gate and enter Megha's family plot. The yellow cone of the porch light beckons, a lighthouse in the still mist.

They lock the door behind them, slide the latch shut. The house is old and cramped, built by Megha's great-grandparents back when Santiniketan was more forest than town—a university haven surrounded by lurking wilderness. It is chilly inside, predictably like a tomb, for all its low cobwebbed ceilings and framed portraits of dead relatives embalmed in monochrome and glass, glazed by the antiseptic brightness of humming fluorescent lights. They close the windows against the mosquitoes and the whispers of the thick garden around the house, which is demarcated by a grove that falls into the slopes of the shallow valley behind the property. The train tracks run through that valley. Days and nights in the house are punctuated by the rhythmic clatter of trains on their way to and from Bolpur Station.

Once they've shut the windows, checked the doors, Megha can tell they've run out of silence. Aditya is looking at her, and he smells sharply of anxious sweat. He's worried about her, and it makes her feel small. A damsel. She knows he wants to talk, so she switches off the lights in the bedroom and takes off her clothes in the dusky nocturnal glow of the curtains.

He tries saying her name, to remind her that he's there for her, but she doesn't want to hear it. She kisses him, and he's salty. He tastes of fear, which seems a silly thing to think, but she feels it in the sourness of his saliva, the re-

sisting twitch of his lower lip as it hardens against her mouth. He doesn't resist long.

They fuck in that dim light, under the ghostly veils of the mosquito net,
put up earlier in the day by Ashok and Anjali, the caretakers paid to look after the house when no one's around. The caretakers are also the ones who left
rooti, daal, and chicken curry on the tiny dining table in the kitchen. It's cold
and uneaten. The ancient bed groans and creaks under their bodies. Megha
finds herself distracted from pleasure by the flimsy wooden bed, disconcerted
by how much it sounds like something hiding underneath, a decaying throat
sighing in rhythm with their sex. She almost stops, her entire body prickling
with goose bumps at the thought of something breathing, smiling under the
bed. She licks Aditya's stubbled chin instead, and grinds against him harder.

The house is small, and sound travels easily in its cramped rooms. The bedroom is by the living room. The front door is in the living room.

Megha can't sleep, and she's wide awake when she sees a shadow cross the
curtains of their window. At first she thinks she's imagining things, just mistaking the patterned shadows of the trees against the window for some other
movement. But then, with a hard, cruel inevitability she realises the front
door, in the next room, is rattling.

The man is here.

The man who would put a wild tiger cub in her lap.

Aditya snaps up, the bed sending a painfully loud crack through the room.
"Fuck," he whispers. "Fuck. Fuck someone's at the door. Megha."

"Shh baby. Please, they'll hear," Megha whispers, holding his arm tight.
"Maybe they'll go away think we're not here," she says, so soft she's not sure he
can hear her.

"They must. Have followed us. Fuck, fuck, fuck."

"Baby shhh please I need you not to freak out please okay? Don't freak out.
I need—"

There is a bang as something slams against the front door. They can hear
the heavy lock shudder on the latch. The wooden bed frame snaps again.
Megha's chest aches as she sees a giant spider of shadow against the frosted
glass of the window, behind the parted, still curtain. A hand against the window. A faceless darkness as someone pushes their head against the glass. A
squeak. The man has brought his friends. There is a sharp crack of something
hitting glass from behind the bathroom door, which is just a few feet from the
bed. There is a window in there too. There are metal grilles on the inside of all
of the windows in the house, thankfully. The front door shakes hard again, the
lock on the inside banging against the wood as if in response to the intruders.

Bodies take over. Megha can still smell the wet latex of the condom, tied in a knot and tossed to the cold floor. Their sweat. Their spittle, drying on skin. Her stomach is throbbing, and she's afraid she's going to shit the bed. They're both shaking, rigid against each other. With a trembling hand Megha grabs her phone and turns it on under the quilt so there's no light visible, or so she hopes. Aditya's phone is dead in his backpack because he's so much of an artist he doesn't give a shit about phones and doesn't care enough to charge it. Megha realises she has no idea what the number for the police in Santiniketan is, or if there's even a thana nearby. Perhaps in Bolpur. Snapping at the heels of that realization comes the memory of all the news stories in which police laughed away women harassed at night, called them liars, sided with rapists, were the rapists.

The door rattles again, loud. The sound of bones in a casket, waking. Aditya is frozen next to her. "Call, call the. Call someone," he whispers. I can't, she doesn't say. The men outside will hear. Maybe they'll just go away. Who'll come and help them here, in the countryside, at this time? The next houses are several plots away on either side, and possibly empty. Behind the house a valley and railroad. Megha thinks of her parents, but she can't find them on her contact list, absurdly. She tries to select names, but she can't, her fingers jerking across the screen. Then she sees the NO NETWORK in the corner of her phone screen. Of course—no reception out here; sometimes out in the garden or the dirt road. No Wi-Fi in this house. Landline's in the living room, probably long disconnected, feet away from the front door, the men behind it. She's paralysed under the blanket, little girl waiting for the creature in the dim room, the dead thing with broken feet turned backward sliding across the floor, features upside down so its face is an unrecognizable leering mask of alien motives, creature coming toward the bed any moment now, fingers against the blanket pushing down to skin. She's seen it before, by the half-light of broken sleep and rotting dream, crawling over the bed to sit on her chest while she's unable to move. Her fingers are shaking so hard she can't dial or do anything.

The screen goes dim. "Fuck," she whispers.

Little girl waiting for the man in the room, the man she knows is her older cousin but is somehow not at this time of night, can't be because cousin-brothers aren't supposed to be lurking by her bed so late like the bhoots, the backward-footed ghosts he'd delighted and scared her with stories of, face contorted and torch held under his chin. No sign of a torch in his hands to tell her this wasn't real, no exaggerated expressions—just a blank hunger. Something else, something awoken behind cousin-brother's dead eyes.

He crawled over the bed.

Megha untucks the mosquito net and rolls off the bed, landing hard on the stone floor with a slap. Closing her eyes tight she crawls underneath, shivering and cold and naked on the stone floor, waiting for the backwards-footed thing underneath to grab her. The bed groans and shakes. She hears the thump and squeal of flesh on floor, and a hand touches her. Her muscles are flooded with adrenaline, and she feels her fist crack against bone before she can even register that she's lashed out. She hears Aditya make a noise like a loud cough. They lie there together, like Adam and Eve, unclothed and revealed to the world. The rusty scent of blood pouring out of Aditya's nose from the punch. "I'm sorry baby I'm so sorry I don't, I didn't mean to," she tells him. He hisses like a snake and she recoils, and she realises he's trying to shush her, comfort her, hold her. She can't stand the clammy texture of his arms around her. They're both too sweaty despite the cold. The phone is in her hands. She doesn't want to switch it on for fear of this coffin-like space keeping her safe and trapped, she doesn't want to see Aditya's face in that pale blue glow, the blood marking out a crimson grin in a ghost mask, she doesn't want to see that he's not Aditya at all, but something else, that ancient god behind dead eyes, animated by the rutting of horrible men from across time. Her fists are clenched.

"Oh god I wish I were more of a man," he sobs in the dark. "If I were big and an asshole no one would come near you. I could I could protect you oh god. If I were a fucking frat boy with big muscles no one would—"

"Please, please shut the fuck up. Please shut up they'll hear," she says through chattering teeth. She has never hated Aditya more, nor loved him more, for the honesty of this sickening confession, for making this about him. Like every man in her life. He wants succour from her trauma. He knows what happened to her as a child. He knows what Megha's cousin-brother, six years older and beloved by the family, did to her at night. He has seen himself take care of her, but he wishes he had a girlfriend without PTSD. She knows he does. Of course he does. Who wouldn't? Poor, sweet Aditya, who thinks being a man is being big and strong and hard as a fucking crowbar whenever she wants, who sometimes apologises until he's near tears when he can't get an erection, and thinks it's a weakness, that he's letting her down, when she wants nothing more than to fuck him right there and then because of it, to take his flaccid cock into her mouth when that happens, and she does, and he grows hard in her mouth and she loves those moments so much but in that love is a shard of hatred for his yearning. Not for her, but for that masculinity her family worships, that the world worships, that everyone around her worshipped and prayed to and appeased when they told her she was lying about her beloved cousin-brother in her bedroom at night, lurking like some dead thing, some backward-footed morally rotted soulless thing out of a story instead of a human being. She has lived in the world of men. She jerks at the squeaks and taps from the window, innocuous birdlike sounds that aren't, that are the fingers of men. She has lived in the world of men with this man who thinks he's not enough of a man, and she has loathed and loved him for it, and she can admit this in this coffin, this cave, finally. Here they are, a shared sacrifice to that god he prays to, that masculinity that has cursed him with an average, unathletic body and what he calls an effeminate artistic sensitivity God fucking forgive him. God almighty, she feels so close to Aditya as he drools blood next to her here. She grabs him in the darkness, tight, and holds him close to her.

"I'm so sorry," he blubbers.

"It's not your fault," she whispers. It's not your fucking fault, stop making me fucking say that you asshole, she doesn't whisper. She wants to tell him so many things. It's okay to not be a man amongst men. It's okay not to be big and strong. It's okay to not be the manly dickhead all the girls supposedly go to because nice guys come last, don't they, you fucking dick. Just like you came last when the woman you wanted so bad but so hesitantly courted with tales of exes breaking your heart fell in love with you despite it, and stayed with you, and now you're stuck with her and her baggage, Mr. Nice fucking Guy.

The darkness is jagged now with claws and fingers, spiders and black bloated lips that smack at her thighs as her skin glues to the floor with cold sweat. Every scratch on the window an electric current through her body. The front door shouts out to the darkness, explodes, it rattles their bones, so splittingly loud in the rural hum of nightfall. Aditya says, barely able to articulate the words because of his shaking body, "I, I can go open the door, hit him. I can go distract them you go out the back door get help." Trying to be the man. "No no you stay here, they'll hurt you there's more than one, please. Adi I don't fucking care, just stay with me." She kisses Aditya hard, teeth snapping as her jaws spasm with his, sinking into tongue and raising more blood, hot in their mouth. She holds her lover close and hopes and prays for this to end, for it to just stop, or for the man who would take her to his cave and never let her leave to just break the door open and enter, wait at the curtained doorway of their bedroom, his locks cascading shadows against his shoulders, his features inverted, mouth a slit in the forehead, eyes soft and rolling like tiny toothless mouths below, the corrupted face she's seen so many times upon half-waking paralysed to hypnagogic hallucinatory shadows of her dear cousin-brother crawling over the bed. Then this will be real again, with a man at the door, in flesh, an intruder, one she can run to, whose face she can look at and recognise as a man she met hours ago, not the undying ghost of a living relative she cannot hurt. It will be real, it will be a thing to fight and flee, rather than this, being trapped here in this coffin with Aditya, barely able to move in amazement at this nightmare, at this thing that is happening to her and her boyfriend that cannot possibly be happening except in a movie, to a couple who've just fucked of course, the girl haunted by a traumatic past. Fuck you, god, God, you unoriginal shit, and she thinks of God as a man with an oily beard and a languorous smile.

The front door rattles again, and holds.

Something is squirming in the cradle of Megha's legs. She is in a cave, and it is freezing. There is a creature, damp and pungent, coming out of her. Its fur is sleek, and it is snarled in serpent or umbilicus. Outside the cave mouth, a hurtling wind breaks its icy teeth against endless mountains, screaming and screaming as the world crumbles. She knows there are terrible things out there, trying to get into the cave. They laugh with the mouths in their foreheads. They stumble in the wind like clockwork because of their feet, twisted backward on their ankles. The wind keeps them cowed despite their laughter, despite their seething masses crawling like insects across a vast continent, across the world. She can feel the great black monuments of the mountain she's inside collapse in this apocalyptic wind, the dead-eyed god-men of aeons past shattering to reveal the ancient bones of the earth. She places her hands on the creature in her lap.

Megha wakes with a man next to her. She flinches back at the blood on his face, encrusting his mouth and chin. There is light to see by, though dim. They both wear wedding veils of cobwebs, the sagging wooden beams of the bed inches above them. She peers over his shoulder at the room, the still curtains of the door, the shining floor dully reflecting early light diffusing through the frosted windows. The air is thick with drums, fast, her heart. She feels acid churning at her throat, scalding her chest. She can't see any stray shadows moving in the room. She searches and sees no feet, backward or otherwise. She strains through her thunderous heartbeat to listen to the house, but it is silent. Only the telltale chirp of birds outside to announce the coming morning. From what seems very far away, she can hear a train coughing across the tracks in the valley, carrying people going about their lives on the outside, travelling across the dawn-bathed landscape. If the man is inside the house, he is silent, hiding somewhere. Would he have dragged them out from under the bed by now to do whatever he wanted to do? Maybe it's just been an hour or so since they tried breaking in, and they are waiting outside. She doesn't want to turn on her phone, lying black and silent between her and Aditya, to check the time. As if the man will see its beacon even through walls. But daylight must be near, if the birds are out.

She looks at her naked boyfriend, his erection lightly touching her leg. His snoring is a gentle whistle. Her knuckles throb—she wonders if she broke his nose last night. She dreads the moment he will wake up. She dreads him asking her if she's all right, and wants him to. She dreads emerging from their stinking coffin, which smells like death, their shared death. The floor under them is sticky, and there is a reek of ammonia in the air. She feels a burning between her legs. Probably a fucking UTI.

The silence, so profound and calm after what they went through just hours ago, washes over her. She wants to remain in it forever.

She dreads talking again, breaking the silence. Talking and listening. To Aditya. To her parents. To her family who denied her truth once, and surely can't this time, because they have a male witness. She dreads leaving this tomb with Aditya, and entering again the real world, where this happened to them. She dreads making their relationship work, rebuilding it from scratch after this night of rebirth. She dreads the train journey home, if they get that far and don't get their throats slit by a man in the next room. She dreads the men they will eye on the three-hour journey from Bolpur to Howrah Station, looking for that familiar bearded face, that oily smile. She dreads going back to Kolkata, and the men among the millions who will stare at her for the rest of her life, try and touch her on the streets and in buses, try and hit on her at parties and repeatedly offer her drugs, drinks, and rides home even after she's said no. She dreads putting on her clothes, and seeing Aditya in his, to know that they've both eaten from that fleshy, squirming fruit, and forsaken their moment of awful innocence.

She looks at her man with blood on his mouth, blood born of terror, blood spilled by her hand. His eyelashes are long in sleep, his long hair unbound and draped over his neck, stubble framing his soft mouth stained livid by her violence, his arms loose and slender, the slight, smooth sheath of fat over his gut resolving into the smallest of Bengali potbellies. After two years of treating her like a glass figurine, he has broken. In one night, her trauma is now his too, she realises, and wants to throw up, a rapturous, horrible glow deep in her gut, crawling up from her womb. He has never looked more beautiful, in this moment of peace, before he wakes to a new and terrifying world.

Looking at Aditya, Megha knows what she must do.

She slides out from under the bed, slow and careful, phone in her hand. She desperately hopes Aditya doesn't stir. She isn't ready. She wonders if the man slipped something in their tea last night, or whether it was just the adrenaline crash that sent them plummeting into sleep despite imminent danger. Aditya keeps snoring through his hopefully unbroken nose. Megha winces as her hip squeaks against the floor, and gets up, her knees and joints spasming with pain from being coiled tight all night, skin itching with mosquito bites. Her throat is dry as she looks around the room, her eyes adjusting to the dimness. Shadows against the window, the speckling of leaves. She gasps, and breathes out as she realises it's just their quilts under the mosquito net on the bed. She turns her naked body, feet imprinting a circular rune against the chilled stone, checking each dark corner for an inverted face, lurking. She can feel the tremble of spiking adrenaline returning, encouraged by the cold. Padding barefoot, avoiding the tied condom, she picks up her panties and T-shirt from the floor where she'd dropped them last night, and hurriedly puts them on. She wants to wear the jeans sprawled on the chair in one corner, needs to go to the bathroom, but knows that would wake Aditya. There's little time.

Holding her phone tight like a weapon in front of her, she walks out of the bedroom and into the living room. Bracing for hands to emerge from either side and grab her throat, her breasts. She flinches, ignores the sparks flying through her body on nerves. The living room is empty. No crouched figure grinning at her from under the glass tabletop. The front door is shut, the heavy lock and latches still intact. She has never been more grateful for her parents' fear of the house getting burgled while it stands empty most of the year. Megha turns right and through the curtained doorway leading into the kitchen and dining room. Walking through the silent house feels like swimming through an undersea wreck, the light from the pulling windows a liquid blue. Megha puts the phone down on the dining table, where their dinner still sits uneaten. Flies crawl frantic over the mesh food covers that entrap the congealed dishes and rubbery rooti. A flash of guilt that they've wasted the caretakers' efforts. Her stomach growls and sucks at the rest of her, but she doesn't feel like eating at all. At one end of the kitchen, the back door to the garden is also shut and locked. It's tempting to just slip into the normalcy of these undisturbed rooms, pretend that nothing at all happened last night. Wipe it from her memory entirely. She knows from experience that it's not so easy.

Glancing at the living room doorway for the man, for her man, for any man, Megha turns on the gas stove on the stone countertop. The click of the knob, thump of blue flame is like an explosion. She winces, waits for Aditya's voice to pierce the silence in a panic. Nothing. Silly. It's not actually that loud. The doorway from the living room remains empty. Each time she looks, the curtain resolves into the hanging shawl of the man waiting, standing and biding his time watching her. Megha forces her breathing to slow, suppressing the urge to sprint back to the illusory safety of the space beneath the bed, right next to Aditya. The heat of the stove's fire caresses her belly through the T-shirt. Something runs across Megha's mind like a tiger through the wilderness, a memory from the depths of sleep, gone before she can glimpse it. She fills the kettle on the counter with water, tilting it and not turning the tap all the way to keep the thrum of water on metal muffled.

Kettle on flame, she waits. In the December morning chill, she draws close to the comforting heat of the stove, which distracts from the burning discomfort between her legs. She turns and finally allows herself to check the phone on the dining table, squinting against its light burning the tender murk. 5:13 A.M. So close to sunrise. The empty doorway to the living room gapes at her. Just the curtains, still. Aditya is silent, and therefore asleep. The sleep of the dead, as they say. Stay dead, my love. She wishes she could have bound and gagged him as he slept, left him there while she takes this time, to do whatever it is that she's doing. The thought of Aditya bound by her hand unfurls like a humid flower, releasing an aching longing to make love to him again, to his helplessness, mirroring her own, to let him know how fraught with desire is his vulnerability. She'd asked him once if he'd like to tie her up in bed, and he'd acted almost offended, not taking the hint, making her feel vaguely ashamed. He has always feared his desires, and hers, caught in the undertow of what once happened to her. Steam begins to emerge from the spout of the kettle, the bubbling water sloshing against metal. Megha turns off the flame. She takes a glazed terra-cotta cup from the drying rack, and pours the boiling water in. Inside the ancient fridge with its icicled freezer, she finds a browning lemon. She slices it into two with a knife from the rack, drops one squeezed wedge into the cup of hot water.

Megha takes the key ring on the dining table, mashing the keys in her fist so they don't jangle. She walks to the back door, unlocks it, and slowly slides back the latch with teeth clenched. Her heart is drumming again, pounding the silent air. The house is unlocked. She has no protection. The man could be pressed against the unlocked door, listening, a foot away from her separated by wood. She opens it a few inches, allowing a crack of the outside to throw a line of light against the kitchen floor. Watching for bony fingers curling around the edges of the door, she places the lock and keys on the dining table, beside the phone. She picks up the knife and the cup of hot lemon water, and walks back to the door. Megha places one foot against the rough, chipping green paint covering the wood, and takes a deep breath. Using her toes, she leverages the door back. It opens with a groan of rusty hinges. Pearlescent light pours in.

Deaf to the world, her blood thundering in warning, Megha walks out into the dawn to meet the man, if he has waited for her. It is the birth of day, blue like sorrow clinging to the trees of the garden, the dew and dirt rough and damp both under the soles of her feet. Between the grass and flower beds of the garden is the signature red soil of Santiniketan, bruise-dark in the morning. The cup steams into fresh air untainted by the smog of the city. In Megha's stiff fingers, the cup feels heavy, an entire ocean trapped in terra-cotta. She looks toward the shallow, unseen valley behind the garden's trees, that red earth running down to the railroad, and thinks of the shrubby slopes seething with men, their many eyes dead of feeling in upside-down faces, all crawling toward her, limbs entwined and hitching insectile over that ochre soil tinted by the blood of thousands of women through the ages. Her legs are unclothed, calves waiting to be grabbed by the terribly gentle hands that held her own last night, and read misfortune across her palm. She has no armour but a T-shirt and underwear. She has no weapons but the heat in her cup of water, the blade of her knife, the teeth in her mouth, and the fear in her sinews. She can't help, at that moment, but think of her cousin whom she hasn't seen in so long, who now has a wife and child he must be sleeping next to, hundreds of kilo-metres beyond this garden. His wedding was the last time she saw his face in flesh. She hopes his wife and daughter have never seen the dead thing she saw awaken behind his eyes, the sign of that ancient god of men.

Megha stands with bare feet on the damp grass, waiting.

If out of the bitter dawn air, glittering with mist, comes a man, she will throw the hot water in his face, smash the cup across his skin-clad bones as hard as she can, and sink the knife into his body with all her strength, making a red rain upon the red earth. It doesn't matter if the man's face isn't inverted, like the ghosts of her cousin-brother that have visited her over the years and nights, doesn't matter if the man's feet aren't turned backward so he lurches toward her in a hitching dance. She will still find his throat and dig her fin-gers into his eyes, shove her knee into his testicles. She will run to the road and scream as loud as she has wanted to all her life, finally, teeth bared and streaked in blood at sunrise.

If no man emerges from the mist and trees that fall toward the train tracks, if only birds move in this temporary paradise, this limbo between life and death, she will wait for the heat to leave her cup, and drink the warm lemon water to soothe her fear-swollen throat, until Aditya wakes and finds her, and she will ask him to sit beside her on the doorstep and not say anything, for the love of everything in the world now tainted by last night. But there is a secret sliver of hope buried somewhere in her shivering body, isn't there. That the man *will* appear from those trees. The birds are choral in the gloaming, and the sun flares across the edge of the world, invisible but for the roseate bleed of clouds to the east. The water in Megha's cup sloshes with its little tides as her hand shakes. Her knife is a slit of reflected dawn sky in her hand.

From behind her in the house, she hears the sound of bare feet on floor, approaching.

SIOLAIGH

by Siobhan Carroll

1658, Scotland. "Works of Navigation do all agree that the Siolaigh Serpent is of a vast magnitude, namely 200-foot-long, and over 20 feet thick; and is wont to live in Rocks; and will go alone from his holes on a clear night and devour Calves, Lambs, and Hogs. At sea he puts up his head on high like a pillar, and catcheth away men, and devours them."

A man's severed arm lay in the surf. When the wave retreated, she saw it clearly: the blue spidering of a tattoo on the forearm, the four fingers curled up to the sky. A wave swept back in, covering the arm with a rush of foam.

"That's three abandoned," Brian was saying. "This time last year, we had four fulmar chicks." He put a hand to his eyes, shading them against the unexpectedly bright sun.

The sea sucked the wave back again, exposing the arm. *It's an optical illusion,* Fiona thought. *A tree branch caught between rocks.* She felt lightheaded, like the top of her head was a specimen jar whose lid had just been unscrewed.

"Do we head to the broch next? Or the point?"

The broch, Fiona thought. *Then the colony at the point.* They'd already lost a precious week of data to the storm that had trapped them on the mainland. With only a single research assistant this summer, she'd need to work overtime to complete the egg count before the chicks arrived. They didn't have time to mess about on the tide line.

And yet her feet carried her into the wash of dark water, across the lurch of pebbles, to the impossibility in the foam. The wave slid out, exposing glistening bladder wrack, a hollow tube of kelp, and the unmistakable fact of a human arm. It ended just above the elbow, in a red tuft of meat and jutting bone.

"Is that more goddamn plastic tat?" Brian clambered over the rocks to join her. His breath sucked in. "Jesus *Christ.*"

Something like relief flooded her. "Yeah," she said. The skin on the arm still looked firm, unmottled; it couldn't have been in the water long.

"What do we do? We need to do something, right?"

Fiona stooped, putting out her hand to the arm. It was cold, as might be expected, but the skin stayed intact. She raised the arm, gently working it free of the seaweed tangle.

"*Jesus,*" Brian repeated. "Should you be doing that? Won't the police want to . . . It could be a crime scene, right?"

"Nearest police officer's on Barra." Siolaigh lay too far east to be properly considered one of the Outer Hebrides, but she knew what government services were available would be based on those more populated islands. Holding the arm as delicately as she could, Fiona gestured for the first plastic bag. "The tide will take it before he gets here." She triple-bagged the arm, as she would for a dead bird, and wiped her hands off on her jeans. "Or the gulls."

Brian held the bag gingerly as he took it from her, his eyes wide. *It's just another body,* she thought, and then clamped down on her annoyance. As with many of his generation, Brian's reactions seemed excessive to Fiona, like he was acting in a play she'd been dragged off the street to watch. And she wasn't interested in managing his emotions for him; the thought appalled her.

Still, she reminded herself, *he's a graduate student. And very young.* "Remember, you intimidate them," her chair had said in the annual appraisal. *Take a breath,* she thought. *Think about it from his point of view.* This wasn't a bird they were looking at.

"Put it away," she said, because Brian was still looking at the arm with a sickened expression on his face. "And mark the coordinates."

She pulled out her cell phone to see if she could get a bar, but as usual there was no signal. Flipping the phone over, she took photos of the tide line at their feet, the rocky beach, the steep cliff climbing up to the broch. She doubted this was a crime scene, but she wanted to preserve what they saw, just in case. At the top of the cliff the silhouetted figure of a lone walker paused to look down at the scenery, oblivious to the confusion below.

"Do you think there's . . . more?" Brian said faintly.

Fiona put her phone away. "Probably a fishing accident. Those new boats have a lot of heavy machinery on them." There was a good chance that person hadn't survived, but she didn't say that. It was a tragedy, but not one she or Brian could do anything about.

"So . . ." Brian said when they'd stowed the arm in the ice chest. "Do we go to the point?" He flushed as she looked at him. "I just thought . . . What do you want to do?"

"What I 'want' doesn't matter." Her tone came out more harshly than she'd intended. She tried to modify it. "What I *want* is to finish our count on schedule, before the weather changes." She resisted the urge to rub her face, feeling the slick of gravewater on her hands.

What needed to be done? They could stop by the Trow's Hole, the tiny general-store-cum-island-pub, and call the Stornoway police from the satellite phone. It wasn't that far a walk, and with the approach of summer, the days were beginning to stretch. One of them could still visit the fulmar nesting grounds at the broch tonight.

But Tuesday, she thought. *Tuesday might be different.* She doubted the police would make a special trip out here for the washed-up remains of a fishing accident. They might have to go to the station for an interview, and that would mean taking the Tuesday ferry. If the weather turned, they could end up stuck on the wrong island for weeks.

"Shit," Brian said, his thoughts now running on the same track as hers. "We're not going to get a complete data set, are we?" There was a saying in field biology: "*The first year you come for the experience, the second for the paycheque, the third because you don't fit anywhere else.*" Brian was in his second year on the project, his mind on the meagre paycheque that justified spending a dull, rain-soaked summer on a remote island. But she was being unfair: her last two grant apps hadn't got anywhere, and she didn't have another funding stream in place yet. Without funding to cover his line, Brian might not get a third year.

Her assistant looked at her expectantly. For a second she wondered if Brian's silence was a kind of proposal: *Let's just leave the arm here. Let's pretend we never found it.*

"We're taking it in," she said.

"Of course," Brian said. He sounded like he was mollifying her, and that made her angry. She handed him the tripod and started the march up the rocky path to the sky.

...

1793, Maine. A captain bound for the West Indies reports seeing a sea serpent swimming beside his vessel. He estimates it to measure about "55 to 60 feet in length," with a brown, horse-like head that it kept elevated above the water. Its "eye was perfectly sharp, black and piercing."

The Trow's Hole was housed in an old croft cottage, its insides gutted to make way for a pub room and kitchen. Jim Clesich, the owner, had returned to Siolaigh after living some years in Edinburgh, one of the few "young men" of the island to return to the shrinking community. This perhaps explained the intense nostalgia of the pub's few gestures toward décor—its insistence on black-and-white photos of whalers and hollow-eyed children in straw capes, the triangular stones of elf-shot perched over the cottage doorway, the line of resin spoons over the cash register that no one would ever buy.

A small, glass-doored fridge contained the general store's perishables; a handwritten sign said that hen feed could be purchased out back.

"Ah, the birders," Jim said as they walked in. "How're the fulmar today?"

"Fine," Fiona said, though the fulmars had been restless. Jim didn't care, anyway; this was just talk, of the resentfully cheerful variety that filled up the slightly cool, beer-sour room. In the corner, a group of locals nursed their pints. A pair of elderly men stooped over a game of chess. A couple of young men, probably unemployed, squatted in front of a flickering, old-fashioned television, watching a match.

Behind the counter, Magnus, Jim's eight-year-old son, beamed at Brian. "Did you see Auld Horgan?" Although Magnus went to school on Barra, his voice was tinged with the local accent. "Wullie Keilo said he seen 'em, just this morning, chasing seals. He said he was just like in the photie, black and *unkan*, with his heid big as a car."

Normally Fiona would have been interested in an appearance of Siolaigh's legendary sea monster, but not today. She leaned forward, signalling Jim, while Brian talked to the boy.

"We need to use your sat phone," she said. "And we need ice."

Jim's forehead furrowed. "Oh aye. We'll set you up."

The pub's tiny kitchen reeked of cooking oil and yeast. Under the bright overhead light Brian's face looked almost green. He'd taken the backpack off and was dangling it at arm's length away from him. Fiona took it off him.

"Can you make the call?" she said. "I'll see to this."

Brian hesitated, then shuffled off. He had the GPS coordinates of where they'd found the arm. He could handle talking to the police, surely.

"We found something on the beach," she told Jim in a low voice. "An arm. We need to get it on ice, quickly."

Jim's eyebrows shot up. "Oh?"

God knows what kind of Hannibal Lecterish visions were in the man's head. "It was probably lost in a fishing accident, washed up on the beach. Brian's going to call the police and let them know." Jim's eyes flicked to the doorway Brian had just left through. "We'll need to keep it. Do you have a corner of a freezer we can use?"

"No." Jim's voice was absolute. "Health regulations." He studied the kitchen, the shadows on his face growing longer. "I can give you a cooler," he said. "And ice."

"That'll do," Fiona said. "I think we can fit it in the freezer back at the cottage."

She stood uselessly to one side while Jim rattled around in search of the cooler. In a lab, she would have taken the arm out to prepare it for travel, but the shining metal surface of the table in front of her was for food. *It's all just meat,* she thought, not knowing if she agreed with herself. The squeak of chairs and a low murmur of voices drifted in from the pub room. She wondered if the arm had belonged to someone from the island, someone the voices talking outside all knew.

"Will the police be coming over, do you think?" Jim straightened a fish cooler on the floor. It looked like the right size.

"I doubt it," Fiona said. "We'll probably have to take it to Stornoway ourselves."

"Robbie MacIver is heading over in the morn," Jim said. "He can take it over for you."

"Is he?" Fiona was surprised. In the summer the island's women might sometimes book the Tuesday ferry to Barra, but the men rarely took their boats over except when delivering their catch. "Today?"

"Aye." Jim didn't look at her. "His auntie's in the hospital. Poor thing."

Fiona made a sympathetic noise. Which fisherman was Robbie? Brian would know. He went to the pub almost nightly and he was good with names. She wouldn't trust a man she didn't know with the transportation of a specimen, but if Brian could join him, that would be better than booking the ferry.

"How long is he staying?"

"Oh, only overnight," Jim said vaguely. "His auntie isna in *that* bad a way. I'll put a bag of ice in the bottom," he said of the cooler.

Fiona unzipped the bag. The fact of the arm was still there, where she'd left it. Through the plastic film she could see the black hairs on the back of the tanned arm, the blue knotwork tattoo, the disquieting white gap where a wristwatch had once resided. Jim, mercifully, said nothing as she stowed the arm in the cooler.

As she closed the lid he cleared his throat. "Och, those accidents on the water can be terrible." Jim was filling up silence the way people did when they didn't know what to say. Fiona never knew what to say herself, so she was sympathetic to that.

Brian's shoes scuffed on the linoleum. "I talked to them," he said to Fiona. "They said to put it on ice and bring it over, soon as you can."

"We've got a lead on that," Fiona said. "Jim knows someone who's heading over to Lewis and Harris tomorrow. Robbie . . ." She looked at Jim.

"Robbie by the Shore," Jim said. "Him you saw playing the fiddle last week."

"I thought you could take it over," Fiona said to Brian. "Since you talked to them." As PI, she should stay on site; if Brian got trapped on the Long Isle for a week, it wouldn't be a hardship for him. He'd no doubt welcome a change.

"I'm not so sure if Robbie can do that," Jim said. Fiona looked at him.

"Why?" she said. "You said he was going over? And he doesn't want to spend time dealing with the police, I'm sure. Besides, we can't give it to someone else to carry," she said, in case that was what Jim was assuming.

"Oh aye," Jim said, looking away. "I just didn't want to speak *for* him, is all."

"Is that all right?" She belatedly realised she should have asked for Brian's input.

The graduate student shrugged. "I can do it."

"When is Robbie leaving?"

"Tomorrow," Jim said. "Crack of dawn." He looked at Brian. "I'll let him know you'll be joining him?"

Brian nodded, and Fiona let out a breath she didn't realise she'd been holding. The sooner they parted ways with this arm, the better.

...

1817–1819, Massachusetts. Over three hundred people report a sea serpent swimming off Cape Ann. In July 1818, eighteen people watch as the serpent attacks a whale, striking it with "tremendous blows" that echo across the waves.

"Did you hear the talk about 'Auld Horgan'?" Brian said, trudging up the slope toward the cottage. The world around them was wind and sky.

Fiona mentally kicked herself. She didn't enjoy listening to superstitious tales, but serpent sightings were frequently based on something real. "No," she said. "I should have followed up. Did it sound legit?"

"I think so," Brian said. "Magnus said two of his classmates saw it off Point Ninian. Three black humps in the water, moving together faster than their boat could travel. He said some of the fishermen saw it too."

It sounded like the classic description of a sea serpent: the head of a marine beast, humps rising and falling in its wake. "Did he say who?"

"Sam Berry and Wullie Keilo." Brian shrugged. "Maybe they were messing with the kid. They seem like the type."

Fiona didn't know the names, but this wasn't surprising. She had no reason to interact with the locals outside of Jim and Connor Leisk, who rented them the cottage.

"We should have called it in while we were there."

"You think it's a 'string of buoys'?"

"Has to be," she said. Minke and humpback whales were frequently spotted near the island, and it was perfectly possible for them to become tangled in the "ghost gear" of Siolaigh's struggling fishing industry. Overfishing and the new EU trade agreement had hit the local fishermen hard, forcing them into different waters in pursuit of different fish, and these shifts had consequences. *Shit.* "We'd probably need confirmation, too, before they'd send someone." And she still had data to collect. And there was this business with the arm.

"I can go back," Brian offered. "Call the SPCA or whoever's interested, go back to the broch to finish the nest count." He'd adopted her clipped way of speaking. He was trying to please her, she knew, but it was irritating.

She checked her watch. It was after five, and the subarctic sun was still high in the sky. "If you do that I can check the nests at the point," she said. "Are you sure you don't mind making the call?"

"Nah. I'll probably stay at the pub for dinner; learn more about 'Auld Horgan.'"

"Maybe one of the fishermen can check it out," she said. They'd asked a lot of the locals already, but it was worth a try. "Call NatureScot," she said. "They coordinated that rescue last year. Their number is at the front of the tour guide. You can leave them a message."

Brian nodded. She couldn't tell, sometimes, if she was explaining things too much or not enough. If Brian didn't remember the number, it wasn't like he could call her to find it out.

"And if Robbie Whazizname is there, confirm that he can take you tomorrow."

"I'll head over now," Brian said. "Maybe I can catch someone before the office closes."

The agency office had likely been closed for over an hour, but she didn't say that. "Don't be too late," she warned him. "Remember the boat in the morning." She sounded like a mother and despised herself for it.

She stood for a while and watched Brian trek back toward the pub, before hefting up the ice chest herself. She probably should have asked Brian to carry it down, but he was right about placing the call quickly.

The cottage's kitchenette fridge was just wide enough to accommodate the arm, packed with Jim's ice. Fiona took out the packets of minced beef and put them in the sink to defrost. She could eat some tonight, cook up some more for tomorrow.

She'd need to disinfect the fridge once the arm was gone. *It's just meat*, she told herself, but still. On her own, with silence creeping in on all sides, the fact of the arm unsettled her.

Luckily there was still work to do.

...

1922, South Africa. Two whales are seen fighting an enormous, white-furred sea monster. Waves later wash the monster's dead body to shore. Locals prod its forty-seven feet of gristle and snow-white fur, take photographs of its carcass.

The trek to the point was uneventful. The sun was still high in the sky, the wind furrowing the grass around her, and it was possible, in the ongoing rumble of sea-sound, to forget about the strangeness of the day.

She set up the spotting scope at the cliff's edge. Cold ground jabbed her ribs as she squinted through the lens at the snow-white birds cackling to each other on the ledges. Fulmars were a hard species to monitor: one of the breeding pair always stayed on the nest, guarding it from Fiona's lens. They could be aggressive too, vomiting orange stomach oil at humans that came too close to their nests, a charming habit that had earned them the name foul-gull in Old Norse. *Fulmar.* When the chicks came, they'd become easier to count.

Fiona's fulmar study had been going on for six years now. The number of nests had remained steady, but chick mortality appeared to be on the rise. The culprit was probably plastic: the unfussy fulmars scooped their food up from the surface of the ocean, gobbling up party balloons and wet wipes along with squid. Plastic could make seabirds feel full when they weren't, could perforate their bowels, could affect the kidney function of their chicks, and that in turn might lead to an increase in chick mortality.

Might. As always, direct links were hard to demonstrate. The black lines in Fiona's notebook were clear enough, but lately, they refused to coalesce into the clear, linear story rewarded in grant applications. She could, perhaps, speculate; could force connections; could make the kind of rhetorical flourishes her colleagues seemed to excel at; but Fiona didn't want to. The data was solid. It should speak for itself.

Fiona reviewed the position of the established nests and scratched down the location of a couple possibles. Occasionally a stiff-winged bird floated back to the cliff, descending to a rock shelf to shriek at its fellows. The mating pairs nibbled each other's neck and bill, their large black eyes reflecting nothing.

Someone's watching me.

It was a strange thought. She never experienced this sensation before, the cold tingle at the back of her neck, the sudden silence of her surroundings. Fiona turned to prove herself wrong, and, in a rush of cold, saw that she wasn't. A black-eyed woman, clad in grey, stood about forty feet away, watching her.

A tight knot formed in Fiona's throat. Was this a local? The island rarely had tourists at this time of year, but the woman's pinched face didn't look familiar. The wind whipped her black hair in long coils, fluttering the edges of her dress, which seemed weirdly close-fitting for the island. She wasn't wearing a coat.

"Can I help you?" Fiona's voice creaked out of her. The woman remained silent, still as a stone. She looked young, maybe in her mid-twenties. Warily, Fiona shifted her weight, closing her notebook.

The woman turned, abruptly, a burst of motion. To Fiona's relief, the stranger began walking away in a curiously straight line. She watched for a while as the woman's figure receded across the bleached hill. The woman did not look back.

1942, Scotland. The remains of a 50-foot sea monster wash ashore. The military prevents locals from taking photographs of the body, the smell of which "grows hourly." The beast is dissected by the local sanitary inspector, who finds "a small portion of what I took to be a seaman's jersey" in its stomach. He keeps hairs from the beast's body in his office drawer, where they dry out and "coil up like bedsprings."

Back at the cottage, Fiona lit the oil stove, chopped some onions, tried not to think about the arm. Brian had said he'd stay at the pub for dinner, but she made extra portions of fried mince anyway. They could have it tomorrow.

Fiona turned on the television for noise and typed up her notes on her laptop. She drafted one email to her fisheries colleague about the "Auld Horgan" sighting, and another to the SNS's Wildlife Management people, just in case Brian's message got mislaid. When she clicked SEND, the cursor swirled uncertainly for a long time. Good thing she'd saved the drafts.

The Airbnb binder included a woodblock image of "Auld Horgan," serpent-headed and looking somewhat cross-eyed. On the opposite page was a handwritten list of sea monster sightings. She took a photograph of that, too, for atmosphere. Before the divorce, she'd have sent it to Tom. She'd send it to her fisheries colleague when she got a cell phone signal, she decided. For context.

She checked her email again, but the app wasn't loading. She closed it and went back to drafting the latest grant application. "*Demonstrating the effects of climate change on the northern fulmar population will help raise awareness . . .*" She deleted the sentence. What could "awareness" do, anyway? People were already "aware."

Something scuffled outside the kitchen's tiny croft window. When she looked outside, she saw only a patchwork of blacks and greys. She expected Brian to stumble back inside at any moment, but he didn't. If she'd had a full complement of research assistants, the house would be an easier space to occupy. She wouldn't have felt quite so much pressure to interact with Brian when he was here, and the silence wouldn't have felt so bristling, so quivering with unheard life.

She turned the light off and listened for a moment in the dark. The wind whistled through a gap in the door. A bell jangled somewhere on the slope. The ancient fridge-freezer hummed beside her. A floorboard creaked. Out of nowhere, she remembered her mother, standing in that awful avocado-coloured kitchen, with the fridge door standing open, the milk carton and cans stacked up around her bare ankles.

Fiona closed her laptop. She'd take another look at the grant in the morning.

The tiny lamp in her bedroom cast a welcome, yellow light on her twin bed.

The book on the wooden nightstand was a popular trade piece about whales, something interestingly close to and comfortably far from Fiona's work on fulmars. She settled in to read about sperm whales, keeping one ear open for Brian's return.

In Spain, a sperm whale washed up with an entire tomato greenhouse in its stomach, tarps and flowerpots intact. A whole different scale from fulmars, but similar problems.

She turned the page. In the open sea, a dead whale usually wouldn't be found. Its enormous body would float, for a while, like a mysterious island, then slip downward into sunless depths. A mountain of flesh sinking into the dark.

In the desert spaces of the abyssopelagic zone, a whale corpse would land like a life-giving nutrient bomb. There was a name for such events: *whalefall.* Sea scuds would writhe through its ribs, albino crabs would colonise its carcass. Species that lived only on the bodies of dead whales would appear, spewing larvae that would, in turn, drift the currents in hungry hope.

Fiona glanced at the print on her bedroom wall: a fuzzy black-and-white grid of maritime images that looked like they'd been rubbed off some medieval stonework. On the far right, a man raising a harpoon toward a square-headed fish. The Age of Whaling must have been a paradise for the whale-devourers of the ocean floor. She imagined strange reefs blooming in the wake of whale ships, cities of mussels and pale worms birthed out of discarded bones. When people halted whaling, *whalefall* must have slowed too, leaving entire species to starve. That was the problem with ecology: you couldn't alter one thing without affecting the system. *Even our mercy brings death.* A cheery fucking thought to end the night with.

As Fiona went to turn out the light, she noticed that one of the print's squares depicted a sea serpent, maybe Auld Horgan itself, writhing under the waves. In the corner of that image, a figure with his arms and legs awkwardly splayed stood in the centre of a pointing crowd. She hadn't noticed it before.

Probably asking for fish, she thought, plunging herself into darkness. The Airbnb binder claimed the islanders petitioned the serpent for their harvests, treating the creature like some kind of laird who might, if flattered, make a good return. She could see the appeal of such myths in uncertain times, the idea that, if you said or did something the right way, nature would provide.

It's a pity the National Science Foundation doesn't accept human sacrifices, she thought. Although they did, in a way: the sacrifice of headspace, of her aching fingers, of yet more hours of life poured into another failed grant application.

Fiona sank into uneasy dreams, in which an arm lay on a beach, its fingers twitching toward the sky.

1959, Hebrides: two shark fishermen see a large, hump-backed creature approach their boat. It has "no visible nasal organs, but a large red gash of a mouth which seemed to cut the head in half." It has "two, huge round eyes like apples." When it opens its mouth, they see "a number of tendril-like growths hanging from the palate." Across the thin strip of water that separates them from the beast, they can hear it breathing.

The next morning, Fiona felt more optimistic. The dawn light outside was bright and clear. Without the distraction of the arm, of Auld Horgan, she could regain some lost ground.

The door to Brian's room was open, but he wasn't there. Had he already left? If so, he hadn't eaten; the sink was remarkably clear of dishes.

She glanced at the freezer. Her stomach clenched as she pulled it open, but only frosted emptiness confronted her. The arm was gone.

She made herself some coffee. Brian must have headed out very early, for her to miss him. Early morning departures weren't that surprising on the island, but she was surprised he'd returned and left again without waking her. And yet, the arm was gone.

She checked her email—no luck—and her phone—no bars. She reviewed the grant application before heading out to the broch.

Like the Cat people who gave their name to Shetland, the first tribe of the island had vanished long before the Vikings arrived, leaving only their Iron Age tower behind. The Siolaigh broch had collapsed long ago, its stones pillaged to build cottage walls and the ruined church on Point Ninian. Weeds tangled its ancient floor, and its rust-coloured stones slid in a slow drift toward the dizzying cliff and the wheeling, shrieking bird colony. Beyond the broch lay the curve of the silted bay, the carcasses of the old whaling boats still visible, rotting in the waves.

Fiona began her count at Plot A, noting the tightly packed guillemots and a cluster of gannets on the rocks below, the odd puffin tucked into a rocky alcove. She clicked her counter in a rapid staccato, her right hand scratching down the positions of resting fulmar, their necks arced back regally, their black eyes watching the sea.

Something set the birds off, flushing the gannets and guillemots up in a volcano of wingbeats. The sky became birds, hundreds of them arrowing upward, a thunder of bodies and cries. Pencil poised over her notebook, Fiona looked for the source of the disturbance. Something huge and black, diving beneath the waves.

Her breath suspended. *Orca?* She scanned the grey waves, looking for debris, the telltale sign of motion. Something black cut the water about a hundred yards away, but that could be a seal monitoring the spectacle. Siolaigh translated as the "Island of the Seal People," after all.

But nothing else disturbed the rhythm of water, not for a long time.

...

1990, Hebrides. "It had what appeared to be a head at one end, a curved back and seemed to be covered with eaten-away flesh or even a furry skin."

Her phone pinged on the walk to Point Ninian. Fiona pulled it out, foolishly relieved that it had found a signal, and even more relieved to see that the text came from Brian. A "thumbs-up" emoji flashed across the screen, followed by a *"guess what i saw."*

Did u take arm, she typed, though that was stupid. She deleted the text and began again. *did u talk to police?*

A string of texts pinged through. *looks hungry lol* and *pub has bottles now did u want some* and, dismayingly, *don't know if u saw but students not arriving until June.*

Her heart sank. These must be old texts, sent on their first week on the island, before they'd learned that the undergrad research visit had been cancelled. Shit. Still, at least Brian's phone had a signal now. Or was it hers that had a signal? She hadn't realised, until her phone started pinging, how urgently she'd wanted to hear from him.

Email when you are done with police, she texted. This was what her chair would call "micromanaging," but the silence of the island had suddenly grown oppressive.

She stopped off at the Trow's Hole to grab some lunch, which she never did, but the door to the white-walled pub was locked. A cardboard sign propped in the window said CLOSED TODAY.

Sheep drifted grumbling up the nearby hill. A few early lambs, graffitied with green letters, bobbed at the centre of the herd. To her left there was the sound of metal hitting wood. She walked in the direction of the sound, trudging through mud and the rank smell of peat.

One of the locals crouched by the side of a gate, hammering a plank back in place. An older, crevice-faced man, in a rumpled jersey. She wasn't sure if she was supposed to know him or not.

"Excuse me," she said. "Do you know why the pub's closed? Did something happen?"

The man put his hammer down and looked at her. "*Ciamar a tha sibh,*" he said. She thought he sounded angry. "Dinna ye mind Clesich, he's about. But no pub da day."

"Do you know why he's closed?"

"Ah no. I tink he hae a reffelled hesp ta red."

Farm chores, Fiona guessed. She'd never been good at following the local dialect. "Do you know 'Robbie by the Shore'?"

"Robbie by the Shore? Oh aye."

"He took my assistant to Stornoway today." Her tone sounded uncertain, even to her. "Do you know if they got off all right?"

"I wouldna ken." The man frowned. "That's unkan business."

"Well," she said. "Thanks. If you see Jim, tell him Fiona stopped by to see him."

The man studied her speculatively. "It'll be a coarse night," he said in a warning tone. "Mind ye stay in."

Fiona nodded, feeling oddly dislocated. "I will," she said, because it seemed the thing to say.

Staying in wasn't a problem, of course. Brian would be occupied for much of the day; he'd email her when he could. She might have a message in her inbox even now.

But, when she returned to the cottage, her inbox was still empty, and her messages from last night had failed to send. She'd have to hope that Brian's call about Auld Horgan had gone through, that whoever was supposed to know about such things, already knew.

...

2018, Russia. The body of a beast resembling a "hairy octopus" is found lying on the sands of the Kamchatka Peninsula. Its discoverer takes video of the body, showing us its grey-white strangeness, its "tubular fur." YouTube comments include such gems as "WTF," "maybe its trump's hair," and "what da hell was that?"

When Fiona was nine, her mother had taken to cutting up newspapers. She'd find the words that spoke to her and lay them out on the kitchen floor. Angels were sending her messages through the stained words. She had to search them, and assemble them, to understand.

Her mother's messages lived inside a queasy pit in Fiona's stomach. As with her mother's strange bursts of crying or laughter, she knew better than to mention it to her teacher, or to the landlord. Sometimes, her mother made Fiona help by stealing greasy pages out of their neighbour's trash can and sorting through them, peeling apart the slick photos of celebrities in an endless search for miracles, but Fiona was useless at distinguishing between the blurred, human words and the ink-stained angelic ones her mother snatched from her.

Once, Fiona had returned home to find her mother crouched in front of

Fiona's bedroom, blocking the door. A tower of Campbell's soup can labels teetered on the floor. Fiona knew better than to say anything. She watched her mother's illuminated face for a while, listening to her stray whispers, waiting for her mother to notice her.

Eventually, she'd said something. She was hungry, she needed to go into her room, her mother was scaring her. The woman who turned on her wasn't familiar, her face drawn in hard lines, eyes glittering. *"Don't interrupt."*

So Fiona turned around and walked out.

2020, Massachusetts. A shaky iPhone video captures a long, serpentine shape turning away from the hull of a sailing boat. Somewhere behind the camera, a man's voice shouts, "Did you get that?"

But here's the thing about sea serpents. They don't exist.

On some level people want *them to exist*, Fiona thought, closing the Airbnb binder. She pushed its scrawled distractions to the other side of the table and opened the laptop. Her mangled grant application stared back at her. People didn't want to hear about garbage-eating seabirds. They wanted sea serpents. They wanted them in the same way they wanted miracles, in the same way they wanted "Nature": the pure wildness of distant forests, the frosty peaks of unclimbed mountains, the abyssal depths no human will ever see. The nature of a thousand "Nature is Healing" memes: ancient, mysterious, and resilient, offering escape, or sublime inspiration, or just a relief from the relentless crowd, the endless contaminating *me me me.*

But there is no such thing as "pure" nature. Fiona moved her cursor over the document, adding in the obligatory reference to "the Anthropocene." The forests were withering, the untrodden mountain peaks were bathed in pollution, microplastics glittered on the floor of the deep sea, in places that hadn't seen sunlight since the dawn of the world. A few years ago, she'd read a nice article about the hemp ropes used in early fishing industries. Apparently such ropes could survive intact for months after being washed loose by storms. Apparently they could entangle marine animals with the same lethal efficiency as modern plastics. Apparently they had been doing so for centuries. Sea serpent sighting mapped horribly well onto the maps of old fishing grounds. A white-furred animal fighting with a whale? Try a whale trying desperately to escape the rotting clutches of a net. Humps in the water? A trail of buoys. Glittering eyes? Glass globes from an eighteenth-century fish trap. A red gash? Blood.

The word "monster" comes from a Latin word meaning "to warn," as in a sign from the gods, as in a warning against future action. Where sea monsters were concerned, humans had misread the warning. "Here be monsters" didn't mean "Here no humans tread," but "Here you already are," your technology already tangling the waters, your influence already spreading across a godless globe.

Fiona didn't know if Brian had succeeded in raising interest in the "Auld Horgan" sightings. If someone at NatureScot was interested, if they received confirmation, they could perhaps reach this year's "Auld Horgan" in time. They had divers who could assist in detangling whales from ghost gear, if they could find the whale. She'd done what she could. Hadn't she? With this and with the arm.

She checked her phone again. She checked her inbox. She paced the kitchen, stretched her back, peered out the window at the darkening valley. Heavy clouds were rolling in from the sea; there'd be a storm tonight, for sure. Brian might be staying in Stornoway for a while.

She opened her notebooks and reviewed her solid lines of data, the number of birds observed, the number of nests identified. The whistle of the wind under the door was beginning to get on her nerves. She laid a jacket down, noting the muddy footprints on the laminate, a trail of dirt as though something heavy had been dragged across the entrance. Some white-looking hairs were caught on the edge of the door. The fibres were straight and felt very stiff, almost bristlelike.

She retraced her steps into the kitchen. Yes, the floor was muddy, but that didn't mean anything. For no reason, she opened the freezer door. The arm was still missing.

There was a sound outside; something metal clattering to the ground. The wind, knocking over one of the rusty tools propped up against the cottage's stark white wall.

Fiona went upstairs to read her whale book, old wood creaking around her. The storm chased shadows across the wall. She leaned close to the print showing Auld Horgan and his worshippers, the whaler poised with his harpoon, a woman standing amid a group of seals. The square near the door showed a man cut into pieces, giant body parts arranged around a shape that she recognised as that of the island. His huge, stone-cut eyes stared ahead blankly.

Grave rubbing from Tomb of Cailleach, Siolaigh, said the legend at the bottom of the poster.

Rain lashed the window, which rattled in the wind. She closed the curtains, then waited, listening. The sound she'd just heard repeated itself: a woman screaming.

It's just the wind, she thought.

She went down the stairs anyway, feeling her way to the yellow light. The sound of the rain absorbed everything. Except, outside the door, a scrape against stone. And that sound again, like a woman howling in the dark.

Fiona thought, for some reason, of the woman in grey who'd watched her with the cold black gaze of a hunting animal. She thought, for some reason, of her mother, standing in the glaring light of the refrigerator, crooning to angels only she could see. She thought, for some reason, of the print upstairs, the man split into pieces, each part where it should be, a leg for each pebbled beach, a head staring out at the ocean.

I don't need to open that door, she thought. *It's a coarse night, I should stay inside. There's nothing out there to see.*

The doorknob was cold underneath her hand. She creaked the door open. Wind-driven water darted into her eyes, and still she thought, as the warmth of the house bled outward, *It's not too late—*

But then something hard yanked her forward, and it was already too late.

...

1701, Siolaigh. It is said that in bitter seasons the heretics will send a man to petition this Serpent to send them all manner of fishes to their nets; and that this man will not return but will be cast about in the old way.

She knew the broch by the sound of its birds. Disturbed by the storm, the sheltering gulls threw liquid calls to each other. The fulmars cried on their ledges. Waves smashed the rocks below, thunderous and strange.

Blinding rain cut into Fiona's eyes and mouth. The hands pinning her arms were still there, strong and implacable. She thought she could still feel the weight of her cell phone in her back pocket, though her skin had long since gone numb with cold. She could reach it, maybe. There was a chance.

If she got free, she'd need to remember these things: the precise posture of the man against the glow of a flashlight, his hands raised in a pose that was stomach-twistingly familiar. The man clutching her smelled of old fish, his breath like rotting seaweed. A local, she thought; but of course they were locals. Somewhere deep in the pit of her body, she'd already known.

A white shape twisted through the darkness in front of her, the woman from the point, walking straight ahead. Fiona couldn't tell if she knew anyone else here, whether Jim Clesich or Connor Leisk or the man from the gate shuffling through the rain beside her. She couldn't say she'd blame them if they were. She was an outsider; she'd been warned.

Say something, she thought. *Now, before anything happens.* They hadn't gagged her; she could still speak. She could appeal to their better natures, to their shared humanity, or to their fears. But there was an empty space inside Fiona where the words should be. She'd never been one to plead.

The iron smell of blood saturated the air. Twisting her neck, she saw the head of a bearded man set on the broch's triangular slab of stone, another man sawing at the leg. Discrete facts separated by lightning flashes. A volunteer, of course, for the ritual. Not Brian, which was something to hold on to. Brian was somewhere else by now; the dark centre of the circle, the same place to which Fiona was being drawn, inexorably, like a weed in the tide.

A ritual interrupted might need to be repeated, to be set right. She held on to this thought too, setting it alongside her other observations. Like, the fierce pressure of wind on her face. Like, the arms at her side pushing her forward. She wondered, for a moment, if she was going to be pushed onto the stone. But no, the arms were suddenly gone, the world turned to air around her, a falling sensation jabbing up through her stomach—

Fiona fell, and as she fell, she saw it: the arcing neck, the massive, snake-jawed head, the huge, luminous eyes that stared, indifferently, at the tiny thing plummeting down to the waves.

The ocean hit her like a wall. White-hot pain filled her vision, and the freezing water rushed in.

Hold your breath, she thought, watching a string of silver bubbles trail up over her head. *Hold your breath,* as though that was an instruction she could give.

The twilight moment stretched; and then she sank, down to the gaping dark, down to the pitch-black cold. And as she sank it floated across her mind, a shimmer of thought, to wonder what strange life her body would birth down there, what manner of reef, what kind of marvel.

WHAT IS LOVE BUT THE QUIET MOMENTS AFTER DINNER?

by Richard Kadrey

Caleb was beginning to think that dinner might have been a mistake. He'd been on the dating app for months and, while he'd made connections with some other women, Patti was the first he'd actually agreed to meet, as his loneliness finally won out over the wariness that defined almost every aspect of his life. So far, though, the evening had been painful. He'd mumbled all the way through the appetizer and wasn't doing much better when their dinners arrived. Still, Patti chatted on as if he wasn't the stammering fool he felt like.

Picking at her honey smoked salmon, she said, "It must be so interesting being a journalist."

Caleb hesitated before answering, but fed up with his fear of human contact he said, "It's fun, but I shouldn't have said journalist. I'm just someone who freelances to a few magazines and papers. Mostly music, film, and book reviews."

Patti raised her eyebrows. "Ah. You're a 'film' person."

"Because I said film instead of movies?"

"Yeah."

He felt a little flutter of panic in his stomach and said, "I hope it doesn't make me sound hopelessly pretentious. It's just a leftover from all the film . . . movie magazines I read growing up."

Patti smiled brightly. "It's okay. I say film too."

"If I understood your ad right, it's your job. Digital film restoration?"

"That's right. Though I don't work with the film itself. I get digitized files and clean them up, frame by frame."

"That must be fun."

"Sometimes. A few months back, I got to restore some new footage for Fritz Lang's *Metropolis*."

"Okay. You can't deny that was fun." To Caleb's surprise, he began to relax as they talked about their jobs. He'd originally been interested in Patti because she worked with movies. He was sure if he kept the subject on that, he'd be all right.

But she wasn't so easily pinned down. She said, "I suppose it was entertaining. But enough about work. What do you do for fun?"

Caleb froze again. What *did* he do for fun? The things he wrote about used to be fun, but now they were just how he passed his nights.

"I can see I stumped you," said Patti. "That's okay. I'll go first. I like hunting."

Caleb looked at her. "You mean animals?"

Patti set down her fork, frowning slightly. "Was that the wrong thing to say? I'm sorry I brought it up."

Before Caleb could reply, the waiter appeared and asked if they wanted dessert. Neither did, so he left to get their check.

Knowing he had to say something to try and salvage the evening, Caleb said, "I'm sorry. I just never met a hunter before. Well, one, but I didn't like him."

"I can see I upset you," said Patti. She reached across the table and put her hand over his. "Come back to my place and let me make it up to you."

That's a surprise, he thought. With his clumsiness earlier and his reaction to her hobby, he was sure he'd ruined the whole evening. Still, part of him wanted to bolt and head home, but Patti was genuinely interesting. He wondered if maybe things would be easier somewhere less public. "Okay. Yes. I'd like that."

Patti wiped her mouth and said, "Great. How did you get here?"

"A cab."

"Perfect. I drove. We can take my car without worrying about yours."

Since he'd invited her out, Caleb insisted on paying for dinner. Patti led him outside to a sporty-looking Mercedes GT and opened the door for him. Once she got behind the wheel, she steered the car at breakneck speed all the way across town, blowing through red lights and letting the tires squeal around corners. Caleb wanted to look relaxed when she glanced at him. Smiling tightly, he tried to think of small talk. "How long have you been restoring films?"

Patti wagged a finger in the air. "No more work talk."

"Then what should we talk about?"

"You'll see."

She lived in a condo complex out by Ocean Beach. The neighborhood looked expensive and Caleb wondered briefly how well film restoration paid if she could afford a Mercedes and a bungalow out here. He theorized that she might have inherited the place from a relative or maybe she made good stock investments. He could ask her for some tips. It wasn't much in the way of conversation, but it was something.

However, once they were inside the apartment, Patti didn't leave any room for small talk. She pushed Caleb down on the sofa and climbed on top, straddling him. Shy as he was, when she kissed him fervently, he kissed her back just as hard. The feeling was both glorious and achingly sad as his loneliness clashed with the joy he felt at being with someone—anyone—after so long alone.

They'd been kissing and touching for several minutes when he felt Patti shift position. Still on his lap, she leaned away from him, pinning him in place with one hand. Caleb didn't see the other hand until it was too late.

She drove the butcher knife into his chest up to the hilt, pulled it out and did it again. Over and over, she drove the knife into him, a wolfish grin on her face the whole time. Caleb started to double over in pain, but gathered his strength and shoved her off hard enough that she rolled across the coffee table and onto the floor. Before she could get up, he pulled the knife from his chest, jammed it into the wall, and broke off the handle. He tossed it to her mockingly as she got to her feet and said, "I guess this is what you meant by hunting."

"Bright boy," said Patti. She ran to an easy chair across the room and pulled out an axe hidden behind it.

Caleb said, "How many people have you done this to?"

"That would be telling." He waited for her to rush him, but she stood where she was, looking at him and his clean shirt. Finally, she said, "Why aren't you bleeding?"

Now *he* smiled. "It's not in my nature."

"Everybody bleeds."

"Not me."

Patti frowned. "You have some kind of disease?"

He laughed. "People like me, we don't get diseases. We don't bleed and we don't die."

Even though she was holding the axe at shoulder height, Patti looked less certain of herself. "What are you saying? You're some kind of vampire or something?"

"You've never heard of anyone like me. And that axe isn't going to help you."

Patti took a nervous step back. "Are you going to try and kill me?"

"I'm not a killer. A killer is a wretched thing."

"Then what are you?"

"I'm leaving now."

"You can't. The door is locked and I've hidden the key. What are you?"

Caleb tried the door and, indeed, it was locked. He turned back to Patti. "Fine. You want to know? I eat the dead."

She made a face. "You're a cannibal?"

"You wouldn't understand."

"Try me."

"I told you what I am, and you know you can't kill me. Open the door so I can go."

Patti lowered the axe to the floor and gave Caleb an odd look. "Are you sure you want to leave?"

He laughed. "Now I'm suddenly interesting enough for you not to murder?"

She shrugged. "I'm a funny girl."

"Please open the door."

Patti left the axe against the easy chair and took the keys from her pocket. As he left, she grabbed Caleb's arm. He whirled, but before he could hit her, Patti said, "I'm sorry about your shirt."

"Good night."

At home, Caleb poured himself a tall glass of scotch and drained it all at once. He set the glass on the kitchen counter, removed his ruined shirt, and threw it in the trash.

What the hell was I thinking?

He went over the evening in his head for the tenth time.

There are so few like me, and most of us are loathsome. What kind of relationship could I ever have with a regular person? No. I'm just a bug scuttling around at night, bribing morgue and funeral home lackeys for food. It's worse when they smile or try to make small talk. I can smell their terror, even as they take the money. No. No more fuckups like tonight. No friends. Never love.

Two nights later, Caleb received an email telling him that he had a message from Patti on the dating app. At first he ignored it, but the more he thought about it the more unsettled he became. In his anger, he'd said more than he'd intended. What if she told someone? Or worse, what if Thacker had gotten to her? He logged onto the app and before he could check his email, a new text came through from Patti. It read, "I've been thinking about you. The things you told me about yourself."

He texted back, "Trust me. I've thought about you too."

"I want to see you again."

"That sounds like a bad idea."

"I promise it will be different this time."

"Why should I believe you?"

"Because of what I know now. To do what happened last time would be pointless and just spoil the evening."

Caleb typed, "Then why?"

"I told you. I can't get you out of my head."

"Maybe it would be better for everyone if you tried harder."

"See me. Tonight. No funny business. I promise."

"Why would I do that?"

"You said you'd been thinking about me. See me tonight. If the evening displeases you, I promise to leave you alone."

As much as he wanted to keep his distance from her, Patti was the first person he'd felt any interest in for so long. As it had on the night he met her, the loneliness welled up inside him. She was beautiful, and she was interesting.

She knows she can't hurt me, and if she tries I could be ready.

He typed, "I can't say I'm not tempted."

"Come at ten. Not my place. At a hotel. Here's the address and room number."

"I'll have to think about it."

"See you at ten."

Tense and fairly certain that he was making a mistake, Caleb arrived at the room number Patti had given him at ten minutes after ten. He hesitated a moment before knocking and slipped a hand into his jacket, taking hold of the snub-nosed .38 he had hidden there. He might be foolish enough to show up, he thought, but he wasn't dumb enough to get stabbed twice. And there was the Thacker question in the back of his mind.

Finally, he knocked. A shadow passed over the door's peephole and he heard locks opening. A moment later, Patti was standing before him. She was nude except for nitrile gloves and a pair of disposable hospital booties. She was covered in blood.

"What the hell . . . ?" said Caleb.

She put a finger to her lips and said, "No questions yet. Here. Put these on."

Patti handed him disposable booties like hers. When he hesitated, she dropped to her knees and put them on over his shoes, then pulled him inside.

It was an ordinary businessman's room, functional and forgettable—except for the body lying on a plastic tarp spread out over the floor. Caleb lifted the edge of the blanket covering it and the smell of blood filled his nostrils and made his stomach growl.

He looked at Patti and said, "My god. Did you do this because of me?"

"Maybe," she said coyly. "Partly. Show me. I kept him warm for you under the blanket. You must like them fresh, right?"

Caleb shook his head. "This is insane."

"Show me," said Patti as she pulled away the blanket to fully reveal the body. He too was nude and his clothes were folded neatly on a corner of the tarp. The smell of the fresh meat was overwhelming. Caleb hadn't eaten properly in a week. There was just the old woman from the morgue where he had an understanding with one of the attendants. There had been so little of the woman that she was mostly bones. Hardly a meal at all. Except for the slit across his throat, the body on the floor of the hotel room was in the prime of life.

He tried to stop himself, but the hunger was overwhelming. Caleb took off his jacket and shirt and tossed them on the bed. Then, as Patti watched, he slid his fingers into the flesh above his sternum and pulled himself apart. His torso parted easily, becoming a gaping maw lined with a row of sharp, ragged teeth.

From close behind him he heard Patti say, "Yes. Yes."

Caleb turned around to check that she wasn't armed. When he saw she wasn't, he knelt over the body and fed it into his jaws quickly, starting with the man's head.

He'd been so hungry that the feeding only took a few minutes, and when he finished he fell onto his back panting as strength returned to him. He hadn't realized how drained he'd become. Caleb looked up at Patti standing over him. Her expression wasn't fear or disgust, but one of pure wonder. Before he closed his chest, Patti reached down and ran her fingers lightly over his torso's lips and teeth. Caleb looked down at himself. He was almost as bloody as Patti now. When he tried to get up, she pushed him back onto the tarp and pulled off his pants, sliding down onto his cock. They thrust against each other for what to Caleb felt like a delightful forever until Patti groaned and dug her fingers into him. Falling on top of him, she kissed him hard.

Patti turned on the shower for him because he wasn't wearing gloves and she didn't want him leaving fingerprints. As he washed, she folded up the tarp and blanket, put them into the dead man's suitcase, and set it by the door. Then she joined Caleb in the shower and they scrubbed each other clean.

Lying together in bed, Patti said, "The other night, you said that killing people was a wretched thing. But you're wrong. It's easy and it means nothing."

Rolling onto his side so he could get a better look at her, Caleb said, "Do you really believe that?"

She nodded and held out her hands, making a rectangle with her fingers. "Killing is easy because people don't exist. They're like frames of film. I can see right through them. Their death is just editing out frames here and there."

"Can you see through yourself?"

"Oh yes. I'm not here either. But here's the thing. Why I asked you here tonight."

"So you could watch me feed."

"That too, but mostly it's because I can't see through you. You're real. You exist. I've never met anyone like you before."

Caleb laughed once. "No. I bet you haven't."

Patti crawled on top of him and kissed him again. "I want . . . I want to know you. I've never felt anything for anyone."

"Because they didn't exist?"

She touched his face. "Yes. But you. I actually feel something," she said. "Stay with me. I'm not afraid of you or anything I saw tonight. I know you're lonely or you wouldn't have come here. Please. Take a chance and see what wonderful things we can do together."

Caleb stared up at her. She was so beautiful. Her skin was warm, unlike the dead, who were the only other bodies he'd known in years. A part of him wanted to run from the room, but another, stronger part of him held him where he was. He pulled Patti down onto his chest and said, "I suppose we can try."

She sat up and smiled at him. "Yes? That makes me so happy."

He looked up at the ceiling. "I was wondering something. These men you kill, do you steal from them too?"

Patti smiled. "You mean how can I afford my Mercedes? Of course I take their money. Killing them means nothing, why should going home with some trinkets?"

"I thought so. That brings me to the other thing I need to say."

"What? Tell me."

"If we're together, you can't kill people anymore. You'd have to be content helping me gather bodies. It's not always easy. Maybe that would be adventure enough for you?"

Patti looked down, her brow creased and mouth drawn down. "I thought you might say something like that, so I thought it over before I got here. And, yes, I promise to try."

"If the urge hits you could always, I suppose, do things to the bodies before I feed."

Patti brightened. "Yes. I think I'd like that."

"And don't worry about money. The kind of work I do doesn't pay much, but I have an inheritance."

She wiggled her body against his. "I guess we're an item, then."

Caleb chuckled. "I guess we are."

They kissed for a few minutes and got dressed. Patti put their booties in the suitcase with the tarp and as they were leaving, she looked serious for a moment. "Is this what love feels like?"

Caleb kissed her. "It's the beginning, at least. We'll know if it's love soon enough."

Smiling, Patti said, "Take me to your place. I want to see it."

"All right."

She drove them out to the ocean first, where they walked along a rocky cliff out of sight of the road. In the darkness, she threw the dead man's suitcase into the churning water below. They waited until it sank beneath the waves, then drove to Caleb's apartment, where they made love the rest of the night.

After a month without a kill, Patti grew restless and began going to martial-arts classes. For all its power, aikido turned out to be too passive for her, while judo was too much groundwork and didn't possess the aggression of kicking and punching that she craved. She soon moved on to tae kwon do and Krav Maga, where pummeling and being pummeled gave her something like the excitement of the hunt. She soon declared herself Caleb's bodyguard and accompanied him on all his runs to the morgue and funeral homes, looming quietly in the background in shades and a long coat, wishing she had a knife in her pocket, but satisfied with knowing how much damage she could do to any rogue attendant who attempted to deny Caleb his meal or try to shake him down. Back at his apartment, she never tired of watching him feed.

One evening after dinner, he said, "I never asked you this because I didn't want to pry, but how long have you been killing?"

Patti thought for a moment and said, "My whole life, I suppose. I can't remember a time when the urge wasn't there."

"How often did you feel compelled to do it?"

"With people? Never more than once a month, and always on different days, using different weapons. I wanted to avoid having too much of a pattern for the police to follow."

"Do you miss it?"

Again, Patti took a moment. "I thought I would, but between the martial arts and sneaking in and out of morgues with bodies, I don't really."

Caleb smiled. "That's wonderful to hear. Still, I feel guilty for asking you to stop doing something so fundamental to you."

"But that's what I mean. Things are different now. I can't see through you and I can see myself more and more."

"I never wanted to try and tame you."

"Trust me, you're not. You should come to class and watch me toss people around. I love feeling them hit the ground."

"I'd love to see you in action."

Sitting on the sofa, Patti put an arm around him. "Can I ask you something?"

"Of course."

"You don't get sick. You don't get hurt. You don't die. So, how old are you?"

"That's a hard question to answer because I don't know," said Caleb. "There weren't really countries back then. Just snow and tribes of people who kept on the move looking for game. I'd drift from group to group, trying to settle down. With the cold and lack of game, death was much more common back then, so if the tribe couldn't feed, I still could. Sooner or later, though, when enough bodies disappeared, they'd realize what I was. Some tribes wanted to kill me. Some wanted to worship me. I didn't like either, so I stayed mostly to myself."

Patti kissed him tenderly and said, "You don't have to be alone anymore."

When she went back home the next day to pick up some clothes and her mail, there was a bald man waiting for her on the sofa. He kept a hand in his pocket like he might be hiding a pistol, but Patti had dealt with enough prey that she prided herself on picking up on facial and bodily cues enough to be fairly certain that it was a bluff. Before she said a word, she went to the easy chair and took out the axe hidden there. The stranger immediately shrank back and his hand came out of his pocket. She'd been right. It was all an act. But he wasn't too frightened to speak.

He said, "Don't do anything stupid, lady."

"Like breaking into my apartment?" she said, advancing on him.

"Thacker put me onto you two. You and your freak show boyfriend."

Patti frowned. "What the fuck are you talking about?"

The bald man sat up a little straighter. "But I don't want him. He's Thacker's problem."

"Who the fuck is Thacker?"

The man ignored her. "Worry about me. Brubaker. I know who you are and I know what you've done. I have photos. Dates. Names. All of it." When he finished, he reached into the pocket she thought might have held a gun, took out a pile of photos, and tossed them on the coffee table.

Patti kept the axe as she looked over the shots. Brubaker wasn't bluffing now. There were photos of her with the last three kills she'd made the month before she and Caleb had become lovers and she'd sworn off murder. "Did you take these?"

"Does it matter?"

"What do you want?"

"A hundred thousand dollars."

She held up the axe a little higher. "You think I have that kind of money lying around?"

"Sell that pretty car of yours. Take out a second mortgage on this place. I don't care."

Patti kicked the coffee table out of the way and swung the axe down so that it embedded itself in the sofa frame between Brubaker's legs. He scrambled back a bit and shouted, "Don't even dream about killing me. Thacker has copies of all the files. If I disappear, he goes straight to the cops."

She knew she needed time to think, so she said, "When do you want the money?"

"Tomorrow night at eleven. Meet me at the Blue Cuckoo." Patti remembered the place. It was a shabby little tavern she'd shown some of her wealthier victims who wanted to see a real live dive bar.

Pulling the axe out of the sofa, Patti said, "I don't know if I can put it all together by then."

"Ask your boyfriend. He has money stashed away."

Patti spun the axe in her hands a couple of times while thinking. Brubaker said, "Don't do anything suicidal. All I want is the money."

"Who's this Thacker? I want to talk to him."

"No," said Brubaker flatly. He got up slowly and inched across the apartment to the door, never taking his eyes off Patti. "Tomorrow night at the Blue Cuckoo or the cops get everything."

Brubaker backed out into the hall. Patti hated letting him go but looking at the photos that had fallen to the floor, she knew the man was serious. She put the axe behind the easy chair and called Caleb.

"Can you come over?"

"What's wrong? You don't sound good."

"Please, just get over here as soon as you can. I'm in trouble."

A half hour later, Patti let Caleb inside.

"What's wrong?" he said.

She handed him the photos. "A man named Brubaker was waiting for me when I got home."

"Do you know him?"

"I've never seen him before. He wants a hundred thousand dollars or he'll send these and a lot more to the police. I have to kill him before he can do that."

Caleb took her hand and led her to the sofa. "I think killing him would be a bad idea. If he got in here without you knowing, I'd guess he's resourceful enough to be ready for an attack."

Patti looked concerned. "Have you heard of someone named Thacker?"

Caleb shook his head. "That idiot. He's mixed up in this?"

"Brubaker said he's working with him. Who is he?"

"Some mad vigilante character. He's been after me for a long time."

"Is he dangerous?"

"Potentially. But I've been dodging him for years, so I'm not too concerned."

"Should I pay Brubaker?"

"We. You're not on your own in this. And no, we can't pay him. He'll just come back for more. Why don't you let me handle this?"

"What are you going to do?" Patti said. She grinned. "Are you going to eat him?"

"No. I don't eat the living. But he doesn't know that. I'm just going to inform him that he's not just dealing with you, but with the two of us."

Patti put her arms around him. "I love you, baby."

"I love you too."

Patti frowned. "Be careful."

"I promise."

"I'm coming with you."

"All right. But once you point Brubaker out, let me handle things."

"Deal."

It was a long night and day waiting for eleven P.M.

They arrived at the Blue Cuckoo at ten and found a table in a dim back corner of the bar. Caleb bought them drinks and when he returned to the table, Patti's hand was resting on top. She had a stiletto in her hand.

Caleb sat and put a hand over hers. "You should put that away before someone sees."

"I can still kill him," she said. "It would be so fast and easy. No one would ever know."

"You agreed to let me handle things."

"I know, but . . ."

He put an arm around her. "It's going to be all right. I promise."

She slipped the knife back in her coat pocket and sipped her drink.

At eleven on the dot, she sat up straighter. "He's here."

"Which one?"

"The bald guy at the end of the bar."

"I see him. Wait here."

"Be careful."

Caleb came up behind Brubaker and put the .38 in his pocket against the man's back. "You should come with me," he said.

Brubaker stiffened. "This is a dumb move."

"Walk over there. To the men's room."

"Whatever you say, Dirty Harry."

Once they were inside, Caleb jammed a metal trash can under the doorknob so no one could come in.

Brubaker leaned against the wall, seemingly unconcerned. "Let me guess," he said. "You're the boyfriend."

"Leave Patti alone."

"Did she send you here to scare me? This is so cute. But she must have told you where the information goes if anything happens to me."

"She told me. And I'm telling you again to leave her alone."

Brubaker jabbed a finger at him. "Fuck you. You aren't going to shoot me. I can tell you're not the type. Besides, the whole bar will hear and the cops will be here before you finish wetting your pants."

Caleb let go of the pistol and took his hand out of his pocket. "You're right. The gun was just to get your attention."

"If you're not going to kill me, then get out of my way."

Brubaker tried to push past, but Caleb shoved him back so that he fell against the wall. He said, "I'm not going to shoot you. But I might eat you."

The bald man made a face. "Fuck off."

Caleb unbuttoned his shirt, dug his fingers into his flesh, and pulled himself open. The ragged teeth around his maw shone grayish green in the men's room's flickering fluorescent lights. Brubaker pushed himself against the far wall. "Oh shit. Oh god. What is that?"

"Leave Patti alone or I'll swallow you down a piece at a time. I can make it last hours."

Holding up a hand, Brubaker said, "Get the fuck away from me, you freak."

Caleb grabbed the man's hand and shoved it between his torso teeth. "How does that feel? Want me to snap it off?"

Brubaker froze. "Oh fuck. Please stop."

"Leave Patti alone."

The man nodded. "Okay. Fuck. Just get away from me."

"If you're lying, I'm not going to give you a second chance."

"I'm not. Just please leave me alone."

Caleb went to the door and shoved the trash can out of the way. "Get out. I never want to see you again."

"You won't," said Brubaker, rushing out of the room.

After buttoning his shirt, Caleb returned to where Patti was sitting.

"How did it go?" she said anxiously.

"He won't bother you again."

She laid her head on his shoulder. "Thank you. Thank you so much."

"Don't thank me. We're in this together."

"Let's go home."

They walked out of the Blue Cuckoo hand in hand. As they turned the corner to go to Patti's car, a man stepped out from behind a light pole. Thin to the point of being gaunt, he wore a long black silk coat and round wire-rim glasses. He said, "Hello, Caleb."

"Thacker?"

The gaunt man slid a hand from his pocket and shot three times. Caleb stumbled back, bounced off a fire hydrant, and fell to the ground. Thacker took a couple of steps toward him when Patti charged, her knife out. She stabbed him once in his shooting hand and again in the arm. He dropped his pistol and fell back against a car, setting off the alarm. Patti kicked the gun into the street and pulled Caleb to his feet, shoving him into her car and speeding away.

When they reached her place, he was weak enough that she had to put an arm around his shoulders to walk him inside. He finally collapsed on the bed, pale and sweating. Patti put a hand on his forehead and felt him cold and trembling. She sat down next to him and took his hand. She said, "I don't understand. Why are you hurt? Nothing can hurt you."

Caleb opened his eyes and said, "It's Thacker. He knows how to kill people like me. He put something on the bullets. Some kind of poison."

Patti squeezed his hand. "How can I help?"

He shook his head. "You can't. I need to feed, but it has to be fresh. Nothing from the morgue. Normally, if something like this happened, I'd scour the alleys looking for a recent death, but I'm too weak now."

"This has happened before?"

Nodding, Caleb said, "Thacker isn't the first who wanted me dead. There have been a few others."

Patti stood. "I'm going to get you something."

He reached for her as she got up. "No. Please stay with me."

She pulled out a box from under the bed. It was lined with purple velvet and full of blades. Selecting a bowie knife and an old bone-handle dirk, she pushed the box back and put on her coat. "I won't be long."

Caleb tried to call to her, but his voice was hoarse and weak, so she didn't hear.

Patti was opening her car when something hard smashed into her back. The pain was sharp and deep, numbing her whole body so that she fell to the ground. Stunned, she felt hands roll her onto her back. Long legs stood astride her, and when she looked up, she recognized Brubaker. He was leaning casually on a baseball bat like it was a cane.

"You put that maniac onto me?" he said. "Fuck both of you. Thacker's got the freak, but I've got you."

The feeling came back to Patti's arms as he stood and held the bat over his head. She slipped the bowie knife from her coat and shoved it through Brubaker's left calf, giving the blade a twist before yanking it out. He groaned and collapsed onto one knee, so she stabbed him in the right calf before he could push himself up. Falling flat on his back, Brubaker swung the baseball bat wildly at her, knocking the knife from her hand. While she stumbled to her feet, her knife hand aching, Patti kneed Brubaker's bloody leg. This time he didn't groan. He screamed at the top of his lungs and swung the bat again, but she dodged it and kicked him in the groin. He rolled onto his belly and started crawling away, shouting for help at the top of his lungs. Up and down the street, lights came on in homes and apartments. Before Brubaker could make it to the corner, Patti dropped her knees onto his back, pulled the bone dirk from her coat with her uninjured hand, and jammed it through the back of his skull until she heard a satisfying crunch. Brubaker made a gasping sound and kicked a couple of times, his hands grasping at the air. However, a few seconds later he was still. Patti pushed herself to her feet and grabbed Brubaker's collar, hauling him to her bungalow, ignoring the trail of blood his body left on the pavement.

A few minutes later, she went into the bedroom and helped Caleb to his feet, walking him into the living room. When he saw Brubaker's body he stopped and Patti had to hold him to keep him from falling over.

"Baby, what have you done?"

"It's okay," she said, gently lowering Caleb onto his knees. "He attacked me this time. It was self-defense."

Caleb reached down and pulled the dirk from Brubaker's neck. "I'm not sure that's what the police will say."

"Worry about them later. Now shut up and eat."

He kissed her. "Thank you."

Taking off his shirt, Caleb pulled himself open and leaned over Brubaker's corpse. He fed the man's head into his chest first, then tilted the body to swallow the left shoulder, then the right. Feeling heat and his strength returning, Caleb tore into the rest of the body, swallowing it all in under a minute. He remained there on his knees breathing, feeling Brubaker's raw meat absorbing the poison in his system. As he stood, he saw the blood trail leading from the door. Patti helped him to the sofa. She put her hands on his cheeks and looked into his eyes. He put his hands over hers and said, "It's okay now. I'm feeling a lot better. You saved me."

Patti put her arms around him. "What else would I do?"

Eyeing the blood trail seeping into the carpet, Caleb said, "Did a lot of people see you?"

She sighed. "Probably everybody on the block. The cops will be on their way. We have to get out of here."

In the time it took Patti to get to the bedroom, tires squealed, and bright red and blue lights pulsed through the curtains. "Turn out the lights," Caleb said. When the room was dark, he went to a front window and peeked outside. "Fuck. Thacker is with the cops. God knows what he's told them about us."

Patti shook her head. "I'm not going to jail and leaving you."

"No one is going to jail."

She went to the kitchen and looked out the back door. Blue and red lights flared off the walls. Back in the living room she said, "We're surrounded."

"They'll want us outside soon. That's if they want us to come out at all."

"What do you mean?"

Caleb pulled Patti away from the window. "I mean that Thacker will have told him a story. That we're maniacs or terrorists. Someone beyond negotiating."

"You think they'll listen?"

"They're cops. What do you think?"

Patti went to the bedroom and came out with a Marine Ka-Bar in each hand. "Fine. Let's take them on together."

Caleb said, "Maybe we can . . ." and glass flew into the room as all the windows exploded. Metal canisters landed on the sofa and easy chair, while a couple rolled under the curtains. A choking mist filled the room and Patti began to cough violently.

"Tear gas!" shouted Caleb as he grabbed her, pulling her into the windowless bedroom. While she sat on the edge of the mattress, still coughing, he stuffed her bathrobe under the bottom of the door to keep out the fumes.

They could hear the cops, shouting something at them through megaphones.

Catching her breath, Patti said, "What happens now?"

"I don't know. I have a feeling if we went out now, they'd just gun us down."

"That's okay. You could save yourself."

"But it's not okay for you, so no one is giving themselves up."

Something in the air changed. A second scent mixed with the caustic tear gas fumes. Caleb touched the door and snatched his hand away.

"What's wrong?" Patti said.

Caleb opened the door a crack. The paint bubbled on the outside as heat and smoke poured into the room. "The canisters," he said. "They've set the whole place on fire."

Patti put a terry cloth robe over her nose so that she could breathe.

"Cover your eyes too and give me your hand. Get ready to run."

"The smoke doesn't bother you?"

"I'll be all right. Just follow me."

She put out her hand and Caleb led them in a dead run down the hall and into the bathroom. Inside, Patti coughed and wiped her eyes as Caleb pressed towels at the bottom of the door. "Why are we in here?" said Patti. "Could we stand in the shower, so the flames don't get us?"

Caleb shook his head. "If the cops haven't turned off the water, the pipes will burst soon enough. The shower won't save us."

"You've been through this before."

"Something like it."

"With someone else?"

"Yes."

"Did they survive?"

Caleb didn't reply. Stronger than the smell of tear gas now, smoke snaked and swirled from under the bathroom door. The paint began to blister.

"Do you still have your gun?" Patti said. "I'm not going to the cops, but I'm not burning either."

"We could go out that window," Caleb whispered, thinking.

"But they'll shoot us if you do. That's what you said." Patti coughed as the room grew hotter and the choking smoke began to fill the place.

"There's still something," Caleb said.

"Tell me!"

He took Patti's hands and looked at her hard. "Do you trust me?"

"Yes."

"Do you want to live forever?"

"With you?"

"Yes."

"Then I do."

Caleb took a breath. "I told you once that I don't eat the living."

"I remember."

"There's a reason for that. The dead are just food. My body absorbs them and that's that. But for my kind, to eat the living is to have them inside you forever. Fused to you, body and soul."

"We'd be one person? Forever?"

"Forever."

Patti took off her clothes as the bathroom door turned black with heat. "Do it," she said.

When she was nude, Caleb held her to him and began to feed.

When the house was fully engulfed, the police pulled their men and cars back from the conflagration. Covered in flames, Caleb kicked out the bathroom window and ran westward toward the sea. A sniper on a roof nearby spotted him and shot a volley of bullets into his back. At the end of the block, Caleb found a deep puddle and rolled in it until the flames were out. By the time the police had their searchlights on, he'd rounded a corner and dashed for the beach, where he dove under the waves. The police soon found his footprints and followed him there. They searched the shoreline and sent divers down into the cold, churning water. They brought in helicopters and search dogs. They called in forensic experts and the FBI, but found nothing in the apartment except for a charred box of knives. No bodies. Nothing. One police officer fell off a cliff during the search and landed on a cluster of boulders below. By the time his companions scrambled down after him, the body was gone. When the police searched Caleb's apartment, they found his clothes closet empty and an unsigned Valentine's card on the living room table.

No one ever saw Caleb or Patti again.

THE ISLAND

by Norman Partridge

There was an island that was not, and it was in the middle of the sea. And it drew ships with cargoes strange and passengers stranger, for that was how it lived.

Its tools were the wind and the fog and the sea. The fog was the island's eyes, and its gaze tracked passing ships for signs and portents. When these were found the fog spilled over quarterdecks, exploring cabins and holds like a soft wet shadow. And though the things the island prized were well-practiced in the art of obscuration, nothing could hide from the fog.

In this way monsters were discovered and revealed. Not always, perhaps rarely, but as often as often could be. And then the fog whispered to the sea, and its waves crested like glass mountains, tossing those who walked above deck or hid below. Soon thoughts they only recognized in dreams whirled free as in a tempest, and in time quite brief both thinker and thoughts were cast to wave and water.

And delivered to an island that was not, in the middle of the sea.

When the vampire broke through the locked cargo hold hatch, the crew was spiking his sisters to the deck with harpoons and boucan knives.

The three women thrashed like fish trapped in a net, already past saving. The vessel pitched and rolled as waves piled over the gunwales, flooding the deck with salt water and blood, but the vampire did not slow his tread at the sight. Neither did he spare a glance for the thrall who had spilled his secrets, kicking heels as he swung from noose and yardarm, for that man was beyond the Count's vengeance now.

Others were not. The first mate turned, harpoon in hand, and the vampire tore out his throat and voice box along with any answers those simple constructs might have conveyed. The men standing behind the first mate were the kind who had no answers at all, so the Count killed them just as quickly, their weapons clattering uselessly against the deck in his wake.

He was closing on the lone sailor who stood at the ship's wheel when a man appeared through a slashing wave, a Colt Single Action in his hand and one finger tight on the trigger.

That finger moved faster than the vampire.

The bullet shattered the Count's shoulder and ripped it from its socket.

Lead, he thought, barely stumbling as the wound healed. *Not silver.*

In a moment the gunman was in his grasp.

In another the vampire had consigned him to the sea.

The helmsman would have dived over the side at the sight, but his shackled wrists were chained to a bolt in the wheel hub. And then the Count was on him, spitting words in halting English: "Your captain . . . tell me where—"

The helmsman's only answer was an unspoken glance over the vampire's shoulder. The Count whirled just in time, his cloak wrapping the charging captain like an enormous shroud. The big man struggled, but it was like trying to fight a shadow.

The vampire drove him backward and they crashed to the deck as one.

Faces inches apart. Eyes locked.

"The fourth woman," the Count began.

"The one with gold hidden in her coffinbox, and hair just the same?" The captain smiled. "Both precious cargoes, but we only kept one."

The vampire struggled to make sense of the Englishman's words, and with that simple pause the captain drove a stake through the Count's ribs, tearing arteries, missing the vampire's heart by the slimmest of margins . . . and then the two rolled together as the ship was tossed by another monstrous wave, but the stake was still fisted in the captain's grasp and he drew it out and drove it in again, the shaft splintering as it scraped between the vampire's ribs, and—

The Count slammed the captain to the deck, tore the stake from his side, and buried it in the bigger man's shoulder.

"Where . . . is . . . she?"

"In Davy Jones' locker, down on her knees with a crew of dead men. We'll be there with her soon enough, you bastard, and—"

Before the captain could utter another word, the Count pulled the stake from his shoulder and drove it through his heart. Ruddy lips that had spit words now spit gouts of blood, and then the ocean sprayed hard needles across the bow and washed both blood and words away.

But the words rang in the vampire's ears even so. His ribs felt as if they'd been levered by a crowbar, and the world and all the things in it bled before his eyes—the hanged thrall swinging above him, the tearing mainsails and buckling deck, planks spitting nails as the storm ripped them from beams and carlins. The only thing fighting to remain stationary was the helmsman, still chained to the wheel, straining against its power and the power of the raging sea.

In that moment the Count should have moved. But the wind whipped him like a fury of bats in the sky above his castle on *Walpurgisnacht,* and the waves were avalanches now, and together they raised a mammoth hand of tide and terror from the sea. The Count watched it come, and it closed over the helmsman like a fist and flung him over the side, leaving nothing behind but a wheel spinning madly and a shackled pair of severed hands beating against the deck.

And then the watery fist returned, crushing gunwales, shattering ribs. Cargo spilled from the hold as jetting fingers ripped it open, and the hand raised the ship above the sea. The living and the dead swam in its palm, and gold coins from a woman's coffinbox sliced through its whirling vortex, scoring the flesh it found there.

The hand clenched tightly around it all.

Plowing over shoals, spilling away the gold.

The rest it threw high and washed low as it hit the shallows.

Finally the hand was empty, and it bled into the sea as surely as the Count's world.

The wave that was a hand was only one of the island's secrets, but it had a single absolute secret of its own: It brought things to the island, but never did it take them away.

So the hand left the Count on a shoreline of thick rocks which armored the island like a dragon's scales. And though the vampire was a creature of the grave, the island felt his presence, and much more deeply than the mortal chum that had washed ashore unbidden in his wake.

Yes. The island felt what it felt, so it exhaled a breath from a cave that hid high on a rocky tower cloaked by the fog. That breath washed over jagged stone paths to the edge of a cliff, and then it set its course on the wind. It threaded treetops and was sliced by the pointed crest of a pyramid fashioned from shells and bones, but even that eldritch structure could not give it pause. And finally it whispered to the sea itself, for the cave was very deep and its breath came from a place deeper still.

The vampire was just as deep, but not as a cave. He was a vessel fashioned from dead flesh for eternal use. He contained countless lives, carrying them the way the living carry secrets, but the weight the dead man bore was so much heavier. For the river running through his veins pulsed with the blood of a thousand others, and it whispered to the island in the same way that the island whispered to the sea.

The music of sword and shield swam in that river. Its currents carried the screams of warriors impaled on pikes and the percussive crack of an executioner's axe against chopping block. In it flowed the blood of sultans and boyars long dead, and sailors killed a scant hour before, and Saxons and slaves who had fallen in battle when the vampire had been but mortal himself. And whether they had died by undead fang or mortal fury, their fates rested on the Count's shoulders still.

Other fates he carried in his heart.

His three sisters, slaughtered on the deck of the ship, their corpses now churning in the sea, destined to be devoured in its depths before the morning sun.

The fourth woman, his wife, undead still, sinking slowly in a box sheathed by chains.

Trapped beneath the waves, as the island demanded.

Her coffin now nothing more than a lockbox for her screams.

The English vampire slayers played a cadence over the vampire's corpse with hammers and stakes.

Of course, this was only a dream. The slayers who'd stormed his castle had themselves been slain by the Count weeks ago, before he was forced to flee his native land. But even as the dream faded fresh stakes drove down, piercing the vampire's flesh, pinning him to the shore.

They were the stony legs of crab-like creatures hunting for wounded prey in the wake of the shipwreck. The things swarmed from rocky wedges, carving the vampire's flesh with barbed claws, sawing for his arteries. One discovered the hole between the vampire's ribs, and it tore through garments and savaged the wound. And now the vampire thrashed like a man on the rack, for this fresh pain made the captain's stake seem a gentle memory. He tore the creature from his ribs and crushed it against a rock, but a larger crab dug in its claws just as quickly. Again the Count ripped the thing away, but the night was alive with the steady percussion of scrabbling legs as a dozen more crabs joined the feast.

And then a different rhythm—the sharp click of claws over rocks, followed by a smear of shadow that washed over the vampire's face.

A larger creature loomed above him in the fog.

Its teeth flashed. Its jaws snapped wildly. Salty meat splattered the Count's face as the crab's shell shattered, a monster's breath behind it. In an instant the vampire understood that it was the breath of a meat-eater, and a blood-drinker, and a hunter, and now the creature ate its fill. And when its work was done the wolf howled, and the sound was as long and terrible as the night itself, and the Count surrendered to the darkness.

He awoke as the wolf's jaws clacked closed over his collar. The beast pulled him across the rocks, away from tide and shore. It left him in a spot buried by a low fog, where the scaled earth beneath him seemed as unyielding as fallen tombstones in a cemetery.

And then the wolf was gone.

The fog remained.

Silence hung within it, lingering for a long, long while.

In that silence, the vampire's wounds began to heal.

Slowly . . . and all but one.

Many monsters had washed ashore in the island's lifetime, each one as different as the wind and the fog and the sea. Some had been fashioned by fate, like the black wolf who rescued the vampire from the strange crabs. Others were walking relics bearing ways (and curses) forgotten long ago—witness the dead Egyptian who had washed ashore in a box stolen by an American museum. In time, there had been many dead things that walked due to vagaries of chance, and cursed things just the same. One in particular was a creature born from unbridled curiosity. It was not a man at all, but made from them and by them. And, like the island, the simple fact of its birth charged it with a secret understood only by nature herself.

And ships had brought them, and the sea had brought them, and the hand that was a wave had delivered them. But there were others here that had not come from the sea. The stone-shelled crabs had fallen from the stars in ships that glowed like icy coals, and those ships had dug through the island's scales as easily as clams burrow through sand. Below those scales the fallen ships excavated tunnels, and in those tunnels the crabs' masters attached to subterranean walls and grew tentacles, and this was why the island's inhabitants learned not to stray close to blowholes or burrows.

Once learned, the knowledge was simple enough to retain, as were most of the island's lessons. And the simplest lesson of all was the subservience of its inhabitants to the island itself. So it mattered not the lives they took, or the things they devoured, or that they themselves were devoured. Neither did it matter if they lived or died or feasted or starved. What mattered was that the island reaped the bounties if there were bounties to be reaped, and this was done without satisfaction or celebration.

For the island was as constant as the seasons, though it did not care for time. In spring and summer, in fall and winter, the island simply was. Time was marked by the things the island held prisoner, both great and small. The dark eucalyptus trees that shed scented leaves in the winter, and the one sickly pear tree that dropped black fruit on the same fall day each year. The stony crabs that baked beneath the summer sun until their rocky shells burst, then slithered into shadowy blowholes and grew fresh armor while wrapped in the tentacles of the creatures they served. The enormous bats that feasted on fireflies and ship's rats each spring, then nestled in the corpses of dead men in winter, dreaming of warmer days.

And as the seasons were weighed, one thing and one thing only cared as little for time as the island. That was the monster which was not a man at all, but made from them and by them. It was frozen in ice in a place that was always cold, high on a winding path above the rocky tower. The creature had been trapped there long ago through the ill-intentions of the black wolf. And though the monster's actions more than warranted those ill-intentions, the frozen thing did not mark time in recognition of its fate, but in defiance. A single finger was all it could move, but that finger was enough. For it was encased in a scant pocket of water as cold as the monster's gaze, and it beat a rhythm on the ice as steady as its hatred, tapping . . . tapping . . . tapping . . .

Tapping as it bided its time.

A woman walked out of the fog dragging a sailor with a bite missing from one cheek.

She dropped the man at the vampire's feet. "You can have this coat," she said. "You can have what's in it, too."

The Count did not say a word. The woman wore rough clothes, and moccasins fashioned from reptile skin. It came as no surprise that a wolf's eyes and grin were hidden among the tattoos on her face.

The sailor tried to rise and the wolf gave him a kick. "He doesn't look like much, but be careful with this half-shingled bastard. He came at me with a billhook but didn't much know how to use it, so I taught him some manners. He might maybe still have a little gumption left in him, though . . . so watch yourself."

Again the vampire nodded.

"Damn, mister. You do know how to say *thank you,* don't you?"

"I do," said the Count, but he said no more.

"Sweet Christmas." The woman laughed, and the shells braided in her dark hair clacked lightly as she knelt to meet the vampire's gaze. "It's sure enough some kind of battle getting a conversation started with you."

This time the Count did not nod at all. He was too busy staring at a trickle of blood that traced the path of a muted blue artery along the sailor's neck.

To the vampire's eye, the trickle seemed as wide as a raging river.

He licked his lips.

"Okay," the wolf said. "You're a little distracted right now. I understand that, so let's not waste time. Way I see it you can cinch up the favor I did for you last night along with this hunk of meat wrapped in an oilskin coat, and we have ourselves an arrangement. As in: I don't try to kill you, and you don't try to kill me. Not that you could roll the dice on that endeavor right now, but you know what I mean. Hell, maybe we even try to help one another once in a while if you manage to get back on your feet. How's that sound?"

The trickle of blood disappeared beneath the collar of the sailor's coat, leaving only a drying trail. A single fresh droplet remained, beading on the man's torn cheek. But that droplet was growing . . . larger, then larger still.

Soon it would fall.

The Count's mouth watered at the sight.

"You do speak English, right?" the wolf asked. "You understand what I'm saying?"

"I understand," the Count said. "And I will . . . endure."

If the woman replied the vampire did not hear it, for the blood bead on the sailor's cheek was larger now, too large to bear, and—

In an instant the vampire had the man in his grasp, and his teeth scraped over cheekbone and tore a path down his neck.

The wolf watched, but only for a moment.

"Enjoy your supper" was all she said, and she rose to leave.

And then the only sounds were the vampire taking his meal, and the slow whisper of the waves, and the soft music of the shells braided in the wolf's hair as she vanished in the fog.

The first monster to tread the island's shore arrived chained in the belly of a longboat, crewed by those with braids and painted faces who looked like monsters themselves. But they were only men and women, warriors born in a land of snow and ice.

The thing they delivered was like nothing they had seen or slain. They only knew that it was dead, and its skin was like a rock that had rested too long at the bottom of a stagnant pool, and its gaze was unsparing. And though they had killed it many times, and buried it and burned it on a funeral pyre, it never remained dead for long. Like many things it lingered longest in memory, and that was a land from which it always returned.

"What can we do?" they asked around night fires.

"We are people of the oar and the sail," their chieftan said. "That is what we know. Where can we find a prison among the waves?"

"There are no shackles in the sea," a man said.

"There are shackles everywhere, and all can be closed," an old woman said. "An island is a shackle. Distant enough, barren enough, it holds no key. Curse it with hunger—as this creature is cursed—and it will suffer no release."

As a shackle weights a chain, the chieftan knew that these words were heavy with truth. And so sails caught wind, and oars were driven through water, and the old woman traveled the waves with nothing more than hammer and chisel and knowledge that had been whispered to her on cold winds. And her people found an island, an ungainly collection of rocks with a tower that reached high into the clouds and wore a cloak of frost and snow.

The old woman climbed that tower.

She put hammer and chisel to work in an empty cave.

Runes were carved. Spells were cast. And that night the island drew its first breath.

An exhalation followed, combing through the woman's long hair like a lover's whisper.

The woman dropped her hammer and followed that whisper into the darkness.

Miles below, just beyond the shoreline, a monster howled in the depths of a longboat, for the crew had set their ship on fire. Not knowing why. Not understanding. But the island knew. It breathed, and breathed again. And the monster stepped through the flames, and it breathed the breath of the island, and its was the first footfall on a land quickly growing rocky scales.

The monster looked to the cave nestled high in the rising fog, and it smiled.

The old woman had not understood shackles, or hunger, after all.

She had not understood that an island could have a mouth, and a woman with her powers could serve as a meal as surely as a monster.

The Count would have drunk longer, but he did not want to drain the sailor. So, thirsty and unsatisfied, he rose and dragged the man along the rocky shoreline.

Gulls screamed high in the dismal whiteness and waves whispered over the path traveled by the Count, for the tide was coming in. Occasionally he noticed another sailor's corpse levered between the rocks, but the dead were past use to him, and he already had his next meal in hand.

Of more interest were wrecked vessels trapped on heavier shoals. Some had rotted to the waterline, while others had been stripped to ribs and rigging so that they resembled the desiccated corpses of great leviathans. Ultimately, he passed these as easily as the dead sailors, for mere remnants held no possibility of use.

In time he came to a ship which invited careful attention. The masts had collapsed and crushed much of the bow, while the aft section had survived with little damage and was trapped on a sandy spit.

He crossed an oily bog—later he discovered it sprang from broken barrels in the ship's hold—and the sailor did not stir as the Count leaned him against the battered rudder. Climbing on deck, the vampire discovered a block and tackle. It proved much more troublesome than the sailor, but the Count soon had it in working order. As darkness fell the man rose easily, cradled in a cargo net. This the Count hung belowdecks with the sailor still in it, as a spider would hang cocooned prey.

With these tasks completed, the vampire searched the ship and discovered a cabin nestled just below the quarterdeck. Judging from its appointments, it might have belonged to the captain. Much in the room had gone to rot, including a lone book resting on a small table. This was Marcus Aurelius' *Meditations,* but the condition of the volume did not trouble the vampire. Long ago, he had committed to memory Aurelius' ideas with which he agreed. The rest he had ignored, and would ignore still.

So he turned his attention to a sealed chest beneath the cabin's ornate window. Breaking the lock, the vampire discovered clothes which provided a reasonable fit, though they had obviously belonged to a simpler man. There were also charts of regions far to the north, and two journals—one belonging to a scientist who was entirely absent responsibility and personal fortitude, and the other an explorer whose notions were marred by a sense of the Romantic. Men like these mattered to the Count not at all, so he cast the journals to a corner and made the empty chest ready for his purposes.

Of course, his own coffin had been lost in the tempest, along with his native soil. There was no escaping that, just as there was no escaping the incessant pain from his wound. So the vampire did as circumstances demanded, and soon his task was complete and the chest was ready.

Exhausted, he sat in a sagging chair that stunk of silence, holding a small locket he had discovered hidden in the chest. Fortunately, it was gold, not silver. The locket contained a picture (smaller still) of a blond woman who might have been the captain's wife. It shone well in the dim moonlight, and the Count stared at it for a long while. Then he closed the locket in his palm and thought of his own wife, and the waves just beyond the ruined ship, and the sea beyond that, and a coffin that might rest in the hidden chambers of its depths. And it was easy to think thoughts like this, alone in this place, for the room was small and fashioned with a door that had both bolt and bar.

Hours later, he awoke to the squealing and scurrying of rats. For a moment he imagined that he was in his castle and the previous night's kill had become a banquet for lesser creatures, but this was not so. A brief examination determined that the sailor was still alive, still hanging in his net. So the Count beat away the hungry rats that troubled his prey and drank again, and with each swallow fresh pain scalded his wound.

He returned to the cabin. The chest was no coffin, but certainly it could hold him and his thoughts . . . and the locket. At present that was all he needed.

He raised the lid and stepped inside. The rocks he had collected from the beach were as cold as the armor he had worn in another life, and the black sand beneath them grated like grist in a mill. And the Count thought of the island, and the chance experiences that had brought him here, and things that might happen tomorrow or might not happen at all.

The pain in his side faded. And so he closed the lid of the chest and curled in among scales and sand. For a moment he remembered a tale from his youth—a lost boy finding comfort while nestled against the scales of a sleeping dragon's coiled tail, his fingers black with the grit of bones baked in the monster's fire, his belly full.

Thinking these thoughts, the vampire held tight to another man's locket.

This was how he slept.

Of course, the island slept, too.

But even in sleep, it was true to its nature. The island was indeed a prison, just as the old woman had believed. It shackled monsters as well as men, for these were the things it needed to survive. But there were things that shackled the island, as well.

They took much or they took little. The eucalyptus trees, burrowing simple roots beneath its scales. The black pear tree doing the same. The sailors who chopped and sawed the eucalyptus trees to make boats that never sailed and coffins for their dead, and the shovels those sailors used to cut graves in the island's flesh. The tentacled things within the island's body, still drawing nourishment from its blood as they clung to its rocky walls. Even the dead Egyptian, who had built his pyramid's foundation from the island's scales and rocks, bracing its walls with the bones of fallen monsters which the island had nurtured and fed.

And through all this the island was patient, for it knew a price would be paid in the end. It accepted the taking with the same patience men employ while butchered meat hangs on a smokehouse wall, waiting for time to season the meal.

So the island gave of itself, even to those who were shackled. But the things it never shackled were their dreams. For the shipwrecked sailors, these dreams were simple fantasies of survival or escape, neither of which was a possibility. And in truth, the monsters' dreams were just as simple. The wolf, dreaming of a mother and father who walked in her every action. The dead Egyptian, rebuilding a land he would never see again in a place it could never belong. Even the frozen monster tapping against the ice—shackled more surely than any other— its dreams of wrongs suffered becoming more dreadful each time they cycled through its brain.

The island had its own dreams, of course, but these had never been shared. For the island was solitary. Its only real companions were little more than tools—the wind and the fog and the sea. And tools did not dream.

But there was another now.

A woman with nowhere to go, and time to listen.

A woman chained in a coffinbox beneath the sea.

So the island whispered to her.
The island told her everything.

One morning the vampire lanced the wound that would not heal with a scalding iron shaft, raising black blisters on his flesh and charring ribs. The ultimate results of this effort carried the realization that he would never truly heal, for he could never be free of the wooden slivers lodged close to his heart. After all, he could not drive a scalding lance close to the muscle itself and survive.

So he did what he could, using hot iron and time as his weapons. By the time repeated treatments sealed the wound with a feeble scar, pale sunlight had begun to bleed through the fog. Once again, the Count began to move from the chair in his cabin to other parts of the ship. Fortunately, the sailor had not escaped his net, but he had grown pale and listless as disease took hold. Perhaps this was a result of the rats' bites. The Count did not know.

So he found a coal scuttle belowdecks and descended the ship's ladder to the rocky shore, employing care as he crossed the oily bog. He walked the beach, eyes on the water's edge. Stony crabs—smaller, newborn—had been smashed by a wild incoming tide the previous night. Some were dead and others were not, but all were dead when the vampire dropped them into the scuttle.

It was not challenging work. The sun began to rise, and the scuttle filled, and the Count's gaze traveled to a place usually shrouded in the fog—the rocky tower at the island's center. For the first time, he noticed a cave set high among crags that jutted like broken teeth.

Then the cave was lost in silhouette as the sun rose behind the tower, casting a long shadow which stretched to the eucalyptus forest on the opposite shore. As the sunlight spread, the trees' narrow shadows fell across the shipwrecked sailors who sawed and chopped at the forest's edge.

"They always do that." It was a woman's voice. The wolf.

"To what purpose?"

"None, really. It's just their nature. They start off making spears, bows and arrows, weapons they figure will protect them from us. When that doesn't work out they figure they'll escape, and they try to build boats. But that's no good, either. Those eucalyptus are as heavy as a fat man's coffin, and the shipwrecked fools wear themselves down to nothing trying to work with the wood. In the end it just means the meat is harder to chew once I run 'em to ground, and then they have to build coffins for a sackful of leavings."

"They are chattel. Nothing more."

"Good goddamn, but I do love the way you talk." The wolf laughed. "All high and mighty, while you're carrying around a chum bucket and collecting sea-guts. What happened to that fat sailor I gave you, anyway? You give him up for clams and seahorse stew?"

"He is not as fat as before . . . so I must feed him."

"Then give him a treat," she said, rolling a large rock and revealing mussels that clung to its dark pockets. "These'll go down easy."

The Count said nothing as she skinned the gray creatures and dropped them into the coal scuttle.

He tried to lift it as the sun grew brighter, and his shadow fell across the large rock.

Suddenly dizzy, he nearly joined it.

The wolf steadied him. "Looks like we need to get you out of the sun, Your Majesty. Way I heard the tale told, a day like today should be curling you like bacon on a hot skillet."

"And it is said that my kind cannot cross running water, yet I have swum in the sea. I have seen my reflection in broken mirrors on the ship, as well. So it seems this island is barren of absolutes."

"Absolutes?"

"Unbreakable laws."

"Seems like. I don't even need a full moon here. I change damn near every night, and some days twice before breakfast if those idiots decide to sharpen their spears and go on a hunt."

"Did it begin for you . . . here?"

"No." The wolf cracked a couple of mussels and ate them. "I'll give you the dime novel version. I won't tell you who my mother was—that's not for talking about with a stranger—but my father was a buffalo soldier. You won't know what that means, though I figure you understand the soldier part."

"Yes. I was a soldier once."

"Not too surprised about that. Anyway, I came across the pond with Buffalo Bill's Wild West—you won't know what that means, either. But I worked with guns and horses, did things most people can't do with both. We did shows in England, Italy, and Germany—that's where the bad things happened. I took to the ways of the wolf and then some worse things happened. For a time I had hunters and German lawdogs on my trail. Even some gypsies, too. Took every dollar I had but I booked passage on a cargo ship out of Rotterdam heading back to the States. Figured things out West would still be wild enough for a creature like me . . . but hell, I might as well have just spit in the wind for as far as that notion got me. I ended up here, same as you."

These were not all words the Count understood, but he understood enough of them.

"What about you?" she asked.

He considered the question. It seemed there should be something he could say in reply, for the wolf had said so much. But it also seemed that everything he had worth sharing was contained in a box at the bottom of the sea.

So he said, "The story is long, and I am past telling it."

"That's pretty close to a mouthful for you. But maybe you'll come around to it one of these days . . . say next year, or the one after that."

"It seems we have time."

"Yeah. Seems that way."

They sat for a while longer, until the light began to thin.

"You'd better get back now," the wolf said. "Good news is we don't get too many sunny days around here, but it might not be a good idea for you to come out tonight, either. God's little lumberjacks over there gathered all the black pears from that sick little tree a few weeks back, and they've been making their yearly supply of skull-blaster. Tonight they'll get drunk and dance around the fire, and then they'll start singing sea chanties. If they don't get all weepy and sentimental after that, they might light torches and go out for a little hunt. Their spears aren't much different than stakes, so . . ."

The Count nodded but did not rise.

"I will consider that."

The wolf was already up, moving down the beach. "You do that, Your Majesty," she said. "In the meantime, take better care of yourself. Seems like I'm starting to enjoy your company. And besides, we've got ourselves a deal."

"I have not forgotten."

"Good. Now go feed your sailor. Have a drink. You'll feel better after that."

The Count said nothing, but he followed the wolf's suggestion. He stumbled under the coal scuttle's weight more than he should have, and the return journey to the ship took longer as a result.

Once on board the ship, he felt better until the stench of the sailor hit him. At first the Count believed the man was writhing in his net, but the man was not moving at all. It was the net that was alive, crawling with gigantic flies and bigger rats, all feasting on the sailor's corpse.

The Count looked down at the chum bucket in his hand.

He spilled its contents on the floor.

If there was to be a feast, it might as well be a grand one.

Flies and rats buzzed and squealed over the carnage. The vampire returned to the deck and tossed the coal scuttle over the side. Across the island, torches glimmered faintly in the sailors' camp, and within that light there was laughter and music.

The vampire rarely smiled, but he did that now.

Tomorrow he would hunt.

So the wolf and the vampire stalked the island in sunlight or shadow, often taking fresh prey as soon as ships and crew washed ashore. The dead Egyptian spent many nights standing silent in the eucalyptus forest, hoping for a drunken sailor to mistake him for a shadow. The crabs and tentacled things waited for opportunities without risk, clinging to burrows and blowholes, hunting as they had always done.

But the island did . . . nothing. It lurked in its cave and it thought, and its thoughts were of the woman in the sea. And when patience strained it spoke to her, and it did not need the tools of the wind or the fog or the sea.

In truth, the island did not end where it met the waves. It spread beneath the sea itself, for there was only one land beneath the waves, and that land contained the island and the woman's coffin. So the island built a path from shore to chained box with its own scales, and that proved no great challenge at all.

And one day when the island had told the woman everything but one thing, it shared its final secret: "Your Dark Prince walks like a skeleton now. He is no longer for you. He is for me. And when I finish him, I will bring your coffin to my shores and begin with you."

"If that is the truth you will never begin with me," she said. "For I will be your end."

"Ha!" the island replied. "I command the sea and the ships on it. I am master to the wind and the fog. You are a dead woman locked in a box!"

"The fog has deserted you. When have you seen it? And the wind will go with it, or perhaps it already has. One day soon you will follow them both, and another will take your place. Perhaps it will be me."

"You? Impossible! I can drown you. I can bury you. I have buried you beneath the sea!"

"Have you talked to the sea? Does it still listen?"

"It will listen. All will listen!"

"I have listened to you. I have heard every word. But you have never listened to me. I know secrets you can't imagine, just as the woman who birthed you with hammer and chisel."

"I swallowed her whole and will do the same to you!"

"In this box, you can never touch me . . . and you will never touch me. The runes in your throat have faded, and there is no woman to carve them again. Soon the runes will disappear like the fog and the wind have disappeared. And on that day I will do as my nature demands."

"And what is that?"

"I will drink your blood, and I will take your life, and that will be an end to you."

The woman waited for a reply, but there was none.

The island had fled the sea.

And now the currents did as they would.

One evening the surf washed three dead sharks onto the beach, each one clawed and torn and bitten. And then the sea washed up something else—a creature with webbed hands bigger than most baskets, and shoulders armored like a turtle's shell, and teeth that gleamed like a sackful of razors.

The creature did not move, so the wolf approached and gave it a kick. And then the monster's gills fluttered with effort, and it sucked a dry breath between its awful teeth.

"Amphibian," the wolf said.

She watched the creature struggle for another breath.

Then she smashed its head with a rock.

"I don't like seafood, anyway," she said.

"It is an acquired taste," said the vampire.

"Well . . . I'd like to acquire something with some taste in it right now, Your Majesty. My belly's cinched down as far as it can go."

"It is said that the tide raises all ships."

"What?"

"You must be patient. The hand of the sea will bring another vessel. It always does. And there will be a creature like us upon it. And there will be men, and perhaps women, and—"

"Hasn't been a ship in a month. Maybe longer. And have you watched the tide lately? Notice anything?"

"It is different . . . calmer."

"Other things are different, too. I haven't seen a crab in weeks. Haven't seen one of those tentacled things in a month of Sundays."

"That is a long time."

"You don't have to tell me," the woman said. "My belly knows."

The Count said nothing.

"Damn, I wish we still had that sailor."

"There is no value in wishing."

"Right about that," she said. "And the men left on this island look more dead than alive . . . so I guess it's like the sailors say, 'Any port in a storm.'"

The wolf drew a knife from her belt and went to work on the dead amphibian.

Blood spilled on the beach. A red sun fell toward the horizon.

And a warm wind rose from parts unknown.

And this was a different wind than the one the island had mastered, for it did not whisper to the sea. No. That wind was gone, just as the woman beneath the sea had promised. In its place came another wind, this one born of sun instead of shadow, and the island had never felt its like.

For days the wind howled and blistered.

For a week it did not yield.

And then another.

The island's scales grew hot as in a furnace, curling beneath the wind's power. And though the island implored the sea, it would not soothe the scalding shore. Instead the tide retreated, and the water in the blowholes boiled, cooking the crabs and tentacled monsters that had lived there for centuries.

The island called to the wave that was a hand, but the wave was gone. So the wind rose, and it had a hand of its own that did not care for fog or sea or island. It tore the pear tree from its roots, and stripped the bark from eucalyptus, and the bark caught fire as it cycloned through the forest. And the forest was a whirl-wind of ash and flame, casting burning shards to the wind, and this was what the air became, as did anything that dwelled within.

The dead Egyptian, a walking pyre.

Shipwrecked men, boiling in their own flesh.

And when it had finished with sand and shore, the heat and the ash and the fire rose up, scorching the tower's face. And then the ice above it began to melt, and it ran down the jagged path like the tower's tears.

Soon the ice was gone.

And that was why the next monster to tread the island did not come from the sea.

No.

It came from the tower.

And the ice.

The wolf's belly burned beneath the midday sun.

Her skin burned as well. Nature had shorn her of her pelt for more than a month, despite the appearance of a full moon just one night before. The last of the fog had been shorn from the heavens that night as well, leaving only stars and moon to shine down on the useless silhouettes below.

In the blind light of morning those silhouettes were revealed to be the simple dead things they were. Fallen eucalyptus trees stripped and chopped for boats that would never sail. The bones of the men who'd cut down those trees, savaged and gnawed in a time when the wolf had laughed over the island's bounty and joked about things that ate chum.

Now her belly growled at the simple idea of such fare. Everything that had washed ashore in the last few days had been riddled with maggots that writhed under the sun's rays.

And there was no fog to comfort her, and no shadows to hold her. So she sat in the sun, and she stared at her hands. Her fingers were as long as they had always been, her nails just as sharp, her skin now as dark as her father's. And that skin held the sun's warmth, and she remembered the warmth of her father's hands, and for a moment that memory calmed her.

But her father must be long dead by now. The woman's own hair was longer, with more shells woven through its silver strands, more bones, too. The seasons had gone 'round again and again; the years had traveled by. Even the vampire seemed older.

She had not seen him, since . . . when? She could not remember.

They had laughed over that dead creature on the shore. She remembered that. Laughing the way cursed things laughed. But now the memory made her stomach knot, and she went down on her knees, and a crab scuttled from between the rocks, and her hunger twisted inside her now and—

A whisper, behind her.

From the cave?

The wolf turned and looked to the stone tower. Skinned of fog, the mouth was a naked hole now. She had never told the vampire about the cave—in truth she had diverted his attention when he first noticed it—but she had been in it. She had stood among carved runes, and felt the whisper of its breath, and heard the words that had drawn so many others into its depths. And sometimes she had wondered what it would be like to take a little walk down that throat as those others had done, down as far as her feet might carry her, to a place where mysteries were revealed and she could see whatever it was that—

The wolf's senses stirred.

Now she heard something breathing. Ragged, raspy . . .

She heard it clearly.

And for the first time she realized that the tower above the mouth was black. The ice was gone. Hunger had dimmed her senses, and she had forgotten about the ice . . . and the monster.

Behind her, a laugh.

She turned, and the monster standing there was not a silhouette or a shadow.

Its eyes were yellow, and unblinking.

It held an axe in its hands.

It did not wait to use it.

The woman beneath the sea was alone now. The island did not speak to her. The sea did not whisper. And the hand that was a wave did not hold her chained coffin to the ocean floor.

No. Those things were dead now, or free. It did not matter to the woman which. For the waves were different now, and they seemed of another time, like the waves that had carried the people of the oar and sail.

Beneath those waves, her coffin began to stir.

Driven by sure currents that roared like fire.

Some distance away, another fire roared. Its sparks spit at a monster's face, and ash clung to the wolf's blood splattered there. But the monster did not care.

It hovered over a spit in the moonlight, turning a slab of wolf meat above a blazing eucalyptus fire. And it muttered to itself while the meat cooked, fingers brushing a scalp knotted to its belt, and with each stroke shells and bones woven through the hair made music in the darkness.

The creature removed the spit from the fire. It touched the meat, for it longed to know the feel of it when cooked. And the monster continued speaking as it did this, spilling words locked too long in its head. It did not fall silent until it tore the meat with its teeth and savored the taste of blood.

That was when the vampire stepped out of the shadows.

The monster reached for its axe, but the Count did not retreat so much as an inch.

Instead he stared into the creature's yellow eyes.

"I have something that you want," he said.

The Monster's fingers worried the bloody scalp, for he did not like this place. Neither did he like the dead man, who had disappeared belowdecks. The only solace the creature could find was considering what trophy he would take when he killed the vampire. Perhaps he would wear the vampire's withered heart around his neck on a chain. Perhaps he would make a cup of his skull. There were possibilities.

And so the Monster tapped the axe blade against the wooden gunwales, just as he had tapped his finger so many times against ice, but the blade rang far too loudly. The Monster had dwelled in silence too long, and every sensation unleashed a small torture. His own breath seemed as raspy as a rusty saw, and the steady sound of oil from the bog dripping against the deck was as awful as the stink of it in his clothes. Even the warm night wind brushing his cheek seemed a punishment, for the bright moonlight was as cold as ice and could not free the night from darkness and shadow.

And the thoughts that had spent so much time locked in the Monster's skull now spilled from his lips along with those raspy breaths. The words were barely a whisper, for his voice had been stilled for far too long. But the circle of his thoughts ran 'round as it always did, whether waking or sleeping, and he remembered a father who was not, and a bride the father had made but killed, and a journal that held every secret the man had known.

The axe came down, marking time, its blade spitting splinters. Again and again and again.

And then there were thoughts of the island, and the wolf, and the ice.

And the axe came down.

And as the cycle began again, the Monster realized he had stood here, years ago, in this same spot. He recognized it, even though the ship had fallen to ruin. The doorway just ahead stood in his memory, and he knew the room behind it, and the book that rested on its table. Marcus Aurelius. *Meditations.* And he saw the man who had come through that door long ago, a man named Walton who was the ship's captain, and—

Another man came through the doorway now. The vampire.

He held a tattered volume in one hand, and a torch in the other.

"This is the book you desire," the vampire said. "Your doctor's journal."

Stunned, the Monster dropped the wolf's scalp on the deck and stepped forward, raising his empty hand.

The Count touched torch to journal, and the pages flared as surely as eucalyptus bark. And then he tossed the book at the Monster, and it struck his clothes, and the oil there flared alive. But the Monster came forward even so, and each step he took was a path for a memory, and he walked it surely and quickly, wrapped in an inferno now, the axe still gripped tightly in his hand.

He raised it, ready to strike. The vampire thrust the torch in his face, but that would not stop him. Nothing would stop him. So the axe swung wide, as in the circle of the Monster's thoughts, and it struck home beneath the vampire's raised arm.

Its blade finding a wound that had never healed.

And then the Monster struck again, and the blade fell in the same place. The vampire faltered and fell, and the Monster did as well. Timbers caught quickly as the fire spread from the writhing creature, making the rats scream.

The Monster screamed with them.

In an hour, maybe two, he screamed no more.

By that time smoke rode high in the sky, and the moon was full and red, and all that remained of the ship was a charred ruin.

The vampire sat on the beach, an axe in his hand.

He looked to the moon and a wave broke before him.

It sounded like a wolf's growl.

Long ago, the first ship had burned—the one brought by the people of the oar and sail, and the old woman who had carried hammer and chisel to carve runes in a cave's throat. And now a final ship had suffered the same fate, charring to the waterline with a monster in its grasp.

But the island did not watch. It was deep in its cave, far down a throat lined with faded runes that could no longer protect it, barely breathing . . .

So the island did not see the woman's chained coffinbox wash ashore, or the man with the axe rise to meet it. And it did not see that axe fall—once, twice, a dozen times—as the man spent his last efforts and the blade cleaved the chains.

It did not see the man fall next to the coffin as the lid was raised.

It did not see the woman step onto the empty shoreline to find him dead.

Neither did it see her sit with him as smoke from the ship painted the sky.

It did not feel the red coal of the sun rising over it, or know that the wind was warm as it had been long ago when she was young, or understand that the things she remembered were things that she would never speak.

And it did not see the fog wrapping the tower in a shroud as it did her bidding, or the wind rising to carry her words. But the island felt them. And it heard the sea crashing behind her as her feet traveled a jagged stone path and she climbed the rocky tower with an axe in her hands.

It heard her as she entered the cave's mouth, stepping surely into the darkness.

It heard the scrape of the axe blade against the runes.

And it heard her call its name.

FLAMING TEETH

by Garry Kilworth

I couldn't find reference to the island anywhere. The discovery of a new island in a remote southern corner of the Pacific Ocean, well clear of normal shipping routes, is remarkable enough in an age where we can see the earthwork of an ancient king's burial from space. How had it remained unknown? True, we had passed through a forbidden area, a nuclear test zone, but we had been taken against our will by an unmanageable storm and Chris informed us that it had been many years since those tests had taken place.

My first thoughts were that it might have appeared recently from the ocean depths. But then, the landscape of the island was thickly forested and was abundant with wildlife. The two explanations that we all liked best were that it had been shrouded in mist for eons or it had slipped through a portal from a parallel world. Mystery takes mastery over pragmatism on a planet that is rapidly going to wrack and ruin through selfishness. At that time we didn't know that it had for centuries been deliberately hidden from stray shipping, due to the savage nature of the island's only inhabitant.

The lagoon was stocked with fish with a hinterland that seemed almost primordial. We were prepared to stay there until the lawyers tried to oust us. I imagined at the time that every mother's country would want to wrest it from us. In fact, it would only take a few muscled bouncers to throw us into a boat and send us packing. We agreed among us that if it had to be given to any nation, it should be the nearest Polynesian archipelago.

The yacht belonged to Jill and me, but we had guests on *Hilda:* two other couples. We were in the for'ard berth, while the other two couples had twin berths aft, one either side of the ladder to the top deck. There were James and Sally to port and Chris and Juliana to starboard. We found the whole adventure quite exciting. Within a short time we had separate huts spaced out along the beach and began to live suburban lives. Naturally, there were times when we got together, for a barbeque or an evening's entertainment, but it was a similar arrangement neighbours and friends have who live in the same street.

James and Sally were a very private, respectable, upright pair, only ever married to each other. James was in insurance and Sally in local government. Acquaintances, they took a four-month unpaid vacation to come with us when they heard we were sailing round the world. Chris and Juliana were not married. He was an engineer, a world traveller with his work, and had been married three times. She was Italian and had worked in a variety of jobs from shop assistant to restaurant manager. Chris had answered my advertisement for a competent sailor. We needed another experienced navigator and helmsman on board in case I got sick or fell overboard. He told me he was between projects and would enjoy the voyage. That left Jill and me. I am a retired ex-serviceman and Jill an artist, a painter and sculptor who could work anywhere. Neither of us had been married and to my knowledge neither of us had any intention of becoming so. We had been together for almost three years.

After a week on the island it became clear we were not alone.

"There's a wide track which runs through the rainforest, just two miles east," said Chris.

"What sort of a track?" I asked. "Wheel ruts?"

He shook his head. "No, nothing mechanical. It's just flattened undergrowth. Trees broken, here and there. Too uniform to be a storm or anything like that. Something has blundered through the rainforest."

Juliana asked, "Are there great beasts on these islands?"

"An animal? You mean an elephant, or rhino, something like that? Borneo once had a small rhinoceros, but I'm sure that's extinct. We've killed 'em all off. There won't be any elephants, unless imported."

James chimed in here. "Natives? I mean, a local tribe?"

Chris shook his head. "There were trees that'd been snapped. Not cut but broken. In fact, I didn't see any signs of machete use, anything like that."

"Some of us will go out with you tomorrow, Chris, and have a closer look."

Chris's mouth tightened. "You're not satisfied with my assessment."

"Yes, of course I am. I'm not doubting it. But several heads are better than one. If we've been blown off course to this island, maybe someone else has. I just hope we got here first and that means it's ours. I mean to keep it. *We* must keep it," I added quickly. "Chris, you're a reasonable sailor. How about this. New Zealand's about seven days' fair sailing. You take the *Hilda,* sail to Auckland and register our claim. You need to tell them we wish to retain sovereignty but are willing to come under their national umbrella. I'm sure the Kiwis have some sort of arrangement with the Cook Islands like that. What do you think?"

Chris looked at Juliana. She shrugged as if to indicate that it really didn't matter to her, one way or another.

Turning back to me, Chris said, "Let's go into the forest tomorrow and I'll show you what I saw. Then we'll discuss what to do about it."

I nodded in agreement and we all went back to our huts for an evening meal. Sometimes the group ate together, but tonight we needed to discuss the situation with our partners. Once the lizard we were having as our main meal was cooked and put on our banana-leaf plates, Jill told me she understood Chris's annoyance.

"He thinks you don't trust his judgement," she said.

"Well, he's a bit too sensitive for my liking," I replied.

"I think you chose him to be the one to leave because he's the biggest threat to your leadership. Are you sure you want to let him have the *Hilda*? We'll be trapped here till he gets back. What if someone falls ill or has an accident?"

"In which case I'd use the sat phone to call for help. The boat wouldn't be of any use in an emergency. They can reach us much faster than we can get to them."

Nothing more was said on the subject. The next morning Jill, me, and Chris set off for the area where the forest had been levelled. It was a good three miles from camp and I was glad Chris and I had cut a path on previous hunting expeditions. Forcing a passage through a dense, virgin rainforest is a slow, exhausting business. On arrival at the "track" I could see that it wasn't easy to decide what had caused it. The undergrowth had been flattened, but not uniformly, and the odd tree had been broken, but none of the hardwoods with strong buttresses. It looked as if an animal had blundered through, not caring about what was in their way. Were we in Africa, I would have suggested one of the pachyderms or a small herd of ungulates, but since neither of these were to be found on a coral island I was completely mystified. I fell back on my theory of intruders.

"What do you think?" I asked Jill. "Human destruction?"

"But what with?" she asked. "I'm puzzled about the broken trees. As you said last night, Chris, there's no vehicle tracks."

"Balloon tyres?" I suggested.

"In the jungle?" said Chris, scathingly. "Come on."

For the next two hours we followed the track, until we came to a river. There on the muddy banks on either side were large prints, but of what we couldn't decide. The mud was too sloppy to retain the shape of feet. It was simply a few holes about twenty-five to thirty centimetres deep. Even so the creature must have been huge and heavy, though it was difficult to guess the actual size. The only scenario I could come up with was that it was a large creature of some kind, possibly an elephant. Maybe one or more had been imported to the island at some earlier time. However, that would have meant we were not the first to put foot on these shores, which unsettled me.

"You don't think," asked Sally, when we got back to camp, "something from another era could have survived the passing of time?"

James snorted. "A dinosaur?" he scoffed. "No, I don't."

"What about crocs, then? They're from that period."

"Well yes, but . . ."

"Well yes and no buts. You can stop sneering now, Mr Know-it-all. What about mammals?" she persisted, ignoring the glare he gave her. "Australia was roamed at one time by huge marsupial lions—in prehistoric times."

Jill replied, "They weren't big enough to cause such damage to trees, Sally. I had to provide artwork once, to an Australian museum, on their marsupial 'monsters' as they called them. The lion was the largest and it was the size of the boars we have today. Now if you were talking about mammoths, then yes, the destruction would be consistent with such a creature. But really? A herd of hairy mammoths surviving all the changes the world has gone through over thirty thousand years? I doubt the island is even that old. It's surely one of those volcanic islands that's risen from the seabed without being detected. However, I have a good idea what this creature is—it's so obvious I wonder none of you have thought of it too."

"What's that?" I asked.

"A giant."

We all stared at her. It was me who broke the silence.

"That one they found in the Amazon basin was supposed to be the last unknown giant."

"There was another one found recently in Low's Gully, in the barely explored rainforest area below Mount Kinabalu. Let's face it, giants have been with us since the first cave woman gave birth to a baby. They've mostly kept to themselves, where they could, but with the human population growth there's been confrontation. It's only a couple of centuries since we stopped killing them. So long as we don't bother this one, it might not bother with us."

She was right. It was possibly not the only explanation for the tracks in the rainforest, but I couldn't think of another one.

James said, "They're not always placid vegetarians."

"No," I replied, "but there's a lot of false information about giants. You get it when people aren't familiar with a creature. Wolves for instance. I read the other day that there wasn't a single person killed by wolves during the last century, despite the increase in numbers of packs. Most people have never come across a giant. The media feeds on ignorance. They like a sensation and print stories about giants killing and eating humans."

"I hope you're right," said James. "All the same, Sally and I want to go back with Chris on the yacht."

"Whoa!" cried Sally. "Who said I wanted to leave?"

James shot her a fierce but hurt look. "Well, I'm going and I assumed my wife would support my decision on the matter."

She appeared indifferent to his anger.

"Jimmy, daaarling, if you think I'm going to rush back to that stuffy old office in Broad Street, Bury St Edmunds, you're very much mistaken. This is the adventure of a lifetime and I'm not going to end it prematurely because you're frightened of a silly old giant. I'm staying here."

James set his jaw. "Well, I'm going."

As it happened James had a bad case of diarrhoea that night. A man given to eating too much and already overweight, he had continually been down with stomach problems since we left home. At home, Sally could control his diet, but not on board the boat, and certainly not on the island. By the time he managed to stagger out of his hut the next morning, Chris and Juliana had sailed. He railed at Sally for a while, then started on me, but he was in no condition to keep up a tirade of verbal abuse and finally went back to his bed. I wondered if we would have trouble with him once he threw off the stomach troubles, but in fact two days later he was as meek as a lamb. There was almost a spark of enthusiasm about him which made me think that maybe he was glad he'd been overruled by his wife and was now prepared to experience an adventurous time.

Three days after Chris and Juliana had left, we needed to go hunting. We had stores, but I only wanted to use those in an emergency. We went into the rainforest in a careful and vigilant manner now. There was no way we wanted to disturb a giant, if giant there was, especially with a surprise party. If Jill was right about there being one of those early offshoots of the human race, then it was best we gave it a wide berth. To be on the safe side, I had a rifle with me. I had brought it with my personal gear onto the island from the yacht. It was only a small-bore weapon, but hopefully it would deter any attacking giant.

The women stayed in the camp to keep it occupied in case a boat or ship came by. James and I went out to forage and hunt for edible wildlife. This time we found a glade where there were three blackened lumps of wood. One of the stumps was still smouldering. Here we found definite prints of a barefooted man whose feet were around five times the size of my own. That would make him going on for ten metres in height. A big fellah, by any standard.

"What do you make of that, James?" I asked. He did not like "Jimmy" or "Jim" except from his wife. "It seems to be a giant and this is probably where he had his fire."

"Very small fire." His tone was grudging. It seemed he had gone back to being angry with me for not waking him before the yacht left.

"True." This much was puzzling.

"Well, at least we know we have a giant here. I hope to God he's friendly," said James, frowning. "Hadn't we better get back to the girls? They may be in danger."

I told him the women were quite able to take care of themselves and that I'd left Jill with a hand axe, but actually I realised it wouldn't be of much use. It was illegal to harm giants anyway. They had the same status as Homo sapiens. If a giant attacked one of us, we could claim self-defence, but there would be a lot of messy courtroom dramas to go through and the LPG wouldn't let it rest. There would be bad general media coverage, bad social media coverage, and probably a great deal of street harassment to contend with. Actually killing a giant was only one step down from strangling a baby orangutan. They were an endangered group along with the Oceanian pygmies and others.

I managed to shoot a pig and we went back to camp, and of course found Jill and Sally alive and well. We told them about the footprints and the smoking charcoal and they both took it well. We had a good meal, which included fish as well as the pork, Sally having caught a red snapper on a line. We still had some vodka and whisky, and so ended the evening feeling satisfied and jolly. However, I had trouble sleeping and went for my usual walk along the beach when it occurred. It was, as always, a balmy night with the waves from the lagoon lapping at the shore. The moonlight picked out hermit crabs going about their business. I could hear rustlings and murmurings in the undergrowth above the sands, but all this was normal. There would be creatures moving around and there would be plants waving in the wind. Then, at the end of the bay I found myself smelling the smoke of a fire.

I climbed some rocks on the headland, to see where the smoke was coming from. It was rising from the same area where we found the three charred stumps. Cautiously, I made my way along a narrow path we had fashioned ourselves and emerged on the edge of the clearing. Looking into the glade, which the moon lit up like a cosy living-room in a Suffolk cottage, a jolt of fear went through me. Sitting there about to raise the carcass of a whole pig to his mouth was a huge man. He was covered in hair except for around his jaws where the beard was singed or had been burnt clean away. There was a thickness about him: his torso and limbs. And his feet and hands were huge. The strangest thing about him though was his mouth. Flames were licking and hissing from it as they would from a small fire fed by unseasoned wood. Open as it was, I could see burning logs for teeth. It was the most frightening sight I had ever witnessed. My legs shook and my heart thumped.

Freeze or run? The two choices of a terrified creature.

I froze.

The next moment, he rose to his feet. Up and up and up he came. I knew he had seen me even though I was partly hidden by shadows. He peered at me with reddish eyes as if he were witnessing a phantom emerging from the night. Though he was monstrously huge to my idea of an ordinary man, in a forest where some of the yellow meranti trees were eighty to ninety metres in height it was not surprising that he'd remained hidden until now. He was almost completely naked, except for a thick bamboo pipe which sheathed his penis. It was held in place by a cord which encircled his waist. For a moment I couldn't take my eyes away from that extremity. The size of it caused me both to shudder in awe and want to laugh at the same time.

The pig was dropped and he took a step toward me, but he still seemed unsure of what to *make* of me. I think he was as much bewildered by my presence as I was by his. Suddenly I thawed and *now* I ran. I took to my heels and ran like an athlete back along the track toward the camp. Although the blood was pounding in my ears and I wouldn't have heard an air raid siren at that point, I had the feeling he wasn't following. It was a good thing, because my lungs became unbearably painful and the breath caught in my throat. After a while I had to stop, gag, and suck in air. Looking back, there was nothing crashing through the undergrowth after me. By the time I walked into camp I had gathered myself together and was, to outward eyes, fairly calm.

Sally and Jill were up and tending the fire, it being close to dawn by this time.

"I've seen the giant," I croaked.

That day we tried to fortify our position on the beach, burying sharpened spikes around the hutted area, dragging large tree trunks and covering them with thorned creepers, digging pits and laying grass trapdoors over them, but I—having seen our possible enemy—knew that anything we built would not stop the creature from attacking us if it wanted to. By the evening we were exhausted, and James was talking about building a raft.

"I don't think that's feasible," I said. "It would take a great deal of time and effort, and then we'll be abandoning a place of sufficiency for possible starvation and thirst on the largest ocean in the world."

"You're the sailor," he snapped. "You can do it."

"I'm not sure we can build a craft sturdy enough to keep it together for very long. One squall would probably be enough to tear it to pieces. A bamboo deck and pandanus sails? I'm no Captain Bligh."

"What's a mutiny got to do with it?"

I believe James was thinking I was questioning his motives.

"The mutineers set Bligh adrift in a small boat and he navigated his way over four thousand miles to Timor. All he had was a sextant and charts. But the boat was a sturdy craft and he was a brilliant navigator. I rely on electronic devices to tell me which way to go. It's not on, James. We have to dig in and wait for Chris and Juliana to return."

Luckily, an hour later, Chris managed to contact us on the solar-powered sat phone for the first time since he'd berthed in New Zealand. Our phone hadn't been working since James dropped it into a tide pool. Drying it had taken several days and only now were we able to get a signal.

"What's been the problem with the phone?" he asked first of all.

"It got wet and even when it was thoroughly dried out, it wouldn't take a charge at first. I think it's serviceable now."

"Good. Okay. Now listen, we're on our way back. I reckon a few days should do it. How are you coping. Food? Water? Any sickness?"

"All fine, but we've got company. A giant. One that seems to breathe fire. He hasn't bothered us yet, but we don't know his disposition. We've tried fortifying the camp, but the barricades are pretty flimsy."

There was a short period of silence where I thought we'd lost Chris, but then he came through again.

"Ah, I was hoping he wouldn't be anywhere near you. It's a big island. He's known to the authorities. That's why the island is uninhabited, and no one wants it."

I swallowed hard, knowing the other three were listening. The fruit bats were gliding overhead, going to their roosts for the night. They gave the evening an ominous spooky feeling.

"So, is he dangerous?"

"The Kiwis wouldn't commit themselves. They just said to get you off there as soon as possible. Just try to keep out of his way. He might not be interested and may wander off to some other part of the island. The good news is, the island's yours—ours—though whether we want it or not under the present circumstances . . ."

"They can keep it. It's his. Just get us off as quickly as you can. Can't they send a faster craft for us? A helicopter?"

"Expensive. Very. Do you want to lose your nice big house?"

I looked at Jill and she shook her head firmly.

"No," I replied, hollowly.

"They'll come if you ask for them. If it looks like he might get hostile, that's the time to put out a Mayday. A Pacific Islander did go missing in the region a short time ago, but that could have been anything. Storm, hidden shoal, accident, anything. The guy was in a small canoe—a *va'a*—those things can be upset by a big fish. Anyway, I'm on my way. Talk again in a couple of days."

"Okay. Before you go, does he have a name? The giant?"

"Name? Oh, yeah. Hold on, I'll have to read it to you. Juliana, where's that bit of paper, sweetheart? Thanks. Yes, there it is, they call him Yameyame Vakasequruqurubati. I'm sure I'm not pronouncing it right."

"That's a bloody mouthful. What's it mean in English?"

"Flaming Teeth."

"Huh. Why use one syllable when ten will do."

"Yeah," Chris said, "anyway, when a tooth burns down to the gum, he rams another lump of wood in its place. It has the advantage of cooking his food as he's eating it."

Sally said, "He must be the biggest mammal on the earth."

"No, that's the blue whale, Sal. Good try though."

"Don't be sarcastic. Just you hurry up and get here."

Shortly after Chris had cleared down Jill let out a cry.

"What's the matter?" I asked, thinking she'd been bitten by something.

"There—there along the beach!"

The rest of us turned to look. The bay was concave and was around a mile long. There at the far end, almost on the point, stood a huge silhouette with a fiery face. I knew now that it was only his mouth that burned, but from a distance as darkness fell it looked like his whole face was alight.

"My God, he's big," breathed Jill with awe in her tone.

I was tempted to ask her whether she meant the whole man or some special part of him, but it was no time for flippancy.

"Is he coming this way?" asked James with a trace of fear in his voice. "I can't tell, can you?"

So far as I could ascertain he was as still as a beacon.

"I don't think so," I replied.

"We need a guard," James said, quickly. "I'll take the first four hours," and he picked up the rifle.

"There's only a couple of rounds left," I told him. "We've used most of the ammo hunting our food."

"Well, that's pretty stupid," he retorted, "with a bloody giant on our heels."

It was useless to argue that we'd only just learned of the presence of a giant, so I left him thinking he'd scored.

Jill said, "Not four hours. Two. We can all take a shift."

James shook his head. "Sally doesn't know how to use a gun."

"Then you'll have to show me," said the woman in question. "It can't be that hard."

"But," argued her husband, "you have to know how to use one—you know, safety catches, how to aim and . . ."

"Jimmy, how many guns have you fired in your life?"

"Well, I had an air rifle as a boy. But a man, you know . . ."

"Don't say it, James," came in Sally. "Just don't say it."

I let them get on with it. The darkness came down like a shutter, as it does near the equator. We piled branches and logs on the fire, to light up the perimeter as much as we could. I got the yacht's fire axe, but it was merely a comforter. I knew that I couldn't fight a giant with a hand axe. I don't think any of us got much sleep. In the morning, we had a surprise waiting for us. There on the sands, not thirty metres away, was a pile of fruit and a haunch of wild pig.

"The giant's left us a gift," cried Sally. "He wants to be friends."

James replied, "How did he get so close when we had a watch?"

Flaming Teeth had managed to get within thirty metres of the camp without being heard or seen, which since he had a mouthful of fire—not too difficult to see at night—meant that one of us had fallen asleep on duty. I said nothing though, since everyone was hanging on their nerves.

The "gifts" were welcome however, since the hunter-gatherers amongst us didn't want to go into the forest. Our water source was a stream that trickled from the top of the headland just a few metres away, so we were able to stay together in a tight but nervous ball and wait for the yacht. We had the choice of a Mayday, but it had to be a life-or-death situation. So far it seemed he was a tame giant. We could hear him moving around in the forest, doing something with trees and branches, but so long as he didn't enter the camp I wasn't too worried.

As the hours passed, I began to reflect on our time on the island. At first I had been full of optimism and enthusiasm. We had found a very valuable piece of real estate by accident which might change our lives forever. There was lush rainforest in the interior which led to some spectacular volcanic peaks that had been fashioned by an eruption. You could see bird and animal shapes in the frozen lava—and anything else your imagination allowed. God or science was an extraordinary sculptor, depending on your beliefs. The beaches were remarkably clean for the century. One or two plastic items had been washed up, but there was a swift current out in the deep which I think took most flotsam and jetsam past the island and on to somewhere else. It was an idyllic setting in a garden of plenty and it was such a shame we had to leave it.

The next three days passed without any serious event. Food was left for us almost on a nightly basis which saved us from having to go into the forest to hunt. Sometimes we could hear him breathing fire, but the closer we came to leaving, the more I felt positive. The *Hilda* was getting nearer all the time. Chris called every evening and he felt that things were in hand.

"*Alles in Ordnung*," he would joke, in a German accent.

Then one night Jill wandered further than usual into the edge of the rainforest. She came back with a frown on her forehead.

"Hey, Dougie, what were those deadwood fences called, on that New Zealand farm?"

"Thorn fences. Why?"

"Well, I think the giant's built one, just inside the rainforest."

The hairs on the back of my neck rose.

"He has?"

James looked up from the fire. "Has what?"

"Nothing. I'm not sure. I'm just going to check on something."

I picked up the rifle and went to investigate. I came back a while later after following the thorn fence both ways.

I went back to the camp.

"He's built a pen," I said. "A bloody cattle pen, ten feet high. It's all the way from one headland to the other. We're trapped inside."

James went white with fear.

"He's got us corralled." He was quiet for a minute or two, then he added, "The food he leaves. He's fattening us up."

"Oh, my God," murmured Sally. "Oh, my God."

I tried to calm things. "Chris will be here in the morning. We have to hold out one more night. Flaming Teeth won't know we have a rescue boat coming. We have to be ready to walk out to the reef in the morning, during low tide. We can't wait for Chris to bring the dinghy in to shore. Hopefully Chris can manoeuvre the yacht close enough to the reef for just a short swim."

Sally said, "He'll see it first, if he's looking out to sea. The giant. He can see much further than us."

"You're right," I replied. "Tell you what, I'll call Chris tonight. He's very close now. He should get to us before dawn. Thank God the tide will be out at that time. We'll wait for him on the reef. Hopefully the boat will be hidden by darkness till it reaches the reef. Then we can swim for it."

I called Chris and told him the plan. We spent a restless few hours waiting for the right time and around three in the morning we set out over the shallows of the lagoon. It was slow and tortuous going without torchlight. There was a gibbous moon, but it kept ducking behind a cloud and leaving us in darkness. We held hands, forming a string. Everyone was wearing thick trousers and boots to prevent coral lacerations. Once or twice someone trod on something squashy—a moray eel or octopus caught in the shallows—but the boots kept us safe from dangers like stonefish spines, which are deadly.

Eventually we made the edge of the reef. Beyond the coral rim that fringed the island was deep water. A coral cliff plunged fathoms down to the ocean floor. Down there were monsters. Large man-eating sharks, manta rays, massive lion's mane jellyfish, sea-snakes with venom many times more deadly than a banded krait's. Staring into the dark, we took off our boots and held hands for the next three hours on the precipice of the solid world.

The water began to rise as the tide came in, until we were up to our waists. There was a quiet panic amongst us. It was a half-awake beast that threatened to suddenly jump up and cause havoc. Then darkness slipped away suddenly. Within minutes it would be bright sunshine. We would be fully visible to anyone on the shore. James was peering fearfully at the forest pale, muttering a prayer, while the rest of us stared out to sea.

I was terrified.

And then there it was, the *Hilda*, ploughing through choppy waters. Chris would have the engine full on and as much sail as the yacht could take.

"He's coming!" said Jill. "Come on, Chris. Come on."

We were all willing the *Hilda* on and always, always when you're watching a vessel hull-up out on the water, mentally urging it to reach you, it seems not to be moving at all. In the words of Coleridge, which only came to me while writing this account, it was like a painted ship upon a painted ocean. My gut was taut and I was shivering violently. On, on it came, painfully slowly to our eyes until suddenly it was there, closing on us, some thirty metres from the reef, where it swung round and presented its starboard to us.

At that moment there was a loud roar from the beach. We looked back, almost as one. Flaming Teeth stood on the edge of the lagoon. His cavernous mouth was blooming red-and-yellow fire. Smoke poured from his nostrils. Then he began wading toward us, the now deeper water of the lagoon slowing his progress. His weighted penis swung back and forth like a pendulum. Without another word we all leapt into the water and began to swim toward the *Hilda*. Chris was on the deck, aiming a rifle at the giant. However, he didn't fire because, as he told me later, he thought we were safely out of the monster's reach at that point.

Jill reached the yacht first. She was always swifter than me. Chris had thrown a scrambling net over the side and she was trying to climb it, exhausted by panic and the swim. Chris put down the rifle to lend her a hand. I got there next. Looking back, I could see Sally nearing the boat. James, though, was struggling with his poor ability as a swimmer. Flaming Teeth had reached the edge of the reef. It was obvious he wasn't going to follow in deep water.

Hanging on to the net I reached out for Sally to pull her up. During that time the giant undid the cord from his waist. He pulled the bamboo piping from his penis and swung it round his head like a bolas. He was obviously an expert with the weapon. It flew out and wound itself around James's neck. James let out a gargled scream and was pulled rapidly toward the reef like a hooked fish. The giant reached out and grabbed his victim by the hair and waded swiftly toward the shore.

Chris grabbed the rifle from the deck and began shooting, but the yacht was bouncing on the heavy chop and destroying his aim. Flaming Teeth looked back at us and his fiery mouth roared like that of a dragon. I swear it was a shout of triumph. Smiling, he held the squirming James by one leg, dangling him above the ground. Next, he let go of the poor man, pretended to try and catch him, but then let him fall to the floor. James was on his feet in a second and running. The giant let him get almost to the water's edge before stepping forward. James screamed and tried to climb into the hollow of a driftwood tree-trunk, but Flaming Teeth plucked him out like a mouse from his hidey-hole. He dangled the wriggling man at eye level by the head and huffed into his face.

Finally, one of Chris's shots hit Flaming Teeth in the shoulder. The giant jerked and grunted, but remained standing, still staring at us. Then the nasty smile came back as he put James between his burning teeth. We watched the pale figure going into the furnace, squealing in terror, writhing in pain. A second later Flaming Teeth bit down on his victim, taking head and shoulders. The torso and the legs fell, to be caught in his left hand as he chewed. Several of us screamed at that moment, both men and women, at the horror of the spectacle. In a blink the giant was gone, into the dense rainforest.

"We have to go after him," cried Sally, frantically. "My poor James. We have to save him from that monster."

The rest of us looked at one another. It was one of those times when shock warps what has actually been seen. James was dead meat, charred dead meat, we had all witnessed it, but Sally's recollection had stopped at the point where James had been struggling in the giant's grip. Jill and Juliana tried to comfort her, but she became hysterical for a while and had to be taken below for a sedative.

Chris and I were left on deck, staring at the island.

"No point in making a landing," said Chris. "We'll just have to report it."

Six months later, at the inquest the coroner informed us that the island had been removed from the charts over a hundred and eighty years ago.

"Giants live a long time. He's been there for over four hundred years. Perhaps they knew he had acquired a taste for human flesh?"

Chris said, "They'd have been a lot wiser to put out signs, warning people to stay away."

"Well, it was a long time ago. Maybe they did have signs at one time? Who knows? People did things differently then. There'll be warnings now, but sadly in your case, too late."

Sally asked, "What'll happen to him? What will they do to the murderer?" Naturally, she sounded quite bitter.

"Nothing I imagine," said the coroner, tidying his desk, probably to hide his embarrassment. "What prison could they put him in which would be more secure than where he is now?"

And so the whole episode came to an end, at least for everyone except Sally, for whom it would never come to an end. She said she would spend the rest of her life in the determination to have Flaming Teeth punished. How she hoped to achieve that, or what sort of punishment she envisaged, she didn't say.

The other day I spent a few pleasant hours in my garden. Jill and I had weeded and planted some new species in the flower beds, then we took out the sun loungers and both read our books. However, our cat disturbed us when she came out of the hollyhocks with a mouse in her jaws. She dropped the terrified wriggling creature on the lawn and played with it, before picking it up with her teeth and breaking its back. She then returned to the hollyhocks to eat it.

I ran into the house and threw up in the toilet.

STRANDLING

by Caitlín R. Kiernan

1.

It is not easy for me to conjure up the words to *properly* describe the thing. If it were, I would more likely be home in my office, sitting at my desk, at my typewriter, not standing here in the frigid April morning wind blowing in off the bay. If the words would come easier—indeed if the words would come at all, if the words would simply *come*—I would not have been walking the beach for the last hour and a half, pretending this is exercise, that I am doing my body a favor, a half-assed apology for the cigarettes and the bourbon. And I most certainly would not have to try not to see (and see anyway) all the crap that washes ashore with every high tide. Plastics, mostly—Styrofoam cups that once held coffee someone paid too much for, Styrofoam boxes that once held take-out fish-and-chips or chowder or a burger and fries, polyethylene terephthalate water and soft-drink bottles by the dozens and dozens and dozens, a stray pink flip-flop, cigarette butts, the eerie, vaguely insectile fluttering of plastic bags from grocery and convenience stores, the occasional discarded syringe, plastic bottle caps, bright red swizzle sticks and paler drinking straws, and on. And on. And on. The hydrocarbon debris of a thoughtless world. I try not to think about the deadly confetti of microplastics I cannot even see.

But I have gotten off topic, haven't I? I was saying, I look at the thing lying there half buried in the gray-white sand, surrounded by all this filth, by all these castaway carcinogens, and I know if I simply had the words in me to *describe* it, I would not be here *seeing* it. I do not mean the words merely to set down its *appearance*. Sure, I can *do* that. Any competent fifth grader could do that.

If it were not dead—and I am fairly certain that it is dead—I would say that it is looking up at me. The exposed part is at least four or five feet long. The back end is buried, so it may well be much longer. Its eyes are the size of dimes and silver as spilled mercury, except for the pupils. Those won't last long, the eyes. The gulls will have taken care of those in another hour or two. The gulls will eat anything. The gulls even eat the plastics. With my own eyes I've seen them doing it. But yes, dead silver eyes with small black pupils. Its skin looks like black latex stretched over the frame of a kite. That is almost exactly accurate. Latex pulled taut over a frail balsa-wood skeleton. The thing's back has not been entirely buried, and I can see the dorsal fin, spines or quills as long as my hands linked one to the other by translucent webbing that has been torn and tattered. The thing's skull is short and almost round, and I would be lying if I did not admit there is something very vaguely human about it. I would be lying if I did not say that it almost seems to have a face. Sure, I might only be committing a lie of omission, but it would be a lie all the same. The black thing's mouth is partway open, and I would swear those teeth have been sculpted from some inorganic crystalline material—quartz, maybe, or calcite. Or maybe they're glass. Maybe they are only some other sort of plastic. Behind the head, there are gill slits, like sharks have. There are three on the side I can see, so presumably there are three on the other side, as well. Bilateral symmetry and all. Just behind the gills, where I imagine there should be pectoral fins, there are tiny jointed appendages that make me think of stunted arms more than fins. A rubbery black fish with tiny arms (again assuming bilateral symmetry and that there is another "arm" on the buried side of the body), and I tell myself, well, mudskippers *sort* of have arms, don't they? This certainly is no mudskipper, but at least mudskippers have conveniently set a precedent for what I am seeing. The fish world is not without pseudo-arms. Along the exposed side of the carcass, I can see the suggestion of ribs through the taut latex skin. It gives the impression the thing was hungry when it died.

And it has some manner of parasites clinging here and there to its body. Looking at them, I think of whale lice, great masses of whale lice seething over streamlined cetacean anatomies, but *these* parasites are not whale lice. They are nothing *like* whale lice. The parasites attached to the thing in the sand are the color of raisins and resemble nothing so much as common, garden-variety slugs, but with their heads embedded in the flesh of the dead black thing. I count at least twenty of the parasites on the visible portion of the carcass, and I wonder if they're what killed it.

I stare at it up close for as long as I can stand to stare, and then I turn away and walk several yards back from the strandline, well out of reach of any stray waves and whatever load of toxins they might carry, and I sit down on the sand and pull my navy-blue peacoat tight about me and stare at the thing. I think, *I can describe you perfectly well, but so could any biologist, and I am not a biologist. I write novels and short stories.* Or I did, when I still was writing anything much at all. Before I took this cabin on the bay, got it cheap because the waters have been closed to swimming for three years now, ever since a Portuguese supertanker got turned about in the fog and struck a submerged outcropping, ripping its steel hull wide and vomiting its load of dodecylbenzene into the sea. Two million gallons or something like. As a result, now even writers on the bum can afford an oceanfront view, if they don't mind the smell. Van, she doesn't mind the smell as much as I do, and me, I don't complain, so we're happy campers on the shores of Hell. See? I can describe the strangest fish I ever have seen and at the same time I can be glib, but I cannot meet a deadline, or an extended deadline, or a deadline that has been extended until the beleaguered publisher finally, quietly, politely, mercifully has had enough and stops bothering to ask when I'll have a manuscript ready. I'm like a Swiss Army knife with everything but the actual knife blade.

I'm tits on a boar.

I look back out across the garbage-strewn sand, at the thing half buried in the sand, the black latex, kite-boned thing, and I wonder where it came from. It looks—at least to my eyes—like something that ought to dwell very, very far below the oily surface. It looks like something from an abyssal trench seven miles down, where the water pressure is more than fifteen thousand pounds per square inch and the all-but-freezing water is unimaginably, inconceivably dark. If you ever glimpse light down there you've made it yourself, or you've stumbled across some other bioluminescent creature. I imagine the dead thing not yet dead and lurking between the chimneys of towering black smokers, skirting the scalding geothermal vents, picking off unwary albino shrimp and crimson tube worms. I imagine it crouched down there, it and all its kin, unseen for a hundred million years until some submarine catastrophe sent it tumbling upwards into that ever-brightening sky to finally wash up here, on this plastic-littered beach at the edge of the poisoned bay. I think, in some sense, I have never seen anything so lost and broken. I think it almost seems to be smiling. And then I turn and march back through the cold toward the cabin. It's almost lunchtime.

2.

This is the next morning. Van is at the old gas stove cooking bacon and fried eggs. We take turns, and this morning is her turn, and just like always I will not complain that she overcooks the yolks of my eggs. I like them runny, and she says that isn't healthy. I am sitting at the kitchen table, looking out the window framed by the yellow walls, looking out the window at the beach and the place where I found whatever it was I found the day before. I cannot help but wonder if it is still lying there, or if the tide has carried it back out to sea to be eaten by sharks and small fish or to wash up somewhere else farther along the coast. I did not go for a walk this morning, and when Van asked me why, I told her about what I'd seen on the beach.

"You should use the trails," she said. "That's why they're there, so people don't have to look at all the filth on the shore." She means the sandy footpaths that wind between the wild tangle of blackberry briers and wild grapes, poison ivy and Virginia creeper and beach roses. The trails lead around a shallow salt pond surrounded by the shrubland and the dunes. There are often swans there, and ducks, and if you're patient you can see the backs and the peering heads of painted turtles breaking the surface every now and then.

"I don't like the trails," I told her. "There could be snakes." That was a lie. I don't like the footpaths because they remind me of a hedge maze, and when I was very young I once got separated from my parents and lost inside the hedge maze at the botanical gardens in St. Louis. I have hated them ever since. "I worry about snakes," I lied.

"It's too cold for snakes this time of year," she said, as sensible as always.

At the stove, Van pokes at the sizzling bacon and flips the eggs. I can tell mine is already overcooked.

"I wish you'd taken a picture of it," she says.

"I didn't have the camera with me."

"No, but you had your phone. You could have used your phone to take a picture of whatever it was."

"It really wasn't anything I wanted a photograph of," I tell her.

"But I could have posted the picture online and maybe someone could have told us what it is. An ichthyologist or marine biologist or someone like that."

"You can be morbid, you know it? My wife is a morbid woman."

"Why the hell would you say a thing like that?" she asks and glares at me over her right shoulder. There are bags beneath her eyes because she never, ever gets enough sleep, which is another reason we left the city and rented the cabin by the sea.

"Because only morbid curiosity would make someone want to see that thing."

"I can be curious without it being morbid curiosity, can't I?"

And sure, I might be inclined to agree, obviously. But more than once I have seen her pause on the beach to poke with her walking stick at something dead, because dead things are always being dragged in by the tides, even if they're not usually monstrous fish with tiny arms and kite-frame bones and black latex skin. Usually it's just sea bass and flounder and scup all rotten with tumors, the stray shark, gulls and cormorants tangled in fishing nets. One time, there was a small humpback whale, and Van braved the oily stench to poke at it for half an hour. No, it's not for nothing I call her a morbid woman.

"I just wish you'd taken a picture, that's all. It might have been an anglerfish. It sort of sounds like an anglerfish, especially those teeth, or something like an anglerfish."

"It wasn't an anglerfish," I say, even though I suppose that's possible. I have only ever seen photographs of them in books.

"And maybe the parasites were those horrible isopods that eat out the tongues of fish and then live in their mouths." She flips the eggs again. They must be shoe leather by now, but when your wife is dying of cancer, you do not complain about how she makes your breakfast.

And there's the truth of it: we did not take the cabin by the poisoned bay because I'm having trouble writing, or to help her sleep. We took the cabin because she wanted to die near the ocean, because she was born in Oregon, not far from Coos Bay. There's the vicious, razor-sharp truth, and it's much, much worse than what I found washed up and half buried in the sand. It's much easier for me to pretend we are here for almost any other reason in the world.

"They weren't isopods, the parasites. I don't know what they were. They were more like slugs or something."

"I can't stand those things."

"Slugs?"

"No, I'm fine with slugs," she says, plating the overcooked breakfast. "The isopods that parasitize fish. I cannot stand those things. And there's not just the tongue-eating kind. Some burrow straight into the body or embed themselves in the nostrils or live in the gills. But somehow they never kill the host fish."

"You know an awful lot about this stuff," I say.

"I read a book this one time," she tells me, and she smiles and sets the plates on the table. I put salt and black pepper and Tabasco sauce on my eggs, and just like always she tells me I need to watch my sodium intake. I wonder who will say shit like that to me when she is dead and gone and buried in the ground? When she's dead, I can smother myself in salt and no one will give a good goddamn.

"Well," I say, "that's gross, and I really didn't need to know any of it, but what I saw clinging to that thing were most definitely *not* isopods."

"You know that for a fact."

"I do."

She sits down across from me and doesn't salt her eggs.

"Because you know everything."

"I read a book this one time," I say.

3.

It often seems that there is anger in me more than there is anything else. More than there is sorrow. More than there is fear at being left alone when she is gone and I am finally, truly alone, when her death is no longer some hypothetical, future thing. I lie awake at night, listening to the sounds of her pain, the sounds she makes sleeping and half awake, terrible *small* sounds, like the torture of foxes and cats and birds muffled, as if I am hearing them through a thick wooden door. There is some truth to that, I think. I am hearing them muffled by the doors of sleep, and in her sleep she must be screaming. I think how I should be there with her, and then I find myself wondering if I meant that or if I am thinking that only out of some sense of duty, because she has been so selfless and uncomplaining and over the long years done so very many things for me. I know this is why I cannot write now. How can I write in the midst of her pain? How can I do anything so ordinary, as if life were still the way life once was, in a life that seems as if we lived it long, long ago? How could I do anything so superficial, so frivolous, so ultimately meaningless? No, I do not want to hear any arguments to the contrary. Not ever. I lie here in the dark and listen to her hurting, small animal sounds and her labored breathing, and I will not hear any arguments that *fantasy* is necessary, not in the face of this horror sleeping fitfully beside me, rotting from the inside out.

And minutes pass.

And minutes pile up until they are hours.

I do not sleep much anymore. Which only seems fair.

"I was dreaming," she says, so I know she's awake.

"Are you thirsty?" I ask, because I can hear the papery dryness in her voice, like hornets thrumming inside their papery hives.

"A little," she says, and I hold the plastic cup for her, the cup with the plastic straw built into the lid, and when she's done I set it back on the table next to my side of the bed. It was her mother's table, and before that it was her grandmother's. There's a mark on the underside that says it was made in Vermont in 1887. When she dies, it will be mine, and someday, when I die, it will be no one's.

"That's better," she says, lying down again, though she doesn't sound much better. I can still hear the hornets between and beneath her words. "I was having the strangest dream," she says.

"Is it something you want to talk about."

"I suppose, if you want to listen."

"I'm not doing anything else."

"You should be sleeping," she says.

"Tell me your dream. How was it strange?"

"Aren't all dreams strange?" she asks. "Isn't there something about dreams that renders the most mundane thing slightly strange?"

"Sure," I say. "I never thought of it that way."

"I was walking on the beach with you, and we were picking up all that plastic litter and putting it into plastic garbage bags, and I was talking about how ironic that was, and how futile it all is, how the plastic will wind up in a landfill, and the toxins will leach out into the soil, and poison forests some-where else, and—anyway. We were trying to clean the beach, at least a little bit, even though, you know, we both understood the next high tide would just dump more garbage on the sand. You were talking about a writer I've never read, that I've never even heard of, and I was trying to pay attention, but the sky was so full of gulls, and they were very, very loud."

"At least we were making an effort," I say. "Fighting the good fight."

"Hmm?"

"To clean the beach, I mean."

"Oh, right," she says, and then the pain gathers all its strength, rising up like a mighty rogue wave and slamming down, an oily black fist hitting her so hard that she can't say much of anything at all. I give her more water when she will take it. I check the clock on that table that has traveled here all the way from Vermont and 1887, but there's still half an hour left before her next dose of morphine. I hold her, instead.

"We were walking on the beach," she says, when she can talk again. Her voice is as thin and dry as the hexagonal walls of a hornets' nest.

I hide in the anesthetic of my similes and metaphors. They keep every-thing partway at arm's length. They render everything a little softer.

"We were picking up all that plastic shit," I say. "They gulls were so loud you were having trouble following whatever I was saying, which probably wasn't worth hearing, anyway."

In the darkness, I feel her frown.

"They were very loud," she says.

"And then what?"

"And then I looked out across the bay, and I was thinking about the day you told me that if you traveled that way in a straight line for long enough you'd be in Africa, and that story you wrote, 'Oranges from Africa,' and I saw something coming up out of the water. It was enormous. At first I thought it was only a whale, but then I saw that it was so much bigger than a whale.

It was bigger than a dozen whales. It was, I don't know, a mile or so out, but I could see the water spilling off its flanks, and I could see the sun shining wet off its black skin. Its skin looked like rubber, and I thought at once about the thing you found dead on the sand, but this thing, *this* thing was—I don't know—a hundred times bigger. Two hundred times bigger. It was huge. We were standing there watching it—by then you'd seen it, too, but you didn't say anything—and I was thinking how nothing alive has ever been *that* big—not a blue whale, not the largest dinosaur that ever lived. It was *vast*."

"I didn't mean to give you nightmares," I say, and I hold her more tightly, like maybe I can smother the pain and the cancer and the terrors in her dreams.

"No, no. It *wasn't* a nightmare. Maybe that's what made it so strange. I wasn't afraid, seeing it. It was amazing. It was possibly the most amazing thing I ever had seen. It was just sort of floating there in the sea, and I think it was staring up at the sky, because maybe it never had seen the sun before. Imagine living your whole life at the bottom of the ocean, living in complete darkness for so long you grow *that* goddamn big, but you've never seen the sun. You've never even *imagined* the sun."

"What happened next?"

"I said, 'That's awe. On its face, that's awe.' And you said that if it had a face, you couldn't see it, and then I could see the parasites, just like you described them. Even though it was a mile or two away. There were hundreds of them. Maybe thousands, dangling like black slugs from its skin. Hanging there perfectly still. I was about to say something about them, but that's when I woke up."

"Well, at least you weren't afraid."

"No, I wasn't. I wasn't afraid at all."

I hold her until it's time for the morphine, and then I hold her until she's asleep again, and I can see the first dishwater light of morning leaking in through the slats in the blinds.

4.

And these are mine, because not only dying women have strange dreams. So do the wives of dying women, and minutes seem to last hours or days in the space between gray dawn and bright, full morning. I meant only to rest my eyelids for a moment. Surely I had no chance left at sleep, not that night. But then, not knowing I am no longer awake, but in another world believing that is precisely what I am, it is the night that Van and I met. I was signing in a wretched little bookshop that smells of dust and paper and slightly of mildew.

She's wearing the white dress printed with small yellow flowers that she won't buy for another ten years, but it has not been my experience that dreams have much regard for the inconvenient, and possibly only apparent, linearity of time, chronology, narrative accuracy. I know what I mean. I am sitting behind a metal folding table, and she is sitting on the opposite side from me. The table, the sort brought out at family reunions and church socials and such, is stacked high with copies of my most recent novel. She is the only person who has come to the reading slash signing. In all the wretched little shop there is only herself, the old man behind the cash register (who occasionally glances suspiciously my way, as if I have no business being there), and myself. My Waterman fountain pen is also lying on the table, the pen my father gave me when I finished my undergraduate degree, when I still intended to work toward an MA. Things that didn't happen. Dreams are one of the places we keep things that never happened, but this is not *that* sort of dream, not exactly.

"Is it always like this?" she asks me.

"More often than not," I reply.

"But you keep doing it."

"I do."

She watches me a moment with eyes that are still clear and blue and not stained with the perpetual bruise of sleeplessness. She is smiling, but in the softest way, a smile that seems like an intimacy between us, a smile that is almost a secret.

"Then you must love it," she says.

"I really don't."

"May I?" she asks, pointing to a copy of the latest collection of my short stories that isn't selling for shit.

"That's what they're there for," I say.

She picks up the book and stares at the cover for what seems like a very long time. But maybe it isn't. Maybe it's only an instant. She opens the book, but I can't tell if she's actually reading the words or just looking at them to be polite.

"I have never wanted to be a writer," she tells me, turning pages. "I have been an avid reader all my life, but I have never wanted to write books of my own."

I tell her how relieved I am to hear her say that. I tell her how men and women come to me, as if I am a priest in a confessional booth, to tell me how all they ever wanted was to become an author, but this happened, or that happened, and they want me to reassure them how exciting and romantic and fulfilling it must be.

"I like this story's title," she says.

"Which one?"

"'Oranges from Africa,'" she replies. "But it isn't, is it? I mean, it isn't exciting or romantic, being a writer."

"No," I say. "It isn't. I sit alone in a room almost every morning and afternoon, typing, typing, typing, hoping I'll have at least a thousand words to show for the day's efforts. I write books that sell just barely enough that someone will deign to publish the next one, which, by now seems like a sort of punishment. It has ruined my eyesight. I'm beginning to have symptoms of carpal tunnel and my back hurts all the time."

"It's as bad as that?"

"I am a writer," I say, in this dream, that is only almost what actually happened that night. "Everything I say is a lie. And that's the truth."

She laughs, and it's a laugh that makes me feel better about being there in the wretched bookshop, less humiliated and discouraged and angry at all the readers who cannot be bothered to appreciate what I do.

"If I buy this, you'll sign it?" she asks me.

"That's how it works. Actually, I'll sign it first."

And she tells me her name, and I tell her mine, even though it's printed right there on the dust jacket and title page and the headers of every page of the book she's holding.

And then we aren't in the wretched little bookshop anymore.

We're standing in the dunes, among the beach roses and blackberry briers, and she's talking about rabbits and foxes and all the other animals that are hiding in the underbrush, watching us. She's telling me how she wanted to be a veterinarian when she was a girl, before she knew she couldn't stand the sight of blood or the thought of putting an animal out of its misery.

"I don't care if it's mercy," she says. "I wouldn't be able to do it."

There are high cirrus clouds, and the air smells like the sea and like the small pink and white roses sprouting from the deep green tangle on either side of the sandy trail. I think about all those rabbits and foxes watching us, and for some reason it frightens me.

"They're more frightened of you," she says.

"I would save you if I could," I tell her.

She stoops down and lifts something from the sand and holds it out for me to see—a bleached and broken conch shell, bleached white by the sun and sea, broken by waves so that the spiral running through its center is exposed.

"I would fix this, if I could. But I can't, and I won't beat myself up because I am not a woman who can restore broken shells."

"Do you think I'm beating myself up?"

"Do you believe you're not?"

I take the shell from her and turn it over and over in my hand, as if there's something more there I'm supposed to see.

"I have always hated feeling helpless."

"You think maybe there are a lot of people in the world who enjoy it?"

"Have you never heard of a masochist?" I ask her, dropping the shell back onto the sand, not asking her if she might want to keep it and take it home and set it on one of the windowsills with all the other things she's found beach-combing, the things that *should* be here, that are not plastic litter.

"No," she says, as if I *have* asked the question. "I get what I came for."

And that's when I see the black sluglike body protruding from her neck, gently pulsing, glistening in the daylight. There's another on her left forearm. I wonder how many there are that I cannot see, and I'm about to ask her that when I wake up with the sun in my eyes.

5.

April becomes May, inevitably, as it does even to people whose lovers aren't dying. The days became warmer and longer, the nights warmer and shorter. I stared at the typewriter in my small office, but I didn't write. I stared at the diminishing balance in our joint bank account. Days blurred one into the next. Days began to smear. Insomnia will do that. Insomnia and waiting, and by the beginning of May I understand more fully that I was simply waiting now, waiting for Van to die. Even after all this, it would be sudden. It would be unexpected. Even after all these months, somehow it would still take me by surprise. Even now, I was unprepared.

One day early in May she asks me to drive her into the village at the edge of the bay, the village that used to make a living fishing, before the waters turned to poison. There are a lot of empty houses and boarded-up storefronts with FOR SALE signs out front. I do not like going into the village, but Van said she needed to go to the library—yes, the village still has a public library, though it is small and, near as I can tell, has only one employee, a dour woman with cat-eye glasses who looks like she fell out of 1960 and a Shirley Jackson novel. The library does not have any of my books, but I don't hold that against it. While she prowls the shelves, I sit at a computer terminal—there are seven in this small library, and it's obvious that the people left in the town are more interested in the internet than the stacks—and I read news articles and revisit two-month-old email from agents and editors and friends that I still have not answered. Half an hour passes, maybe a little more, and she comes back with her walking stick and an armload of books, everything from a Peterson field guide to fish of the Atlantic to an old parasitology textbook to a cheaply printed paperback with the unwieldy title *The Ecology of Deep-Sea Hydrothermal Vents and Their Role in the Origin of Life on an Iron-Sulfur World.* I don't ask her why these books. I don't ask what the common thread might be. I do not think of nightmares and the kite-boned carcass I found on the beach almost a month ago. On the drive back to the cottage, it begins to rain again, and by the time we get home the shower has become a deluge.

It rains for three days, and I stare at my typewriter, and Van reads her odd assortment of library books.

I don't ask questions.

Then one night we are eating Campbell's chicken and stars soup and saltines, because it's one of the few things she can still keep down, and Van says, "What if they weren't really parasites at all?"

I have to ask what she's talking about. I honestly have no idea.

She makes a face like I'm being dense on purpose.

"The slug things attached to what you found. You called them parasites, but maybe they were something else."

"You mean maybe they were part of its body?" I ask, and she shakes her head.

"No, I mean, yes, maybe they were separate organisms that had attached themselves to—whatever it was—but they might not have been detrimental. They might have been symbiotes of some sort. They might actually have been beneficial."

"Aren't symbiotes technically parasites?"

"They can be, but not necessarily. There's mutualism, where both organisms benefit by the interaction, like butterflies pollinating flowers. There's also commensal symbiosis, where one organism benefits, but the host isn't harmed, but also doesn't benefit. Like the way remoras attach themselves to sharks."

"Okay," I say, and I have no idea where this is going, but now I see that the library books were part of some sort of mental jigsaw puzzle she needed to try and put together for herself. "Okay, maybe they were symbiotes, the slug things. They might have been."

"And maybe they were the helpful sort," she says. "Maybe if it really did come from very deep down in the ocean, maybe its blood was full of toxins that pour out of those fissures in the seafloor, the metals and all the minerals dissolved in that superheated water. Hydrogen sulfide, for example, which normally kills most anything, but there are bacteria at those fissures that live off it. But maybe the things clinging to what you found, maybe they eat hydrogen sulfide. Maybe they clean it from the blood of other animals, the fish and whatever else lives way down there. If so, that would be mutualistic symbiosis."

"That's an awful lot of maybes," I tell her.

"Yeah," she says. "It is. But that doesn't mean it might not be true."

"No, it doesn't," I agree. "But there's no way to ever know."

She stirs at her soup with her spoon. She's eaten maybe four or five spoon-fuls and one cracker. She has grown so thin, so frail, I am afraid to hold her at night, afraid of breaking something. She stirs at her bowl of chicken and stars and says that maybe if I'd kept what I found that day we could have taken it to a university or an aquarium or somewhere and they could have figured out what the slug things were. There's an unmistakable note of judgment in her voice. She's saying that I *should* have hauled that hideous rotting thing back to the cabin. She's saying I made a mistake by *not* doing that.

"They find new medicines in the rain forests," she says. "Maybe there are new medicines down there, at the vents, waiting to be discovered. Maybe the slug things could clean the blood of sick people, the way leeches can help with osteoarthritis and varicose veins and help with healing after surgery. They sort of looked like leeches. You said that. That they looked like leeches or slugs."

"You should eat," I say. "Your soup is getting cold." I finally know where she's going with this, why I drove her to the library that day, and selfishly I wish she'd kept it to herself. I think how, to a dying woman, hope can become a psychosis. I think how hope can be irrational and sadistic and can lead desperate minds down the bottomless rabbit holes of obsession.

She says, "Maybe another one will wash up. Maybe they wash up here all the time, and no one notices, or they're so common that no one pays them any mind."

"Maybe," I say.

"We could go look tomorrow morning," she says, "after the tide goes out."

"Sure," I reply. "We can do that. But I really don't think we'll find another one."

"But you don't *know* that," she says.

"No," I admit, "I don't know that."

6.

The end of it, which, of course, is really only a different sort of beginning, years later it will seem that it comes in fits and starts, stuttering, days and nights broken up by holes in my memory, by sleep, by what is simply forgotten. But also by a strange tumult that seemed to seize my mind there in the cabin at the edge of the continent, on the shore of the poisoned bay. The end of it, I will look back and it will seem as a flashlight in a very dark room, the walls adorned with moments and hours and weeks, revealed only in sweeping and incomplete glimpses.

I will write two of them down, two and only two, and make an end to this.

A conversation, one of our last. Van growing too distracted by the pain to be bothered with words, too weak from medicine and illness alike, too locked up inside her fear and her weariness of fear. But there were still sometimes conversations, and this one happens in the unbreathing, still heart of night:

"Do you think much about being alone?" she asks.

"I try hard not to," I reply.

"You should think about it. It's coming, and it shouldn't catch you off guard. There isn't any reason it should. You *should* think about it."

"I would rather not waste what time we have left making plans for how it'll be when you're gone."

"You should, though."

I'm silent for four or five minutes, or that is how I will remember it, briefly confounded by her insistence, and then I say, "I was alone before we met. I'll get the hang of it again. It's probably like swimming or riding a bicycle."

"I think about it all the time," she says.

"About me being alone?"

"Yes, about that, but also about the perpetual darkness at the bottom of the sea, and how lonely a place it must be. How empty and lightless and lonely. Do you know about anglerfish?"

"I know what they are," I reply. "Those ugly things that are all head and teeth, and there's that sort of bioluminescent lure that dangles from their head to draw in prey."

"All that's true, but do you know how alone they are?"

"It's nothing I ever thought about."

"Well, they are so alone down there in the cold and the dark that it is very infrequent that one anglerfish ever finds another anglerfish, and then only by accident, I suppose. And because of this, the males are very tiny, and when they finally find a female they latch on to her with their jaws and they actually *fuse* with her. They become *part* of her, eventually, not much more than an appendage. I think about it, and I cannot imagine a more perfect marriage."

"I didn't know that. About anglerfish, I mean."

"I don't *want* you to be alone," she says, and I can feel her breath on my face. "I don't want you wandering the lightless oceans of the world all alone."

I don't think that's actually what she said. But I'll remember it this way.

"You should sleep a little bit," I say.

"What you found on the beach," she says, "it seemed a bit like an anglerfish, didn't it. We talked about that, didn't we, and all those slug things growing out of it, maybe they were actually its lovers."

"Maybe," I say, and the thought gives me a shudder.

And then, a few days later, a few days later just before sunset, and I'm sitting on the porch that faces out on the bay. She's walking the beach, gathering up plastic litter and putting it inside a white trash bag. At the very end, she's become obsessed with trying to clean the beach, trying to clear it and keep it clear, and she expends what strength is left to her this way, in an act of utter futility. I do not try and stop her. It is the ending of her life, and she should spend it as she wishes, and who am I to say any different? She comes to me one evening with an old issue of *National Geographic,* and there's a story in it about the Great Pacific Garbage Patch, hundreds of thousands or millions of kilometers of floating plastic refuse churning in the gyre of currents, increasing in size by tenfold each decade since 1945.

"It might only be as big as Texas," she says, "or it could be the size of Russia."

There is a grisly photograph of a dolphin with its belly split open, its guts packed with trash, with fishing line and netting and water bottles, a toothbrush, a baby bottle.

Anyway, I'm sitting on the porch, watching the sun go down over the bay, the early-summer sun like a fireball, the sky smoldering and molten. I watch Van as she stoops, dislodges something from the sand, and drops it into her bag. And does that again. And again. And again, moving slowly away from the cabin. *She might as well be trying to gather up all the sand with a teaspoon,* I think to myself. *She might as well be trying to hold back the tide with a mop.* I want to call her home so badly that it aches, that it throbs like a rotten tooth, that longing to make her stop this. But I don't, because of what I've said already. I will *not* tell her how to spend her last days.

It's getting dark, and what happens next, I will never be sure what it is that I actually see. It might never have happened at all, but I'll spend my life trying to forget that it *might* have. I'm sitting there alone on the porch thinking about how it will be dark very soon now, so she'll surely be heading back of her own volition before much longer. And then it seems—*suddenly*—that she is not alone, that there is something moving along over the sand beside her, something only half her height or less, a lurching, hunched-over sort of a thing, hardly more than an ink-black silhouette in the fading twilight. She seems to be speaking with it. She reaches out a hand and touches its face. I'm getting to my feet to shout a warning to her to *please* be careful, that it might be dangerous, whatever it is, but I'm also absolutely *certain* that all the weeks of sleepless nights have finally caught up to me and whatever I *think* I'm seeing, it's surely only a hallucination. I stand, and I go to the porch railing and open my mouth to call out to her, when Van's dark companion turns away and lurches into the sea. She watches it go.

My heart is a hammer of flesh, pounding blood. My mouth is dry as dust. *Do you know how alone they are?*

And then she's coming slowly, unsteadily, up the back stairs, and then she's with me on the porch, breathless and setting her trash bag down on the weathered gray boards. I hold her like a drowning woman clinging to driftwood. Neither of us speaks. In silence, we watch the bay together, and the night coming on.

THE SPECIAL ONE

by Chịkọdịlị Emelụmadụ

There had been no portents to mark Joy's conception and birth. No dreams or visions, foreshadowing who was to come, no prophecies, no thunder shaking the earth, or lightning rending the skies, or rain threatening to drown out the year's harvest, its floodwaters carrying many a carelessly placed foot to a watery end. Her mother's pregnancy had been perfectly ordinary, culminating in a safe, predictable labour.

They named her Joy, an ordinary name for a child who became extraordinary, at least in childhood.

Joy spoke full sentences while her mates were still babbling babyspeak, wrote independently before she turned two, and could read and memorise whole passages by the time she was five. Her parents trotted her out in front of priests and professors alike, varying her recitations to suit her adoring audience: the Bible or *Encyclopaedia Britannica*, it made no difference. She'd pore over the minute print, picking out the words with a toothpick in her hand, mouthing diligently, only to regurgitate everything she'd read hours later. Her parents praised her, called her "The Brain," and fed her eggs and chicken thighs in excess, foods which were denied to other children for fear that it would turn them greedy. So sure were they of her genius, they spared no expense in her education. Probed, they would not have been able to name the "It" for which they prepared their daughter. They only knew that it would happen, their years of sacrifice coalescing into something astonishing.

What Joy had not realised, however, was that in billions of households around the world, other parents were telling their offspring the exact same thing.

She grew up, waiting on her greatness.

In the meantime, she fancied herself in love with a man and married him, and, for a while, her destiny seemed to have converted to producing the right type of children for her husband and his grateful family. Boys marched out of her like soldier ants from a cracked anthill, leaving destruction in their wake;

first to her brain, then her body, which drooped and sagged, emptied of its precious cargo. She forgot things—was Kilimanjaro in Kenya or Uganda?—and scoffed when her husband suggested she stop torturing herself and use Google, for chrissakes, like a normal person. She accepted the compliments of strangers:

"Nne, you are blessed o. Four boys, just like that! I use you as a point of contact for my own blessings." They rubbed her hands, her skin, hoping for a bit of her good fortune.

The skin around her mouth hurt from smiles stretched too far, held in place for too long. The boys, her children, they made a mockery of the belief, burning in the folds of her psyche like a wound that surely, she was made for better things than the endless sleep, eat, shit, that characterised her life.

Greatness arrived in the form of a python.

The family had gone to spend the Christmas holidays with her parents, who had retired to the village. Crammed into their three-bedroom bungalow, Joy woke with it coiled around her supine form. She relaxed into its embrace. The next instant, she was up, the dry, scaly warmth warning her of the anomaly. It was not the arms of her youngest son, who still slept beside her, nor his father, who had chosen to remain behind in the city "tying up loose ends" but ostensibly to have time away from his pack of wild children.

The blood sang in her ears. Here was the moment for which she had been made. A python-child in her bed. She'd been chosen by the goddess Idemili herself. Joy woke her mother.

"Ah," her mother said, crossing herself. "Let me get your father, after all this is his village. I don't have anything to do with pythons."

The old man was roused and, ever the gentleman, came without a fuss. "Ah," he said. "I will call someone to chase it outside, it's okay. Or maybe we could just tell it that we are Christians and it will flee, like in that Achebe book, what is it again?" He'd phrased the question as he always did, from habit, expecting her to respond.

Joy despaired. Saliva congealed on her tongue as she prepared to disappoint him with her rubbish memory.

"*Arrow of God*," she replied. The answer surprised her because she knew it was right. She'd remembered a book, one of those she memorised over twenty years ago. It was a sign. In the book, Oduche had tried to imprison the sacred python in a box, to prove his zeal for the church. Joy would do no such thing. After all, what had decades of being in thrall to the church wrought but misery and division?

The python's eyes followed her, singular in its purpose. Not everybody was deemed worthy to be visited by Eke, the royal python, and by extension, Idemili the goddess whose totem the snake was. The visit was a message: Follow me.

"It is here for me."

Ignoring their concerns, Joy grasped her baby and walked, expecting the creature to follow, which it did. She popped the bolt on the gate out of its hole in the ground and it crunched on the sand as she pulled it open. Once outside, she and the snake switched places. It led, and she trailed it in the early-morning sun, the patterns on its back, bronze and ochre and copper, undulating as it went. Onlookers gawked. The older ones bowed their heads in reverence to the totem. The younger ones jumped off the narrow laterite pathway and into the bushes, dirtying their Christmastime outfits.

The shrine to Idemili lay at the boundary between Joy's village and the next, half-heartedly surrounded by corrals of corrugated zinc sheets, wood, and bare concrete. In places, white plastic seating and banners were the only things which marked the borders between one church and the next, on land donated by converts hoping to receive everlasting life. Upon sighting the snake and the woman who followed it, they cursed at them with Bible verses, revived from draining, all-night vigils by the sight of what they perceived to be an ancient enemy. Joy baulked, her old, people-pleasing instincts revived. These congregants showed no compunction about violence.

"Blood of Jesus," they spat.

They kicked the air in front of them and hollered in tongues. Someone threw a sachet of water at her and it exploded in a pop of wet plastic and sand. When one of the pastors rushed at her, Joy raised a hand on instinct, gripping the baby tightly in her other arm. The man's face connected with her forearm and his nose began to bleed. After that, Joy glared at them, renewed with power. She'd never hit a man before, much less made one bleed, and she knew now that a force was with her, guiding her steps. She took deep gulps of air and unfurled her shoulders, which had curled up protectively around her chin. Nobody could touch her.

At the shrine, all was quiet and calm. Trees swayed, the dawn chorus sang. The python led her to the door of a hut and slithered inside. It had worn a deep groove in the loose sand of the compound. Joy hesitated at the threshold. Although she was certain of the call, the weight of her destiny gave her pause. The morning was balmy and a stream of sweat trickled down her spine. Her baby began to cry.

"Who is there?" A voice, sharp despite the hour.

"It is me," replied Joy.

"Are you man or spirit? What kind of name is 'Me'?"

An elderly woman emerged. She was small and upright, eyes shiny like the python's. She looked Joy up and down.

"He is not here," she said.

"Who?" asked Joy.

"Who are you looking for?" The woman crossed her arms in front of her, readying for a battle of wills or wits, whichever came.

Joy transferred her baby across to her other hip, the loose skin of her belly jiggling as she rocked it to silence. The woman was a gatekeeper, the sphinx perhaps, with a riddle. Joy knew enough to recognise that she had a role in the hero's quest. Tamping down on her irritation, she tried again.

"Good morning." An obsequious bow. "My name is Joy. The python came. Is there a message for me?"

"I said Isi-Idemili is not here. The man you are looking for, the chief priest."

Why then would the python come for her if there was nothing to tell, Joy wondered—and just like that, the answer came to her. A test, to judge if she was worthy.

"I will wait," she said, nose in the air.

The woman shrugged. "Take off your shoes before you come in."

Joy sat with her baby on her lap, picking dry skin around the bed of her big toes to pass the time. She pulled and picked until the skin showed pink and tender under the old, flaky grey. It started to hurt. The old woman spoke or sang softly to herself. Sometimes, the timbre of her voice varied, and Joy found herself looking up, but she was not addressed after that first exchange. Her son fretted and fussed in her arms until she set him down on the floor, worn shiny by the passage of many feet. He crawled to where the python lay by the fireplace, warming itself in the embers. Joy held on to his foot to stop him, a maternal alarm warring with her belief. The baby started to cry again. She let him go. He crawled, bubbles and threads of his clear drool dotting the floor.

"Azuka, come back here," she coaxed. Azuka sat right in the middle of the snake's many coils, giggling.

"What did you say your name was again?" the woman asked, eyeing the boy. "An English name," she sneered. "You know, Our Lady gives many things: wealth, beauty, even suitors, but not children. Are you sure you are in the right place?"

"How do you mean?" Joy's nostrils flared. The ancient one, ignoring her, gestured to the animal skulls exhibited on the wall, bleached white from the sun. The mark of sacrifices, a display of wealth. Meant to show that people continued to seek the goddess's favour even with the churches encamped about the shrine.

"Oh, yes, Idemili herself married and had children, but she does not give children, you know." The old woman spoke to herself.

"I do not want for children, I have many sons. This one you see here is my fourth." The nose again, raised like a dog's. Even so, the woman's words rankled. Joy waited as the sun walked across the sky, until the boy fell asleep on top of the serpent, until her stomach growled with hunger and she could smell yesterday's skin on her body. She got up, picked up her son.

"Please tell Isi-Idemili that I will be back for my message," she said.

Somewhat diminished, she made the journey back to her parents'. However, she could not be kept down for long. Her spirits bobbed and danced, buoyed on top of the currents of drudgery which would have previously pulled her into its depths. Joy sang as she did chores. Her mother watched and pretended not to.

"So, what did they tell you in the place where you went?" asked her mother, when she could no longer bear the suspense. Joy only sang louder, a secretive smile on her lips. She heard the rustle of a page turning as her father read one of his dusty, outdated books, holding it up to his nose to make out the minuscule print. An intake of breath told her he was about to speak.

"You should be careful," he said. "I hear talk of Isi-Idemili being sick."

Joy paused. "What is his issue?" she asked.

"Old age. The same sickness all of us have sooner or later." He turned the page slowly, feigning nonchalance. "He may soon go to sleep."

Joy's ears picked up an unusual inflection. *Go to sleep.* Her father was saying the old priest was at death's door.

"Just be careful. A man like that dies, and it is not only animals that are killed to accompany him to the afterlife. Sometimes, people have to go too."

Joy's mother clicked her fingers over her head, in a gesture intended to ward off misfortune.

"Human sacrifice?" Joy chuckled, disbelieving. "Impossible." Inside, Joy began to connect the dots and her mind exploded with possibility. Could it be that she was next-in-line to serve the goddess as priestess?

She tried not to think of the path that had been revealed. This had not been how she'd imagined she would end up, a priestess to the oracle. Her mates might mock her for entertaining such unsophisticated notions—a priestess, living in a village, walking around barefoot, listening for celestial voices, and tending to provincial matters. How narrow-minded they would find it. How . . . local. She imagined their lips twisted with bitter mirth as they gossiped.

Once, everybody thought with her brains she would make a fine doctor, but Joy found the whole process tedious and often fell asleep in classes which demanded rigour. Besides, if every other Nigerian was a doctor, who would be left to treat? With a flair for the dramatic and an ease in the limelight, she knew she was more suited to the arts anyway where her skills at performing would be appreciated, but even university had left a bitter taste. She had hoped for a challenge, a chance to hone her craft, to show off her remarkable brain at learning lines and delivering them, but did not meet anyone she considered her equal. Her lecturers were dull and dowdy, the infrastructure ancient, her programme underfunded. And the classmates in her theatre arts course were all obsessed with Nollywood while she dreamt of Emmys and Oscars and Juilliard. So, while they had gone off into one "home video" or another, Joy had kept the faith.

On the day that MTV decided it would hold auditions across Africa for stars for its new show, Joy, standing in line, had met one of the producers, the man who would become her husband. He had the right lines, and she was hungry for a fairy tale. He swept her off her feet and into his home. From there, she watched classmates churn out films, win awards on television, and get endorsement deals. Her envy swelled as far as her pregnant bellies would allow.

Now, it seemed her patience would be rewarded.

The python returned the following night and the next, no matter how tightly the doors and windows were shut and barricaded. Joy's mother feared for her chickens. Joy, craving its warm embrace, offered their eggs to the snake as one would a lover. Her father showed signs of worry.

"You know, one cannot go forward and then suddenly start moving backwards," he said. "Some things die off for a reason. Civilisations evolve. Our forefathers were born in darkness and died in darkness. We who know better must surely do better, not so? Leave pagan things for heathens."

"Have you thought about going after a Ph.D.?" asked her mother. "I'm sure you will do excellently well. You are just bored. It is not wise for a woman to make a job of her own children. Do something else."

"Mummy, we are hungry," cried her sons. "We are bored, we are tired, Ugonna's nose is running and Amala has wet the bed again."

Her husband rang. "I hear you are leaving the children hungry and abandoned. What the hell is wrong with you?"

Joy responded to them all with equanimity; she would bring the goddess into the twenty-first century, maybe, divinations on apps. Who said Idemili, like Joy, had not grown too big for the confines of an earthen shrine? And what use was a Ph.D. if her paper would just sit in the dust of some university library? Joy shooed her children, bade the older ones care for the younger, and to her husband she retorted in renewed confidence, "What am I supposed to do, feed them my own flesh?"

"I can see you are finally going mental," her husband replied, surprised at her brand-new boldness. He was much older, and when he married her straight out of university, it was to avoid this very thing.

Joy knew he did not understand, not really. They had studied the same subject and would have ended up in the same industry had Joy not gone the domestic route, but that is where their similarity ended. He was a man, subject to the privileges afforded his gender. She was not. Joy had found herself by accident of birth and anatomy in charge of childrearing when they both knew she was the special one in the relationship; the one made for big things. She ignored the telltale rustling of sheets on his end of the line even though he was supposed to be in his office.

Joy trekked again and again to the end of her village.

"Oh-ho, it is the one who wants to follow a great masquerade with empty hands," said the old woman. Joy had grown tired of her taunts and riddles. After years of waiting, she had become the legendary tortoise who had fallen in a cesspit for seven days, only to bristle with impatience after help arrived. She wanted to come into her inheritance.

"Can you please tell me when Isi-Idemili will be in? The python keeps coming for me but there is no message."

"In or out, all the same. He is in his house, dying as we speak. When he is gone, a new one will take his place."

"It is true then?" Joy asked, her tone bearing none of the reverence with which people spoke of death.

The woman turned her head, a quick movement, like a bird sighting prey. "What did you bring, or is it just your mouth?"

"Who are you and why do you speak for Isi-Idemili?" Joy frowned.

"I am his wife, or maybe his mother. Doesn't matter, doesn't matter." She waved a hand. "You know, those church people you see around us, they like to bother Eke, the goddess's python, but none of them will dare to touch it. Who amongst them can afford the expense of burying Eke like a chief, according to custom? The firing of cannons? Palm wine flowing like rivers? They surround the shrine but they are afraid to touch it."

Joy made a sound in her throat, fidgeted. "I don't understand what you are talking about. Speak plainly."

The woman laughed. "'Speak plainly' she says, as if she is a child." Her eyes were upon Joy again, all traces of mirth gone. "I am telling you that we have cow heads and goat heads and heads of ram with horns curling like pods of akidi beans. What did you bring in tribute? Following Idemili is not for the poor and the stingy. That is why the churchgoers no longer speak to you. You have no . . ." The woman looked Joy up and down ". . . grandeur to your steps. Idemili is an important goddess. In the world of gods, she is a giant. You cannot come to her with nothing."

Joy thought about the question on the walk home, turning it over with the mindfulness of prayer beads. The churches came alive in the evening, prepping for spiritual battle with things that roamed in the night. Growling generators powered fluorescent bulbs nailed onto wooden poles, jabbing blades of harsh light into the darkness. Loudspeakers magnified worship songs to distortion. The old woman was right. After Joy's initial visit to the shrine, the church members no longer harassed her, shouting Bible verses about damnation and spitting. They did not bother her as she came and went. It was as though she had become invisible.

With blind hands she washed her children and put them to bed.

Joy waited all night but the python did not return. Sleep fled. She stayed in bed the next morning, fighting the grittiness in her eyes, the fever which burned in her blood.

She sensed a challenge, one to which she had no worthy rejoinder.

"Please do not go to the shrine again, people are beginning to talk," her mother begged.

Joy turned away from her and into the glare of the sun coming from windows whose curtains had not been drawn. She bore the scorch to her eyes, a penance for what, she did not know. Her mother begged and pleaded and when Joy said nothing, she went away to tend her grandchildren. For three days Joy lay there, questioning, while the children ran her poor parents ragged. She would not stir, could hardly do more than sweat and try to swallow the thick saliva clinging stubbornly to her throat. Her mother placed glasses of water on her bedside table. The sun bounced off them, casting rainbows on the wall.

The answer came to Joy on the fourth day. The town crier sounded his gong and announced his news; Isi-Idemili was dead. There would be a burial, of course. He was an important person and there would be animals slaughtered, a feast, a celebration. Joy climbed out of the damp indentation that had formed in the mattress. Her hair was matted, her breath rank. Her children eyed her warily, wondering if she would curb their fun, but she barely paid them any attention. Joy's mother kept her company as she finally ate, cramming her mouth full of palm-oil jollof made over smoky woodfire, dried fish and fried plantains cooked by her house girl.

"I was worried. I hope you did not catch germs in that place," she said, stroking the face of her only child. She combed her hair, drew it into a bun the way she did when Joy was a toddler.

Joy kissed her mother, peppered her with reassurances. Her mind whirred. Of course, she knew all along. Idemili did not give children, the old woman had said. A big inheritance demanded a worthy sacrifice.

She fed her children from her own hands as she herself had been fed, bathed them, and rubbed the powder from roasted white clay around their already-sweaty necks. Joy drew patterns in their skin, whorls on chests, a cluster of dots around the eyes, four arcs, four bows like an upside-down rainbow. The children's eyes sparkled at this new game, trailing her fingers, encouraging her.

They delighted at this new mother, the lightness of her touch, her spirits as buoyed as theirs always were.

Joy put the children to bed and watched them go gradually into sleep. One by one their eyes dimmed and shut, their breathing growing even. She walked on silent feet into the kitchen and pulled out a cleaver, made sharp by the constant ministrations of the house girl at the whetting stone, and went back to her children, singing quietly under her breath.

DEVIL

by Glen Hirshberg

All the way back to the Conservancy Centre, Tim kept the van windows cracked open despite the cold and the drumming rain. "So you can hear," he told the Americans in the back, and watched them all—father, mother, kids—swivel to the nearest windows to stare hard into the Tasmanian dark. Already, Tim knew, they were reframing those moments even as they relived them. Embalming and enshrining them. Turning them into stories.

From the passenger seat, Mika caught his eye, wrapped her arms tight to herself. Didn't wink, might as well have. At the end of tour-days like this, when they'd actually glimpsed one back there in the bush, when the woods seethed with weather and all that life they hid, and the tourists who'd hired them were interested and ready to be wowed, Mika was practically a walking wink.

Except . . . how many tour-days like this had there been, lately? When was the last time they'd even spotted a devil in the wild? Let alone one with whatever it had just devoured still dripping from its jaws?

Was it just the devil sighting that had created those last moments? That sense of the woods shifting around them, tricking them, turning into other woods, so that the third time the teenaged boy asked Mika if she was positive this was the way they'd come—which, sure, was mostly just an excuse for him to talk and walk next to Mika some more—even Tim had found himself holding his breath. Awaiting her answer.

Which had turned out to be a laugh. Possibly even a nervous one. Instead of "Yes."

Which had led him to increase their pace, more than he'd realized. So that at the end—the path clearly their path, now, the van not quite visible but less than a hundred meters away—at the exact moment son, then daughter, then mom and dad had all started sprinting, Tim had barely had to speed up. He'd watched them run, flinging glances over their shoulders like spent rocket fuel, watched Mika charging in front of him, watched her glance back, felt himself do it, saw trees and shrubs surging in the whistling wind and whipping rain, and further back, up on the hill, the taller trees tipping almost all the way over as if crouching to take wing, as if the whole forest was about to lift off and flee, or else swoop down and take them. When he'd dropped the keys trying to click the van open, lost and then fumbled for them momentarily in the underbrush, even Mika had wheeled on him, snapping, "Oh, beauty, Tim, come on!" before grabbing the family's gear to hurl it into the back.

Actual wild moments. His wildest in years.

For Mika, too. He'd seen it in her face, though he knew her well enough to suspect she was already in the process of reclassifying. Denying.

"Sssh," she whispered now to the tourists. To the boy who whipped his head around to her. "Listen."

Recognizing his cue, Tim slid the Fabulous Diamonds CD into the deck. The music would of course drown out any actual forest sounds that the van motor didn't. And yet. Played way down low, these tracks perfectly accentuated these nights. Rumbled and rolled like the road beneath them, amplified. Gave a beat to the rattling rain. Transformed the sighing wind caught in the window openings into black kites, keening.

Most nights, he played this music to sustain the Tassie-ness of the day for the tourists. But tonight, it was also weirdly comforting. It settled and slowed his heart.

Still shuddering, the boy glanced from the window to Mika and back, gape-mouthed as a five-year-old.

She's not even pretty, Tim marveled for the thousandth time, and for once, he was absolutely sure this wasn't just their year-old breakup talking. Coiled there with her knees to her chest and her muddy boots caking new layers of sludge atop the caked sludge on her seat, wet-dirt hair whipping around and across her round, freckled face, she really did look like some sort of dwarf pine, stumpy and solid, the laughter erupting from somewhere way down inside her like birdsong. As though Mika wasn't her body at all, but a wild thing nested in it.

"Should we?" she stage-whispered, to Tim.

Tired, he was about to say, swerving suddenly as a wallaby materialized just ahead, eyes glinting in the headlights. He stayed on the wrong side of the road to avoid the already-dead thing humped a few hundred feet further ahead, body curled neatly in on itself like raked leaves. Possum, possibly. By the time he remembered Mika's question, he'd missed his moment.

"When we get back," she was already saying. Addressing the parents, hardly even glancing at the boy. Having herself a grand Mika time doing that. "You want to come along to the Den? Join us for a beer and a slice? To celebrate?"

"Slice of what?" the mother asked, and Tim smiled to himself.

"Slice. It's like cake."

"Damn right!" the boy said immediately. But not as fast as his mother, who clapped her hands and thanked them.

Which made Tim like this whole group all over again. Mika, too, and why not? They'd gotten along all week. They had a proper Roaring Forties windstorm blasting and juddering around them outside the van, the Fabulous Diamonds on the CD player, a night alive with eyes and rain. And they'd seen a free-roaming devil, bloody-mouthed and scurrying half up a tree before turning its face on them: ears pricked, deceptive teddy-bear eyes wide. No tumors ballooning from its cheeks. Cuddle-thing cute in the second before it yawned, opened those still-healthy jaws and went on opening, the teeth seemingly studded all the way down its throat like piercings, like the teeth of the trees themselves, and they'd all shivered in place, held still. Not one of them even saw for sure where it went, whether up or around back or down into the ground or the brush. Which meant they'd gotten not only an actual devil sighting but that delicious before-we-had-brains dread of being stalked.

Which, Tim thought, was almost certainly what the devil had experienced, too. Startled surprise. Then dread.

Do devils dread?

One thing was certain: he himself apparently still did. And that was *before* they'd all lit out running for the van.

A night worth celebrating, for sure, now they were safely out of it.

"How about a game 'til we get there?" Tim heard himself say, and caught Mika's surprised grin out of the corner of his eye. Sexiest thing about her. Rare as a devil sighting when they were alone, now. Which was almost never, anyway.

"You know the license plate game?" Mika asked the family, falling right into their old rhythm.

"Don't you need other cars for that?" murmured the dad from the back.

It was, Tim realized, the first sentence the guy had spoken since they'd returned to the van. He'd spent the whole ride staring into the dark. Taking it in. Settling his nerves. Or stealing some rare family vacation musing time. Either way, Tim liked him. Good family, this.

"Right, mate. This one's the Tassie version." Automatically, he swerved again to avoid the next carcass on the asphalt ahead. It always unnerved him, the way wallabies seemingly stretched out as they got hit, or in the split second before they got hit. As though prostrating themselves. In the road, when they were dead, their corpses looked laid out like meat on a table. Ready for carving.

Mika explained the rules. One point per roadkill spotted.

"High-scoring game," the dad murmured.

Which meant he really had been paying attention. Tim nodded even though he didn't think the guy could see him. "There's still a lot of life out here."

"Dead life."

"Same thing."

"Annnd he's back. Have-a-Whinge Tim," Mika chirped, then stuck out her tongue in the old, pre-breakup way. The way where she still liked him. Where he still liked himself with her.

Apparently, both things held true tonight. Devil-magic. Post-dread comradeship.

"*Two* points if you spot something alive in time for Tim to avoid it."

"Extra points if you can name the species," said Tim, swerving for fun, and the mom and son yelped, and the daughter grinned, and the dad caught his eye in the rearview. Shared a dad moment with him, even if Tim wasn't one. Which felt nice. "Possum's worth one point. Wallabies are two."

"Birds three," Mika said, primarily so the son back there could say, *Birds?*, which he promptly did. "Lot of birds out here, mate."

"What about a devil?" the mom asked abruptly. Apprehensively. In a way that suggested she understood just how awful and stupid that would be, given the whole island's—the whole nation's—conservation efforts, the attempts to wall off and save this last, wild remnant from the face cancer devouring the entire species.

Tim nodded appreciation at her. "Negative points. Happens a lot, unfortunately. They're carrion eaters first, remember. This highway's like a hundred-kilometer buffet table for a devil."

Another swerve, real this time, the wallaby already dead but still unfurling into its legs-outstretched corpse pose, as though the accident had just happened even though Tim hadn't seen a single other vehicle coming or going since returning to the van. As though whatever had hit it had fallen on it with the rain.

"Platypus, ten," said Mika, and both parents started guffawing, then stopped when Mika just stared at them. "Think I'm kidding? Am I kidding, Tim?"

"Sadly not. After rains like this, lots of times, they come right up out of the creeks."

There was a silence. The glorious Tassie kind, wind howling and rain drumming and the Diamonds churning and melting in the speakers like magma. Then the daughter yelled, "Wallaby!" and Tim swerved, and Mika awarded her two points and held out her hand for a down-low slap.

A long time later—they were almost back, the ground rising as the trees fell away, the space between dead things elongating as the numbers of invisible

live things out there declined—the boy stirred in the back. He'd been obliterated by his sister in the game, and Tim had taken his silence for sullenness.
But the wonder (and at least a little of the fear) was still in his voice when he
spoke, and he kept straining against his seat belt to get a last look back the way
they'd come. There was something endearing, childlike about the way he did
that. Tim half-expected him to wave.

"What about people?" he asked.

"People?" The sister settled back in her seat, regal in triumph. "Mom, he's
doing the babbling thing."

"Do people ever get hit out here? It's so dark."

To his own surprise, Tim felt himself grin. He modulated his voice, slowed
his cadence. Even to himself, he sounded uncannily like the Old Damper
from the Den. Mika had always teased that Tim would one day become the
Damper. Assume his mantle, live out his days camped in a folding chair in
that room's back corner, waiting for tour groups to come in from the brush
so he could tell them stories. Right then, in the van, there seemed worse fates.
"Do people get hit? Na, mate. People just disappear."

There it was again, the shared dad-thing glance with the father. The
mother laughing, the kids, too. He half-turned to Mika for the wink he'd
surely earned.

But Mika had her lips pursed, her gaze in the sideview mirror, aimed behind them. Back the way they'd come. After a hesitation so slight it might not
even have been one, she shrugged.

Five minutes later, the streetlamps surrounding the low cement buildings
of the Conservancy Visitor Centre swam up in the windshield, bleary and
flickering, as though projected from an old Super 8. For the first time in ages,
Tim felt a twinge of disappointment. Like when he'd just been ordered out
of his childhood community pool in Brisbane so the adults could swim laps.
Playtime over.

Because the wild really had been wild, today. And they'd seen a devil, for
the first time in almost a year.

"Could you all check to make sure any headlamps or thermoses or gear we
lent you gets stored with the rest in the back?" he asked as he parked next to
the Conservancy's three other vans in the corner of the lot. "Mika will check
you out. Then we'll lead you around back to the Den."

"For your secret celebration slice," Mika said, and *now* she winked, not at
Tim but at the poor kid back there. Her freckles seemed to blaze from her face
like little meteors.

Quite a night this kid was having.

The rain hadn't lightened, but the wind slackened at least temporarily. The
family all danced and shivered beside the van as backpacks and ponchos got

sorted and checkout forms signed, but neither Mika nor Tim so much as bothered wiping wetness out of their eyes. Point of pride, and also habit. Weather like this barely qualified as storm, here. Rolled through and down them as though they were trees.

"Right." Slamming the back door shut, Tim gestured around the side of the visitor centre. "Denward."

They were maybe three steps from the van when the shriek erupted.

It poured down from the hillsides beyond the buildings, but also bubbled up from the tarmac, the echo almost preceding the sound, the whole thing curling over itself like a wave breaking. It just kept coming, too. In the end, it didn't so much die as shut itself off like a kettle removed from heat. Or a hawk having struck.

"*What?*" the father hissed, frozen mid-step the way they all were, and hunched, too. As though hunted. About to be. Tim thought again of that unfurling wallaby in the road they'd just traversed.

Even Mika looked right at him. Mouthed, *Wow*.

Mother and daughter had thrown their arms around each other, but now the daughter shook free, raked rain out of her hair as she stared past the centre into the dark beyond it. "You have the most amazing birds here."

Mika's answer was immediate, dictated by the tone of this whole day, the nature of this specific guided group. Plus the fact that she was Mika.

"We do." Beat. "But that wasn't one of them."

"*Drop bear!*" the son shouted, and his sister shoved him.

"Not real."

Even as he waved everyone forward, Tim had to give the whole family credit, again. Not a single one of them had hunched into their jackets or whined about cold or wetness. The parents, in particular, were clinging to this night. Imprinting all of it—devil, Roaring Forties, Fabulous Diamonds, Tassie dark, terrifying mystery shriek, their children, everything but Tim and Mika—into memory.

"Now, think," Mika was teasing. Flirting. Though even she kept stealing glances toward the hills. "Why would a drop bear make that sound?"

"To claim territory," the boy said immediately. "Alert anything and everything about who's boss."

"Thereby defeating the whole purpose of being a drop bear, yeah? Lot easier to drop out of a tree onto someone's back if they never know you're there."

By now, they'd reached the overhang, and the sister's laughter reverberated down the paved breezeway between concrete buildings. Tim gestured toward the restrooms, and all four family members broke off, leaving him and Mika alone for just a moment under the tin roof, in the drumming rain, looking at each other through the shadowy dark. Which was how they had always seen each other. Would always. It was the way *they* were imprinted.

"They're cute," he said, gesturing toward the laughter echoing out of the restrooms.

To his surprise, Mika reached up and brushed a wet curl off his forehead. "You, too. Sometimes."

"You three," he murmured.

"Hey, Tim?" She glanced down the breezeway, out the opening at the far end toward the back lot. "What *was* that?"

The family returned. The sister cut in front of the boy, marched right up to Tim. "Please tell him, once and for all, there's no such thing as a drop bear."

Pressing his lips together, Tim shrugged. "Do not mock the drop. But . . . hey, what's that on your shoulder?" Lunging past the sister, he made a furious sweep at the son's jacket. The kid flinched, stumbled back.

"That's not funny," he snapped, while his sister laughed.

"Not laughing, mate. Never mind drop bears. We have spiders here that could chew your arm right off."

Mika joined in immediately. "Octopi as small as your palm that can shut down your whole neuro-system with one sucker-touch." She stuck out a finger, and the daughter ducked back.

"Let us not neglect the poor, hounded Tasmanian devil," Tim said, leading them down the breezeway. "Which, as we informed you before, literally devours entire corpses, of any kind, the second it finds them. Hair, bones, teeth, cellphones, pocket watches, you name it. And it does so in a frenzy so violent that if there are two of them doing it, they will bite *through each other's faces* and just keep right on eating. Which, poor cute devils, is part of the reason we are having so much trouble containing the disease that may literally exterminate them. They're not model quarantine citizens."

As if on cue, the wind kicked up, plastering their wet clothes against their already-soaked skins. Even Tim and Mika shivered, wrapped their arms to their chests and moved more quickly toward the Den.

"They'd really eat a cellphone?" the dad murmured.

"In a heartbeat. Without a thought, if they have thoughts."

"What if they break their teeth?"

"Wouldn't even slow them down."

"Then there's the giant carnivorous snail," Mika said, and they rounded the corner around back of the centre, which got them out of the worst of the wind but set the resurgent rain raking over them.

"Okay," laughed the mother, huddling into her son, "I'm calling drop bear on giant carnivorous snails."

"I'm calling stupid," said the boy, and Mika waggled a finger at him.

"You'd be wrong. They're not *so* giant, I admit, and you actually find them on the mainland. But they *are* carnivorous. You should never, ever doubt. Not in Australia. Especially not on Tassie."

"Except about drop bears," the sister mumbled.

The door to the Den had no peephole, no handle or knob, just a bolt lock that didn't actually have a bolt in it as far as Tim knew. Not one anybody used, anyway. Even as he pushed open the door and stood aside to shepherd everyone in, he marveled again at the effect this place had on him. On everyone. In his mind, the place had a hazy, smoky, firelit glow; in reality, there was no fireplace, not even any light fixtures, just bare bulbs in a straight track down the center of the low ceiling. No posters, no wallpaper. Concrete walls, a few scattered circular white plastic tables with a handful of folding chairs circulating amongst them as trail groups or group leaders came in, pumped themselves with cups of reheated coffee or homemade pumpkin soup from the thermoses on the craft services table, grabbed a slice from under the cling-wrap on the tray Swannie or his ma always dropped off in the morning. Mostly caramel, those slices, though sometimes chocolate mint. Rarely any variations beyond those. The place was really more airplane hangar than pub or even break room. A people-garage.

"Hey," the mother said as she passed Tim. Her family was already across the room, accepting plastic cups and spoons as Mika doled them out, the dad elbowing his son aside and laughing as he unwrapped the slice tray and grabbed a paper plate. She gestured toward the back wall, but Tim knew she was really thinking about the hills out there. The whistling downpour. Same as him. "Do you know what kind of bird that was? For real?"

"Are you joking?" said the Damper from his corner, and both Tim and the mom startled, whirled around.

There he sat where he always sat when he was here. Which hadn't been so often, lately. He'd been sick, word had it. Sick*er*. The gravel in his voice box running riot down his throat, through his glands.

He also looked genuinely surprised to see them. Alarmed, almost. He cleared his throat, and his too-prominent Adam's apple bobbed under his thin skin like something he'd just swallowed.

"You weren't really out there, Tim?"

The question surprised him. "It's just rain, Damper."

"You didn't have *them* out there?"

"You appear to be out here."

"I'm *in here*. For the company."

Glancing around the room, just to make sure he hadn't missed something as they entered, Tim nodded. Felt a ping of free-floating sadness. "The joint is jumpin'."

Judging by the crumb-strewn plates in front of him, the Damper was well into slice number three. His Dodges Ferry football jumper looked ridiculous on him, at least three sizes too big, the giant red shark logo seemingly just burst from his ribs. The beanie on his head was even more ridiculous, its fire-red cross logo tilted and glowing over his left eye, as though he'd just been branded.

"Jesus, Damper. Who bought *you* a Dark Mofo hat?"

The Damper was still staring at him out of those perpetually leaking, yellowy eyes. Cat eyes. Finally, he shrugged. "Everyone on the booking committee got one."

Never failed. Tim felt his jaw unhinge. Half drop, half slip sideways in the direction of grinning. "*You* were on the Dark Mofo booking committee."

From across the room, Mika burst into laughter. "Surprised, Tim? You know a darker mofo? Excluding your own fine self, of course."

"What's a dark mofo?" the sister asked, and the dad started to shush her, and Tim waved him off.

"It's a . . . actually, it's kind of hard to describe. An arts and music festival."

"But dark," Mika added.

"Like . . . death metal?"

"Yeah. No. Sometimes. It's a Tassie thing. In a kind of . . . new-old way. Pagan. Performance art. There's *some* death metal, most years. Also really, really good food. And some . . ." Finally, Tim gave up. Ceded the Damper the drop-mouthed grin he apparently craved. "Ask him. He apparently books it."

"Ask me anything you like," said the Damper. "Just be sure you want to know."

The Damper was not grinning. Mostly, he was still staring at Tim. The pallor of his cheeks was probably illness. The shake of the head might have been tremors.

Does the Damper have tremors?

If he did, Tim had never noticed them. Given how many nights they'd spent together in the past three years, it was amazing how little Tim knew about the Damper, except that he came here ridiculously often, as though the Den were an actual pub. Soup and coffee and slices poured down him. Words spilled from him. As though he were a record player, almost. Console radio. Thing in the corner that you switched on, settled near, and listened to. Not always for comfort, just because it was there.

That's how they all treated him, Tim realized. And now here was his own sadness again.

And *still*, the Damper was staring at Tim.

It was the son, surprisingly, who skipped them past the moment they'd apparently gotten stuck in. Not only set down a plate and cup for himself but brought one of each, unasked, to the Damper. For the first time, the old man seemed to notice him. He nodded at the kid in what Tim first thought was thanks, then snapped, "Hear it?"

The kid glanced toward his mom, then Tim. Then the ceiling. "The rain?"

Lifting the cup the kid had brought him, the Damper poured liquid down his throat. Greasing the gears.

Here it comes, Tim thought.

The kid retreated to another table a good ten feet away, out in the middle of the room. One without even chairs, he had to go get one. He even brought one for his sister, which Tim suspected meant the Damper had gotten to him, too. Once his sister was there, though, he kept his eyes glued to the old man.

"You mean that screech? The one from a few minutes ago?"

Easing the Dark Mofo cap up his skull, the Damper revealed his single, protruding bat-ear. The one on the right. The left one wasn't there anymore. If the Damper had a story about where he'd lost that, he'd yet to tell it to Tim.

"Heard of the Dish?" he said.

From the tray table where she was still filling cups of soup, Mika laughed. Both kid and Damper ignored her. "What's the Dish?"

"Big satellite antenna," Tim said. "For listening to space."

The Damper tapped his one good ear. Possibly, he was grinning, now.

Even so, Tim found himself listening harder to the room. The barrage of banging overhead as rain pummeled the roof, which had all of them automatically raising their voices. He gazed around the bare, concrete walls. Loud as it had been, Tim was surprised the Damper *had* heard the screech. Caw. Whatever it was.

Mika appeared at his side, handed him a soup cup. "The Damper has mad skills," she said. It wasn't clear to whom.

The old man turned his leaky cat-eyes on her. Stared the grin off her face. "Like listening? Like respect for where you are? Like common sense?"

She opened her mouth, either to laugh or answer. Which is why, for one insane second, Tim thought the new shriek exploded from *her.*

Then they were all—the Damper, too—ducking, flinging glances up at the ceiling, around the walls as sound reverberated everywhere. Actually, it *wasn't* reverberating, Tim realized, there wasn't any echo in here, nothing to bounce off or from, so all this raging, blaring smoke-alarm shriek was *the sound itself,* happening now, which made it even crazier, drove all other thoughts but reaction out of his head except for the impossible idea that if anything, it was *louder* in here.

As if it were in here with them.

Then it wasn't. It also wasn't anywhere else. No echo or reverberation. No sound anywhere except rain.

"When you were out there today," the Damper said immediately, hand sliding off his ear to pull down his cap as he settled back in his chair. He grabbed up his coffee and blew on it. "Did you come across any tracks?"

Everybody else still had their hands near their heads, their shoulders hunched. It took them a few seconds to uncoil. To trust that the noise had shut off. Stopped.

Tracks? Tim thought, right as the dad said it.

"Tracks?"

"Railroad tracks."

Obviously. Tim shook his head at himself. "On the way to the cave," he said, then had to say it again to be heard. Mika was standing right next to him, but not leaning in. Not in their usual, comfortable way, even post-breakup. He gulped some soup, which was miraculously hot, as always. Thick pumpkin taste coated his mouth. "Remember the signs?"

"Crossing Not in Use," the daughter said immediately.

"Observant one, you are," said Tim. "Good on you."

"Flirt," Mika murmured.

"Not those tracks," said the Damper, and just like that, he had them, the way he always did, sooner or later. There was nothing for it, even if they'd wanted there to be. Unfolding a chair, Tim started to offer it to Mika. But she'd already grabbed her own. They sat.

The Damper didn't look at any of them, but into the air over their heads. As though consulting winds. Conjuring not just memories or visions but the crystal ball to contain them.

Or else just scanning.

"The tracks I mean . . . these two, they know . . ." He waved a hand toward Tim and Mika. "These tracks haven't been in use for almost fifty years."

For a second, Tim wasn't sure he *did* know. Then Mika said, "Oh. Those." Quietly.

And Tim realized he did. He watched his former lover cradle her soup. If either of her hands had been free, he might have given it a squeeze. Which was probably why she kept them around the cup. So he addressed the Damper instead.

"We didn't get that far back. Or up. We're not totally insane. We didn't even need to, believe it or not, we actually saw—"

"So you're not complete drongos, then," said the Damper.

The family members, of course, were spellbound, in exactly the way they'd hoped to be when booking this day. All four of them watched the old man and said nothing.

"Laid more than a century ago, the tracks I have in mind." The Damper took a forkful of slice, shoveled it into his mouth. Went right on talking.

"Narrow-gauge. For the gold rush, such as it was. There wasn't so much actual rush in this corner of Tassie. But then there was the logging. The mines that popped up, operating way back in those woods, up on those craggy hillsides. Not for long, not any of them. Not there."

Pausing abruptly, he aimed another long glance at the back wall of the Den. Eventually, he inclined his head as though genuflecting. Or acknowledging dominance. Both.

"Those places," he said. Slice crumbs flecked his lips and cheeks. "After a while. They . . . reject incursion. Hmm."

"Gilding the lily a bit, Damper," Tim muttered, meaning to tease, but even as he said it, he heard how he'd somehow fallen into rhythm. Filled his preordained slot in the Damper's call-and-response spellcasting.

The old man mopped at his face with a napkin and somehow managed not to dislodge a single crumb. "Doesn't make it less true. It's a marvel, honestly—a testament—that those men even got those tracks laid. On inclines that steep." He made a near-ninety-degree slope with his hand. "Through rocks rooted in place, strangled in roots, immovable except when they all decide to move at once. Just drop down and obliterate everything. Not to mention the storms up there. The ones that seem to rise straight up out of the mountainside, like a tsunami of snow and ice, except sometimes the snow and ice aren't even *visible*. They're just on that wind. *In* that wind. They bury men right where they die, right there in the open. Killed by nothing. By nothingness. That's a real Tassie storm for you."

"Lily," Mika said. On her cue, Tim thought. He wondered if she realized it, too. "Gilding."

"And the *wildlife*," said the Damper, sliding suddenly forward, waving his hands and spreading them wide. "So much wildlife, we can't even imagine it, now. Or *you* can't. You have to have seen it."

"We saw all the roadkill," the mother said.

"I saw the most," said the daughter, and the Damper snorted.

"Roadkill. Now imagine before there was road, girl. Back then, in those woods, on those hills, at night, there was so much movement, it was like the planet was blowing bubbles. Wombats and kangaroos springing from a forest of their own shadows. Tree trunks crawling with so many snails and frogs and possums and squirrels that their bark seemed made of 'em. Everything, everywhere, jumping, foraging, *moving*. Fleeing."

"Fleeing what?" the father half-whispered.

The Damper spread his lips. Maybe he thought he was grinning. Teeth full of cake crumbs. What teeth there were. "Just so. Ask ten men who worked up there then—assuming you could find ten anymore, and assuming they'd talk to you—and you'd get ten different answers. I've heard people mention foxes fast as cheetahs, big as bears. Actual bears, as big as pine trees. I've heard wolves."

"Drop bears?" the kid piped up, and the Damper slammed that gaze down on him. Shut him up tight.

"But *officially* . . ." The old man waved a dismissive hand, not at the back wall this time, but toward the door. In the general direction, Tim knew, of Hobart, but also the rest of Australia. Civilization, period. "We don't have foxes here. Or wolves. Or bears." He did his spread-lips thing at the kid. "Drop or otherwise. Now, three of my grandfather's bunkmates, they came back from the woods one night swearing they'd seen a pack of thylacines tearing a screaming pademelon in half. Did you know pademelons can scream?"

After a few seconds, the mother whispered, "Which ones are the pademelons?"

"Like wallabies," Tim murmured, at the exact moment the daughter asked, "Is that what we heard?"

In response, Tim expected a full-force Damper glare. Instead, the old man laughed. At least, Tim had always assumed that was his laugh. Tonight, especially, it was closer to smoker's cough. Mostly scrape.

The son bobbed again on his seat. "Thylacine. Tasmanian tiger!"

"Just to be clear," said Mika, leaning back toward the wall, and for one startled, sweet moment, Tim thought she might do as she used to. Grab his hand with her warm, wet one and anchor him. "In the interests of science. The last thylacine died in a zoo on the mainland almost a hundred years ago."

"Herbert Murphy," said the Damper, turning his gaze on her, and whatever Mika was about to do with her hand, she stopped.

"What about him?"

"He had them on his cabin roof. Not five years ago. A month before he died." Into the Damper's mouth went a last shovelful of slice. The mouth chewed.

Bullshit, Mika didn't say.

So Tim said it for her. But the Damper ignored him. Ignored them all, really.

"Mostly, though, there were devils." Picking up his coffee, he held it to his mouth for a punctuation sip. But he never drank, didn't even blow, just left it there. He stayed that way a long time, staring at the back wall as though looking out a window, until the boy got restless. Or just excited.

"How many devils?"

"Oh," said the Damper. Steam rose from his cup, subtly distorting his face. The Den equivalent of a flashlight held under a chin. "So many, son. Like the bushes had mouths. Creatures would just fall into them, there'd be a clamor and snarling—you heard that snarl? Like a pig with a lion in its throat—and then that creature wouldn't be there anymore. Would be gone."

"Once again, for clarity," Tim said, "he means creatures that were already dead. Devils are scavengers, remember."

"Mostly," said the Damper.

Tim started to nod, caught a glimpse of Mika's face. Still weirdly hooded, frozen somewhere between smile and something very much else. The Damper noticed, too.

"Not that that was much comfort if you worked out there. Lived out there. To have your dog, say, just vanish one day, so completely that you never even found its bones . . . as if it had never been alive at all . . . They had to build fences to bury their dead. Otherwise, within days . . ." His fingers popped open. "Poof. Erased. That's the world we all decided we should strip. Plunder. And we succeeded. For a while. Those narrow-gauge tracks you didn't quite see? They're the fossilized remains of a whole human network. A monument to endeavor. For a few decades, we went up into those mountains and came down from the crags and ravines with logs, tin, zinc, silver, a little gold. It was like the whole region was a storehouse to raid. Ours for the taking. That's the world I grew up in. The cabin where I lived. People think of it as silent, now. Remote and barren as Mars. I still think of it as the loudest, most *living* place I've ever been.

"And then, the summer I turned eleven . . ."

Right in the pause, before the Damper said the words, Tim realized what the shriek—the one that triggered tonight's performance—really had sounded like. Sounded *exactly* like.

"That train," Mika said. As though reading his thoughts.

The Damper nodded. "The first one? The Wee Pandani? It was hardly even a train." Pushing his plate and cup away, he sat back, folded his arms. The movement looked mechanical and jerky, as though the guy was animatronic. "Those tracks. They could bear more than you think, but not much. Not what you have in your head as a freight train. Mostly, they were for getting crews and supplies up and down. Surprisingly sturdy, though. They'd been using that line since before the turn of the century. Through blizzards, Roaring Forties, hail so hard it punched holes in tin roofs. Up and down those slopes. There were stoppages every now and then, sure. A few derailments, nothing spectacular. Not one person dead, though. Not from the railways. Not one."

All four family members were leaning toward or into each other. The dad flashed a look at the mom. Amazed. Grateful. A family that understood their luck. The night they'd been gifted. Tim saw this, wished Mika would at least turn toward him. Then she did. Cup in hand, held at her waist. Face blank as the Damper's.

"Now, the Wee Pandani. It was just an engine and a passenger car. The passenger car empty, at least that night. Just an engineer and a stoker, making their way down to bring people back up. There was no storm. Bright moon. Nothing like this night."

"You tell it like you saw it," Mika snapped abruptly.

The comment seemed ridiculous to Tim, and also surprising. Of course the Damper told it that way. Secret of his magic.

So why accuse him of it now?

"No, no." The Damper didn't look at her. And yet, Tim had the uncanny sense that he was talking to her, alone. "No, I didn't see it. But the boys who did—out hunting late, when they shouldn't have been—they all told the same tale. Said they saw the Wee Pandani wind its way down the mountainside, as normal. Every now and then setting off its whistle, like it was waving."

Pursing his lips, taking a long, bumpy breath, the Damper unleashed a hoot. It came from the back of his throat, equal parts hum and hiss, as though he couldn't quite hold the tone or get it to catch.

Except that that was *exactly* what those trains sounded like. Tim had heard them in museums. Had even let Mika take him on one of those Christmas summer holiday excursions once.

The tourists had no basis for evaluation. But right as the Damper's sound gave way—seemingly melting into an echo that wasn't actually there, then splintering in the pounding rain—the father clapped. The mother, too.

The Damper didn't so much as lower his gaze. "The boys all said they saw the Pandani drop into those myrtle woods, nice and slow, just as it was meant to. Threading between the gorges and ravines the way it had a hundred times before.

"But it never came out. Never arrived in Hobart. Was never seen—by anyone—ever again."

As on so many other Damper nights, Tim felt simultaneous twinges of annoyance and comfort. This was the way the old man's stories always ended. Campfire-disappointing and strangely satisfying all at once.

Except tonight, the old man was still glaring right at him. As if this was less a tale than a prosecution.

"What?" Tim finally said.

"Did any of you even search?" Mika snapped. She, too, sounded angrier than the moment seemed to warrant.

Tim could almost hear those old lips stretch, like a seam popping open. "Search. Meaning what, exactly? Did we outfit mountaineering expeditions and rappel down cliff-faces, take our machetes, and hack to the bottom of those chasms—assuming they have bottoms—in the hopes of finding bodies? Wreckage? We did not. You want the cold, awful truth? What had we lost? Two cars. An engineer and a stoker. Tragic. Less loss than an average logging week in those woods, though, to be honest. At least in winter. In storm. Hardly worth the effort."

Again, the old man glanced toward the back wall. "Not like the second one."

Tim folded his arms across his chest, then felt ridiculous. What, exactly, did he need to defend? And from whom?

The Damper saw, though. Drilled those eyes into him.

"This was eleven years later. I wasn't even on the mountain by then. I was on the mainland. So all I know is what other people say they know. This train—the second—had a crew of miners on it, heading down for the summer holidays. Its engineer was old Levingston, the longest serving on all of Tassie. Half Aboriginal, with railroad ties for bones. Capable of blowing coal to life with his breath. So they say.

"That train was last heard just above Russell Gap, blowing whistles to the midmorning sunlight and the wheeling birds. There's barely even a curve there. Plenty of gorges, mind. Rivers emptying down falls into pools so deep, no one's ever plumbed them, or bothered trying. Until then. So, theories abound. Anything *could* have happened. But if you're asking—and yes, young Daughter of the Hills, I see you are—what actually *did* . . ."

"Goddamnit," Mika muttered, starting forward again as though she might . . . Tim didn't even know what. Throw coffee at the Damper? Burst out laughing, turn, and bow?

The parents shared another look. Gratitude. Self-congratulation. Amazement at being together backstage at the factory where memories get imprinted. Holding hands while rain drummed. If the shriek had gone off again, Tim would have been sure he really *was* in a play, or a dream. Something the Damper had magicked up, for his birthday party, maybe.

Except that now the Damper was glaring at Mika some more. "So you know. You knew it happened right around this time. You knew there was a storm coming. And yet, out you went."

"Is that why they stopped using those tracks?" the son asked, oblivious.

Another few seconds passed before the Damper returned his attention to him. "Oh no, son. That wasn't until the third one. The last one."

"That's enough," said Mika. So quietly that Tim was sure only he heard it. He stepped forward, touched her elbow, but she edged away.

Guilt whisked through him. About what, he had no idea. Regret, too. For this relationship that had almost worked. For this whole island world he'd decided on a whim to come to after uni, and discovered he loved. Even imagined himself part of.

Which seemed ridiculous, suddenly.

He watched the Damper. Ensconced in his chair, the old man seemed almost to emanate light, as though he were a projector. This whole place his movie. Shadows—or the ghosts of shadows, there being nothing in here actually to cast any—leapt around him. Ghost-wallabies of the air.

"This was long after most of the mines had closed. The logging camps packed up or just abandoned. The effort-to-yield ratio had grown too great decades before. So, no, son, none of this has anything to do with why those tracks stopped being used. It doesn't have anything to do with anything. Except to the people who were on the train. And the people who still live here and care for their memory." Once again, the rheumy gaze swung to Mika. Taloned as a bird, threatening to sweep her away.

The Americans noticed nothing. They were too wrapped up in the story they were already telling themselves about the night they heard this story.

"Let's go," Tim whispered to Mika. "We don't have to stay. We've done our jobs."

"*You* go," she hissed back.

"Sightseers, this was," the Damper said. "Like yourselves."

Meaning not just the Americans, of course. Even Tim felt a *fuck you* bubbling up, and not just in Mika's defense. But saying it would have been like cursing a cliff or a fogbank.

"A holiday excursion train. One car. Mostly mainland tourists, but some so-called locals, too. Ho-BART-ians. Out for a romantic weekend jaunt.

"This was so long after that second disappearance, almost no one even remembered it. Why would they? It had involved no one they knew. Twenty-six tourists. On a bright sunny day, at least down here. Up there . . . they say there were clouds, although I don't really know who 'they' are, since no one saw it happen. They say there might have been a freak mountain storm. One of the rare kind that boils up on those hillsides even in midsummer, like this one here tonight, except worse. Wind everywhere. Ice and snow flying around like the whole world is chipping apart.

"They made the top. Up above Russell Gap. Afterward, a surveyor up there found a backpack one of the tourists had apparently forgotten, with a camera in it. Intact roll of pictures inside. All those happy people picnicking on the rocks. Whole families. Just like yours."

He grinned at the Americans. There was nothing kind in it, Tim knew. Nothing happy, or mean either. The facial-expression equivalent of wind.

"A carefree afternoon exploring old mining camps. Daring each other into the mouths of the mines themselves. Wandering in and out of abandoned sheds where actual people had lived. As if this were all an attraction. Set up just for them. And *their* tour guides. Tasmania. All those animals. The trees. The gorges. The birds. But there's one shot. It's on the wall behind the circulation desk down in the Hobart Library, along with all those other historical snaps no one ever looks at. A group of twelve or so people, just about to reboard the train, in a sloping field of tall, wild grass. The sky stone blue, completely clear overhead. But on both sides, ringing the mountain, those black clouds. Whipping whorls of ice. As if they're all about to light out into the mouth of a wormhole. Trailing the thylacine into wherever it went. By steam-gauge rail."

Once more, the Damper glanced toward Mika. Transfixed her. "Maybe you've seen such things," he said.

"Maybe I have," Mika answered. Her voice wavering. But not her answering glare.

"Hey," said the father, seemingly awakening from his trance, noting for the first time that there was some other story being told here. And it wasn't for them.

The Damper ignored him. Went right on. "Down they came. Into the maelstrom there must have been, given those clouds. Can you imagine? Actually, I think you can, given the night your intrepid guides chose to march you into. So there would have been wind sound. Maybe hail and rain, too. But also . . ."

Jerking with surprising speed to his feet, the Damper sucked in a deep, shuddering breath, rocking on his own legs like an engine clinging to tracks, and let loose.

He didn't quite get it right, Tim thought, even as he flung his hands over his ears. He couldn't come anywhere close to the volume, for one thing. But he *did* get overtones, somehow. Like one of those Tuvan throat singers. The top of his voice splitting into a shriek, the bottom all but disappearing into his throat and out the bottom of his feet into the floor, where Tim almost believed he could feel it. Half earthquake, half roar. The whole family startled back, collapsing toward each other.

Only Mika didn't move. Stood there staring. Tears streaming down her cheeks, as irrelevant to her as rain to rock.

The Damper did it again. Better. Louder. Still not quite right. Definitely closer.

Then he fell back into his seat. Almost tipped off it, clutched the table, and sat there heaving like an old man.

Like the old man he was.

There was a long pause. Not nearly enough of one.

Then the kids burst out laughing. "You're so good!" the sister said.

"That's what you're saying we heard?" said her brother. "The last running of the great Tasmanian ghost train?"

At Tim's side, Mika leaned in again. Held on as the Damper gasped for breath, glanced at the back wall, the roof still thrumming and bucking as the rain hammered down.

"I thought you told me they showed you a devil," the old man finally said.

"They did!"

"And they told you how it eats?"

"Bones, claws," the boy chirped. "Keys. Cellphones. Everything."

One last time, the Damper smiled. Flat, ferocious smile. While the forest they'd fled barely two hours ago rose up in Tim's memory. Surged around him. Everything—devils, pademelons, wallabies, trees—up and roiling, raging. Running.

"No, son. Not the ghost of a train," the Damper said. "The ghost of what that train was running *from*."

Then he folded deep into his chair, crossing his arms over his chest. He closed his eyes as his Dark Mofo cap slid forward. The record player clicking off, Tim thought. Console shutting down.

Which should have been comforting. Would have been, if he could have gotten the woods out of his head. That primal, overwhelming need to *get clear* of them.

Overhead, rain drummed, though the wind had slackened. No more howling. Just drumming.

The father was the first to stand. He seemed to be fumbling with his smile, trying to get it to catch. One of the kids—Tim couldn't tell which—murmured, "Thanks." Tim also wasn't sure whom the gratitude was for.

"Best walk them to their car," said the Damper, without opening his eyes.

But Tim was already up. Mika, too. Together, they shepherded their charges out of the Den and back down the breezeway to the parking lot. Free of that room, the old man's spell. The family was already chattering to each other. Laughing again. So they probably never even noticed Tim, then Mika, then both of them at once, glancing back at the hills they could no longer see. All those lives, animal and otherwise, marked and forgotten, predators and prey, tucked up for the night behind their curtain of rain.

CRICK CRACK RATTLE TAP

by A. C. Wise

The baby is hungry again.

The wail comes like tiny, scratching fingernails prying Kiersten's eyelids wide. She knocks her phone to the ground trying to grab it to read the time—12:47 A.M.—and once she sits up to retrieve it, there's no point crawling back under the covers, hoping the baby will stop.

It never will.

Because the baby is always hungry. Because Kiersten is never allowed to get a single fucking hour of uninterrupted sleep. Because she's a mother now, not an individual human being.

She fumbles on a robe. The wail continues, rising and falling in time with the storm, matching the wind until it suddenly drops out of synch. There's a moment of unnerving silence, followed by a series of pathetic, broken sobs. To her sleep-deprived brain, they sound fake, spiteful, like the baby is mocking her and proving it is in control.

Kiersten knows that babies cry. They get hungry and gassy and need to be changed. It's not their fault. But knowing this rationally, and feeling charitable toward the baby in this exact moment, are two different things.

Since Nick left—since she kicked him out—her life has been a blur of waking and sleeping in fits and starts. Exhaustion, her brain mush, time lurching forward, crawling, then rushing ahead again. She can't help the petty thoughts or the inappropriate anger bubbling up now and then.

It's only been three weeks since her maternity leave started. Already, her life before seems like something that happened to someone else. She holds in her head an idealized version of that time, so much so that she almost misses the faculty at the university seeing her as no more than administrative support, fit only to fetch and carry and fulfill their requests at a moment's notice. Not unlike the baby, but at least their requests came in the form of email rather than screaming her awake in the middle of the night.

Kiersten pushes open the nursery door.

Tick tick tick tick.

Ice pellets rattle against the glass. The baby snuffles, a miserable sound. Shadows the color of a darkening bruise cluster, seeming deeper where the night-light next to the crib has burned out. The wind sounds louder at this end of the house too, making a hollow wooing noise as it rounds the corners. She pulls her robe closer, and peers into the crib.

She can't help bracing herself every single time—expecting the baby blue and cold, strangled in its sleep, breath stopped. But it kicks chubby limbs, lungs healthy, mouth wide. As if cued by her presence, the baby ramps up its cry—a painful scream, the kind that leaves a throat raw.

Kiersten lets it go. Just for a moment. Just to prove she has some measure of control too.

And immediately, she feels cruel.

"I just fed you, didn't I?" She lifts the baby with a sigh. "Are you really already hungry again?"

The only answer is another piercing wail. She sets the baby against her shoulder and carries it downstairs. At least in the kitchen she's muffled from the wind, the storm duller and farther away.

Kiersten doesn't bother to turn on the lights. The act of heating bottles is second nature now; she could do it with her eyes closed. The shadows here are blue-gray, the kitchen floor chilly underfoot. She regrets leaving her slippers tucked under the bed. She just wants to get this over with and go back to sleep.

Kiersten yawns and brings the warmed bottle to the baby's lips. The baby responds by squirming, turning its head away, nearly wiggling itself right out of Kiersten's arms. The bottle is knocked from her hand, hitting the ground and splashing milk in an arc across the floor.

"What do you want, you little monster?" She clenches her teeth until her jaw aches.

The baby lets out another ice pick shriek. A frustrated whine bruises Kiersten's throat. She wants to shout *fuck you, fuck you, fuck you* in the baby's face. She wants to smash the baby's head against the counter as hard as she can.

And wanting those things, even for a brief, uncontrollable split second, makes her feel like the monster.

Tears overflow her lids. She snatches a dishrag from its hook, drops it over the spilled constellation of milk, but makes no further move to clean it up. She clutches the baby hard—Violet, her daughter's name is Violet, not *the baby*. She is a good mother, and she would never ever do anything to hurt her little girl.

Kiersten racks her brain for a soothing rhyme, a lullaby dredged from the achy spaces of her mind. She's so fucking tired. She just wants to sleep. A wave of dizziness, a sense of dislocation takes her. A door has opened somewhere and she is—

A baby girl in her crib, not yet two years old. A blanket, blue-gray and worn thin, is held aloft by a pair of hands. A woman stands behind the blanket, her dress visible below its hem. Her feet are bare. The hands drape the blanket over the unseen face, the unseen head. Mama? The woman-shape sways, shuffling her bare feet over the floor. She dances, and beneath the blanket, she sings.

"Crick crack, rattle tap, creaking through the storm." Kiersten's mouth opens, echoing the words, unwittingly carrying them forward from the past to the present as the kitchen snaps back into place. "Bones knit, you little shit, clicking all night long."

For a terrible moment, she's viciously proud of the stupid rhyme, and just as quickly, she's horrified. She claps a hand over her mouth.

Crick, crack, Rattle Tap, creeping through the storm. Sleep, sleep, Mama weeps, wishing you weren't born.

Kiersten bites down on the meat of her hand, digging her teeth into the ball of her thumb. The small pain helps center her; the hand crammed into her mouth keeps her from screaming. She breathes around the panic, desperately telling herself that children don't form memories that young. It's only a weird product of her sleep-deprived brain. A half-remembered nightmare, nothing real.

Surely Kiersten's mother never danced around her crib with a blanket draped over her head. She never sang a terrible lullaby, wishing for Kiersten to be taken away. And even if Kiersten repeated it unwittingly now, it's just a silly rhyme. It means nothing.

She focuses on the concrete weight of the baby in her arms. *Her* baby, she reminds herself, *Violet*, who peers up at her with watchful eyes. She's quiet now, and even though her face is red and blotchy from crying, her eyelids are starting to drift closed. How quickly babies forget trauma, hunger, pain, living entirely in the moment. When they want something, it is the only thing in the world, and then an instant later, it is forgotten.

But Kiersten's pulse still thumps, erratic and jittery, and she clutches Violet close, too tight, drawing an indignant squawk. She forces herself to relax her hold, carrying Violet back upstairs to the nursery door.

Click.

The sound freezes her in the hall. She left the nursery door open, didn't she? Now it's all but shut, with only a sliver of the room visible between the frame and the door. Kiersten shifts, not pressing her eye to the gap, but trying to see as much of the room as she can before stepping inside. There, in a slice of the room, stands a woman with a blanket draped over her head.

No.

No no no.

Instead of backing up, some impulse makes Kiersten shove the door open, angry. She breathes hard, but there's nothing there. The *tap tap tap* is only ice pellets hitting the glass. The *crick-crack* only branches outside bending in the wind.

If Nick was here . . .

No. If Nick was here, he'd make things worse. If he bothered to try to soothe her nerves, he'd do it in a way that condescended while pretending to be kind. He'd feign sleep when Violet cried, leaving Kiersten in the same position she's in now, dealing with the baby alone. Calling him on it would only lead to a hurt expression, the implication that him doing any share of parenting at all was already a favor to her, making her feel unreasonable, demanding.

Kiersten strides across the room and puts the baby back into the crib with an almost-forceful shove. She expects another cry, but the baby simply watches her with wide, solemn eyes.

"Go to sleep now." The words are a little harsher than she intends, and Kiersten hears an echo, a reply, even though her mouth is firmly closed.

Go to sleep, or Rattle Tap will get you.

A prickling, unsettled sensation crawls across her skin. The feeling of being watched. The feeling she isn't alone. Kiersten turns sharply on her heel. She can't stay in the baby's room a minute longer. In her uneasy, exhausted state, she's afraid of what she might do.

Her mama ran away when she was less than two years old. That's what her daddy said. She wasn't a good mama. She was a bad mama and she ran away during a storm.

As tired as she is, Kiersten finds herself sitting up in bed, blanket wrapped around her. The wind makes an anxious sound, sawing at her nerves. Less than two years old. All she has is her daddy's word as to what her mama was like. Kiersten doesn't remember her at all. She remembers—

Hands holding a blanket aloft. An unseen figure, swaying and singing.

She digs her hands into the sheets, twisting the fabric, an anchor to keep her here. The wind isn't only testing the boards of the house, it's testing her, trying to pry her loose. She's—

A little girl, five, nearly six years old, creeping down the hall in an exaggerated attempt to stay quiet. She wants a glass of water. She's thirsty, woken by the howling wind.

She finds another sound in the darkened kitchen, and it stops her in the door. A weird, rhythmic scraping, a hollow, metallic sound. It's a moment before the mass of shadow at the kitchen table resolves into her father, and she sees he's turning a beer can round and round against the table's wood.

"Can't sleep, baby girl? Did you have a bad dream?"

She shakes her head. Her throat is dry, but she's suddenly afraid to ask for the glass of water. Her daddy's voice is so strange.

"I had a bad dream," her daddy says. "I dreamt your mama came back."

The little girl's throat goes drier still. She wonders if she's still in bed, if she really is dreaming. Scrape, scrape, scrape goes the aluminum can.

"I dreamt your mama came back like a ghost, but we don't want that, do we, baby girl? She ran away on a night just like this one, because she was a bad mama. Lucky for you, I'm a good daddy. I'd do anything for my baby girl."

When he taps his cigarette, the ash scatters everywhere. A row of empty cans lines the edge of the table. He takes a long swallow of his beer, and sets the final can down with an empty click.

"Go on back to bed now," he says. "Scoot. Get."

The cry is an alarm-siren, a tornado-warning, an air-raid sound. It jerks Kiersten back to the reality of the baby and the storm and she almost falls scrambling out of bed. She only just sat down. She only just put Violet to sleep. What can the baby possibly want now?

She runs down the hall. And finds Violet with her tiny fingers curled into fists, one pressed against her rosebud mouth. Every line of her is soft, round, lax with sleep. Her eyelashes cast shadows on her cheeks, and she isn't making a sound.

Did she imagine the cry? Is she dreaming?

Tap tap tap.

Kiersten whirls to face the sound, and a flicker of motion catches her eye. A reflection in the nursery window. Dirty gray hair and a long, pale face. No, not hair. A blanket draped over a skull.

Kiersten startles backward, banging into the crib. Despite the jostling motion, Violet doesn't make a sound. The sudden conviction fills Kiersten that if she turns again, she'll find the baby gone.

A thing with long, boney legs as delicate as a deer's, cricking and cracking inside the storm, will have taken her baby away.

Breath clogs in her throat. She squeezes her eyes closed. Rattle Tap isn't real. There's no reason to check the crib. No reason at all. Violet is still there. But shouldn't she look, just in case? She's a coward. She flees down the hall, not looking, and slams her bedroom door.

She snatches up her phone to call—who? The time shines at her from the screen, 1:15 A.M. No signal bars.

"Shit."

The small × sitting in the corner of the screen deflates her, and Kiersten sinks onto the bed. There's no one to call anyway. She scrolls through her contacts, and pauses at Nick's name. She can't help the familiar swoop in her belly, a visceral response like hope and disappointment rolled into one. She should delete him. She should. She scrolls on, past names that blur in her tired vision, a meaningless jumble of letters.

Before the baby, before Nick, she would go out for drinks with the other office admins. They would complain about the faculty members they didn't like, and gossip about even the ones they did. Looking at their names now, Kiersten can't think of a single one she would call. Co-workers. Acquaintances. Not friends.

Before Nick and before the baby, she used go to brunch at least once a month with a group of friends she'd met at summer camp years ago. But none of them have children. Their lives, Kiersten imagines, are untethered, gloriously carefree. What would she even say to them now?

Before Nick and the baby, she was a different person.

She'd thought the two of them were being so careful. Once she'd gotten over the initial shock, though, Kiersten had surprised herself; she'd actually been excited about having a baby. As her due date grew nearer, that excitement had only grown. She wanted a baby, right up until the moment Violet was born.

Somewhere in the haze of pain, in the nebulous space between the final push and Violet being placed in her arms, something had shifted. A door had opened. A flood of memories she'd forgotten or buried had returned. It wasn't just a matter of simple recollection, though. She's found herself somewhere else.

In another nursery, in another house. In a darkened kitchen, her daddy scraping a beer can across wood.

In a place simultaneously aching with brightness and utterly dark. Flickering between both. Not her memory, but something more primal. A collective space where nightmares are born. And something had emerged. Something shaped like a woman, but not a woman at all. Narrower, clicking and rattling in the dark. A blanket draped over its head, and instead of a face, a long animal skull.

Had her own mother ever seen it? Had other mothers, stretching back to the beginning of time? A creature with an offer, a bargain, an exchange to be made? *Please take this baby from me. It's too much, too soon, I'm not ready, I can't handle it alone.*

Rattle Tap. A thing summoned by a rhyme, existing outside of herself, and just under the surface of Kiersten's skin. Her and not her, a convergence of the two. And in that moment, she'd hated the child they laid against her chest and tried to push it back into the nurse's arms.

"These things take time," the doctor had reassured her. "Be patient with yourself. Be patient with your little girl. Get to know each other."

Three weeks later, she's still waiting to feel the bond all mothers are supposed to feel. She's waiting to feel that overwhelming, transformative love. And she has no one to ask if her experience is normal.

Nick hadn't wanted them to join any of the parenting classes being offered locally. Despite the books and the articles he'd shared with her, he'd scoffed at the idea of mommy blogs and chat groups and forums for new and expectant mothers. He trusted doctors writing books more than women actually experiencing pregnancy. He'd told Kiersten they could do this on their own, they didn't need any "new-age, feel-good crap," as he assumed the parenting classes to be.

Kiersten had briefly considered joining on her own, at the end, but it felt too late. If she had, she might have someone to talk to now. But like always, she'd gone along with what Nick wanted, let him convince her, let him cut her off from outside support, leaving her to rely solely on him.

Maybe what she's feeling is something all parents feel; maybe she's just built wrong.

Your mama was a bad mama. Bad down to the bone.

Kiersten wonders what her daddy would say about it, if she could ask him. But her daddy had had a heart attack the year she turned eighteen, and even if she could have asked him, she isn't sure he would have told the truth. He always looked after her, but they'd never really been close. Instead of the loss of her mother drawing them together, it was as though her mama had remained, a ghost, a shadow between them. Her absence was a physical thing, and it made her daddy strange.

It was like he found a way to become two people wrapped inside one skin. Some days he was all smiles, and others he was distant, jumpy. She had loved him, of course, but she'd been frightened of him too.

When he died, there had been grief, but also a kind of guilt-laced weight lifting from her shoulders.

His life insurance policy had made it so Kiersten hadn't had to worry about the cost of his funeral. It wasn't until she'd been seated in the law offices of Grundy and Peele, awkward in a black pencil skirt she'd bought for her senior choir concert, wearing black pumps that pinched her toes and her heels, that she'd learned that she'd been left a house. This house. The house her father had grown up in.

Like she'd never known her mama, she'd never known her grandparents either. Her daddy had a falling-out with them, but even so, she learned, they'd always meant their house to go to her, their only grandchild. They'd left it in trust, in a way that made it impossible for her daddy to sell it or do anything else with it until she came of age.

Kiersten scrolls back, and hovers over Nick's name again. She presses the phone icon, her pulse jumping at the thought the call might go through. Relief, with a hollow feeling tucked inside, washes through her when the phone doesn't respond. She should delete his number. She should. She returns her phone to her bedside table, lays it facedown.

She thinks of how Nick chided her when she'd so much as mentioned the idea of bottle feeding. How he'd left parenting books lying around, forwarded articles, and linked to websites. He'd been so full of opinions about what she should and shouldn't eat while pregnant, what she should and shouldn't do. He was always ready with unsolicited advice, couched in kindness, all without modifying his own behavior, as if the entire weight of child-rearing should fall on her alone.

She reminds herself she doesn't need him. She was right to kick him out. And she wonders—did he ever even want a child, or did he just like an excuse to tell her what to do? Was the baby only ever an extra lever of control?

He'd barely fought her when, eight months pregnant, belly straining, ankles painful and swollen, she'd asked him—told him—to leave. Threw him out. Changed the locks. But in a moment of stupid weakness, she'd stopped short of deleting him from her phone.

Kiersten unfolds herself from the bed and creeps to the window. Across the white expanse of snow, the trees look like a solid wall. Anything could be hidden there. The trees closer to the house are sheathed in ice. The wind rattles them, making a dizzy patter and she is—

Ten years old, playing in the scrubby field behind her house. Cars frequently pull into their cul-de-sac under the cover of night and dump trash—empty bottles, worn-bald tires, and once a whole mattress, torn and water-stained. She isn't supposed to play there, so she walks with her head down, switching a long branch at the dried grasses that crackle underfoot, pretending she doesn't see how far she is from the house.

Then all at once, the sense of something watching her is so strong that her head snaps up. A deer's skull, long and narrow, sits atop two branches—pale and stripped of leaves—lashed together like a cross and planted in the ground. A ragged gray-blue blanket drapes overtop the skull.

A wind kicks up out of nowhere, lifting the blanket to ripple in the air. Light pinholes through it where it's worn thin, like a field of stars scattered against a dirty sky. And for a moment, it isn't a skull atop a cross at all. It is a woman with impossibly thin arms stretched wide to embrace her, to snatch her away. Her bones go crick-crack, crack-crack and rattle in the storm.

She runs.

Pelting away from the skull and the buzzing sensation crawling across her skin. She knows the thing in the field somehow, and worse, it knows her. Her foot catches where the pavement begins, and she goes down, skinning her knee. She's too startled in the moment to even cry.

Later, though, there are tears as she tells her daddy what she saw. She'd meant to hold it back, not only because she was playing where she shouldn't have been, but because there's something terrible about the cross and the skull she can't name. The image sits at the back of her mind and she has to tell him, spitting the words out like an exorcism.

Her daddy gets a glassy look in his eyes. He swabs her knee, and covers it with a bandage decorated with mermaids. He ruffles her hair, pressing his fingers into her scalp a little too hard, and tells her she has an active imagination. It was probably just some sticks in the ground and she conjured up the rest.

She knows this isn't true.

Later, much later, she creeps back to the field. She's scared, but she needs to see it again. She knows the thing in the field and it knows her. It wasn't her imagination.

She searches all up and down, every part of the field. She finds nothing.

Kiersten's breath comes unevenly, as if she is still in that field, running from the cross and the skull and the blue-gray blanket.

Crick crack. A sound tucked inside the ice rattling against the glass. Kiersten's breath tangles in her throat, like the cold slipped inside, freezing the air in her lungs.

She steps back from the window.

Click. A sound like two knitting needles coming together in the dark.

She scrambles up onto the bed, tucking her feet under her. She still feels exposed. Kiersten drapes the blanket over her head, covering her hair, wrapping and tucking the trailing ends around her like a cocoon. Rattle Tap is coming for her and she needs to hide.

The cold wakes her. Kiersten's neck aches, her body folded at an awkward angle. She must have fallen asleep hiding under the covers, and at some point, kicked half of them off. Part of her is still wrapped, the other half not, and the sudden image comes to her of a blanket-draped figure with boney hands standing over her, peeling the covers away as she sleeps. She pushes the image away, working her other arm free to turn her phone over. 2:33 A.M. Still no signal bars.

"Fuck." She murmurs it quietly.

There's no one to hear her. No one to admonish her and look at her with wounded, puppy-dog eyes, as if her foul mouth reflected badly on him personally. As though Nick himself never swore.

"Fuck!" She yells it, as loud as she can, a cathartic release, and for a moment, it feels good.

The feeling doesn't last. The house stretches around her, grows extra spaces filled with bruise-dark air. The storm is louder, more insistent—the sound of someone on the roof throwing handfuls of stones.

But the baby is quieter. There's no piercing yell. It's only as Kiersten listens that she becomes aware of a hiccupping whimper. A small, brokenhearted sound. How long has Violet been crying, while Kiersten failed to wake?

Crick crack.

She freezes, halfway to crawling out of bed.

The rhyme wants to come to her lips, rising under her skin, filling up her throat with itself and taking possession of her. *Crick crack, Rattle Tap, creeping through the storm . . .*

Violet's whimpering cry rises, need and guilt worming their way toward her, and Kiersten feels a fresh surge of unreasonable anger.

Crack.

Only a branch snapping in the storm. Or snapping under the weight of a delicate hoof as a blanket-draped thing totters on legs as thin as lashed-together branches at the edge of a field.

Sleep, sleep, Mama weeps, wishing you weren't born.

Crick.

Kiersten can't make the sound be anything other than bones coming together without the benefit of cartilage or skin to cushion the sound. A scream builds in her throat. She needs to go to the baby, her baby. She needs to protect it. It's what a good mother would do.

Only maybe she isn't a good mother at all.

Kiersten storms down the hall. She shoves open the baby's door. Light from the hall seeps in behind her and a shadow peels itself away from the crib, a woman with a blanket draped over her head. Something old and terrible, clicking every time it moves.

The shadow slides along the wall and slips behind the curtain. Kiersten seizes a board book with thick pages from the dresser near the door and hurls it. It bounces harmlessly off the glass, stirring the curtains, showing there's nothing there.

Startled, Violet cries louder, a hook buried in Kiersten's skin dragging her into the room. Tears sting her eyes, frustration, embarrassment at her stupid behavior. She wants to add her cry to Violet's own. The wind sighs, a disappointed sound, and Kiersten forces herself to step closer.

She lifts the baby, and waits again to feel that swell of love. Instead, she feels a surge of vicious resentment. The baby can sleep whenever she wants, eat whenever she wants, nothing is expected of her.

"I wish Rattle Tap would take you." She squeezes the baby's arm, not a full pinch, not enough to make her cry. Just enough to get her attention, to widen her eyes and startle her into silence, her breath a little gasp interrupted on the way to another shout.

Immediately, Kiersten hates herself; she needs to make it up to the baby somehow.

A warm bath, maybe? She carries the baby down the hall to where the white porcelain tub crouches on claw feet over cold black and white tiles. She turns the tap on hot hot hot, steam filling the bathroom until condensation streaks the window and mirror. Kiersten sits on the closed toilet seat holding Violet, listening to the tub fill.

She hums to herself, an old and terrible rhyme, half dozing to the soothing rush of water. She twitches, a convulsive motion, like starting to fall asleep and jerking awake again. Kiersten is utterly disoriented. She remembers thinking about calling Nick, but her phone had no signal. She doesn't remember bringing Violet into the bathroom.

She stares at the tub and the surging water. The air is wet and heavy and she can barely see for the steam filling the room. The water is far too hot for a baby. The tub yaws dizzily at her, and she almost loses her balance as she stands, tilting in its direction. It is long and shaped like a grave. It pulls at her, wanting to tug Violet from her arms.

There are countless stories of mothers drowning their babies out of desperation, out of frustration and fear and exhaustion and a sadness they can't name. Some of them even go on believing their babies are alive afterward, hearing them crying, with no memory of the terrible thing they've done. There are other, quieter stories—sudden infant death syndrome, breath inexplicably stopped in the crib. There are stories of monsters stealing babies away in the night, wicked faeries leaving changeling bundles of sticks in a baby's place, and weeping ghosts pulling them into rivers to drown. Is one story a kinder version of the other, and if so, which is which? She—

Sees the blanket drifting through the air, held aloft by disconnected hands. Like a game of peekaboo, only the blanket descends, a vast, fluttering thing. Covering the baby girl in her crib, swallowing her whole. Tight, tight, too tight, and when she tries to scream, the fabric is in her mouth and she can't breathe.

Kiersten jerks back from the tub. Violet squalls. The back of her onesie is damp—with curling steam, or did Kiersten actually dip her into the water? Violet's dark, sparse hair clings to her scalp and she kicks wildly. Like she's trying to run away. Like she knows her mama is a bad mama, right down to the bone.

Crack.

Kiersten wrenches the tap off. It drip drip drips and her pulse matches it, erratic. She carries Violet back downstairs to the kitchen. She is not a bad mama. She would never drown her baby. Never wrap a blanket around her head. She would sooner wish a monster out of the storm to take her baby away than personally do her harm.

She fumbles for the light switch. At least the power is still on, even if the storm has stolen her phone signal. She takes a tentative step into the kitchen, and stops. A bottle lies on the floor, surrounded by a constellation of spilled milk. The sense that someone was in the room just before her is overwhelming. A woman with a blanket draped over her head. A woman with bare feet, and she . . .

No. Kiersten dropped the bottle herself, and failed to pick it up. She remembers now.

She used to be able to trust her own mind. In college, she could read the material for an exam the night before and recall it photographically the next day. But when she was growing up, it wasn't just the cross and the deer skull in the field that her daddy told her weren't real. Frequently, her memories jarred against his, like a vase broken and ill-repaired. Stupid, little things—she wore a blue shirt instead of a yellow one when they went to the park; she got chocolate chip ice cream, not cookies and cream. Memories that meant nothing. But were those little things meant to erode her confidence in the bigger one? To cast everything she thought she knew into a shadow of doubt?

She sets the bottle in the sink to clean later. She heats milk for the baby and for herself, and carries her daughter to the front room. The curtains stir, but Kiersten refuses to look at the hem, to check for feet, for a woman hiding behind them, her face covered.

She turns the TV on, but leaves it muted, letting the flickering images wash her with multicolored light. And she wakes to a cracking, crashing sound. She jumps, forgetting the baby, catching Violet just before she hits the floor. For once the baby doesn't cry at all.

Kiersten reaches automatically for her phone, but finds her robe pocket empty. She must have left it upstairs. What time is it? Did she doze for an hour, or only blink her eyes? The images on the TV screen blur. She can't make sense of them, doesn't remember if they are the same as when she sat down.

She forces herself to cross the room, twitch the curtain aside fast like pulling off a bandage. Just a tree branch down, snapping under the weight of ice.

Rattle. Shhhh. Rattle. Shhh. Crick. Tap.

A sound like dice in a cup, passed from hand to hand. Jaws clicking and bones tapping.

Your mama left us on a night just like this. In a storm. She was a bad mama. Bad, bad, bad down to the bone.

Her daddy had been a healthy enough man, right up until the end. He didn't drink or smoke except on nights when it stormed, and then, almost always, he'd say the same thing. He'd remind her how her mama ran away, sometimes with a cagey look in his eyes, sometimes like he expected another one of those moments when her memories scraped jaggedly against his own. Sometimes, it almost seemed like he wanted her to contradict him, and other times, he simply looked afraid.

She remembers his foot tap-tap-tapping under the table, his leg bouncing up and down, and him peering at the shadows like he was waiting for something.

Waiting for the night his heart finally stopped. Like a hand reached right through his chest and squeezed and squeezed and squeezed the life right out of him.

It occurs to Kiersten that Nick and her daddy had a lot in common. The way Nick always had of reassuring her she had things wrong, he hadn't meant what she'd thought he'd meant, she'd misunderstood. She was making a big deal out of nothing.

Had her daddy talked to her mama like that too?

People called her daddy brave for raising her all alone. If he'd been the one gone and her mama had stayed, would they have said the same thing?

Up until the moment she'd thrown Nick out of the house, Kiersten had believed the things he told her. Or she'd tried to. She couldn't shake her daddy's voice in the back of her head. "You don't want to turn out like your mama, do you? She used to be different, she changed."

She'd never asked her daddy what he meant by that. What did he think her mother had become?

A monster in a long line of monsters. A thing born in that primal nightmare space in the dark, where mothers discovered the thing rising beneath their skin and the thing outside of them and had to choose between them? Become the monster, or be afraid of it for the rest of your days.

Kiersten shakes her head, shaking the thoughts free. She's tired, and once she sleeps, she'll be able to think clearly again. She climbs the stairs, and lays the baby back in its crib, clean and fed and warm and dry.

"Let's both try to get some sleep, okay?"

The baby says nothing, blinking moon-owl eyes, turning its head uncannily to follow her all the way back to the door.

Kiersten wakes with panic rattling in her chest. 4:18 A.M., almost two hours since the baby last woke her. Something must be wrong. The baby is gone. She left the door open and it crawled into the storm. She carried it outside and set it down for just a moment, but then she forgot and came back inside alone. Rattle Tap took the baby away.

She's a bad mother. Just like her own mama.

Silence pounds like a headache. If she doesn't check, the baby will be fine.

If she doesn't see the empty crib with her own eyes, it isn't her fault, she didn't know. Kiersten tiptoes down the hall, holding her heart in her mouth, dreading and dreading until the moment she opens the door to find the baby sleeping, delicate eyelids tight-closed, mouth sucking on nothing in its dreams.

She wants to slap the baby awake. Shake it and scream in its face. How dare it scare her that way?

Tears—relief, anger—smear under her palm.

Ping!

Her phone in her pocket chimes an alert. A dozen more tumble in its wake, a cascade of sound as a flurry of texts come through all at once. The signal finally breaking through the storm.

Shh. You'll wake the baby.

She scrambles to open the phone, to silence the noise.

Nick—12:32 a.m.—Thinking bout u.
Nick—12:35 a.m.—Miss u.
Nick—12:40 a.m.—U asleep already?
Nick—12:57 a.m.—Baby keeping u up? I could keep u up.
Nick—1:01 a.m.—I miss fucking u.
Nick—1:35 a.m.—wtf? U ignoring me?
Nick—1:36 a.m.—Bitch.
Nick—1:37 a.m.—Fuck u.
Nick—1:38 a.m.—Bitch.
Nick—1:40 a.m.—Fuckin Bitch.

She scrolls through the messages, eyes stinging, blurring, hands shaking. Message after message, a scream building inside of her.

"No, fuck you!"

She claws the window open, icy wind tearing in, and throws the phone as hard as she can. It spins, illuminating the falling snow, and drops, vanishing.

Shit. Shit. Shitshitshit. What if there's an emergency?

Kiersten half runs, half falls down the stairs, gripping the banister and barely keeping herself upright. She shoves her feet into unlaced boots, doesn't bother with a coat, and plunges outside.

Its like wading through a rising tide, snow up to her shins. Between the wind smoothing everything and the still-falling snow, she can't pick out where her phone landed.

Shit. She couldn't have thrown it that far. She drops to her knees, digging. Freezing pellets swirl in cross-hatching patterns, making it even harder to see. Grains stick in her hair like beads of glass, rattling when she moves.

Crick crack.

Kiersten's breath steams in the air. The sound comes again and she makes the mistake of looking over her shoulder. A figure steps from between the trees.

Crick.

Long legs and a body so light its narrow hooves don't break the crust of ice. A ragged blanket flutters in the wind.

"Please," she whispers. "Please don't. Please—"

The little girl is carried through the storm, small body jostling with each step. She cries and cries, but the running doesn't stop. A gray-blue blanket, worn from multiple washings, clings to the shape of a face, a head. A suggestion of eyes, a suggestion of a mouth. Something terrible and unseen.

Then hands rip her away violently from the monster trying to steal her. The little girl is not the one screaming anymore, just emitting quiet, heartbroken sobs. She doesn't understand what's going on, only that everything is wrong, wrong, wrong.

Crack. A wet, heavy sound.

The scrape, scrape, scrape of someone digging.

Crick. The brittle snap of branches or bones and the scent of turned earth and wet leaves.

"—don't take me. Take the baby. Take it, not me, please."

The words emerge, a ragged blur of sound that Kiersten is barely aware of making. Tears burn her cheeks. She scrabbles at the ice-covered snow, breaking her nails. She needs her phone; she needs to get back inside. Bone on bone bends at the knee. Click, click, click. Joints knitting through the dark while wind sighs through the empty sockets of a skull.

Shhhh.

Mama's here, Mama's home, there's no reason to be afraid.

Kiersten bites back a scream. Fingers at once numb and freezing stub against her phone. A choked sob of relief. She wrestles it free, bolts back toward the front door. Which stands gaping wide.

Did she leave it that way? She can't remember.

Crick, crack, Rattle Tap, climbing up the stairs. Hooves clack, Mama's back to sing you through the storm.

Kiersten lurches forward, scrambling to get inside. Her toe catches the threshold, and the world goes out from under her. She sprawls, phone flying, wrist crunching painfully as she hits the ground.

The baby. She has to get Violet. Kiersten tries to push herself up, but a pure, hot spike of pain shoots from her wrist all the way to her shoulder. She collapses, panting. She wants to curl into a ball, cradle her wrist, never get up.

She wants to.

She can't.

She isn't allowed to want things for herself anymore.

She pushes herself up, deliberately putting weight on her wounded wrist as punishment, reveling in the pain. Her wrist throbs. Under the skin, her bones go *crick crack, crick crack* as she crawls her way up the stairs.

Gray light seeps through the curtains. It's 8:07 A.M. The baby never lets her sleep this long. There hasn't been a sound since . . .

There's something wrong.

Kiersten lifts her phone in a shaking hand, double-checking the time. A crack bisects the screen. Nick's voice sounds in the back of her mind, reminding her how much the phone cost, never mind that she paid for it, that she's the one with a job, and the house is in her name. Never mind that he lived here for almost a year, rent free, while she cooked and cleaned, did the laundry, did everything while he sat on the couch and played video games.

I'm trying, but the job market is really tough right now, babe.

And the dishes?

I don't know where they all go. I'd just put them back in the wrong place.

And the laundry?

You're so much better at it than I am. Remember I shrunk your favorite sweater? You cried for like a week.

Kiersten's head pounds, a hollow, distant aching, like a hangover, though she hasn't touched a drop of alcohol in longer than she can remember. Not while she was pregnant, of course. Not while she's pumping.

She doesn't remember coming back to bed after . . .

She unlocks the phone to scroll through her messages. She's sure there were messages. Did she delete them? Her phone is cracked where she threw it, or where she dropped it on the floor.

It didn't happen that way, baby girl. I don't know what you remember, but you're wrong.

Kiersten presses the heels of her hands against her eyes, digging them in against the hollow pain. She tries to hold it all straight in her head.

Your mama was bad bad bad and I did what I had to do.

She dug her phone out of the snow. She came back inside. Locked the door. Put a towel down to soak up the mess tracked in on her boots.

Your mama went away on a night just like this one, disappeared into the storm. I dreamt she came back, creeping through the dark.

Kiersten presses harder against her eyes, against the pounding blackness, trying to hold on to her truth and not let it slip away.

She closed the door and climbed the stairs. She checked on the baby, because that's what good mothers do.

You don't want to turn out like your own mama, do you? Bad, bad, bad.

She crawled into bed. Pulled the covers over her head, wrapped tight so nothing could find her. And she fell asleep. Slept all the way past 8:00 A.M., and the baby never woke her.

Kiersten listens to the silence.

She gets her slippers, pulls on her robe. There's an odd soreness as she feeds her arms through the sleeves. Maybe from digging in the snow? She looks at her hands; they're rough, chapped from the cold, but not abraded. Did she throw her phone out the window?

She does remember digging. A weight in her arms. But maybe she's just remembering carrying the baby around. It feels as though she's carried it for miles. All the way across the yard. All the way into the trees. Cricking and cracking her way through the ice, through the storm.

She was a bad mama. A bad. Bad.

You don't want to turn out like your mama, do you, baby girl? We all do what we have to do.

She looks out over the lawn. Her body aches from carrying, digging, carrying, digging.

Sun gilds the ice and snow, a pale golden color. The wind no longer rattles the eaves. Downed branches lie stark on the lawn. Black scribbles of ink on white. A blanket, smoothed by the wind. There's only one tiny hump in the snow, far away, at the very edge of the trees. She has to squint to see it, and even then, she isn't sure. It might not be there at all. A tiny hump in the snow, no bigger than a sleeping child.

Kiersten creeps down the hall, pushes open the nursery door. The curtains sway in the draft, a shadow like a long-fingered hand from a tree branch outside rippling out of view.

Shhhh.

She listens for breathing from the crib.

Crick.

The curtain sways.

Crack.

A faint smell like wet leaves hangs in the air. Like earth, dark and freshly turned.

Tap tap tap.

Kiersten stands over the crib and peers in. A mounded shape lies under a blanket, like the hump in the snow outside. The blanket is blue-gray. Tattered. If she held it up to the window, the light would shine through. Like a field of stars against a dirty sky.

She considers draping the blanket over her head, hiding.

Crick crack, Rattle Tap, creaking through the storm.

There's a dark smudge on the white crib rail, like a dirt-smeared hand rested there briefly as it laid something down, or took something away.

Shhh.

Shhh.

Kiersten peels the blanket free. The baby lies utterly still. The baby, whose soft curves and pudgy kicking limbs have been replaced by sticks and mud and leaves. The baby whose pouting, rose lips have been replaced by the weathered teeth of a deer's long skull.

Crick. Crack. Rattle. Tap.

In the corner of the nursery, a woman with a blanket over her head raises a finger to her lips.

Shhh.

Kiersten understands. She's not allowed to scream. She's not allowed to be afraid. She's not allowed to want things, or feel her own emotions anymore. She has the baby to consider. And she's a good mother.

Gingerly, she lifts the child and holds it up for a better view. Dark, solemn, empty eyes gaze back at her.

Crick. Crack. Rattle. Tap.

Eyes like her daddy's. Eyes like her mama's. As much as Kiersten might want to deny it—deep in the part of her that's screaming, tamped down so she doesn't make a sound—the baby is hers. She's the reason it's here. She is responsible for it.

Crick. Crack.

The baby doesn't breathe.

Rattle. Tap.

Kiersten settles the insubstantial weight against her shoulder and hums a nonsense rhyme.

The baby is hungry again.

CHILDREN OF THE NIGHT

by Stephen Graham Jones

Tol never won the lottery, he never got an accidental second order of fries with his burger, and if he ever dropped his glasses, it was a sure thing they were breaking, but for once, for this one time only, he knew, he was in the right place at the right time.

More than that, he was even tuned in to the right band.

His Bigfoot hunting crew was spread out over ten square miles of this part of Montana outside Lincoln. Since this was going on their fourth year, most of them had geared up by now, had the night vision goggles, handheld audio dishes, forceps and probes for hair and scat. And of course all of them carried plaster kits in their packs, in case of a footprint.

And tonight, they were going to need them all, they knew.

The weekend before, a couple out to see America from the front seat of their RV had supposedly seen a tall, hairy form moving from one side of the road to the other. It had only been in their headlights for a second, a second and a half, but that was enough to get them on the six o'clock news.

They were calling it a "dog man," but Tol and his crew knew better, of course.

The reason he was in the right place at the right time, though, and nobody else was, was because it had been his turn to drop everyone off, and then man the two-way. He hated just sitting there, being the mom in the minivan, but he knew that this was part of it. It can't all be glorious.

When nobody was checking in every fifteen minutes like they were supposed to, he turned the radio down, squelched into the CB band to try to glom on to some juicy trucker gossip. Well, some trucker talk, anyway. Gone, pretty much, were the days when there'd been anything actually juicy. Any PG-13-rated content nowadays went into Bluetooth headsets and cell phones. The CB band lately had pretty much just been general heads-ups about state trooper locations, traffic backups, and weather.

Still, it was getting pretty lonely in the minivan.

Tol had been listening for what he guessed couldn't have been any longer than ninety seconds, was still dialing for a station with voices, when one came through: "*I hit it, I hit it!*"

Tol leaned forward, staring into the two numbers on the front of the CB unit.

"Go on," he said, just to himself.

"Mile marker, um, um," the woman was saying then, "just past that Aspen Grove place! Just east of that! It just ran right out in front—"

"Ho, ho," a deeper voice came back. "You hit what, pretty lady?"

"The dog man," the woman said, which is when a semi barreled past, straddling the lines. As if its driver was on the CB or something . . .

Tol looked up to the sign right in front of the minivan: ASPEN GROVE CAMPGROUND.

He was breathing hard, his face cold.

It was finally happening.

"I'm coming," he said, still just to himself, and started the minivan, strapped his seat belt across his chest, and, after checking his mirrors and then physically looking over his shoulder like he'd been taught, he pulled out onto the two-lane and floored it in the direction that semi had just come from.

He expected the rear tires to spin in the gravel, but of course the minivan was front-wheel drive—which was even better: those two front tires grabbed, rocketed him out to what he'd always known his fate was going to be.

"Shh, shh," he said to no one, and only realized a half-mile later that he was talking to himself. To his heart, maybe.

Because this part of the road was so windy, switching back and forth on itself to get up the mountain, there was no way a truck with a fifty-three-foot trailer had found a turnout. And he couldn't see any other headlights either—not in his mirrors and not through the windshield.

Even better, just like that trucker had said, there on the shoulder, its legs in the ditch, its upper body on the asphalt, was the bigfoot.

Tol turned his lights off, eased in, and—thinking ahead—backed right up to it, the back hatch already rising like a slow mouth opening.

"You can do this, you can do this," Tol told himself, and stepped down, stiff-legged it back there.

The bigfoot was of course huge, a *mound* of huge, and heavy, and nothing but dead, stinky weight, but Tol was so excited he could have loaded a horse, he was pretty sure.

He knew this wasn't the time for analysis, but he couldn't help but notice the simian face, the sloped-back forehead, and how there was no fur on the hands, but the orangutan-colored hair on the arms was almost like sleeves, coming down to neat cuffs.

There wasn't any blood, either.

Tol swallowed, and allowed himself to take just one selfie, squatted down at the bumper, this mass of dead bigfoot piled into the minivan behind him.

The flash blinded him, and he was sure that would be his undoing, that this bigfoot's mate was surely out there, waiting for exactly this kind of opportunity.

Instead, headlights crested.

Tol scrambled into the front seat, dropped into gear, and eased away calmly, turning his headlights on once he was straight in the lane. He was just another late-night traveler—nobody here, no reason to stop.

All the same, the big rig touched its brakes as soon as it passed Tol.

Tol hissed, accelerated, and turned his headlights off. With luck like he was having tonight, he figured, no headlights probably meant he was about to hit *another* bigfoot, right?

He laughed out loud, barely made the right turn, and was on a steep grade now.

Halfway down it, his crew getting farther and farther away behind him, he slowed, stepped up onto a runaway-truck ramp.

It was dirt and fine gravel, for slowing a truck that can't slow itself, but the minivan was light enough, even with the bigfoot, that it didn't sink.

Five minutes later—it had probably had to go a mile or two to find a place to turn around—the big rig blasted past, its brights on. Tol huddled over the steering wheel, begged nothing on the outside of the minivan to glint, please.

Once the truck was past, wouldn't be coming back until it made it all the way into Lincoln, Tol screamed into the horn button, which turned into crying, and then laughing, and then just hugging himself.

Nothing else ever having worked out in his life was worth it, now. He was even glad that nothing had worked out, if it meant that *he,* Tol Oliver, and not any other bigfoot hunter or researcher or believer, was going to be the one to prove to the world that it had been wrong all along.

Eat that, Rachel, he said inside.

Rachel was the newest member of the club, which was what Marty was using as his excuse for her getting out at his drop-off, so he could make sure all her tech was in order.

Yeah, likely.

It's a *bigfoot* club, not a singles meetup. Tol would never use it that way, anyway. Sure, like everybody else—bigfoot club was all male—he was working up the exact phrasing for the dinner invitation he was going to extend to Rachel, but that date would be during the week, not the weekend. The weekend was for . . . it was for *this,* for what Tol had *done:* bagged a bigfoot.

He held his hand out and couldn't stop his fingers from trembling.

He nodded to himself, breathed in deep and held it for a four-count, and then he opened the door, stepped out, the dome light announcing him to all of Montana, it felt like.

He pushed the door shut then caught it at the last moment, sure he was about to lock himself out. With the keys securely on his belt loop, he rounded the back of the minivan, stood there steeling himself for what would probably go down in history as the first ever authentic undeniable examination of a bigfoot, a sasquatch, a yeti, a skunk ape, a wild man—maybe a Gigantopithecus, maybe some remnant offshoot of Neanderthal . . . nobody knew! That was why this was so amazing!

But Tol had to be scientific. Analytic. Calm.

He smoothed his hair down, tucked his shirt in, which felt like a weird affectation even to him, and was probably about to retie his hiking boots with double knots when he had to admit that he was stalling, that he was being an idiot, like Marty was always saying.

Like Marty was going to be able to keep Rachel's interest when Tol showed them *this*.

He clicked the fob at his belt loop and the hatch hissed open, the dome light glowing on again. Tol rushed up to the dashboard, rolled the interior lights roller until it clicked, and then reset his thinking as best he could: all his hard work had been worth it, his faith was being repaid . . . his whole life had come down to this singular moment in time.

Some of the small gravel and sifty dirt under his boots shifted, making him have to adjust to keep from falling over.

"You're still stalling . . ." he told himself, and, telling himself that this was how Marty would do it, he stepped forward, his phone already out and recording.

"The Dogman of Lincoln," he narrated. "He caught the grille guard of a truck going sixty, trying to get up a head of steam for the climb, and, well. Here we are, people. Bigfoot." Tol flipped the phone around to himself, even though the glint of his glasses was probably the only thing getting recorded. "And, this is the culmination of years of hoping and wishing," he said solemnly. "But let's not forget that this, this . . . it's dead now. And it walks on two feet like us, doesn't it?" He turned the phone back around, angled it down onto the bigfoot, going up and down its length and breadth, then flipping the manual light on above it, doing that top-to-bottom side-to-side pan again, but slower, because every frame of this monumental recording was going to be pored over, he knew.

Every word Tol was saying here, it was history.

"Shit," he said, then covered his mouth, closed his eyes hard.

But he couldn't go back, start over. This couldn't look staged, like all those bigfoot costumes that show up in freezers all over the south.

And—no.

Tol winced. There *was* blood. Of course there would be blood. You don't get slapped by a semi and not burst something.

But . . . weird.

The blood was only on the hands? The forearms?

Maybe this guy had gotten hit and then tried to catch itself on its hands, scraped all its skin away on the asphalt.

Had to be that.

Tol stepped up to document it better. And to be sure none of that blood was getting into the carpet. Cindy would have his hide if he messed her mini-van up again.

Tol touched the fob again and the kid-door on the passenger side slid back. He came back from it with two of the canvas shopping bags they used. He worked one each over the huge bloody hands, the phone recording from where he'd leaned it, meaning it must have seen when he couldn't get the second bag on as well as he wanted, had to twist the bigfoot's arm while lifting it.

Which was when the arm came *off*?

Not the whole thing, just . . . from the elbow down, anyway. And, not "off" so much as it got weirdly looser.

"No, no," Tol said, and backed off fast, hitting his head on the dome light he still had clicked on. Its plastic shell shattered, the shards in his hair now, the bare filament sputtering in the cool air, then fizzling out.

Tol stepped down again, shook the foggy white shards from his hair on the way to the front seat again, and just turned all the interior lights on, screw it. Like anybody's going to see a dim glow a quarter of the way up a runaway ramp at ten o'clock on a Friday night and stop, go see who's smoking what up there.

"Now," Tol said, and stepped back into the cargo area, careful not to put any real weight on the bigfoot anywhere. Because . . . who knew, right? Maybe that forearm and hand coming loose was how all the bigfoot never left any remains. It could be that when they die, they start to fall apart. Give them two or three hours, and they're just a few stray tufts of hair, maybe some teeth.

Instead of inspecting that arm—Tol didn't want to pull it again, have blood spurt—he went directly to the head. After working his right hand into one of the latex gloves he carried, that everybody was always making fun of him for, making out like he wanted to be a CSI tech, he worked that hand into the bigfoot's wide mouth.

It stopped at the throat. And it wasn't that in death the throat muscles had clenched, and this wasn't damage from the impact.

The mouth, quite simply, had no opening back there.

Dreading what he already knew to be true, Tol twisted the big head side to side, worked it up and . . . off, off the head *underneath* this costume.

Which was some bullshit.

"Your winning streak continues," Tol said to himself.

Except, the head underneath this high-dollar bigfoot costume was . . . the same? Sort of?

"*What?*" Tol said, pushing back.

Not exactly the same, but pretty damn close. There was long stringy hair, maybe a bit more brown on each side of the face like muttonchops, and the eyebrows were bushy, and when Tol used his blue fingers to work the right eyelid back, there was a big yellow contact lens. It had to be. It was striated, was just as expensive as this bigfoot getup must have been, but—

"Werewolf," Tol said, obviously. Disgustedly.

Taking a mechanical pencil from his chest pocket, Tol tapped on this dead person's eye.

Instead of the *tink* he was expecting, though, the eye was . . . soft?

Tol sucked his breath in, held it, suddenly sure that if he made the slightest noise, it would be his last. There was no movement, though. No breathing. No flinching from that tap on the eyeball, which surely no living thing could help.

He'd thought this was a person pulling some Scooby-Doo gag, but . . . no, it couldn't be.

An *actual* werewolf?

Tol had never stopped to consider whether he believed in them or not.

He sat beside the dead thing, whatever it was, and considered this from all angles: if—if bigfoot could be real, then why not werewolves, too, right? Really, who's to say that they aren't one and the same? Maybe it had been werewolves running around in the woods for centuries, and they'd just started getting called "bigfoot" in the twentieth century? Granted, bigfoot was a lot taller, at least in the stories, but, the same as the camera adds fifteen pounds, Tol had to admit that the human memory might add a foot or two of height, too.

And werewolves probably liked this, didn't they? The more "bigfoot" could take the heat, the less heat werewolves had to.

Which could all lead to a werewolf dressed up in the family bigfoot outfit, taking its turn out here on the highway, to perpetuate the big lie that preserved their way of life. Probably, this werewolf hadn't even been shifted into wolf-form when it had pulled this bigfoot head over its own. Chances are it tried to shift at the last moment, right before that fast-moving grille guard caught it, but it was too late, so it only managed to shift this much.

So?

One way of looking at this was that that Tol had failed at proving bigfoot to the world. Another way of looking at it was that he *did* have a werewolf corpse, here. And, unlike in all the stories, this one wasn't dialing back to its human form in death.

Tol couldn't bring it in like this, though—in costume.

Moving methodically, sweating in the cool night air, he peeled the boot-parts of the costume off—the rubber feet were mostly padding, were comically big, practically snowshoes—found the zipper on the torso, and then when it caught, had to work the chest-piece and shoulders up over the head.

It took the muttonchop on the right side with it.

"Hunh," Tol said, rolling it between his fingers, and holding it up to the dome light that wasn't shattered.

Instead of roots, this hair had . . . some clear, viscous excretion?

Tol flinched, tried to shake the hair off his fingertips but it was stuck. He rubbed his fingertips on the headliner, just left the hair up there, which Cindy was definitely not going to approve of, but this was life and death. Well, life and grossness, anyway.

Before he could tell himself not to, then Tol rubbed the pad of his thumb against the pad of his index finger, and took a sniff.

Instead of the gamey, musky scent he was expecting—

"*Glue?*" he said.

He turned to the head of this "werewolf," pulled at the *other* muttonchop, and it peeled off just the same.

"Oh, come *on*," Tol said, and scratched at an itch in his hair. His latex blue fingertip came away bloody. Evidently a shard of that dome light housing had punctured his scalp, and, as everyone knows, scalps like nothing more than to bleed and bleed, and then bleed some more.

Tol did not have time for this.

He held this dead *human* face between his hands and rotated it to look directly into it, as if he were going to scold it.

Without the muttonchops, he could see now that this wasn't a man, like he'd for some reason been thinking, but a woman.

Of course there would be female werewolves, he said inside, reminding himself immediately that this was *not* a werewolf. It was some human in werewolf makeup, which—

Tol shivered, pushed away from the body.

He'd never been this close to a dead *person*.

One who had, evidently, gone to all the trouble of gluing on a werewolf disguise, and then . . . putting a bigfoot costume on over that?

Seriously?

Marty was probably to blame, Tol had to assume. All bad things were Marty's fault, one way or the other. This was part of some showing-off stunt intended to make Rachel swoon, to make Tol look bad.

Or, it was supposed to have been. Until someone died.

"Backfire, Marty boy . . ." Tol said.

The big hilarious prank had an unfunny body count, now.

This would probably go down as an unfortunate accident, maybe reckless endangerment on Marty's part if his masterminding it could be proved, but . . . who even was this?

As far as Tol knew, Marty had ostracized every woman he worked with, and no way did he have the money to hire someone for a stunt like this.

Meaning?

"Do you even *know* Marty?" Tol muttered.

The dead woman didn't answer, of course. But one of her fangs was hooked over her lower lip, making her look like she was considering saying something. Because he wasn't a bad guy, didn't want her to be having to make that face, Tol reached a timid finger out, to either push that plastic fang back or pull the lip forward, but forgot about the blood from his scalp that was smeared on his blue latex finger.

It dabbed onto this woman's flat front tooth.

"Evidence," Tol recited from all his crime shows, so he jabbed his finger in again, to just remove those fangs altogether, throw them away, nobody would know they'd been there.

It would have worked, too, except the woman's dead hand had come up, took him by the wrist, made his hand stay right where it was.

Next her dead *head* snapped forward, and one of the costume fangs bit into his index finger.

It wasn't plastic.

Tol screamed, pulled back with all of his weight.

It didn't matter.

This woman's striated yellow eyes fixed on his, and her lips sealed around his finger, and, and—

Tol screamed, but this was a runaway ramp late on a Friday night in backcountry Montana. He kicked, but this woman's muscles were steel.

The veins on his forearm stood out and she brought her other hand around to catch his fist, the one sailing toward her face in what was going to be the first punch of Tol's life.

"No no no, Tolly boy," she said, both her hands holding both of his.

Tol felt all the certainty in his life fall down inside him, scatter on the floor of his heart.

"R-*Rachel*?" he managed to get out.

How had he not recognized her, when he'd spent so much time fantasizing about her?

Then he saw, got it: at the meetings, she'd always had so much makeup on, hadn't she?

Now, though, with the werewolf sideburns off, she was pale, almost ivory.

"Thanks," she said, then did her hand to indicate the ribbon of blacktop down below them wherever, "getting hit by a truck like that can really take it out of a girl, you know?"

"*What?*"

"No, I mean, we're not indestructible, we can—"

"*What!*" Tol repeated, not sure how much longer his mind could hold on, here.

"Your blood," she said, leading him into this. "I didn't take any from the others. That stupid mouth on that bigfoot costume, right? I didn't even think of that. But . . . well, as you can see, it doesn't take much. One drink and I'm right as rain."

"Rachel?"

"I thought you would figure it out faster, though. Aren't you supposed to be the smart one? Marty said you were kind of like a brain on legs." When Tol still couldn't make words, could hardly even see out of his eyes in a way he trusted, Rachel shrugged like this was the obvious part, said, "I'm a vampire, Tol. I drank your blood, it healed me? You thought I was dead before, didn't you? I was, you were right. I mean, I *am* dead, I have been for about three hundred years."

"But, but—"

"Yeah, this," Rachel said, scooching back to sit up, hold the bigfoot head up as if still impressed with it. "I thought it would be more . . . more poetic like this, yeah? Bigfoot comes for the crew out hunting him? Think of it like a—like a gift. I mean, you all had to die, you were dead the moment you left Helena, you were dead the moment I wrote that email asking if you needed any new members. But, I mean—the look on Marty's face? That was worth the six hundred dollars this cost."

"But you were . . . under that, you were—you were—"

"Oh, yeah, that whole . . . you know your buddy Jance? I mean, ex-buddy. Anyway, I know your crew's all against guns, would never *shoot* a bigfoot, but Jance . . . yeah, sorry to have to tell you this. He had a taser in his fanny pack. And, in this ridiculous thing"—the bigfoot costume—"I can't move like I usually can, and these claws aren't real. I figured he might get lucky and actually knock me down with a jolt of electricity, right? So, as soon as I told Marty I had a little nature call to make, could he give me a few minutes please, I was wolfing out with the spirit glue. So if Jance zapped me, pulled my fake head off, he'd find another. Electricity only knocks my kind out for a few minutes, I mean. That's all I'd need to freak him out for."

"Your *kind*?" Tol managed to say somewhat coherently.

"I'm not the only vampire, Tol baby," Rachel said. "But, that's cute, really."

Tol figured he was sort of crying here, but he couldn't feel his face anymore, so didn't really know.

"But, but *why*?" he asked.

"Because I can?" Rachel said. "Because it's fun? Because, after three centuries, if you don't do shit to keep it interesting, you kind of go off the deep end?"

"No," Tol corrected, "I mean, why are you telling me all this?"

"Oh, yeah," Rachel said. "When I probably didn't tell Marty and Jance and Chuck, and . . . who's that other one?"

"Deaner."

"How have I lived so long without ever hearing that name?"

"I—I don't know?"

"'Deaner,' 'Deaner,'" Rachel said. "I think he made it up. He has to have. Who would name their kid that?"

"You're not answering," Tol told her.

Rachel sighed, shrugged one shoulder.

"I got most of the license plate of that truck," she said, and turned to show him what she meant: her shoulder had an imprint of partial numbers and letters, reversed. "Can you write it down before I heal?"

Tol got out his journal, his write-anywhere pen, and cribbed the four characters down, tore that page out, handed it to her, kind of watching himself do all this while he was doing it, as if he could maybe watch it through again later, make it make better sense.

"Appreciate that," Rachel said, and folded the page over, tucked it into her bra, it looked like. Which was a thing Tol had never considered: Vampires wore underwear?

"Cindy's gonna kill me," he said, looking around the back of the minivan, where he'd autopsied a bigfoot, shaved a werewolf, and fed a vampire.

"*Well* . . ." Rachel said, squinching her three-hundred-year face up like she hated to disagree, but—

Tol turned to see what she meant, and standing there, impossibly huge, most definitely larger than life, blotting out most of the night sky, was Bigfoot.

Tol opened his mouth but no sound came out.

"Why I had to take your crew out?" Rachel said. "It was this idiot. He got seen when he shouldn't have, so . . . call Rachel, the one-woman cleanup crew."

"Hey now," Bigfoot said, his voice so bass it made the fine hairs on the back of Tol's neck tremble.

He swallowed painfully, batted his eyes at way too rapid a rate, and then, because it was easier this way, allowed himself to think that he'd fallen asleep on mom-duty, that he was actually parked on the side of the road having a nice dream where he was getting to play with all the monsters he could conjure, that the radio was probably spiking with Marty and Jance and Chuck and Deaner's pleas to come pick them up already, but he couldn't, because, look, he'd found out that vampires were real, and he knew now that Bigfoot could speak, and speak *English* at that, and, and—

With one big hand, Bigfoot twisted Tol's head around backwards, so that the last thing he saw was Rachel, her lower lip pushing up past her top lip as if in apology, or regret, but she was right, wasn't she? No, Cindy wasn't going to kill him.

Bigfoot was taking care of that.

THE SMELL OF WAITING

by Kaaron Warren

On her fourth birthday, Andrea and her parents had a picnic by the settling pond. Her brand-new birthday dog bit at her ankles, making her laugh, as she and her mother laid out a blanket under a tree near the edge of the pond and her father traversed the area, collecting bones, clearing blockages, skimming off dead birds, and testing the water, performing the mysterious tasks that "kept them in the money."

She and her mother ate sandwiches and cake and talked about many things. Andrea didn't always understand, but still she nodded, aping adult conversation, something which made her mother laugh and kiss her cheeks and give her treats. If her mother looked away for a minute Andrea would be at the water's edge, trying to paddle her fingertips, reaching down to cool her wrists. The new dog, tied up to the tree to keep him from disturbing the wildlife, strained at the leash to join her.

Her grandfather already despised him. "Stupid dog for the bush," he'd said that morning, which made Andrea laugh but her father cross. He wasn't wrong; the dog was a golden cocker spaniel, whose ears were already tangled with bush weeds and whose fur was matted with red dust. He wore a pink collar studded with diamonds that Andrea coveted for herself. The dog wriggled loose, dashed toward the low-flying birds circling the pond, and in he went. And sank. Andrea remembered this as if she'd watched it a dozen times; he disappeared so quickly it was like something tugged him down into the water. She remembered the sound of her own scream ("Dad! Save him!"), knowing even at that age that something was terribly wrong, that the dog should not be in the water.

He hadn't even had the chance to learn his name. She called him Sunshine because he was golden, even though they all said that wasn't a dog's name. His bones were down there, somewhere, sunk deep in the mud.

• • •

She herself almost drowned, in that same pond, when she was six.

She still went with her dad to check the pond, but her mother mostly stayed at home. Her mum had a baby in her tummy, which was annoying and took all the attention, so Andrea liked going with her dad.

As he pulled up at the pond, he swore. "Bloody campers," he said.

"Bloody idiots," Andrea said.

Her dad laughed, put his finger to his lips. "Don't tell Mum we swore!" he said.

Her dad hated campers. They ignored the signs warning them not to swim, the big yellow sign saying BEWARE: HEAVY METALS IN WATER. He repainted the "s" a dozen times, but gave up after that. Too many heavy metal fans coming all this way to make the joke.

They were stripped off down to their undies, stupid enough in this heat, and jumping into the pond as if they were at the council pool.

"Oi!" her dad said. "Oi, it's not safe, that water. Don't swim in it, mate."

One of them climbed out, then the others, three of them approaching Andrea and her dad. A big golden dog stood with them, as high as their thighs, and Andrea, hiding behind her father's legs, peeked out. She loved dogs and wondered if they'd let her pat it. The men didn't seem to like their dog, though; they waved their arms at it, swore at it.

"It's all good, mate, don't worry. This fucken heat, though, right?" one of the men said.

"Don't swear in front of my daughter, please." Andrea didn't know what the word meant, back then. "And this water really isn't good to swim in. You should go a bit further up the road, you'll find a campsite up there."

"What, with a swimming pool nice as this?" They were close, now. She could smell them, and the dog, muddy, stinky. "That's just a precaution, right? Look at that water. Beautiful."

So quickly her dad couldn't react in time, one of them lifted Andrea up and tossed her in the water. She gasped; it was warm on top, but ice cold underneath. She squeezed her eyes shut as she sank, and instinctively flapped her arms. She'd use this, later, as a joking weapon against her parents; *you should have taught me to swim.* She took a breath, swallowed water, began to cough but couldn't, looked up, saw a glint of sun then shadow then a tug as she was dragged out by the big dog.

Her dad wrapped her in the picnic blanket they kept in the car. The campers were gone, driving off in their colourful red and blue campervan the minute they threw her in the pond. "Wish I'd had the chance to shoot the bastards," her dad said, squeezing her tight.

"I'm alright, Dad! I liked swimming." Andrea stood up and did a little dance to prove it, and the big dog spun in circles alongside her.

"Good country girl," her dad said. He looked out over the pond. "Are you okay for a bit? I've got to finish up." She nodded; she'd been for a swim! She'd loved it! "Don't watch," he said. One of his jobs as caretaker was to put the fish and birds he found gasping near the water out of their misery.

"Don't tell your mum about going in the water," he said. He gathered up dead fish and birds, pulling some out of the water, gathering others from the side of the pond. He spread them all out amongst the rocks in the baking heat. The dog hung around, fascinated, sniffing at the carcasses and bones, pushing at them with his snout before running off to catch rabbits. "Where'd you come from, Pongo? Big Fella? Good dog," Andrea's dad said. "Your grandad would approve of that one."

The dog deposited a rabbit at her feet. There were rabbit bones and small corpses all around, she noticed, as if he'd been here for a while and this was how he fed himself. She was a bit scared of him; he was so big and he smelled funny. Her dad finished his things and picked her up to put her in the truck.

"What about their doggy?" she said.

"I don't think he was theirs. He's a stray," he said.

"Grandad will like him," Andrea said, putting her arms around the dog's neck. "He's not like my other dog, is he?" Although strangely he was, with the same golden fur, the same lovely brown eyes. Her dad shook his head, but then took a piece of rope to leash the dog. Pongo, her dad had already named him. Because of how bad he always smelled, no matter how they washed him. The name never stuck, though. You don't call a dog like that Pongo.

The truck had been parked in a clump of trees for the shade, and was cool to the touch. The doors weren't locked so her dad strapped her in and the dog jumped on the tray of the truck. Her dad went around to his side, climbed in, swore.

The campers had stolen the truck keys. He swore a bit more, then grabbed their water bottles and said, "Quick hike home, Andrea? Not too far!" He used his "hurry up" voice, but calm, not wanting to panic her. He checked the glove box and swore again; they'd taken his wallet, too. "Lucky I had me gun with me," he said.

It was a half-hour walk for a grown-up, so it must have taken hours. Her father carried her for a bit, and the dog trotted along beside them. He was so big she could ride him like a pony; at six she was light as a feather. The ride was nice at first. His fur had dried soft and golden in the sun, and he moved slowly and carefully. After a while she didn't like it, though. She felt as if he might run away with her and her dad would never find them. Her dad was anxious, keeping one hand on the dog's shoulder. He found the farm truck keys sitting on the roof of The Lemon, the car they used to go into town, and he picked them up and thrust them in his pocket. He stopped, staring at the house. In a calm voice he said, "Let's go see your mum."

The dog ran ahead and began sniffing around, the rope trailing behind him. He barked, a loud, anxious sound that made Andrea cover her ears.

"You wait here for a bit," her dad said to her, but when the dog snarled, she was allowed inside.

The door was swinging open, the flywire off kilter, and the buzz of flies inside was loud.

"Georgia?" he called out. There was no response; no sound at all. He walked through into the kitchen and there she was, Andrea's mother, lying on the floor, blood pooled around her, her face battered, her arm bent strangely, flies buzzing over her lips and her eyes, which were narrowed but open.

The dog barked, sniffed at her, and her father tied him to the table, where he barked hysterically.

Her dad fell to his knees, panting. Andrea squatted beside him. Was her mother asleep? Did she cut her thumb with the sharp knife? Her father moaned, an awful sound, and Andrea found it hard to breathe. She could smell the dog; wet, hairy, chemical, like the truck's tank when it was just filled. A pretty golden ribbon of smoke came out of her mother's mouth. It was so pretty she ran her hands through it, and the dog, next to her now, thrust his large snout into it, breathing in. Andrea leant forward and breathed it in also. The smell was sweet, like barley sugar, and her mother coughed. Sat up. "What?" she said, her voice cracked. "The baby," she said, as she wrapped her arms around herself as if protecting her unborn child.

Andrea hugged her mother, squeezing as hard as she could.

"Oh, darling," her mother said, hugging back, but then she laughed and said, "Oh, you stinky girl!" and turned away.

Her father kissed her mother. "I thought you'd died. Oh god. I thought we'd lost you." He embraced her, holding her so tight she winced. Andrea snuggled onto her mother's lap until her dad turned his head. "Bath night tonight for you, Pongo the Girl," he said. "You smell as bad as that dog does." The dog licked Andrea's arms and she giggled at the feel of it. "And, you, Pongo the Dog, you're going outside." The dog obediently followed orders. All of them not sure what had happened, but in that moment it didn't matter.

It was the campers who'd done it. Her mother remembered that much but little more; the last thing was the approach of a campervan, noisy, pulling up in front of the house. "I thought about how far away you were," she said. "But that's the last thing I remember." Her father phoned the police to alert them and then they all bundled into The Lemon together, leaving the dog tied up with a bowl of water in the shade. They stopped first at the doctor's, marching straight through into his office past the receptionist who was the world's worst gossip.

The doctor tut-tutted as he patched her wounds (shoulder dislocated, bruises on her face, a deep gash in her neck that had already closed and just needed a few stitches) and checked her vitals, checked the baby, side-eyeing her father as if he'd done it. "You're lucky to be alive, I'm not going to lie. Injuries like this. Lucky for the baby as well."

"We're going to the police after this," her father said. "Bloody bunch of campers did it."

"Did they?" the doctor said. He smiled at her mother. "All right?"

Her mother said, "I could do with a good bowl of hot soup! Vegetable soup, thick, with fat white bread and butter," and they all laughed although Andrea didn't see what was funny about it. As an adult, she'd understand that sometimes you laughed to alleviate a difficult situation, whether the joke was good or not. "I'm hungry too," she said, although she wasn't, really. She felt ill, as if her stomach was full of golden syrup, sticking to her ribs and making it hard to breathe.

It felt like half the town watched them walk into the police station. Andrea walked proudly beside her parents, quite enjoying the attention. Her skin felt a bit tight and she rubbed at it. It was like that one time they went to the beach and the salt water dried on her cheeks, making them feel stretched.

She sat on her father's lap while they spoke to the policeman. The policeman asked if she'd like to go do some drawings out with the desk sergeant but she didn't, and her parents didn't mind her staying.

"These men are known to us, Reg," the policeman said. "Well-known. These are men who are known thieves and have a number of suspected murders to their names." He whispered the word *murder* which made Andrea very curious to know what it meant. He said that what they'd done to her father, stealing his keys and wallet, going to the home, they had done more than once. He asked for a list of belongings stolen. It was jewelry, money, and other small items of value. He said all alerts had been sent out and they'd catch the mongrels, he was sure of it.

"You're lucky to be alive," the policeman said. It wasn't the last time they'd hear this. People would say, *Why didn't you race home,* and her dad would say, *I didn't panic until I saw the keys gone. They seemed bad but not that bad. And I had the kid with me. You can only go so fast.*

Andrea wondered if anyone would talk about the dog, and the golden smoke, but no one did so neither did she.

When they got back home, the dog barked and yelped, straining on his leash, although when her dad went to check it was loosely tied and he could have run off at any time. Her mother wanted a big rest so she lay down on the couch, while Andrea, taking advantage of her parents' distraction, took a bag of potato chips out of the food cupboard and slunk off to one of her favourite hiding spots—a large crate facing the wall—in the loft in the barn. It was a spot her parents never found; they'd call and call and she would only crawl out when she felt like it. She could peer through a gap in the wooden wall, watching the world. So she saw the dog, off his leash, sniffing around as if following a trail, and then trotting straight to where she was, barking below the loft because he couldn't climb up the ladder.

She shushed it, not wanting her parents to discover her spot, and slid down the ladder, pretending to be a firefighter as she liked to do. He sniffed at her, licked her, and she ran as fast as she could into the house.

In the morning, when Andrea looked out the window, the leash lay on the ground, no sign of the dog. Her dad was gone too, on the quad bike, to get the farm truck, she thought, and she could hear her mother crying, sitting up in bed with the covers tucked under her chin. She blinked when Andrea came in. "Do you want some breakfast? I'm so tired," she said. So Andrea went and got a box of cereal, and the two of them sat up in bed with the sun coming in all warm, eating the cereal.

"Where's Dad gone," Andrea said. "Is he taking the dog away?"

"They're on a little hunting trip," her mother said. "That's all."

Her dad and the dog came back around midday the next day, the dog sitting up in the front seat like a hairy man. Her mum was up and about by then, making them sandwiches for lunch. Andrea was building a bed for her pet chicken, and suffering pecks and scratches for her troubles. Her dad drove up, but didn't get out of the farm truck for a bit, not until her mum went over to the window and reached in and kissed him. Andrea ran over too, clamouring for attention. He held tight to her mother and to her. He smelled bad, like when he killed the lamb for Sunday Roast, and his clothes were sticky and dusty, his hands the same. Andrea looked in the back of the truck to see what they'd caught, but there was nothing. The dog jumped out of the front seat and nudged her, as if asking to be petted.

Her father tied the dog in his spot, *Let Leash the Dogs of War!* he said, and her parents both laughed. Her mother's laugh was croaky, like the crows that flocked in when they threw the vegetable scraps out the back door. Her dad drank a beer, her mother drank fizzy water, and they danced around barefoot together, laughing. Andrea sat and watched for a while, feeling left out, then to get their attention she pulled her mother's shoes onto her feet. She'd done this before, to great laughter (although her mother hated it. *Don't ruin my shoes!*), and she danced around for them until her father lifted her up and all three of them danced together. Andrea would remember that safe and comforting feeling of being sandwiched between them.

They were noisy in their bedroom but Andrea was too tired to check. She fell asleep with her clothes on, which she loved to do, because in the morning she wouldn't have to pick new things to wear, she'd just keep wearing these ones.

She was woken up in the middle of the night by a bad smell. The scratch of nails on wood. She called out for her dad. "It's the scary dog," she said.

"It's okay, he's leashed in the yard," her dad said, pulling back her curtains. "And he's a good dog. Best tracker there ever was. You must have been having a bad dream." The dog sat there chewing on a boot, but nobody went to take it from him. She knew she hadn't dreamed that smell or the sound. That dog had come to her bedroom somehow.

That dog came as he pleased from then on. He liked staying by the settling pond, mostly, living off the rabbits he caught. It was dry, and insects worked fast. There wasn't much you could leave in the dirt that would still be fleshy a week or two later. Andrea had her chickens, and sometimes baby rabbits as pets, but they always died.

The night the baby was born, her mother paced up and down the hallway, breathing weirdly, just making noise, until, an hour or so before dawn, her father came into her room.

"The baby's coming!" He told her to bundle into warm clothes and grab her Thing bag, which was full of snacks and things to do.

They packed into The Lemon, even though her mother argued for the truck, and took off at high speed.

As they turned in to the road at the end of the driveway, Andrea thought she saw the dog stand in the dawn shadow of the large ancient pine tree. He opened his mouth but she didn't know if he was yawning or snarling.

Her grandad was waiting at the hospital and he took Andrea's bag and put his heavy hand on her shoulder. They watched her mother and father disappear from sight and he said, "What's the bet she'll make such a fuss we'll be able to hear about it downstairs?" They went to the café, sitting outside even though there was no sun. They had hot chocolate and pineapple donuts, and Andrea chatted away. She talked about the dog ("You don't say," he said) and her mother's golden smoke ("You don't say") and where she wanted him to help her build a little house.

The next time she saw her parents, she had a little sister. Her mother sitting up in the hospital bed, red-faced, holding a dear little baby that Andrea felt love and affection for. A nurse took her mother's hand and squeezed, something Andrea could see gave her mother comfort.

Andrea hoped she could stay home and help look after her mother, that she wouldn't have to go back to school now the baby was born, perhaps until the baby turned five or six. But no; her father laid out her school clothes, and set out her lunchbox, ready for the morning. Sadly, sister or no sister, Andrea had to go to school. She was not a pretty child. Her hair was thick and limp, no matter how often she washed it. The kids at school called her Greasy and said she smelled. Later they called her Easy Greasy, pretending that she'd have sex with anyone who asked. "Stinker," they called her. She sucked mints all day so at least her breath would be sweet.

She was a heavy-boned girl, her mother said, heavy-boned.

Still, each day she showed up at school, doing the right thing, being dutiful. Sometimes, the dog would go with her, and later be waiting patiently at the school gates for her to finish her day.

Just before her tenth birthday, she smelled that particular smell, the smell of waiting, as her grandfather called it.

The sky darkened and the air chilled. A group of children had been playing a game they called Traitor, with Andrea watching, an outsider. It didn't look at all fun, to her. It started to rain, and they all ran inside, leaving the "traitor" tied to the tree. She began to cry.

Andrea, used to knots on the farm, untied her. The girl pushed her, *Leave me alone, Greasy,* and ran, right across the football field, except halfway there she was struck by lightning.

Andrea's heart almost stopped. Somehow the rain paused and Andrea ran to the girl, falling to her knees beside her. She remembered her mother's smoke; where was this girl's smoke? She pressed on her stomach.

There. There it was. Andrea breathed it in, catching fresh air as well, taking it in, in gulps.

The girl gasped, sat up. The dog gently licked rainwater off Andrea's arms and legs. "Come on," Andrea said, "or we'll get in trouble for being late." She took the girl's hand and squeezed, mimicking the nurse she'd seen.

That night, Andrea told the story of what happened. Her grandfather said, "There's no such thing as that dog!," one of his favourite jokes. But her sister, three now, golden-eyed and cute as a button, loved that dog. She was obsessed with all animals, but loved the dog more than anything else.

Andrea found it hard to sleep. Her skin was dry and flaky; her mother gave her lanolin to rub in and that helped a bit, but the itch kept her awake most of the night.

At school, they avoided her even more. One of them told her about stories that came back from the pub. Men drinking at the bar were often a source of gossip. "My dad says your grandad says you can bring people back to life because you're a witch. Witches are evil so you must be evil."

"He wouldn't."

Another said her grandfather made up his stories at the pub for free beer, that he made fun of her and made everyone laugh.

Her grandfather laughed until the day she saved his life and he became a true believer.

She was eleven then. Her parents and sister were on a shopping trip for soccer boots, but as Andrea reached home after exploring with her dog she expected her grandfather to be there. Instead, she entered a silent house. The dog waited by the back door and howled until she let him in.

She climbed the stairs to where her grandfather lay breathing shortly, his fingers shaking. She looked at him. His breathing slowed, seemed painful. She thought about how mean he was to her mother but he liked her cooking, and his beer, and was out there with her dad at the settling pond (the unsettling pond, they liked to call it) and surrounds, helping out. He did Andrea's homework for her sometimes. The dog sidled in and pressed up against her legs. He felt soft and warm and she gave him a hug. He nudged at the golden smoke (really closer to yellow, she thought) that rose from her grandfather and she sat on the side of the bed. She leaned over and breathed it in. It tasted of dirt, and the way beer smelled (she had stolen a sip once, so in all honesty knew what it tasted like). It was disgusting, slimy like mucus.

Her grandfather sat up. "Wait," he said. "Wait wait wait." The dog patiently licked at Andrea and she let him, stretching her legs.

"He likes the salt, I think," she told her grandfather. "Gross thing he is." She tousseled the dog's hair then patted her grandfather's arm. "I'll call Mum." But her grandfather picked up his walking stick and hit the dog as hard as he could, so hard the dog went yelping out of the room, pushing his way through the wire door downstairs and away. Andrea started to cry.

"He looks like your shitty little dog grown into a monster," he croaked.

"He's a ghost?" she said.

"He's a monster."

Her grandfather headed out with her father the next day to the settling pond, just to lend a hand, he said. He liked to be useful but mostly, Andrea thought, he didn't want to help around the house.

She knew a bit more about the pond now, and the mine it had served. She'd learned how much land had been cleared for the mine, how little of the money reached the local people, how poisoned the land became. Still, her father was paid good money to keep it clear, and that was fine. The toxins were better resting at the bottom rather than rising to the top.

Andrea begged to go with them, and her sister did, too. Andrea hadn't been out to the pond for a while and she wanted to check on the dog, to see if he was okay. "Grandad hit him," she said. "After I saved Grandad's life."

There was silence at that.

"Why would Grandad do that?" her father said, as if that was the most important thing.

"I don't know," Andrea said. She started to cry.

"Because he's an angry, fearful man," her mother said. "And I need you to help here, Andrea. How about we make a nice cake for when your dad gets back?"

Andrea's sister started school at five and it was nicer then. They caught the bus together and Andrea could look after her, make sure she was okay, and then home again on the bus for scones for afternoon tea or cereal if everyone was out.

One day when they got home, a pink studded collar sat on the kitchen table. "Ooh, a necklace!" her sister said.

"That looks like Sunshine's collar!" Andrea said. "Where did you find it?"

"In the dog shelter we built your wild dog out by the pond," her father said.

Her grandfather said, "I bloody told you. It's that shitty little dog. The water did it. The water changed him."

"Don't be stupid," her mother said.

Andrea went outside and threw sticks for the dog. He loved to play fetch.

Andrea was fourteen when the first request came. Looking back now, she was surprised at how long it took. Once it started, though, it never stopped. People believed she brought her mother back to life, and her grandfather, and the student. And there was the time when one of her friends choked on a bone (and did anyone else smell that dog/that wet dog smell and hear the sound of the long nails on floorboards/and hear the small whimper he gave?). Andrea leant over her and breathed in her smoke, feeling it cut like glass. The friend shook, shivered, and spat out the bone, now turned to jelly, pink and nasty.

The locals already knew about Andrea's spill in the settling pond (a cautionary tale because of her crocodile skin and the way she smelt like plants left soggy and in the dark for too long) and for a while, this is what they thought, that it was the pond. The Unsettling Pond. Her father had to patrol the pond with a shotgun, because people came in droves to swim in the poison pond, messing up the settling. They thought somehow they'd be able to save lives, too. But all that happened most times was they'd get sick, and end up at the hospital. Meanwhile her grandfather was at the pub every day, taking those free beers and talking about her as if she was some kind of miracle sent to the town to save them.

The first one who showed up on their doorstep was the pub owner. He'd listened to the story so many times he believed it. He said, "I'll pay you a hundred dollars a day to sit by my wife's bed and save her when the time comes." His wife was sick with pneumonia and the doctor gave her a week, less, to live.

Andrea already had in her mind she wanted to leave this place and she needed money to do it, so she said yes. Her dad said she shouldn't take the money, but her grandfather told him to shut his idiot mouth, of course she'd take the money.

It was only two days' work in the end. They held hands at times, and Andrea took comfort in that herself. Andrea was glad the wife couldn't talk, but at the same time was unnerved by the constant attention, the almost-unblinking stare the wife laid on her. Those eyes widened at the last minute, went grey, and a loud scratching at the door meant the dog needed to come in.

This woman's smoke was brownish-gold and tasted of sweet tea.

The pub owner never paid her; no one did. She sucked up people's smoke time and time again, giving them new life, but if she mentioned payment they'd recoil as if she was some kind of evil. Her sister was always there to cheer her up, bring her a warm blanket, bring her a soft cloth to wipe her skin clean. Bring her hot drinks or beer stolen from the fridge, anything to make the taste of the smoke go away. Her mother was increasingly absent, focusing on what she called good works and volunteering at the fire station. Her father and grandfather always had outside business to attend to.

She saved a baby. The taste in her mouth was awful but with a baby powder sweetness.

When she was seventeen, Andrea tried to leave. She planned it out, working at the local supermarket, to save money and gain experience, planning to find the same sort of job in the city, in a place where no one knew her. She bought a bus ticket, prepared her Thing bag, and said goodbye to her sister.

But as she approached the bus stop, the dog gently held on to the hem of her trousers with his sharp teeth, and the people of the town showed up, because someone had realised and spread the word, probably the man who'd sold her the bus ticket. *You stay with us,* they said. They had armfuls of gifts for her, things she didn't want and wouldn't use. They had tins of toffees, boxes of chocolates, they had skin care. All of it placed a distance away. She was swollen, and her hair sparse. She didn't think she smelled bad but they seemed to; they gave her perfumes and oils and all sorts of things.

Her money for the bus ticket found its way back into her bank account.

She saved a sexy man the day after she turned eighteen. He'd lost his way and his footing, and ended up unknown in the gutter but still a gorgeous man. He was the most grateful anyone had been and he treated her like a goddess. He said, *Let's go, let's go to the city and I'll treat you like a goddess for the rest of your life,* and this is what she wanted to do. She knew from experience (from watching her mother) that there was little to identify a once-was-dead, but sometimes there would be a blankness of eye and a coolness of skin, but those things would soon pass.

Andrea craved new people, energy, noise. She was tired of saving the dead. They were brought to her day and night. Some way past helping, and yet people wanted her to try. Some were dug up from the grave, some were dead only minutes. She couldn't bear to look at herself in the mirror; she was greenish. If she cut herself, it smelled like a rotted limb, but there was nothing wrong with her—no broken bits, no need for amputation.

As she was checking her Thing bag for the hundredth time, the town librarian drove up in her beat-up car, a desperate look on her face, *Don't tell.* She parked next to The Lemon. Andrea's father taught her to drive in that car when she was about thirteen, and she'd had her official license for six months. The sense of freedom it gave her, the "I actually could," made her feel light-headed.

Nausea overwhelmed her and she had to sit down and rest for a bit, closing her eyes, breathing slowly, calming herself. She didn't know how many more times she could do this; hopefully this would be the last. If she could run, then this would be the last. The dog followed closely at her heels.

Andrea heard crying as she neared the car, something she was very used to. The librarian was dusty, tear-streaked, clothes askew as if she'd dressed quickly and in the dark. "Please!" she said. "You've got to help him!"

Lying on the back seat was a man Andrea didn't know personally but she knew for a fact wasn't married to the librarian. All he had on was a pair of woman's tracksuit pants; apart from that, bare-chested, bare-footed. Still warm, and there was the familiar yellow smoke rising off him. Andrea held on to the back of the driver's seat with one hand and placed the other on his chest. She leaned in and sucked the air, feeling it cut her throat, the scent of it sweet but sickly. *Last one,* she thought. *This is the last fucking one.* She breathed harder; his smoke was thick, distasteful, and she gagged. He coughed, and Andrea stepped back to allow the librarian to tend to him. They both bent down and cuddled the dog. Everybody loved him. He had adoring fans; those saved were devoted beyond measure. Were they different, on awakening? Certainly she was; each time she felt it in her bones, the flavour of their smoke sitting in the back of her throat before nestling in the pit of her stomach, like lumps of chewing gum.

No one changed much after she saved them. Beyond knowing, at all times, where the dog was, they were mostly the same.

Andrea went inside, not waiting for a thank-you. They didn't always come these days. She needed a shower, and about a gallon of water to wash out her insides as well.

This was the one that Andrea hoped was the last one. It was bad and she felt it in her bones more than ever.

When her father and grandfather came home, they found her slumped on the couch, in the dark, unable to move.

"The librarian's boyfriend," she said, by way of explanation.

"This can't go on. We have to get you away," her father said. "It's enough."

Her grandfather shook his head, saying, "Bloody nonsense. Get on with it. This is your role in life, so get on with it, girl."

"It's hurting her," her dad said. She was swollen, now, her insides pushing against her skin like a ripe plum.

"Some ice cream'll fix her," her grandfather said, as if she was six and he could bribe her into doing something. So the three of them, with the dog in the back with her (he wouldn't go near her grandfather—and who could blame him?), piled into the truck to head into town. There was silence, until they neared a dirt road. Like a dog who saw a rat once near the fence and always goes back there, the dog always strained and barked whenever they passed this place in the road.

"He knows there are bones that way," her grandfather said, chuckling.

"What bones?"

"Not your business," her grandfather said. "Man's business."

But she knew it was her business. The dog wouldn't let her go; she belonged to him, so anything to do with him was her business. Her grandfather thought he owned her too, day by day trapping her there (*What if I need a wake-up again and you're not here? Your dad? Your sister?*).

It wasn't until a week later she could take The Lemon. She wanted to keep on driving, heading for the big city, but the dog sat beside her, growling at a low grumble, nudging at her, and she wanted to know what was at the place her grandfather said was full of bones.

She drove to the dirt road and let the dog out. He ran ahead of her and she drove slowly after him, alert in case he stopped suddenly. His nose twitching, he led her until he reached a grove of trees that concealed a massive pile of large rocks. Then he stopped.

She climbed out of the car. It was hot out there, so hot she dripped sweat and she felt her skin constricting.

The dog climbed onto the rocks and howled. She could see a glimpse of colours, red and blue, and as she rounded the corner, she saw it was a camp-ervan.

The dog circled her legs as she walked toward it. As she approached, she saw what she feared. Three skeletons sitting across the front seat.

These were the campers who had killed her mother.

Covering her face (although there was no smell; they were long past that) she approached the van. The driver's door hung open and she could see a bird's nest in the corner, evidence of wild dogs in the dirt.

The dog tried to leap at the first skeleton but she held him back. She man-aged to tie him to a stump in the shade, ignoring his howls as she looked into the van.

They had been chained to their seats. Around them, dark stains, long since dried, told her they'd been alive when left there. One of them must have had an arm free, because there was a handwritten note, scrawled on the back of some registration papers:

sorry for dropping the girl in the water
sorry for killing the lady
Please save us
Please let us go to heaven not hell.
God bless the hell hound and god save us

Andrea squatted in the dirt. The dog sniffed as if looking for golden smoke but all there was, surely, was heat haze. Staring in at the skeletons, she called her father, finding cell phone reception.

"I'm in the place. They're just bones now," she said.

He choked and she wasn't sure if he was laughing. She thought he was probably crying.

"I couldn't remember where it was to go back there. To get them."

You didn't try very hard, she thought. "The dog brought me."

"They killed your mother . . . they almost killed your mother. And you. They almost drowned you."

"They're just bones now."

"I should confess, shouldn't I? It's time. Their families need to know."

"You know they don't have families. You know no one cared they went missing."

"Stay there. Stay there. I'll come, we'll call the station. It's meant to be, An-drea. You know it." The phone felt hot against her ear. "I was so angry. And the dog . . . I swear he wanted it too. I shoulda shot them. I know. I'm weak. You know how much I hate killing things. And there was something. The begging. Hearing them beg; that sounded good. It made me feel better."

It didn't make Andrea feel better. "I love you, Dad," she said. "But I'm taking them to the settling pond."

She found a sleeping bag in the back of the van and gathered their bones. They came away easy, no sinew left, no connecting tissue. The dog leaped around, he wanted those bones badly. She thought about giving him the evidence to destroy, but had another idea. One that might distract him long enough for her to get away.

Her father met her at the settling pond. It was shallower since she was last there, and the water thick and brown, barely covering the debris resting, half-sunk, in the quicksand that lay beneath the surface.

Part of her wished she was still a child, that she knew nothing of the world. Andrea thought about the fierce, determined child she'd been. That was back then, before they'd taken everything from her. When her skin was smooth, not cracked and oozing . . . she rubbed at her cheeks, feeling them stretch in the sun.

Andrea gazed at the bottom of the settling pond. It was murky, cloudy; lord knew what sort of shit that was. Tree roots sticking, and bits of metal, and she shuddered to think what else. She instinctively collected some of the bones around the edges of the settling pond, adding them to the piles and piles of bones her father had collected over the years.

There was a smell of ozone in the air, that "smell of waiting." Dark clouds overhead meant a storm was on its way. She hoped it hurried. She circled the settling pond, her nose wrinkling at the dank, oily smell. She felt no desire to throw off her clothes and swim.

Andrea opened the boot and dragged out the sleeping bag that held the campers' bones. Her father was a good man; no manner of investigation or confession should change that. She dragged the bag to the water's edge, the dog leaping and sniffing at it. She couldn't say exactly why she was doing it, but at the same time she lived in hope; if she did this, if she offered enough of the bones, added enough to the pond, perhaps the dog, the one that stood guarding every avenue of escape, would let her go. Would be happy with her offering and let her leave for the city, to the anonymity she craved. Perhaps he would be distracted enough so she could run.

She squatted at the water's edge, peering down. She'd done this many times over the years, wishing that Sunshine, her little gentle dog, had never drowned and feeling as if she should have saved him somehow. Her father arrived, parking the truck haphazardly and walking quickly toward her. He didn't argue when she told him what she wanted to do.

The bones rattled in the bag. "I'll chuck it," her father said. He lifted the bag high so the dog couldn't reach it, then he spun around as if he was about to throw a discus. It was such a ridiculous sight Andrea laughed, the first genuine laugh she'd had in a long time, and he threw the bag a good distance toward the centre of the pond.

The dog splashed in happily, head high out of the water, tail wagging.

"I need to get out of here, Dad. Look at me. Every day I'm more filled with poison."

"You go. Go get your Thing bag, and git."

She had her Thing bag already.

She felt happier than, perhaps, that day long ago when she got Sunshine the cute dog for her fourth birthday.

Driving The Lemon, she composed a letter to her mother and sister in her head, knowing she could call for her sister to come once she was settled. The rain hadn't paused and the roads were wet, and she could almost hear her father say, "Careful." She pulled onto the main road that would take her out of town, heading toward the big city. It was a five-hour drive to get there; she'd stop for a burger on the way. She'd heard about this; people did this sort of thing, and now she'd do it. She'd stop for a burger, then drive into the city and find the hotel she'd booked herself into, and then figure it out from there. That handsome man; she'd call him, perhaps, or perhaps not.

Standing in the middle of the road, near the Milly Molly Café, was the dog. Massive, twice the size or more from the day he saved her from the pond, his head forward, guarding the way out, wanting to keep her in. People on the side of the road pointed at her, looked at each other; they didn't want her leaving, either. Who'd suck up their death if she was gone? Who'd save their lives?

She veered slightly to avoid the dog but he stepped that way and this, this way and that, always in her path, and if she got around him he ran ahead, far faster than she was, and would stand there. In the end she tried to drive straight through him, thinking he wasn't real, but the car spun sideways on the wet road, lifted off the ground, flipped, skidded, smashed into the one and only traffic light. She hadn't been going fast but somehow the impact was as if she'd been going four times the speed limit, and she was thrown forward and back, no airbag in this old piece of shit, banging her head so hard it knocked her out, before the car was crushed with her in it. Another car veered out of control, right into the path of a young boy. The dog collected him with his jaws, then with a flick of his head, tossed him to safety. Another life saved, all of this flashing before Andrea's eyes. She could see the child's future because it was her own life—she had been saved like this, been given a "gift"—and now she was sure the boy would have this gift, this curse. But there was nothing she could say or do as the dog came and licked her face, then with his teeth gently gnawed at her throat. The smell of oil and transmission fluid and brake fluid and the smell of ozone. Andrea watched as cars stopped and the people stared at her. Every one of them owed her for saving a life. Not one of them would pay what she wanted them to pay: her freedom. Helping her leave, to have a life outside.

Instead, they loomed over her like a many-limbed monster. The dog sat nearby, scratching fleas, and then, as the smell of ozone rose, he leapt off and loped away. That smell—and she could hear someone say, "That's the smell of waiting. Waiting for death."—it was a smell of burning wire, of chlorine. It was sweet, and clean, and it brought the rain.

No one would come near her; her flesh had split like a ripe plum and the stink of her, the reek of all those deaths, made them turn from her. She stretched out a hand, hoping at least for that small comfort she'd given so many of them; a warm hand squeeze. No one came near, all the people whose lives she'd saved or their loved ones, and the dog, already moving on, trotted over to the young boy, leaving her to die alone.

NOW VOYAGER

by Livia Llewellyn

The untold want by life and land ne'er granted,
Now voyager sail thou forth to seek and find.
—Walt Whitman

THE PRINCESS

A princess stands on her bedroom balcony, silver-tipped furs draped around her shoulders yet still shivering in the early-morning cold. There are many thousands of windows in the castle, but none so low in the thick walls that anyone can see out of them. This is by her design, and the design of her brothers and sisters. There are only nine balconies. This one belongs to her and no one else. From here she can see what her siblings see on their private balconies, what none of their countless servants over the many centuries have ever seen, save a privileged few. An autumn sun is rising over the edges of the massive caldera that is their private estate, catching at its ragged edges and spilling onto the western ridge like honey dripping down from the mouths of sated gods. By midday it will shine upon all four flanks of the inner cone, across all the countless rooms and passages of the circular castle that snake across its surface, over the rustling forests and meadows, until no inch of the ancient volcano's interior resides in darkness, except for what lies at the very center. All across the lush caldera floor, birds will sing and soar in full-throated glory, glossy-coated animals will prowl and prance and crunch their dinner's bones, leaves will detach from trembling branches and cascade to the ground in waterfalls of glorious reds and golds. Life, straining one last time toward the sun before the days begin to darken and shorten, and everything decays and disappears with the first of the winter snows. The princess places her elbows on the balcony's stone edge, cups her face with small, knotty hands, and chokes out a sob as deep and melancholy as a moan.

She is not an ordinary princess, this indelicate creature violently rubbing her bulbous eyes and pinching the snot from her nostrils, she is not a princess of fairy tales or tapestries or troubadours' courtly love songs. Barely taller than a child, with dark cratered skin that has survived numerous plagues. A jawline and mouth too wide even for that oversized head. Short, coarse hair as unruly and tangled as a bear's, and a single brow protruding from her face like a canopy. Her stance is regal but her body is muscular and thick, the body of someone who spent a good portion of her early life fighting to stay alive with all the blood-soaked, calculated savagery of any other hunter, only to see her people's place in the world usurped by a lesser branch from the evolutionary tree. She is not ashamed of her face, however. She knows what she is. The princess has heard all of the cruel names given to her over the centuries by each wave of servants brought into the castle, and they suit her better than the string of long-forgotten sounds that was her original name. She and her brothers and sisters are indeed frightful and grotesque, and they were given a frightful and grotesque task, long ago in their earliest days on the planet, a task that would have broken any human being. Of course, it has broken them, in countless little ways, of that there is no doubt—but. But. Now it is to those soft, inferior humans they must turn for the continued existence of the Camera. This has been a long time coming, and all their efforts to stave off this day have come to naught. The Camera of the Gods is finally dying, and their gods demand a replacement, and they do not like to wait. There is still so much in this world they wish to see.

The princess lets out another soft sob, and breathes in the crisp air. It smells like cedar and ancient rock and the lingering chemical tang of last night's storm. All this pain, all these fears and doubts, all the burden of their sacred work, all this will pass like the storm. And what they strive to accomplish today will bring them one step closer to what she and her family all yearn for, what they only ever receive once every several centuries: that singular, explosive, numinous moment when their distant gods bend their ancient gaze into her and her siblings' minds, hollowing her out until all she sees is what they see—vast alien creatures and landscapes and planes of existence so far removed from the limited vocabulary and experiences of her true primitive self that she has never been able to remember little more than disjointed flashes of dream-like images. Incomprehensible, terrifying, more addictive than any drug. A third and final sob escapes the princess's lips, but this one is pregnant with longing and the anticipation of a distant lover's arrival.

"It's time." Her eldest brother stands at the door. She no longer remembers his name, and his features are always somewhat unfamiliar to her (they have all become so much alike in their collective eternal hideousness), but knows he's the eldest by the white hair crowning his head, and by a deep scar along the side of his face, still an angry purple-red despite having healed while much of the world had once been covered in ice. Behind him, the princess glimpses the rest of her family gathering. The servants are right, they really do all look like hobgoblins, she ruefully realizes.

"We have chosen our novitiates. Their albums have already been collected from the vaults, the novitiates must be collected. You cannot hold off on this decision any longer. You must choose your novitiate so we can proceed."

"I will never be ready," the princess replies. Her words are labored, each one forced from a throat and mouth that were never meant to utter any language at all. Another gift from their gods. "If it does not work—if we cannot create the new Camera . . ."

The prince places one hand on her shoulder, and points with the other to what lies at the center of the caldera. Its blackness, its immensity, its cyclopean size, the absolute and definitive absence of life pouring up from it in hard shimmering waves that distort the rays of that autumn sun—her family has bled its entire existence out over the passage of hundreds of thousands of years, protecting and serving what her brother, in this infinitesimally small sliver of a moment in their lives, reaches out to, his twisted hand steady in the bright morning sun.

"We are not gods. We do not create," he says. "We merely stand at the open door of the divine. Creation alone knows how to make its way inside."

The princess stares at him, only for a second, but for what seems like until the end of time.

THE CAMERA

Deep in the center of the caldera, in the sleeping forests of night, the Aperture opens.

. . . *once upon a time,* **THEY** *signal to the Camera in her tortured fever dreams, nightmarish dreams mushrooming from the broken ruins of her epoch-spanning body, dreams now commingling with their desires, their all-consuming need to see see SEE*

. . . *once upon a time, a familiar phrase, a welcoming, a command, and like a broken yet loyal dog the Camera submerges into* **THEM** *and the painful dying spasms of her body subside in an ocean she has never fully reached the bottom or surface or sides of, an ocean of vast cosmic sentience she swims through like a microcosmic speck*

[::are there others like me? i cannot be the only one::] The thought overwhelms the Camera, sending her decaying body back in the waking world, into massive seizures—

*. . . once upon a time, once upon a time, **THEY** chant, casting through the darkness of **THEIR** astral subconscious as they calm the Camera once more into complete submission, and now she slithers mindlessly like an unseen current of wind through all the labyrinthine layers of the castle, each corridor a passage of a hundred years, each room an album of **THEIR** memories*

*. . . once upon a time—**THEY** hear a familiar voice singing back through the starry indigo static of this astral highway, and **THEY** wend the Camera's dreaming mind down into flesh so young, bones so supple, velvety plump folds of brain, once upon a time they whisper to this potential new Camera through the mind of the old Camera, and in the waking world*

a young woman in a small stone room slowly curls onto her bed, closing her eyes as she tries to will the edges of an oncoming headache away. Colored lights flash and spark behind her drooping eyelids. She drapes her forearm over her head, blocking the afternoon sun, but the sudden darkness only intensifies the pain, makes the colors sharper and more intense. Wind whistles and moans through an unseen crack in the walls. Her limbs grow heavy, dragging her into sleep, dragging her down to that hidden place inside where the knocking has never relented for a single second since she first stepped inside the massive black keep, the entrance to the caldera and her new life in the castle beyond. Seven months of knocking, seven months of opening that door. The young woman floats through it and down and down and down until she is with **THEM** and in **THEM** and filled with **THEM**, and the relief of not fighting it, of letting **THEM** take control once more, is the most profoundly satisfying sensation she has ever known. And now, once upon a time, **THEY** sing to her through the primitive language of the Camera as they flutter through the woman's memories and desires and dreams, and *once upon a time . . .*

Once upon a time, there lived a young orphaned woman trapped in an isolated and abandoned village, one of many that dotted the valleys and foothills of a silent chain of long-dead volcanoes crowned in forests and snow. A young woman so crippled from a life of poverty and hunger that she ate her younger siblings, one by one by one. Every day from the front step of her dead parents' small stone house, the young woman stared up at the jagged horizon and longed for a better life, dreaming of the day she would escape her village—

—no, I don't want to think about that anymore. That's my old life, it's over.

Once upon a time, there was a powerful and feral girl with the sight of the divine beyond all time, a girl not quite human, who had been born to a sorceress in a far-off inland sea of tall grass. But one day the girl was kidnapped by a family of evil goblins and spirited away to live in servitude to their dark gods in a prison high above endless cold forests, because—

—no, that's not my memory, and that doesn't make sense at all.

It's the story I tell myself, my own creation myth. You'll have your own some-day.

Once upon a time, there was a woman who lived in a strange, museum-like castle, more like a collection of beehives rich with all the plundered treasures of the world, at the heart of a massive chain of long-dormant volcanoes on the oldest continent on the planet, in the final days of the human race. The woman was the chosen vessel of the gods, cursed and blessed to be filled with the orgi-astic power of their vision from beyond the edges of space and time, and to act as their eyesight in a world they could never fully enter or control. But she was growing old, and in her death throes, she cast out and found a girl who could re-place her, who had the power to assume the mantle of divine sight and journey up and out of the volcanoes into the great wild world, to view and catalog every convulsion and death rattle of this broken world—

—this is not my memory, this is not a dream . . .

*Your memories are **THEIRS** now, as are mine. Your eyes will be **THEIRS**, and it will be the greatest gift you have ever known. Watch this with your own eyes, a final time.*

Once upon a time in the waning days of the world, when life everywhere was circling the drain but had not yet begun to slip forever away, a malformed-looking woman traveled from the stronghold in the highest ridges of the caldera and over all the outcroppings of the newly built castle nestling in the forested hills of the dormant volcano, down to a small cluster of long-abandoned homes at the outer edges of a system of caves. The last of the snowy storms had departed from the skies, leaving the numb land bright and hard and cold under the clear light of approaching spring. In a room far older than the stronghold, she sat at a table in the glow of a multitude of lamps, her pens and her pots of inks be-fore her, the massive, single glass lens perched on the remains of her nose pol-ished and focused to a precise and perfect degree. With great delicacy, she pulled a pristine sheet of paper out of a packet and sliced it into a rectangle, shaving away the edges with a fine blade again and again until they matched in size to the label affixed on the front of a sumptuous crimson leather album crammed with an inventive new form of imagery. The air trickled in and out of the crum-pling remains of her nose, the bridge long collapsed as her eyes grew larger over the centuries, swelling and stretching toward each other as they slowly merged and formed a single lidless orb. It took time and patience to ink the words in the exact manner as the year before, something her prehistoric fingers still strug-gled with—many blotted and botched rectangles piled up over the hours until a perfect one emerged, which she carefully glued onto a new, empty album. The crackle of candle flame and creaking of bare branches in the afternoon wind kept her company as she cleaned up the supplies, putting everything back in its place until next year. And now all that was left on the table was the crimson al-

bum, the white label affixed to its smooth face, and a matching label across the ribbed spine. Both labels said the same thing, in black ink flecked with bits of pure silver: AD 27592.

—this memory is from the past. Your past.

And it is a vision of your future. Attend.

Behind the table, a built-in bookcase lined the entire wall. Row after row of albums sat on the shelves, all shining in the soft light like polished bones. AD 27591. AD 27590. She ran her ancient, crooked fingers along the spines, across the bookcase, onto another bookcase, in another room, and another room. The hallway, the kitchen, the bedchambers—all filled with bookcases and albums. She followed the gleaming rows of leather from wall to wall, deep into the cave system, backwards across the centuries which merge into millennia, until they directed her to a steep flight of stone stairs leading into a warren of cellars and storage rooms, where the albums gradually morphed from leather binders of the crude, mechanically produced images of this century, and the watercolors and sketches of the last, to illustrated books of hours, to scrolls of parchment, to leaves of papyrus nestling in boxes of cedar and gold. As always, she stopped at the edge of the third flight of stairs, never descending further, never venturing past the delicate rolls of drawings that count their way down to AD 1—the first album to be given a name and number, by some long-dead and forgotten poet, but not the first collection of images, no, not at all. Deep in the lowest reaches, in the hollows of old lava tubes, rested hieroglyphic and cuneiform descriptions scratched out on clay tablets, buried beneath stone chests filled with long hematite and carnelian cylinder seals, one chest for each full suite of seasons under the sun, one cylinder seal for each image of what she saw those nights so many eons ago. And these were not even the oldest records—scattered across the world, lost in the passage of time, pictographs and ochre stencils and crude scratches slowly faded from the sides of megaliths, barrows, other caves. She had never sought out those sites for the same reason she never opened an album or unfurled a scroll once it was filled. Not because she was afraid of disturbing long-lost memories, but because they were not her memories. She captured and cataloged the images at the command of her protectors and patrons, for their grotesque and illicit pleasure long after the acts had been committed, but she knew they were not truly memories for anyone on this planet to relive. The images had been spoken for long ago by something else, something lurking at the earliest edges of the Pleistocene, when she woke up from her mother's arms one evening to see it staring down at her from behind the rim of the sparkling black sky . . .

No matter. The only memories she wanted to relive—those short, blissful moments in her life before they broke through the membrane of space and took everything away—were never recorded in those books, or anywhere else in the world. Like her mother, her home, her life: they were gone.

THE NOVITIATE

Slack-jawed and daydreaming, Eliana raises her head and stares at the high vaulted ceiling. Little soap bubbles silently pop off the horsehair brush and melt into the gray flagstones she's been hypnotically scrubbing while trying to recall the unsettling cascade of images that had once again flooded her sleep. Sitting back on her legs, she raises her head and listens. The cathedral-sized passageway is one of two radiating out of the original keep and through a massive V-shaped canyon in the dead volcano's walls, into what has over the last five millennia gradually become the labrynthine castle that she and a thousand other servants crawl through like ants, perpetually cleaning and maintaining for the cold, imperious family—the patrons, as they prefer to be called—who hold dominion over all those stones and souls. Always, echoes of footsteps everywhere, no matter where you are, the clack of shoes against stone, voices bouncing down stairs and throughout rooms large and small, the slosh of water and clatter of cleaning carts, the constant heavy rumblings of delivery wagons and trucks up and down the passages, their horns sounding out like church bells, morning, noon, and night. Always, except for this first time, not here, not now.

Eliana stiffly lurches up to her feet, adjusting the fat pads of wool protecting her knees and smoothing down her damp skirt with pruny hands, before standing as still as the high walls around her, waiting. Somber faces from tapestries and building-sized murals stare down at her, stare into the distance, stare at nothing at all. Old battlefields, old countries, old monarchs, their names and their victories lost to time. Afternoon sunlight pours through high arched windows in thick, dust-flecked beams. This corridor is so long and wide there are special horse-drawn carriages stored in the keep for the castle's occasional private guests, so as to make their way in relative comfort down the miles-long river of stone. This afternoon, though: not a sound at all, except for the distant moan of the late-summer winds, fleeing the mountains in advance of an even warmer fall. Eliana opens her mouth in a sigh that ends in a yawn, a feeling of deep, intense peace washing over her. She feels like the only person in the world left alive.

"Eliana." Her name ricochets down the passage—she gasps and turns, slipping on the wet stones.

A phalanx of servants is walking toward her, all of them forming a curved wall behind a small figure dressed in dark clothes, holding what appears to be a small photograph. Wild animal fear explodes inside her, and it feels like she's being hollowed out inside. She knows who this person is.

It was in that sliver of season between winter and spring that Eliana first met her. She had been answering a proclamation of employment opportunities within the castle and its vast private forests and lands, carrying with her samples of her sewing and embroidery skills; but she was young and hopeful for adventure as well—travel, mystery, maybe even love. One of the princesses had overseen the recruitment within the dark circular interior of the keep, not a tall and willowy beauty wearing a golden crown as she had expected, but a plain-clothed, muscular woman no taller than a child, with unsettling, perfectly round eyes that seemed to burn in her square-jawed face, a goblin-like creature who looked older and harder than the mountains themselves. Eliana still recalls the fizzy panic flooding her body at the knowledge that even behind these inpenetrable walls, she would not escape the ugly decay and disappointments of life. The princess had carefully inspected her samples with no expression, pocketed them, asked her a few vague questions—to which Eliana gave her replies to the lady-in-waiting at her side, as instructed—then motioned for a pock-faced house manager to load her on a cart with the others picked for a new life in the castle. Eliana was given a bedroom the size of a large closet, with a wooden trunk for her new work wardrobe and personal possessions, and two thin pocket-sized boards, each carved with maps showing common rooms for servants and where she would be allowed passage to her assigned cleaning areas. Eliana remembered expressing dismay on that first morning of her new life that she hadn't been given work more suited to her specific skills and dreamy ambitions. The house manager had simply shut the door in her face as a response, leaving her to sit at the edge of her new bed immobilized by the terror of having committed an unpardonable crime. Early evening came, and the door opened once again to reveal the imperious little princess, with what looked like a small photograph half-hidden in her right hand. She beckoned to Eliana, who followed her out the door and through myriad bare stone passages, until she suddenly slipped through a hidden door. Eliana followed her out onto a small balcony. The sight was so shocking, she gasped. The caldera, in all its colossal glory, and the equally magnificent castle sprawling like a thousand glittering cities along its lofty circular heights.

Do you see that? the princess had said in a ragged-edge growl of a voice, stabbing at the frosty air with a tiny finger. Eliana nodded: they were in one of the higher areas of the castle, looking at the curved side of the caldera down to a covered stone bridge on thick arches that ended in a squat, circular tower capped with a row of glass windows that floated like a diamond bracelet in the purpling skies. *Now, look down, directly below the tower, and follow that road through the forest into the center of the caldera,* the older woman had said. *What do you see down there?*

Eliana's gaze followed the broad slash of brown dirt, cutting through miles of emerald forests directly into the center of the bowl-shaped valley. It must have been incredibly large to be seen from such a distance and even at their height, this feature within the landscape that was so large and wide and black, so agressively empty against all the brilliant verdant shades of the temperate rain forest that for a moment Eliana couldn't comprehend what she was see-ing.

It's—it's a hole?

That "hole," as you so simply put it, the princess moved behind her as she spoke, placing a worn hand on Eliana's shivering back, *that crater, the Aper-ture, and what waits inside both it and the observatory at the end of that bridge, are our real work. It is why the patrons came to this place and built all of this. It is why we are here. I have seen it. I have seen what happens, once in my lifetime already, many lifetimes ago. And when the time comes again, and believe me when I say it will, all you fresh new things will understand why you were chosen and brought here, and you will understand what your real work is. And if you survive, you will never complain about or question your life's purpose again.*

A fierce and terrible fear had risen up in her at that moment, followed by exultation at the great mystery of it all, at the sweetness of the undiscovered, the unknown. And then she forgot everything about that evening, as if she had dreamt it, as if she had been asleep all this time like a real princess in a real fairy tale, until the princess called out her name, here, now.

"Eliana of Wolfton Run."

"Yes."

"Come with me."

THE THRESHOLD

There are rooms within rooms in the castle, stairways that lead to junctions where even more stairways shoot out like tentacles into yet more rooms. The effect is that of a jigsaw puzzle box—all the pieces jumbled together, half-connected, half-separated, flashes of order within the infuriating yet intoxi-cating mess. The princess walks before her guards, but slightly behind one of her many ladies-in-waiting, taking a small amount of pleasure in letting the woman sort out the directions from a set of wooden placards that she contin-ually shuffles in her gloved hands. Long ago, the princess would have taken pride in knowing exactly where she was within the sprawling stone hive, but for the past five hundred years or so, she's become sloppy, relying on servants and the many small maps piled in corners of each of the rooms to jog her memory. The castle must always grow, the treasures must always increase, pleasures and perversions and every experience of the flesh must be available on command so that the Camera has endless possibilities before it, at all times, for all time. Not so much anymore; with every decade, the Camera's abilities have decreased in increments large enough to notice, and with her decline, so has the procurement and staging of amusements. *Even with the help of the gods themselves, mortal beings are not substantial enough to forever wield their appetites, their powers, their curiosity, their desires,* the princess muses as they approach the doors to the most heavily guarded of their many libraries and studies. *They are an unstoppable ocean, pulverizing us all into sand.*

Behind her, she hears the fearful sighs and half-sobs of the young woman, smells the sweat pool and sour under her soapy, damp clothes as the guards guide her through the thoroughly alien landscape of the castle: she probably thinks she's being led to her death. In a way, she's not wrong. The princess's own hand has become somewhat damp as well, and she slips the photograph into her skirt pocket before surreptitiously wiping her fingers against the thick brocade. It wouldn't do to return it to the front of its album in such a damaged state. A sticky and viscous emotion is settling inside of her, but she has no name for it, she doesn't recall ever feeling it before. Everything about this place saddens her, the realization comes to her like a clarifying bolt of lightning. Overhead, crystal chandeliers twinkle and glow, so beautiful against the murals of the ceiling. Fresco angels fly in mathematically perfect formation, spiraling around the benevolent ripeness of their ancient, eternal creator. What cathedral in what century had her family ripped this masterpiece out of? She has no idea, and that was always the point. Outside of the caldera, was there anything of beauty left in the dying world? And what did it matter?

Several more novitiates, both male and female but all equally young, have joined the procession, each escorted by one of the siblings and several house guards and private servants. They walk together as a single serpentine unit, their footfalls muffled by thick carpets and animal skins. Behind her the princess hears breathless questions—some of the novitiates, shock and curiosity overcoming their apprehensions, are asking the private servants about everything now surrounding them: salons stuffed with velvet sofas the size of produce wagons, oil paintings as large as the sides of buildings hanging over carved fireplaces that could hold her entire room. Silver and gold gleams above, below, on every side table, cabinet, and console. They stream past a pale room filled solely with ancient, vaguely human statues, followed by a stately inner courtyard displaying geodes taller than trees, their jewel-bright insides sparkling in the ambient light. The entire contents of museums, of countries, of centuries, flow around them.

"So much beauty it almost hurts," the young woman, Eliana, blurts out.

"It does, sometimes," the princess replies. "And what you have seen is not even the most extraordinary of what we have."

"It would take hundreds of lifetimes to view everything, I imagine."

"Or one endless lifetime," the princess says, a sad lilt to her gravelly voice.

Through a series of double arches, the princess spies a far-off room that looks to be encased in glass, filled with strange flowers and other flora undulating in misty air—or is it water they float in? She makes a mental note to return someday and find out. And now the main library, its two-story-high doors open wide to provide them with views of thousands of books, in long aisles that spread out along right and left wings, as well as an open central tower lined with staircases and railings all the way to the ceiling several stories up. The princess spies some of her siblings and their novitiates gathered at the middle of the space around a large circular table. She leads the group inside, walking through the high arches into a cathedral of knowledge gathered from every corner of the planet, from places and peoples that no longer exist except as bones and ruins crumbling away under winds and rain. All conversations have stopped, and a heavy malaise blankets them as they file around the table. The princess motions to her lady, who leads the young woman over to one of ten leather-bound albums placed on the table. The princess slips the photo out of her pocket and affixes it to the front, just above a series of numbers scratched below in gold ink—the month and year each novitiate entered service. Each date is the same: it is a date from earlier in the spring. Each photograph is also much the same, the princess notes—that of a young and earnest person, fresh out of some unnamed collection of ramshackle buildings that calls itself a village, anxious and eager to take on their new position in the castle and make a better life for themselves. Each face has been photographed up close, as if in the dark, without the knowledge of the subject. Their pupils are wide and berry black like the eyes of night animals, their skin bleached into whiteness tinged with a faint wash of red, as if glowing from the light of a harvest moon. They look alien and wild and beautiful, as if they are the faces of a fabled and mysterious species, never before seen until now.

The eldest prince motions with his hand: the ladies and gentlemen-in-waiting melt away from the table to the edges of the open space. Only the novitiates remain, each standing before an album the color of wine, with a prince or princess behind them. A preternatural silence envelops the library. The princess notes how each of the young men and women trembles, the breath in their chests shallow and erratic like frightened horses. So much hope and terror battling in those expectant mouths, those dark eyes. So much powerful beauty in their youth. As she did on the balcony so many months ago, she places a hand at the small of the young woman's back.

"Open your album, child," she says.

Eliana of Wolfton Run runs her cracked fingers across the front of the album, then slowly lifts the cover. All around the table, the other servants do the same. The princess watches the woman's face as she peels back the delicate sheet of tissue covering the first photo in the book. There she is. Eliana's face, rising out of the dark of the keep. Skin radiant, mouth slightly open as if her lips had just brushed up against an invisible hook. The princess feels her stoic resolve crumbling under a sudden wave of sorrow and melancholy for herself, something she rarely indulges in. What would it be like to be that enchanting, that youthful and alive? If given the choice, would she trade all that she has experienced, for a mere twenty-some years of burning life? If some other divine entity of creation had broken through to this existence, how different would all their lives have been? Infinite gods, infinite versions of herself exist, she is certain of it—but she is here, immortal yet stuck in her life like a dead fly in a flat glob of amber, forever destined to remain on a path that leads eternally to nowhere.

The young woman turns the page. "These are from the keep. Who took these?" she asks, turning to the princess. The princess remains silent. Another photo of her, this time turned slightly away from the camera, eyelids closed so that the lashes cast feathery shadows against her skin. The princess feels her bowels twist in anticipation of what is coming, as Eliana turns yet another page. Now she is speaking to someone, her eyes and mouth open, one hand caught mid-flight to the side of her face as if about to brush stray curls back behind her ears. The next page: she is turning again, this time her face a smear of pale strokes against the preternatural night. The next page: the camera has drawn back up, Eliana has been photographed from the waist up, her left arm curving up to slip the strap of a worn travel bag over her shoulder. Behind her, the faint shadows of other people in the keep hover, indistinct as trees in evening fog. The next page: another close shot, Eliana looking up, her lips pursed and unsmiling, as if contemplating her voyage into a future she cannot quite comprehend. The next page: closer. The next page: closer. And the next, and the next, and then just her eyes, every photo from the middle of the album to the last page focused on her eyes, a single eye, the rich animal brown of her iris, the soft black of her pupil, until . . . Eliana flips through the album to the last page. The photo is completely black save for a few bright dots scattered across the square of paper, like tiny stars swimming in the vast of space. The princess feels her breath catch in her mouth—this is the photograph that made her certain she had found the right novitiate. Eliana squints. At the center of the photo, a slight lessening of the black, a soft faded smear of jewel-like colors, like the shell of a beetle, or oil pooling across water, or the ambient light of the space reflecting off the slick surface of a large lens, or—another eye, an eye within her eye . . .

From within the photo: movement.

Eliana of Wolfton Run stands before the image now, her arms at her sides, a certain soft slackness in her face. All around the table the other young servants are assuming similar positions: head slightly bowed down over the last image in their albums, pupils wide and seeing yet not seeing. Ten bodies, compliant and ready. Ten open doors. The princess feels a rustling at her side, and looks down. Eliana's fingers are seizing, ever so slightly, grasping out against the air as if searching for a lifeline, a way out. Resistance. The princess smiles; she knows the fight that's taking place inside the young woman's mind. This is a minute of her life that is the longest minute of her life, a minute that is stretching back through all the minutes and days and years, to some inconsequential moment when she felt or said or did something that created this door that she now feels inside her soul, a door to a place whose vastness she already feels gathering at the lintel, readying itself to pour into her until she is both obliterated and created anew.

"Shall we take the bridge, or go up through the library tower?" the eldest asks. His question rouses the princess out of her reverie, and she gathers herself up as she motions for the servants standing back in a ring to come forward.

"It is the same distance, either way," a younger sister responds. "Your decision?" She gestures to the princess.

The princess looks up. Directly overhead, the library tower ends in a domed ceiling comprised of hundreds of intricately carved wood panels, each depicting some now-dead field of science or art. Directly above that ceiling sit another ten windowless stories, filled with laboratories, medical rooms, and studies crammed with the blackest instruments of magic ever assembled in the history of humankind's futile race. Above all that, the top room with its bank of windows looking out over all the caldera. Originally built as an observatory, it was eventually turned into a sumptuous bedchamber, a panopticon fit for a queen. The princess made sure of it; it was her greatest delight to comb the world and seize its most precious things, bringing them back to the caldera for the pleasure of the Camera. Now it's a surgical theatre. Soon, it shall be a mortuary, and soon after a nursery. In a century or two, it shall become a bedroom again.

"Preparations are underway to wake the Camera, the tower will be too busy," the princess says. "We shall take the bridge. Let them see the caldera the way it was meant to be seen. From above, as the instrument of a god."

THE VASTATION

Once upon a time, a rebellious group of servants, among them a young woman named Eliana, stole several bottles of wine and descended into the vast subterranean basements of the castle. Flush and full with the still-new thrill of working within such a magical, magnificent castle, they drank and danced in ruby-lit rooms that hadn't been entered in a thousand years. They burned drugs and writhed within the milky clouds of smoke, ran their hands over dusty paint- ings and sculptures, so old and forgotten that some crumbled at their touch, the paint floating off in little feather-like strips that they caught with their mouths and swallowed. They piled themselves onto lush furs and fucked like frenzied animals, fucked like they were dying and would not live to see morning light. And as they dozed off in the wine-soaked heat, the crimson lights flickering overhead, Eliana overheard the whispers of a lovers' conversation, a bedtime story, about a terrible, hideous living eye of the gods hidden away in the castle, an eye that could see into your soul, imprison it or crack it apart like a fragile egg and fill it with all the horrors and wonders of the universe. It was the most terrifying and thrilling story Eliana had ever heard.

"Camera," Eliana softly snarls, twisting her head as she struggles to work through whatever drug or dark enchantment is floating through the air about them, making her body feel so distant, so not her own to command any lon- ger. "The Camera."

Beneath her feet, the stone floor ever so slightly trembles.

Once upon a time, a young woman named Eliana said she would be hon- ored to work at—no, she was never asked if she would like to work at the cas- tle, she was asked if she would accept the work. Would she accept the work if chosen, the goblin-faced princess had asked. And she had said yes, she would accept the work, and somewhere in the pitch black of the keep, the Camera cap- tured her face and the dilation of her pupils like two miniature supernovas, and something, some thing, had watched her face and the faces of all the others, and it chose her. It saw all the terrible things she had done to her mother and her father, her poor innocent sisters and brothers, it recorded those images of her memories and shunted them back to wherever in the universe something, some things, sated their curiosity off the images, the atrocities, fed off all the possibil- ities of her.

Once upon a time.

Once upon a time.

Once . . .

Eliana has lost her shoes, but she can't remember where or when, only that the worn flagstones beneath her feet are cool and dusty, and they should be scrubbed. Her ears ring slightly, a single low-pitched note like some woodland creature enchanting her off the path with his witchy flute, or maybe it's just the wind. They are walking down a passageway lined with fluted stone columns that hold up the roof over their heads. From either side, Eliana sees the sway- ing tops of the forest, the glint of lakes and small streams, and the ouroborus that is the castle, surrounding all. She wants to turn to the princess at her side, the patron of her work and new life, she wants to say, *Oh yes, this is the bridge you spoke of! I remember that day, you put your hand on my waist as though we were friends and you showed me the great hole, the . . . crater thing in the middle, and the bridge.* The bridge. She feels flattened, as if an invisible weight is pressing against her face and chest while unseen hands pull her legs and torso forward—she wants to stop walking, she wants to slow down her uneven pace to a halt, turn and quickly slither through all bodies behind her, back down the hundreds of stairs and hallways, back to her little room in the lower levels of the castle, or further down, back to those forgotten storage rooms carved deep in the flanks of the caldera, she wants to bury herself in a mound of cobwebbed antiquities and sleep there, unseen by anything in the world ever again, unseen until she sinks into the final oblivion that's peaceful and quiet and from where no one can retrieve her, from where she can never return.

"The more you resist, the less control you will be given. When you cease to fight it, you will be free. Remember this." It's the princess, speaking softly to her as they reach the end of the bridge. A spasm of primal fear crashes through Eliana's body, and she feels herself shake from a million miles away. One at a time, each patron ahead of them takes the arm of their chosen servant, and is admitted through the heaviest metal door she has ever seen, while the personal servants and guards who escorted them turn and begin the long march back down the bridge into the castle. Eliana catches a glimpse of oily black marble walls and floors before the doors close.

"Come." The hand of the princess slips around her forearm, and a sliver of herself screams *no no no* even as her body walks itself through the opening slab of steel, and she catches the look of one of the guards and it's a death sentence in a single glance, and the door closes and they are in the vestibule, a single seamless cube of marble, and where before has she seen those winged and bearded figures carved on the walls, where has she seen those muscular arms, was it deep below the castle in the plumes of smoke or was it within the eyes within her eye in that last photograph, and the door behind them has shut and now the second door swings open and everything changes. The world bursts into light, followed almost immediately by a stench of chemical decay so overpowering that Eliana swears she can see the air shimmering.

"NO—" She manages to push the one word from her lips, but it costs in so much pain and pressure that for a second her bones feel like they've been liquefied. Immediately, though, the pain disappears and her body comes to a complete standstill. It's not just whatever is opening up inside her, it's the chemicaled air, working its way through her lungs into her blood. The hotness of her fear cools and dims. Everything is a dream, again, as it has always been in this place. She feels the hand of the princess pushing her forward, and realizes she's floating, her big toes brushing against the slick marble floor. The room is larger and small all at once and the ceiling rises and lowers in slow waves, sending pulses of afternoon sunlight through the circle of windows. Eliana calmly opens her mouth, and a stream of vomit pours down her clothes, hitting her feet as it splatters on the floor. Others are vomiting as well, some of the novitiates floating sideways as if they've gradually lost control of their center, while a few simply sway back and forth like grass stalks in a slow breeze as little jets of regurgitated food squirt out of their mouths and nostrils. No one is sobbing, no one is screaming, but she can see it in their eyes, just like she saw it in the eyes of every member of her family, that look of incredulity that there is such madness and ugliness in the world and that it laps at them like dogs, that they cannot evade it, that they will choke and drown in their own fear and vomit and blood, and she will eat it up because to be the eater is to be alive.

She lets go.

Her body grows limp, and her feet touch the floor. She laughs.

A novitiate in front of her drops to the ground, his head cracking against the polished gray floor. Several more novitiates pass out, their bodies slumping as if someone had suddenly flipped an off switch. And then, the rest.

Eliana blinks once: twice. Burns the image onto her retinas: the cracked heads and split faces, teeth sprinking pools of vomit, the long spatterings of blood. Shudders violently. Throws back her head so hard the snap of it quiets the room. Lets out a long, tortured, strangled howl, matched by another howl from somewhere in the room. Tiny lights burst across the edges of her vision, eating the room away until it is gone, until there is *nothing but the setting sun, and she is falling into it. Her mind is traveling across the antediluvian forests, brushing the tips of the trees, frightening the birds into death mid-flight, leaving all the animals, the wolves and black cats and all the predators with no names quaking in their tracks, and she is sailing over the edges, she is being pulled, she is pouring over and into the ancient crater that is no longer a crater, down its sides and down until there are no sides left, there are only slender ropes of bone-like rock that burst into long clouds of stars that fall with her, spiral then expand out as they vomit her out into a cosmic expanse that contains beings so beyond her comprehension that little parts of her mind crumple into themselves and disappear, and then she disappears and there is nothing left but the image, she is the image, and THEY take her in, and she is in THEM and she is THEM and it is forever and—*

Eliana's head snaps back into place and she falls to all fours. She opens her mouth so wide that the corners tear her cheeks apart, heaves once, twice, and from somewhere inside, not her stomach but a new organ, a new series of pulsing biological pockets of flesh and pus and blood and other substances forged in another universe, a stiff square of paper is extruded up through her newly expanding esophagus and slides out of her mouth in a rush of clear chemical liquids. The square lands on the floor between her splayed hands. With trembling fingers, she lifts it up, exhausted, bleeding, triumphant, to the princess and her nine siblings who stand before Eliana. The princess takes the drying photograph and hands it to the eldest, who places it in a massive photo album labeled *AD 68427.*

The princess places a trembling hand on her aching head.

"You are the Camera," she says.

Eliana looks up at her and speaks, the words garbled and wet, completely clear.

"I know."

THE VOYAGER

You remember when you first arrived at the keep, how you felt being driven down the imposing passage into the vast expanse of the castle, how you felt when you saw the jewel-like interior of the caldera for the first time, the undulating green of the valley and the far edges of the dead volcano at the horizon, gloriously untouched and glowing in the setting sun. You think of all the places in the labrynthine castle you have never seen. You will see them now. All the places in the world you have never seen. You will see them now. You remember your first sight of the Aperture, black and lifeless against the trees. The Aperture is in your soul now, a little version of the void, tendrils of broken stars and cosmic decay rising up its steep sides, pressing against the door of your soul until it buckles and submits. This is how you want to see the world: crying out as it buckles and submits.

You stand in a room located three stories beneath the observatory, a room that has never seen the light of the sun. Your patrons stand beside you, their faces racked with grief. You take photographs, one by one, each image an explosion of divine, numinous pleasure and pain that sends you back into the roiling, hungry abyss and out again. Already the lips of your newly widened mouth are healing, the eyes in your head bulging, expanding, coming together to work as one. The patrons are astonished at the speed and strength of your physical powers, at the voraciousness of your visual appetite. You will astonish them, you promise yourself, you will astonish them all the way to the end of time.

In the center of the room, someone is howling, a series of deep guttural moans and inhuman screams. The howls are emanating from a bed surrounded by men and women in white coats and masks that give them the appearance of flies, while the patrons hover to the sides. In another life, the bed with its intricately carved posts might have been beautiful, the silk sheets pristine and elegant—a resting place fit for royal blood. The bedposts are draped in rubbery cables that look like intestines, all of them leading to various barrels and copper tubs and pulsating machines—the sources of the unbearable smells. The sheets are slick, dripping with a clear amber liquid that also covers the arms and chests of two of the white-clad physicians who are carefully shearing away the edges of a thick, viscous substance that partially covers the withered, misshapen legs of the old Camera. These are her death throes. This is her end. She is traveling to the place you and your dark gods cannot follow, slipping off her divine mantle and voyaging into a beyond from which no light or darkness escapes, the only place in all creation you cannot follow. You will never know what she knows. You will never see what she sees.

A sharp ringing fills your head, and the edges of your vision blister into blackness as another image is sent off into the cosmos. You stare, unflinching, unblinking—you couldn't stop yourself if you tried. You don't want to. You drink it in.

The woman on the bed, the creature, rears up and screams from a toothless mouth that stretches from one side of her head to the other. Just above the bleeding lips and a misshapen mound of flesh that had once been a nose, her face disappears, as if something has eaten away the upper front and top half of her head as if it were a soft dessert, leaving behind the ravaged remains of her brain. From out of that gray matter, purple and red filaments pulse and writhe and squirt, all surrounding one massive lidless eye, an eye almost the size of the head itself, bloodshot and straining against its mangled cage. The intestine-like cables that wind around the bedposts are attached all over her body: two large men and women hold her quaking limbs as an equally large doctor grabs the end of each cable and twists until it pops off her flesh, sending unidentifiable liquids and waste spraying. With each detached cable, the creature lets out a sound that makes you feel as if your soul is being dragged closer and closer to the edge of some invisible cliff from which you might never return. It will be over soon. They kept her alive as long as they could, but once your gods lose interest in you, find another, fresher body with which to view the world from, what use is it to struggle?

Several boys in oily overcoats are already mopping and hosing down the floors, pushing the filth and liquids toward large metal drains. Two of the patrons leave the room, indecipherable looks on their faces. The screaming has subsided into mournful, child-like sobs. The end is here, now, she knows it, they all know it. You cannot explain why, but the sobbing is worse. It is the loneliest sound in the world. The patron who spoke to you on the balcony, the oldest of the little princesses, stands at the foot of the bed now, and you position yourself so you can see her face. She stares at the creature, the dying old woman, just an old woman now, no different from her, really. She does not grieve, her face is stone, but a mysterious emotion hovers almost imperceptibly at its corners, in its ancient folds and cracks ... The images flow through you, flow back through your mouth and into the hands of one of your now many personal servants, a young woman with the pinched and haunted look of someone who knows her face will one day be captured in those photographs, her pain and terror immortalized both here and elsewhere in the universe. She should be so blessed.

"Is—is it done?" The eldest male patron is speaking. He places his hands on his eldest sister and they step back as the limp body slowly rises to a sitting position, rivulets of matter dribbling out of the puckered wounds and down the grayish limbs, clotting into thick rivulets that mimic veins. The last of her life is leaving through the eye, you realize, as it shudders in its ruined casing, struggling as if to propel itself into the world, free from the dangling remains of flesh. You position yourself, the image coalescing into place in the crackling folds of your brain, and then: the eye lowers, swiveling to meet your gaze with its unbearably large black pupil, two conjoined pupils swimming in a wet jelly sea of entangled brown irises flecked with the most vibrant emerald you have ever seen, still somehow fighting for one last glimpse of the world through a tangle of decaying flesh. For that brief second before the eye deflates and collapses onto the bed with the body, the room and the world and all the stars above bleed away until it feels like you and she are the only beings in the universe that can see and be seen.

THE END

It is night, and the inner walls of the caldera sparkle and glitter with light spilling out of thousands of castle windows, as if a starry arm of the galaxy had drifted down and caught against the jagged slopes. The princess always enjoys this quiet hour alone, after the evening meal and before ... before whatever secret wonders and horrors the darkness holds begin to reveal themselves. Sometimes they stay hidden, however, and the night is quiet and uneventful, almost ordinary. In a way, those are the best of nights.

From her balcony she sees the circle of windows of the observatory, a titan's liquid gold crown floating over the bowl of the caldera. Soon the new Camera will make her way into the castle, where she will view whatever monstrosities or delights await her in any of the thousands of rooms at her disposal, or perhaps she will roam the forest floor, where she will hunt down and record the eyes of a dying animal or human; or perhaps she will make her way to the middle of the caldera, stare down into the endless obsidian void of the Aperture, letting the cosmic visions of those distant beings break through the membrane of the world and roll through her like thunder. The princess was never one to miss an excursion, but the old Camera reveled in rapturous beauty most of all, and it is clear that this new Camera will require the ugliest, cruelest, most painful mysteries of the world to watch and record; and the princess doesn't yet have it in her to cater to what will be excruciating demands. She rubs her hands, remembering the feel of the soft, cooling flesh of the old Camera as she reverently wrapped her body to be taken away for destruction without ceremony. The loss of the creature felt familiar, as though she had lived it before, and that disturbs her greatly. She knows her duties, and she will perform them. Tomorrow she will start a search to replace those servants-turned-novitiates who did not survive the ceremony to create the new Camera, tomorrow she will gather up lists of the few places left in the world her brothers and sisters can plunder and dismantle, but tonight, just tonight, she must be alone.

The princess retreats into her candlelit room—some of her siblings prefer electricity to light their private rooms, but she has always favored the ancient and pure beauty of fire. She makes her way over to an ornately carved vanity and sits at the small chair in front of its silver-streaked, six-millennia-old oval mirror. In the flickering light, her reflection shifts between grotesque and sublime. The princess opens one of the wooden drawers and pushes aside a stack of faded woven cloth squares, leather pouches filled with glossy river beads, several crudely carved stone figurines, and pulls out a small flat box. A true secret, her only one. She opens it, carefully moving aside layers of archival paper to reveal an unframed oil portrait on a board, which she leans up against the mirror, so that she might view her face and the face in the painting at the same time. In the powerful commingling of the night and the undulating flames, she and the face appear to exist again in the same time, in the same peaceful, ageless moment. It is the face of a very young girl, with a face very much like hers. It is a copy of a copy times tens of thousands of copies, a face she has tried to recreate on and from every conceivable material throughout the ages, an imperfect memory of a face she fiercely fights every day to remember, though if she were forced to admit, she could not say that the face she redraws is anything close to the original. But she no longer knows who this girl is—that knowledge quietly disappeared from her mind eons ago, like an old animal slipping off into the forest to die. She knows she once knew the name of that girl. She knows the girl was meaningful to her, was a powerful, essential part of her, she feels it deep in the untouched, primal core of her soul. Everything else about her, though, like the girl herself, simply . . . disappeared.

The princess wraps her crooked arms tight around her flat breasts as a rush of tears blur their faces into one, the face of a being both ancient and new, long dead and long alive, eternal and ephemeral as dust. Her sorrow cleaves back all the hundreds of thousands of centuries, and a sudden memory of a particular scent and weight against her chest rushes throughout her body, milky and warm and sweet, and with it an emotion so perfect and complete that she would kill everything in the universe to have it in her arms again, forever.

"I created. I was a god once, too."

She whispers so softly that the forbidden thought barely escapes her lips, always fearful that something will hear her taboo words and wake up, rush across space and time into the world and inside her, that same monstrous something lurking at the earliest edges of the Pleistocene, the night a young Neanderthal mother woke up to see it pouring into her daughter from behind the rim of the sparkling black sky . . .

. . .

The memory is gone.

THE LAST DROP

by Carole Johnstone

I'm going to tell you a story and it's true. But it's full of lies.

I visited her first before the trial. I didn't want to go—or at least I wanted to go less than I wanted to stay away. But I was curious, and that's why I went. I think it's why any of us do anything. I'd been expecting something like the Tower of London pictures in old schoolbooks; Mary Queen of Scots praying on her knees in a cold stone room with no windows. But it wasn't like that. Mary Timney's cell was small, but morning light was bright through a window crossed by only two bars. She sat on a narrow bed with a straw mattress and blanket, and I sat on the only chair, next to a low wooden shelf.

That first time, she didn't say much of anything, and I found myself rambling about the weather, the rising price of sugar in every grocer in Dalry. Her face had that empty look she sometimes got, more often when Francis was away and she and the kids had to fend for themselves. But maybe that's only because it was at those times I most often saw her—if I had food or money or clothes to spare, it was then I would take them.

"It's not so bad here, aye?"

Her laugh was quiet but savage. It made me wonder if the guard was still standing outside.

"What I mean is—"

"I know what ye mean. Suppose after all these months, I'm used tae it some. Belly's full enough, at least." She turned toward the light of the window then, and I couldn't see her face.

"Does Francis visit often?"

She bowed her head as she shook it. And when her shoulders began to shake too, I found my suspicions torn equally between crying or laughing. She would do that—laugh at the wrong things. Or cry at a thing so small as to be barely seen.

"You know they were at it? The pair ae them?" She looked at me then, nodded so hard, I heard her teeth clack twice, eyes narrowing down to slits. "I never seen them, but I know they were."

"You'll be glad to have the trial start though? To have it all be over with." Which was less a question than just something other to say.

"Why d'ye come, Nancy?"

And the smile that turned up only the corners of her mouth was one I remembered too. It was as savage a smile as her laugh. Worse. Her eyes would glitter with it.

She knew why. Even though she'd not prise that truth from me, not even with a butcher knife or poker.

I wanted to know if she'd done it.

The next time I saw her was the first day of the trial. The town was busy as a gala day, and with that same high nervous feel on your skin; like the air before a spring storm.

The judge, all the way from Edinburgh, came down from the station at Lockerbie. Was accompanied to the Court-House by the Provost, Sheriffs, Magistrates, and militiamen. All of us lining the streets to watch the parade. He had a cold look about him, the judge; his nose, hooked like an eagle's beak but still pointing up to the sky, beady, close-set eyes looking neither left nor right.

As if his shite doesna stink, someone said nearby, and enough of us laughed that the judge's chin dropped just for a moment.

By the time he took the bench at ten o'clock, the Court-House was so packed to the rafters it had the look and sound of the cattle market at Newton Stewart. By early afternoon, it had the smell too. It only got quiet when they brought Mary in. You could have heard a pin drop as she was put up to stand at the bar. She wore a dark dress and a white cap, her long hair tied away out of sight. Since I'd last seen her, she'd put on some much-needed weight and her cheeks were pink. In the *Dumfries and Galloway Standard,* the next day, they wrote *she is about twenty-seven years of age, slimly made, and with a countenance by no means repulsive.* I think I saw the reporter down in the front on that first day, sitting with hunched shoulders, paper and nib pen; his coat ill-fitting, hair greasy and balding in the back.

But even as Mary stood stiff and still, she wore that empty face. Even as the room gasped and muttered at the charges they already knew were set against her.

"Mary Timney, wife of Francis Timney, road surface-man, Carsphad, Kirkcudbrightshire, you are accused of murder, in so far as, on the thirteenth day of January 1862, within the house lately occupied by William Hannah, tenant of the farm Carsphad, and Lockhart Paterson Hannah, labourer, you did wickedly and feloniously attack and assault the now-deceased Ann Hannah, sister of the aforesaid, until she was mortally injured and died. And was thus murdered by you, the said Mary Timney."

And still that empty face even as she said not-guilty in a low, steady voice.

By the time they called me to the box, my palms were clammy and my chest tight. I didn't look at Mary as I passed, only the jury alongside—fifteen men; farmers and grocers, I imagined, and from Dumfries or Lockerbie most likely, though I recognised William Hunter who has the big pig farm out at Sundaywell, and a tobacconist from Minnyhive. I didn't look at them either.

And then I was there, and the judge with his too-close eyes and eagle's beak nose was making me swear to tell the whole truth and nothing but the truth, so help me God, and that's all I could think of as I stood there and waited for the question with my clammy hands and my tight chest, and my heart beating away like a pipe band drum. Help me, God.

"Miss Nancy MacDonald, can you describe to the court how you came to discover the body of Ann Hannah, the deceased?"

It's a lonely place, Carsphad Farm. I never liked it even before that day. Set back only a few yards from the turnpike between Dalry and New Galloway, it's always felt to me as if as soon as you set foot on that farm track and go down that hill into that valley surrounded by grey hills and black-green forest, you're alone. The sky is always clouded. The ground is always boggy. The birds are always quiet. And in the whole world, all that's left are those two stony buildings less than fifty yards apart—mean and small-boned like crouching rats in the dark. My father says that's fanciful talk born of what I found that day, but I know it's not. I've been friends with Ann Hannah for years; have known the Timneys at least two. And not once did I look forward to going down that track and that hill into that valley.

I'd only gone that day at all because Mary's oldest, Susan, had come calling at Kells, asking if I would come to the house and bake for her mother as Francis was away again and she was poorly. And I went not because I wanted to and not because I liked Mary, but because Susan at nine was skinny as a girl half that age, her big sad eyes as anxious as an old woman's. And because I felt guilt. It would be a lie not to say so.

I walked the lonely road to Polharrow Bridge, turned onto that track, walked down into that valley. It was only one in the afternoon, but the sky was the colour of old slate and the path as muddy as ever. I had to pass the farm to reach the Timneys' smaller cottage fifty yards beyond, and had meant to stop in on Ann first, but the moment that I turned toward the farm a thing gripped at my throat. Cold fingers that choked my breath enough I put up my hand to prise them free. And found nothing. I stood there awhile, coughing, a little bent over—though not enough to leave me blind. I felt hiding eyes on me; felt fear like a hollow inside my throat and chest. A cold hole.

One of the farm's paired wooden doors was open. I knew the Hannah brothers were working out at Greenloop. I glanced once at the Timneys' cottage, but all was quiet save for the grunts and snorts of the pigs in their house behind. Something in the way they sounded—not unsettled, but angry like Spanish bulls poked with pikes—made that hole inside me stretch wider. I nearly ran to the farm door. But there I stopped. I couldn't go in because I'd smelled it by then. A smell like hot pennies. Or the sky just before summer rain. Or the Kirkdale Slaughterhouse in Gatehouse of Fleet.

But I saw Ann's feet just inside the door, and I had to go in then. Even if all I wanted to do was run. I pushed through the door and into the kitchen. She was lying in shadow on the floor, away from the window, near to the gable wall with the fireplace and her close-bed. There was only one other room, I knew—the bed, where the brothers slept—but I couldn't find the courage either to leave Ann or push through yet another door.

"Ann?" My voice sounded too loud, and flat with no echo. I crept as close as I could bear to—but the smell had raised the skin from my bones and I could hear my teeth chattering against each other like a tattoo. "Ann?"

She lay on her face, her two hands crossed underneath her, her forehead on newly washed wet clothes. A washing-tub was near the window, next to an upended dish and scattered wrung clothes. Her hair, long and always pulled into a bun behind her neck, was down and bloody. I could see blood on the clothes beneath her forehead. Loose flaps of skin at her crown; a deep and terrible wound between them. Blood was all over the flagged floor—sitting in rainlike puddles or still running in downhill rivers through the joins and holes between stones.

The knife I knew Ann was never allowed to use because it was the one used to butcher the pigs, lay bloody on both blade and handle next to the cold fire. And its poker lay next to Ann's right hand, covered in black clots of blood and long dark hair. The furniture was not moved or disturbed, but all sprayed and splashed with blood and blood and blood.

"Ann?"

When she moved, I screamed. Conceded what little ground I'd made, the open door banging hard against my spine as I retreated. Ann raised her head slowly like a corpse waking up from its grave, found and then fixed me with one working eye, the only part of her face not painted red.

"Oh dear," she said. In entirely Ann Hannah's voice. "Oh dear."

"I'll get help! I'll get help!" I said in a voice nothing like my own, and I was already running back out into the air as I did.

And I left her there to run to the Porter's Lodge at Knocknalling more than quarter of a mile away. Because nothing could have made me stay in that slaughterhouse with her. Nothing—no one—could have made me go down to that dark, crouching cottage fifty yards beyond. And its grunting, screaming pigs. Or those hiding eyes that I knew were still fixed on me.

The postmortem came after. And it was gruesome enough that several in the gallery fainted or had to be carried out by the militiamen. It had taken Ann eight terrible hours to die. There had been ten wounds to her head. Three slashes to her face—left temple, eyelid, and nose—from the butcher knife. Three blunt blows to her forehead from the poker. And four to the back and sides of her head, all of them bad enough to cause fractures. The worst of them the one I'd seen—one and a half inches square—and so deep it had exposed skull and vessels and even the brain beneath. So severe it had split Ann's skull clean down its middle. The police found a heavy wooden beetle covered in blood and hair behind a meal barrel in the Timneys' cottage, the surgeon said, pausing while the Court-House gasped and muttered. And hidden in its loft, a tartan dress and petticoat wet with water but still covered in blood.

And through all of it stood Mary. Blank empty face in her dark dress and white cap as she looked at nothing.

If anything, the next day was worse. A long procession of folk from Dalry pronounced Mary a thief and a scrounger. One with whom you dared not even pass the time of day for fear you would be propositioned for a loan or begged for a handout. A constable, who the week before Ann Hannah's death was approached by Mary, who claimed to have neither money nor meat and asked for a loan of sixpence, which he did not give her. A grocer's wife, from whom Mary begged a shilling, which she did not give her. A dairymaid, who witnessed Mary asking Ann Hannah for some tea less than three days before her death. Which she did not give her.

When William Hannah took the box, his hands shook. I knew him little more than to say hello, but he had been Ann's favoured brother. And his was the name on the lease for Carsphad Farm; it was he who had sublet that smaller cottage to the Timneys.

"I had lent Francis Timney half a crown that morning, about seven o'clock," William Hannah said when the Advocate Depute asked of him the same questions as all those folk from Dalry. "He said he was going from home, that there was no money in the house, and he wished to leave some with his wife."

William never once looked at Mary. Leaned hard from her as though standing against a fierce wind, like an ear of wheat in a field.

"Mrs Timney was in the habit of borrowing things from my mother. After she died, Mrs Timney also borrowed tea and sugar from my sister, and sent the children to borrow. Latterly, my sister refused to lend her anything. They also had words about the carrying away of firewood from our farm about four or five weeks before. My sister objected, and I did so too. There were also a great many turnips in our garden that were pulled up and missing."

He leaned and he leaned. Until he was almost bent over. His shaking hands drawn into white fists.

"There ought to have been tea in the farmhouse," he said. "Some was bought on the Tuesday before. The sugar was gone too. My sister had money the Monday; had used only some of it for the plate on Sunday. She ought to have had a purse we never could find."

The woman sitting in the gallery to the left of me tutted and leaned forwards, fat ringless fingers tapping the shoulder of another in front. "Her man works. How is it that she needs tae steal? Eh?"

Because steal she did. John Robson, police constable, told the court that when he searched the Timneys' house after Ann Hannah's death, as well as that bloody wooden beetle behind a meal barrel and the bloody tartan dress and petticoat in the loft, he had found tea and sugar mixed together in a cloth. And seven shillings and sevenpence on the dresser-shelf inside a glove. William's half crown. And a threepenny piece, four pence in coppers, the rest in six-penny pieces.

The Advocate Depute looked at Mary. He stood with squared shoulders and a muscle working inside his cheek. A tale of two women, said he. A good and generous Christian, whose kindness had been abused and charity mocked. And a grasping and greedy thief who had turned to brutal and bloody murder.

That's when the *Dumfries and Galloway Standard* started calling her a monster.

The second time I visited her only because she asked for me. I took her some bread, some tea, though I wasn't sure it would be allowed. All of that was guilt too. Partly because of what I'd said in court. Not against her, but it felt that way all the same.

But it was also because I still didn't like her. Was never likely to like her. Mary *was* grasping and needy; she'd take from you until nothing at all was left, and she'd feel no worse for doing it. And sometimes she'd turn to you with those eyes, that savage laugh, and you'd shiver down to your bones. But now I was as afraid for her as I'd been for Ann. And not one part of that wasn't guilt. In more ways than she would ever know, I had always very much been against Mary Timney.

But it was a very different Mary waiting for me inside that small, bright cell. Sitting on the straw mattress bed. She flinched when I entered, took to her feet straightaway. Her eyes were wide and wild, glittering with a bad excitement.

"I didna do it, Nan! Ye never asked, but I'm telling ye I didna. Not ever." She paused for mere seconds, pacing the room so furiously, I didn't enter it any farther. "You dinna believe me!" Though she had scarcely looked at me at all. "You see, you *see*? *No one* will believe me. No one will believe the truth!"

"That you're not guilty?"

She whirled toward me, and I flinched away. "That I know who is. I know who *is*!"

"You know who is?" There had been no one in that valley away from the world that morning. No one but Ann and Mary. And Mary's four wee children. "But you never said—"

"I know what I never said," she scowled, though her eyes stayed wild bright. "I was protecting her, right? I didna want her tae hang. She's my mother. D'ye know what they call him, the judge? Lord Deas? The constable told me—"

"Your *mother*?"

Mary blinked. Sat down on the bed as if her strings had been cut. "Aye. She came down from Dalry that Monday morning to wash some clothes for me. I was sick in bed with the baby, and afore she started cleaning she said she would have tae put off her good frock that she had on. She put on my green tartan dress, my petticoat too." Mary talked too quickly and too low; I had to strain to hear her as she stared down at the stone floor. "She seen Ann Hannah coming out ae the yard, and said tae me—I swear it, Nan—*Mary, I've a mind afore I leave this world tae give Ann Hannah her licks for stealing yer man away and setting him against ye*. I told her no' tae go. That Ann was too strong and would fell her. But she went anyway. And when she came back all over in blood, she confessed tae me what she'd done. She took off my frock and petticoat and put on her own. Washed her hands and face in my tub. She dared me no' tae tell any person that she'd been at my house that day. No one seen her as she came, and she went back by the riverside." She looked up at me again. I could see the whites of her eyes all around, her pupils big and black. "She'll no' even bring my weans tae visit—she'll no' even bring me my babies. But still I didna tell the police 'cause I dinna want her tae hang. D'ye know what they call him, Lord Deas?" She jumped up, returned to her pacing. "The constable told me, the one outside—they call him Lord Death. That's what they call him, Nan. And I'll no' have her hung! I'll no'!"

And yet, something must have changed her mind, because the next day that became her new defence. Her lawyer, a stringy man who looked no more than twenty and struggled to carry a beaten case packed with papers into the Court-House every day, tried to talk her out of it. But she wouldn't be moved.

In her mother, Mrs Samuel Good, came. Fat and infirm, leaning heavy on a stick and wheezing sharp breaths. She looked at Mary only once as she denied all her daughter had said. And was followed by neighbour after neighbour, all of whom testified she'd not been from home since harvest.

Mary shook back and forth at the bar that day, her eyes still bright wild and glittering. I saw flashes of her teeth once or twice, like a polecat set to pounce.

When Susan, poor wee Susan, was made to stand in the box, Mary never looked at her once. Not even when Lord Deas fixed Mary's daughter with his too-close beady eyes to tell her it was wrong to lie and the Devil would take her if she did. Over and over again until the child burst into tears and said that yes, she'd seen her mother go to the farm that morning. She looked over at the bar and sobbed and cried sorry so wretchedly that the Court-House hummed with uncommon sympathy; some even shouted to the judge to leave her be. The woman with fat, ringless fingers turned tutting to me and those in the seats behind. "Poor wee bairn. No' as if she was the one tae split a skull in two, is it?"

And the neighbour to the other side of me, a man in Sunday suit and black tie and dirt under his fingernails, shook his head once and sharp. "She'd have her mother swing and her wee girl risk the fires ae Hell tae save her own damned neck."

That's when the Court-House—and then the country—started calling her a monster.

After the summing-up, the jury went out to deliberate. I stood in the cool spring air of Buccleuch Street while I waited; the stink and noise of the Court-House was becoming more than I could stand. I tried to think of Ann Hannah—the sight of her feet inside the farm door, that smell like hot pennies, and the terrible hole in her head, bloody down to the white-grey beneath. But all I could think of was Mary. And poor Susan. Those hiding eyes that had watched me, and could just as easily have had a mind to blame me instead. Perhaps with better success.

In less than half an hour, I heard an almighty roar go up—loud enough to set my heart banging against my ribs. And then I felt it drop down into my stomach. Because I knew what it meant.

By the time I managed to push and shove my way back to the front of the gallery, the judge was already passing sentence. I looked to Mary, and all of the blank empty had gone from her face. It was grey-pale as she grimaced as if in great pain, her white fingers gripping hard onto the bar.

"The jury, an intelligent and attentive jury, have unanimously found you guilty of the crime of murder," Lord Deas said, expressionless. "It was impossible for anyone who heard the evidence to expect that there should have been any other verdict. There now remains only for me to pronounce upon you the last sentence of the law." He paused. "The time of all of us in this world is short, with most of us it is uncertain, but your days are numbered. They must indeed be few."

"No, no. Give me anything but that!" Mary cried out, her hands reaching toward his bench. "My lord, it was never me. It was never me!"

The Court-House gasped at her cry—so changed, so high and harrowed.

"I recommend you to use the short time you have still in this world to make your peace with God," Lord Deas said, unmoved. He looked at her, it seemed to me, as if she were a mayfly caught in a web. Of no consequence to anyone but the spider.

When he put on the black cap, he did it slowly and deliberately, as if making an entertainment of it.

"No, my lord! Give me forever a prison. Dinna. Dinna do that!" Mary was sobbing now. Pulling at her hair in quick snatches, pressing fingers over her face hard enough to leave long red marks.

"Mary Timney, you are to be removed from the bar to the prison of Dumfries, therein to be detained and fed on bread and water till the twenty-ninth of April; and upon that day, between the hours of eight and ten of the forenoon, to be taken to the place of execution of the burgh of Dumfries, and there, by the hands of the common executioner, be hanged by the neck upon a gibbet until you be dead—"

"Oh no, my lord!"

"May God have mercy upon your soul."

It took three militiamen to take Mary away from the bar and down to the trap. She was screaming by then, her face blotched angry red between deathly white. Her cap askew, hair wild. She screamed and screamed so long and so loud that we could still hear her twenty minutes later, when the jury had been discharged and the judge had left for the station. When no one else looked to be minded to move, the landlord of The Commercial Inn announced a free hour of drinking. And within minutes there was no one left in the Court-House to hear Mary's screams but me.

I went the last time to see her the night before the execution. She'd had, by then, a little over two weeks to prepare for what was to come. And I'd held off as long as I could, even knowing that the longer I waited the worse it would be; the closer she'd be to her end. Because I'd known I *would* go, I couldn't not.

I was almost shaking as I stepped into her cell. It was nearly evening. Finally, her prison looked like a prison—gloomy with cold comfort and mean shadows. She was sitting on the straw mattress again. A tallow candle, thick with smoke, obscured her bowed head and clasped hands. The sight of her white cap reminded me of her screams as Lord Death had donned his black.

When she looked suddenly up, I flinched.

Her expression was neither blank nor savagely sly. Her eyes didn't glitter with wild excitement; they were bloodshot and dry. Her skin was waxy-pale and she was clammy enough that I could smell her—the kind of sweat that isn't clean; that's born of fear and dread and no way to escape either. And everything in her was so tightly clenched, so rigid, that my own spine straightened sharp and my hands drew into fists.

"It wasna me, Nan. I didna do it."

There was no pleading in her voice, no entreaty.

My nails bit into my skin. "Then who?"

She smiled a smile so gentle and brief I wondered if I'd seen it at all. "The monsters."

When I said nothing, she unclasped her hands, placed them carefully in her lap. Looked out of the dark window crossed by two bars.

"The monsters hate my mother. Hate her 'cause she'd no more rescue me from this death than this life." For one moment, her composure cracked with her voice. "And what life have I given *my* babies? No better."

When she turned back to me, that strange smile had returned, and I tried not to shiver from looking at it.

"The monsters hate my husband. Feckless and always gone. Always giving me babies, and then leaving me tae watch them starve. And they hate the black eyes and high noses ae all those folk who think they'll never starve. Who think it's greed has me grovelling in the mud at their feet."

I can hear the grind of her teeth. In the gloom, the shadow of her is distorted and contorted against the cell's stone wall.

"The monsters wanted tae hurt all ae them in the Court-House nearly the worst ae all. 'Cause they said it was firewood when it was sticks. I was gathering sticks, Nan! That came down by the flood. How can ye steal sticks? And when Ann Hannah took them out ae my hands and called me a thief 'cause most likely her ugly pigs had taken her bloody turnips, the monsters wanted tae kill her there and then." She nods once, solemn, as if saying a vow.

"The monsters never cared about her and Francis. She coulda had him and welcome if he brought her anything at all but misery. No. The monsters hated her fat belly and her thin lips. The smirk on her face when she said no. Lording it over us when she was barely any better—were it not for her brothers, she would have starved worse than me, the fat, ugly, old spinster!"

I stepped back then, nearly to the door but not quite. Because the bad light had returned to her eyes. The savage smile to her mouth.

"They're just sins, Mary," I said, glad that my voice didn't shake. "Only envy, wrath, pri—"

"No."

She got up from the bed then, reached me in three short steps. I tried not to cringe from her, but I know that I did.

"No. They're monsters." Her eyes glittered. "Have ye ever had a hole in your belly so big ye think your stomach's eaten itself? Or a hole in your head so wide that ye stare at walls for days and think ae nothing at all? Or a hole in your chest where your heart should be? Where it used tae beat?"

I shook my head, even though it was a lie.

"They hide in corners, in empty cupboards and hearths and in the holes in me. In forests full ae sticks and fields full ae turnips. They hide in folk's eyes when ye ask them for help. And in their mouths when they tell ye no."

Her smile vanished as her lips trembled and her hands started to shake. "I hated Ann Hannah 'cause I was the only person in the world she could look down on. But the monsters— " She swallowed. "The monsters promised that I'd be the one looking down on her."

The silence then was an unwelcome one. I wanted to cough against the stinking pig fat smoke, but I didn't dare. When Mary grabbed hard hold of my hands, I almost screamed and certainly cried out. Until I felt the warm splash of her tears against my skin.

"I'm scared, Nan. The chaplain says God will forgive me if I want tae be forgiven. D'ye think that's true?"

"Yes," I said, and I didn't know then nor now if that was another lie. "Aye, Mary. I do."

And then her smile was the worst of them all—filled up with so much sorrow and so much fear. Her tears ran over my wrists and between our fingers.

"But they're still here, Mary," she whispered close to my skin. "They're still here," she tapped her temple, "and here," her breastbone. "How can God forgive me them?"

And I offered her scant comfort then, I'm ashamed to say. I took back my hands. Dread stirred cool air against the hairs on the back of my neck. I feared her monsters were there, in the corners of that small, cold cell choking with shadows. And I only stayed longer because I feared that they would follow me home.

As the constable was taking me back down the corridor toward the exit, suddenly there was Francis. Walking with another guard I didn't recognise toward me, toward Mary's cell. The shadows under Francis's eyes were nearly black, his beard grown grey. His shouts to little Margaret as she ran on ahead were hoarse and feeble. The baby, John, struggled in his arms, mewling like a cat. Susan followed behind him, head bowed, shuffling her feet as though walking to the gallows herself. My heart pricked for her, but then Francis was saying my name once, twice, was awkwardly reaching out a hand to touch me. I recoiled from him the way I'd wanted to recoil from Mary.

"Maggy! My sweet wee Maggy!" I heard Mary cry. In a voice I'd never once heard before, and so had chosen to believe didn't exist.

The revulsion that shot through me was enough to make me taste bile, and I wanted to spit it between us. I wanted to slap the hurt from Francis's grey, confused face. That I'd ever let him touch me. That any part of letting him touch me had led to that terrible day in that terrible valley. To this. To what would happen tomorrow.

I arrived at the junction between St David Street and Buccleuch Street at seven o'clock. So early, I hardly expected a soul, and was instead confronted by a crowd of hundreds. I pushed to the front, though few obstructed me. I'd read about hangings in London and Glasgow—raucous, almost celebratory affairs—and I'd been dreading being confronted with the same. Instead, the mood was subdued, almost reverent, as if we were standing in front of a pulpit instead of a gallows.

The scaffold had been procured from Edinburgh. It had sat at that junction for nearly three days. I'd wondered more than once if Mary could see it from her little window crossed by two bars. William Calcraft, the executioner, had arrived from London yesterday, said an old man with yellow eyes and wires of grey hair growing out of his nose. He nudged me hard and grinned with only two teeth.

I looked up at the scaffold. It smelled of fresh-cut wood, and I thought of Mary's *I was gathering sticks, Nan! That came down by the flood. How can ye steal sticks?* The noose I found I couldn't look at, at all. Every time my eye was drawn up toward the gallows, I'd squeeze them shut or gaze at a point somewhere beyond, so that all I could see was its outline; the vague idea of what a noose should look like.

Soon it started getting busier and louder. By a quarter to the hour, the crowd behind had swelled to what must now be thousands. There were swarms of policemen and militiamen, and perhaps a few hundred more special constables, gathering around us like a perimeter wall. I heard laughter, some shouting, even singing—the reverence of less than an hour ago gone. My heart had begun beating too hard and too fast, and I pressed a fist against my breastbone, willing it to calm. I was here for Mary. Whether she knew it or not, saw me or not. I was here for Ann Hannah. And I was here for me. I'd left them both there, inside those two stony buildings less than fifty yards apart—mean and small-boned like crouching rats in the dark.

When the clock on the New Church struck eight, I jumped. Let out a sound loud enough to attract the yellow eyes of my neighbour.

"Here we go," said he, rubbing his palms together as if cold.

I shivered and looked away, turned toward the prison door. When no one came through it for long minutes, the crowd grew restless and louder. Something like hope sprung to life in my chest. Many had petitioned on Mary's behalf; a deputation had even visited the Home Secretary to plead for clemency. Perhaps there would be no hanging here today at all.

And then the door opened and Calcraft came out. Dressed in black and wearing a skullcap, his expression hidden inside a white bushy beard. Calcraft favoured the short-drop, everyone knew. His victims more often strangled to death than broke their necks; sometimes he even swung from their feet to entertain the crowd.

My fingers began to tingle, my breath growing shallow and quick. I'd not been able to stomach breakfast, and my belly felt hard and empty. *Have ye ever had a hole in your belly so big ye think your stomach's eaten itself? Or a hole in your head so wide that ye stare at walls for days and think ae nothing at all?* Nausea rose up into my chest and my mouth began to water enough that I wanted to spit.

And then Mary.

I heard her before I saw her. Her cries, plaintive and so full of horror—*No, no! Please!*

The crowd inhaled and bellowed and turned toward the prison door as the chaplain came out with Mary behind, struggling between two constables. Thin now again after her days of only bread and water, dressed in a long, black frock and that same white cap.

"Mary," I whispered, heat rushing into my eyes. And when the vile old man looked my way again, I gave him back a glare so cold, so full of eager fury that he stepped quick backwards out of my reach.

The constables dragged Mary, still screaming, still begging, onto the scaffold. They'd pinned her arms to her sides with leather straps; her hands closed in and out of frantic fists. When she saw the noose, her body became rigid, and then as quickly lax. So quickly, in fact, that the constables almost let go of her as she fainted.

The crowd muttered a little, less entertained than disquieted.

When Mary came awake again, that blank empty look had returned, but only for a second—only until she remembered where she was. And then all in her face seemed to fall, to crumple like kindling as it burns. And she resumed her piteous entreaties to us, to the chaplain, even to William Calcraft. Tears streaming down her face and off her chin, turning her bodice blacker still. Her hands twitching and squeezing at her sides. My own hands were fists. How I longed for her savage laugh. Her glittering wild eyes.

Let it be done, I thought. God, just let it be done.

The constables, their faces drawn and pale, dragged her over the trapdoor. When they let her go, she swayed once, twice. The executioner walked toward her, nodded once at the crowd. No cheers or shouts were offered up to him, and I was glad to see his head dip and his shoulders sag.

When he brought out a white hood, Mary cringed and sobbed, looked up into the sky.

"No, please. Oh, my weans. My weans. Oh, oh, oh. *Please.*"

And at that, the crowd didn't only go quiet, it went silent. Until all that could be heard was Mary, the chaplain's muttered prayers, and the April wind singing through the junction and into the main street beyond.

Calcraft looked discomfited enough to glance away from us and briefly up at the sky as he covered Mary's head with the hood and secured the noose around her neck.

I turned to stare at all the faces behind and alongside me. Many of them stared back. And maybe, like me, they all knew what it was to have a hole in their bellies, their heads, their chests, because they started calling Mary's name. They started begging for mercy, for her life to be spared. The shouts and cries grew like a chorus. And Mary still led them, her wails, her pleas neither diminished nor weakened.

Calcraft retreated to the hangman's lever, and the chorus grew only louder, louder. My throat was raw with it; my ears rushing with noise as though underwater. I shouted Mary's name until it was all that there was in the whole world. And I thought of those cold fingers gripping at my throat. Fear like a cold hole inside my chest. Hot pennies and screaming pigs. Francis's palm hot against my skin. The want that is always there. The monsters that are inside every one of us.

And then—then—Mary Timney, *about twenty-seven years of age, slimly made, and with a countenance by no means repulsive,* was dropped down through the trapdoor and into the space beneath, where she hung, not moving, neck broken.

The silence returned, save the slow long creak of the rope's swing.

William Calcraft nodded his head. The two constables stared at their feet. The chaplain closed his Bible.

And as one, we turned around and left that junction between St David Street and Buccleuch Street. We didn't look at one another. We didn't look back at the scaffold. We said not a word. We made not a sound. Just like all of the birds inside that lonely and terrible valley surrounded by grey hills and black-green forest.

———————————

Mary Timney was executed in Dumfries, Scotland, on the 29th of April, 1862. Although she was almost certainly guilty and was initially condemned as a monster for her brutal crime, the sentiment of the media and local community quickly changed, and there was a great effort to save the poverty-stricken young mother from the gallows. When this didn't succeed, there was a countrywide outcry, and no woman would ever again be publicly executed in Scotland.

Although the character of Nancy MacDonald is entirely fictional, all trial testimonies are taken from abridged transcripts, first reported in the *Dumfries and Galloway Standard* and the *Wigtownshire Free Press*, on the 10th of April, 1862.

THREE MOTHERS MOUNTAIN

by Nathan Ballingrud

In early to mid-May of every year, in what the locals call blackberry winter, the witches of Three Mothers Mountain come down from their little cabin to sell their wares to the people of Toad Springs, North Carolina. The date is never fixed; you know by the weather. When the last cold snap before spring frosts the grass and strangles the columbines in their seeds, people drift toward the field out beyond the Stonewall Jackson High School baseball field, where the witches set up their stalls at a respectable remove from each other. They arrive in the morning and remain there until the sun touches the peaks of the Smoky Mountains which surround them, at which point they pack what remains unsold and walk slowly back up the only known path to their hut, where they resume their mysterious works in isolation until the following year.

It's called Witches' Day, and it's a day of celebration.

Mother Margaret, in her fifties, is the youngest of the three. Only the faintest streaks of silver highlight her sun-blond hair; by natural luck or by uncanny means she has retained the appearance of someone twenty years younger. She smiles easily and receives all her customers with genuine welcome. Her stall is a sturdy table set up beneath a forest-green awning. She sells delectables and potted delights. Scuttlefoot Pie, Fruitfly Cake, and Pickled Pillbugs—these are only a small assortment of the wonders she brings down from the mountain each year. These dishes stanch tears and ease the pains of living. They fill the heart with the trickle of forest streams and blow a cool piney wind across heated thoughts. Frog Song Soup is her most popular dish, emitting a melodious concert of croaks and cheeps once simmering; this not only fills the night with a chirping beauty, but bequeaths soothing dreams to every child and frog in a mile radius.

Mother Ingrid is older, though exactly how much is a matter of conjecture. She brings with her a wagon pulled by a bony-legged mule, the same she has used in anyone's living memory. On its journey down the mountain, the wagon is covered with a patchwork quilt—a gift from an earlier generation of Toad Springs. It will be folded and carefully stored for the return journey. The quilt shifts and bulges as it rolls into place; when pulled off, the results of Mother Ingrid's labors turn their black eyes to the sun, taking in with wonder the absence of crowded maples and the firelit beams of a low roof. These are the homunculi which she grows in little clay pots, animated with a sigh of life. They are hideous creatures: standing between four and eight inches tall, they are composed of bundles of thorny vines and serrated leaves; gnats and wasps cloud around them, forever crawling from their dark and sticky interiors. They stink of offal and sometimes leak blood onto the floor. And yet they speak with beautiful voices and perform their services well. Some help clean the house; others offer good advice or shore up one's confidence with kind observations. They live for six months, give or take. They are well-loved.

Mother Agnes is the crone. She looks as though she crawled from every child's dream of witches, as though she ought to ride down astride her crooked broom, scarved in phantoms. She carries her wares in a great cupboard of blackened oak strapped to her back. She balances with a heavy walking stick that flares into spindly, finger-like branches at its apex, each bristling with autumn leaves of red and gold. After thumping her cupboard onto the grass, she undoes the lash which binds shut the doors and opens them to reveal the glistening jars of ghost preserves. These are made from the spirits she is said to harvest from her garden, which she cultivates in a half-acre of earth hacked from the mountain's dark wood. Each jar is half the size of fruit preserves you might buy at the local grocery, and each sheds a small, pale light, though you might not notice this under a midday sun. Some of the jars have labels affixed to the sides, but many—the most popular—do not. These are to be selected based on whim, or instinct, or compulsion; what it will do for you is not for her to say, nor anyone else's business to know. Of the three witches, Mother Agnes is the one most likely to return to her cabin with unsold inventory—though there have been dark years when the demand for her goods outpaced her ability to satisfy them.

There are other services the witches perform for Toad Springs, but these are not conducted in the sunlight, nor are they discussed in person. Letters are exchanged, contracts signed, payments made. Results are always guaranteed.

Witches' Day is not about those arrangements. It's a lighter, lovelier affair.

And so, the population of Toad Springs awakes to frosted air and a cold fog curling through town; those with the means and the desire brew coffee, perhaps stoke a fire in the hearth, dress in their heavier clothes, and make their way through town—on foot, never by machine, because that is the rule—until they arrive at the open field behind the high school, where the witches of Three Mothers Mountain are already waiting for them, each behind her stall, as still as a painting.

One year, Tom Bell and his little brother, Scotty, arrived with them. Tom was thirteen years old; Scotty was nine. They wore jackets too light for the weather. Their hair was uncombed and their faces unwashed. Scotty came with Tom, and Tom came alone. He had an emptiness in his heart and he was trying not to fall into it.

They were here to sneak up the path to the witches' hut and smash everything in it.

Tom and Scotty roamed the edges of the field for the first hour. In that time the first sortie of people from Toad Springs ventured into the orbit of the witches' stalls. They performed their interest as a kind of dance: they congregated in small groups and stood at a distance from a particular stall, speaking quietly to one another about who knows what. Then they shuffled to the next stall in sequence and repeated the charade. After a few moments of this, one of them approached the first stall—Mother Margaret's, naturally—and took up an item from the table, turned it this way and that, asked a question, smiled shyly and returned it to its place. Throughout this process the witches remained patient and quiet, speaking only when directly addressed. Eventually this long flirtation came to an end, and someone bought something. The dam broken, business was conducted as normal throughout the rest of the day.

"Which one is it?" Scotty asked.

Tom pointed to the crone. Her stall received the least traffic, just as it did every year. The morning fog, burnt away as the sun rose, never seemed to leave her stall completely. Nor did the sun illuminate her the way it did the others, though she had nothing to shade her. Darkness crowded her like a favorite pet.

"That one," he said.

"She's scary," his brother said. He delivered this information gravely, as though it were difficult news he was obliged to share.

Tom did not react to it. He'd been afraid of her once, too. But a year ago their wise and loving father, who drove a four-hundred-mile route delivering restaurant supplies from here all the way up to Hob's Landing and back, lost control of his truck on the downslope of a mountain less than an hour away from home. The truck punched through a guardrail and rolled eight hundred feet down the mountainside, tearing through spruce and pine and collapsing in a crushed and inverted heap, half submerged in a creek at the bottom of a ravine. His father had survived the crash only to drown in the shallow water, his body pinned in place by crumpled metal. By the time he was discovered, crawdads and catfish had cleaned the flesh from his skull and his hands, and his body had surrendered to the heat and the flies. But somehow his wedding ring had been retrieved from the corpse—Tom's imagination returned, again and again, to the image of someone lifting his dead father's hand out of the rushing water and twisting the gold from its finger—and returned to his mother. She delivered it by mail to Mother Agnes that same year, who planted it in her garden.

Three months passed, during which they watched their mother descend steeply into a bleak, interior country. She stopped going to work, stopped feeding her children or herself, stopped bathing. She sat in the cold kitchen, her head hanging, her dirty hair hiding her face. The boys still went to school, eager for something steady and reliable, but Tom especially began to lose his way. He skipped classes, he stopped paying attention or doing his homework. He got into fights, coming home split-lipped and bruised.

And then their father came back home.

Tom and Scotty discovered him while heading out to the bus stop one frigid morning. He'd been waiting on their front porch, perhaps all night. He was bloated and black as jet; his skin seemed to be damp and molting beneath his tarry clothes. Flies celebrated him, rising and falling like breath, filling the air with their hum. The boys would not have recognized him at all, but he fixed them with his loving eyes and he smiled at them with shining teeth. "Boys," he said.

They led him inside. Tom remembered entering the kitchen, the sun cresting the eastern mountains and spilling light through the room. Everything gleamed, even the unwashed dishes and the floor sticky with dirt.

Their mother gasped. She shouldered them aside in her rush to him, enfolding him in her arms. She was enfolded in turn.

Their father lived in the house again then, smiling on the couch, watching television, asking the boys how things were going. But things didn't go back to the way they were. They only got worse. He couldn't work anymore, of course, and their mother didn't go back to work either, choosing instead to spend all her time with him, leaning into the softness of him, the sticky black residue of his body staining her clothing and her skin. The flies surrounding him crawled over her face, lodged wriggling in her hair.

"She's not scary. And if you're too scared then you can go back home."

Scotty whipped a fearful glance at his brother before fixing his gaze back on Mother Agnes with fresh determination. "I'm not scared."

"Good. 'Cause I need you today, Scotty. You understand that?"

Scotty nodded.

By then it was late morning, and the field was starting to fill up. Some people had brought picnics. Later that afternoon there would be portable grills, the smell of charcoal fires and cooking burgers filling the crisp air. Tom remembered when they'd been part of that once. He remembered sitting on the grass, a messy hot dog in his hand, watching the lights come on in town behind them, watching the witches in their stalls, spicing the evening with miracles.

He tugged his brother's arm. "Let's go, then."

Scotty resisted. His attention had wandered to where some of his friends were playing tag, running and laughing raucously in the otherwise quiet morning. "Can I play for a little first?"

"We didn't come here to play, Scotty."

His brother looked at him with naked yearning. It irritated Tom; he hadn't even wanted to take Scotty with him, initially, but he'd been swayed by this very same forlorn expression. And now here the kid was, blinded by friends and toys when there was dark work to be done.

But these friends were the last anchor to sanity Scotty had in the world, aside from Tom himself. Scotty looked forward to going to school because it was light and clean, and because people cared about him there. Tom feared something vital was being leeched from his younger brother every morning he woke up in that house, and sometimes his inability to protect Scotty left him gasping for breath in the middle of the night. Scotty deserved whatever scraps of happiness he could find.

"Half an hour," Tom said. "That's all. I'm serious."

His brother beamed. "Thanks, Tom!" And he was off like a cannonball, barreling toward the other kids. As they opened their ranks and accepted him into the group, Tom felt a sudden welling of relief and sorrow.

Tom walked out to the bleachers and waited. He kept his back to the market. He watched the stream of cars out on the highway, sunlight glinting off chrome and glass. Once, his father would have been part of that traffic, steering his rig gently through it, a tender goliath. But he never left home anymore. The boys couldn't recognize their father in the thing that lived in their house.

He gave his brother an extra fifteen minutes. He approached the gaggle of kids slowly, reluctant to interfere. Scotty, in mid-lope, saw him coming and came to a reluctant stop. "No, please? Ten more minutes?"

"It's now or never."

Scotty's face clouded. Tom felt a wave of unreasonable anger. But it wasn't his brother's fault that they were abruptly poor. It wasn't his brother's fault that Tom himself didn't have friends, that this loneliness at home was absolute and all-consuming. It wasn't his brother's fault that their father was a monster and their mother was crazy. The anger dissipated almost at once, replaced by something sad and sweet.

He didn't need to take him on this trek. Scotty belonged to the sunlight.

"Tell you what. Stay here and play. I'll pick you up when I'm done."

Scotty surprised him. He turned to the other kids and said, "I have to go." And to his brother he said, "You need me today."

Tom felt a flush of pride. It was not a feeling he was accustomed to. "Okay," he said. "Let's get to it, then."

No one noticed them leaving the baseball field; people came and went all the time. The road leading up the mountain was empty. Nobody lived up there but the witches, so there was no need for anybody else ever to walk up that way. It was getting on toward ten o'clock. The sun was bright, and the air was cold and clear.

Soon the market fell out of sight. The path ascended around a steep bend, and then Toad Springs was obscured by the woods. They walked fast, making good time. Soon they were sweating with exertion despite the chill.

By the time they'd been walking for an hour or so, Scotty was making a show of his weariness, leaning over as he walked, swaying his arms dramatically. "I'm too tired, Tom!"

"Come on," Tom said. He kept trudging, though he was starting to feel worn out too.

"I can't!"

Tom stopped, turned around. Scotty was sitting flat in the middle of the dirt road, his legs splayed out before him and his hands resting palms up, as though he were offering himself up to whatever might come along to collect him. "Get your ass up, Scotty! You can't just sit in the middle of the road!"

"No cars come on this road," he said, and lay straight back to underscore his faith in this point.

"Fine." Tom turned and continued his climb. "You know who does come on this road though? Witches."

In moments, he heard his brother's feet slapping the ground behind him. He permitted himself a little smile.

The path darkened as they walked. Tom no longer had a sense of what time it was, and he felt a flutter of fear in his gut. Common sense told him it couldn't be any later than two o'clock, two thirty at most. And yet the light filtering through the trees seemed diffuse and weak. This might have been due to the sun pursuing its course above them, and it might have had something to do with the heavy tangle of branches crowding them from either side, but he knew instinctively that the cause was something else: they were entering the Witch Wood. Darkness was an animal, and this is where it lived.

"Come on, we gotta hurry."

They doubled their pace, Scotty huffing and pouting behind him, until they came at last to a place where the road narrowed and split three ways. One wended in a slight decline to the right, where the trees thinned and sunlight dappled the way; one rose sharply straight ahead, a path composed more of stacked rock than packed earth; and one bent toward the left, into deeper woods. This left-hand path was straight and level, though the trees grew tight and mean around it, hoarding darkness. It was obviously the path to the Mothers' cabin.

"Come on, Scotty." He took a few tentative steps, feeling the temperature drop a few more degrees.

His brother slipped a hand into his, and they continued their walk, suddenly reluctant to get where they were going.

On the second week, while seated at the kitchen table, their father opened his chest. His rib cage was fashioned from cedar branches; suspended by a red thread in its center was a jar of ghost preserves of the kind Mother Agnes sold at market, its interior gray and mold-thick, sparkling with an interior light. He reached into himself, took it into his hand, and offered it to their mother. It steamed when he opened it. Careful not to snap the thread, she took it into her hands. It was hot to the touch, and she winced. She scooped her fingers into the jar and pressed them into her mouth. Their father remained silent and still, his smile radiant. Tears gathered in their mother's eyes, and she closed them, drawing a deep breath.

"I missed you," she said. "I missed you." Then she clutched Tom's sleeve. "Come here. You too."

"No." He jerked his arm away.

She reached for Scotty instead. "Scotty. This is your father."

Scotty backed against the refrigerator. Revulsion crawled across his face. "No! I'm too scared!"

Their father put his own fingers into the jar, scooping out a thick dollop, and extended it to Scotty. It dripped onto the carpet, a mixture of preserves and the black, greasy residue of his skin. Scotty edged further away.

Their mother's face curled in anger. "Scotty! Take it! *Don't you want to know your father?*" Her voice escalated into a shriek, a piercing dagger of sound. Scotty bolted from the kitchen, his footsteps thundering all the way to his room. The door slammed shut and a keening wail floated back to them.

His mother's head dropped into her folded arms, and she sobbed. She held the half-depleted jar loosely in one hand, the thread still connected to the cedar ribs, the fingers of her other hand still smeared with its contents. Her own crying mingled with Scotty's mournful howl into a noise that filled

Tom with a desperate self-loathing. Maybe he could stop at least one person from crying.

"Mom?" He touched her shoulder. "Mom?"

She lifted her head. Her eyes were swollen, her whole face leaking. It was the worst he had ever seen her.

"I'll try it."

She gripped his forearm so tightly that he knew there'd be bruises later. "*Yes.* Yes, Tommy. I knew you would do it. He always loved you best."

He felt a spike of guilty pride, and then a fresh wash of grief at having lost him, this man who had apparently loved him better than anyone else in the world. He noticed that Scotty's crying had ceased, and he wondered if he'd heard her say that. He half hoped so.

"You're just like your dad, Tom."

Maybe, by consuming this awful substance, he could accept his return. Maybe he would recognize him in the entity sitting at the table.

He went to the utensil drawer and retrieved a spoon. His took the jar into his own hands, staring into it. Faint screams lifted from it, like a sound drifting down the mountain, carried by the wind from a far place.

"Mom? Is Dad in Hell?"

She pulled back slightly, surprised. Her lip trembled halfway between a grimace and a smile. Her eyes shone like cracked glass. She put her hand on his cheek, and suddenly all he could see in her face was love. Boundless love. "No, honey. No. He's right here. He's right here with us."

The father-thing opened its mouth into a bright grin.

Tom ate.

The cabin was nestled in a copse of blackened trees, each curled like a finger around its white-painted walls. Bright flowers were painted on its doorframe. Little pots of herbs were suspended from hooks along its gabled roof, and a trellis leaned against the wall beside a curtained front window, heavy with roses in unseasonable bloom. A small lantern hung from a hook by the door, spilling a warm nimbus of light. Only then did it occur to Tom how late it had gotten. It seemed impossible that evening should already be settling over the mountain, yet here it was.

Scotty clutched his hand so hard it hurt. Tom extricated himself and made his cautious way to the door. He put his ear against the wood and listened.

"Are they home?"

"You know they're not home. They're still at the market."

Tom glanced at the road behind them, not at all sure this was true. Any moment they might materialize from around the bend, Mother Agnes with that great cabinet strapped to her back. He thought he heard a sound even now: *tuk . . . tuk . . . tuk . . .* Her walking stick punching into the earth, dragging her up the path.

He turned the doorknob. The door swung open silently. The lantern light illuminated a dusty wooden floor, spangled with divots where Mother Agnes's walking stick had gouged the wood. An end table was just inside, littered with little white pellets that made him think of knucklebones. The interior of the house radiated a kind of thrumming energy, setting his nerves jangling. But it was quiet as sleep.

The boys entered, and Tom shut the door behind them. He felt his little brother tense at the abrupt plunge into darkness. He reached into his pocket and removed the lighter he'd taken from his mother's purse. It popped its little orange flame, giving them just enough light to maneuver by. When Scotty saw the lighter, his eyes widened.

"You're going to get in trouble!" he hissed.

"She's never gonna know, shut up."

They pushed further into the cabin. It seemed to have more rooms inside than it should, although every one of them was cramped with tables, chairs, a couch in one room, cabinets and chests of drawers. And shelves, everywhere they turned. Freestanding bookshelves stretching to the ceiling, small knick-knack shelves hanging on the walls, glass-cased shelves in the living room, shelves of spices and ingredients in the kitchen crowding a narrow cutting table and a potbellied stove.

What struck Tom's attention, though, were the items stored on the shelves: on some, miniature wooden figures fashioned from entwined branches and fleshed with mud, most still awaiting the breath of life, but one of them staring back with eyes like pinprick red cinders, a cockroach sliding out of its mouth like a tongue; on others, endless jars of various sizes, all of them full of glittering, moldy, pearl-colored preserves, all of them shedding a sickly light. They were like jars of rotting stars.

The strange energy he'd detected was radiating from them; although they were still, they projected a sense of shuddering movement, of imperceptible vibrations, as though each one housed something living and desperate to get out.

"Ghosts," he said.

Scotty grabbed his hand, squeezing hard again. This time Tom did not protest.

"We need to hurry," Scotty said, and Tom knew he was right. He had come here to destroy. Ever since he'd eaten the preserves, he could feel his father in his brain, like something long asleep starting to uncoil. The first time he'd experienced it, he wept with relief. It was as though his father was couched in his every thought, as though the weight of his arm around his shoulders would never leave again. He felt confident, protected, and loved. But it kept uncoiling, kept pushing for more space, until he started to feel other things too. The brush of his mother's hand through his hair released complicated yearnings. Once he awoke to find himself standing over her as she slept, his hand poised to pull down the covers. The father-thing reposed beside her, his pale eyes fixed on his son, his grin like a light in the lightless room. Tom fled the room and pounded his own head onto his dresser until the world swam. Looking into mirrors produced a sense of disjunction which made him nauseous and filled him with self-loathing; he avoided them now. He was filled with an anger hotter than he'd ever experienced. Something elemental. Maybe an adult would know how to restrain it or to channel it; maybe not. But he had come to the Mothers' cabin to deliver his revenge.

And yet, faced with these shivering spirits, he was transfixed. He wanted to grab the edge of the closest bookcase and topple the whole thing over, but he couldn't bring himself to do it. It would have been like desecrating a church.

Scotty yanked his arm. "Tom, they're going to be here soon! We need to hurry!"

"Wait, wait. Let's look at their labels. Maybe we can find one that can help Mom."

A single shelf was affixed to the wall on his immediate right, and he peered more closely at the jars it held. Each small label was marked with an elegant cursive script. *Indian Summer. All Hallows' Eve. Skullpocket Fair. The Yuletide Weeping. Hannah's Underground Wedding.* They were all times or occasions: no indication of who was inside or what it would do to you if you ate it. Which ones could be taken as they were, or which were destined to be the hearts of creatures like the father-thing.

Scotty grabbed the nearest jar—a big one, like the one that held pickled pigs' feet at the gas station—and hurled it with all his strength across the room. It hit the dappled wallpaper with a soft crunch and fell behind an easy chair. They both stared at the place it disappeared in silence, waiting for whatever had been trapped inside to make itself known.

"Why did you do that?"

Scotty looked at his brother in terror. "You said! You said that's what we're supposed to do!"

I changed my mind, he wanted to say. *I'm scared now too.* "I know, but—"

"You *said*!" And he grabbed another jar.

But Tom grabbed his wrist, staying his throw. "No," he said, and pointed. Light was streaming in from between the closed curtains.

Moonlight.

Someone was on the other side of the front door, huffing with effort.

"Hide!"

In a house this cluttered there was an abundance of places, yet they stood paralyzed for long seconds. Finally, Tom hustled them into the kitchen. The potbellied stove squatted in the corner like an evil goblin; Tom's mind flashed to an illustration from *Hansel and Gretel:* a stove with children's legs thrashing from its open grate.

There was a back door at the kitchen's far end, but he feared they'd be seen through the window if they went for it. He opened the pantry closet and pulled his brother inside with him. It was cramped and dark, but he thought they would be fine as long as they stayed perfectly still. As long as the Mothers didn't open the door.

Around them were shelved all the instruments of Mother Margaret's art: cloves of garlic, soup stock, onions and potatoes and jars of crickets. Coiled salamanders and sleeping toads, red peppers and racks of spices, a burlap sack sealed with clothespins that shifted slightly as if it were filled with rats or snakes. The smell was giddy and overwhelming. One of the toads opened a sleepy yellow eye and regarded them with patient curiosity.

The witches entered the cabin. The boys heard a grunt, followed by the heavy sound of Mother Agnes's cabinet thudding onto the floor. Footsteps shuffled through the small home. When they spoke to each other it sounded like the language of abandoned wooden shacks, creaking and squeaking in the wind.

"The fat one was rude again today."

"Put a goblin's tooth in her pie next time. A civil tongue or no tongue at all, is what I like to say."

"Did you see the Owens boy? So fetching before, but now he looks like an ox. I knew he'd grow up stupid."

Occasionally one of them would laugh or cluck disapprovingly.

Eventually, they exhausted their chatter and the cabin fell into silence. Tom began to wonder if they'd gone to bed. He had all but made up his mind to open the pantry door when he heard one of them enter the kitchen. She was breathing heavily, humming quietly to herself; from time to time a word or a phrase breached the surface: an old song Tom had heard on the radio before, one his mother liked, though he couldn't place it. A country ballad. He tried to imagine a witch listening to popular music on a radio but it was too strange.

Scotty whimpered. Tom locked his hand over his mouth and squeezed tight.

A soft light flickered at the bottom of the door. The tap at the sink came on, and they listened as the witch filled a kettle.

The water cut off. "What?" she said.

The boys looked at each other, Tom's hand still over his brother's mouth.

They heard something else moving in the house: scuttling like a centipede. A very large centipede.

A voice came from another room: "Ingrid! Look at this!"

The witch—Mother Ingrid, the one who made the homunculi—left the kitchen. After a moment they heard a chair being dragged from its position in the other room.

"Who did this?"

The shattered jar.

"Let's go!" Tom hissed. "Now!"

He opened the pantry—the kitchen was bathed in warm light coming from the stove, and from a lamp on the cutting table—and bolted for the back door. He knocked into the table in his haste and its legs scraped loudly over the floor. He didn't care anymore; he only had to get out of there. Let them see him through the window, let them leap onto broomsticks or send a flock of vampire bats through the night after him. He just needed to be out of this cabin.

He reached the door—unlocked!—and banged through it. He leapt down the stoop and hit the grass. His heart lifted—free! The trees surged against the full night sky. The moon burned.

He skidded to a stop.

He stood in Mother Agnes's garden.

It was a modest parcel of land, no wider than the little house itself. A small white fence—only up to his ankles, purely decorative—surrounded it. Inside it were four ghosts. They were tethered to the ground just beneath the earth, bright white scraps of light whipping and shivering like flags in a hurricane wind, though the air was still. The ghosts did not make a sound, but Tom felt a welling of nausea and grief. They froze him in place.

Behind him, his brother said, "Tom?"

He turned. The witches stood at the top of the stoop, the three of them together a huge black shape, the dark rags of their clothing fluttering like crows' feathers. One spindly hand gripped Scotty's shoulder.

"You left before the tea was ready, child," said Mother Margaret. "Come back inside."

The brothers sat at the small table with Mothers Margaret and Ingrid. There were five chairs and five empty clay mugs. Had the table been set for five before? Tom couldn't remember. The lamp had been extinguished, so the only light came from the red-orange belly of the stove and the eerie luminescence of the ghost jars. They waited meekly while Mother Agnes shuffled about in the other room, moving furniture and making clucking noises. She was trying to capture the escaped ghost.

"Come here, love. You're not fit to be out yet." When this didn't work she started to sing. Her voice was old and weathered, but it carried a melody with surprising ease. Tom found himself lulled by it. His fear started to abate. Scotty's eyes were half-closed and he seemed to be studying the mug in front of him with a sleepy intensity.

In a moment the singing stopped and the witch came back into the kitchen, her expression clouded. "It won't come," she said. She paused by the table and glared at the boys. "That's bad business," she said. "Why are you here?"

With the song stopped, fear bubbled up inside him again. Tom wanted to answer her, but the words wouldn't come.

The kettle began to whistle, and Mother Margaret made a shushing gesture. "Wait."

Mother Agnes grasped the kettle with unnaturally long fingers—hands which only minutes earlier had clutched Scotty's shoulder, those sharp nails so close to his throat—and poured. Their mugs billowed steam like little cauldrons. Mother Margaret dropped a bag of herbs into each. "Five minutes," she said. "Any more, any less, and there will be dark results."

"I want to go home," Scotty said.

Mother Ingrid looked at him, her lips curled in distaste. "We'll see," she said.

Mother Agnes seated herself at the table and looked at Tom. "Well?"

"My mom sent you a letter."

"I get a lot of letters from a lot of people, in case you didn't know. Do better."

"It had my dad's ring in it. She sent you his ring."

"A wedding ring?"

Tom shrugged. "I guess."

Mother Agnes laughed. It was not a pleasant sound. "I remember her. She seemed sweet."

Anger flashed through Tom's whole body. "You ruined her life. She can't do anything anymore. She doesn't work anymore. She doesn't care about us anymore. Only Dad. And he's . . . not the same."

The witch fluttered a hand. "So what. She's haunted. That's what she wanted."

Scotty started openly weeping. He lowered his head, his eyes screwed shut. "Mom's haunted? Is Dad a bad ghost?"

Mother Agnes looked at Tom. She winked. "What do you say, boy? Is your daddy a bad ghost?"

Tom felt the foreign presence shift in his head. That knot of urgency, desire, thwarted want. That bubbling anger. His father had never been an angry man at home. Tired and harried, impatient sometimes, yes. But never angry. Never a hard word for his family. So who was this thing Tom felt crawling inside him now? Why the urge—the need—to break bones, to crack wood, to burn this whole mountain down to black earth?

What had his father kept locked away? Had he ever really known him at all?

The freed ghost stepped in from the other room, filling the doorframe. It looked like a curtain of flame, and it shed a cold radiance. It pinwheeled where it stood, billowing silence. It wore multiple heads.

"Look what you've released, you stupid child. I can't get it back now." Mother Agnes stood from the table and teetered to the back door. It was hard to believe this frail woman had walked up and down a mountain with a six-foot cabinet strapped to her back. Opening it, she thrust a pointed finger outside and addressed the ghost. "Go, wretch. You're not welcome in my home."

The ghost was still for a moment; then it lunged for the door in a frigid rush. It passed over the brothers and seemed nearly to pull something from the center of them in its wake; they were left vertiginous and a little ill, as though they had almost walked off the edge of a building. Mother Agnes shut the door with a grunt of disgust.

"It is unquiet, and will stay that way. Whatever it does now is your fault. Remember that."

Mother Ingrid tutted in disappointment, shaking her head.

Scotty rose from his position at the table. His tea was untouched. He looked scooped out, exhausted. "I'm going home now."

"Wait for me, Scotty."

Mother Agnes resumed her seat and looked at them both. "You don't get to break into our home and vandalize it, then leave at your whim. Answer the question I asked you. Why did you come?"

"To break things," Scotty said. "I'm sorry I did it. I just want to go home now. Mom's going to be mad."

"Darling," Mother Margaret said. "No. She won't."

"You have to help me," Tom said. As he said it, he knew it was the real reason he'd come. The witches had to get rid of their dad. Not for his mom or his brother, but for himself. He felt the terrible weight of the betrayal even as he thought it.

You're just like your dad, Tom.

The father-thing opened its mouth into a bright grin.

"She's feeding us from the jar," he said, his voice quavering. "Is that safe?"

Mother Margaret was delighted. "Some people think the heart is delicious!"

"Nothing in this world is safe, boy," said Mother Ingrid.

Mother Agnes took a sip from her tea and seemed to think about it. "People come to me for what grows out in that garden. I don't make any promises about what it will be like for them, or whether they'll be better for it. *Caveat emptor*, boy. Do you know what that means?"

Tom shook his head.

"Ask your mother. She knows."

"Please," Tom said. Tears burned his eyes. "I can't be like this anymore."

Mother Ingrid frowned at him. "Your mother made an honest transaction," she said. "Do you think we're cheats?"

Scotty started to cry. "Please just let us go."

Tom watched as his little brother lowered his head and sobbed unselfconsciously, his cheeks flushed red, tears dripping from his eyelashes. It was a plain, uncomplicated sound; almost musical. Once they left this mountain and returned home, there would be nothing uncomplicated about his life again. He would grow up in the shadow of their grief-wrecked mother and the bizarre presence of the father-thing, their house filled with the stink of a love gone mad, the air choked with flies. Tom felt his father's darkness percolating inside him; but maybe Scotty could be spared.

"My brother," he said, finally.

The witches leaned in, smiling. "Yes, child? What about him?"

"If you can't save me or my mom, save my brother."

"From what?" said Mother Margaret.

". . . from the dark."

Scotty stared at him, shivering in fear.

She reached across the table and took Tom's hand into her own. "Poor boy. Poor, dull boy. It's far too late for that. No one is spared."

That was it, then. All was lost. He closed his eyes. He couldn't look his brother in the face.

The witches whispered, and then Mother Ingrid said, "Well, perhaps we can do something. Your mother paid. Will you?"

Thank God, at last, a window. Yes, he would pay. Yes. "Yes."

"You'll have to make friends with the dark," Mother Margaret said. "Do you have the heart for it?"

He nodded.

"We'll see."

"Don't fret," said Mother Agnes, staring at his little brother. "The sweetest things grow in the dark."

The ghosts trembled in their jars. Weird light shivered over their faces. Tom felt a creeping hope.

Scotty walked out the door. Tom stayed behind.

He stayed behind for fifty years, each one spent in servitude to the Mothers. He was given many tasks and performed them all dutifully. He ventured into the woods to gather ingredients for Mother Margaret's recipes: scraping beetles from the undersides of rocks, tending mold farms, catching cricketsong with a net made from the woven strands of a bog hag's hair. He lost two fingers obtaining the hair, but under the ministrations of Mother Ingrid, flexing twigs grew in their place.

For Mother Ingrid he cut and whittled branches of cedar trees, the ideal wood for the housing of spirits. He maintained the cellar full of spoiling meat and offal, where the vermin so vital to her efforts thrived. The homunculi caterwauled from their clay pots, scratching and biting viciously when the time came to cut them from their warm roots.

He tended Mother Agnes's garden, where the ghosts whipped back and forth under a sky frozen with stars. Mostly they grew from trinkets brought to her from the people of Toad Springs; but sometimes they grew on their own, straight from the corrupted earth, like Hell's questing fingers. These were untamable and he cut them loose to drift away and do their work upon the world.

When he complained, he was beaten, and he accepted these beatings. When he grew older, he submitted to the dark advances of Mother Margaret, surrounded by the crawling walls of her bedroom. Eventually his skin grew old and loose, his eyes turned opaque, his bones bent beneath the weight of his labors. He knew that if they ever dismissed him from service, he would be too old, too broken, too strange to be of worth to any living thing in the world.

He never learned whether or not his mother missed him, or if she even knew that he was gone. He hoped not.

He asked the Mothers what had become of his brother when they turned him loose that night, bewildered and alone—what kind of freedom Tom's sacrifice had bought for him.

They wouldn't tell him. Maybe they didn't know.

But each blackberry winter, when he felt the encroachment of despair most acutely, he remembered the night he agreed to this price. They gave Scotty one of the jars that night, and he ate from it at his brother's urging. He remembered Scotty's face as it released him: from his heart's shackling to his parents, from his brother, from a household in love with its own doom. Released finally into the dark, glittering wood, where, Tom liked to imagine, the pin-wheeling ghost they'd freed became Scotty's protector, his guide, his howling companion in a hundred eerie adventures. Scotty could never escape the darkness; but he could love it, and it could love him back. They ran together with abandon—into the Troll Wood, the Werewolf Wood, the Witch Wood, the full moon resplendent above.

Tom remembered, in the season's last frost, and was glad.

WIDOW-LIGHT

by Margo Lanagan

The hunter's daughter was never much good at girling. She didn't cook or clean any better than the most slapdash lad would. Her needlecraft never rose above a woodsman's proficiency with twine and leather thong. She sang only rough campfire-songs. So she was the right degree of useless.

And it was the time of year. *Some* girl must go up the hill to his castle. And all the others the proper age were suddenly affianced to town boys or to distant cousins, or not yet given to bleeding. Or they were too ugly—the town did not want to insult him.

Some girl, passably handsome, *must* go, else he would come down and choose a wife for himself, and who knew whose daughter he would take? Best to decide, while the choice was theirs, which young woman they could spare. Which girl did they not much care to see again, or to mention, or to mourn?

She fought tooth and nail. There was no one else to fight for her. The hunter was dead of the fever that had kept him home that season—and kept her home, too, tending him as best she knew how. No one knew where her brothers were. But they'd been gone long enough for people to forget how fearsome they turned when ganged together over a grudge.

The townsmen had to truss the girl up and gag her. But you could hardly deliver a bride all bloodied like that, in stained hunting clothes, tied mouth, hand, and foot. To such a groom, she must seem to go willingly. She must be clean. She must be dressed right.

Grimly they carried her, bound to a stretcher, up the mountain, in the latening afternoon. The spring wind caught the women's skirts, and played the girl's hair like dirty brown flames about her head. Behind the stretcher-bearers went men and boys carrying all the town's ladders.

The castle spread down the slope from its uppermost tower, which was pressed into the slant of the mountain peak. The party skirted the ramparts and paused at the tower's foot. There the ropemaker and his sons joined the ladders foot to head, with strongest lashings of good cord.

The older women washed what they could of the girl, and cut and combed the worst snarls out of her hair. Then snip, snip, went they with their scissors between the ropes that held her, cutting to pieces the good stout coat and the shirts and trousers the brothers had grown out of. They swaddled her in a blanket to keep her decent among the men, and gave her into the keeping of the second-eldest of the stonemason's daughters, a hefty, dull-eyed piece.

The men raised the ladder to a small diamond-paned window high in the tower wall. The town's best climber then danced up, secured it to a hole in the sill, and slithered down again.

Up then went the stone-daughter, carrying the girl in the blanket. The prisoner had struggled somewhat, but when asked should they knock her unconscious she had subsided. Now she lay like a sack of meal over the stone-daughter's shoulder, her face bouncing against the woman's belt.

After them climbed the priest, shaking like a poplar leaf in a breeze. At the top he took out his book, and gabbled the ceremony over the girl, who was slung across the sill, head inside the tower and washed feet motionless over the abyss, pale in the waning light.

Then the stone-daughter snatched off the blanket, bundled the girl into the window, and sawed away the knot behind her neck that all the bindings led to. The hunter's daughter dropped to the floor and fell against the wall.

The priest scrambled down the ladder, and the mason's girl stumped after. The climber scurried up with the bag of bride-clothes, cast it into the tower room, shut the window, untied the ladder-head, and skipped down again.

They broke the ladder into its pieces, then. Unlashing and putting away the cords, they grew cheerful, the ropemaker whistling. With a last look at the high, closed-fast window, they turned and began to pick their way down the path. The spring feast awaited them in the town, and honor from their fellow townspeople, and general relief. They had kept away the threat for another year.

The ropes had fallen from the girl when she landed, taking the snipped cloths with them. Cold, damp, stone-trapped air attacked her on every side. She sat and shivered and stared at the bag of bride-clothes. Diamonds of late sunlight crept up the stone wall.

She was married now, by church and by law. She had never wanted to be a wife, even to the most amiable man of her own choosing. She liked the hunting life. And the solitary life, too, since her father died.

Now she was not only wedlocked but sworn for life to some *thing* that she had never seen. Worse than a violent man, worse than a wastrel or weakling, worse than the farthest-gone lunatic. Hardly a man at all, if you believed some

tellers. More of a dragon, or a wild boar, or a vast toad, or some unholy mixture of the three. No one she knew had seen it, but that did not stop them telling of it, and each gave it the shape of their own greatest fear.

Below her massed the castle. She was used to sensing nearby living creatures. She could read oncoming weather from the merest shifts of air and predict how the wild things would meet it. But nothing lived here besides that
creature, her husband—not rat or beetle or bird. No space had ever felt so dead
to her, so drear. Wherever he was within these walls, no sound of his voice, no
movement, no scent of him reached her.

Now the diamond shapes had begun to slide across the rough-plastered
ceiling. While there was still light, she reached for the dress-sack and tugged
at the knotted cord. Out burst the bridal costume, multicolored, textured, and
trimmed. The best weavers, dyers, stitchers, tasselers, and lace-makers in the
town had toiled through the year on these garments. Some of the cloth was so
fine that the threads snagged on the girl's rough fingers. "Tut-tut!" she said,
pulling them free. She had never in her life handled stuffs as expensive, or as
impractical.

The foolish shoes she kicked aside. The headdress she threw across the
room—it clattered and snapped against the far wall. She put on the under-
shift, the stockings, and the drawers. It was like donning cobwebs, no protection at all from the cold.

The air thickened, then, a very slight curdling that none but a hunter
would notice. She crossed to the door and listened, trembling in the thin un-
derclothing.

It is only from cold, this shivering, she told herself, told the brothers and the
father who had raised her, whose good opinion she had always sought.

Hmph, said the brothers.

The father stayed silent.

Nothing approached or noised outside. The tower stairs spiraled upward
and downward, empty.

She went back to the pile of clothes. She tore the bodices from the petticoats and the dress, and layered them onto herself as shirts, thinner to thicker.
Then she wrapped the skirts around them, crissed and crossed so that she was
well covered shoulder to thigh. She tied the clumsy assemblage to herself with
the bag-cord.

By then she was panting, for the air had pressed closer as she wrapped herself, and chilled further. She had never felt anything like it in all her nights
among the mountains. Some enchantment was surely building in the castle's
air.

She left her tower room and crept down the stairs. The reddened sun
blinked at her through the western arrow-slits; red-and-purpled clouds flowed

past the eastern ones. Soundlessly she descended through the dimming fortress, first the clustered roomlets where the servants had slept, then the more spacious apartments below, the king's and the queen's and the other nobles'.

The beds were turned down ready for their royal sleepers, the curtains looped back, candles unlit beside them. Here and there, on a carpet or in a corridor, lay remains of a chambermaid or manservant. Bending to make out their shapes as the light waned, *Look,* she said to her brothers and father, *how the bones are grouped: the skull here, shaken free of the rest, the ribs and limbs scattered. But nothing has gnawed on them. He likes to tear his prey apart, but not to eat the pieces.*

Strong, then, said the brothers.

Take care, said her father. *Watch. Listen.*

She came to a broad stone banister and leaned there, dragging in breath after thick, cold breath. A grand staircase swept away before her, pale stone curving down to chaotic shadows. Her clothes hung heavily, as if soaked by a fog. The inner layers, those cobwebby nothings, clung to her like an icy extra skin. Stranger still, the stockings, and the sleeves of the bodices, now glowed with a faint blue-greenish light. And the colors and ornaments of the outer skirts were fading, as if bleached by the sun over many ages.

Her very mind paled, as she examined her garments, as she gazed down at the shapes strewn on the lower stairs and across the floor. Her brothers stood stupidly within her now—what did they know of bride-clothes, of glowing enchantments? Her father was dead, remember? How could he be of any use to her? She was entirely alone in this treacly trap of cold magic.

And why should she care what might happen? *He* awaited her, more powerful, and doubtless more magnificent, than any beastly foe she had ever fought or outsmarted. Long ago he had struck a bargain with the townspeople; it was her duty to keep their side of it. For their sake, to keep them from being torn apart like the royal servants, she must submit to him.

But what did submitting mean? She sat on the uppermost stair, for her shaking legs would no longer bear the weight of the sodden clothing. She sat, and her arms and legs glowed, and her jaws ached, and her eyes grew strange in their sockets—colder, wider, less inclined to blink. She touched her face, and her hands did not recognize the shapes there, and her eyes did not see her hands as hands. His power, his nearness, were giving her a new form. She would lose not just the life she was used to, not just her kin, but her own familiar body, her very self. Her fate was to merge with him, to become his kind, to live out her life as this cold creature, crushed and deformed.

Stair by stair she lowered her heavy, changing body toward the shadows. Gradually the light from her clothing revealed scattered weapons and dented armor-plate. Darkness splashed and streaked the pale walls where bloodied body-pieces had been thrown and slid to the floor. All this had happened too far in the past for anyone now alive to recall. The dry mountain air had turned flesh to leather. Once-plump faces were now tight masks, with hollow eyes and lips shrunken in against teeth. Hands were made bony gloves. The guards grasped swords they no longer had sight to wield or legs to carry into the fray. These would be her company, once she met her man and was remade in his image. These would be the only people left in her world.

On the bottom stair she paused. A page at her feet cried silently for help, his limbless torso draped in rotted silks. She must raise herself to standing. She must move on through this charnel house, find her husband, achieve her final form. But the clothing was heavier than armor now—and cold, so cold!

A halberd lay angled up the stairs. She stood it on end, and by great effort used it to pull herself upright.

Many rooms opened from this vestibule, but it was the tall doors tilting toward her, attached only by their lower hinges, that drew her eye. Bodies of nobles and soldiers had fetched up in that doorway thick as sticks in the pinch of a flooding stream. Fetched up as they fled from the room beyond, as they crowded and wedged themselves, as they fell.

Slow as an ancient, on glowing legs, on clumsy feet, she stepped toward them over bone and weapon, over the shadow-eyed and hollow-mouthed dead. When she reached the doorway she had so lost her will that she did not hesitate for a moment before climbing the teetering mound of piled carcasses, steadying herself with the halberd. Her groom, her husband, her master was beyond them somewhere, beckoning. She had no choice but to obey.

Beyond the corpse-mountain opened the great hall. The merest measure of dusk-light fell from the high windows. By her own feeble sleeve- and stocking-light she pieced together the awful drama that had unfolded here. Some of the remains were shrouded with gold-stitched velvet and silk banners, torn or decayed from their poles high above. Others lay in postures and fragments whose piteousness, through familiarity and the dread enchantment all around, left the girl quite unmoved. They were powerless, unbeautiful; they were not what she sought.

At the head of the hall stood three thrones. The king, the queen, and the crown prince had been snatched from them, and tossed no doubt to the corners of the room. Exhausted, the hunter's daughter sank into the king's cushioned seat. As a last hopeless measure against the cold she drew her limbs inside the chill weight of the tied-on cloth, concealing their light. Her husband must be very near; her old self felt to be almost disappeared. Her breath as she sat there slowed to almost nothing, and her head drooped forward.

Her eyes had begun to sink closed when a wordless, unwavering song roused her. A blue-green luminance swelled forward over her, brightening the shredded banners and tapestries, the battle scenes and portraits on the flaking walls, the fat pillars soaring to a vaulted ceiling painted with crests and gilded foliage. All had been grand and splendid, but grander was arriving, and more splendid still.

His shadow slid across her. High in the hall above, the curve of his vast jaw slowly covered those painted shields, those leaves. His shape followed, widening, afloat on the curdled air, finned or raggedly cloaked at the sides, trailing pennants and threads below. His dim throat, patched with pale growths, swelled downward to almost brush her head. Filaments rayed out from it, curving at the air's resistance. Their tips touched the floor, ran lightly over the objects there. Ran lightly over her, closing her eyes in momentary ecstasy.

The bright, cold light glimmered down on the hunter's daughter through his branched tail. A flight of creatures glided above him, like fish, like birds, like pale rags spread upon the air, some spreading longer than others. The light came from them, and the singing—that high, heartless, pauseless chorus.

She was caught between yearnings. *Oh take me, envelop me, dissolve me!* But also, *Oh, turn! Let me feast my eyes on you in the last moments I can call my own!*

Then he was past. Past forever? Surely not! She leaned after him, mouth open.

He passed out of the hall. His fin-tips curled lazily against the wide doorposts; his filaments stroked the dead, up the mountain of them and down the other side. The hall dimmed, and the hunter's daughter extended her shining limbs from her coverings—

—to find that they did not shine so brightly as before. The weight of the cloths had eased from her shoulders, too, and their inner layers did not cling as they had done, did not chill. The air—stale, dry, deathly as it was—moved more readily into and out of her.

She stood and stared after him, her thoughts returning, sharply. That tail. It was no branched plant, no fin, indeed no *tail*. It was a man's body. Boneless, wavering, it flowed after the bulk of the finned and filamented head—a mere pigtail, an empty glove, a scrap of scarf, long bereft of volition or activity.

This was no wild, mad beast of fancy or forest. It was but a man. A man of great magic and power, maybe, but a man withal. And those singing creature-lights were women, her fellow townswomen, the yearly brides brought here to appease this man-gone-monstrous. His nearness brought that light out of the bride-cloths. The women's shapes—their misshapenness—came from their having dressed in all the layers given them. Her own inner costume had transformed as it should—chilling, adhering, brightening. But the dresses and petticoats, torn apart, had not done as intended. She was not trapped completely, not quite overcome. In destroying them, she had prevented their glowing, prevented the groom seeing them; she had thwarted his magic.

She stood and freed the cord binding her clothing. She cast off the many skirts, and peeled away the underclothes. The last of the air's congestion eased; it did not compress her as before, did not frighten her, weaken her; now it was only cold as a spring night is cold.

It was also quite dark, all light having departed from the sky outside, and the moon not yet being risen. She picked up a stocking, rolled it into a ball, grasped it in a fist. It began to glow with a weak, bluish light.

She took up the halberd and set off naked down the hall, avoiding by the light of the stocking the unhappy obstacles strewn on the flags. She climbed the ghastly mountain in the doorway. She could not believe she had scaled it before without a qualm. The cold bodies gave underfoot with leathery squeaks, with gristly crunches, bony snappings. How lightly he had floated over these souls, how idly he had fingered them! Still she longed to see his face, but not to feast on the sight—now she needed to vent her rage upon it.

She paused in the vestibule. The only sound—distant singing, draft-blown, momentary—came from above. She mounted the stairs—so easily now!—and silently stalked the halls above.

Floor by floor, hall by hall, the insect hum of the brides' chorus led her to the tower doorway. The song flowed down from the high room where the town had abandoned her.

She sprinted up the stairs. The song grew louder—but then exploded, discordant. She shrank against the wall. A deeper voice bellowed among the shards of song, and the tower trembled from blows to its stone fabric. She climbed on, more slowly.

Bride-light played on the landing outside the doorway, on the stairs angling up to it and on those fanning away beyond. The balled-up stocking—sodden again, cold as a winter stream—shone brightly now; her aching fingers looked melted into its light.

The brides' song swelled higher and more anxious. Chattering sounded within its hum. The husband's temper thundered out again—his voice, his blows. The dust of his thrashings floated into the stairwell.

She grasped the halberd in both hands. She clenched her teeth. As soon as the noise ceased, she leaped into the doorway and gave a shout. Every creature in the room spun to face her. The brides' song soared in alarm.

The magicked air buoyed their robes, behind their appalling faces. Their eyes were huge and white, their mouths thick with pointed teeth. From two brides' jaws hung the bridal shoes; from a third's dangled the broken headdress.

Their pulsing light lit the groom, his lichen-crusted face, his vast mottled lips down-slashing around the glassy teeth, his small pale eyes, empty of even such life as a toad's or a boar's would betray. A jewel in his forehead sent an icy beam through the stone dust.

The hunter's girl bent into the beam and rolled the stocking across the floor. Its light quickly dwindled. The brides fell silent; the groom hung still. The dust churned in the shaft of jewel-light.

Quicker than thought she sprang up the stairs. As she sprang she turned; as she turned she tilted the halberd; as she tilted he engulfed her.

His jaw passed under her airborne feet. His top teeth but brushed her bent head, her curled back. As she landed on the cold slither of his tongue, as she slid toward his throat, she thrust upward. He clamped down hard, and together they drove the halberd's point, its thorn and its blade, through the ribbed roof of his mouth, and into whatever form of brain such a man, such a creature, possesses.

The magic broke; the air uncurdled; they fell. Inside her husband's icy mouth, her legs in his gullet, the girl clung to the pole. He slid down the tower stairs, round and round, flailing around her as he died.

At the bottom, she waited inside him, waited out his spasms. Between his slackening lips came the clatter of bridal shoes down the stairs, and the voices of women exclaiming, laughing.

Gingerly she loosened the halberd—the women cried out, clattered back, seeing the beast move. She forced apart his jaws, and they cheered to see her, framed by his teeth. They drew close again and she stepped out into their circle. Their faces were patterned on those she had met all her life in the town. Their bodies, whether youthful or bent with age, were arrayed alike in the richest bride-finery, still softly aglow.

Naked she had fought him, and naked and filthy she brought him in. She laid him on his side and, walking between his parted jaws, pulled him along by the braced pole on which he had impaled himself.

The women came with her, clapping and singing, all the women that the town had sacrificed since he killed the king and took over the castle. They had smoothed their bride-dresses and straightened their headpieces, and combed out their hair, which had grown in great sheaves while they were bespelled. Just as they had flocked around their husband when he lived, so they formed a procession for the girl and her kill, and their songs were town songs, wordy and warm and sweet.

Children and dogs ran out to meet them, then fell back from the ghastly face, from the trailing body's empty glove. All the townspeople followed them to the square. Even there they did not approach, even those who recognized a sister, daughter, aunt among the brides. For the women were made strange by time, and by their freedom and exhilaration—and their savior's nakedness and ferocity were also new sights to shrink from.

The leading townsmen tried to disarm the women with windy congratulations. All would be restored, they said, to the way it had been—only without a king, for had they not managed without a king, untaxed and untroubled, for many a long year now? The brides would be returned to their families, and the families would show them proper gratitude for the sacrifices they had made to keep the beast at bay, and finally to so bravely kill him.

No, said the huntsman's daughter. They would do no such thing. The town had cast these women out and taken from many their best years. For recompense they would have the castle, and all the treasures therein. They would live there and rule themselves—they would not submit to husbands, to fathers, to brothers. Any woman who needed refuge from a man that beat her, or who preferred to live unmarried, was welcome to join them on the heights. She stood be-slimed with sweat and blood, as proud as any naked wrestler at the yearly fair, and she shamed the town's leaders, and she told them how things would stand. She delivered the brides their final freedom, and no one looking at such a face, at such a body in the jaws of such a beast, could deny her any thing that she demanded.

SWEET POTATO

by Joe R. Lansdale

A soul may find its way back from the corners of darkness
by becoming part of a common thing.
—From *Everyday Items of Darkness*

There's only so much a lonely man can do, so much TV that can be watched, books that can be read, so many moments of masturbation, before buying a rototiller and gardening seems a realistic consideration.

Though he had a good retirement plan, Tyler hadn't expected his job to end so abruptly, the boss having gone to prison for ass-fondling and grubbing money from the public trust. But there it was. She went and the business went, and now here he was, out in the wilds of unemployment, living off his considerable savings (thank goodness), and submerged way down deep in the cold-ass nothing.

Dreaming for a while was so fine. No alarm clock, living in pajamas. What he liked best, at first, was that things that seemed silly in real life seemed fine in the dream world. He could be an old-fashioned hero in his dreams. Much younger, washboard abs, a baseball-bat dick, and balls like grapefruits. Carrying a sword, brave and relentless, six foot five and forever young. And then, one night, down in a dream, there was a soundless shift.

He was cruising along beneath the quicksilver light of triple moons, in an open self-operating flying craft with a drink in his hand, an olive in his martini. He had fought for and rescued the fair maiden, but somewhere in his dream, Morpheus had dropped her off, as if after a date, and he was alone. He stood in his open craft as the wind lifted his hair and he sipped his chilled drink and chewed his olive, felt as happy as a twelve-year-old with the summer off from school and plans for a trip to the carnival.

A long-shadowed moon licked at the split in the alley of trees that was his path. Leaves the size of his palms blew about, brown and gold and crackling in the air. Then at the far end of the wooded and shadowed corridor, a door in the world cracked open, and a shadow oozed out. And brave and resourceful a hero as he was, he felt a rubbery shift in his spine, a melting of re-solve.

The sensation was so upsetting, Tyler couldn't hold the old dream, and awoke in his bed. He felt certain whatever came out of the doorway came back with him, blending with the shadows in the room. He could feel it, cold and damp like a water-swollen sponge, lurking. The central air hummed. The moonlight through the curtain was cloudy like infected urine. Though out-side was dry, there was a sensation of a recent rainstorm having passed in the night, leaving behind electric sizzles and reverberations from thunderous roars.

Tyler sat up, turned on the lamp beside his bed.

Nothing.

It had all been a dream, perhaps a dream within a dream. Or had the shadow found a mousehole?

He decided right then, he had to find something to do that would give life to his life, not just life to his dreams, for even his dreams were growing stale, and perhaps even precarious. Or at least he had begun to feel that way. De-cided it was a mental health consideration.

After that night, he no longer remembered his dreams. He slept with the light on. But he still had the sensation of a crawling thing lurking in the dark recesses of the walls, the flooring, the ceiling, ticking at his bones, trying to get inside of him.

A week later, while walking through a farm and ranch store, he bought some jeans, a chambray shirt, and decided on a rototiller and a gardening book. He decided he would break the ground in the spring after loading it with compost over the summer, fall, and winter. When the time came, he would plant sweet potatoes.

He was uncertain why he had chosen sweet potatoes, other than as a child he and his mother had liked them baked and split and coated in butter and cinnamon. But sweet potatoes were his choice.

He broke the ground behind his house with the rototiller, churned the grass under and heaved up the dark, dank earth and exposed it to the sun and wind and any rain that might come its way.

It felt good to be doing something physical. The tiller rocking his body like a gyrating lover. Muscles aching pleasantly, sweat glistening on his forehead like sugary doughnut glaze.

His next-door neighbor, an old woman, Carrie Baker, who looked to have one foot in the grave and the other on an oil slick, shrouded in a white cotton housedress, hair white as well, observed him from her backyard with squinted eyes while filling her bird feeder with seeds that rattled against it like gravel under truck tires.

Over the years he had never seen her other than alone, dressed in that housecoat. She would fill the bird feeder, then retire to a chair on her back porch, hidden behind flower trellises which were without flowers or vines. She would sit there with a BB gun, in a kind of duck blind, waiting for hungry birds to arrive at what they assumed was a free buffet, only to be shot for her entertainment.

The air rifle would huff, a bird would fall, and old Ms. Baker would hoot with satisfaction. She was a good shot. Killing birds was like her morning coffee.

She bagged three or four a day, except on Sunday, a time of rest and abandonment of her white cotton nightdress. She garbed herself in ancient clothes, dark skirt, blouse and shoes, a block hat made of cloth and straw that was bedecked with a yellow band with an enormous bow. She would walk off late morning with a massive Bible tucked under her arm, on down to the church at the end of the street. A few hours later she marched back again. She never lifted a hand or spoke in greeting. She merely eyed him like she was taking aim at one of the birds on her feeder, perhaps hearing in her head the puff of her air rifle.

As for the dead birds, she would gather them up, and with a trowel, dig little holes. Their bright-winged corpses ended up beneath mounds of dirt in her side yard, like clay goose bumps on the ground.

No one came to visit her. The post lady dropped the mail in the box and ran away for fear of an encounter. Tyler found this understandable. Birds, however, were slow learners. The survivors failed to spread the word.

At night, Tyler felt as if the escaped shadow from his dream was stirring about the house, searching for something. When he burst awake and turned on the light, there was nothing there.

He would then turn off the light and once again he would feel an uncomfortable feeling. He flicked it back on.

That was better. He would leave it on.

Next day he bought powerful light bulbs and used them to replace the old. At night, the inside of his home was lit up like an airport runway.

All through the winter he laid out a pile of hay and sawdust and horse manure he procured from a stable, table scraps, and even added a dead cat and a dead possum to his mound. It was his view, from what he read, that even the little corpses would break down sufficiently, heated in his compost bundle to such a degree there would be nothing left but nutrients for the soil.

In the spring, Tyler heaped his winter compost over his quarter-acre garden (he thought of it as his mini-farm). The soil was black from the compost.

No animal bones, cat or possum fur. No discernible food scraps, no offensive horse manure smell.

He bought sweet potatoes and cut them in half and placed them in large containers of water until green slips sprouted from them. He removed, rooted, planted the slips, and pulled compost around them. He built a standing frame around his quarter-acre enterprise, covered the sides with cheesecloth, roofed it with the same. He made a door with simple hinges and more cheesecloth, so that he could enter into his bird-protected mini-farm and tend his sweet potato flock, as he liked to think of it.

Ten long rows were sunned through the cheesecloth, watered by the rain and a water hose when days were dry. He saw the slips grow firm and green. He knew that beneath the ground the sweet potatoes were swelling and filling with nutritional goodness. They would become so big and ripe they would beg to be split open and stuffed with butter and cinnamon.

He bought a book on sweet potato recipes. He bought a metal gardening shed and filled it with his tiller and gardening tools he most likely didn't need.

One summer morning, already hot, white clouds flowing across the sky like soapsuds, Tyler went outside with a lawn chair. He entered his miniature farm, placed the chair at the end of a row, and sat and gloated over his greenery. He would have plenty to eat and plenty to sell to the farmer's market. He had visions of buying land, expanding his farm and becoming a professional sweet potato farmer. He might add corn and tomatoes. But he was worried about one section of his plot that seemed to have rejected the compost. The potato slips there sagged like an old man's dick. They were beginning to turn yellow. He had applied the same amount of compost all over, but that section refused to respond. The books suggested a lack of nitrogen.

He was thinking about all of this when he noticed what looked like a deflated human-sized doll lying in Carrie Baker's yard. He viewed it for some time before leaving his chair, walking over to the line of grass between his yard and hers.

As he grew closer, Tyler saw that the deflated doll was, in fact, a decimated human lying facedown in the yard. He recognized the housedress and the shock of gray hair. It was Carrie Baker, and she wasn't imitating a snake. She was dead. A bag of birdseed lay spilled beside her. She had a spade in her hand. A hole was dug and a dead bird lay beside it.

Tyler peered down at her for a long time. Her housedress was damp and she had begun to flatten and smell. Insects crawled in her hair. She must have been lying there for quite a few days. The bird was wormy and bug-chewed too.

Why hadn't he noticed?

The self-asked question was answered immediately by his subconscious, yelling over miles of synapses. Because he didn't like her and didn't care.

Didn't want to see her kill birds and snarl across her yard at him. He hadn't seen what he didn't want to see. Or perhaps he wasn't that observant, caught up in his own concerns and newfound hobby.

It was likely she had been seized by a heart attack, perhaps even as he tended his potatoes. He could imagine her clutching at the air, reaching in his direction for help, trying to speak, but finding her mouth stuffed with vomit and phlegm, her head with goodbye memories, likely all of them mean and stale and wearing a housedress.

As he was about to return home and call the police, he was struck with a thought. Who was she, really?

It wasn't as if she was in need of immediate attention, and if he hadn't found her, she would merely have faded into the grass, her cotton dress rotting around her like melting snow.

He went to his garden shed, grabbed his thick, new gardening gloves, and used them to open her unlocked back door. He was already thinking like a criminal. Leave no prints. All he really wanted to do was see inside her house, see what she was about when she was away from her bird-hunting blind, though sometimes he did see her on her riding mower, rolling over her yard like Patton rolling through Italy. Perhaps she dreamed of the mower chopping gopher heads.

Tyler slipped inside.

It was humid inside and dark. The air felt empty of life. Where there was light streaming through the windows dust motes swirled like alien parasites.

Unlike most grandma houses, there were no knickknacks or grandkid photos on shelves, or silly slogans framed and placed on the wall. The house wasn't piled up or nasty, but it felt that way. There was very little furniture, and when he opened the kitchen cabinets, he found a plate, a bowl, a glass, a cup, and one saucer. In the utensil drawer there was only a knife, a fork, a spoon, and a spatula. There was a frying pan and a little pot on the stove.

The refrigerator was empty except for a jug of water with greasy lip stains on its mouth. Another cabinet was full of instant oatmeal, a bag of sugar, a box of salt, a shaker of pepper, many economy-sized cans of pinto beans, enough to produce abundant intestinal gas that could fart her north of the moon.

In the bedroom there was only a bed, a dresser, and in the closet, on a hanger, were her church clothes. On a shelf, her hat with the bow. He wasn't sure why he did it, but he picked the hat up and held it while he punched a hole in the crown. He replaced it on the shelf.

He opened the dresser drawers. They were stuffed with photo albums.

Inside there were no family shots. Just newspaper clippings of hospital deaths, all sudden, all men. In that same album was her nursing license, one photo of her in a white nurse's dress, wearing one of those hats they used to wear. What wowed him was that he could tell it was her, but she was young and pretty. No. Beautiful. The kind of woman you dreamed of, twisted up in the sheets with her legs locked around your ass. Yet those eyes, then and before her death, were still the same. Not so nice, near insane. Cat eyes in the moonlight.

There were marriage certificates arranged next to death certificates. Her name was on the marriage certificates. Four husbands were on the death certificates. All had died of a heart attack, and in their prime. Insurance documents were also there. The poor widow had received quite a windfall. A lot of people seemed to have signed their savings over to her.

"Shit," Tyler said aloud.

Good lord. He could envision her sitting on her bed with her scrapbooks and photo albums all around, her hand on her crotch, rubbing while reading of medical deaths and insurance payouts that she had somehow manipulated.

A black widow, an angel of doom, had lived next door to him, finishing out her golden years eating beans and shooting birds.

Tyler dug the hole. Made it deep and fairly wide, poured in some lime, not just for her, but to even out the soil. He had tested it there, and it was far too benign. It needed some acid and a corpse for the worms to grind.

Down in the hole he stacked compost on the lime, then he laid in Ms. Baker. Another coat of compost, a bit more lime, then he stood back and looked down at his work. It seemed fine. Come next spring he would put in a few more sweet potatoes. Let them grow up from her bone dust, withering skin, and his rich compost.

That night, when he lay down, all the lights on as was his custom, he thought of the old woman down in the ground. She had been awful, of that he was certain, so it was only fair that she should contribute to the rebirth of soil and vegetables. A good deed in place of all the people and birds she had killed. Surely, that wasn't so bad.

Tyler waited to feel guilty. He waited to feel sad, or disappointed in himself. But he hadn't killed her. He had merely composted her.

But once she was beautiful. Had she always been conniving and mean? He had sexual dreams about her youthful self, and then at some point he popped awake, having felt as if he had been having sex with a barbwire doll with a shadow-black heart.

Visiting a friend from work, who was also out of a job with time for the coffee shop, Tyler said, after their conversation began to falter, "Have you ever had a dream that seemed real?"

The friend, gray and heavy with lips like two red earthworms, rocked back in the booth and sipped his coffee before answering.

"Of course. Though mostly they don't make sense when I wake up. But now and again, they feel real, could be real. Some of the most outlandish dreams seem real at the time."

"Just for curiosity's sake. Have you ever felt something in a dream come back with you, being there when you woke up?"

"No. Though I've heard of it. Some people believe your soul lets go sometimes and comes right out of you when you breathe awake. One moment you're breathing asleep, the next, you're breathing awake."

"Your soul?"

"If you believe in that sort of thing. Maybe a piece of your soul. Or something worse. A demon. A succubus, which is a kind of sex demon that rides in and out on your essence while you dream, fucks the shit out of you and takes your energy, borrows your soul, and finally keeps it. They can be created by your subconscious, or they can be night riders."

"What's that?"

"Loose souls looking for a place to light. A place to suck the energy out of. Men can be incubuses, you know."

"I don't know."

"Male sex demons. The succubus in reverse. I think succubuses and incubuses can switch-hit when it comes to sexual matters. You might even have to put Scotch tape over your dog's asshole if one of them is around."

"I don't have a dog."

"That's one less worry, then."

"How do you know all of this?"

"I read a lot. I found golf too tiring."

"Well, I could use a sex demon actually," Tyler said.

"I wouldn't mind one either. But it might be like that old saying about how you have to be careful what you wish for."

While Tyler slept, the lights stayed on through summer, fall, and winter. Come spring, he felt strong, and one night he turned all the lights out. The darkness seemed immediately stuffed with something he couldn't define.

It was as if the universe were expanding inside his room. He felt stifled. But he didn't turn the light on. He was stronger than that, he decided. Stronger than being foolish about shadows and lights. Still, the sensation of the room pressing against him was so overwhelming, that without really thinking about it, he opened a window as if to let it out.

In that moment he glimpsed a wave of darkness roll out of the sweet potato patch, out of the area where the old lady lay rotting beneath dirt and plants, beneath the cheesecloth. He had an impression of something rushing past him, like a great shadowy bird taking flight. Something colliding with the fullness in the room.

Next moment he was in bed without remembering lying down. The shadow shaped itself and mounted him, and he could feel it moving against him, and it felt good, and soon it felt better. It was draining him not only of night emissions, but something that wiggled desperately in the back of his mind, then slithered away.

"What the hell?" he said, sitting up in bed in the early morning, his pajamas around his knees, a wet spot on the sheets.

As far as Tyler knew, not one soul had asked about Ms. Baker. No one from the church. No one from anywhere. He assumed seeking her out might be like seeking out a virulent strain of flu. The mail lady ceased to bring mail to the old lady's mailbox. Birds ate from the bag of spilled seed all winter, then ceased to come when spring bloomed. They were singing in trees somewhere safer, or so Tyler liked to presume.

In the garden the slips grew fast and spread their vines, twisted over the earth and climbed the cheesecloth and the board frame and made everything within emerald green. Tyler had never seen such vines, thick and pumping as if with arterial blood, puffing up little spurts of dust between the vines, as if down below the potatoes were desperately breathing, like a reformed cigarette smoker coughing out nicotine tar.

He couldn't bring himself to dig there, in the place where he had seen the dark shadow. He took smaller potatoes from underneath other vines. He baked them and split them and buttered them and dusted them with cinnamon. They were delicious.

At the beginning of each day, getting out of bed became difficult and strong cups of coffee might as well have been water. He hesitated to go to bed at night, but welcomed it as well. He would open the window and let the air and the night and the winged shadow in.

The dreams had become good, and he could imagine the younger Ms. Baker mounting him like a show pony, running him through his tricks, urging his best performance. In those moments, he felt simultaneously close to death and ecstasy.

When it came time to harvest the sweet potato section where he had buried Ms. Baker, he discovered that the earth had swollen high and rounded like an enormous burn blister filled with dark pus. Raking back the soil, he saw the orange skin of a single, massive sweet potato. One vine that grew out of it was thick and green, like an arm tipped with pea-green fingers.

Leave it alone, he told himself, or dig it up and chop it up, burn the remains. Sow the ground with salt so that nothing will grow there.

But there was something so appealing about it. As he scraped dirt away, he saw the potato was in the shape of a human. His thoughts went in a different direction. What if he dug her up and brought her in the house, placed her next to the bed?

Tyler had no idea where such feelings came from, and he walked away, ducked in the house, and killed time watching television. He didn't remember a thing he watched. When night fell, he took the shovel from the shed, went to the sweet potato bed, and began to dig the human-shaped sweet potato completely free.

When he broke it out of the ground, there in the moonlight, he could see green and gold vines had clustered where the top of the head would be, and there was the same where the legs parted, growing there like matted pubic hair.

Tyler hacked loose the umbilical cord vines with the tip of the shovel, then dragged the surprisingly heavy sweet potato out of its lumber and cheesecloth home. Pulled it through his back door, trailing a swath of dirt across the floor.

He dropped it on his bedroom floor. He sat in a chair and looked at it. He was sick of eating sweet potatoes. He was sick of gardening, but this amazing product of the soil and of flesh intrigued him. Even hacked up, it would take a few days for him to eat it. He wanted to consume it in the way disciples of Jesus wanted to taste his blood and flesh via wine and wafer.

Rising from the chair, he walked to it and touched it, and ran his fingers over it. Its skin was soft and thin, even warm to the touch. It looked less orange in the light, more golden. The appearance of legs and arms, head and body, was more pronounced. He tugged it into the bathroom, filled the tub with warm water, hustled the potato up and into the bath. He stripped off his clothes, climbed into the tub, and rubbed the potato gently with a rag. The skin trembled under his touch. Dirt darkened the water.

When he felt he had cleaned it as best as possible, he pulled it out, dried it and himself off with a fluffy towel. Still naked, he lugged it into his bed and nuzzled up beside it, feeling its warmth and soft skin. He put his arm around it.

For the first time he felt he wanted the lights out, wanted to be in the dark with his companion. He rose, turned off the light, and crawled back into bed and pulled the covers over them. The moonlight through the window was like a highway to heaven and the softness of the potato was like a woman, and now the vines that sprayed from the head of the potato were softer than before, and sweet smelling, and all the darkness around them was soft like silk.

Fingers touched him. Lips kissed him. Skin warmed him. And finally, he was making love to a woman, not a sweet potato, but a woman. The younger version of his next-door neighbor.

He could hear her breathing and grunting, and himself doing the same, and they tumbled and rolled and loved together.

When they were done, he lay with his arm around her. He felt her move and throw back the sheets, and then she crawled out of bed with her hands touching the floor first, pulling the rest of her away from him. He could hear her crawling, slinking along the floor. It was then quiet for a time and then she rose up at the foot of his bed. The moonlight had shifted, but he could see her clearly. She was indeed the woman next door, in youth. Her features were cut with shadow. Her eyes were flat and black and looked like tiny holes in the ground. Her skin was the color of a golden sweet potato.

She began to sway, then she began to dance as if the room were full of music. Swirling and writhing at the foot of the bed like a snake finding position to strike. Her legs lifted. Her arms fanned. Her head cranked left, then right, then back and forward. It was sexy at first, and then he had an empty feeling. The sudden realization that the source of him was moving away.

Everything was dark. Tyler collapsed into deep but jagged sleep. As he tumbled, down, down, a silhouette of a giant sweet potato passed him, touched him lightly, damp and cold, and then the bottom of his dream fell out and he shot shamelessly into a cosmic abyss containing stars and moons and planets. Then there was nothing but the dark and the smell of butter cinnamon.

And then there was nothing at all.

In the morning the young woman moved naked in the light. Her skin was smooth and pale. Her hair was thick and hung to her shoulders and was the color of a lion's mane. There was the lip-smacking aroma of baked sweet potato in the air.

On the counter, next to a cleaver, lay hacked sweet potato parts. They were shaped like amputated arms and legs and there was a head with green knobs where eyes should be; sprigs of vines flowed from the head like tangled hair. Two knobby hunks of potato were beside it.

The kitchen was toasty. The woman turned off the oven. She put on an oven mitt. She pulled out the baking pan containing the large wedge of potato-orange thorax and placed it on the counter. She used a knife to split it and butter it. She shook sugar and cinnamon into the split. Now the air really smelled sweet.

She put the baked sweet potato portion on a plate and then on the table next to a knife and fork. She licked her lips and sat down to eat.

After a while, satiated, she walked naked with a swollen stomach. Went out the back way and crossed to the house next door. She removed a simple housedress from the closet, white with blue flowers on it. She slipped it on.

Barefoot, she found the BB gun. She loaded BBs into it. She carried it out on the back porch and placed it on the glider.

Back inside, she removed a bag of birdseed from under the kitchen sink and hauled it out to the feeder in the backyard.

She filled the feeder, and dropped the bag on the ground. On the porch, sitting in the glider, the BB gun lying across her lap, she waited for the birds.

KNOCK, KNOCK

by Brian Evenson

I. The First Death

The first time it happened, Hakon thought he had been mistaken, that he hadn't managed to kill his uncle after all, that even though it had seemed like the man was dead he wasn't. True, Hakon had checked his uncle's pulse right after he stopped moving. True, he'd rolled the body into the muddy water, where it had floated facedown for at least a minute before Hakon fled. But maybe it was that very action, the shock of the cold water, which had brought his uncle sputtering back to life. Hadn't that happened before: someone seemingly dead who, as it turned out, wasn't? It was, so he told himself, just possible his uncle had, somehow, survived.

That first time, after rolling the body into the water, Hakon had been horrified by what he had done. He hadn't meant to kill his uncle. He had only meant to scare him away. But his uncle, he should have known, was not the sort of person to respond well to threats. In a manner of speaking it had been self-defense, Hakon told himself as, breathless, he hurried away from the pond and back through the woods. True, his uncle hadn't been armed, but when he'd seen the gun he hadn't acted sensibly. Instead of putting his hands up, he'd crept closer and closer to Hakon until he was close enough to knock the gun out of Hakon's hand. And then he struck Hakon in the face and fell on top of him and began to strangle him.

Something like that anyway. It was a little unclear now to Hakon what had happened after. How had it come to be that his uncle was on the ground and Hakon was on top of him, a fist-sized rock in his hand that he had groped off the ground? He was striking his uncle's head with it. When he stopped, the rock and his fingers were bloody. Hakon looked at his hand, looked at the rock. It was perfectly round, polished, two holes and a slit on it seeming to form a crude, swollen face.

. . .

Afterward, Hakon had checked his uncle's pulse, dragged his body into the water, and fled. He was already far from the pond before he began to slow down. His breathing was still ragged, and he was moaning a little. He needed to calm down.

He placed his hands on his knees and bent over. He made an effort to slow his breathing. The saliva in his mouth felt too thick, congealed. He stared down at the path that he and his uncle had crushed through the grass on their way to the pond. *Have I forgotten anything?* he wondered. Hakon straightened, patted his pockets. Of course he had: the gun.

He grew cold. For a moment the earth jolted a little and Hakon felt himself beginning to pass out, but he caught himself. He'd have to go back.

By the time he reached the pond, even though only a few minutes had passed, the body was gone—sunk into the muddy water, Hakon assumed at the time. He would have to wade out for it later, find it, drag it out, and dump it somewhere less incriminating than the woods behind his house. The house that up until now he had lived in against his will with his uncle. The house his uncle refused to surrender his hold on.

Hakon searched for the gun. Where had they been when his uncle had slapped it away? Over there? Or here? He moved in slow circles, parting the underbrush with his hands and looking for the glint of metal below.

It was his father's fault really, Hakon told himself as he looked. His father was happiest, for some incomprehensible and no doubt reprehensible reason, when those closest to him were at odds, pitted against one another. It made him feel important. After his wife, Hakon's mother, had committed suicide, the only people remaining for his father to persecute were Hakon and his uncle. But this had been enough to keep Hakon's father entertained. He had told Hakon one thing about who would inherit the isolated house and its surrounding forest (Hakon) and had told Hakon's uncle another (Hakon's uncle), ensuring that they would remain in conflict well after his death.

Hakon hadn't found the gun. Did it matter? It was humid here, rained a lot. How likely was it the gun would ever be found? And even if it were found, who cared? The gun hadn't been used to kill his uncle. It was just a gun.

Hakon kept looking anyway.

There was the stone again, its face staring upward. It was still spattered with his uncle's blood. It felt like the stone was staring at him, the eyes so small and piggy that Hakon could not be sure how much it actually saw. Still, he rotated it with his fingers until the face was pressed to the ground. Then, on a whim, he picked it up, hefted it, and tossed it into the pond. With a plop it disappeared.

Immediately he regretted it. It was evidence—he'd have to find that in the pond as well and dispose of it elsewhere.

Perhaps the gun, too, had ended up in the water. Perhaps it was in there somewhere, sunken into the mud and silt just as his uncle's body was. If so, he would leave it for now. He wasn't up to wading in barefoot so soon after the murder, feeling for it and the stone with his toes in the silt, with each step braced to tread on his uncle's corpse. No, he would come back later, tomorrow perhaps, once he felt more himself. For now, he would go home.

Hakon shucked off the muddy boots outside, sprayed the soles clean with the hose. He left the boots on the porch to dry. Before the door was even shut, he was already stripping off his clothing. He balled everything up, dumped it into the washing machine, turned it on. Naked, he made his way from the utility room across the kitchen and up the stairs to the shower.

A reason, Hakon thought as he stood in the shower stall, the steam rising up around him. The heat of the water made him groan. He would have to come up with a reason for his uncle's absence, something he could tell people when they asked where his uncle had gone. *A trip*, he could say, though that would simply postpone suspicion rather than dispel it. Eventually Hakon would have to come up with a reason for why his uncle hadn't returned from his putative trip. *We had a fight and he left*, he tried, but knew that when after a few weeks nobody heard from his uncle suspicion would fall on him. Maybe just *He left. I don't know why*. They had never been close, people knew that: it was certainly conceivable his uncle would finally get fed up and leave.

He toweled off. In his mind he kept sticking on that moment of blankness. He could clearly see his uncle looming above him, choking him, and he could clearly see the situation reversed and him battering his uncle's head with the stone, but how he had gotten from one situation to the other was still unfathomable. It was as if there was a gap, a time when he wasn't in his body.

Something shook him from his reverie. From downstairs came a low thudding sound. It lasted a few seconds, then stopped. This confused him. He held his breath, waited, listened. When the sound came again, Hakon realized it must be someone clumsily knocking at his door.

Quickly and silently he got dressed, slipping on a clean T-shirt, a pair of shorts. Maybe they'd go away, he thought. But the knocking kept recurring at regular intervals, every thirty seconds or so. He started down the stairs. *My uncle just left, I don't know why,* he practiced. At the bottom of the stairs he stopped long enough to examine his face in the mirror. He changed how he was holding his mouth to look less guilty, and then he opened the door.

But as soon as Hakon saw who it was, he forgot all about controlling his expression.

"Hello, Hakon," his uncle said. The man's clothes were soaked and streaked with mud. "May I come in?"

II. The Second Death

Normally his uncle would never have asked for permission to come in. To do so would be to tacitly acknowledge he didn't have a right to the house. His uncle claimed the house was his rather than Hakon's—his brother had promised it to him!—which was why a month ago, shortly after Hakon's father's death, the uncle had forced his way in, taken over Hakon's father's room, and refused to leave.

"Your father wanted me here," he told Hakon. "He told me so himself. Many times."

Hakon doubted this. His father didn't want either of them to have the house. The only thing his father had wanted was struggle and conflict, and his father had arranged, even though he was dead, to get it. He was probably laughing in his grave.

"Don't worry," Hakon's uncle had said. "I'll let you live here. At least until you find a new place."

What followed was a month of agony. Hakon felt more and more miserable until finally, at wit's end, he took his uncle out into the woods on the pretense of showing him around the property, threatened him with a gun, and killed him with a rock.

An uncle standing dripping on the porch asking politely to come in seemed not at all like Hakon's actual uncle. It felt wrong. He wondered if this was some sort of trap. If his uncle was up to something.

"Well?" the man said, tone acerbic this time. "You going to invite me the fuck in or not?"

This was more like his uncle. Stunned, before he could stop himself, Hakon did.

His uncle immediately went to the kitchen and began opening cabinets. He'd open one then close it, open another and close that, then return to the first as if he'd forgotten he'd already opened it. Hakon just watched.

When it began to feel like this could go on endlessly, he asked his uncle what he was looking for.

"Tea," said his uncle. "Where's some goddamn tea?"

"We don't have any."

His uncle offered a look of disgust. "Sure we do. What about that dark brown stuff?"

"Dark brown?"

"You know," said his uncle. "That one tea that comes from beans."

Hakon just stared at him. "Do you mean coffee?" he finally said.

"That's the one," said his uncle.

Hakon got out the mugs and the pre-ground coffee and the filters and the teapot to boil the water. Leaving his uncle to make coffee, he retreated to the living room.

Something was wrong with his uncle. Something must have come loose in his head when he had nearly died. He wasn't himself. It seemed, too, he had no memory of Hakon trying to kill him. Either that or the man was faking amnesia, waiting to take his revenge. Well, Hakon could pretend too.

Still, Hakon wished he still had the gun. He went to the fireplace and lit the kindling there, added a log to it. He opened the nearest window to provide a good draw. As an afterthought, after stirring the fire he leaned the poker against the wall beside his easy chair, within easy reach.

The teapot whistled. A moment later his uncle came out of the kitchen, holding the steaming mugs. He extended one to Hakon, who took it.

It was almost too hot to hold. It didn't smell like coffee at all. He looked into it, saw only hot water with a heap of loose grounds floating in it.

Across from him, his uncle raised the mug to his lips and drank the whole thing quickly down, chewing the grounds as they slid into his mouth. Steam drifted out as he chewed.

"Damned fine tea if I do say so myself," his uncle said.

Hakon just stared. This was a dream. It had to be. He raised the cup to his lips, but the water was so hot that the slightest sip scalded the inside of his mouth.

No, he thought, tongue throbbing, *no dream*.

For an hour Hakon and his uncle sat there staring at one another, not speaking. Occasionally the man made a little mewling sound that was more like an animal than a person. Hakon ignored this. He just sat there as the light drained out of the room, waiting the other man out.

"Getting dark now," his uncle said at last.

Hakon nodded.

"I'm going to sleep here," his uncle said. "Which bed should I take?"

What was his game? "The usual," said Hakon.

His uncle gave a barking laugh, if it was a laugh, then abruptly stopped.

The man stood and wandered around the ground floor, opening all the doors and peering into the rooms beyond. He even peered into the closets. Finally he came back into the living room and shrugged.

"No beds," he said.

"What's wrong with you?" asked Hakon.

"What do you mean?"

But Hakon just shook his head.

His uncle stood there, eyes darting around. At last, they landed on the stairs. He made his way to them. He reached out very carefully, as if palpating the first tread with the tip of his toe, then finally let his foot settle, slowly bringing his weight onto it. He continued up the stairs that way, slowly, tread by tread, by feel, as if he had never walked up a flight of stairs before.

Eventually, though, he reached the top and disappeared from view.

Hakon got up from his own chair long enough to fetch a bottle of vodka and a shot glass. He settled back in, rocking slowly back and forth, staring at the empty chair his uncle had been in and, before that, his father.

He poured a shot, drank. Had another. Outside, the darkness settled in completely. Hakon waited, wondering when the right moment would be, or even if there was a right moment. *You killed the bastard once,* he told himself. *Now all you have to do is kill him again.*

When it was very late indeed and Hakon had finished nearly half the bottle, he armed himself with the fireplace poker and climbed the stairs. He would have more to clean up this time. The first time he had used his hands, now he was using something that allowed him to kill at a slight distance. *If I have to do it a third time,* he told himself absurdly, *it should be more distant still:* a gun maybe. But the gun was lost. *If there is a fourth time,* he thought as he reached the top of the stairs, then stopped himself: there wouldn't be a fourth time. Or a third. Only a second. Which was really the first, he tried to tell himself, since his uncle must not have been dead that first time.

Moving as silently as he could, Hakon made his way to his father's room. The door was closed. Slowly he twisted the knob, opened the door, and entered.

The room was very dark. He couldn't see a thing. He adjusted his grip on the poker until it felt balanced. He crept forward until he was just beside the bed and then stopped, held his breath, listening for the sound of his uncle's breathing.

Nothing.

Haken waited, listened, slowly releasing his own breath and drawing air in again. He reached out, moving his free hand in a slow rhythmic circle over the bed, slowly bringing it lower. But he felt nothing, no lump of his uncle's body, only air. Maybe the bed was set lower than he remembered. He kept doing that, drawing wandering circles in the air and slowly lowering his hand, until the hand brushed against the coverlet. No matter where he touched, it was flat, smooth. The bed hadn't been slept in.

Hakon left the room, shaking his head, and made his way toward his own room. Before he reached it, he noticed a thin red glint coming from under the door.

For a long time he hesitated. He was confused, didn't understand what his uncle was up to. But in the end, not knowing what else to do, he opened his bedroom door.

Inside was his uncle. Something was wrong with him. Physically this time. His body had become red and swollen, as large as an ox. He looked like he was full of too much blood and was about to burst. The bed creaked beneath his colossal weight. Worse, the glow Hakon had seen beneath the door was coming off his uncle's skin, like a kind of sweat, but made of light.

Carefully, Hakon approached, moving into the red glow. His uncle seemed to be asleep. His features were so swollen that the eyes were little more than piggy slits. It seemed impossible his uncle could see through them. It reminded Hakon of the stone he had killed his uncle with the first time.

The bed creaked as the chest rose and fell, but what was missing was the sound of breathing. Even when he held his own breath, Hakon couldn't hear his uncle's breathing at all. Had he heard it earlier? He tried to think back, to when his uncle had just come in the front door, but couldn't recall. But why would he have been listening to hear if his uncle was breathing? That would have seemed crazy then. Now, though, he wasn't so sure. Nor was he, come to that, convinced that this was actually his uncle.

His uncle—if it was his uncle—stirred and shifted a little to the side. The bedframe popped and threatened to give way. Hakon brought up the poker and swung it down as hard as he could at the swollen head. It made a soft, wet sound, like hitting a sodden sponge, and stuck. When he pulled it out, a rivulet of blood followed, and spread down the side of the bed. His uncle—if it was his uncle—gave a moan and covered his face with his hands, but that was all. Hakon brought the poker down again, breaking some of his fingers, unloosing more trickling blood, then a third time, then a fourth.

The creature tried to sit up and Hakon beat it back down again. It seemed partly deflated now, no longer so swollen, verging on flaccid, the skin that remained flabby and jiggling. He struck it again, then again—or would have if the thing that he no longer thought of as his uncle hadn't darted its hand out and grabbed hold of the poker.

It hissed at him, like air from a slit tire. Hakon yanked on the poker, but the creature wouldn't let go. It managed to get one foot onto the floor and was now trying to stand, to rise to its feet.

It wrenched the poker away and cast it clattering to the other side of the room. For a moment they stared at one another.

"What *are* you?" Hakon couldn't help but ask, astonished.

It smiled with its bloody broken mouth. "Why, I'm your uncle," it said. "What else could I possibly be?"

And then Hakon dived for the door.

He managed to get through and slam the door closed, heard a wet thump as the creature struck it. Blood, or something not unlike blood, oozed out under the door. Hakon held the doorknob tight with his hand, felt when the creature tried to turn it, but its hand, what passed for a hand, must have been too flaccid and too slippery with blood to get a good grip. Hakon managed to hold it closed.

It tried again, then gave up, began thumping against the door with its body again.

Hakon let go of the knob and as quietly as possible crept down the stairs. He would leave, he told himself, abandon the house to the creature that had taken the place of his uncle. Above him, the wood of the door creaked, threatened to give. *But will that be enough to placate it?* he wondered. He had, after all, just tried to kill it, and had maybe killed it earlier as well, unless that first time hadn't counted because that had been his actual uncle.

He was still a few steps from the bottom when the door above exploded. Hakon fell the rest of the way down. Above, the creature was starting to swell up again, to bloat, but was still seeping where he had struck it, though less so now. It placed what served as a hand, though it could hardly properly be called a hand now, against the wood-paneled wall at the top of the stairs. It left a bloody mark that did not resemble a handprint at all. It was more like a hoofprint.

Now it'll kill me, thought Hakon. *It will rush down the stairs and slaughter me. Now it's my turn to die.*

The creature did indeed place a foot on the first tread, but only slowly did it bring the second foot down to meet it. It was just as slow going down the stairs as it had been going up.

Hakon scrambled to his feet. He rushed to the door and out through it, but slowed, stopped before his feet left the porch.

No, it would come after him, he could feel it. And it would be faster once it was down the stairs. He had to take care of it now. Here. He had to go back and kill it once and for all.

Or, at the very least, for a second time.

He burst back through the front door. The creature was almost down the stairs now, still moving in that trancelike tentative manner, feeling each tread into being. It was so swollen now that it rubbed the walls on either side.

"This one won't last," it said in a wheezing voice, when it noticed him. "I need a new one." It looked at him. "I need you, Hakon."

It came down another step. Hakon cast his gaze desperately around the room.

"You killed this one, then hurt it badly enough that I had to bloat before I was ripe." It felt for the last step with its bulbous, splitting toe. "That's on you, Hakon. You owe me yours."

"How can you still be alive?" asked Hakon.

It gave a stuttering wheeze which Hakon guessed was supposed to be a laugh. "Who said I was alive?" it asked.

Hakon backed toward the fire. There was his easy chair beside it, there was his tumbler, the bottle of vodka. There was the fire, nearly out, but its coals still hot and glowing.

"Hakon," said the creature, and gave a wheeze. "Don't make this more difficult than it has to be." It stepped off the last step and onto the floor. "I don't want to break you. I need you."

Hakon picked up the vodka bottle and threw it as hard as he could. It struck the ground at the creature's feet and shattered, splashing his legs.

The creature smiled. "Missed," it said.

But Hakon had already twirled around. He grabbed the fireplace shovel and plunged it deep into the coals, then spun quickly back around and dashed the coals at the creature.

For a moment nothing happened and Hakon thought he had failed. Then the floorboards where the vodka had splashed shimmered with a bluish flame, the creature's feet and legs too. The creature didn't seem to notice, just kept moving ponderously forward. Hakon placed himself behind his chair, watched it come.

Isn't there supposed to be a moment of realization? he thought vaguely. *Some brief moment when I understand what this is and how to defeat it?* No, this wasn't a story, nor was it a dream. Nobody was going to help him.

It reached the easy chair. The flames had spread now up its body, and Hakon was beginning to smell its flesh cooking. He was mortified to find himself salivating. The creature grabbed the chair with burning fingers, and by the time it had set it to one side so as the better to get at Hakon, the chair was aflame.

It reached for him and he dodged it. Hakon shoved the chair out of his way and into the wall, and the drapes there caught flame. The creature was sidling ponderously, cornering him. Coughing now, Hakon threw himself out the open window.

He rolled off the porch, the wind knocked out of him. He scrambled to his feet. Inside, the creature stood at the window, trying to force its way through the frame, but it was too big to fit.

Flames were rising all around it now, the whole house catching. Hakon backed away from the heat. Inside, the creature took hold of one side of its chest and dug its fingers in. Fluid began to ooze out and the creature began to deflate. Soon that half could fit through, but the other half still could not. The creature's burning fingers sizzled as it sunk them into the other side of its chest.

Abruptly it was hidden within a great wall of flame.

It roared. Hakon ran.

III. A Last Death

In the dark, out of breath, Hakon heard the sirens and circled back. There it was, the town's only fire truck, the town's lone police car alongside. When they saw him, someone draped a blanket around his shoulders and a policeman put him in the back of his squad car. For a while they sprayed water on the blaze, but then they ran out of water. One firefighter drove off to refill the truck's water tank, the other two simply waited and watched the house burn.

The policeman opened the car door and asked: "How'd it start?"

"My uncle."

"Careless of him. Where is your uncle?"

Hakon just shrugged. "Probably inside," he said.

The policeman nodded. "No chance he got out?"

God, I hope not, Hakon thought, but instead said nothing.

The fire truck returned. They were no longer trying to put out the fire. They were just trying to make sure it didn't spread beyond the house.

He fell asleep after a while, there in the back of the squad car. It seemed impossible that he could under such circumstances, but he did.

The police officer shook him awake. It was over, the fire put out, the danger past. Hakon climbed out of the car, blinking in the daylight.

There was little left of the house beyond a few charred stretches of semi-collapsed walls. Puddles of water were everywhere, clotted with ash. The town's three firefighters wandered through, making sure everything was really out.

"Did they find my uncle?"

"There was a lot of heat," said the policeman. "Maybe there's nothing left to be found."

Hakon nodded.

They watched until the firefighters came back out of the ruin. One, the chief, gave a thumbs-up and then all three climbed into the truck and drove off.

"Want a ride back to town?" asked the police officer.

Hakon shook his head. "I want to see if there's anything worth salvaging," he said.

"There's not."

"I know there's not, but I still need to see."

The policeman clapped him on the back and left without a word, leaving him alone.

Heat still rose from the ashes, not much, but enough to notice. He made his way across the sudden charred remnants of the porch, careful with his footing. Out of habit, he entered through what had once been the front door. He wove through the ruin, careful not to hurt himself, careful not to fall through the burnt-out portions of the floor. He was keeping to the edges of the room, feeling out each step before taking it.

Near where the window had been, Hakon could see a dark stickiness on the floor, perhaps from where the creature had torn itself open. Where the floor had fallen through he peered down into the basement. It was hard to see much beyond water and piles of debris. If the creature was down there, it was buried.

Where the ceiling had been was open sky. The only remnant of the upper floor was part of the stairwell and a jagged stretch of blackened wall. The kitchen had burnt to the ground. Hakon searched through the piles of debris, found a fork twisted and deformed by the heat. He examined it, tossed it clanging aside. He dug a little deeper, but it was still too hot within the pile to touch much. Probably he shouldn't even be in here yet.

He heard a knocking sound and thought *Someone's at the front door,* but when he turned he remembered there *was* no front door. But there, standing where the door used to be, was the thing pretending to be his uncle. Hakon could see the way its skin hung wrong and sloshed with inert fluid, could see the strange mixture it was of puffy and flaccid. Its skin was blackened and burned, splitting open in some places to reveal a dull red surface within.

It lifted a mangled hand and rapped at the air and Hakon heard again that sound of knocking that seemed to come from nowhere.

He began to be very afraid.

"Knock, knock," the creature said, almost singing the words. "Anybody home?"

"Go away," Hakon said.

The creature ignored this. "Can I come in?" it said.

"No."

"No? Is that any way to treat your uncle?" But it made no move to enter.

"You can't come in," said Hakon.

The creature smiled. "Well, then," it said, "I guess that means I'll have to wait for you to come out."

Hakon watched the creature prowl the ruin's perimeter. A few times, he picked his way from one side of the ruin to the other, trying to do so unseen, but the creature was always there, just waiting for him to step outside the boundary of the ruined house. *I should make a run for it,* he thought, but he knew, unless there were stairs for the creature to navigate, that he couldn't run fast enough to escape it. And as he watched, with each step the creature was becoming quicker, more agile. But it apparently would not or could not enter the ruined house without being invited.

Hakon wrapped his arms around his belly and, hunched over, paced. Once his foot broke through and he almost fell into the basement, but he caught himself in time, survived with little more than a gash on his leg.

The creature seemed to smell the blood. It sniffed the air and gave a lop-sided smile.

He coughed. He paced, trapped. He was very hungry, very tired. As he walked he had stirred up the ashes, and now he was covered with them, gray as a ghost.

Eventually he would have to do something. He couldn't stay here forever.

But what would he do? He wasn't sure. The only thing he was sure of was that nobody was coming to help him.

The injured creature loped back and forth outside.

He would just have to try something, take a risk and hope whatever he tried would lead him to something else, and that in turn to something else, all a perfect little chain that would allow him to escape. Even though he knew it probably wouldn't.

Any moment now, something would come to him. A potential way out.

Any moment now, Hakon told himself, hours later as darkness began to fall.

Any moment—

"Knock, knock," said the creature, somehow rapping on the inside of his head now. He could hear muffled in its voice the sound of his dead uncle screaming. "Anybody home? Mind if I let myself in?"

WHAT IS MEAT WITH NO GOD?

by Cassandra Khaw

This is how the body dies again:

Artillery fire slurrying flesh, the meat within the armor rilling down the honeycombed front of the breastplate. Amazing what close-range cannonade can do to a body, especially given what enchantments were worked into the iron.

Get up, get up.

We are not done yet.

More amazing still is what the body can do when it is wefted to a will immortal as war. We are not done yet. We get up. The body rises as best it can, the vestibule of its belly become refuge for shrapnel: bone and bits of shattered bullet. It staggers first onto one knee and then another, collapses as there is not enough muscle on which to scaffold the action.

So, the body crawls, mailed fingers sinking into the cool black earth, finding purchase in the sediment beneath that good soil. It drags itself forward toward the soldiers who'd gunned it down, forward to the army shuffling unsteadily in place, who look now to their generals for answers as to how a body can move when there is so little left of limb and sinew.

Sometimes, the brain takes a minute to realize it's dead, says a moustached lieutenant, bayonet-lean, a cigar between his teeth, its cherry rendering his pupils the orange of a senescent evening.

Are you sure? They said there were holy warriors in this place, says a rawboned private, the words murmured like a blasphemy, his eyes round, only pupil in its fear.

Holy? chuckles the lieutenant.

That's what they say, he replies.

Nothing holy about those things. They're war-engines powered by little boys and girls, says the lieutenant, stubbing his cigarette on a wall.

No, that isn't how it works.

But we will not tell them that.

Instead, the body gets up.

It gyres in place. In the clearing smoke, this is what the army sees: a lone figure in sacramental armor; the platemail corroded, black. A single ragged red feather streaming from the helm, its vanes jellied with brain. We shake our head, adjust the angle of our hand and how the heel of our palm sits on the pommel of the body's weapon, that ruinous thing. The body's right arm is notated by fractures from when it first trained with this weapon, when the body was smaller than its hulking armament, egret bones, and a face to which you could still pinion a name.

The body steadies.

It lifts its head, cocks a thoughtful look at the waiting army, and then impossibly, it hefts its blade atop a shoulder, the chest beneath felted with gore now dark, now of the consistency of jam left to crust on the mouth of a bottle.

Shit shit shit shit, it's one of those things. Those fucking things are real, says a corporal, shucking his helmet although he knows better than to do so, *his* face unmarked, its eaves unmarred by scars.

There is no time for his expression to shed its bewilderment, not before the body's sword cleaves through his neck, severing vertebrae, the brain stem's tail. His head tumbles onto the wet dirt, still wearing its careful wonder.

There is no time for anything at all as the body accelerates, and the army is unmade into a fine burgundy mist.

This is why the body dies again, and again, and again, and again:

It was given to a god when it was nineteen, the country of its bones unbroken, its acres holy still. They wreathed the body in summertime blossoms: lilacs and lilies, thin tufts of lavender, dahlias, daisies, hydrangea in such volume, they drowned all sight of the body's face. But that was all right.

In days, it would not matter.

When a body is given to a god, to this god, in particular, this lord of the smithy and the secret places only the dead know to go, it is a kind of marriage. The body is wedded to the god's armor, its name given away like a bride. And it will not eat from there on. It will neither sleep nor speak. The body will take no sustenance save for the rich lard of the god's will, and it will be enough for the body, for what tool has needs outside of its wielder's wants?

The body does not know this yet.

In days, this will change.

This is what the body remembers:

It had a brother once. The memory is as rusted as the cartilage of our armor, details flaking, dried eschar rubbed from skin. But there was a brother, that much the body is sure of. We are sure of this too and assured in turn by how the brother pulls at us like the north dragging the needle of a compass.

Dusk buries what remains of the army in a bruise-blue dark, the sun between the mountains like a lidded eye. The body exhales, steam geysering from the camail veiling its mouth. Already, flies have come and the air seethes black with their wings. We tip our head back, drink the quiet. The body remembers as do we what it was like before our world died, and there was purpose and there was our god, and there was our god's voice in the body's ear, and it did not hurt so much to be a holy thing and it hurt even less to be alive.

But as with all things, like civilizations, like the clarity of early memories, like childhood, like hope, this will pass too.

The body is dying, but the god hasn't yet said that we may rest.

Offal slicks the road toward the enemy city. They are the adversary, the reason why our god now rots beneath the burnt corpse of the capital where the body was born. The smoke from the desecration clogs the air, and miles away, what is left of the body's people wail for their god.

The god is dead.

But the body is not.

So, we take our sword, we take this gore-lunged body with its gutted throat, its stoved breastbone, its dripping innards; we take the votives of its wounds, the offering of its ruin, and we place it on the road to the enemy city, and we begin to walk.

There was a brother once whom the body loved.

We will find him.

We must.

This is what we remember:

In the beginning, there was the Word and the Word was War.

This is what the body remembers:

A damp white rag laid over its forehead, set there as the body is coffined in restraints.

What are you doing? it said softly, turning, afraid although it knew it should not be, that the pain to come was what would make it holy, that its god would be there, that it would be all right, that it was safe, it was safe, it was safe. A hand spooned its jaw, steered its face so it was gazing again at the ceiling. Around wrists and ankles, the soft cups of its bended elbows, leather is tightened. It hurts. The air drones with prayers that the faithful are sure we know, but we are only holy because they made us so.

Don't look, said a woman's voice. You don't want to look.

Why, said the body.

Don't look, said the woman again.

We woke when the body disgorged its first scream.

This is how the body dies again:

A bullet trepanning the body's skull, burrowing into brain, and the force of its entrance purees the delicate tissue, turns it nearly liquid. The body drops immediately, folding onto itself, onto its knees, head bent as if in worship. It rocks in place, the bullet smoldering, cooking the fat of the brain. On the battlements, a woman looks sidelong to her sister-in-arms, lowering a rifle kept oiled and oilslick black.

What the hell was that? she said.

Get up, get up.

A dangerous relic, says her companion. Don't stop shooting. Those things don't die easy.

Get up. We are not done yet.

As before, as it has always done, the body lurches upright again, blood drooling from its visor. It will not stand straight, its neck so broken even we cannot compensate for its pain. But we can move the body, we can guide its shambling tread forward, while the soldiers atop the parapet look on with mounting dread.

How is it moving, we hear someone whisper.

The body aches to breathe, but its lungs are silted with carrion. When it tries to breathe, what it does instead is choke. We take our sword as the body gurgles. We look up at the enemy faces and we forget, for a sliver of a moment, that we are destitute, without our god and without our people, without the orisons that told us we are more than just a weapon, without anything.

What are you all doing? we hear someone bellow. Take it down. If it gets past the walls, we are all dead.

There is so little left of this body, but we do not need much; we have subsisted on much less. As we ready ourselves for battle, the body heaves up a name. *Alfonse Alfonse Alfonse*, it shrieks to us. There was a brother once whom the body loved and he is there, our Alfonse, waiting for his turn to be blessed.

This is what they will remember:

We left nothing alive.

This is what we see:

He is old now, this brother, face cragged by the years, the skin drained of all softness, lesioned with disease, the sum of him leached of the swagger the body remembers. But the eyes are the same, as are his magpie gestures: the staccato quickness of his movements, how he tilts his head one way and then another.

Alfonse, weeps the body, one last time, and we reach a hand to the brother. "What happened to you?"

If the body could still speak, we would have had it say: a god happened, you were there when they gave the body away. We are too late for such conversation, however, and we say nothing as what is left of our people stream past, all of them starved to brushstrokes. If there were priests still, if there were larders dizzy with grain and cured meats, if our god was not ashes, we would have led them home. But there is nothing left, nothing but us and the memory of when we were as holy as hope, and the brother's hand, so small in the palm of our own.

"I'm so sorry."

Sludge blooms from our visor: reeking, viscous as tar, this emulsion we have made of the body. It dribbles first from the mouth of the helm and quickly, it becomes a deluge, until we are black with the substance, the darkness crawling up, up, up the brother's arm, as though somewhere in the muck, there is enough of the body to remember what it is like to seek a sibling's warmth.

We pay no attention as the brother screams, too exultant in this moment. How long have we dragged the body along, how long have we ferried that dying mass. Now, we are done. There is no more need for the body, not when the brother is so close.

In a different time, they would have garlanded the brother with summertime blossoms, and there would have been feasts, and there would have been a woman telling him to not look as they tore him apart so he could be something holy. We drag the brother closer, and he squirms and wails, as we fit him into us, one fistful of flesh at a time.

He dies before we can finish the work.

But that is all right.

This is only the first death. There will be many more before we are done.

BITTEN BY HIMSELF

by Laird Barron

1.

I was named after my granddad, Charles Custer Poe. Chick was a sprout when he marched off to fight in the War of Western Expansion alongside a whole army of wet-behind-the-ears blockheads. Dad's words, not mine. At the Battle in the Tall Grass, a Peloki warrior castrated Gramps and peeled his scalp. King Crockett's men sent the remains home in a pinewood box. Thus was the legend of my father's father, who left behind a pregnant wife and a couple of snot-nosed whelps.

Time passed.

We Poes squatted on a homestead plot a stone's throw from the Big Forest. Hunters, trappers, and gillnetters. My family eked out a squalid existence. Harder and meaner than average, and possessed of more kinship with woodland critters than with our fellow man. "Trespassing" upon our swampy paradise was the last mistake many a fool committed. Peloki skinners had nothing on Dad and his jawbone knife. Observing people in extreme circumstances taught me everything necessary about human nature.

Mom and Dad kicked in the winter of '65. I inherited their worldly possessions, which included a flea-bitten coonskin cap, well-traveled buckskins, and a Green River knife. Strapped that blade on my hip, opposite a homemade tomahawk. Sharp as hell, the pair. I honed those suckers against a black whetstone which I hauled at great risk from the muck of a creek bed the way our ancestors did. First time I used the knife in anger, I sliced an eel farmer's hand off at the wrist in one lick. To be fair, the hand was still hanging by a tendon as he recoiled, but I'm counting it. The knife was built for infighting, balanced to a frog's hair and of sufficient weight it could surely chop through a neck, although I never put her to the test. I endeavored to ambush my enemies and stab the kidneys or that divot at the base of the spine. "Up to the Green River!" was a euphemism for burying one's knife to the company stamp on the hilt. And did you know, there's a major vein in the rectum? Now you do! One nick and a piker will be shitting his way into the next world.

I got away with murdering the eel farmer on account of no witnesses. Alas, a lord caught me poaching rabbits on his demesne. Since there was trouble brewing with a neighboring territory, the authorities gave me a choice: hang or get my marching boots on. Well, you bet I did a tour in the army, just like Chick. Served as a long-range scout with Royal Reconnaissance. Didn't win any medals or particular distinction. On the other hand, I didn't get castrated or skinned alive. Folks don't understand the reality of scouting, which generally amounts to lying in wait and holding one's piss for hours and hours. Scouts do their best fighting while the enemy sleeps, jugular vulnerable to a quick slash. There's not much honor in scouting. Whole lot of *valor,* if you consider that discretion and cowardice are damned near interchangeable. Got cashiered with a pocketful of gold doubles, which I squandered in nothing flat. I bunked at the family homestead until it fell down around my ears. Eventually, my traplines and hunting routes carried me far afield. In due course, I picked a cave, or an abandoned hovel, or a hollow log, to curl up in at night.

Time passed.

The Poes had cultivated an unsavory reputation, thus I kept my surname under my cap. Most folks recognized me by my mild-mannered persona, Chick, a hermit trapper who'd act as a wilderness guide for a pouch of silver and a snort of awerdenty. Wrinkles and seams and snowy beard came early, lending me a false appearance of agedness. This lulled rubes and professional manhunters alike into complacency. Nobody looks twice at a decrepit codger, much less suspects him of feats of athletic villainy. Camouflage is a hunter's second-greatest advantage after patience. None guessed that their scrawny, wizened associate went by more colorful sobriquets, such as the Ghost of Wolf Vale. The Mad Trapper of North Fork. The Hunting Man. And my sentimental favorite, Black Moccasins. A wounded Peloki tribesman gave me those moccasins as a peace offering. Thanks to cunning refined by dint of time, trial, and comfortable footwear, I prowled whisper-soft through the Big Forest and environs wreaking havoc with blades and snares.

Some philosopher claimed men are inclined to madness when separated from the tribe for too long. He probably figured hermits and wise men proved the rule. Certainly, the storyteller would've gotten a kick out of me. Preferring the remote fastnesses on the edge of the kingdom, serenaded by birdsong and the choruses of coyote yips, I answered right back to the critters in their own dialects.

Occasionally, I was drawn to civilization for basic supplies, hooch and hellraising at the tavern, and, if silver jingled in my pouch, an evening in the arms of a comfort gal. Tavern drunks might comment upon my thinness.

Sinewy as a puma! Or they'd remark upon my flesh, pallid as whitecaps. *Not much sun in the Big Forest!*

The more perceptive of the merchants, whores, and drunks considered me kin to a wolf or coyote who crept near the fire and accepted scraps. Fearful of my fangs, even the wariest of them inevitably grew complacent, forgetting that savagery often bides beneath a docile veneer.

Sometimes even I forgot.

2.

One night, while roving the Big Forest, I was bitten by myself.

High on a dose of skunkweed, I'd strapped on knife, tomahawk, and my moccasins, and set forth to poach a deer from King Dick's own private reserve. Unsanctioned hunting is a perilous endeavor, best undertaken in the dead of night to avoid the peeping eyes of man-catchers and wardens. Alas, traveling by the dark of the moon presents its own set of challenges. Dire entities awaken with the pearly dusk. None are pleasant to encounter.

Pausing for a swallow of awerdenty, I noticed a dim flame ahead. After a bit of creeping, I parted the bushes and beheld two figures locked in mortal struggle in a glade by the light of a fallen lantern. Well, one figure mainly squirmed while the other chuckled as he stabbed with a boar spear. The man nailed to the ground was none other than Warden Dudley; I knew him by his fine cloak and badge of office. The king's personal henchman, Warden Dudley had seen to the hanging of countless desperate woodsmen. His name was a curse upon the lips of so-called scofflaws and scoundrels within fifty leagues.

The man driving the spear (wrested from the warden, I believe) was my very own spitting image. *My* coonskin cap, tattered cloak, stained breeches, and moccasins. *My* bulging eyes and lank beard. Sinewy, veiny, ruthless. Exactly, unerringly, wholly me. The only difference? He wore a filthy scarf around his neck, neatly wrapped and knotted. The feeble light made no difference—his identity registered in my bones.

The Other Me knelt, reached down the warden's throat, and gripped a hank of flesh. He pulled mightily while his victim uttered glottal moans. I had no idea a tongue could stretch so far! Perhaps I chuckled in amazement. My double's head swiveled. Our gazes met and he leaped upon me whipcrack-fast, teeth ripping a chunk from my neck as we tumbled. His fingers closed like steel traps on either side of my head. And his breath . . . Saint Hasselhoff's tits, it could've blistered paint. Black stars spun in my vision and the white rime of chaos covered the world. Truly, I thought it was curtains and me with so many ill deeds yet uncommitted.

He released me and settled on his haunches. Blood dripped from the point of his beard. "Hello, old me."

I couldn't speak. It felt as if I were inhaling fire.

He rocked and gnawed his thumb. "The hierophant was right, damn him. I'm shedding." His rocking and gnawing became more agitated. He regarded me with an expression of devilry unsurpassed.

I knew an instant before he uncoiled that he'd decided to finish the job. The shitbird couldn't dodge midair, so I caught him between the eyes with my desperately flung tomahawk. Other Me thrashed in the leaves and went still. I crawled over to receive his muttered last words, "Time is a ring . . ."

I searched both men. Warden Dudley carried a pouch, which I pocketed. Sure as horse turds roll downhill, more of King Dick's lackies would come sniffing around. Best to make myself scarce. I left the corpses for the turkey vultures and slunk away to nurse my wound.

3.

Time passed.

Illness possessed me. Foam curdled in my beard. I howled at the moon. Sickness coiled in my guts like hookworms bloated with slimy, unwholesome eagerness. There were bad days and worse days. Fugues stole countless hours and deluged me with apocalyptic visions of colliding moons that cracked in half and crowds of men boiling in the gut acids of an eternal god that lived in one of the half-shell moons. All the men wore my blistered, screaming face. Thusly afflicted, I raved and thrashed in my bed of moss inside a hollow log.

Worst of the worse days ended with me suddenly clearheaded, naked as a jay (except for my moccasins), clinging to the tippy-top of a sentinel pine. Scratched in a dozen places, I gawped at the Almighty's creation spread far, far below. A throttled sloth dangled from my fist. Sloths belonged to the far southern jungles of Florida and Mexico and were rarely seen in the temperate north. I took it as an unlucky sign.

"Well," I said to the limp sloth, "it can't go on this way." I climbed down, found my britches, and tramped through the hills for the nearest outpost of civilization to seek counsel. A village barber saw me straightaway. He had scant choice as I jimmied a window and let myself into his bedroom while the white-cold moon egged me on.

Aggrieved protestations notwithstanding, the barber leeched me and tasted my urine. "Headaches? Hypnogogic interludes? Irritability?"

"Yes. Maybe. And more so."

"Aversion to water?"

I shrugged.

"It's not a trick question," he said.

"I don't drink it."

"Don't bathe in it either. May I inquire what you *do* drink?"

"Hooch!"

The man, yet in his robe and nightcap, paged through a moldy grimoire and muttered forebodingly. "You've contracted the rabies," he said at last. "What bit you?"

"Does it matter?"

"Death has you by the shorthairs, I aver." He unrolled a parchment scroll and dipped a quill in ink. "I'd love to record the facts for posterity."

There was no sane way to explain the inciting event. I wrung my coonskin cap and asked how long and he allowed I might hang on for another fortnight, plus or minus. The second week would be hellish and not worth the suffering. He graciously offered to administer a hemlock tonic to ease my crossing of the threshold into King Pluto's ballroom. Also, did I mind donating my brain for the advancement of medicine?

"Nah, I'm good."

"You're not *good*. You're dying. Can't you smell that smell?"

"Everybody's dying, leech." I paid him a handful of grimy coin I'd taken from the warden. Then I trotted over to the tavern and acquired a flask of awerdenty with the remaining coppers. Fortified against persistent woe, I returned to my flop in the hollow log and got drunker than ever. This proved to be of no real help, although it dulled the edge for a while.

Time passed: swooning, blurry, indeterminate.

As I tossed in febrile slumber, a behemoth slouched toward my lair.

you killed my boy! Oh, shit; this probably referred to that sloth I'd throttled. Small trees cracked and popped as they were shoved aside. The presence snuffled at a knothole; rancid breath cool as corpse gas against my face. *smelled your blood. followed the snail trail through the forest. smells good.*

Its voice (voices?) circled inside my skull; warped and skipping the way a gramophone needle scratches against a wax disk. Though the interior of my hidey-hole was night-blacked, an image of the visitor coalesced with nightmarish clarity. A vision, one might declare. The creature was shadow-cloaked, enormous as a grizzly—two grizzlies!—hunkered atop the log, claws lightly digging into mossy wood. Its glaucous eyes wobbled in opposite directions. Slugs and cockroaches cohabitated within its matted fur. Slack jaws oozed clabber, and its mottled, suppurating tongue knew the names of all men.

In turn, I knew it to be an avatar of the Black Sloth (yet no sloth by any sane measure), Lord of the Eighteen Hells, patron of hunters, thieves, gluttons, and assassins. Otherwise known as Zellig the Creeper, Sneak Boots, and locally,

Slaughin, a corruption of the Peloki term, Slow Skinner. By whatever name, it was a prehistoric god whose worship transcended tribal superstition and was favored by confabs of evil men across the spectrum of society. The cult had even infiltrated Empress Innocent's own court if such profane tavern gossip were credited.

Further, I intuited that however large Slaughin's avatar appeared, its true form was titanic.

this realm is colder than i favor in this aspect. no bananas. no guava. meat? meat's fine in a pinch. fingerlings. eggs. chicks. It clacked jagged fangs and licked the knothole, tasting the stink of my sweat. *you slaughtered my child. repay me with your soft innards.*

Maggots squirmed free of the sloth god's tongue; pattered through the knothole, wriggling down my cheeks and into the festering hole in my neck. I choked; mute, blind, and paralyzed. *or we can forge a pact. hunt your little friends. hunt them and send their souls to me. obey and i'll gorge upon you last.*

Although not sure precisely what he meant by "hunting my little friends," how could I possibly refuse? Those dagger claws were casually scraping ever closer to my flesh. Taking my gurgles for assent, the terrible presence eventually withdrew. The maggots did their miraculous work.

Time passed.

Ravaging fever subsided to dim coals that nonetheless altered my nature both physically and otherwise. I existed in a state of high-functioning malaise. Hangdog and moribund, yet galvanized with interludes of preternatural vitality. Nor did the hole in my throat properly seal despite the magical maggots' diligent efforts. The raw edges puckered and assumed a rigid, leathery texture. Somewhere along the line I acquired a handsome scarf. Couldn't have leaves and twigs and flying bugs dropping in there whenever I tilted my head back for a snort of hooch.

4.

Before the infection settled into my blood and bones, I was, to put it charitably, a murderous asshole. After the bite, I transformed into a raving, murderous asshole. Contrary to the barber's gloomy prognosis, the disease didn't kill me, although it certainly kindled my longing for death. Alas, raving assholes don't follow the moral course of ending their own lives no matter how bleak the outlook; they visit their misery upon others in the guise of vengeance and necessity.

Wicked old Slaughin had bid me hunt, and I hunted.

The Big Forest spreads across a third of this continent and only its contours have been fully mapped. Its interior is a Here Be Dragons legend on a map. No home for the faint of heart, but a fitting home to the heartless. Every tree and every bush resembles every other tree and every other bush. A tenderfoot is liable to lose his way and die of exposure or get eaten by a catamount or a cave bear. Or worse. There's always worse. Cannibal hillmen are worse. Tribes of Fomorians and troglodytes who inhabit the caverns beneath the roots of the massive firs are also worse. Wily creatures (namely Jumping Jax spiders and two species of malevolent, flightless birds) imitate human voices as a lure. Some predators wear the skins of men like ill-fitted costumes. Then there are seemingly ordinary folks cast as perfect doubles—accurate down to the mole on your ass. Yea, these latter are truly insidious in that each believes his or herself to represent the genuine article.

Hunting my "weaker halves" became an obsession motivated by an atavistic revulsion to the very notion of their existence. I crossed paths with them in the woods and in the city at my bucket o' blood haunts. Acquaintances (fellow scofflaws, mainly) unwittingly assisted my efforts—*Didn't I see ye in Ball Cutter Alley this very morn?* Or, *Hail, Chick! I thought ye were renting a cot in the West End? Strange to meet ye here* . . . Folks reported seeing me chopping logs on the edge of the Big Wood or selling ill-gotten coneys to a river village butcher, or simply lurking in one hedgerow or another. In each case, I laughed at their poor eyesight, then immediately rushed to the named location, ready to ambush these imposters, these loathsome imitations. If the ambush went well, I might enjoy an opportunity to interrogate them with heated pliers. I wanted to know who they really were and where the hell they came from, mainly.

The doubles reacted to their imminent demise the same as I would've—they fought, begged, swore oaths to make a nun blush, and at the end, expired sullenly. Before dying, each claimed to be in the service of darkness, tasked with tracking the false Chick Poes and delivering their miserly souls to the Black Sloth, Zellig the Creeper, or Slaughin, depending.

As you might surmise, these sincere assertions confused and enraged me. Matters went hard for the imposters. Oh, very hard indeed. Once I'd done my worst, I whistled a culling song retrieved from a vivid nightmare of the void. On such occasions, fetid smog billowed, dimming any nearby light source. A doorway to hell yawned at my shoulder. As a final breath escaped my victims, monstrous claws breached the shadowy portal to pluck them into oblivion. I always turned away and covered my ears to block the awful crunches and gulps. Even I, uncouth and untutored, don't chew with my mouth open.

5.

Time passed.

On Midsummer's Eve, I shared a campfire with a girl named Ferris. Agitated cries of birds alerted me as I emerged from a hunting blind and observed her in a dirty gown stumbling about the glade. Lost and alone, she was overjoyed to encounter another human being. I deduced as much when she leaped into my arms and wrapped her legs around my waist. Damned strong for a girl.

Ferris had fled an arranged marriage—literally dove out a window and run for the hills while her betrothed sobbed at the altar. Uncharacteristically mellow, and a trifle lonely, I gave the lass a slug of awerdenty to calm her nerves. I roasted a rabbit haunch and regaled her with a flattering version of my life story thus far, to which she inquired why I'd chosen the existence of a hermit. An honest question only the pure heart of youth could pose so baldly. The warmth of hooch in my belly compelled me to rejoin with equal candidness.

I confided that I'd known a sublime love. The object of my desire was a maiden named Threnody. She resided in a village on the edge of the Big Wood. A furrier's daughter. Flaxen-haired, blue-eyed, and winsome. I first spied her at the market in the spring after I'd finished my tour with the Royal Reconnaissance, and again that winter as I brought pelts to the Fur Rendezvous. Our attraction was instantaneous, albeit measured in glances rather than words. We locked gazes when I sold her father my best ermine and fox pelts with a bit knocked off the top.

Two years I pined for the object of my affection. Pine was all I could manage since she'd long been promised to a jeweler. Wealthiest man in the entire county next to the nobles.

My wiser angels counseled that this could not end well. Better to lay my sights on a tavern wench or scullery maid. Alas, wisdom is useless to a fool trapped in the throes of desire. Unrequited love turned my brain to mush and stripped me of whatever common sense I possessed. Love compelled me to sing romantic ballads under her window at night. Love inspired me to hunt down small, exotic critters and hang their fresh corpses upon her garden trellis as tokens. Love dulled my natural wariness and I was taken unawares by a band of thugs in the pay of my rival, the jeweler. They beat me raw with clubs. Crushed my back, my legs, and lastly, my skull. My blood flowed upon the dirty leaves. The brutes left me dead.

"*For* dead," Ferris said, morbidly attentive. "They left you *for* dead."

"Fair enough, girlie. Mayhap I imagined my skull getting stove in and this dent above my ear too."

"Indeed? Hold fast a moment." Her eyes flared hot as the flames. She muttered, "Hmm. Inconclusive scan. Previous cranial trauma. Elevated pulse. Unusual brain-wave patterns. Near-death trauma can initiate aberrant neurological activity . . ." Then to me, "Congratulations, Mr. Poe. You've the indicators of a unique specimen."

"Specimen?" I liked not the sound of that.

"My master is keen on fresh subjects for his research experiments."

The Green River knife practically jumped into my hand. I kicked coals at the girl and leaped backward. Ferris's wedding gown went up in a woosh of flames that scorched pine needles and sent them zinging. Though I reacted with the speed of a puma and the alacrity of a lake pike, it was of no avail. Dainty fingers, hard as bark and crushingly powerful, clamped my throat before I could whistle for my monstrous pal, the Black Sloth. She shook me insensible then grabbed a handful of my greasy beard and dragged me away to meet her maker.

6.

Howard Campbell dwelt in a hillside cave above a bend in Shiver Creek. The infamous Green Druid was a fellow I'd done my level best to avoid, as did most denizens of the Big Forest. Hoary and wrinkled, clad in ragged hunter-green robes; a disgraced hierophant of the Hemlock Grove who haunted the region, abducting animals and men for unspecified, purportedly profane, rituals. His glasses were tinted, his teeth snaggled, and his flesh was as pallid and spongy as the toadstools that flourished in the deeper, endless caverns. He lighted his stone honeycomb with rare luminescent crystals. Bones and pelts of men and beasts decorated the lair.

Chained to a damp granite wall, I was at leisure to assess my surroundings. Badgers, martens, and songbirds languished in iron cages. Exotic creatures too—birds-of-paradise, ornamented lizards, monkeys, and sloths. The fellow had trekked widely to obtain his specimens. Like me, his apparent age belied a vibrant, predatory vigor.

"Ah, you recognize my hawkish mien and holy garb. Welcome to my laboratory. I pretended to be a druid for nigh on twenty years. Pagan nonsense. An extended foray into anthropological drudgery." Campbell relished answering unasked questions. He also enjoyed soliloquies, monologues, and musing aloud in general. Good thing too—I sure as hell wasn't keen to indulge him.

He lingered at a workbench laden with vials and smoldering beakers. Alcoves were carved into the opposite wall. Nude men and women stood within the niches. Their eyes were frozen and lifeless. Ferris, upon locking my manacles, retired to the leftmost indentation and became inert. Campbell referred to her and her kind as simulacrums, which I interpreted as a fancy word for golems. Intuiting my thoughts, he cheerfully explained that they were devised by engineers of his homeland, akin to clockwork automatons, except vastly more sophisticated. The simulacrums served as spies and gatherers; donning costumes as appropriate to the given task. Knights, merchants, peasants, run-away brides . . .

I feigned lassitude, eyeballing his every move, patiently waiting for a mo-ment to escape as he drew samples of my humors and poked arcane instru-ments into the hole in my throat. I noticed that several of the animals behaved oddly. A monkey and a lizard regarded one another through bars, grunting and hissing in bestial conversation. A sloth hung amid the branches of a pot-ted bush, drooling as it raptly observed the monkey and the lizard.

"A rift in the lower caverns emits a psychomagnetic frequency," Camp-bell said. "Quite possibly a bifurcation in the space-time continuum. Mayhap a fracture, in the worst-case scenario. Typically, such phenomena exist in re-mote space. Bursts from neutron stars and wormholes. I've not encountered a terrestrial source until this one. The emanation attracted me and has be-come the focus of my research. Genius loci, my homicidal friend. Spirit of the Place." He described the anomaly as a coagulation of dark matter that bent light and gravity and by logical extension, time itself. He'd briefly introduced subjects to the rift—the aforementioned monkeys, lizards, and sloths. Their resultant aberrant behavior was a mystery he hoped to unravel.

The hierophant gently wrapped my throat in the scarf. "Your blood and tissue are irradiated with an energy quite similar to the samples I've extracted from test animals that survived exposure to the rift. Ditto your vital signs. And the mania in your bulging eyes! Exciting and unsettling. A simian can only relate so much of its experience. Human trials are in order." His wink was terrifying. "I could ask for no more uniquely qualified candidate than a durable shithead such as yourself."

Ferris and another simulacrum named Elmer animated and conveyed me (kicking and cursing, any pretense of docility abandoned) along a series of tunnels that descended far below the hierophant's cave. We navigated by a chain of those glowing crystals. Red, yellow, blue, down into the black. It grew oppressively hot. Water seeped and steamed.

We arrived in a grotto of weird mushrooms and dripping stalactites. A fault split the rock floor. An oily sheen glimmered within the chasm. Nearby sat a wooden cage attached to a gee pole and a crude windlass. The intent was plain—lock me in the cage, swing it over the rift, and lower away. I thought about those drooling animals in Campbell's laboratory.

"What the hell is that?" I pointed at the rift and its contents.

"Behold primordial ooze," Elmer said.

"Afterbirth of the cosmos," Ferris said.

Though I'm not smart, cunning will often do in a pinch. I appealed to reason, for once. "Wouldn't it make more sense for one of you golems to test this ingenious loci thingy? I'm fragile."

"Indeed," Ferris said as she fussed with the windlass. "Alas, Elmer and I are invaluable. *You* are eminently replaceable."

"Corruption of our systems would pose an unacceptable risk to the master's work." Elmer guided me toward the cage with an avuncular pat on the back.

"Remember the monkeys." Ferris unlatched the door.

"Later, fuckers!" I ripped free of Elmer's grip and hurled myself headlong into the pit.

Hard to say whether this impulsive gambit took them by surprise or if my "escape" was part of their larger plan to document my exposure to the forces of the rift. Whatever the case, plunging through the membrane, I promptly regretted my life decisions.

Mucus poured into my orifices. I flailed, an ant sinking into a honeycomb, a flea pissed into extinction by a god. Crushed and ripped apart simultaneously. Absolute cold numbed my extremities and slowed my heart. Momentary blindness smote me, followed by a cascade of celestial fire. My mind's eye catapulted into the eternal ether that enfolds the star fields winking across every night sky. The membrane absorbed flesh and thought. On the opposite side, I gradually apprehended many secrets of the universe and its filthy, carnivorous nature. This wisdom included much of Campbell's esoteric theories and scholarly nomenclature. None of that did me a lick of good.

Does it ever?

7.

Upon falling a short distance, north and south reversed. I felt as if I'd been yanked out of the rift to be deposited at its precipice, soaked in slime. Everything was the same, but different. The simulacrums weren't in evidence, nor was their contraption. My vision blurred and the cavern contracted, expanded, and seemed to multiply. I fled down vermiculate passages in a maze of rock guided purely by instinct or the illogic common to dreams. The pitter-pat of a multitude of feet synchronized with my own swift steps. Light and dark shuttered rapidly. The slime was potent as any snuff or hooch; it curdled my mind with a familiar, albeit more intense, madness and caused the wound in my throat to throb and writhe.

Campbell's voice pursued me: *Every living creature sheds its cells. You shed universes, Charles Poe! Come back and permit me to dissect you!*

Brambles tore my face. Now I loped pell-mell through a version of the Big Wood that doubled and redoubled like a gallery of mirrors. Dull yellow and cracked, the moon beamed upon a ridge of jumbled rock that dominated a meadow. I climbed, nearly insensate with panic. Bats shrieked from a vent in the earth. Except, these weren't bats, but tiny, humanoid figures jerking and jittering on leather wings. The mass tumbled around me, then heaved upward. One snagged in my beard and I grasped it reflexively. I saw myself, albeit deformed and in miniature. Beady red eyes and needle fangs. Naked, shriveled, utterly mad. The bat-thing sank its fangs into my thumb and blood welled. I crushed it like a handful of wet twigs, flung its corpse into the night, and stumbled onward, gibbering. Dense forest closed around me, a gauntlet of thorns and whipping branches.

Campbell cried, faintly now: *Incalculable numbers of universes! Your every speck of spittle, flake of skin, drop of blood!*

I instinctively realized that motion was illusory. Whatever memory popped into my head manifested in the physical realm. No sooner had I considered it a shame to perish without once embracing my love, the furrier's daughter, than trees thinned and there, like magic, stood her father's manor.

Propelled by inchoate longing and rising terror, I clambered through a window into her room, where a lamp beckoned. She lay beneath a sumptuous quilt, long hair flowing over pillows. I gently grasped her shoulder. She stirred, rolled over, and gazed at me. Her nubile form indeed belonged to the girl I'd yearned for, but the face was mine—shrewd, ancient eyes, rabies-stained beard, and evil grin.

The warped mirror effect returned and my gorge rose. The flesh between my shoulders spasmed, bulging until it split like a sausage on a griddle and birthed another me, cojoined and hollering his outrage in perfect harmony with my own. The chamber telescoped to impossible dimensions while an ever-lengthening daisy chain of Charlie Poes screeched and struggled. Skull from skull, spine from spine, our colossal chain wrenched apart in a spatter of severed taffy strings. Once free, my doubles scuttled in all directions across identical bedchambers and flung themselves out of identical windows.

And me as well.

8.

Mystics have argued for millennia over the matter of free will versus predestination. Even now, I can't tell you who is right. Dream navigation persisted to carry me forward without any discernible pattern. I blundered into a glade and lantern light hit me a heartbeat before Warden Dudley cursed and smote a blow across my chest with his spear haft. He dropped the lantern to get a double grip on the spear. Too slow and too weak. How could he reckon my crazed, bestial power?

When the original me stumbled upon the murder scene in progress, I was too far gone to initiate a rational exchange. Knowing what was to come (or what had already occurred?) helped not a jot. I was reduced to primal instinct and foaming with cosmic rabies. The narrative unraveled with the certainty of water pouring over a cliff.

Here came his (my) tomahawk to bury itself in my forehead.

Though I can't settle the debate regarding free will and predestination, I *can* confirm that sages are correct to assert that consciousness persists for some brief duration following bodily death. I lay near the corpse of Warden Dudley, helpless except to stare past the canopy into a sea of glittering stars.

As fate would have it, the warden's men never discovered us. Our bloating carcasses attracted carrion birds and small animals. Beetles polished our scattered bones. I lost track of Warden Dudley. My thoughts became untethered; they drifted in an interstellar vacuum, ever forward and backward. Moments or eons passed until my astral self plunged into billowing, reflective clouds shot through with strokes of red lightning. These clouds had obscured much of Creation in the earliest moments of material reality.

9.

Time doesn't pass anymore.

I walk a plain of doom. A filthy bundle of nerves drags in my wake. Reminds me of Ferris and her fake bridal train clotted with dirt and leaves. At the distant end of this umbilical cord is a hollowed corpse, an aborted twin of myself bumping along, almost weightless, its features scraped and disfigured by stones.

The frayed cord abruptly snaps, which means I'll enjoy a brief respite. Merely a respite, because the cells of my lower back will soon boil and churn and mark the beginning of a new struggle for primacy with a lumpen tumor, a fetus, that will rapidly enlarge into another conjoined me. We'll do battle, tooth and nail. The victor will drag his yoked twin until the cord breaks again and so on. The trick is to wait to destroy my false self at a precise moment. Act too soon, I'll forever lug a fetus anchored to my spine. Wait too long and one of the bastards will do unto me.

Meanwhile, I endure an endless procession of days shuffling toward the horizon; a black welt that pulses and fades with the crash and tumble of blood in my temples. Alien skies loom as imposingly as a demiurge's obsidian hand mirror. The ground is dim. I squint to see my feet kicking in the ashes of fallen stars. I lost my moccasins somewhere. In truth, none of this exists; my thoughts create a physical realm and give it shape. I navigate purgatorial twilight by the compass and charts of my diseased imagination. Suffering and pain are the signposts. Lest tedium prevail eternally, bellows of a gargantuan beast, presumably Slaughin or his avatar, roll behind me across the plains of dust and dead sea forests.

Nights here are cold. I build campfires of petrified wood. The fires blaze pure darkness. Squatting upon stony earth, I think strange thoughts and wonder darkly as a man does when he's got nothing to do but scratch his balls and listen to the breeze crooning. I rub my hands over the shadow flames, pronouncing a litany of oaths against the powers that be. *You fuckers again!* I mutter into my beard, salty with tears and snot. Nay, the powers at large care nothing for a flea such as myself. This must be one of Slaughin's Eighteen Hells and my punishment for a life of iniquity.

A whisper answers out of the vault where spare galaxies are kept:

You fucking idiot. There is no afterlife. No Heaven, no Underworld. No punishment except of your own devising. Suffer for an hour, an eon, or eternity.

Being or nothingness. To gaze ahead is to gaze backward at the hole from whence all matter exploded. There is no difference.

These words are either a memory or a prophecy half-formed in my stewed consciousness. Their meaning is plain—the monster that pursues me also awaits my arrival. In brief snatches of slumber, I dream within this dream that I'm slogging through the immortal guts of the Black Sloth itself. That pulsing black welt on the invisible horizon is a godly asshole. Ultimately, I'll be expelled into the material world; a chewed-up soul reduced to a turd upon a festering pile in some prehistoric swamp. And start again as a mold, a tadpole, a simian. Perhaps the delusion of hope is the last spark of intellect to get snuffed. Because the core of me that hasn't yet divided into imbecility suspects heat death and extinction are the actual likely outcomes.

The cells along my shoulders are in full riot. Not one fetal lump, but two.

Time doesn't pass. It repeats.

BURIAL

by Kristi DeMeester

Mara was thirteen the first time she whispered her hatred into the ground, her fingers earth-stained as she tore a squirming, pink worm into smaller and smaller pieces.

"I want her to hurt," she said and then dug until her fingernails cracked, the delicate skin beneath raw and bleeding, before dropping the pieces into the hole one by one. "I want her to hurt." Again and again, she said it until the words felt like honey on her tongue. Like a balm for all her mother's barbed words. Those false promises.

Whatever slept beneath her feet shifted and opened its maw. Gobbled down her insubstantial offering and watched as Mara trudged back to that shitty house with the overgrown yard and nicotine-stained walls and the never-ending bleating of the television and her mother's voice. Always her mother's voice gobbling up the silence she so desperately wanted.

"I told you I needed you to watch Bethie." Her mother exhaled a stream of smoke as she squinted at Mara. "I got to go to the store."

"So take her with you," Mara said, barely a stream of breath, barely a sound, but still her mother heard, her hand darting out so quickly Mara only had time to blink before the slap landed across her cheek.

"Who you think puts those clothes on your back? I'm out there working myself to death day and night, and you sit up here like a damn princess, always running outside to wherever the hell it is you go to do nothing. Watch her," she said and slung her pocketbook over her shoulder.

Outside, their car rattled to life, gravel crunching under the tires, and Bethie toddled over to Mara, her hair a carroty tangle, her face sticky with apple juice and dirt.

"Let's get you cleaned up," she said, lifting Bethie in her arms as the television blared that stupid fucking purple dinosaur singing about happy families or some shit. She snorted and turned it off instead of driving her fist through the glass.

Bethie whined as Mara passed a damp washcloth over her face, and then fully screamed, her face going red when Mara tried to comb her hair.

"Fine," she said, setting Bethie back on the floor, where she immediately found something to shove in her mouth. When Mara tried to fish it out, Bethie bit down. Mara swore as she rubbed at the imprint of Bethie's four tiny milk teeth and then closed her eyes and told herself she loved her sister. Even with the dream she couldn't stop having. Even with the sensation of dirt still on her skin as she scooped handful after handful over her mother and Bethie's still, pale faces.

There were dishes in the sink. Crusted plates, smudged glasses, a mug with a cigarette butt floating in the coffee her mother hadn't finished that morning. She knew that later her mother would yell at her for not cleaning the kitchen. It was her responsibility. The only thing she asked Mara to do, for fuck's sake.

Bethie clawed at her legs as Mara washed the dishes, and she gazed out the window, her vision blurring. She drifted, verdant smears transforming into dark earth, until Bethie's voice was far away, and the water flowing over her hands felt cold as if it flowed from some subterranean place rather than from the rusted tap. Outside, the trees bent toward her, the branches reaching as if they could pierce through the walls like paper and reach into the thin shell of her chest and draw out her heart. She leaned forward, her breath fogging the glass, her body aching with the need to offer herself to this thing that called to her, and there, amid the shadows, she imagined she saw a hand emerge from the earth.

Behind her, there was a sudden crash, and she whirled, the vision broken as Bethie let out a wail. She'd hauled herself onto one of the kitchen chairs and fallen.

"Where does it hurt?" Mara said, her fingers frantically poking and prodding at the soft bits of Bethie's body that could be so easily broken. The girl offered up her left arm, her sobs hitching as Mara examined it.

"You're fine, baby. I think it scared you more than anything else." She hoisted Bethie onto her hip, and the girl immediately nestled into her. She carried her to the couch, Mara humming as she ran a hand over that tangle of hair until Bethie's breathing grew deeper, her arms going slack as she fell asleep.

Mara eased her onto the couch, surrounding her with cushions so she wouldn't fall off the edge.

Later, when Bethie woke, Mara fed her, let herself be led around the house by a finger as Bethie pointed out the small things that made up their world. *Bed. Clock. Stove. TV.* Round and round they went until the afternoon went golden, the sunlight streaking through the windows and turning Bethie's hair into flame.

And then night fell, and she curled herself into Bethie, sharing her tiny bed rather than risk waking Bethie by going to her own, and tried not to listen as her mother's car finally pulled into the driveway, the door slamming open as her mother tumbled inside.

"Shit!" Her mother's voice was slurred, and Mara squeezed her eyes closed. At least she was alone. Most nights there was another voice—yet another man her mother had found at the bar.

Too many times, Mara had woken to heavy breathing and the fecund scent of sex, the sensation of someone sitting on the end of her mattress. She'd keep her eyes squeezed closed, praying he wouldn't touch her, that he wouldn't force her body still with his own, that he wouldn't go to Bethie's bed instead.

I want her to hurt.

Outside, in the earth, something stirred.

At sixteen, Mara fell in love. She met Ryan at the Quickie Lube while she was waiting for her mother to get her oil changed. His hands were stained and callused, but they looked gentle. He'd smiled at her, a chip missing from his right incisor, and her heart had ached with the effort of looking at him.

She'd buried so many parts of herself underground. Three years of holes filled with her rage and desperation, with her wish that she'd come home and her mother would be someone else. Every one of her mother's indiscretions whispered into the dirt and filled with whatever carcass or bone she could find. Worms. Birds. Deer. To speak death into the ground required an offering—a reclamation of what death had already taken. There were so many places where her hands had torn at the soil, hoping for an end. But now there was Ryan and looking at him felt like finding something precious amid the dead leaves and dirt.

It didn't matter that he was twenty, and she was still in high school. That she'd been fired from the two jobs she'd managed to land because her mother had stuck her with Bethie, promising she'd be home in time for Mara's shift, only to appear hours later, drunk and angry, and there were only so many times a person could be understanding. But it didn't matter anymore. She could drop out, get her Good Enough Degree, apply to beauty school, and they'd get married and live somewhere that wasn't where they were from.

For a long time after she met him, she was able to put her mother into a faraway place that couldn't touch her. She didn't go to the woods, didn't press her lips to the earth as her anger poured out of her, a curse wrapped in soil. Her body was fire and water, air and sky. It did not need earth and the dead things gone to ground. Not anymore.

She didn't invite him out to the house. Didn't want to risk her mother coming home, her smile gone predatory as she took in Ryan's broad chest, the dark hair curling at his neck.

Instead, there were stolen afternoons in the bed of his truck, the oil on his hands marking her hips, her arms, her neck, but it was never enough. His was a feather touch when she wanted teeth and claws.

Two weeks after their first time, she put his hands around her throat and leaned into him, breathed into the cup of his ear. "I want it to hurt," she said, and he froze, his hands dropping as he blinked at her.

"The fuck?"

She lifted herself off him and tugged her skirt down, her cheeks heating. As if he hadn't already seen every part of her. As if she hadn't placed herself before him like an offering. A thing to be devoured.

"Sorry," she whispered. He stared into the distance, and she watched him, wishing she could crack open his skull, turn the slick parts of him over in her hands until she understood why he didn't want her in that way. Why she wasn't good enough.

"I ain't into that weird shit, if that's what you want." She didn't respond, and he slid away from her. "You should get on home now."

He left her sitting in the truck bed, her knees tucked under her chin, and when she didn't follow, he started the truck up anyway and drove her back to the house where her mother waited.

"Mara," he said when he pulled up to the house, but she didn't respond and tumbled out of the truck, her vision already blurred with the tears she refused to let fall.

"Aw, fuck this," he said, and he revved the engine, the gravel scattering as he threw the truck into reverse. Mara didn't look back and let herself inside.

Her mother and Bethie were sitting in front of the TV, their gazes vacant.

"You keep runnin' around like a whore, and you'll end up just like your mama," she said and then bared her teeth at the tears Mara couldn't blink away. "Or maybe he couldn't get it up. God knows I could teach that boy a thing or two."

"Fuck you."

Her mother cackled. "Looks like I'm the only one gettin' fucked round here."

Mara spun back to the door, her knee catching against the frame before she fell through it, her hands scraping against the gravel as small dots of blood appeared on her palms. Her breath caught painfully in her lungs, but she pushed herself upright and ran and ran until the fire in her chest felt as if it would consume her.

Once she could no longer see the house, she slowed, the trees a blurred canopy above her. She imagined the sky beyond as a foreign, unseeable blank. That whatever existed there had turned its eyes away, and she knelt, her palms stinging as she drew up handful after handful of soil.

It was like filling her lungs with breath after centuries. Like sun after so long in the dark. The scrapes on her hands opened further, and her words came choking out of her, a long, garbled string of regret and shame and the anger she'd buried under what she'd thought was love.

Her slumbering creation woke, tasted the blood Mara did not realize was a prayer. A seed planted deep. If Mara had dug further, she would have seen the faint gleam of teeth—a mouth widening in hunger, in a smile. It had waited so long for her to open herself fully, for her offering to be of her own body, her own blood.

"Please. Both of them," she said, and it was enough. The earth fed on her, knew the violence wrapped in her skin. There was no need for anything else. Her body. Her blood. An unholy Eucharist spoken into the land Eve had liberated from the impossible good.

Beneath her, the earth trembled, and she pressed her body to it, writhing as her hands did what Ryan would not, the skin on her throat parting beneath her nails as she gasped, her mouth coated in grit as she screamed and screamed and screamed.

The house was silent when she returned. No pale blue flicker from the television. No light in the windows.

She drifted inside. Bethie was already asleep, her mouth open slightly, the thin blanket crumpled at her feet. Mara passed a hand over her sister's face, marking her with an earth-dark smear.

"Not her," she said.

She lay atop her own bed, not bothering to take off her dirt-smeared clothes, and let herself drift into sleep. She dreamed of blood. Of bone. It was beautiful.

When she woke, it was still dark, but the air had gone warm and damp. As if the door had been left open, and the night had crept inside. In the hallway, something drew a single breath.

She would keep still. Would let it pass over them. But she would watch. Her eyes strained with the effort of looking through the dark, every part of her attuned to what she'd made. What she'd commanded.

The click of a door opening, and *keep still.* Her eyes watered, but she did not blink, and then a single footstep echoed through the house. Another. Beyond the doorway, the darkness seemed to gather, and she stared into it. Stared as a form moved into view and then paused, the head turning, and it would *see* her watching. Her heart stuttered, the blood surging to her face, her neck, as those eyes took her in, and then turned away.

Her breath streamed out of her. Her mother. It had only been her mother. Mara could make out the faded robe she always wore, the way her shoulders curved, the shadow of her hair tumbling down her back.

She curled her fingers against the damp of her palms and let herself blink. Only a second. Her mother was still in the doorway, already moving past to go take a piss or smoke a cigarette, her back the only thing still visible, when there was another movement. Another body.

Mara's skin went cold. It was her mother. *Another* mother. Something wearing her mother's same robe. Something wearing an approximation of her mother's body. A doppelgänger made imperfectly. The head sat slightly too low on the shoulders. One arm grew too long, the fingertips sweeping the floor as it walked—the gait too oiled, too smooth to be human. The eyes were a rind of white on a face that had no mouth, only a row of sharpened teeth. It smiled at her, this thing she'd made of earth and hate and lack and want.

From her bed, Mara smiled back. Then she rose and followed them into the kitchen.

Her mother did not scream when the second mother peeled back her skin. She only stared at Mara, her mouth opening and closing as if she could somehow finally speak into life the remorse she'd never had, and then the second mother slipped inside her, sighing as this new skin settled over her. She reached for Mara, beckoned to her new daughter, and together, they lapped at the spilled blood from that false mother, and it burned, it *burned*, but it was sacrament, and outside, the sun rose for what Mara hoped was the very last time. It was more lovely to move through the dark, through the earth that wrapped over you and held you like a womb.

"Darling girl," the new mother said, and pressed a bloodied hand to Mara's cheek. "You called for me, and I came. To make them hurt. To take their place."

Mara sat still as the new mother licked her clean.

"Mama."

"I won't leave you. Never again."

They buried what remained of the false mother deep. Sacrilege to do anything other than feed her to the earth she'd spent so long defiling. There would be no rebirth from the ash of what they'd scourged.

Hand in hand, they walked back to the house where Bethie still slept, her damp hair spread over the pillow. There would be a new home under the earth for them all, a crown of bones placed on her head, but there were still things to finish. Promises to keep. If Mara had learned anything at all from her false mother, it was the importance of keeping a promise.

They made breakfast with what there was. Stale cereal. Milk mixed with water so they could each have a small bowl. Bethie watched them, her small hands fisted on the table.

"TV," she said and pushed the bowl away. Milk and water sloshed, and the new mother tutted as she sopped it up with a paper towel.

"Not today," the new mother said, and Bethie's eyes narrowed. This was not her mother. Her mother did not sit at the table, did not have breakfast. Only coffee and a cigarette as she flicked on the television for Bethie, who could pour her own cereal.

"TV," she said again, her voice pitching higher, and the new mother leaned across the table and grasped Bethie's lips between her fingers and squeezed. The girl's eyes went large and damp at the corners, her chest hitching. Mara shifted toward them. Licked her lips.

"Mama loves you, darling." Bethie whimpered as the fingers pinched tighter. "Someone should have cared for you. I will care for you now, yes?"

Bethie nodded, and the new mother released her and traced a crimson-stained finger over her lips. The pink tip of Bethie's tongue darted out and lapped at the blood the new mother had given her. "Sweet girl. My two sweet girls," she said.

"Mara and I have a last thing to do, and then we can all be together. I promise." The new mother cupped Bethie's cheek, and that word, that *promise*, filled Mara up until she thought she would stop breathing.

The new mother shooed Bethie outside, and then led Mara into the bathroom. With careful fingers, she washed Mara's hair and brushed it in slow, smooth strokes. She painted her lips a dark pink, trailed a line of perfume over her neck. An unspoken ritual between mother and daughter Mara would have never had. Mara did not bother to hide the tears that fell down her cheeks.

"They should have seen you. That boy. Your mother. How lovely you are," the new mother said, and Mara heard the teeth in her words. The blood. How Mara's body ached for it.

They drove in silence, the windows down so they might smell the earth, feel the dust on their arms, their faces, their hands twined together, the air heavy with the threat of rain.

The lot was empty as they pulled in, the engine bays abandoned in favor of the shitty television and vending machine inside the office. Mara could see Ryan alone at the desk, his feet propped up, a can of Dr Pepper beside him. She waited for the heat to surge between her legs, for her heart to expand painfully in her chest, but she was empty. She'd given all of herself for too long now. Always hoping, always longing for someone to want her for something other than what she could give them. Wishing that even in the giving, they would want what it was she'd offered.

"But he didn't," the new mother said, her eyes the color of pastures, of leaves in the height of summer, of moss as she looked inside Mara and *saw*. All the things she'd been denied.

"No. He didn't," Mara said.

"You opened yourself. Spoke what you wanted into the earth, and I came for you. He won't dismiss you again," the new mother said.

Ryan barely looked up when they entered. "Help you?" he asked.

"I'm sorry. I shouldn't have . . ." Mara trailed off as he snapped his gaze to her, taking in the lipstick, the dress that was too short, too tight. His Adam's apple bobbed as he swallowed, and she pictured ripping it from his throat with her teeth. She bit down on her tongue so she would not laugh.

"You look nice," he said, and she smiled, perfectly contrite.

She glanced over her shoulder, and the new mother stepped forward. "This is my mama. I wanted you to meet her."

"A pleasure," she said and trailed a finger over her throat, her collarbone. Ryan's gaze followed the movement. "You were right about him, Mara. So handsome." Her painted mouth stretched into a smile—a bloodied streak of skin against white teeth—as she reached out a hand.

He stood then, his hands brushing through his hair, against the permanent stains on his shirt as if he could wipe away how small he was. How insignificant. He took the new mother's hand and lifted it to his lips.

"And a gentleman," she cooed and took a step closer. The snake in the garden. Temptation wrapped in earth and flesh. She cupped his flushed cheek and leaned into him. "We were thinking . . ." She scratched a fingernail down his neck. "That maybe we could show you what it feels like to be *bad*."

Already, he was fumbling with the buttons on his shirt; already, he was hard. Mara sneered as she took her place beside the new mother, her hand winding through his hair as she tugged it backward to expose that pulsing vein in his throat.

"I should lock the door," he said.

"What would be the fun in that?" Mara said, her tongue already painted in the salt of him.

"Keep still," the new mother hissed. He let out a nervous laugh as her fingers reached into his mouth, her knuckles scraping past his teeth.

"You don't want it to *hurt*, do you?" Mara said, and then he was gagging, his eyes going wide as he tried to pull away.

"Mmm. What will you taste like when we pull you open?" the new mother said. He clawed at her arms, but she only reached deeper into the core of him. The ruined shell of his body arched, a thin scream working up and out of him.

Beside them, Mara waited. A good, dutiful daughter. She hoped he would taste of rain. Of earth. Of the nocturnal places where her new mother had slept before Mara had spoken her into life.

It was a relief when he finally went quiet, when his body parted beneath their hands, those soft, animal parts of him laid bare.

Her mother placed small pieces on Mara's tongue; fed her as the false mother had never done. In the corners, flies droned, not daring to approach the blood smeared on the linoleum. It was not meant for them. Not yet.

They left him on the floor—a carrion offering. They went back to Bethie, fed her with the velvet of their mouths. Maiden, mother, and crone painted in blood and moonlight as they walked together into the forest.

"Look," the new mother said as the earth opened itself for them, as it reached to reclaim what it had lost.

Mara stepped down, Bethie's hand closed in her own.

"It won't hurt," she said. "It won't."

BEAUTIFUL DREAMER

by Jeffrey Ford

There was a knock at the door. It was my neighbor, Hank, the farmer. He owned and worked all the fields on the other side of the road as well as the ones around our property and then off into the distance for a few miles. He stood there, a little slouched, wearing his usual sleepy expression. In one hand he had a semi-automatic rifle with a scope, maybe an AR-15, and in the other hand some kind of revolver.

I said, "I don't care what you do, I'm not voting for Trump."

"East Coast liberal," he murmured.

I stepped aside and he came into our kitchen. He laid the guns on the counter, and I asked him if he wanted a beer. It was autumn, past harvest, but we went out on the porch and sat in the two chairs on the eastern side of the house. The wind usually blew from the northwest. It was cold and the trees were changing—orange leaves on the oaks out on the property line.

He lit a cigarette and said, "I'm lending you that .38. And you need to listen to the reason why."

"What's the rifle for?" I said.

"It'll all be clear in a minute." He flicked his cig and launched into it. "My cousin, Tommy, you met him, the cop?"

I nodded.

"Tommy told me there was an explosion at Ballet Corp three days ago. You know the place? Right?"

I nodded. "Underground facility where they make the weaponized anthrax?"

"Yeah, and from what I've heard, a heck of a lot more," he said.

"When I pass it, I see a guard gate and then that one poopy little whitewashed building in the distance."

"That's just the entrance. The facility is only fifty yards beneath the soy and corn and supposedly goes on for miles in every direction. Anyway, Tommy told me that Avrel Hughes, who has a farm just a mile or so out of town, was in the middle of one of his fields Tuesday evening, and not but one hundred yards from him, the dirt exploded. He said the impact nearly knocked him on his ass, and it rained clods of earth for a quarter-mile radius. A crater was left by the blast, smoke coming out, a halo of flames. Avrel was still off kilter from the bang when he saw some kind of animal crawl out of the hole and dash off due west, into the coming night."

"What kind of animal?" I asked.

Hank glanced out to the end of the driveway. "Well, old man Hughes is getting on, so I don't know how much credit we can give him, but he said the thing looked like an albino hyena, a muscular animal with the strangest head of long platinum-blond hair. He told Tommy, the thing's face had wicked racks of sharp canines, but at the same time, looked—he swore to this—like the guy who used to run the post office a couple years back."

"I remember that guy," I said. "Whatever happened to him?"

"Nobody knows."

"So I'm guessing, whatever crawled out of the hell of Ballet Corp is still on the loose and that's why you're carrying the rifle."

"Correct. You should carry that .38 everywhere you go until they catch this thing or kill it. Tell Lynn. Don't let her go out without you."

"I should just give her the fucking gun," I said. "She's more likely to use it and hit something other than herself. Guns make me nervous."

"Your wife is not gonna carry a gun. You know that. You need to man up," said Hank. "Tommy tells me a cow, two pet dogs —big ones, a shepherd and a pit bull—an old lady who lived alone in a tiny place at the end of a mile-long dirt driveway, and a kid in his backyard have all been attacked by this thing and partially devoured. They supposedly saved the kid but had to amputate both legs at the hip. Ballet Corp is paying off people to the tune of millions to keep them quiet, and everybody on the police force has been given the order to track the creature down. Meanwhile, they're not telling any of us civilians squat and the thing is still out there, maybe sneaking right up below this porch right now. What would you do if next time you go to your freezer in the garage to get a pizza for a late dinner and the blond hyena pops out of the shadows? What would you do?"

"Probably crap my pants."

"That ain't gonna get 'er done."

"What the hell is up with an albino hyena? Who knew they were messing with animals down there? That's heavy Dr. Moreau shit. You sure this isn't the latest QAnon conspiracy? All it's missing is space lasers and pedophiles."

"They're making America great again," said Hank and dashed off the rest of his beer.

"Jesus."

"Tommy said he wouldn't put much stock in Avrel's description. From the couple of other reported sightings, he thought it sounded more like some kind of big cat."

"I'll keep an eye out," I said. "But how do you shoot the gun?"

"It's a Colt Cobra double-action .38 Special. Point it and pull the trigger. It'll give you somewhat of a kick so be ready for that, but there isn't a hell of a lot more to it. You've got six bullets." He reached into his pocket and brought out a fistful of bullets and dropped them on the porch table. "Here's six more."

"You better show me how to load it and so forth," I said. He went and got the guns and brought them back outside.

When Lynn got home, I was waiting for her on the porch, gun in hand. I got up and took the three steps down to the path that led to the driveway and scanned in all directions looking for the ridiculous creature described by the old farmer who lived near town. It was already dark, but there was a good piece of moon, and I could actually see some way out into the fields.

She got out of the car, and the dogs mobbed her. I called in a whisper, "Hurry up."

"Why are we whispering?" she asked and then saw the gun in my hand. She stopped in her tracks. "Is that a real gun? What are you doing with that?"

"You're never gonna believe me," I said.

I ushered her up the steps and inside, and took one long look around at the field off that side of the porch before calling the dogs. When they slid in around me, I slammed the door and locked it. I gave Lynn a bowl of the rice and beans I'd made her, grabbed her a bag of corn chips out of the closet, and poured her a glass of wine. We sat at the kitchen table, the gun between us.

"Where'd you get it?" she asked. "For a split second I thought you'd gone nuts and were ready to shoot me."

I told her everything Hank had told me. She listened and punctuated my exegesis with brief interjections—"Ridiculous," "What the shit?," "Come on . . ." When I was finished, I asked her if she wanted to learn how to shoot it and reload it.

"I'm against guns," she said.

"Me too, but I'm also against being partially devoured."

"It's so far-fetched."

"You realize Ballet Corp isn't making doilies down there. We know they're in the business of bioweapons. Say we don't go with the albino hyena in a Debbie Harry wig theory, but just that it's some big cat as Tommy said, something they were doing experiments on."

"I hate stupid conspiracies," she said.

"People have been killed by this thing."

Finally, with my haranguing, Lynn gave in and let me walk her to her car when she went to work and came home. On Saturday, we took target practice in the backyard. We each got three shots, seriously depleting our bullet stores. The idea was to stand at the base of an old pear tree fifty feet from the garden where the past summer's scarecrow still stood. Lynn, being a nurse, had made it in the image of Florence Nightingale, her hero. She didn't mind if we wrecked it as she made a new scarecrow each year. I stood with the gun stretched as far from me as possible. After I aimed, I closed my eyes before firing. Lynn held it with two hands like the cops on TV. Both of our first shots missed completely, as did my second. On her second, she blasted the playground ball with the face painted on it. My third put another hole in Florence's head. Lynn's third severed the central stick and sent Our Lady of Grace of the Order of St. John toppling onto the frozen mud.

"Baby, you're dangerous," I told her.

And then early Sunday morning, Lynn got a call from Hank's wife, Barbara. It was about the retired cop who used to plow the snow from everybody's driveway all the way up the road to the Baptist church. He kept a horse in a stall in his barn. The Ballet Corp creature got into the stall and was literally tearing up and eating the horse. I can't remember what the guy's name was. He was a nice guy. He heard the commotion and went out there with his shotgun. The thing bit through his neck, nearly severing the head, and he never got a shot off. Splattered blood everywhere.

I drove the fifteen miles to town to see if I could find a newspaper carrying the story. There was absolutely zero online about any of the recent deaths. It was impossible for me to believe that none of this was getting out. We were in the sticks, but not like we were on a desert island. When I passed the church, the sign out near the road read, SATAN SUBTRACTS AND DIVIDES. The words made me think of William Blake's Urizen, plumbing and dividing. I knew it had nothing to do with the sign, but that's all I could muster in my imagination. First time I met Hank, I told him I was a writer, and he said, "I don't read." I thought he was kidding but apparently, he wasn't.

In the years I'd lived in Ohio, after moving from Jersey, I never really got the humor, certainly not the politics. All my neighbors had Trump signs on their lawns during the 2020 election, even the lesbian couple a few houses down the road. All of them owned an arsenal of guns. Nobody brought up politics at any of the barbecues we were invited to. Once I asked Hank as he passed my porch on the way back home from his field, "How could you vote for Trump?"

"I couldn't vote for Clinton. Don't trust her. I did, though, vote for Obama," he said. None of it made much sense. They all knew we were lefties, but Hank plowed our big garden every spring and put in a wellhead for us with his cousin. The other guy, who got mauled by the creature, did the driveway when it snowed. A young fellow stopped by with a chainsaw when a tree fell in a storm across our driveway. Being fresh from Jersey I tried to pay him, but he said he couldn't take any money. I wondered for weeks what his angle was. An old woman up the road brought us pies and cookies at Christmas. They waved when they drove by. What made less sense than all of this was that upon reaching town and buying the two local papers, there wasn't a shred of news about the Ballet Beast in either one.

That night the cops came by. One of them was Hank's cousin, Tommy. First he told us the thing attacked a moving car on Modan Pike, punched in the back window and tore a child out of its car seat. The creature took off with the little boy under its arm like a rolled-up newspaper. I tried to picture how some kind of panther could carry a kid under its arm. And right after that Tommy's partner pulled me aside and told me there was some money in it if I was the one to kill it.

"What kind of money?"

"A year's worth of money," he said and nodded.

The money sounded like a bullshit story. On their way out the door, both of them said, "Stay strong."

"We gotta watch out for ourselves," I said to Lynn once she closed the door behind them.

Maybe 3:00 A.M., I got up for my fourth piss of the night. After I went and I'd turned the bathroom light out, I was on my way back through the dark to bed. I just happened to glance at the windows looking north through barren branches, and I saw something glowing a quarter mile out in the cut autumn field. I gave it my full attention and saw that it was a pickup truck with its lights on. A moment passed in which I focused on the distant headlights, and then it became clear to me, from beneath the sounds of the wind, the distant blare of a car horn. After a few minutes, Lynn was next to me.

"Somebody's stuck out there. Can you hear the horn?"

She cocked her head and a moment later nodded. "They must be in trouble. We have to do something."

"Like what?"

"Like go out there and see what's going on."

"You gotta be joking . . ."

"They're in trouble. They need help. I'll take the first aid kit, you take the gun."

"Fuck this," I said and put on my sweatpants. "I'm not running unless I have to. Why don't we take the car?"

"I'm not driving either of our cars out in that lumpy, muddy field. They're in bad enough shape as it is."

We put on our autumn jackets and I wore my Cleveland Browns cap, Lynn her knitted hat with earflaps and two long ties that looked like it came from the Andes. She wore mittens, but I only had on a right-handed glove since I was carrying the gun. It felt only slightly less impossible against my bare skin. The creature could have popped out of anywhere, and I was shivering, trying to breathe deeply, stay steady.

Finn, the black Lab, insisted on escorting Lynn. We tried to put him back in the house, but he wasn't having any of it. Finally, I just said, "Fuck it, let him come." The old pit made no such move. She had a bad back leg and would never be able to run away if the shit hit the fan. It was freezing and the dead leaves rattled in a persistent wind. We carried flashlights against the dark. There weren't even any stars.

By the time we hit the boundary between our place and the fields, the horn from the truck in the distance sputtered and died out. The headlights still shone. We crossed over and headed for them.

"What are these people doing out in Hank's field?" I said.

"Maybe they were hunting the Ballet Beast. It's been sighted around here quite a bit lately."

"Looking for a year's worth of money. The Ballet Beast, I like it."

Lynn was walking fast, and I was out of breath. At the halfway point I told her to chill. "You gotta give me a breather. I don't want to have to get saved when I'm saving somebody. Where would we be then?"

"You got a minute."

I caught my breath and turned in circles, making sure the thing wasn't sneaking up on us. That minute went fast, and before I knew it we were outside the truck. The flashlights glared on the windshield and side windows, and we couldn't really see what was leaning against the wheel.

"There's somebody dead in there I bet."

"Cover me," said Lynn and she went to the driver's door. I stood behind her with the gun pointed at her back. As she touched the door handle, I said, "Wait. If something comes out of there snapping and clawing, I'm gonna shoot you. Move to the side and open the door so you're behind it."

She went right to it, and I gasped. The truck door yawned open on shrieking hinges and the beam of my light hit a seated massacre. Blood and organs and a headless corpse. The other side window had been smashed out and that's how the Beast got in and out. There was another corpse beside the one at the wheel—as far as I could make out, also headless and ripped open from stem to stern.

"I think I'm gonna puke," I said.

Lynn reached in to check for any signs of life I might have missed. "They must have been hunting it," she called over her shoulder. "There's a pile of guns in here along with the guts. Fuckin' grim."

"Call the cops."

She nodded and took out her phone. I hoped they wouldn't expect us to stay by the truck while they got there. The Ballet Beast could be just far enough away to be cloaked by night, waiting to pounce. The gun wobbled in my grip. I wanted to split so badly, my legs moved around with a strange energy, and I probably looked to the creature watching from the dark like I was tap-dancing.

Lynn hung up and told me, "They want us to stay."

"Fuck that," I said. "Come on. That's not worth a year's worth of money. Let's get outta here."

That's when Finn, who I'd completely forgotten about, growled and the growl slid into barking. "Shit," I said, looked right and then left. I looked down at the dog and he was looking up. I followed his gaze with the flashlight in my gloved hand and saw the thing, in midair, leaping high over the truck. On the descent, I briefly made out a giant red cat head, whiskers that glowed in the dark, and sharp teeth galore. Half a heartbeat later it hit me with both front paws, and I went backward onto the ground. My hat flew off. In the runaway train of my thoughts, I pictured how pathetic it would be if I was discovered, a mangled pile with a Cleveland Browns hat lying next to it. Worse yet, when I hit the ground, my elbow took a banging, and the gun flew out of my grip.

I went into shock when I saw the giant claws and smelled the thing's battlefield breath. The Ballet Beast's eyes were a pure, deep yellow. No irises, no pupils, just expressionless yellow marbles. It fell on me like a faithless lover. As it descended toward my neck something suddenly burst out from within its forehead. Its blood splattered across my face. Before, I'd missed it, but now I definitely heard two gunshots. The way the creature cried out, like a child falling from a tall building, made me believe it'd been hit by both. Finn leaped into the fray, and knocked the beast off me. It growled and hissed at the dog, but couldn't move.

A hand came down and helped me to my feet. Lynn held a huge handgun, covered in blood.

"I saw it coming through the broken window on the passenger side. It took two steps out of the dark and leaped way up, gracefully and totally silent. It was clear the thing was hunting you. I dug through the guts in the front seat and came out with this cannon."

"I think it's a .357 Magnum," I said.

"It almost knocked me over, even holding it with two hands. Was kind of surprised I hit with all three shots."

I put my arms around her. Finn came over to us and jumped up, wanting to get in on the hug. We went back to make sure the beast was dead and found it shivering and rolling back and forth. I gathered up my .38 and put one in its head. The blood splattered across the long blond hair, and that did the job. Its eyes went immediately from yellow to silver like liquid mercury and leaked down its snout. Lynn studied every inch of it with her flashlight. I couldn't be sure, but I think she was sorry she had to shoot it.

"Looks like a really buff mountain lion," I said.

"A psychedelic buff mountain lion."

"I'll give you that."

We looked away from it and saw the cops coming across the field from the direction of town. There were two cars.

Hank's cousin wasn't in one of those cars. In fact there were no local cops among them. There were two guys with BALLET CORP SECURITY on the backs of their jackets and two more in the second car in plain clothes, like they might have been FBI. The two security guys lifted the big cat off the ground, one at the head, one at the haunches, and laid it in their trunk.

Meanwhile one of the agents—if that's what they were—in plain clothes asked us if we knew the people in the truck. We didn't. I wondered aloud if we got the year's worth of money for killing the cat. The other agent in a suit and trench coat came over and stood with us. He was older; a ring of gray hair around an otherwise bald head. "I'm Agent Steit," he said. "You're going to have to keep this quiet. Your neighbors don't need to know."

"What about the money? That's what the cops told me. We get a year's worth of money if we bring it down."

"You get the year's worth of money, if you keep this quiet for ten years."

"What kind of bullshit is that?" said Lynn.

"OK, ma'am. I'm going to have Agent Breadlo take you back to your place. And we're conscripting your husband. The work's not done yet on this."

"What do you mean, you're conscripting my husband?"

"The power vested in me by the federal government allows me to conscript citizens. I wouldn't do it if we didn't need the help."

"It's OK," I said. "I'll just go and help these guys out. You take the ride back."

"I'll walk," she said.

"I wouldn't," he said. "This thing's not over yet."

"There's another cat out there?" I asked.

"Not quite."

"What is it then?" she said.

"That's classified, but it would pay for you to take the ride."

"I don't like it. I don't like you taking him," she said, pointing to me.

"Would you like it better if we threw him in jail for a few months?"

"Take the ride," I told her. She came to me and we kissed as Agent Breadlo pulled up. She got into the back of the car that had the dead Beast in its trunk. Finn tried to jump in with her, but one of the Ballet Corp Security guards blocked him and quickly closed the door. Finn growled and I called him off.

"We'll need the dog," said Steit. "Do you have a gun?"

"I have a .38 with five bullets."

"Better than nothing."

He led me to the remaining car. I got in the back and called to Finn to join me. He leaped in and I moved over to the middle. Steit got in the other door and sat next to me. The Ballet Security guys were in the front.

"What can't the FBI do that they need me for?" I asked as the car began slowly moving out further into the field.

"Who said I'm FBI?" said Steit.

"Who are you?"

"We all work for Ballet Corp. The FBI is the last people we want to know about this. We need you to draw the creature out into the open, so we can tranquilize it."

As I reached for the door handle, I heard the lock engage and eased back into my seat. I could try to pull the gun and shoot my way out, but when I glanced at Finn to see if he was OK, I thought I saw him shake his head as if telling me, "Don't try it."

"I can at least tell you what we're up against," said Steit. "It's called the Beautiful Dreamer. The scientist who bioengineered it out of an albino hyena was unhinged, to say the least, but my bosses saw that he was doing things that had not been done before with animal genetic manipulation . . ."

"Wait. Does it actually have blond hair?"

"Yes," said Steit, nodding and laughing.

The guy driving looked back over his shoulder and said, "It's really fucked up."

"Vicious?" I asked.

"Well," said the guy in the passenger seat, "it ate the scientist who made it."

"You see. It has a very remarkable ability in addition to all its mismatched parts. It exudes pheromones that put human beings into a waking dream state. When the dreamer gets carried away, they are open to attack. They continue to dream while being eaten," said Steit.

"Can I just say how irresponsible and outrageously heinous this whole thing is."

"Say whatever you want," said Steit. "You'll be whistling out the hole in the top of your neck in a couple of minutes. It likes to collect heads. I'll tell you one more thing about it. When you come upon it sleeping on the ground and it has its back to you, it looks for all the world like a naked woman with long blond hair, and it hums in the sound of a human voice."

I looked out through the windshield and could see that the sky was lightening in the east. Ahead of us loomed the seven-acre oasis of white oak and hickory that lay in the middle of Hank's harvested field. I'd asked him what those thickets of trees were for back in the first year we moved in. You'd see them in the middle of certain farm fields and not in others. He'd told me, "You see them in the fields of the old farms. Today, they just clear-cut everything. I don't know why the old-timers did that, but you can bet there's a reason for it."

The car came to a halt at the edge of the island of old trees. They were tall, and even with the sun breaking through on the horizon, they were gloomy as hell. "Get out," said Steit. The door unlocked. I opened it and Finn and I exited the vehicle.

"Does it hide here during the day?" I asked.

"We think so," said one of the Ballet Security guys. He was on his way to the trunk, which he popped open. Inside were all manner of weapons.

"Get two tranq guns," said Steit. "I'll carry the M249 in case killing is in order for either predator or prey."

The black machine gun they handed him looked like it could really rip shit up. "What do you mean, prey? Do I get one?" I asked.

All three of them laughed. I pulled out my .38. They pointed at it and laughed harder. "You'll be dead before you can ever pull the trigger on that. Get moving," said Steit and pointed the dangerous-looking weapon at me. I called to Finn and he followed me. As we passed into the woods, Breadlo showed up and ran to catch us. I looked back and he was also carrying one of the tranq rifles.

In among the trees, it was still somewhat dark, save for the place where the beam from the rising sun passed through like a thin, glowing sword. I was trembling, on the verge of tears, wondering if Lynn really did get back to the house all right. Jittery and starting at every snap of a twig, I calculated if it was possible for me to spin around on them and take them out like Wild Bill Hickok, fanning the trigger and diving for cover. At least I realized that the pheromones hadn't begun working on me yet, 'cause the whole scenario I'd just concocted seemed ridiculous even to me. Instead, I walked slowly ahead, in under the ancient towering oaks, like the columns of an enormous church. They'd been there since at least the inception of the farm, one hundred–plus years earlier. Two deer leaped up and darted deeper into the oasis. A wind had snuck in to the heart of the thicket and dead leaves fell all around me. Finn strode a few paces ahead, afraid of nothing.

A gunshot sounded and I leapt in the air and spun around. Breadlo, who had been bringing up the rear, had dropped his tranq rifle and had a 9-millimeter in his hand. The Beautiful Dreamer had its back to us, long blond hair shimmering in the little morning light there was, white body like a nude artist's model from behind. It didn't stand like a hyena on its hind legs but like a human. It made ferocious noises and the blood sprayed away in a shower.

Steit yelled, "Hit it," and the two Ballet Security guards aimed and fired hypos of tranquilizer. As the darts flew toward their target, the Dreamer swung the lifeless body of Breadlo around and blocked them with it. The weird, pale thing screamed in victory and threw the corpse at the two guards. I took the opportunity to duck behind a fallen tree with Finn next to me, and we peered over the top.

The Beast crept toward them slowly, and I got a better look at it. There was gore in its sizable mouth, dripping down across its white chest. The guards dropped their weapons, and just then I noticed the aroma in the air—some kind of funky perfume that made me a tad woozy on the first inhalation of it. The Dreamer slowly chewed at the face of one guard while the other stared on, unable or unwilling to act. I realized in that moment, it looked more like an old wrestler with long blond locks than an animal. It did have the face of the missing postmaster. Steit yelled "Wake up" to his men, but one was already dead on the ground and the other was staring up at the autumn canopy, pointing to it and saying, "Look at the size of that angel." There was nothing there.

There was a tearing sound, a gurgle and a slurp, and the creature was eating through the abdomen of the second guard while the poor bastard continued to converse with the angel he saw. Steit took the safety off the machine gun and aimed. By the time he pulled the trigger, the thing had fallen to all fours and was charging at incredible speed, now very much like an animal. It dodged back and forth just ahead of the bullets chewing up the forest floor. Then it seemed to simply vanish. When I saw that, I got up and started running. The pheromones tried to fuck with my head but I shook them off and kept sprinting for my life. Behind me I heard Steit give up the ghost while singing opera. Finn barked and I came to, thinking I was running, but was standing still. We bolted for the edge of the oasis and the open fields. I still had my .38 in hand. I could hear the Ballet Beast gaining on me, and it felt like we were running in hip-deep water.

Any moment, I expected the thing to be on my back, biting into my neck, taking off an arm with its wicked claws. I got to the point where I didn't think I could run anymore, and then I saw the bright lights. I ran to them and broke free from the island of trees into the field. The lights were headlights from a dozen or more pickups and cars and tractors.

Standing in front of the line of vehicles were all the neighbors, each one packing heat. Hank was letting loose with the AR-15 the way he did out into the barren field on late afternoons in winter. His wife, Barbara, had a sawed-off shotgun. Jenine and Maxine, the couple from a little way up the road, had high-powered rifles. They all had on clothes with upside-down flags and thin-blue-line flags, Betsy Ross flags, enormous Q's and the roman numeral III.

I spotted Lynn there with what looked like a rocket launcher, saw her pull the trigger and watched the missile speed toward the Dreamer. The old woman who brought us pies, and the kid from across the way who cut our acres of grass, and the pastor of the Baptist church, and even the old guy who cleared snow from the driveways, all blasted the monster with everything they had. Lynn dropped the RPG tube and ran to me. All the truck and car horns started honking in victory. There were fireworks of red, white, and blue in the sky behind us. Finn was dancing in circles on two legs. Then Lynn fell into my arms, and we kissed by the dawn's early light.

BLODSUGER

by John Langan

I

The truth is, although I grew up here, I did so without knowing a lot about the history of New York State. My parents were from Scotland and while my seventh-grade history class concerned the state they had chosen to settle and raise me and my siblings in, I was less interested in the purchase of Manhattan or the construction of the Mohawk canal than I was the Battle of Bannockburn, where the Scottish king, Robert the Bruce, faced down a charge by the English knight, Henry de Bohun, and slew him with his hand axe. Single combat between armored men on horseback appealed to my younger imagination in a way that the patroon system of land ownership did not. During my teenage years, I started to pay attention to the place I was living in as a setting for the horror stories I had begun to write. In this, I was strongly influenced by my discovery of Stephen King's fiction, whose use of his home state of Maine offered a compelling example of how a writer might employ familiar places to make a story's supernatural elements more real. Reading William Faulkner's novels and stories in college deepened and extended the lessons I'd learned from King. Faulkner's concern with the continuing effects of the past—personal, family, local, national—on the present convinced me the history of my part of upstate New York was worth looking into. I was fortunate to be living in Ulster County, which has been rich with incident ever since the Esopus first called it home, and to have available to me books by several outstanding local historians: Alf Evers, Marc Fried, and Robi Josephson. I was equally lucky to encounter a number of women and men willing to share with me anecdotes of their and their families' experiences.

More of these personal stories touched on matters of the strange and even supernatural than I would have anticipated; though I ask myself why I should have been surprised. Such events are exactly what would remain lodged in one's memory, aren't they? Most of these involved brief encounters with the uncanny, some more dramatic than others. There was a city of Wiltwyck police officer who responded to a call for assistance from an address that turned out to be the graveyard surrounding the old Dutch church in the city's stockade area. Certain he'd been pranked, the officer nonetheless left his car for a quick check of the area. While walking beside a grave of such antiquity all of the identifying information had weathered from the tombstone, he heard screams coming from the ground beneath him. He dropped to his knees, pressing his ear to the soil, shouting to whoever was trapped there—a woman, it sounded like—to hang on, help was on the way. Using his bare hands, he started to scrape at the dirt. But it was packed solid and he realized he needed assistance immediately. He sat back, reaching for his radio. As he did, the screaming turned to laughing, the woman's voice deepening, spreading through the ground below him, growing louder, until it seemed to issue from the assembled graves, a rumbling laugh with nothing of mirth to it, only cruelty and mockery. His plans to call for help forgotten, the officer backpedaled out of the place as quickly as his legs would carry him. In his haste to depart the scene, he drove his cruiser onto the sidewalk and almost knocked over a mailbox. Later, he would be half-convinced he had been the victim of an elaborate prank perpetrated by his fellow officers, but no matter which of them he asked, or how many times, his colleagues denied any such plan, for so long and with such consistency he reluctantly decided they must be telling the truth. In years to come, he considered researching the history of that portion of the graveyard, only to reject the idea in favor of essentially ignoring the experience and all it might imply.

(Needless to say, after he shared his anecdote with me, at a birthday party our sons were attending for a mutual friend, I spent a long night online investigating the history of the old Dutch church and its cemetery. When the parcel of land was selected for the construction of the house of worship, I learned, there was already a grave in what was to be the northeast part of the graveyard. The plot was marked by a headstone worn blank. No one could say who was interred in the spot: according to the most elderly residents of the neighborhood, the grave had always been there, its stone always bare. The decision was made to leave the plot undisturbed and incorporate it into the graveyard. Throughout the centuries since the church's stone walls had been mortared, there had been occasional calls to exhume the grave, to attempt to solve its mystery, but those had always come to nothing. I was sufficiently intrigued by the story—or lack of one—to call the church's current minister, but she downplayed my inquiries in favor of encouraging me to attend that Sunday's services.)

II

Probably the most elaborate story I've heard was told to me over the course of two cups of fine coffee and a slice of excellent cheesecake carried all the way to Ulster County from a Manhattan bakery. I was at an annual party my younger son and I have been attending for a number of years now. Held in the early fall at a modest farm about fifteen minutes west of our house, the event brings together a wide range of people to fish at the farm's pond and/or shoot clay pigeons in one of the back fields. It's a potluck affair, the dishes served inside a former barn whose interior has been converted to a dining area, its floor swept clean, its walls and rafters strung with white Christmas lights. David and I know the family through our karate class; they first invited us to their party when they learned what an avid fisherman he is. I don't fish, nor am I much for target shooting, so I tend to pass the afternoon and evening in the dining area, in conversation. Typically, the talk begins with David, whose skill and dedication as a fisherman draw compliments and questions. *It's so nice to see a boy his age outside, instead of at a computer screen. Do you fish? Thank you,* I say. *No, he didn't learn it from me. He's pretty much self-taught.* From there, we proceed to the story of how he became interested in fishing (watching Jeremy Wade's *River Monsters* show on the Animal Planet channel) and to advice from the person seated across from me (most of it concerning the locations of spots to take David).

Occasionally, though, the discussion swerves in an unexpected direction. This was the case several parties ago, on a bright Saturday afternoon whose warmth eased the faint memory of hay from the barn's walls. David was twelve at the time. I was speaking to a woman who introduced herself as Doris when she asked David and me if we minded her sitting and eating with us. She was about a decade older than I was, so closing in on sixty, her white hair short and in fashionable disarray. Of average height, she was wearing a tweed blazer over a hunter-green turtleneck and new jeans. Her face had the deep tan of someone who spends a good deal of time outdoors in a sunny place, which in her case was Key West, where she ran a small charter boat business. "Which one of you is the fisherman?" she asked once she was seated, and after David said he was, the two of them were off on a wide-ranging exchange about favorite fish to catch and the best places to do so in the Catskills. As it turned out, Doris had grown up near Woodstock, and had had the benefit of grandparents who had taught her how to fish, and driven her to various streams and lakes throughout the area. She knew most of the places David preferred, and offered us the names of half a dozen more to try. Their talk was lively and entertaining, and I felt a strange mix of pride and sadness: the former at watching my son demonstrate the knowledge he had obtained through years of practice and research; the latter at realizing how mature he was already and anticipating the day he would no longer be a child.

At the end of their conversation, as David was preparing to return to the pond, he said, "What I really want to try is ice-fishing. There's this big lake near where we live, and when it freezes over, you see guys out on it. Some of them set up insulated tents and spend the day there. But my *dad*," he drew out the word mockingly, "won't let me."

"You're absolutely right," I said, "because who's going to have to go with you, and sit on a sheet of ice for hours in the cold? No, thank you."

The moment David mentioned ice-fishing, Doris's expression changed, all the ease and good humor suffusing it replaced by a tightening of her features into what I realized was an expression of horror. In this moment, she appeared vastly older, the ancient survivor of a terrible calamity. She recovered sufficiently to say, "Well, I'm sure there'll be time for that. To tell you the truth, though, it's not much fun, ice-fishing. You'd be better coming down to the Keys, let me take you out in the boat and try to hook a barracuda."

"That would be awesome," David said. "Can we, Dad?"

"If I write a bestseller, it'll be first on the to-do list."

"It's a deal," Doris said.

After David had taken his gear and set off for the pond, Doris said, "You have a wonderful boy."

"Thank you," I said. "My wife and I are very proud of him."

"You should be. And you're a good father, taking him all over creation so he can fish."

"Thank you. I try."

"But you're not planning to let him go ice-fishing, are you?"

"No," I said. "My wife and I are both too nervous at the thought of him on the ice, which is silly, I know, but what can you do? Maybe when he's older. In the meantime, he can use the winter to work on his fly-tying, right?"

"That's right," Doris said. "Once he's older, you still need to be careful, especially with the lakes in this area. There are . . . hidden dangers, let's say."

"Oh?"

"Yes. In fact," she added, "one of them killed my grandfather."

"I'm so sorry," I said, the explanation for the change to Doris's demeanor now clear to me.

"This was a long time ago," she said. "Nineteen sixty-eight. Before you were around, I'm guessing."

"Just by a little bit."

"I was ten. I was living with my grandparents—my mom's mother and father. Had been for about six months. Prior to that, I'd been an Army brat, moved all over the country with my folks. Then Dad was deployed to Vietnam, where he stepped on a land mine his second week in-country. Mom suffered a nervous breakdown and flew me from Texas to stay with her parents. Up to this point, I had met my maternal grandparents a handful of times, when my folks had taken me to visit them. They had a house full of dogs they claimed they couldn't leave for any length of time. This was unlike my dad's mom and stepfather, who visited every major holiday and a week in the summer, besides. I would have been delighted to go to them, but I gather Mom asked and they declined. Said they were past the child-rearing stage of life, told her to pull herself together and look after her child. It sounds harsh, I know, but attitudes about mental health were considerably less enlightened in those days. Mom expected her parents to echo her in-laws' sentiments, which was why she hadn't approached them to begin with. Instead, they said they would be happy to have me. I left Texas with two suitcases. There was a big one Mom packed with all my clothes. And there was a smaller one I packed with as many of my dolls and stuffed animals as I could jam into it. Mom put me on an airplane in Dallas and my grandparents were waiting for me at LaGuardia."

"It must have been difficult for you—the adjustment."

"You know what made everything worse? The airline lost my suitcase, the one with all my toys. We stood at the baggage carousel until the other passengers had departed. When it was clear no more luggage was going to slide down onto it, I started sobbing. I had dreaded this trip, even though I didn't want to live with my mother anymore, not really. Since Dad's death, she had been lost to me, taken away by whatever the doctor had prescribed to numb her grief. She passed her days on the couch, in front of the television, watching *General Hospital, One Life to Live,* and *Dark Shadows.* Sometimes, I could persuade her up from it to make me lunch or dinner; usually, I was left to fend for myself. My attendance at school was at best spotty. What kid wants to be at school, right? I did—or, I wanted the life I'd had when Mom was getting me out of bed each morning to make sure I didn't miss the bus. I didn't know if Grandma and Grandpa—Dad's parents—would give me that, but I thought it was a possibility. Secretly, what I hoped was that Mom would let me live with my best friend, Morgan Bowman. To the best of my knowledge, this possibility was never entertained. So off it was to New York, to stay with my *Mormor* and *Morfa.* That's Danish for Grandma and Grandpa. They were from outside Copenhagen, had immigrated here after the war. My grandmother still spoke with a heavy accent. I loved them, but I was never comfortable around them, unlike my father's parents—or Morgan and her family.

"Back to the airport. There I was, standing beside the baggage carousel with these old people I hadn't wanted to stay with in the first place, crying my eyes out. It's funny, I call them old, but they were younger than I am now. Give them credit, they knew I wasn't enthused about coming to New York. *Mormor* took me in her arms and hugged me. She was on the stout side, not much taller than I was. While she stroked my hair and murmured that it was all right, everything was going to be okay, *Morfa* spoke to a succession of airport staff in an effort to locate my missing suitcase. He wasn't too much taller than *Mormor*, his round face perpetually red, as if he'd just stepped in from the cold. By the time we left the airport, he was positively scarlet. My bag was still nowhere to be found, nor had the men he'd talked to shown enough concern about it. For the first hour of the drive to their house, he muttered to himself in Danish. I didn't speak it then, but I didn't need to: the tone of his voice let me know the kind of thing he was saying as well as if I understood his every word. Every now and again, *Mormor* would snap at him, also in Danish. I'm sure she was telling him to keep his eyes on the road.

"Not what you would call an auspicious beginning. Almost the minute we arrived at their house, I fell sick and remained in bed with a fever for the next week. Despite *Morfa* making a couple of long phone calls, my suitcase was not found. It never would be. Oh, and then there were the dogs, all seven of them."

"Seven?" I said. "I hope you were a dog person."

Doris laughed. "I was, but it was still overwhelming. They were a rambunctious crew, a pack of mutts *Mormor* had adopted one at a time. Walking them took forever. You had to be sure you took Paprika with Stone Henry and not Caesar; although Henry and Caesar were all right together and if you were feeling ambitious, could go out with Ulysses. What names, right? I can still remember them. Paprika, Stone Henry, Caesar, Ulysses, Lefty, Donner, and Odin. All males. Donner was the biggest, a shaggy dog who looked as if one of his parents had been a wolfhound. Ulysses was smallest, a mix of dachshund and maybe Chihuahua. Even on the hottest summer day, he shivered constantly, so *Mormor* dressed him in little jackets she made from *Morfa*'s old shirts. He was my grandmother's dog—they all were, really. When I came home from school, or *Morfa* from work, a couple of the dogs would wander over to sniff us. But the moment *Mormor* returned from her part-time job at the public library, all of the dogs rushed to greet her, swirling around her in a barking maelstrom. Maybe it was because she was the one who organized their meals, which was another adventure. Stone Henry's teeth were bad, so you had to soak his food first. Odin was missing his right eye, which made him defensive about the other dogs trying to sneak up on him to steal his food, so you had to feed him in one corner of the kitchen, away from the rest of them. Lefty had to have a special diet, or he would have diarrhea—and I mean explosive diarrhea. Giving him the wrong food was a mistake I made only once."

"Yikes."

"Oh, it was pretty horrifying, I can assure you. *Mormor* insisted I help clean it up. 'But it was an *accident!*' I said. 'Of course it was,' she said, but there was still a mess, and we couldn't have that, could we? Poor Lefty. For days afterward, I shot dirty looks at him.

"It was quite the adjustment. My grandparents lived in an old, slightly run-down farmhouse at one end of a long dirt driveway. I think I mentioned they were outside Woodstock, didn't I?"

I nodded. "You did."

"There were dense woods surrounding the house. Our nearest neighbor was over a mile away, an old man who had been a concert pianist until he developed rheumatoid arthritis."

"Ouch."

"Yes, it was very sad. Mr. Rivera. We didn't see very much of him. Directly behind my grandparents' house, a few hundred yards through the pine and maple, there was a large clearing at the center of which stood a grove of apple trees. There were hardly enough to call it an orchard, but during the warm weather, *Mormor* and *Morfa* walked back there to inspect the developing fruit. We had to watch for black bears, which was simultaneously terrifying and exhilarating. I would have loved to see one—from a suitable distance, of course. The closest I came was a pile of bear scat in the center of the apple trees. When fall came, we harvested the fruit, which was a lot of work, and then *Mormor* spent every minute she wasn't at the library (or dealing with the dogs) turning them into pies and jam. One of the local grocery stores sold them for her, in exchange for a percentage of the profits; though she kept a couple of pies and jars of jam for us. The apples were small, green, and tart as lemons. *Mormor* countered this with the liberal use of sugar in her recipes, which made them favorites of mine. Typical kid, right?"

"I still have a sweet tooth," I said.

"Me, too," Doris said. "When I was younger and had a metabolism like a house on fire, it wasn't a problem. Now . . ."

"I hear you," I said, slapping the gut no amount of middle punches and front kicks seemed to be able to shrink. I inclined my head at the slice of cheesecake in front of me, almost done. "And yet here I am . . ."

"Oh, you have to live a little, don't you?"

"My living a little has made a lot of me."

Doris laughed. "Well, someone went to the trouble of bringing this wonderful dessert here. You wouldn't want to hurt their feelings."

"There you go," I said, "I'm being polite."

"Exactly."

"Now, if only good manners burned calories, I'd be set."

"My grandfather—this is *Morfa*—used to have a saying about manners. 'Manners without love is hypocrisy. Love without manners is sloppiness.' I'm not sure where he got it from. At the time, it didn't occur to me to ask. He was always coming out with things like that, sentences and phrases with the sound of folk wisdom. The first six months I was at my grandparents', I heard a lot of them. Except for work, *Morfa* took me with him wherever he went. This was how I learned to fish. He was an avid outdoorsman: fishing, hiking, bird-watching, you name it. He was also a good teacher. When she was my age, he'd taught my mother how to fish. I guess she lost interest as she grew older— didn't pass the knowledge on to me, anyway. At first, I was pretty dubious, but the moment—the *instant*—the first fish took my bait, that was it for me."

"David was the same. I wasn't sure how he would react if he hooked something. Right away—I think it was his second cast—his line went taut. I thought, *Here we go*. I was half-expecting him to throw down the rod. He didn't. And here we are, four years later. He has his own YouTube channel for his fishing videos."

"It's funny, isn't it, how certain things can be such an immediate fit for you? I could not get enough of fishing. Every chance I had, I went with *Morfa*. He was happy for the company, happy to share what he knew with me. 'My little *fisker*,' he called me. I think he and *Mormor* were pleased to have discovered an activity I was so enthusiastic about. It helped to bridge the gap between us.

"Then winter arrived. I can tell you, after four years in Texas, winter in the Catskills was a shock. The mercury plummeted, a strong wind blew up, and snow started streaming from the heavy clouds overhead. It was pretty to look at from inside the big picture window in my grandparents' living room, but something else to venture out into. And venture out into it I had to, several times a day, to walk the dogs. All of them loved the snow except for Ulysses, who shivered madly the entire time he was outside, and Paprika, who was completely disoriented by the snow, running around in circles and snapping at it. None of the clothes in my suitcase was suitable for the weather. I wore the heaviest jacket I had under one of *Mormor*'s old coats and I was still cold. The three of us had to make a special trip into Wiltwyck one Saturday to kit me out in proper winter gear.

"As far as I was concerned, the worst thing about the change of season was the end of fishing with *Morfa*. When I said this to him, he shook his head and said, 'No. Now we are waiting for the lakes to freeze, for the ice to grow nice and thick. Once it is thick enough, I show you how we fish through the ice.' It took a couple of weeks. Every night at dinner, I would ask him, 'Do you think the ice is ready yet?' 'Not yet,' he would say. 'Soon. Maybe tomorrow, maybe the next day.' You know how it is at that age. A week is an incredibly long time, especially if it's standing between you and something you're desperate to do. Two weeks might as well be an eternity. I complained about it to *Mormor*: 'I'm *never* going to get to go ice-fishing!'" Doris laughed. "As if it was the greatest tragedy that had ever befallen anyone. '*Tålmodighed*,' she said to me, which is Danish for 'patience.'

"Well, poor as it might have been, my *tålmodighed* was rewarded early the second Saturday in December. The sky was full of low, heavy clouds. There was snow on the way, a lot of it. Nonetheless, *Mormor* wrapped me up, gave me a thermos full of hot cocoa, and turned me over to *Morfa*. I expected we'd be driving somewhere, but he was standing beside a small sled loaded with a number of long bundles. 'You are sure you want to do this?' he said, an expression on his face as if he was having second thoughts about taking me. I practically screamed, 'Yes!' 'All right, all right,' he said. 'Kiss your grandmother goodbye and tell her you love her.' I did, and so did he. 'Bring back a big fish for supper!' she told me. I said I would.

"With *Morfa* pulling the sled, we set off in the direction of the orchard. We passed among the trees and kept going. Another couple of hundred yards beyond it, there was a low ridge. It wasn't much more than a rise in the earth, but the snow made climbing it an effort, especially for *Morfa* dragging our gear. At the top, we paused to catch our breath. In front of us, a long, narrow lake spread out at the foot of the hill. I had no idea there was so substantial a body of water this close to us. I turned to my grandfather, who knew what I was thinking. 'I keep this place secret,' he said, 'for when we want to go ice-fishing.'

"As we descended the ridge, I asked him what the lake's name was. Always know what the place you are in is called: it was one of his rules for fishing. To my surprise, he said he didn't know. None of the maps he'd consulted gave the lake a name; neither did any of the locals he'd asked about it. He had christened it himself, Gunne Lake, after a lake in Denmark. There was a story connected to the original about a king who loved the countryside around the lake with such passion, he said God could keep heaven, he preferred to stay right there. After he died, he was condemned to haunt the place, riding around its shore at the head of a ghostly hunting party. Seeing the look on my face at the mention of ghosts, *Morfa* added that his choice of name wasn't because of this part of the story, but because of the king's love for his lake. He knew exactly how the man must have felt. This area, where he and *Mormor* had settled and raised their daughter and made their life together, was dearer to him than any other, even the house in which he'd been brought up.

"By now, we were at the edge of the lake. I had never set foot on frozen water before. My previous visits to my grandparents had been during the summer; nor was I much interested in ice-skating. (I can't remember if there was an ice rink near where we lived in Texas.) The wind had scoured the snow from the surface, which looked like an enormous sheet of scratched and scuffed glass.

I was anticipating the ice would be slippery, so much I would have to struggle not to fall on my bottom right away. I also had the idea it would groan the instant I stood on it. It was smooth, but as long as I was careful, I could walk without trouble. Neither did the combined weight of myself, *Morfa*, and the sled elicit the slightest creak from it.

"We made our way out to the center of Gunne Lake. There, *Morfa* unzipped one of the bundles on the sled and began removing a series of slender metal tubes from it. He fitted them together into a frame over which he stretched and tied a canvas cover. He worked quickly, describing each of his actions to me, and in short order had put up a tent large enough to hold the two of us. The shelter finished, he slid it to the side and untied another bundle, removing a decent-sized auger from it. He balanced the tip of the drill on the ice and started turning it. I was fascinated watching the metal spiral into the ice. Once it was a couple of inches down, *Morfa* let me crank the auger while he steadied it. The muscles of my arms burned, but I would not stop until the drill had broken through to the water. 'Very good!' my grandfather said. 'What a strong girl you are!' I was quite pleased with myself. *Morfa* wiped off the auger and replaced it on the sled, then lifted a hatchet he used to enlarge the hole we'd opened.

"When he was satisfied, he returned the hatchet to the sled and unzipped the bag that held the fishing rods. I was surprised at how short they were. He passed the rods to me, along with a small bucket. Holding the tent at one of the corners, he maneuvered it over the hole in the ice. He centered it, then unbuttoned the tent's door. Inside, the air was dim, the opening in the frozen lake a black mouth. *Morfa* unsnapped a smaller flap where one of the sides met the roof, and winter light flooded the tent through a plastic window. He ducked out to retrieve a pair of rolled-up lengths of carpet, each the size of a bath mat, which he untied and spread beside the hole. After a check of the sky, from which a few flakes of snow had started to fall, he pulled the door flap closed. He seated himself on one of the pieces of carpet, reached into the right pocket of his coat, and withdrew a tiny transistor radio. He extended the antenna, placed the radio on the ice to his right, and switched it on. Elvis Presley's voice sang from the speaker, telling us we were caught in a trap. 'A little music helps pass the time,' *Morfa* said. 'Maybe the fish like it, too.' I wasn't especially fond of Elvis, whose songs my mother had loved to sing around the house, but I appreciated having the radio on, and 'Suspicious Minds' was over soon, anyway.

"I don't suppose you know anything about ice-fishing. Am I right?"

"Only what my son has told me," I said. "You drop the hook into the hole and sit there jigging the line," I mimed the up-and-down motion, "until something takes a bite."

Doris nodded. "That's pretty much it. Not quite as exciting as casting your line out and reeling it back in quick as you can, trying to provoke a bass into striking it, but when it's winter and you're desperate to fish, you take what you can get. The bucket my grandfather had handed to me was full of bait, a selection of chicken livers, cut into halves and thirds, most of them several days past their best. The moment he removed the lid, the smell filled the tent. It was . . . well, as *Morfa* said, 'Wakes you up, doesn't it?' If I had any doubt about my commitment to fishing, remaining there with that stink, not to mention sliding a chunk of slimy liver onto my hook, put it to rest. 'The water is cold,' *Morfa* said. 'The fish move slow. We need something they notice.' Which I did not doubt they would.

"Sure enough, the bait served its purpose, and it didn't take long for us to pull half a dozen decent-sized bluegill out of the hole. After we unhooked them, *Morfa* took each by the tail and slapped it hard against the ice. He placed their bodies in a row on the ice behind him. Have you ever eaten bluegill? They're quite nice, fried in butter."

"One time," I said. "David wanted to try them. As you said, I cooked them in a pan with butter, and served them with lemon. They were tasty; although there wasn't much meat on them."

"True. During the summer, we had them for dinner most weeks, along with *ørred* and *malle* (that's trout and catfish). These were the days before the concern about what the fish were absorbing from the water was widespread. I didn't mind killing and cleaning what we caught. Any squeamishness I might have felt was outweighed by the satisfaction of putting food on the table."

"David was the same way," I said. "He was so proud to be providing the meal for us."

"Like an adult, yes." Doris smiled. "Well. My grandfather placed five more bluegill on the ice. For a meal, it was plenty, but I did not want to stop fishing. I had waited long enough to be out here. I intended to remain until the last possible minute. The interior of the tent was no longer cold, or very cold; our breath had raised the temperature noticeably. *Morfa* was inclined to indulge me, but conditions outside had deteriorated. Snow was streaming from the sky in long white lines. A strong wind was blowing, whistling around the tent, every now and again gusting and slapping one of the sides. On the radio, the deejay announced the arrival of the anticipated snowstorm, which was going to be considerably worse than what had been forecast only a few hours ago. Eighteen to twenty-four inches of snow was being called for; amounts approaching three feet were not out of the question in higher elevations. Strong winds would accompany the snow, which might reach whiteout conditions, and widespread power outages were likely. Authorities were advising anyone who didn't have to travel to stay home. The second the broadcast switched over to a commercial, I knew what *Morfa* was going to say: Time's up. As he was opening his mouth, I said, 'One more cast!' Which wasn't really accurate, but he understood my request. 'One more,' he said."

I laughed. "That's what David says every time I tell him we have to leave wherever he's been fishing. 'One more cast!' Which usually turns into another five or six."

"I managed another two attempts. My first, something took my bait and gave a brief struggle before slipping free. *Morfa* consented to another try, and this was when I hooked something big. Whatever it was almost pulled the rod out of my hands. If I hadn't set the drag loose, the line would have snapped right away. As it was, it ran out the reel so fast it sounded like bacon frying. *Morfa* stopped tying up his mat. 'I think you have something there,' he said.

"'Is it a pike?' I said. I was desperate to catch a pike.

"'Maybe,' he said, 'or maybe Mr. Catfish has your hook in his lip.'

"A catfish was less exciting than a pike, but still a respectable catch. Assuming I could bring it through the hole in the ice. I offered to pass the rod to my grandfather, but he shook his head and said this was my fish. Unfortunately for me, no one shared this information with my catch, which was doing everything in its power to free itself from my hook. The longer the fight lasted, the more certain I grew this was no catfish. It was definitely a pike— unless it was a muskie, which would be even more of a thrill. Whatever fish it was, I didn't believe I would be able to land it. It was only a matter of time, I assumed, until the fish broke my line or I made the mistake which allowed it to escape. The wind increased, rattling the tent's canvas. Outside, snow must be starting to pile up. *Morfa*, I expected, would be growing impatient to start for home.

"If he was, though, he didn't let it show. Just the opposite: he kept up a steady stream of encouragement while I gave the fish line and reeled it in, gave the fish line and reeled it in. Gradually, I felt it begin to tire, and then I had it at the opening in the ice. Now *Morfa* stepped forward to help me hoist my catch out of the water."

"What was it?" I said.

"Nothing I had seen before, in either my fishing trips with *Morfa* or the pages of the fishing books *Mormor* brought me from the library. It was huge, four feet long if it was an inch, thick as the trunk of a young tree. The skin was gray, gelid, translucent. There was no dorsal fin, and the pectoral fins were misshapen, bunched against its sides. The tail was similarly twisted. Its head was shaped like the blade of a shovel, its mouth lined with row upon row of teeth like needles. The eyes . . . the eyes were the strangest features on what already was the strangest creature I had encountered. You've seen a fish's eyes. You know what they're like: flat, metallic, gold or silver, with tiny pupils. These eyes might have been a person's, pale blue irises set in white sclerae, large pupils regarding *Morfa* and me with a distinct intelligence. The thing tried to return to the water. I don't know if you're familiar with the way a leech moves. It stretches, elongates from an oval shape to a straight line. This was what this creature did. Its flesh quivered, and it extended toward the fishing hole, its trunk thinning as it added another foot to its length. Let me tell you, I would have been happy to let it go.

"Not *Morfa*, though. As the thing reached for the water, he grabbed the rod from where I had laid it on the ice. The creature was hooked in the corner of its mouth. When *Morfa* pulled up on the rod, it twisted away from the opening, then paused in its movement. Something shifted in its eyes, the subtlest of changes, but . . . Listen. I've been under the water with sharks, big ones—eight, ten feet—with no steel cage to protect me, just a knife in the event anything went wrong. The sharks passed within arm's reach, closer, and it was one hundred percent clear that I was in the presence of pure predators. If one of them decided to turn its teeth on me, there wasn't anything I could do. At the same time, dangerous as the sharks were, there was nothing personal about the danger they posed. What they did or did not do was motivated by the most basic of impulses, hunger, or the perception of a threat. This was not the case with the thing *Morfa* had prevented from returning beneath the ice. In its blue eyes, I saw hatred, malevolence pure and cold as the snow piling up outside. It wasn't the same sort of intelligence I saw in the dogs, it was . . . corrupt, wrong in a deep-seated, nauseating way. I said to *Morfa*, 'We should let this fish go.'

"My grandfather had noticed the effect the creature was having on me. He smiled sadly and shook his head. 'This is a bad fellow,' he said. 'You can see it. We don't want to put him back with the regular fish. This wouldn't be very nice for them, would it?'

"I agreed it wouldn't. 'But what are we going to do with it?' I said.

"'For this,' *Morfa* said, 'we need your grandmother. It is a job for the whole family. You must fetch *Mormor*. I must remain here to keep an eye on our friend. Any other time, I would not dream of sending you out in such weather by yourself. Even if you are careful, it is not safe. But this is a special case. You must go for *Mormor*, quick as you can. This bad fellow will be waking up, remembering who he is, which we don't want to happen.'

"'Can't we bring it with us?' I said. 'We could put it on the sled.'

"'No,' *Morfa* said, 'we cannot. We should not come too close to him. As long as I have him in here, I can keep moving him back and forth on the ice like so. While he was in the water, he was stupid. Up here with us, he is becoming smart, and this makes him a danger. You understand?'

"I didn't, but I said, 'Yes.'

"'There is one more thing,' *Morfa* said, 'a word for you to say to *Mormor*. When she asks you what we caught, you tell her *Morfa* called it a *blodsuger*. Let me hear you say that.'

"'*Blodsuger*,' I said.

"'Excellent,' *Morfa* said. 'We could be standing in the middle of the Råd-huspladsen.' As he was speaking, the thing—the *blodsuger*—stretched, not in the direction of the fishing hole, but toward his voice. He stepped to the left, swinging the rod to the right. 'Look there,' he said. 'This fellow wants to come over to me. He is wondering what it would be like to bite me with his sharp teeth.' He laughed, but in the sound, I heard something off, and understood he was afraid of the creature I had brought out of the water. The knowledge was as awful as the *blodsuger* itself. I had no desire to remain in the tent with the thing one second longer than I had to, but the prospect of leaving *Morfa* alone with it made my stomach churn with dread. 'All right,' he said, his eyes on the creature, 'it is time for your big adventure.' Holding the rod in his left hand, he unbuttoned the tent's entrance with his right. Freezing wind shoved the flap open, filling the interior with a cloud of snow. 'Quickly,' he said, 'quickly, quickly.' I hurried outside, into the mouth of the storm. I took a second to get my bearings, then set off toward home. By the time it occurred to me to glance back to the tent, *Morfa* had already sealed it again.

"It was the last time I saw my grandfather alive."

For a moment, Doris fell silent. I was aware we were the only two in the dining area. Everyone else had left to join my son in fishing, or to walk to the back range for target shooting. Emptied of people, the barn was cavernous, its rafters full of shadows. Doris sipped her coffee, said, "I made it back to the house, but the trek lasted a long time. The wind seemed to fling the snow directly into my face. I raised my forearm to shield my eyes, but I kept stopping to check my course. I was extremely anxious I would lose my way. Conditions were practically blinding, which made maintaining my bearings an ongoing challenge. Fresh snow was piling up on top of what was already there. I reached the edge of the ice and started climbing the rise. What had been a gentle slope on the way down was now considerably steeper. Calves protesting, I struggled up it. At one point, I decided I would sprint to the top, but after eight steps I had to stop, chest heaving. I looked back for the tent, which was hidden from me by the snow. Despite my heavy clothes, I was cold, the wind peeling the heat away from me. Snow clung to my jacket, my hat, my eyebrows. I had done my best to wind my scarf around my nose and mouth, only to have it keep slipping down. I pushed on. The ground leveled, and I was at the top of the rise. I was so excited to have reached it, I tried to gallop down the other side. Right away, I tripped and went tumbling through the snow. As I rolled, I collided with some buried object, a rock or tree stump, which knocked the breath out of me. When I came to a halt, I lay in a daze, staring at the flakes streaming from the sky, trying to draw air into my lungs. After what felt like hours, the tightness in my chest eased. I struggled to my feet. Snow stuck to me. My hat was gone, lost in the tumult. If I had been cold before, now I was freezing. And I still had a long way to go. At the prospect of the distance I had left to cover, my heart dropped. I wanted nothing more than to return to my grandfather in the little tent. What kept me from doing an about-face was the memory of the *blodsuger*'s eyes, those cruel blue eyes, so unlike anything I had encountered in a fish—this and the fear I had detected in *Morfa*'s laughter. I wiped the snow from my face as best I could and went on toward the house.

"By the time I reached the apple grove, I was exhausted. My feet felt as if they were encased in lead boots, which grew heavier with every step I took. The storm had continued to strengthen. The wind shoved me this way and that; it drove the snow in great swirling currents around me. At some point, my scarf had unwound and the wind caught and whirled it away. My face was numb and had been for a while. I was very far from *Morfa* and the monstrous creature, but not yet close to *Mormor* and the dogs. I felt more alone than I ever had, even after my dad had died. I missed my old home, missed Texas, so acutely it filled my eyes with tears that froze on their way down my cheeks. Yes, Mom hadn't exactly been what you would call present, but there had been my friend, Morgan, and her family to watch after me. Not to mention, no blizzards. Since coming to New York, I had heard from my mother on a scattering of occasions, half a dozen awkward phone calls and a couple of perfunctory letters. At the end of every conversation, she said—she *promised* she would see me soon. As of yet, she had made no attempt to visit, let alone to move me back in with her. Wandering among the twisted ranks of the apple trees, the wind roaring about me, I understood I wasn't going to be seeing or returning to my mother any time soon, if at all. To tell the truth, I think I had realized this already, but had been unwilling to admit it. Until this minute, I hadn't considered myself an orphan. I had lost my father, but there was still Mom waiting for me, once she recovered from Dad's death. Trudging amidst the trees, I understood I might as well have lost both parents. Which I will concede was a bit on the melodramatic and self-pitying side, but I was ten, and lost in a snowstorm.

"Oh yes, I had become disoriented in the midst of the trees, veered right when I should have turned left—or something, I was so cold it was difficult to keep my thoughts straight—and now I was uncertain which way led home. If I struck out in the wrong direction, I would lose the grove as a point of reference, and the consequences for me as well as for *Morfa* would be dire. I had to keep moving, I knew, but each step brought me further into confusion. I struggled not to panic, squinting at the nearest tree for any hint of the path home.

"And then a figure appeared on my left, trudging toward me through the blowing snow. It was *Morfa*. He was hatless, his fine white hair waving in the wind, his face pale, colorless. His coat was open halfway down his chest, the buttons missing. With his right hand, he was gripping his throat. All of which was strange, in the middle of a storm of this severity, but I was so happy to see him, none of it mattered. I started to run toward him, but already he was backing away, waving at me to follow him with his left hand. I did. Keeping just within view, he led me on a zigzagging path through and out of the trees. It didn't occur to me to doubt the direction he was taking me. We headed across open ground. I wondered what had happened to the *blodsuger*. Perhaps *Morfa* had hauled it out into the blizzard after all, let the weather take care of it. I tried to ask him, but he was too far away, my voice no match for the raging wind.

"Soon, we were walking among tall trees, pines whose branches whipped back and forth in the gale, maples whose trunks were plastered with snow. *Morfa* was gaining ground on me, moving further away, becoming harder to see. Every so often he would pause, half-turn in my direction. I assumed he was checking to be sure I was behind him, but to the extent I could tell, I had the impression he was looking beyond me. I struggled to catch up to him, but try as I might, I could not. The muscles in my legs screamed, my lungs heaved, but I ran after him. It was no use. Already, he was barely visible, a faint shape in the swirling white. I shouted for him to wait, but with the wind and the distance, there was no way for him to hear me. He grew fainter still, and it was as if I was looking at him across a tremendous space, much greater than however many yards lay between us. Even after the snow veiled him, I maintained a sense of him ahead of me. The trees thinned and I was crossing open ground. When the house loomed before me, I assumed *Morfa* had gone into it. In fact, this was the first thing I asked my grandmother, once I struggled open the back door and clomped into the kitchen: 'Where's *Morfa*?'"

III

"She had no idea what I was talking about. She was seated at the kitchen table, reading a book, the dogs spread out on the floor around her. The radio on the counter was on, set to the oldies station, its volume low. Only Stone Henry lifted his head to acknowledge me. Blissfully near the woodstove radiating heat, the rest of the pack didn't stir. *Mormor* removed her reading glasses, took one look at me, and was on her feet, bustling toward me. Questions poured out of her, too fast for me to answer. Where was my grandfather? Didn't he know you had to cover up in a storm? Of course he did, he was *dansk,* wasn't he? Had he forgotten that? As she talked, she hustled me over to the stove and began to strip the snowy, wet clothes from me. I knew the stove was hot, but I was so cold, I couldn't feel it. *Mormor* fetched a quilt from the bed in the guest room, wrapped it around me, and sat me beside the stove on one of the kitchen chairs. Throughout, her stream of questions continued. What kind of man had she married? Did he not notice the storm outside? Why would he send her out in it, alone? What would happen if little Doris had lost her way? Gradually, sensation was returning to my hands and feet, my face. *Mormor* put the kettle on the stove top. She took my hands and rubbed them. She did the same for my feet, clucking her tongue all the while. I had to tell her about *Morfa,* about the *blodsuger,* but as I warmed, I began to shiver, my teeth to chatter, with such force I couldn't accept the mug of tea she prepared for me.

"By the time the worst of the shuddering was past, and I could sip the sweet, milky tea, my grandmother's questions had tapered, her outrage replaced by concern. Of course *Morfa* wouldn't allow me to go unaccompanied through a winter storm without good reason. Through mouthfuls of tea, I told her about the strange creature I had hooked. I described its gray skin, its rows of sharp teeth, its hate-filled eyes. As I did, she grew quiet. I repeated the name *Morfa* had given it. When she heard me say, '*blodsuger,*' she drew in her breath sharply. She didn't stop me, though, so I went on to my trek through the storm, to getting lost, to *Morfa*'s appearance and then disappearance. Something happened to her face as I described my grandfather's open coat, his bloodless skin, the hand at his throat. It grew still, blank. If you didn't know my grandmother, you might have thought she had stopped listening to me, become caught in a daydream. If you did know her, you recognized her lack of expression as what happened to her features when she was struggling with great emotion. They became a dam, behind which her feelings raged. I had never seen the look directed at me, but *Morfa* had been on the receiving end of it a couple of times, and even if I hadn't recognized what the stilling of *Mormor*'s face signified, the way his sentences stumbled and snarled would have made it clear. As I continued my story, relating my struggle up the rise, losing my way in the orchard, her face . . . emptied, drained of color and motion, until by the time I reached *Morfa*'s apparition, I might have been sitting across from a plaster cast of my grandmother. I knew—*Morfa*'s reaction to the *blodsuger* had told me things were serious; *Mormor*'s absolute stillness said they were far, far worse. I thought I knew what that meant—but I didn't want to say so out loud, because as long as I didn't, it remained only a possibility, not yet set in reality. Our shared knowledge hung unspoken in the kitchen between us, like a great ugly bird perched on top of one of the cabinets. To avoid speaking about it, I asked her what the thing I had caught, the *blodsuger,* was.

"She did not answer me. Instead, she rose from her chair, and it was as if a statue had come to life, her movements slow and stiff. She walked to the back door, opened it, and stepped onto the stoop. The dogs raised themselves and hurried after, around, and past her into the yard to do the necessary. Heat emptied from the kitchen. Missions accomplished, the dogs rushed into the house, crowding me, licking my hands, my feet, Paprika angling his head in an effort to taste my tea. *Mormor* remained on the stoop, staring into the storm's whiteness. The kitchen was growing cold, now. The dogs shuffled nervously, Ulysses whining at the drop in temperature. The storm continued to swell. I placed my mug on the stove, leaned forward, and picked up Ulysses, gathering him into the quilt. He was only too happy to snuggle against me. At last, Donner padded to *Mormor* and nosed her hand. With a sigh I heard despite the roaring wind, she stepped inside, pulled the door shut behind her, and locked it.

"The instant the lock slotted into place, *Mormor* hastened to the stove, muttering questions as she went. Some of them were for me: What was this silly old woman doing, standing with the door open in the middle of a *snestorm*? Some were for her: Why didn't that man leave the *mørk alf* on the ice and come with Doris? Squatting in front of the stove, she unlatched its door and slid a couple of pieces of wood into it. Speaking to herself in Danish, she straightened and went to the counter. From the knife drawer, she withdrew the cleaver and carving knife, which she set on the table. I was a little afraid of both implements. My grandparents kept them razor sharp, as they did all blades in the house. I had watched *Mormor* use the cleaver to joint a chicken in half a dozen strong chops. I had sat at the dinner table as *Morfa* shaved a roast to thin slices with the carving knife. I wasn't sure why *Mormor* had taken them from their drawer; though I guessed it had something to do with the creature, the *blodsuger.*

"I had still less comprehension of what she did next. From the refrigerator, she fetched the tub of lard, which she also placed on the table. She pried the lid from it and dipped her right index finger into the fat. She swirled her finger to loosen the lard then, once it was coated in the stuff, used the digit to write on the blades. Going from handle to end, she drew the same five characters on each. I didn't recognize any of them. They looked like trees, straight vertical lines with two or three or four lines branching from them at differing angles. When she was done, she flipped the implements over and jabbed her left index finger on the point of the knife. A bright red bubble of blood swelled from her fingertip. With that finger, she wrote another three symbols on the blades. These were different, circles crossed by lines long and short.

I watched open-mouthed as she washed her hands with soap and water at the kitchen sink and pressed a clean dish towel to her self-inflicted wound.

"She noticed the expression on my face and said, 'What a crazy old *Mormor* you have, eh?' She forced a smile, but it was obvious she was as worried as *Morfa* had been, if not more. I retrieved my tea from the stove top and cupped it in my hands. *Mormor* returned to the chair she had been sitting in when I stumbled into the kitchen. Stone Henry walked under the table and laid his head in her lap. She sighed and rubbed between his ears with her good hand. Her eyes shone with tears she was doing her best not to shed.

"No child likes to see the person looking after them distressed. I understood this was connected to the creature I had hooked and to what had befallen *Morfa*. The moment *Mormor* told me what the *blodsuger* was, I would know what I was part of. My stomach curdled with dread as intense as what I'd felt standing on the threshold of the room in the funeral home where my father's coffin had lain waiting. I wanted nothing more than to forget the thing I had caught, to sit beside the stove with Ulysses curled against me and drink my tea. But the cleaver and carving knife were lying there with *Mormor*'s blood drying on them and I knew I was a long way past being able to retreat from all of this. Like every ten-year-old, I was constantly insisting on my age, my maturity. 'I'm not a baby,' I liked to say. Well, this was what not-being-a-baby consisted of, wasn't it? Facing those situations you not only didn't want to, but would give anything to avoid. I asked *Mormor* to tell me about the *blodsuger* and this time she did."

Doris raised her cup to her lips and saw that it was empty. "Hang on a minute," she said, standing. "Are you going to have anything else from the dessert table?"

"I'm good for now," I said.

"Suit yourself."

Her coffee refilled, Doris resumed her seat across from me. I said, "What did your grandmother say?"

"She started with the *nisse*. These were the creatures she and *Morfa* blamed whenever one of them couldn't find something they were looking for, the car keys, say. 'Ach, what have the *nisse* done with my keys?' *Morfa* would say. The first time I'd heard them mention the *nisse*, I asked what they were talking about. 'The little people,' *Morfa* said. 'You mean fairies?' I said. He nodded. 'Yes, you can call them fairies.' I said, 'Wouldn't the dogs eat them?' He smiled. 'If they could catch them, I'm sure they would like nothing better than a nice meal of *nisse*!' I had seen the Disney *Peter Pan* in the theater and I imagined the *nisse* looked something like Tinker Bell, small, dressed in leaves, with insect wings to let them zip about. Secretly, I started to refer to them, myself, when I was about to miss the school bus because my pencil case was nowhere in sight. 'Stupid *nisse*,' I would whisper, 'you give me back my pencil case *right now*!'" Doris laughed. "It never seemed to work. I guessed the *nisse* weren't intimidated by me.

"Mind, I didn't believe the *nisse* actually existed, any more than I did Santa, the Easter Bunny, or the Tooth Fairy. I had my doubts about religion, too. The previous year, Morgan had let me in on one of the great secrets of childhood, namely, that it's your parents who place the toys under the Christmas tree, who leave the chocolate rabbit in your Easter basket, who replace the teeth you hide under your pillow with money. I was scandalized, even more so when I asked my mother and she confirmed Morgan's revelation. 'You *lied* to me!' I said. Mom had done her best to differentiate between lies and what she called stories, but I would have none of it. If I was sad to learn the world was less magical than I had believed, I also enjoyed the peculiar power I gained from having caught my parents lying to me, and quite extensively at that.

"For all my recent skepticism, though, the moment *Mormor* started talking about the *nisse,* and how there were many kinds of them, not for a second did I doubt her. Everything about the *blodsuger*—especially those eyes—was of sufficient difference from anything else I'd caught for me to accept it wasn't a fish at all. *Mormor* listed a half-dozen kinds of *nisse,* all of whose names I've forgotten except for the *mørke alver,* the dark elves. The *blodsuger* were of this brood. They were taller than most of the other *nisse,* each the size of a child. Their flesh was not solid in the same way ours was, which allowed them to shape themselves to resemble various animals. They were fiendishly intelligent, gifted mimics. These abilities they used to aid them in obtaining their favorite meal, fresh blood, preferably from a human. One tradition said they had come from leeches who had tasted the blood of Odin, the king of the old gods, when he had hung on the world tree, Yggdrasil, in order to obtain secret knowledge. Another story said they were leeches who had feasted on the blood of Judas Iscariot after he hanged himself in despair at having betrayed Jesus. Whichever was true, or if neither was, they were a plague, and should you be unlucky enough to encounter one, you must do everything in your power to destroy it.

"What was one doing in the lake behind our house, though? This was my concern. I had a fearful vision of the water and woods around us full of undersized gray men with a taste for blood.

"*Mormor* understood what I was asking. The *blodsuger* were rare, she said. You might live your whole life without meeting one. As for the creature whose lip my hook had found, *Mormor* was of the opinion we had the British to blame for it."

"The British?" I said.

"Exactly what I said. It was the era of the Beatles, remember. I couldn't imagine John, Paul, George, and Ringo consorting with a bloodthirsty monster. This wasn't who *Mormor* was talking about, though. She had in mind the British of a little less than two centuries before, when the American colonists were waging war for their independence. New York State was one of the principal battlegrounds of the Revolution, you know."

"I do."

"The British saw the Hudson as key to their strategy. If they could control it, they could split the colonies, divide and conquer them. As plans go, it wasn't a bad one. It failed because their army was defeated at Saratoga, which initiated a series of events leading to them losing all of the state down to the City, where they remained until the end of the war. Before news of the loss at Saratoga spread, the British had sent thirty ships sailing up the Hudson. There were a few thousand soldiers on them. The idea was for these men to meet up with the British forces marching south along the river from their presumed victory at Saratoga. On their way, the British ships would create a diversion and perhaps more. They got off to a promising start, destroying a couple of colonial forts on the lower Hudson, capturing one right across from West Point. A little bit below Wiltwyck, the fleet received word of the defeat at Saratoga. With this message, their mission became pointless. To say the least, they were not pleased. Since Wiltwyck was the closest settlement, they visited their displeasure on the city. First, they subjected what was then the state capital to bombardment by their ships' cannons. Last I heard, one of the older buildings uptown still has a cannonball lodged in its basement wall. Fortunately, the city's residents had gotten wind of the ships' approach and had largely abandoned it. Once the cannons were done, the fleet sent several landing boats full of soldiers to shore. Reports vary as to how many redcoats set foot on Wiltwyck Point, with some claiming six hundred, others a thousand, and others still more. For the purposes of this story, the exact number doesn't matter. What does is there were at minimum hundreds of them marching on the city, which was lightly defended, most of the able-bodied men off fighting. The British shot at the handful who showed up to confront them, then set fire to the city. Over three hundred buildings, houses, barns, businesses, and places of worship burned down. The soldiers retreated to their boats, returned to their ships, and sailed for Manhattan, thus concluding their final, spiteful military success in this part of the Hudson Valley.

"Among the soldiers who came ashore that day was a captain, Amos Black. He brought with him a pair of diminutive figures, whom the other troops referred to as Captain Black's little gray fellows. They were part of a group of five such fellows under the captain's command. As soon as it had become clear to the British that the battle against the colonists was not going to be over soon, they had sent across the Atlantic for Black, who was housed with his gray fellows separately from the rest of his regiment. Upon their arrival in New York, the six of them were billeted in a repurposed barn not far from Harlem Heights. From there, they were deployed on select missions, most of which were secret. None of the regular soldiers cared for the captain and his associates.

"As the British troops fired on Wiltwyck's defenders and set torch to its buildings, Black and his two companions kept to the rear. He was a striking figure, a small, narrow man dressed not in the scarlet and white of a regular soldier, but entirely in black, with the exception of an emerald neckerchief. It was as if he was wearing his name, the troops joked. Only when the British were climbing back into their boats did Black take action. Before joining the rest of the landing party, he turned to his undersized companions, uttered words no one could make out, and pointed at the burning city. The little gray fellows turned and sprinted toward it. According to one observer, they ran more like dogs, or wolves, than men.

"In the following days, there were a series of terrible murders in and around Wiltwyck's smoldering remains. Men, women, children, old, young, all were victims. They were killed sorting through the charred wreckage of their homes and businesses. They died attempting to recover what vegetables were left in their fields. They met their end on the road out of Wiltwyck to Hurley, where the majority of the city's residents had relocated. These were savage acts, bodies torn open, entrails strewn around them. Popular suspicion fell on wild animals, a pack of wolves, drawn to the devastated city and made bold by its ruin. There were organs missing from some of the victims, but what was remarkable was the lack of any substantial amount of blood at the sites of the crimes, which pointed to creatures other than wolves. A couple of young men who had spied on Captain Black ordering his undersized companions to remain behind made the connection between those strange figures and the outbreak of murders. The young men—they were boys, really—assembled a group to locate the little gray fellows and put a halt to their attacks. Its numbers consisted of men too old, too young, and too unwell to fight in the Continental Army, as well as a pair of ministers and a widow who had assumed the running of her farm after her husband had been struck down by a British musket ball at the Battle of Long Island.

"Together, these men and women tracked the gray fellows to a barn on the road to Hurley. They circled the barn and attacked. A ferocious fight ensued. Although bloated with blood, the gray fellows were fearsome contestants, terrifically strong, inflicting horrific damage on their assailants with the fangs filling their wide mouths, the claws on their long hands and feet. They killed a full third of the party, and of the rest, no one went uninjured. Finally, the widow—whose name was Emma Dearborn—struck the head from one of the creatures with an axe. For a short while thereafter, his companion continued the fight, then leapt through the ranks of the attackers and fled. The group bound up their injuries, burned the remains of their foe, and set off in pursuit of his fellow.

"For six days, they chased him through the Catskills, occasionally drawing within sight of the gray fellow, though never close enough to do more than waste a musket ball on him. At last, his trail disappeared on the shore of a lake. Assuming he'd hidden beneath the water, the members of the party stationed themselves around the lake and waited for their quarry to emerge. Another four days passed, at the end of which, they decided the gray fellow had either drowned or escaped. A careful search of the surrounding woods failed to turn up any sign the creature had slipped out of the water and through their ranks, so they concluded he had chosen his end in the water rather than at the edges of their knives and axes. They warned the few people living near the lake of what they had pursued into it, advised them to keep an eye out for anything unusual, then returned to Wiltwyck and their separate homes."

"How did your grandmother know this?" I said. "I'm familiar with the burning of Wiltwyck; they reenact it every other Fourth of July. But the rest of it . . ."

"She'd read about it," Doris said, "at the Woodstock library. One of her responsibilities was the local history section, whose shelves contained all sorts of things, personal journals, albums of old newspapers, unpublished manuscripts. She read all of them, in part to figure out how to catalogue the holdings and in part to learn more about the place she and *Morfa* had chosen to call home. Among the papers she examined was a handwritten document titled *Concerning the Terrible and Strange Events of October 18–November 2, 1777*. Fifty-six pages long, it was the work of Emma Dearborn, the widow who'd beheaded one of the gray fellows. During the winter after the battle with the creatures, she set down her account of it. There was no record of the means by which the manuscript found its way to the library.

"When she reached the description of Captain Black's little gray fellows, she recognized the pair as *blodsuger*. How was that possible, right?"

I nodded.

"*Mormor*'s grandmother had come to Denmark from Finland, Lapland, where she had been what the Danes called a *heks*, the Finns a *noita*, a witch. She had taught *Mormor* about the *nisse*, how to distinguish among them, the proper ways for dealing with the more dangerous varieties. Of course, my grandmother didn't imagine the lake behind her and *Morfa*'s house was the lake from Emma Dearborn's story. It would have been too great a coincidence. But she shared the details of the widow's narrative with my grandfather. His father, a blacksmith, had passed along the same and similar folklore to him.

As the one who went off fishing, he was more likely to encounter the remaining *blodsuger*, assuming there was any truth to the tale she had read and the creature had remained in its watery hiding place. Telling him was a precaution of the same order as reminding him to keep an eye out for rattlesnakes when he went hiking on Overlook Mountain. She didn't expect he would meet any of the reptiles on the paths he followed, but better to be prepared for something that never came than surprised by it shaking its rattle at your feet. The only thing neither of them had anticipated was discovering the *blodsuger* in the middle of such a ferocious storm. It was the way of life: you made your plans, and God chuckled at them.

"I was finally warm enough to speak without my teeth chattering. There was one question on my mind: What were we going to do now? Wouldn't the *blodsuger* use the storm to escape into the woods and then the house of an unsuspecting neighbor? Implicit in my words was an acknowledgment of *Morfa*'s fate, though *Mormor* didn't remark on it. Instead, she said we didn't have to worry about the *blodsuger* running off to hunt Mr. Rivera. In the tent with me, he would have gotten my scent, and if there was one thing a creature such as this loved above all else, it was the blood of a child. They could smell it for miles. Even through so great a storm as this one, he would track me, right to the back door.

"You can picture my expression. No, no, *Mormor* said, this was a good thing. It meant we had the opportunity to deal with this creature before it harmed anyone else. I heard that 'else' and my heart contracted. *Mormor* didn't seem to register what she'd admitted. We had laid a trap for the *blodsuger*, she went on. It would be sluggish from its long time in the lake, weak. It would want to feed—not just feed, to gorge itself. Its keen nose would lock on to my smell and lead it through the falling snow and blowing wind straight to the house. I knew how difficult the trek was and the storm had gained in force during the last hour alone, and was predicted to worsen through the night. The wind and snow would make the *blodsuger* slow, stupid, would strip the strength from its limbs. By the time it found us, it would be in bad shape.

"'And then we'll kill it?' I asked.

"'Oh no,' *Mormor* said, 'then we wait.' Frozen almost to death, the *blodsuger* was still fearsome. We would not confront it unless we absolutely had to. No, she said, we would let Lady Skadi, the queen of winter, do the work for us. But it would leave, I said. As soon as the monster realized it couldn't break into the house—which I was hoping was the case—it would seek out someone else, Mr. Rivera or one of our other neighbors. 'You're forgetting,' *Mormor* said, 'the *blodsuger* doesn't know this place. It has no idea Mr. Rivera is sitting in his house not too far away. As far as it is aware, we are the only people around for miles and miles. Because of the cold, its thoughts will be slow. All it will be able to concentrate on is the smell of this young girl's blood—and of the old woman with her, who is not so nice a meal, perhaps, but hunger is good seasoning for bland food.'

"'We won't let it in, will we?' I said.

"'What kind of question is this?' *Mormor* said. 'To think I would let such a creature near my Doris!'

"'But what if it breaks in?' I said.

"Mormor pointed to the door. 'Do you see the doorframe?'

"I nodded. I had never paid much attention to it, but there hadn't seemed any need to. It was a doorframe, three pieces of wood, each about three inches wide, painted plain white. A dull metal cross hung on the wall above the entrance; I thought my grandmother was indicating this, and said so.

"'Yes, the cross is important,' *Mormor* said. 'I am talking about the wood surrounding the door. It is ash, from a very special ash tree. Having it here and around all the other doors and windows to the house makes it difficult for a creature such as the *blodsuger* to enter. Were it full of blood, perhaps it could cross the barrier; though doing so would cost it much effort. Weak as it is now, after a single feeding, the only way it could come join us would be if we invited it in. This we are not going to do, are we?'

"The question was absurd. Nonetheless, I said, 'No!'

"'Good,' *Mormor* said, 'I am glad to hear it.'

"I was on the verge of asking what was so important about the ash whose wood framed the door, but *Mormor*'s features had grown still, as her oblique reference to *Morfa*'s death caught up to her. Is there anything as troubling to a child as seeing a beloved adult upset? I wanted to offer her consolation, comfort, but none of the sentences I formed in my mind seemed adequate. We sat without speaking, the radio's murmur interrupted by occasional pops and crackles, the wind gusting outside. Under certain circumstances, there's an odd pleasure in listening to old songs while the weather rages. This was not one of those times. The bright voices of the singers, the brash music of the orchestras supporting them, sounded bizarre, grotesque. That it did not seem to bother *Mormor* was the sole reason I did not rise from my chair, cross to the counter, and switch the radio off.

"Time crept along, counted off in a succession of songs about not letting the stars get in your eyes, the man who got away, and how to speak to an angel. Several times, I was on the verge of asking *Mormor when* exactly the monster was going to arrive. Part of me was hoping it was not, and I would be spared a second encounter with the creature, this one in its true form. Another part of me thought the *blodsuger* not appearing would be worse still, because this would mean it was still somewhere in the woods around the house, lurking, waiting for its chance to taste my blood.

"The dogs were the first to notice something had changed. They lifted their heads and stared at the back door—Donner first, then Odin, then the rest, Ulysses poking his head out from under the quilt. *Mormor* and I joined them. They whined, shifting from side to side as if uncomfortable. *It's here,* I thought. In that instant, the blank wood door was the most frightening thing I had ever seen. The dogs' whines dropped in pitch, deepened into rumbling growls. Ulysses leapt off my lap to join the others. They stood, heads lowered, teeth bared, ears back, hackles raised.

"Over the dogs' growling, I heard another sound: scratching at the back door, as if someone were scraping their fingernails against the wood. With it came a voice saying, 'Let me in. Please. Let me in.' It was hoarse, barely above a whisper, but I recognized it right away: *Morfa.* Without thinking, I was off my chair and pushing past the dogs. If the blanket hadn't tangled my legs, just about tripping me, I would have been at the door, turning the lock. Hearing *Morfa*'s voice, I was filled with such happiness, such joy, I was light-headed. The blanket caught me, though, allowing *Mormor* time to position herself in front of me. Her expression was blank, her features stilled. 'Doris,' she said, 'this is not *Morfa.*'

"'What do you mean?' I said. 'Can't you hear him?'

"She nodded. '*Ja.* I hear him. So do the dogs. What do they think?'

"Their growling continued. I understood what it meant, but I argued anyway. 'Couldn't they be wrong?'

"*Mormor* shook her head. 'About this, no.'

"At the door, my grandfather's voice went on pleading. 'Please,' it said. 'It's so cold. You must let me in. If you do not, I will die.' I concentrated, trying to pick out a hint of something else, of the *blodsuger,* in its rasping, but all I heard was *Morfa,* begging to be admitted to the kitchen's warmth before he died of exposure. Finally, *Mormor* walked to the door and hammered it with her fist. 'That's enough!' she said.

"The voice ignored her. 'Doris,' it said. 'Let me in, Doris.'

"I didn't know what to say.

"'Doris,' *Morfa*'s voice said, 'why won't you open the door? Don't you know how cold it is? Why are you making me suffer, Doris? Why do you want me to die? Don't you love me?'

"'Yes!' I shouted, overcome. *Mormor* flashed me a cautionary look, raising her index finger to her lips.

"'There's my girl!' the voice said. 'There's my good girl. You're going to let me in, aren't you, my good girl?'

"All at once, I was certain I was going to do nothing of the kind. While the raw voice could still have passed for *Morfa*'s, a new element had entered it, a note of . . . wheedling, I guess I would say. It was as if whoever was speaking to me was engaged in a deception which cost a great deal of effort and so was searching for a way to hurry the process along. At that moment, I knew the presence on the other side of the door was not my grandfather. Horror colder than any blizzard rose in me. Without speaking, I shook my head and retreated to my chair, gathering my blanket from the floor as I went.

"But the voice wasn't finished with me. 'Doris,' it called. 'Doris, hurry up and let me in.'

"'Enough!' *Mormor* shouted again, thumping the door.

"'Stubborn as ever, eh, old woman?' the voice said. It went on talking, now in Danish, too quickly for me to understand any of the words except the simple ones. I didn't need to. From its tone, which was mocking, nasty, the kind of things it was saying to *Mormor* was clear. Although she was the one who had insisted this wasn't *Morfa*, the torrent of invective made her blink and jerk her head back, as if she had been slapped. In no time at all, the wall she had made of her face was quaking, on the verge of collapsing. Every sentence sent another load of bricks tumbling down. I couldn't stand it. Finally, I screamed, 'Shut up! Just shut up!'

"The outburst snapped my grandmother out of the state the voice's words had plunged her into, but it also returned its attention to me. 'Little Doris,' it said. The pleading, the wheedling, was gone, replaced by the same venom it had spat at *Mormor*. 'Why did you leave me in the tent? Why did you leave me alone with the thing *you caught*? Why, Doris? Why did you leave me to die? You know that is what you did, Doris. I was alone in the tent with your catch. The door blew open. I turned to close it and when I turned back, your catch bit my ankle, right through my boot. I fell on the ice. I hit my head. The thing *you caught* slithered up to my neck and sank its sharp teeth into me. So many teeth, Doris. They hurt, they hurt very much. I was alone with *your catch* and it tore my throat out. I died, Doris, I felt the life going out of me. I pissed myself, I shit myself, and I was afraid. This was not how I wanted to die, alone on the ice, away from my wife, abandoned by the granddaughter who made me take her here. Now I am dead and I am out here in the cold and I will never be alive again, Doris, and it is *all because of you*.'

"*Mormor* pounded the door, accompanying her action with a stream of the strongest curses I had ever heard pass her lips. All of it was in Danish. I had picked these up a word at a time from *Morfa*, who was prone to let slip the occasional obscenity while fixing a particularly difficult appliance. I was his assistant, passing him the tools I recognized and asking what this word meant. He always told me, though he made a production of searching for the English equivalent, until he said, 'I know: it is asshole!' or something like that. I would repeat the Danish back to him, allowing him to correct my pronunciation before he swore me to secrecy, especially in front of *Mormor*. You can appreciate my shock at hearing every one of the bad words *Morfa* had taught me, as well as plenty more he hadn't, pouring from *Mormor*'s mouth in all sorts of combinations. The curses didn't stop the voice answering, so *Mormor* snapped her fingers and this released the dogs from growling into full-throated barking. I jumped a little at the racket, but wasn't sorry to no longer hear whatever the voice was saying. While the dogs were filling the air with their barks, my grandmother walked to the radio and turned the volume up loud. Frank Sinatra singing 'Luck Be a Lady' blared from the speaker. *Mormor* called to the dogs, whose barking trailed away. They returned to growling, but she said, 'Okay, enough of that. Go lie down,' and though the dogs cocked their heads at her, they did as they were told, resuming their former positions on the floor and, in Ulysses's case, on my lap under the blanket. Unhappy, they whined and grumbled until *Mormor* said, 'Hey!' and their complaining subsided.

"With the radio's volume turned loud, I could just about ignore the sound of the voice, still talking, growing more angry, more desperate as the hands of the clock counted each hour and the storm gained in ferocity. Ice pellets mixed with the snow; I listened to them rattle against the windows like handfuls of pebbles being tossed at the panes. When the wind gusted, the house creaked, a sound I found especially ominous. From the yard, there was a CRACK loud enough to register over Johnny Mathis crooning 'Wild Is the Wind,' the big oak in one corner losing its top half in a burst of branches and splinters. *Mormor* looked up at the sound, then resumed moving around the kitchen. She was gathering all her large, heavy-duty pots and pans. These were the ones for the big cooking projects, for the joints of meat, for the gallons of stew, for the buckets of chili. Once she'd located them, she tracked down their lids and checked they fit properly. In between her searching, she tended to the woodstove, stoking it, adding another log or two. The dogs remained in their spots, apparently asleep, except when one would raise his head to stare at the back door, and I would realize none of them was asleep, not really. By this time, the voice had dropped too low for my hearing. I half-expected it to return with a shout, but it did not. Having gathered a sufficient number of pots and pans, *Mormor* was now writing on them in lard, drawing the same unfamiliar symbols I had seen before. Once she was done with the lard, she pricked her left index finger and wrote a single figure on each of the lids in her blood. Then, finger wrapped in a clean handkerchief, she began to remove pieces of wood from the woodbox and stack them in half a dozen piles. She did not hum along with the radio as she usually did while she was working. She was distant, preoccupied. I wanted to speak to her, but could find no words to say.

"Impossible as it may seem, I fell asleep sitting there in the chair with Ulysses on my lap and the radio on loud, *Mormor* clattering around the kitchen. I woke to cold air on my face and the back door wide open, admitting the pale, pearly light of early morning. Of *Mormor* and the dogs, there was no sign; even Ulysses had departed my lap. A herd of thoughts galloped through my brain, the pounding of their hooves the pounding of my heart: the *blodsuger* had found its way inside; *Mormor* was dead; the dogs were dead; I was next; I was alone; what was I going to do; what was going to happen to me? I did not want to be caught in a chair when the *blodsuger* appeared, so I stood, disentangled myself from my blanket, and crept toward the kitchen counter, thinking that, if I could wrap my fingers around the handle of a decent-sized knife, I might have a chance of defending myself. Along the way, I noticed the pots and pans were missing from where *Mormor* had set them out, but was more concerned with the knife drawer, which sometimes stuck when you tried to open it. To my immense relief, this time the drawer slid out easily, its jumble of knives clacking as they shifted. I selected the butcher knife, in my ten-year-old hands practically a short sword. I wished I could remember the symbols *Mormor* had drawn on the cleaver and carving knife. The idea of using my own blood to write on the blade made me queasy, but I was afraid enough to do it anyway.

"The click of nails on the floor behind me just about stopped my heart. While I was still steeling myself to turn and confront it, the dogs surrounded me, snuffling me, pushing against me. At the same time, my grandmother said, 'Doris, what are you doing?' She was standing in the doorway, her face red, her eyes bright, bundled in a heavy wool coat, snow boots, thick mittens, and one of *Morfa*'s knit caps. So happy, so relieved was I to find her and the dogs safe and well, I flew across the room to her, wrapping her in a fierce embrace, almost skewering her with the butcher knife in the process. *Mormor* didn't speak, just allowed me to hug her until I felt ready to let go. As soon as I did, however, she took me by the shoulders, bent to look directly into my eyes, and said, 'There isn't much time, Doris. We must act quickly.' I nodded and in short order, she had me back in my winter clothes. I set the butcher knife on the counter while I was pulling on my sweater and my coat over it, tugging on my wool socks and pushing my feet into my boots, slipping my hands into my mittens, wrapping my scarf around my neck and then raising my hood. After I was dressed and *Mormor* was through the door and calling for me to come with her, I retrieved the knife and carefully slid it into my coat pocket. (The coat had very capacious pockets.)

"As you stood facing the backyard, there was a small bluestone patio to the left, about thirty feet from the house. *Morfa* had laid the stones himself and was forever checking to ensure they remained level. The patio was square, maybe ten feet by ten, bordered on two sides by dense green hedges. The third side was taken up by the large brick grill *Morfa* had also built. The remaining side was open to the house. Once the weather warmed sufficiently, my grandfather would fire up the grill and cook hamburgers, hot dogs, chicken drumsticks, and any fish we might have caught earlier in the day. There were a couple of round wooden tables on the patio, each able to accommodate three chairs. *Mormor* would carry out potato salad and coleslaw from the kitchen, I would bring the paper plates and cutlery, and we would eat the food *Morfa* grilled for us as the long days drew into night. There were no tables or chairs on the patio now; they had been carried into the cellar after the temperature turned too cold for outside dining. Because of the hedges and the grill, less snow had accumulated on the patio than on the rest of the yard, which was a field of sparkling white. The record books say the storm brought us a foot and a half of snow, but I will swear on a stack of Bibles there was at least a foot more surrounding my grandparents' house. What snow had fallen on the patio, *Mormor* had shoveled and swept away. She had cleaned the grill, as well, and what's more, had kindled a fire in it, which, despite the occasional blowing wind, was blazing away. She had set one of the pots I had watched her search out on the grill. Its metal was steaming in the cold. There were a handful of other fires on the patio, five in total, each heap of firewood sending flames up the sides of another pot or pan. The lids rested on the stone nearby.

"Although it was no longer snowing, the storm had left the temperature well below zero. Breath steaming out of me, I followed *Mormor* along the path she and the dogs had forced through the snow. The dogs stayed close to us, even the big ones—Donner, Stone Henry, and Paprika—whose heavy coats would have allowed them to bound around us, had they desired to. We walked first to the patio, where the dogs sniffed at the fires until *Mormor* warned them away from the hot metal. She had left the cleaver and carving knife next to the grill. She picked them up and headed out on another trail, this one leading into the yard. I had to squint from the brilliance of the snow. After another fifty feet or so, the dogs, who had trotted around us, halted, turning their heads to the side, looking down. I stopped with them, only to have *Mormor* say, 'Come, Doris.' I did, and saw what the dogs had been reluctant to approach.

"It was a figure—made of ice, I might have said, like one of those sculptures they carve in the cold countries. Up to its thighs in the snow, it was my height, possibly smaller, but with a large, rounded head and long arms hugging its chest. The hands were oversized, like shovel blades. The torso was short, wide, the legs stocky. From its position, it appeared to have been moving in the direction of the lake. Where its face should have been was a cloudy blank. The closer I drew to the form, the more details I noticed. It was less solid ice than a kind of frozen sludge, dirty gray, in whose depths I could see traceries of red. Morfa's *blood,* I realized. I stepped back from the *blodsuger*'s frozen form, bent over, and threw up.

"Under any other circumstances, *Mormor* would have been at my side in an instant, rubbing my back, comforting me. Now, she ignored me in favor of the *blodsuger,* whose head she cut from its neck with two solid blows from the cleaver. She left the faceless globe where it dropped in the snow, moving on to the arms, which she severed at the shoulder with a couple of strikes of the cleaver and some vigorous sawing with the carving knife. Almost no blood escaped from the wounds she made, as if no part of the creature would relinquish the slightest drop of its favorite nourishment. Cutting through the *blodsuger*'s hips to remove its torso from its legs took the most time and effort, and after its trunk fell into the snow, *Mormor* leaned back, her fists pressed against her lower back, her eyes shut. The pause lasted a moment, then she was next to me. She had secreted the cleaver and knife in her coat. Instead of using her newly freed hands to gather me into her embrace, she stooped, scooped up great handfuls of snow, and wiped them up and down the front of my coat and my arms. I was too surprised to complain, and before I could, she said, 'We need to be as cold as we can stand,' and lifted more snow to smear on her coat. 'We are going to carry those,' she nodded first at the pieces of the *blodsuger,* 'over there,' then at the patio with its host of fires. 'Yes?'

"'Yes,' I said. I understood: we wanted the *blodsuger*'s limbs to remain frozen until they were in the pots and pans with the lids securely on.

"'Good. Now quickly, quickly!'

"Together, we carted the creature's parts to the edge of the stone square. The *blodsuger*'s surface was slippery, almost greasy, which meant I couldn't drag the arm *Mormor* passed me, but had to press it against my chest and cross my arms over it. This close, I could smell it, a pungency like spoiled chicken. I was terrified the arm would start moving while I was holding it, which hurried me along. The arm remained motionless, as did the other arm and both legs I placed in a line along the bluestone. As I was moving them, *Mormor* used the cleaver to quarter the *blodsuger*'s torso, the dull clump of the metal breaking the creature's substance loud in the freezing morning air. She brought the sectioned trunk to the patio, dumped it there in a heap, and returned for the head. Throughout all of this, the dogs sat watching us silently, their tails still. Even Ulysses, who hated the cold and snow and would not remain in it one second longer than was necessary, maintained his position. *Mormor* hefted the *blodsuger*'s head, cradling it to her like an oversized snowball, and carried it right up onto the patio, to the grill, where she heaved it into the deep pot sitting there. It hissed on the hot metal. She lowered the lid onto the pot and turned her attention to the limbs arranged next to the patio. With the cleaver, she removed hands from arms, severed the arms at the elbows, separated feet from legs, and chopped the legs at the knees. Though difficult, strenuous work, she performed it speedily, after which, it was one hand and arm in this pot, the other in that pot, one foot and leg in this pan, the other in that pan, the pieces of the torso in the remaining pot. Lids securely on all pots and pans, *Mormor* and I stood in their midst. The heat was nice, but I knew we weren't finished.

"A sound issued from the pot on the grill. It started as the thick murmur of someone waking from a heavy sleep, with notes of confusion and questioning, the confusion becoming frantic, louder, escalating to shouts and then to outright screams. Though muffled by the metal, whatever the *blodsuger* was speaking was neither English nor Danish, but a harsh tongue which sounded as much like the grunting of a boar as it did any human language. I couldn't understand how the creature was making any sound at all, in its present state. After a second, it switched from its feral tongue to English. The first word it uttered was my name. 'Doris,' it said, slowly, hampered by the agony of its burning metal prison. 'Doris, why are you doing this to me?' There was still some of *Morfa* in the *blodsuger*'s speech, but it was mixed with the animal notes of the thing's actual voice, and all it stirred in me was horror. I did not answer the *blodsuger*'s pleas, which slid into abuse. I was a little bitch; I was a little whore; my mother never loved me; she was only too happy to be rid of me; et cetera. Charming stuff. When it had exhausted its wrath on me, it switched to Danish. It didn't waste any time begging *Mormor* for mercy; instead, it went straight to cursing her. I could understand more of what it was saying, all of which was of the same stripe as what it had spat at me. As it went on, its words lost coherence, until it was shrieking its anger and frustration.

"The rest of the pots and pans were beginning to shake, their lids rattling open a hair's breadth to vent the steam building within them. On their lids and sides, the weird characters *Mormor* had drawn in blood and lard had turned black. Fine cracks were visible within each figure, through which a dull orange glow shone, as if the cracks were giving a view of another fire. The lids were clattering and crashing, the *blodsuger* howling. When the lids jumped, I caught a glimpse of gray shapes writhing beneath them: whatever piece of the creature was contained inside reducing to something sinuous. The dogs had moved to the edge of the patio and taken up position in a silent line. There was something about their demeanor—it was more than watchful; it was anticipatory, as if they were ready for something to happen. I slipped my hand inside my coat pocket and closed my fingers around the handle of the butcher knife.

"A second later, I was drawing the blade out. As the pots and pans went on clanking, one of the stacks of wood on which they were set shifted, tilting its pan to one side at the same moment the lid lifted, allowing a portion of its contents to squirm through the opening. What flopped onto the bluestone resembled a gray spider, a collection of long legs about the size of a big man's hand, its flesh steaming from its time in the pan. It writhed on the patio, its limbs flailing bonelessly. I watched horrified, sure it was dying. It twisted around itself, found its footing, then came flapping straight toward me, its legs moving like an octopus crawling over the bottom of the sea. The sight of its rubbery limbs slapping the stone *Morfa* had laid filled me with anger, with fury hot as any of the fires my grandmother had struck. In an instant, the thing had closed the distance between us and was attempting to scale my left boot. I swung the knife toward it, intending to slice it in half. But I misjudged the angle at which I was holding the butcher knife and instead swatted the thing with the flat of the blade, sending it skidding across the patio to land at Donner's feet. Without hesitation, he lunged and caught the wriggling mass in his jaws. In half a dozen bites, he wolfed it down, even as it struggled to escape his teeth. At the end, he lifted his shaggy head to help him swallow the last of the thing, then sat licking his lips.

"Donner remained in place; nor did the other dogs shift from their posts. Only once the *blodsuger*'s screams had disappeared into the burps of steam which escaped its pot, and the rest of the pots and pans had ceased to move with anything besides the boiling of their contents, did the dogs step onto the patio, milling around *Mormor* and me quietly, almost hesitantly. Not long thereafter, Mormor circulated among the fires, removing lids to allow the liquid left under them to steam up into the sky still hung with clouds. Later, while they were still warm, we would rub the pots and pans inside and out with ash we collected from the fires, then use snow to wipe that off. I remember, the blackened symbols on the metal flaked clean with no problem, which seemed odd to me.

"There was so much left to do. We carried the pots and pans inside, where they received a thorough scrubbing with steel wool, Comet, and scalding hot water. We tidied the patio, sweeping up the remains of the separate fires, dumping them into the bottom of the grill, and throwing snow over the bluestone. The dogs had to be fed. We had to eat; though I don't believe there has ever been any occasion I felt less like food. After those dishes were washed, *Mormor* sat me down so we could work out the details of the story we were going to tell the police. I knew we couldn't describe what had actually taken place; although I found the knowledge difficult to bear. 'It happened!' I wanted to shout. 'There was a monster and my grandmother and I killed it!' *Mormor* didn't waste time convincing me. We needed to report *Morfa* missing, she said. We were going to say that he and I went ice-fishing yesterday, not long before the storm blew in. When he saw how bad the weather was getting, *Morfa* sent me home ahead of him. He said he would be right behind me, as soon as he packed up our gear. He had not returned. At first, our story continued, *Mormor* assumed he changed his mind and decided to shelter where he was. She wasn't overly worried. He was *dansk;* he knew what to do in a snow-storm, even one as severe as this. By now, however, he should have returned, and she was growing concerned. Our story was simple, close to the truth, as most good lies are. Anyone acquainted with *Morfa* would have found parts of the story suspicious, especially the bit where he told me to go out alone in the midst of a blizzard, but *Mormor* was counting on none of the police hav-ing been familiar with my grandfather, which they weren't, and any concerns they might have had about his actions explained away by his and her accents. We rehearsed the story until she was satisfied I knew it, then she picked up the phone.

"*Morfa*'s body was found under the tent, which had collapsed on him from the weight of the snow on it. He was frozen. His throat had suffered a massive wound, of the kind an animal's teeth might inflict. There were details of his death I was not supposed to hear, such as his corpse having been drained of blood, and the strange tracks found near his body, and which I pretended not to hear when the police officers discussed them with *Mormor* a couple of days after *Morfa*'s body was carried from Gunne Lake. I was called into the living room so the men could ask me if I had noticed any animals in the vicinity of the tent, either while *Morfa* was setting it up or as I was striking out for home. Truthfully, I could say I had not, which seemed no more than what the offi-cers had been expecting. In the end, after *Morfa* was buried in the Woodstock cemetery following a service at the Lutheran church, one of the men who had interviewed us returned to tell us my grandfather's cause of death had been attributed to an attack by an unspecified animal, possibly a wolf or coyote, or even a mountain lion. *Mormor* thanked the policeman for bringing her the news, which from a certain perspective was not *too* too far from the truth.

"You can understand why I had no further interest in ice-fishing—warm-weather fishing, either, whose connection to *Morfa* was at first too painful. Those months—that year—after *Morfa*'s death was sad, a sad, difficult time. There were moments it felt as if he was in the house with us, in the next room or upstairs or downstairs, and the air would have a kind of charge to it, as if from his presence. There were other times the atmosphere in the house was flat, empty, as if *Mormor* and I weren't truly present, truly alive. Sometimes I would be overwhelmingly happy, surprised by joy, as the poem says, only to have my happiness unravel into guilt and then resentment and then more guilt. Throughout all of this, my mother remained as distant geographically and emotionally as ever. She missed *Morfa*'s funeral, and you can imagine how well that went over with both my grandmother and me. We . . ."

Doris paused, shook her head. "But this is more of my story than I wanted to tell, and I'm sure more than you wanted to hear. I sometimes think Tolstoy got it wrong, backwards, and it's unhappy families that are all the same. We were, for a time, unhappy. Gradually, life improved. Not all the way, but better than it was at its worst. My family patched itself together as best it could. In the warm weather, I returned to fishing.

"Winter, though, the I'm-dreaming-of-a-white-Christmas version of the season you have up here, had lost whatever charm it possessed for a girl who had lived her earliest years in warmer climes. When it was time for me to go to college, I chose UNC for undergrad and Emory for law school. After a couple of decades as a corporate lawyer in Atlanta, I cashed out and continued moving south, until I was the owner of a couple of charter boats in Key West. It's a life I like very much, and I'm glad I found my way to it before I was too old to enjoy it.

"I visit this area every fall. My grandmother has been dead many years, now; though she lived to see me graduate law school. The house passed to Mom, and to my eternal surprise, she chose to retire to it. She's still there, eighty-nine and hanging on. I stay with her while I'm here, in what used to be my grandparents' room. (Mom has reclaimed her childhood room, which was mine when I was living in the house.) I don't do a lot of fishing during my trips. I prefer to cast my line on the open sea, where the waves and currents allow me not to dwell on what might be lurking at the ocean bottom, waiting for an unlucky hook to lift it into the light and air to make its mischief. Aside from this party, the sole ritual I observe is a walk back to Gunne Lake. Do you know, that's its name on the map, now? I have no idea how this came to be, but I like to think *Morfa* would be pleased. I go to the lake in the afternoon, with the sun hanging high and bright above. I remember *Morfa*'s reason for bestowing the name on the lake, as a means of acknowledging his deep love for the place. I also recall the other part of the original story, about the king whose love for his Gunne Lake led to him being condemned to haunt it after his death. I don't know if *Morfa* would have considered it too dire a fate to be bound to the location where he and *Mormor* made their home and raised a daughter and a granddaughter. As long as *Mormor* was alive, he might have been satisfied with his closeness to her, and maybe me, too, while I was staying there. Since she's been gone, and with my mother nearing the end of her life, I wonder if he looks ahead to a time his family will be gone and he will be left to wander the shore of the lake alone. I've no desire to visit Gunne Lake at night, when the moon's light renders all manner of things visible. I'm too afraid I might see him standing beside the water, forlorn, and I'm equally afraid I might not."

IV

"Well," Doris said. "I'd hazard a guess this was not what you expected when I asked if I could sit with you and your son." She laughed.

"You guess correctly," I said. "I appreciate you telling me this, though."

"You're very polite," she said. "If nothing else, you can file it under 'fishing stories.'"

"Those are some of my favorite stories," I said. "I've lost track of the number David has told me."

"None like this one, I hope."

"Thankfully, no."

A consultation with her phone prompted Doris to say, "Oh my goodness, look at the time. I'm afraid I have to be going. My mother gets nervous when I leave her too long." She pushed her chair back from the table.

"I'll see you to your car," I said.

"Stay put," she said. "There's no need for you to disturb yourself."

"Actually," I said, "I have one last question for you. About your story."

"Oh?"

"Yes. The piece of the . . . creature that escaped the pot: you said one of the dogs ate it. Donner?"

"That's right."

"What happened to him?"

"On second thought," Doris said, "you can walk me to my car."

We deposited our trash in one of the large garbage cans to either side of the barn's entrance and emerged from its spacious shadows into an evening of gaudy splendor, round, puffy clouds receding to the horizon like cobblestones in a vast road, the setting sun dyeing them pink and violet. Between the clouds, the sky was blue fading to soft white, the first stars almost visible if you stared hard enough. Closer to earth, darkness had risen into the air, whose daytime warmth was struggling with pockets of coolness. There was no more *crack* of shotguns from the target range a quarter-mile distant, and I supposed most of the anglers would be packing up their gear soon, if they hadn't already. Not David: I knew I would be traipsing around the farm's lake in the thickening night, trying to locate my son so I could tell him, "One more cast." If our history was any guide, the cast was likely to land him a last-minute success.

Past the barn, our cars were parked in two rows on a grassy field. Doris aimed her key fob at a red Mercedes convertible, which chirped and flashed its lights in answer. "Nice," I said.

"She's gotten me back and forth from Key West—I think this is my sixth trip with her? Seventh? Either way: good car. As for Donner . . ." She leaned against the Mercedes's trunk. "The rest of the dogs noticed a change in him before *Mormor* and I did. If we hadn't been so preoccupied with everything concerning *Morfa,* maybe we would have picked up on the growing distance they put between themselves and my big dog. I thought he spent a lot of time standing around, with this distracted expression on his face, his eyes unfocused, his mouth open, tongue hanging out, panting. If he was in the middle of a hall or doorway, which he often was, he would let me push him to the side without complaint. The other hint something was different with him came when we let the dogs out to do their business. During the day, they roamed the yard, visiting favorite trees and bushes, chasing one another around. It could be a bit frustrating if you were in a hurry. Night was different. At night, they trotted out, performed the necessary, and returned promptly. During their final excursion, Donner began to stray farther and farther into the dark, taking longer and longer to come back. I'm not sure if *Mormor* thought anything of it, not at first; I didn't. For a dog of his size, Donner was old, nearly ten, and each of my grandparents had explained to me the relationship between his greater size and a shorter life. As with his distracted standing, I attributed his nocturnal rambling to the onset of senility.

"One night, he wandered into the night and stayed out until dawn. I fell asleep at the kitchen table waiting up for him. The following morning, he was sitting at the back door looking none the worse for wear. All the same, his behavior frightened me. I could picture him wandering all the way to Gunne Lake, becoming confused and drowning; I could also imagine him meandering in the opposite direction, to the road, and blundering in front of a careless driver. From now on, when it came time for the dogs' last toilet, I clipped a leash to Donner and accompanied him into the yard. My plan worked fine until the night he scented something interesting and with a single tug pulled the leash from my grip and bolted into the dark. The rest of the dogs ignored him. *Mormor* permitted me to take a flashlight and venture a short distance from the house to search for him, but she called me in before I had any success.

"Again, he was away 'til morning. This time, he was seated on the back step with his fur absolutely filthy, matted with mud, and leaves, and twigs, and blood, more blood than anything else, really. You would have thought he rolled in it—which was what I guessed had happened. If you know anything about dogs, then you know how much they love sniffing out horrifying substances and rolling in them. In this case, I assumed Donner had come across the carcass of a deer, possibly split open by a blow from a truck, and luxuriated in his discovery. He required an extensive, soapy bath to render him fit to reenter the house, but he submitted to it with placid good cheer. I was late to school because of it, which was fine, since I was only missing math. Over the next month and a half, I was absent for first period five more times, as Donner repeated his nighttime escapes despite my best efforts to keep hold of him, reappearing at sunrise with his coat caked with gore a thorough bathing was necessary to clean. I'll admit, by the last of these early-morning scrubbings, I was wondering how many dead deer there were lying at the sides of the local roads. I didn't recall seeing many from the windows of either the school bus or *Mormor*'s car.

"At last, over dinner one night, *Mormor* said we needed to talk about Donner. After his most recent nocturnal excursions, she had spent the next morning (once I had been dropped off at school) retracing his path, aided by Lefty, who counted some hound among his ancestry. Their first search had ended at the remains of a coyote. Possibly, the animal had attacked Donner; if this was the case, then the coyote would have died regretting its decision, as Donner had torn it to shreds. He had done the same on his last all-night ramble to a doe and a pair of fawns. It was safe to assume his other outings had led to similar scenes of slaughter; it was equally likely he would continue to indulge this bloodlust every time he dashed off. So far, we had been fortunate, in that all of his victims had been wild animals, and not someone's beloved dog or a calf from one of the local farms or, God forbid, a child. The longer we allowed this to go on, though, the greater the risk of tragedy. We had to do something about Donner. The question was, what was this going to be?

"I didn't need to ask *Mormor* for her suggestion. I knew it would involve *Morfa*'s shotgun and taking the dog for a final walk in the woods while the sun was still up. It wasn't that I didn't think she had a point. Donner was a big boy. The prospect of him attacking another animal, let alone a human being, was terrifying. Were the worst to occur, the decision would be taken from us; it might be best to make it while it was still ours. At the same time, the unspoken but obvious cause of his bloody-minded turn, eating the segment of the *blodsuger* I had knocked in front of him, was not his fault, and the prospect of punishing him for it stirred a combination of shame and resentment in me. *Mormor* could see I wasn't happy with the obvious answer. Did I have another?

"After a minute's reflection, I said I did. There was a small outbuilding not far behind the patio. I think it had been a shed. We could turn the shed into a kennel for Donner. If we fenced off some of the yard in front of it, he would have space to move around in. This way, we could be sure he wouldn't run off and kill any other animals. (I admit, a small part of me wondered how safe the rest of our dogs were from the former mainstay of the pack.) 'It would have to be a strong fence,' *Mormor* said, 'strong and high. This would not be cheap, Doris.'

"Without another word, I went to my room, fetched my piggy bank down from its shelf, and brought it to the kitchen table. As *Mormor* watched, I retrieved a hammer from the toolbox under the sink, carried it to the table, and brought it down on the ceramic pig. Mixed in with the shards was my savings for the last five years of my life, ninety-eight dollars and twenty-four cents. For the time, this was a considerable sum. Most recently, I had intended it for the plane ticket back to my mother. I picked out the fragments of the bank, then pushed the heap of bills and coins across the table to *Mormor*. 'I'll work to pay for the rest,' I said.

"So we converted the shed into a doghouse for Donner and sectioned off a generous portion of the yard around it with heavy chain fencing. He wasn't happy to be cut off from the life of the house, particularly *Mormor,* but he adjusted to the new state of affairs. Three times a week, we mixed in a cup of blood with his dinner. Usually, it was pig's blood, which my grandmother bought from the butcher, but once in a while, she added cow's blood or even chicken blood. If we allowed him a small amount of blood on a regular schedule, *Mormor* thought it might help to manage the craving which had driven him into the night. When the weather was nice, I sat beside the fence in a lawn chair, doing my homework or reading. Donner would lie on the other side of the fence, pressed up against it. During the winter, it was difficult to spend time with him. Sometimes, I would look out the kitchen window to see him standing in the snow, his muzzle raised to the wind, and I would feel sadder than I could bear at the sight of him. Then I would bring him one of his bloody dinners and watch the gusto with which he consumed it, the way he licked the bowl for every last trace of flavor, and I would think this might be for the best, after all.

"He lived another seven years, an amazing length of time for a dog his size. There was no warning when he reached the end, no gradual decline. I brought him his breakfast one morning and he was lying in the middle of his pen, legs stretched as if he had been running full stride, lips pulled back from his teeth in a final snarl. We buried him at the edge of the woods, heaping stones over him to prevent wild animals from digging up his remains. *Mormor* wrapped him in an old sheet, and looking at his body lying next to the grave I had dug for him, I felt a surge of panic at the prospect of putting him in this hole in the earth, of covering him over with cold dirt and heavy stones, of leaving him here. I didn't know if I could do it; I almost said to my grandmother, 'I can't.' But I did. I took a deep breath, lifted a shovelful of soil, let it fall on him, and kept going until he was buried. For the next several nights, I thought of him in the ground and sobbed."

Doris shrugged. "Each time I visit my mom, I tend his grave. And now," she added, "I really must be going."

I thanked her for answering my question and promised that, should my bestseller arrive, her charter-boat service would be my first destination. "In the meantime," she said as she put her car in reverse, "remember: no ice-fishing."

"No ice-fishing," I said; although I was thinking, *Yeah, right.* I returned her wave and watched Doris drive away into the gathering night, then started in the direction of the lake where my son was still casting his line, under a sky whose light was dying on its cloudy ornaments from fuchsia and purple to charcoal and gray, my eyes lingering on the mountains on the horizon, in whose valleys and on whose slopes and peaks, in whose streams and rivers and under whose ponds and lakes, dwelled mystery, and wonder, and terror.

For Fiona

ABOUT THE AUTHORS

NATHAN BALLINGRUD is the author of *North American Lake Monsters* and *Wounds: Six Stories from the Border of Hell*. His work has garnered two Shirley Jackson Awards and several other award nominations, and has been adapted for film and television. His first novel, *The Strange*, is coming soon.

LAIRD BARRON spent his early years in Alaska. He is the award-winning author of several books, including *The Beautiful Thing That Awaits Us All, Swift to Chase,* and *Worse Angels*. His work has also appeared in many magazines and anthologies. Barron currently resides in the Rondout Valley writing stories about the evil that men do.

SIOBHAN CARROLL is a Canadian author whose short stories have appeared in venues like *Lightspeed* and Ellen Datlow's *The Devil and the Deep* anthology. A scholar as well as a writer of speculative fiction, she typically uses the fantastic to explore dark histories of empire, science, and the environment. You can read more on her website at voncarr-siobhan-carroll.blogspot.com.

INDRAPRAMIT DAS (a.k.a. Indra Das) is a writer and editor from Kolkata, India. He is a Lambda Literary Award winner for his debut novel, *The Devourers*, and a Shirley Jackson Award winner for his short fiction, which has appeared in a variety of anthologies and publications, including on *Tor.com, Slate, Clarkesworld,* and *Asimov's Science Fiction*. He is an Octavia E. Butler Scholar, and a grateful member of the Clarion West Class of 2012. He has lived in India, the United States, and Canada, where he received his MFA from the University of British Columbia.

KRISTI DEMEESTER is the author of the novel *Such a Pretty Smile*, published by St. Martin's Press; *Beneath*, a novel published by Word Horde Publications; and *Everything That's Underneath*, a short fiction collection from Apex Books. Her short fiction has appeared in *The Best Horror of the*

Year, Best New Horror, and *The Year's Best Weird Fiction* in addition to publications such as *PseudoPod, Black Static,* and *The Dark.* Find her online at kristidemeester.com.

CHIKODILI EMELUMADU was born in Worksop, Nottinghamshire, and raised in Awka, Nigeria. Her work has been short-listed for the Shirley Jackson Award and the Caine Prize for African Writing, and won a Nommo Award for Best Short Story in 2020. In 2019, her manuscript *Dazzling* won the inaugural Curtis Brown First Novel Prize and will be the lead debut for Wildfire Books in spring 2023. She lives in Newhaven, East Sussex, with way too many children and guinea pigs.

BRIAN EVENSON is the author of a dozen works of fiction, most recently the collection *The Glassy, Burning Floor of Hell.* His collection *Song for the Unraveling of the World* won the Shirley Jackson Award and the World Fantasy Award and was a finalist for the Ray Bradbury Prize. He has won the International Horror Guild Award and the American Library Association's RUSA Award, and has been a finalist for the Edgar Award. He is the recipient of three O. Henry Awards, an NEA fellowship, and a Guggenheim fellowship. He lives in Los Angeles and teaches in the Critical Studies Program at CalArts.

GEMMA FILES was born in England and raised in Toronto, Canada, and has been a journalist, a teacher, a film critic, and an award-winning horror author for almost thirty years. She has published four novels, a story cycle, three collections of short fiction, and three collections of speculative poetry. Her most recent novel, *Experimental Film,* won both the 2015 Shirley Jackson Award for Best Novel and the 2016 Sunburst Award for Adult Fiction. Her fourth collection, *In That Endlessness, Our End,* has recently been published; her next, *Dark Is Better,* will be published by Trepidatio in 2022.

JEFFREY FORD is the author of ten novels, the most recent *Ahab's Return* and *Out of Body.* He has published six story collections, including *The Best of Jeffrey Ford* and *Big Dark Hole.* His stories have appeared in numerous magazines and anthologies, from *The Magazine of Fantasy & Science Fiction* to *The Oxford Book of American Short Stories.* His work has been nominated for every major American fantasy and science fiction award and won a number of them. He lives in a hundred-plus-year-old farmhouse in Ohio's farm country and teaches composition part-time at Ohio Wesleyan University.

DARYL GREGORY's novels and short stories have won multiple awards, including the World Fantasy and Shirley Jackson Awards, and have been nominated for the Hugo, Nebula, Locus, Lambda, and Sturgeon Awards. His latest books are the novel *Revelator* and the novella *The Album of Dr. Moreau*. His eight other books include *Spoonbenders, We Are All Completely Fine, Afterparty,* the Crawford Award–winning novel *Pandemonium,* and the collection *Unpossible and Other Stories.* He also teaches writing and is a regular instructor at the Viable Paradise writing workshop.

GLEN HIRSHBERG's novels include *The Snowman's Children, Infinity Dreams,* and the Motherless Children trilogy. His short stories are collected in *The Two Sams, American Morons, The Janus Tree and Other Stories,* and *The Ones Who Are Waving.* He's won three International Horror Guild Awards and a Shirley Jackson Award, and has been nominated multiple times for the World Fantasy Award. He is also the owner/proprietor of Drones Club West, through which he offers online and in-person creative writing classes as well as manuscript editing and consulting. He lives with his family and cats in the Pacific Northwest.

BRIAN HODGE is the author of twenty novels and collections, of which several works are currently in development for TV and film. He lives in Colorado, where he also plays around with music and sound design, sustains lovely contusions from Krav Maga, and has recently taken to climbing the state's 14ers, so far without falling. He enjoys periodic leaves of absence from social media.

CAROLE JOHNSTONE's award-winning short fiction has been reprinted in many annual Year's Best anthologies in the UK and US. Her debut novel, *Mirrorland,* was published in 2021. Translation rights have been sold to thirteen countries, and it has been optioned for television. Her second novel, an unusual murder mystery set in the Outer Hebrides, will be published by Simon & Schuster in the US and Canada and by Borough Press/HarperCollins in the UK, in 2022. She lives in Argyll and Bute, Scotland, with her husband. More information on the author can be found at carolejohnstone.com.

STEPHEN GRAHAM JONES is the author of twenty-five or so novels and collections, and there's some novellas and comic books in there as well. Most recent are *The Only Good Indians, Night of the Mannequins,* and *My Heart Is a Chainsaw.* Stephen lives and teaches in Boulder, Colorado.

RICHARD KADREY is the *New York Times* bestselling author of the Sandman Slim supernatural noir series. *Sandman Slim* was included in Amazon's "100 Science Fiction & Fantasy Books to Read in a Lifetime," and is in development as a feature film. Some of Kadrey's other books include *King Bullet, The Grand*

Dark, The Everything Box, and *Butcher Bird.* He also writes screenplays, and for comics such as *Heavy Metal, Lucifer,* and *Hellblazer.*

CASSANDRA KHAW is an award-winning game writer whose fiction has been nominated for the Locus and British Fantasy Awards. Their short stories can be found in *The Magazine of Fantasy & Science Fiction,* on *Tor.com, Lightspeed, Uncanny* magazine, and *The Year's Best Science Fiction & Fantasy.* They also have two very large cats who are Very Not Smart.

CAITLÍN R. KIERNAN is a two-time winner of the World Fantasy Award. Their novels include *The Red Tree* and *The Drowning Girl,* and their prolific short fiction has been collected in numerous volumes, including *The Ape's Wife and Other Stories, The Dinosaur Tourist,* and *Houses Under the Sea.* Kiernan is also a vertebrate paleontologist and currently a research associate at the McWane Science Center in Birmingham, Alabama.

GARRY KILWORTH has now had forty-one novels and 173 short stories published. He has recently decided to concentrate on short fiction, that being his first love. He does, however, have a fantasy novel forthcoming from NewCon Press entitled *The Wild Hunt,* set in the seven Anglo-Saxon kingdoms of the seventh century. His most recent two publications are *Elemental Tales,* a collection of short speculative stories with a metal element at the heart of each, and *Blood Moon,* a collection of horror, fantasy, and science fiction.

MARGO LANAGAN has published seven collections of speculative fiction short stories, the latest being *Stray Bats,* from Small Beer Press. She has also published two dark fantasy novels, *Tender Morsels* and *The Brides of Rollrock Island.* Her work has been widely translated and anthologized, and has won four World Fantasy Awards, among many other accolades. She lives in Sydney, Australia.

JOHN LANGAN is the author of two novels and five collections of stories. For his work, he has received the Bram Stoker and This Is Horror Awards. He is one of the founders of the Shirley Jackson Awards, for which he serves on the board of directors. He lives in New York's Mid–Hudson Valley with his wife, a houseful of pets, and a pack of feral books.

JOE R. LANSDALE is the author of more than fifty novels and four hundred shorter works, including stories and essays. He is the recipient of numerous awards, including the Edgar Award, ten Bram Stoker Awards, the Spur Award, the British Fantasy Award, and others. His work has been published all over the world and turned into films, TV shows, and animation. He lives with his wife and their pit bull, Nicky, in Nacogdoches, Texas. A cat hangs out named Yoda.

LIVIA LLEWELLYN is a writer of dark fantasy, horror, and erotica, whose short fiction has appeared in over eighty anthologies and magazines. Her collections *Engines of Desire* and *Furnace* have both received Shirley Jackson Award nominations for Best Collection, and her short story "One of These Nights" won the Edgar Award for Best Short Story.

JOYCE CAROL OATES is the author most recently of the novel *Breathe* and the collection *Night, Neon*. She is a recipient of the Bram Stoker Award, the National Book Award, the PEN/Malamud Award for Excellence in the Short Story, the Bram Stoker Lifetime Achievement Award, the National Humanities Medal, and the Jerusalem Prize.

NORMAN PARTRIDGE is the author of six novels and six short story collections. His fiction ranges from horror and crime to the fantastic. A film adaptation of his lauded Halloween novel, *Dark Harvest,* is set for a September 2022 release by MGM. He lives and writes in California.

IAN ROGERS is the author of the award-winning collection *Every House Is Haunted.* A novelette from the collection, "The House on Ashley Avenue," was a finalist for the Shirley Jackson Award and is the basis for an upcoming Netflix film produced by Sam Raimi. Rogers lives with his wife in Peterborough, Ontario. For more information, visit ianrogers.ca.

PRIYA SHARMA's fiction has been published in venues such as *Interzone, Black Static, Nightmare, The Dark,* and on *Tor.com.* Her novelette "Fabulous Beasts" won the British Fantasy Award. Her collection *All the Fabulous Beasts* won the Shirley Jackson Award and the British Fantasy Award. *Ormeshadow,* her first novella, won a Shirley Jackson Award and a British Fantasy Award. More information can be found at priyasharmafiction.wordpress.com. *The Ghost of a Flea* by William Blake is among her favorite paintings, and she has long wanted to write about it.

KAARON WARREN is a multi-award-winning author who has published five novels, seven short story collections, and over two hundred short stories. In 2019, she received the Peter McNamara Achievement Award and was Guest of Honor at World Fantasy Convention 2018, StokerCon 2019, and GeyserCon

2019. Her most recent books include the re-release of her acclaimed novel *Slights; Tool Tales,* a chapbook in collaboration with Ellen Datlow (both from IFWG); and *Capturing Ghosts on the Page,* a writing advice chapbook from Brain Jar Press.

FRAN WILDE is a two-time Nebula Award winner who writes science fiction, fantasy, and horror for adults and kids, with seven books, so far, that embrace worlds unique (*Updraft,* the Gemworld series) and portal (*Riverland, The Ship of Stolen Words*), plus numerous short stories appearing in multiple Year's Best anthologies and listed as a finalist for the Nebula, Hugo, Locus, and World Fantasy Awards. She directs the Genre Fiction MFA concentration at Western Colorado University and writes nonfiction for NPR, *The Washington Post,* and *The New York Times.*

A. C. WISE is the author of the novel *Wendy, Darling,* along with a novella and three short story collections, the most recent of which, *The Ghost Sequences,* was published in 2021. Her work has won the Sunburst Award for Excellence in Canadian Literature of the Fantastic, and has been a finalist for the Nebula, the Sunburst, the Aurora, and the Lambda Literary Awards. In addition to her fiction, she contributes regular review columns to *Apex Magazine* and *The Book Smugglers,* and her work as a critic has made her a finalist for the Ignyte Award as well. Find her online at acwise.net.

ABOUT THE EDITOR

Gregory Frost

ELLEN DATLOW has been editing science fiction, fantasy, and horror short fiction for forty years as fiction editor of *Omni* and editor of *Event Horizon* and *Sci Fiction*. She currently acquires short stories and novellas for *Tor.com* and Nightfire. In addition, she has edited about one hundred science fiction, fantasy, and horror anthologies, including the annual The Best Horror of the Year series, and, most recently, *Echoes: The Saga Anthology of Ghost Stories, Final Cuts: New Tales of Hollywood Horror and Other Spectacles, Body Shocks: Extreme Tales of Body Horror,* and *When Things Get Dark: Stories Inspired by Shirley Jackson.*

Datlow has won multiple World Fantasy Awards, Locus Awards, Hugo Awards, Bram Stoker Awards, International Horror Guild Awards, Shirley Jackson Awards, and the 2012 Il Posto Nero Black Spot Award for Excellence as Best Foreign Editor. She was named recipient of the 2007 Karl Edward Wagner Award by the British Fantasy Society for "outstanding contribution to the genre," was honored with the Lifetime Achievement Award by the Horror Writers Association, in acknowledgment of superior achievement over an entire career, and was honored with the World Fantasy Life Achievement Award at the 2014 World Fantasy Convention.

She lives in New York and cohosts the monthly Fantastic Fiction Reading Series at KGB Bar. More information can be found at datlow.com, on Facebook, and on Twitter at @EllenDatlow. She's owned by two cats.